MW01044965

VISIONS
OF
FLESH
AND
BLOOD

ALSO FROM JENNIFER L. ARMENTROUT

Fall With Me
Dream of You (a 1001 Dark Nights Novel)
Forever With You
Fire in You

By J. Lynn
Wait for You
Be with Me
Stay with Me

The Blood and Ash Series
From Blood and Ash
A Kingdom of Flesh and Fire
The Crown of Gilded Bones
The War of Two Queens
A Soul of Ash and Blood
Visions of Flesh and Blood: A Blood and Ash/Flesh and Fire Compendium

The Flesh and Fire Series
A Shadow in the Ember
A Light in the Flame
A Fire in the Flesh

Fall of Ruin and Wrath Series
Fall of Ruin and Wrath

The Covenant Series
Half-Blood
Pure
Deity
Elixir
Apollyon
Sentinel

The Lux Series
Shadows
Obsidian
Onyx

Opal
Origin
Opposition
Oblivion

The Origin Series
The Darkest Star
The Burning Shadow
The Brightest Night

The Dark Elements
Bitter Sweet Love
White Hot Kiss
Stone Cold Touch
Every Last Breath

The Harbinger Series
Storm and Fury
Rage and Ruin
Grace and Glory

The Titan Series
The Return
The Power
The Struggle
The Prophecy

The Wicked Series
Wicked
Torn
Brave
The Prince (a 1001 Dark Nights Novella)
The King (a 1001 Dark Nights Novella)
The Queen (a 1001 Dark Nights Novella)

Gamble Brothers Series
Tempting the Best Man
Tempting the Player
Tempting the Bodyguard

A de Vincent Novel Series
Moonlight Sins

VISIONS
OF
FLESH
AND
BLOOD

A BLOOD AND ASH/
FLESH AND FIRE COMPENDIUM

As told by Miss Willa

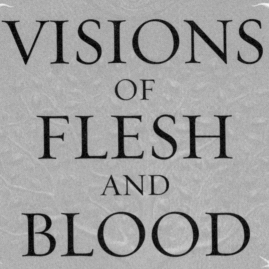

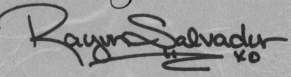

#1 *NEW YORK TIMES* BESTSELLING AUTHOR
JENNIFER L.
ARMENTROUT
with RAYVN SALVADOR

BLUE
BOX
PRESS

Visions of Flesh and Blood
A Blood and Ash/Flesh and Fire Compendium
By Jennifer L. Armentrout and Rayvn Salvador

Copyright 2024 Jennifer L. Armentrout
ISBN: 9781957568836

Published by Blue Box Press, an imprint of Evil Eye Concepts, Incorporated

Cover design by Hang Le

Copyright 2024 Original Works of Art used with the permission of each individual artist:
Alicia MB Art (pages 330, 406, 414)
Amanda Lynn (pages: 202, 206, 331, 415, 457, 472, 506-520, 522-523)
Emilia Mildner (page: 165)
Jemlin C. (pages: front forest, 170, 214, 267, 456, back forest)
Hang Le (pages: 18-19, 166-169, 195, 201, 250-251, 282, 289, 324-325, 398-399)
Kassia Ramos (pages: 11, 293, 489)
Kseniya Bocharova (pages: 38, 142)
Macarena Ceballos (pages: 58, 64, 72, 112, 122, 128, 184, 196, 219, 240, 475, 490, 498)
Steffani Christensen (pages: 274, 474, 480)
Shane Munce (page: 41)
Dana J.K. (page: 332)

ACKNOWLEDGMENTS

Behind every book is a team of people who lend their blood, sweat, and tears to make it happen and shine…

As always, massive gratitude to Blue Box Press—Liz Berry, Jillian Stein, and MJ Rose—for supporting this book idea and making it happen, Kim Guidroz and Jessica Saunders for their unparalleled expertise, Erika Hayden for her assistance in detail gathering, and BBP's awesome editing and proofreading team—Laura Helseth, Stacey Tardif, and Jessica Mobbs. Not to mention everyone else who provided their support and expertise to get VISIONS where it needed to be. Thank you!

We are *so* grateful for Hang Le (@ByHangLe) and her incomparable design, as well as the other contributing artists who lent us their unbelievable talent and made this book what it is: Alicia MB Art (@Alicia.MB.Art), Creatively Agnes (@AgnesArt42), Jenna Pearson (@Jemlin_C), Kassia Ramos (@K_Psps), Kseniya Bocharova (@romannaboch), Macarena Ceballos (@ArtBy.Mikki), Art by Steffani (@ArtBySteffani), Dana J.K. (@Debra.Entendre), Emilia Mildner (@Emilia.Mildner), and Shane Munce (@ShaneMunce).

Appreciation to our agents, Kevan Lyon and Taryn Fagerness, and all those who support us in everything we do on a daily basis—we couldn't do this without you.

We could (and probably should) thank so many others by name, but it would take more page count than we have to spare. So, we will just say, if you are reading this and played a part in keeping us on track or whatever else we may have needed…you know who you are, and we love you dearly.

And last but certainly not least, none of this would have happened without you, the reader. You chimed in on Facebook ages ago that you wanted to see a book like this, and here it is. Without your continued and growing love for these series and characters, it may not have happened. Your support is humbling. We appreciate you, and hope you enjoy this as much as we did putting it together.

DEDICATION

For those who love to live a thousand lives between the pages and enjoy spending as much time as possible with fictional characters... This one's for you.

LETTER FROM
JENNIFER L. ARMENTROUT
INDIGO EXCLUSIVE EDITION

Dear reader,

When I started the Blood and Ash and Flesh and Fire series, I knew keeping track of all the world-building details would be a massive undertaking. One I would gloriously fail at. Thankfully, Blue Box Press has an incredible editorial team who immediately started keeping track of things as each book was released. If I can't find what I need in my notes, I just email them, and they always have the answer, which lets me concentrate on the writing. After a few books, I started noticing readers talking about a series bible and asked in my Facebook group, JLAnders, if a book like that was something they might like to see. The response was an overwhelming yes.

Fast forward to talks with my publisher, where we knew we wanted to do it but didn't want it to interfere with any of the other releases. That was a bit of a conundrum, until we realized we already had a solution. Our Executive Editor had been working with others to create and keep all those files for the series, she'd read every book multiple times, *and* she was already a published author under her pseudonym, Rayvn Salvador. Asking her to help with VISIONS was a win-win.

I was so happy when she agreed to cowrite VISIONS and also super relieved. Your editors often know the book and the world as well as the author does. Sometimes, it feels like they even know it better. Anyway, Rayvn sent her idea for the title to the publisher as she flew home from our business meeting.

For months, she gathered data, sent emails asking questions and getting clarification, and suggested things she thought the readers might like—being a big reader of the series herself.

When the art started coming in, she verified that all aspects were correct, and the two of us worked with Jillian to get the artists what they needed to pluck the images out of my head and bring your beloved characters to life.

And when everything was in place and all put together—the history, character profiles, art, and brand-new content—we all sat back and stared in wonder at what it ended up being.

It's more than we ever could have dreamed, and we hope you love it. It's reference material, yes, but it's also collectible art—from this gorgeous special-edition cover to everything inside. And doing it from Miss Willa's point of view makes it so much more than just a series guide. It also allowed me to leave a few things up to the imagination, reveal some juicy tidbits, and tease about some things to come in future installments. After all, Willa knows a lot, but she doesn't know everything. And even the things she *thinks* she knows are subject to change. You guys have met me, right? *wink*

As Miss Willa would say…

All my best.

Always.

xoxo,

JLA

A LETTER FROM MISS WILLA

Dear reader,

If you are perusing the words between these pages, someone discovered my cache of notes, records, and journals and decided to make at least some of them available.

As you know, I have been around for a very long time—eons, really. As the eldest member of the Council of Elders, I have experienced and borne witness to a lot in my time. As a Seer... I have seen even more. But with that last bit in mind, it bears mentioning that it doesn't always come to me in chronological order. I get bits and pieces from different times or different people and thus need to organize them and put them into some sort of arrangement—for me, of course, but also for posterity's sake.

Occasionally, I experience some of those historic moments firsthand—both the big things and the small, as all are important—as events unfold and thus know when and how they played out. Other times, it's a matter of learning as much as possible about the key players involved and making educated guesses. But I always go where my urges take me. Be they Seer-based or... other. Because, as you know, I never say no to those desires. And I can't ignore the visions of blood nor the fiery pull of the flesh when they call to me.

Which is why what you hold in your hand is a mix of facts, factoids, and observances combined with a personal record of my experiences. I needed to chronicle historically accurate data, things related to my world as it changed, and items specific to timelines and people of note. But it made no sense to do so without interjecting my thoughts and feelings. After all, one should always trust their instincts.

But please remember that these events are ever-changing. As the moon phases change and history unfolds with fulfilled prophecies, the series of events can sometimes take on new meanings. I also wish to mention that I may be spoiling some things for those not present for the past events I detail here. My sincerest apologies. But... I have warned you.

However, now that you are privy to my private collection, you might as well enjoy it. Life is for living, after all. And given that I have a wandering soul with a thirst for exploration, I can tell you that some of these things are delicious, indeed.

All my best.

Always,
Miss Willa

PRONUNCIATION GUIDE

Characters

Aios – AYY-ohs

Alastir Davenwell – AL-as-tir DAV-en-well

Andreia – ahn-DRAY-ah

Antonis – an-TOE-nis

Arden – AHR-den

Attes – AT-tayz

Aurelia – au-REL-ee-ah

Baines – baynz

Basilia – bah-SILL-ee-ah

Beckett – BECK-et

Bele – bell

Blaz – blayz

Brandole Mazeen – bran-dohl mah-ZEEN

Braylon Holland – BRAY-lon HAA-luhnd

Britta – brit-tah

Callum – KAL-um

Clariza – klar-itza

Coralena – kore-a-LEE-nuh

Coulton – KOHL-ton

Casteel Da'Neer – ka-STEEL DA-neer

Crolee – KROH-lee

Dafina – dah-FEE-nuh

Daniil – da-NEEL

Davina – dah-VEE-nuh

Delano Amicu – dee-LAY-no AM-ik-kyoo

Diaval – dee-AH-vuhl

Dorcan – dohr-kan

Dorian Teerman – DOHR-ee-uhn TEER-man

Duchess and Duke Ravarel – duch-ess and dook RAV-ah-rell

Dyses – DEYE-seez

Ector – EHK-tohr
Effie – EH-fee
Ehthawn – EE-thawn
Elian Da'Neer – EL-ee-awn DA-near
Elias – el-IGH-us
Elijah Payne – ee-LIE-jah payn
Eloana Da'Neer – EEL-oh-nah DA-neer
Embris – EM-bris
Emil Da'Lahr – EE-mil DA-lar
Erlina – Er-LEE-nah
Ernald – ER-nald
Evander – eh-VAN-der
Eythos – EE-thos
Ezmeria – ez-MARE-ee-ah
Gemma – jeh-muh
General Aylard – gen-ER-al AYY-lard
Gianna Davenwell – jee-AA-nuh DA-ven-well
Griffith Jansen – grif-ITH JAN-sen
Halayna – hah-LAY-nah
Hanan – HAY-nan
Hawke Flynn – hawk flin
Hisa Fa'Mar – hee-SAA FAH-mar
Holland – HAA-luhnd
Ian Balfour – EE-uhn BAL-fohr
Iason – IGH-son
Ione – EYE-on
Ires – EYE-res
Ivan – EYE-van
Isbeth – is-BITH
Jacinda Teerman – juh-SIN-dah TEER-man
Jadis – JAY-dis
Jasper Contou – JAS-per KON-too
Jericho – JERR-i-koh
Joshalynn – josha-lynn
Kayleigh Balfour – KAY-lee BAL-fohr
Keella – KEE-lah
Kieran Contou – KEE-ren KON-too
King Jalara – king jah-LAH-ruh
King Saegar – king SAY-gar
Kirha Contou – k-AH-ruh KON-too
Kolis – KOH-lis
Kyn – kin
Lady Cambria – lay-dee KAM-bree-uh

Lailah – LAY-lah
Lathan – LEY-THahN
Leopold – LEE-ah-pohld
Lev Barron – lehv BAIR-uhn
Lizeth Damron – lih-ZEHTH DAM-ron
Loimus – loy-moos
Lord Ambrose – lohrd AM-brohz
Lord Chaney – lohrd chay-NEE
Lord Gregori – lohrd GREHG-ohr-ree
Lord Haverton – lohrd HAY-ver-ton
Loren – LOH-ren
Luddie – LUHD-dee
Lyra – lee-RAH
Mac – mack
Madis – mad-is
Magda – mahg-dah
Mahiil – ma-HEEL
Maia – MY-ah
Malec O'Meer – ma-LEEK O-meer
Malessa Axton – MAHL-les-sah ax-TON
Malik Da'Neer – MA-lick DA-neer
Marisol Faber – MARE-i-sohl FAY-berr
Millicent – mil-uh-SUHNT
Mycella – MY-sell-AH
Naberius – nah-BEHR-ee-us
Naill – NYill
Nektas – NEK-tas
Nithe – NIGHth
Noah – noh-AH
Nova – NOH-vah
Nyktos – NIK-toes
Odell Cyr – OH-dell seer
Odetta – oh-DET-ah
Orphine – OR-feen
Peinea – pain-ee-yah
Penellaphe – pen-NELL-uh-fee
Penellaphe Balfour – pen-NELL-uh-fee BAL-fohr
Perry – PER-ree
Perus – paehr-UHS
Phanos – FAN-ohs
Polemus – pol-he-mus
Preela – PREE-lah
Pulus – POO-loos

Priestess Analia – priest-ess an-NAH-lee-ah
Queen Calliphe – queen KAL-ih-fee
Queen Ileana – queen uh-lee-AH-nuh
Quentyn – QWEN-tin
Reaver – REE-ver
Rhahar – RUH-har
Rhain – rain
Rolf – rollf
Rune – roon
Rylan Keal – RYE-lan keel
Sage – sayj
Saion – SIGH-on
Sera – SEE-rah
Seraphena Mierel – SEE-rah-fee-nah MEER-ehl
Setti – SET-ee
Shae Davenwell – shay DAV-en-well
Sotoria – soh-TOR-ee-ah
Sven – svehn
Talia – TAH-lee-uh
Taric – tay-rik
Tavius – TAY-vee-us
Tawny Lyon – TAW-nee LYE-uhn
Thad – thad
Theon – thEE-awn
Tulis [Family] – TOO-lees
Uros– OO-rohs
Valyn Da'Neer – VAH-lynn DA-neer
Veses – VES-eez
Vikter Wardwell – VIK-ter WARD-well
Vonetta Contou – vah-NET-tah KON-too
Wilhelmina Colyns – wil-hel-MEE-nuh KOHL-lynz

Places
Aegea – ayy-JEE-uh
Atheneum – ath-uh-NEE-uhm
Atlantia – at-LAN-tee-ah
Barren Plains – bar-uhn pleynz
Berkton – BERK-ton
Callasta Isles – cah-LAS-tuh eyelz
Carcers [The] – KAR-serz
Carsodonia – kar-so-DON-uh
Cauldra Manor – kall-drah [manor]
Chambers of Nyktos – cheym-berz of nik-TOES

Cor Palace – kohr pal-is
Dalos – day-lohs
Elysium Peaks – ihl-LEES-ee-uhm peeks
Evaemon – EHV-eh-mahn
High Hills of Thronos – hie hilz of THROH-nohs
House of Haides – howz of HAY-deez
Hygeia – high-JEE-uh
Iliseeum – AH-lee-see-um
Irelone – EYE-reh-lohn
Isles of Bele – IGHelz of BELL
Kithreia – kith-REE-ah
Lasania – lah-SAHN-ee-uh
Lotho – LOH-thoh
Masadonia – mah-sah-DOHN-uh
Massene – mah-SEE-nuh
Mountains of Nyktos – MOWNT-ehnz of nik-TOES
New Haven – noo HAY-ven
Niel Valley – nile valley
Oak Ambler – ohk AM-bler
Padonia – pa-DOH-nee-ah
Pensdurth – PENS-durth
Pillars of Asphodel – [pillars of] AS-foe-del
Pinelands – PINE-lands
Pompay – pom-PAY
Seas of Saion – SEEZ of SIGH-on
Skotos Mountains – SKOH-tohs MOWNT-ehnz
Solis – sou-LIS
Spessa's End – SPESSAHZ ehnd
Sirta – SIR-ta
Saion's Cove – SI-onz kohv
Stygian Bay – stih-JEE-uhn bey
Tadous – TAHD-oos
Temple of Perses – TEM-puhl of PUR-seez
The Three Jackals – thuh three JAK-uhlz
Three Rivers – three RIH-verz
Thyia Plains – THIGH-ah playnz
Triton Isles – TRY-ton IGH-elz
Undying Hills – UN-dy-ing hillz
Vathi – VAY-thee
Vita – VEE-tah
Vodina Isles – voh-DEE-nuh IGH-elz
Western Pass – WEST-tern pass
Whitebridge – WIGHT-brij

Willow Plains – WIHL-oh pleynz

Terms
Arae – air-ree
benada – ben-NAH-dah
ceeren – SEE-rehn
chora – KOH-rah
Cimmerian – sim-MARE-ee-in
dakkai – DAY-kigh
demis – dem-EEZ
eather – ee-thohr
graeca – gray-kah
Gyrm – germ
imprimen – IM-prim-ehn
kardia – KAR-dee-ah
kiyou wolf/wolves – kee-yoo [wolf/wolves]
lamaea – lahm-ee-ah
laruea – lah-ROO-ee-ah
meyaah Liessa – MEE-yah LEE-sah
nota – NOH-tah
notam – NOH-tam
sekya – sek-yah
so'lis – SOH-lis
sparanea – SPARE-ah-nay-ah
tulpa – tool-PAH
wivern – WY-vehrn

GLOSSARY OF TERMS:

Before I get into relaying what I know about the world and the important people of note in both this timeline and the one that came before, I feel it necessary to give some background on some of the terms used throughout my notes. I likely use others not defined here, but this should be helpful to those using this in the future.

Abyss: Where souls pay for every evil deed they committed while alive. Houses the Pit of Endless Flames that burns continuously, turning the sky iron-hued from the smoke.

Ancients: Pure energy that fell as stars, creating the realms. They eventually rose to walk amongst their creations, creating the Primals as a way to limit their power and maintain balance.

Arae: Another word for the Fates. They reside on Mount Lotho.

Arcadia: Another realm where the gods take their eternal rest. Denoted by pillars with bright light shining between them.

Atlantians: Citizens of Atlantia with varying bloodlines. Born mortal until the ages of nineteen to twenty-one, upon which time they enter their Culling and mature, allowing their strength and abilities to manifest fully. All Atlantians have two fangs and some shade of amber eyes; however, only Elemental Atlantians have pure gold irises. Must drink Atlantian blood to thrive. They won't die without it, but they become something that is not quite alive. Full-blooded Atlantians are essentially immortal.

Barrat: Large rodent, about the size of a boar.

Blessing: Mortals believed the touch of the Royals had healing properties. They lined up for days for the chance to receive one. It was simply a temporary reprieve from illness obtained by ingesting Atlantian blood—a fallacy.

Bloodstone: Material used to make weapons that can kill Craven, Ascended, and wolven but has no effect on Atlantians or Revenants. Created from ruby-red rocks found on the coast of the Seas of Saion, thought to be the angry or sad tears of the gods petrified by the sun.

Bones of the Ancients: Used to bind gods, nullifying their abilities, and subsequently making them vulnerable to entombment. They can also nullify the Primal *notam*. If made into a weapon, one nick can kill a god or incapacitate a Primal. If left in place in a Primal, they become incapacitated until it's removed. The bones can only be destroyed by the Primal of Life or the Primal of Death.

Ceeren: An Atlantian bloodline that could shift into waterfolk. A large contingent of them lived near the Triton Isles off the coast of Hygeia. Thought to have died out before the war once Saion went to sleep.

Changelings: An Atlantian bloodline believed to be the result of a union between a deity and a wolven. Most are able to shift their forms. Some—though few—can take the shape of another individual, but when they do, they also adopt their mannerisms.

Craven: A creature with four fangs and claws that emerges from mist to attack in search of blood. A bite from a Craven causes the victim to become cursed, thus turning into a Craven within days. The people of Solis led everyone to believe that the Atlantians were responsible for the creation the Craven, a product of their poisonous kiss, and said they were controlled by Prince Casteel as the purported Dark One. In reality, they are what becomes of a mortal when all their blood is stolen through feeding without being replaced. The act rots them, both body and mind, turning them into amoral creatures driven by insatiable hunger...hence why the act of killing a mortal while feeding was forbidden. However, the Craven existed before the vamprys those of Solis know. They were around in the time of the gods, byproducts of the first Ascended feeding without replacing the victim's blood, or a god draining them without replacing the essence.

Dakkais: A race of vicious, flesh-eating creatures rumored to have been birthed from the bottomless pits located somewhere in Iliseeum. Featureless except for mouths full of teeth and slits for a nose. They like to attack from the water and are drawn to eather. The dakkais acted like trained bloodhounds for Dalos, and Kolis treated some like pets.

Deities: Children of the gods. One is rumored to have given rise to Atlantia.

Demis: A mortal who is not a second or third son or daughter and is Ascended by a god. They have godlike powers but are considered abominations.

Draken: The Primals' protectors and guardians. Descended from dragons given mortal form by Eythos, the then Primal of Life. The fire they breathe is the essence of the gods, as is their blood. Only the blood of the draken can kill a Revenant (see more on them later).

Eather: The potent residual power believed to not only have created the mortal realm and Iliseeum (more on the creation of the realms to come) but which also courses through the blood of a god, giving even the lesser, unknown ones unthinkable power. Also referred to as Primal essence and the essence of the gods. The Chosen all have some eather within them. The ones who Ascend have more than most.

Elemental Atlantians: Atlantians with the purest bloodline. Children of the first mortal who underwent the heartmate trial with a deity. They can survive without food for days but require more blood. Most have heightened senses and mental capabilities or gifts.

Godlings: The children of a mortal and a god. Those descended from powerful gods will have powers and abilities, while others are born mortal.

Gods of Divination: Gods able to see what was hidden to others—their truths—both past and future.

Graeca: A word in the old language of the Primals meaning life or love.

Gyrms: In the time of the gods, it was said they were mortals who pledged themselves to the gods or Primals for eternity, becoming Hunters or Seekers. Or souls who refused to enter the Shadowlands at the time of their death, thus striking a deal to serve and ultimately becoming Sentinels. They are all wraithlike beings with stitched mouths and are filled with serpents. In the time after the War of Two Kings, it is said they were not once alive but were instead created from Iliseeum soil and eather, summoned to be soldiers or guards of sacred places. In the time of the gods, they could only be destroyed by a blow to the head. In the time after the War of Two Kings, any fatal puncture wound worked.

Handmaidens: The Blood Queen's personal guards. Not all are Revenants, but many are. Those who are wear painted masks on the upper halves of their faces that look like wings.

Heartmates: Like soulmates. Two halves of a whole. When the Arae look upon the threads of fate and see all the many different possibilities of one's life, they can sometimes see what may come of the love between two or more souls. And in that union, they see possibilities that can reshape the realms by either creating something never seen before or ushering in great change. Almost considered more of a legend. So rare it became a myth for a very long time.

Huntsmen: A division of the army that ferries information between the cities and escorts travelers and goods.

Iliseeum: The realm of the Primals, gods, godlings, and mortals who serve them. Accessed through the Primal mist or a gateway in the human realm that takes the traveler to a specific place in Iliseeum. In the time of the gods, there were access points in Sera's lake and the Bonelands—the area that eventually became Atlantia.

Kardia: The piece of the soul—the spark—that all living creatures are born and die with that allows them to love another not of their blood—irrevocably and selflessly.

Liessa: Means *Queen.*

Meyaah: Means *my.*

Mortals: Born of the flesh of a Primal and the fire of a draken. Most carry a dormant ember of Primal essence within them, except for the third sons and daughters. In them, the ember isn't always dormant. There is no explanation for this, but it is why they were the Chosen used for Ascension.

Revenants: Considered abominations of life and death. Kolis's magical creation. Originally, they were the Chosen who disappeared—those with an ember of eather. They died and came back changed after being given god blood. They can survive almost any wound, even mortal ones, and can resurrect regardless of injury. Their only weakness is draken blood. Kolis called them his "works in progress," saying he needed his *graeca* to perfect them. It was also stated that the blood of a King, or at least one destined to become a King, was needed to ensure they reached their full potential, though that's not entirely true. Callum was the first Revenant, created when he took his life out of grief, and Kolis gave him his blood. Though he is different, given he wasn't a third son. Millicent is also different than other Revenants because she was a first daughter and transitioned differently, as well. Revenants do not need to eat, nor do they need blood or any other comforts, and normal Revs do not have a soul—their pale eyes are like windows to their true nature, showing they are not alive.

Rises: Mountainous walls constructed from limestone and iron mined from the Elysium Peaks and used to protect cities within the kingdoms.

Senturion: The Atlantian warrior lines. Born, not trained. Made up of multiple bloodlines: Primordial (can summon elements during battle), Cimmerian (can call upon the night, blocking out the sun to blind their foe), Empaths (able to read emotions and turn them into weapons, could also heal, were favored by the deities, and feared by others. They were also exceptional fighters—braver and bolder than any other line. Often called Soul Eaters), Pryo (able to summon flames to their blades), Unnamed Others (could call upon the souls of the ones who were slain by the ones they fought).

Shades: Shadowlike souls that refuse to pass the Pillars of Asphodel to face judgment. Because of this, they cannot return to the mortal realm nor enter the Vale. Therefore, they stay in the Dying Woods and are driven mad by unending hunger, thirst, and their desire to live, turning them dangerous. If they are destroyed, there is no redemption, and no coming back.

Shadowlands: The Primal of Death's Court. Contains the city of Lethe and the Vale and Abyss beyond the Pillars of Asphodel.

Shadowstep: A Primal willing oneself where they want to go and then simply stepping into that reality.

Shadowstone: Black stone used in weapons that can kill a god. One of the strongest materials around, if not *the* strongest. Created with dragon fire before the time of the draken. It's what all life forms turned into when burned by dragon fire. Basically, the organic material became like slag and soaked into the ground, leaving deposits of stone. Shadowstone was thought to only be vulnerable to itself and the bones of the Ancients but can be destroyed with eather wielded by a powerful god or Primal. One of the largest deposits in the mortal realm is in Sera's lake, though the Shadow Temples are also made of it. There are vast deposits in the Mountains of Nyktos and the Elysium Peaks, as well.

Sirens: Guardians of the Vale.

So'lis: Means *my soul.*

The Ascended/Vamprys: Mortals who underwent the Ascension. Pale skin and fathomless, fully black eyes. Ageless, unnaturally fast, and strong, they're nearly immortal. They do not walk in the sun and are prone to bloodlust.

The Ascension: The definition varies depending on timeline. In the time of the gods, the process allowed the Chosen to enter Iliseeum to serve the Primal of Life, thus granting them eternal life. It could also be the Ascension of a god into a Primal, or a god into a more powerful god. It was also used to describe the process of a god Ascending a mortal who was not a third son or daughter, thereby making them a demis. In the time after the War of Two Kings, the "Ascension" is still about being given to the gods but is more about allowing those Ascended to engage in prohibited activities since they become vamprys.

The Chosen: Third sons and daughters born in a shroud (a caul), who were picked to serve in the Court of the Primal of Life. It is said the Chosen are born with some non-dormant essence of the gods in their blood, which allows them to complete the Ascension.

The Joining: The bonding process between an Atlantian, his/her/their bonded wolven, and the Atlantian's partner to sync lifespans. Requires a blood exchange and can sometimes be sexual. In order to work, there must be Atlantian blood present in the exchange. Once bonded, if the strongest of the party dies, the others will follow. By Joining, heartbeats and breaths synchronize, and emotions are felt.

The Maiden: One of the Chosen, born in a shroud, the one whose Ascension is said to save the Kingdom of Solis and allow the Ascension of hundreds of Lords and Ladies in Wait.

The Primals: The highest beings of power in Iliseeum outside of the Fates. Each rules a Court and have gods who serve them: Shadowlands (Primal of Death), Dalos (Primal of Life), Lotho (Primal of Wisdom, Loyalty, and Duty), Kithreia (Primal of Love, Beauty, and Fertility), Vathi (Primals of War and Accord and Peace and Vengeance), Thyia Plains (Primal of Rebirth), Sirta (Primal of the Hunt and Divine Justice), Callasta Isles (The Eternal Goddess / Primal of Rites and Prosperity), Triton Isles (Primal of Sea, Wind, Earth, and Sky). They cannot stay in the mortal realm for too long, as their powers begin affecting those around them. If a Primal dies, catastrophic events can occur in both realms; therefore, a new vessel for the eather must be found. They have many abilities that differ between them, but one thing is true of all: If a promise is made, it must be kept.

The Rite: In the time of the gods, it was when mortal third sons and daughters were Chosen to Ascend and enter the realm of the gods to serve. The act of Ascension was highly guarded, but it was assumed that Kolis attempted to turn them into Revenants. He actually turned many of them into Ascended by draining them to the point of death and then using the blood of one of his gods to Ascend them. After the creation of Atlantia and Solis, the Rite was the celebration that took place before an Ascension. The second and third sons and daughters were often offered to the gods during the Rite. However, following the War of Two Kings, it changed to be the time when the children served as sustenance for the vamprys.

The Rot: A plague spreading across both the realm of the gods and the mortal realm, killing the land and creating hardship. Thought to be the result of a deal made between the Primal of Death and the then Lasanian King. It was actually the result of the power shift and lack of balance when Kolis stole Eythos's power. The embers of life residing in a dying mortal vessel only sped up the spread of the Rot. Once the Consort became the Primal of Life in truth, the Rot began to recede.

The Star: A one-of-a-kind diamond known not only for its indestructible strength but also its irregular, jagged beauty and silver sheen. Said to have been created by the flames of the dragons who used to inhabit Iliseeum before the Primals were capable of shedding joyous tears. It sank into the earth where it remained for eons before finally being unearthed by the Fates. Able to hold both Primal embers and souls. It is actually an Ancient turned to stone by dragon fire.

Unseen: Initially created by the deities to serve as spies and soldiers and head off any rebellion, but eventually turned against their creators. They wear wolven masks to hide their identities.

Viktors: Eternal beings born with a goal: to guard someone the Fates believe is destined to bring about great change or purpose. They are neither mortal nor god. Not all are aware of their duty, but the Fates will always put them with the one they are to safeguard. They always reincarnate. When they die, their souls return to Mount Lotho, where the Arae give them new mortal forms and purposes with no memory of their previous lives. However, some *viktors* are predestined to figure out what they are, who they were sent to protect, and retain their memories.

Wivern: An Atlantian bloodline that could shift into the form of a large cat. Believed to have died out.

Wolven: Kiyou wolves given mortal form to serve as the deities' protectors and guides in the mortal realm. When the Elemental Atlantians began to outnumber the deities, the wolven bonds shifted to them. They predate the Atlantians. Their senses are much keener than most. When bonded, they can feel the emotions of the Atlantian(s) they are bonded to, and the Atlantian(s) can use the wolven for energy if needed. They prefer not to remain in their mortal forms for too long.

HISTORY OF THE WORLDS

Our world and the Land of the Gods have both changed considerably over the years. And while I am many, many centuries old, I was not, in fact, alive during the time of the gods. Nevertheless, my Seer powers give me insight into some things from the past that many do not possess, and I have combined that with firsthand knowledge from my lifetime to compile the following list of facts that should help put some things into perspective. Please keep in mind, however, that understanding evolves, truths are always coming to light, and things shift as destinies unfold.

In the Beginning:

Many believe the Primals created the air, lands, seas, realms, and everything in between. After all, little is known about the beginning, and it was better that way for the people to have faith. Easier. Safer. The truth was far more complicated and dangerous because every new beginning carries the risk of a new end.

Our beginning started when there were only stars made of raw, unfettered essence, and it remained that way until Orsus, the largest and brightest of them, erupted. The explosion sent power rippling out, creating barren lands and mountains where nothing but vast emptiness had existed before.

In the millennia that followed, stars began their descent to the no-longer-barren realms. Some fell in areas where great winged creatures ruled the skies, and others in lands separated by vast bodies of water. Those stars buried themselves deep in the soil created by Orsus, feeding the land as the land fed them until they rose to walk as the Ancients.

With their eyes full of all the colors of their beginnings, they were beings of absolute power, neither good nor bad, but they were not welcomed by the great winged beasts who ruled the sky, and their battles nearly destroyed the realms until a shaky truce was established. Peace came, but during that time, ten of the Ancients began to dream of what was to come. They saw the truth in absolute power. It would inevitably corrupt. In their attempt to prevent this, the ten created the first Primals, thus splitting their power with shared bits of their energy among offspring who were designed to be beyond needs and wants to ensure that there would always be untainted balance.

Peace continued, and conception began as the Ancients created beautiful elemental beings and nightmarish creatures birthed from the darkest, deepest parts of the realms. New Primals were created from the ground, and others entered Arcadia for their time of rest. During this time, they never even considered fighting or killing one another, and procreation was purely for the sake of multiplying. Primals gave birth to gods, and the lands flourished harmoniously, but those ten Ancients still dreamed. They knew what was coming.

Some could claim that the downfall of the Ancients and what was to come started with the young Primal of Life and his insatiable curiosity. It was he who created the first beings of duality, solidifying the truce between those who walked and those who ruled the sky. It was he who created the mortals—not in the image of the Primals and gods, but in the way of the Ancients, who were born of stars.

The development of the mortals wasn't as restricted as the Primals. The young Primal of Life wanted them to have what they did not: free will. And with that came the capacity to feel emotion. So, as time passed, and Primals and gods interacted with the mortals, they became more curious and then enthralled by all the things the mortals felt.

They became more like them.

The Ancients were not as bonded to the mortals as the Primals were, but nonetheless, they delighted in them. You see, for eons, the Ancients saw the beauty in everything, but were as old as time itself, and no matter how benevolent or balanced they had been, they began to see only the harsh cost of unbridled creation. As mortals reproduced and spread, crowding the lands and destroying more and more of what came before, the Primals themselves became more mortal-like, eventually developing free will and the ability to care deeply—and nothing is more powerful than the ability to feel and care.

Many of the Ancients started to view their creations, from god to mortal, as selfish parasites. Realizing mortals could not coexist with the land, and that the Primals were becoming unbalanced under the influence of the mortals, the Ancients decided to take back what had been given. They decided to cleanse the realms. But the Primals rose, working alongside the mortals, and the Ancients fell. And while some went to places of rest, others remained behind to ensure balance, becoming the Arae—the Fates.

And evolution continued.

The first Primal fell in love. And the Arae started experiencing emotions, as well. This worried the Fates. They feared those feelings could be used as weapons, so they intervened, hoping to dissuade others, and committed one of their greatest mistakes.

They made love the Primals' true weakness.

But it was too late by then. Another Primal had fallen in love. And another. Eventually, the Primals began feeling other emotions. Joy and sadness. Excitement and dread. Hopefulness and bitterness. Empathy and jealousy. And, of course, love and hate. They began to *live*, and like with all beings that have choices, some became corrupt, uncontrollable, and obsessed.

And what the Ancients had dreamed so long ago continued to play out despite their interference. The balance of the realms grew increasingly unstable as the Primals fought amongst each other, but they were always nothing more than skirmishes—never all-out war.

Never anything that threatened the very fabric of the realms.

Until now.

First on our journey of discovery, let's start with the Ancients…

Note: Some of this information was given in the glossary, but if you did not use that before accessing this file, it's reiterated and expanded upon here.

Ancients:

Fallen stars that created the realms and rose to walk the lands, eventually splitting their power into creations of their flesh—the Primals. As time wore on, they became fed up with the way the Primals, gods, and mortals took care of what had been given to them and decided to cleanse it all. The Primals joined forces with the gods, mortals, draken, and their ancestors—the dragons—to battle them.

Arae/The Fates:

The Fates, Ancients who remained behind to ensure balance, made of pure eather, just *existed* for the longest time. Eventually, they took mortal form. They worried about what they couldn't predict and the unknown/unseen possibilities. But nothing worried them more than unbalanced Primal power. They wanted to have something in place in case a Primal needed to rise but there was no Primal of Life to Ascend them. Obviously, one foresaw what was to come, but none foretold that the very thing they created would bring about that which they tried to prevent.

Enter the Star diamond: a conduit powerful enough to briefly store and transfer embers both volatile and unpredictable in their raw and unsheltered state. It was unearthed from deep within the Undying Hills, and removing the diamond made the land uninhabitable. The Arae erupted half the mountain to find The Star, and the heated rock and gas irrevocably changed the landscape.

Created by the flames of dragons that used to inhabit the realm of the gods long before the Primals could shed joyous tears—which also present as diamonds—it was the first of its kind and known for its indestructible strength; irregular, jagged beauty; and silver sheen.

It's actually a petrified Ancient.

None but the Arae were supposed to know of its existence. While The Star has many uses, possibly the most important is the storage of embers for a transfer. But only an Arae or a Primal has the kind of power needed to force such a thing.

After the events surrounding Sotoria (detailed below), a Fate gave The Star to

Kolis, but it is unknown who or why. He used it to trap Eythos's soul and kept it at the top of a gilded cage made of the bones of the Ancients. Sera eventually rescues it, sets Eythos free, and then uses it to store Sotoria's soul.

Now, let us regress just a bit and speak a little more about the Primals, shall we?

Primal Gods/Goddesses:

Appearance: They look like mortals, but their preternatural appearances vary.

Abilities: Only ten Primals can tear open the realms. Some Primals can taste emotions. All Primals can shapeshift. They can be bonded to draken in their Courts and are thus able to call on them in times of need. Most draken see it as an honor, but some Primals force the bond—like Kolis. They have the ability to heal and can sense magic. They are able to gain access to memories during feeding. They can shadowstep, which is using eather to will themselves wherever they want to go. If in the mortal realm, a Primal's essence can affect the moods and minds of mortals and the environment. They can also power electricity.

Biology: Shadowstone won't kill them unless they have been weakened by love. The bones of the Ancients can put them into a years-long stasis if used to wound. It was always believed that Primals could not have children with mortals. They age like mortals until about twenty years in, then the process slows to a crawl. Primals can go quite some time without nourishment, but if they go too long, they become, well...*primal* and primitive. It takes a lot to scar their skin, and salt must be added immediately to make any ink stay. Primals are virtually endless. The minute they are born or Ascended, their essence begins to change them. They can light fires and move incredibly fast, but it's powered by will and not thought. Bone chains and cells *can* hold a weakened Primal. They will go into stasis if the body is overwhelmed and it needs to heal or recharge; if they do, roots grow and cover them for protection. When Primals fall in love, they develop a *graeca,* which is a word in the old language meaning love or life.

Governing: Each Primal rules a Court in Iliseeum with lesser gods who serve them (Attes and Kyn shared the Court of Vathi, however—more on the Courts later). Each Court is a territory within Iliseeum with enough land to allow the Primal and their gods to do as they see fit. Every Primal has enough power to do whatever they like, but some always want more, and there are always consequences for their actions. Primals cannot make demands of or touch the Fates; it is forbidden in order to keep the balance, though the Arae cannot see the fate of a risen Primal, either. Even speaking of going to war with the King of Gods would be to invite conflict and mean a sentence in the darkest parts of the Abyss. When the Primal of Death takes a soul, no other can touch it.

Habits/Mannerisms/Strengths/Weaknesses: Primals do not need blood unless severely weakened. They rarely, if ever, enter the mortal realm—some go more often than others but are aware of the consequences. It is not easy for a Primal to sense a *viktor*. Rest: for some, it's sleep; for others, it's like retirement. If they do not wish to go into stasis, they can choose to enter Arcadia, which prompts a god to be Ascended in order to take their place as the Primal. If they take their true form in anger, they become something else—a personification of the rage. Intense emotion can force physical shifts…thinning skin, causing eather to glow different colors, etcetera. Primals can see or sense what another is thinking/feeling during blood exchanges—some are more skilled at it than others. Primals cannot feel the presence of others as strongly while in the mortal realm. Using eather weakens them until they complete their Culling. Primals rarely die; if they do, it creates a ripple effect that can be felt across the realms. The only way to stop that is for the eather to go to someone who can withstand it.

During the time of Seraphena and Nyktos, these were the ruling Primals:

Nyktos: Primal God of Death, ruled the Shadowlands.
Kolis: False Primal God of Life, ruled Dalos.
Attes and Kyn: Brothers—twins. Primal Gods of War and Accord and Peace and Vengeance respectively, ruled Vathi.
Embris: Primal God of Wisdom, Loyalty, and Duty, ruled Lotho.
Maia: Primal Goddess of Love, Beauty, and Fertility, ruled Kithreia.
Keella: Primal Goddess of Rebirth, ruled the Thyia Plains.
Hanan: Primal God of Justice and the Divine Hunt, ruled Sirta.
Veses: Primal Goddess of Rites and Prosperity / a.k.a The Eternal Goddess, ruled the Callasta Isles.
Phanos: Primal God of Sea, Earth, Wind, and Sky, ruled the Triton Isles.

I mustn't leave out the other gods…

Gods:
Gods either serve a Primal of a Court or become a Primal themselves at some point. While still with a Primal, they cannot leave the Court they were born into without express consent of the ruling Primal. If they do so without being allowed, defection is punishable by death—the final kind.

During the time of Poppy and Casteel, these were the resting gods:

Aios: Goddess of Love, Fertility, and Beauty.
Bele: Goddess of the Hunt.
Ione: Goddess of Rebirth.
Lailah: Goddess of Peace and Vengeance.

Penellaphe: Goddess of Wisdom, Loyalty, and Duty.
Rhahar: The Eternal God.
Rhain: God of Common Men and Endings.
Saion: God of Sky and Soil / Earth, Wind, and Sky
Theon: God of Accord and War.

Appearance: They appear as mortals, but some have eather that glows in their eyes.

Abilities: Gods cannot shadowstep like Primals can. Only the strongest can hide their appearance from others. Mist and eather are extensions of their will. Some can use compulsion. Some can dig into the mind and read memories. Some can project thoughts. Powerful gods can detect magic. Few—but some—can shift forms. Some are able to gain access to memories during feeding like the Primals can. Only the eldest and strongest gods can power electricity.

Biology: Shadowstone to the brain or heart will kill them, but if they're stabbed elsewhere, and the blade isn't removed, it can paralyze them. If they are even nicked with the bones of the Ancients, it means instant death. All gods need to feed, but feeding from a mortal does the same for them as taking from another god. Gods can go long periods without food, but it will eventually devolve them. The Culling brings them into maturity, slowing the aging process and intensifying the eather within them. Their blood is a glimmering bluish red.

Habits/Mannerisms/Strengths/Weaknesses: Seeing a god in the mortal realm is not unusual—they get bored or are there to carry out their Primal's business. When gods kill mortals, they usually leave the bodies as warnings. Gods find mortals fascinating.

Related: Deities are the third-generation descendants of Primals or the children of gods beyond that. Godlings are the offspring of mortals and gods. Elemental Atlantians are the closest and *purest* descendants of the deities. Many believe that changelings—like me—are the resulting offspring of a wolven and deity pairing, though there is room for argument there. Perhaps it's just having those bloodlines somewhere in the ancestry.

And those are just *some* of the bloodlines descended from the gods. What about the others that came about then? Since the draken resulted from a partnership between a Primal and the dragons, I propose we begin there.

Draken:
A very long time ago, dragons existed in both realms—even before the Primals and gods in the time of the Ancients. When the Primals and gods came to

be, Eythos befriended the dragons. He wanted to learn their stories and histories, so, being powerful, young, and impulsive, he offered to give them mortal form so they could communicate. Some agreed to the dual life—the first being Nektas—and those descended from the first became known as the draken. Nektas and Eythos then went on to create mortals.

Here is some more information about the draken…

Appearance: They look mortal in their god forms—outside of fine ridges on their skin that resemble scales. These scales appear on different places of the body at different times depending on how close they are to shifting. Other times, the draken look like dragons: spiked tail, horns, wings, frills around the head, eyes with vertical pupils, and scales that feel like leather. All draken's eyes were a brilliant sapphire blue until Kolis shifted the balance. After, they turned blood-red. Once Sera came into her power, they turned blue again.

Abilities: They know when the Primal they are close to has been wounded and can always sense the Primals. Draken are immune to the changes a Primal's essence forces upon those around them. They can gravely wound the Primals but cannot kill them. Like the Primals, draken are virtually unending. Their fire burns through anything.

Biology: They have acute senses. Draken spend the first six months of their lives in mortal form, and then shift, typically remaining in their draken forms for the first several years—the shape they're most comfortable in. They mature like a god for the first eighteen to twenty years, then hit a growth spurt in their draken form. They compare shifting to shedding too-tight clothing. Reproduction is complicated, and centuries can pass without a fledgling being born.

Habits/Mannerisms/Strengths/Weaknesses: In their teens and early twenties, they can be killed by a blow to the head or heart, just like a god. Many draken lost their lives when Kolis falsely became the Primal of Life. Draken are not always entirely aware of their surroundings, often leading to furnishings and those around them getting knocked about—though I often wonder if they *do* know and simply choose to seem oblivious. For most, bonding to a Primal is a choice and a point of pride. The bonds don't automatically transfer—when their Primal dies or goes to Arcadia, the bond is severed. Draken are forbidden from attacking a Primal but not members of their Court. Hunters by nature, they will eat just about anything—including gods and mortals. Bone chains have no effect on them. Only draken—and those who have Ascended—can enter the Vale. Their young can sleep through anything—even a war.

Culture: Draken do not have ceremonies for their dead as they know they've moved on. When possible, one close to the deceased burns the body within hours of the death, and each mourns as they see fit. Mating is very much like mortal marriage but isn't entered into lightly, as the bond can only be broken by death.

So, what about the wolven, our other dual-natured?

Wolven:

Kiyou wolves were wild, fierce, and loyal to their packs but driven by instinct, survival, and pack mentality. Everything was a challenge for them, and many didn't survive very long. The kiyou were on the brink of extinction when a Primal—most believe it to be Nyktos—appeared before the last great pack and asked if they'd protect the gods' children in the mortal realm. In return, the Primal offered them human form so they could communicate with the deities and have long lifespans. He asked—didn't demand—and it was not an agreement of servitude but rather a partnership. Some kiyou refused as they didn't trust the Primal, and still others simply wanted to stay as they were.

Once they were of two worlds, they formed bonds with the deities. Those bonds were instinctive and passed down through the generations. Eventually, however, Elemental Atlantians began outnumbering the gods' children, and the ties eventually shifted to them. The wolven numbers were severely impacted during the War of Two Kings, which is why they are so adamant about regaining land now.

Not all Elemental Atlantians or wolven are bonded. For those who are, while they cannot read each other's minds, the bond allows them to sense one another's emotions. If an Atlantian is wounded significantly, they can draw on their bonded wolven for strength. If one of them dies, the other is weakened but will survive. The Joining changes those things slightly, heightening all (see more below). Given the reasons behind the partnership in the first place, the bond means the wolven must obey and protect the Atlantian(s) in all things, even if it means the wolven's death—nothing supersedes the bond. While Atlantians are not required to give their lives for their wolven, most bonded would.

What else can I tell you about the wolven?

Appearance: They look like oversized wolves in their true form and run hotter than normal.

Abilities and Biology: Wolven can heal fast, thanks to quickly replenishing blood. They have extended lifespans—some have even lived as long as I have. Only wolven have keener senses than the Atlantians. They are vulnerable to any wound to the heart or head. Wolven can sense unrest, vamprys, and Primal emotion.

Culture: Scars are revered and never hidden within their culture. Public displays of affection are commonplace.

Habits/Mannerisms/Strengths/Weaknesses: They will do anything to protect their homes and families. Wolven have their own language. Most find clothing cumbersome. Gods hold a special place in their hearts since one made them of two worlds, which is why they feel honored to be in the presence of a child of the gods. No wolven has ever ruled—their pack instinct is too strong.

The Joining: It's an old tradition, not done much anymore, when a bonded pair extends the bond to the Atlantian's partner, thus making the wolven duty-bound to both Atlantians and tying all their lives together. It requires an exchange of blood by all parties. The ritual can become very intimate and include sex, but it does not have to. It is not to be entered into lightly, as the blood bond goes all ways. If one dies, the others die, as well. It doesn't work with mortals—all parties must have at least some Atlantian blood. The ritual must be done in nature with all participants naked. Vows are spoken, and blood is exchanged—the strongest of the party drinks first from the others, then they drink from each other; lastly, they drink from the strongest. An Atlantian blade is used to mark the center of the chest near the heart for those without fangs needing to draw blood. The blood is taken from the wolven's throat as it is a conduit of sorts, a bridge to link the lifespans, and then blood is drawn simultaneously from the strongest partner to ensure they hold the lifespans of the others and become the base.

Other: It takes many decades to raise a wolven; therefore, it's normal for siblings to be born decades apart. It takes wolven at least two decades to gain control of their forms. Young wolven are very accident-prone in their alternate forms, and if injured, they must shift as soon as possible to avoid permanent damage. At a wolven wedding, only the wolven can dance around the fire—or their *Liessa*. Wolven are relatively healthy, but a few diseases *can* fell them—the wasting disease that took Elashya and her grandmother, for one.

Now, let's delve a little bit more into what Kolis did to Eythos and what the consequences were…

The Shifting of Fates:
The story begins with a mortal named Sotoria…

Kolis, the then Primal of Death, used to enter the mortal realm. Those who saw him cowered and refused to look him in the eye. On one trip, he saw a beautiful young woman picking flowers for her sister's wedding. That woman was Sotoria.

Kolis watched her and immediately fell in love. He was utterly besotted with her and eventually stepped out of the trees to speak with her. Sotoria knew who he was—back then, mortals knew what the Primal of Death looked like since his features were captured in paintings and sculpture. She fled, and the chase ended in her falling from the cliffs.

Despite dying young and much too soon, she accepted her fate, and her soul arrived in the Shadowlands, passing through the Pillars of Asphodel and entering the Vale within minutes of her passing. She did not linger. She was at peace with starting the next stage of her life.

Decades after her death, Kolis remained obsessed with bringing her back and being with her. Eythos, the then Primal of Life, warned him that he shouldn't pursue it, but he didn't listen, and knowing the Primal God of Life had the power to do what he wanted done, Kolis found a way.

Only he and Eythos know *exactly* how he managed to do it. One will never speak of it, and the other isn't here to tell. We do know that it involved the Star diamond. Kolis was successful in trading places and destinies with his twin. The act had catastrophic fallout, though, killing hundreds of gods who served both Courts and weakening many other Primals—even killing a few, thus forcing the next in line to rise from godhood to Primal power. Many draken were also killed, and the mortal realm suffered devastating earthquakes and tsunamis. Many places were leveled, and pieces of land just broke off, some forming islands while others sank.

Eythos warned Kolis not to bring Sotoria back, saying she was at peace, and it had been too long. He said if Kolis were to do what he planned, she would not come back as she was. It would be an unnatural act and upset the already unsteady balance of life and death. Still, Sotoria rose, and as predicted, she was not the same. She wasn't grateful that Kolis brought her back; she was frightened, unhappy, and horrified by what had been done to her.

Kolis couldn't understand why she was so morose, and nothing he did made her love him. No one knows how long she lived the second time, but she eventually died again. Some say she purposefully starved herself. Others think she might have started living again and fought her captor, despite his power.

Callum says Eythos killed her that second time.

I have yet to see more that confirms one way or another.

During the time of that second death, Eythos did something to ensure his brother could never reach her—something only the Primal of Death could do. With the aid of Keella, the Primal Goddess of Rebirth, he marked Sotoria's soul, which meant she was destined to be reborn and would never pass the Pillars. Her soul would continually come back, over and over, though her memories of her previous lives wouldn't be anything of substance—if she retained any at all.

Because of what Eythos and Keella did by marking her soul, Sotoria would be reborn in a shroud (as you know both Poppy and Sera were, the most Chosen of the Chosen). Kolis knew this and continued looking for her in the mortal realm. Even entombed, he searched, using his power to extend his will. What Eythos and Keella did wasn't perfect, and some might argue it was worse than what Kolis did, but it was the only thing they could think to do to keep her safe.

Both Eythos and Keella paid dearly for what they did. Kolis grew to despise his twin and vowed to make him pay, eventually killing Mycella—Eythos's Consort—while she was pregnant. He did it because he believed it was only fair that his brother should lose his love just as he had. He also destroyed Mycella's soul, bringing about her final death.

Losing her destroyed a piece of Eythos.

Kolis also annihilated all records of the truth—both in the mortal realm and in Iliseeum. That was the start of the Primal God of Death no longer being depicted in any artwork or literature. Kolis went to great extremes to hide that he wasn't supposed to be the Primal of Life, even when it became apparent that something was wrong with the balance of power. He started to lose the ability to create life and maintain it. The destiny was never meant to be his, just as the powers of the Primal God of Death were never meant to be Eythos's.

It took centuries for the powers to wane, and by that time, Eythos was dead—killed and captured in the Star diamond by his twin—and Kolis had mastered *other* powers, creating the Ascended and Revenants as a way to prove he could still create *life*.

The fallout of what was done was far-reaching. Despite Ash being born into the role of the Primal of Death, what his uncle did reshaped his destiny and caused the balance to shift even more toward death—the end of everything in both realms. And while it should have taken several mortal lifetimes for the destruction to be absolute, it had already started. Two Primals of Death were not meant to rule, and that was exactly what happened because, at his core, Kolis *was* the Primal of Death, not the Primal of Life.

Before his death, Eythos took it upon himself to give Nyktos and the others a chance for salvation. He placed an ember of life in the mortal Mierel bloodline, as well as the flicker of power that had been passed on to Nyktos at the time of his birth. Once done, he just hoped for the best. Still, the unbalance of power progressed in its destruction and caused the Rot, continuing and intensifying when Sera was born because it put the embers in a vulnerable vessel with an expiration date for efficacy.

The bits between Sera realizing that she was the true Primal of Life, Sotoria's soul being placed in the Star diamond, and Penellaphe Balfour being born are a bit hazy, but I gain additional information all the time and will continue updating my files as I am able. What we do know is that Poppy is finally aware that she is descended from Sera and Nyktos and is thus the Primal of both Life *and* Death. And we can suppose that Sotoria's soul will come back into play as Isbeth has awakened Kolis—I mean, have you *seen* pictures of Poppy and Sotoria? There is definitely an uncanny resemblance there. Regardless, things are about to get very interesting for us all.

Forgive me for jumping back there and then surging forward again. I'll try to get the story's timeline a bit more on track linearly.

Where were we? Ah, maybe we should tackle the Ascension. Ascension in the time of the gods meant something entirely different than it does in our time.

Ascension:

Originally, the act of Ascension required the blood of a mortal to be drained from their body and then replaced with a god's or Primal's blood. The mortal completing the Ascension was not always guaranteed, however (more on that later). Those Chosen in the time of the gods were born in a caul and always carried some Primal essence within them, which allowed them to Ascend.

The Rite existed then and was an honored tradition. The Chosen—third sons and daughters—crossed into Iliseeum to serve the gods. They were then given a choice of whether to Ascend and become immortal or not. That all changed when the power shift in Iliseeum happened. Kolis took away the Chosen's free will and brought them to Iliseeum to be treated as objects—used, traded, toyed with, and ultimately tossed aside. If they were *Ascended*, it wasn't like it should be. Either Kolis used the blood of the gods in his Court to transition them, making them what we know now as the vamprys—dark-dwelling near-immortals with an insatiable thirst for blood; or his twisted essence coupled with their mortal death made them into something not alive or dead, turning them into what we know to be Revenants.

In more recent times, the Rite became something very different. The vamprys needed a food source, one that wouldn't be questioned, so they convinced the mortals to hand over their children to *honor the gods*. They even created an entire religion around it, forcing families to turn on each other if one refused to relinquish their children.

During the Rite, the Ascended take the third sons and daughters to feed upon. If they don't drain them dry and kill them, they become Craven—though most are dead before they even learn to speak. All second sons and daughters are used to make more Ascended—this is different than the time of the gods, when the third sons and daughters were those Chosen to Ascend. However, the dirty little secret there for the vamprys is that Atlantian blood is required to complete an Ascension; therefore, the Ascended always have an Atlantian held as a prisoner to use for bloodletting.

All history of the Atlantians was erased within Solis, and the Ascended don't tell people that it is absolutely possible to survive outside the Rise. A crucial part of their control is to create a rift between the mortals who have and those who don't, causing the poor to turn their hatred on the wealthy and never the Ascended. They believe the Ascended are their direct access to the sleeping gods and thus an answer to their prayers, therefore above reproach.

Let's take a closer look at how Ascension ultimately became the start of the vamprys…

The First Ascension After the Time of the Gods:

Atlantian King Malec O'Meer fell in love with a mortal woman named Isbeth. When she was mortally wounded, Malec committed the forbidden act of Ascension in a bid to save her. He drank from her, stopping only when he felt her heart begin to fail, then shared his blood with her. While this should have created the first vampry, it ultimately turned her into a demis because Malec was much more than a King, and Isbeth wasn't a third daughter. Malec was a god, and gods cannot Ascend mortals—in the traditional sense of the word.

After Isbeth's Ascension, King Malec lifted the Ascension ban, and many others followed suit, making the first vamprys. As more were created, many were unable to control their bloodlust, thus creating the pestilence known as the Craven and decimating mortal populations. The Craven are created when a vampry feeds on a mortal to the brink of death—or *to* death—but does not complete the process. Originally, this was thought to be the result of them not feeding the mortal *their* blood, but we have since come to understand that it's the magical missing piece: the Atlantian blood—blood with the essence of the gods.

After Malec was exiled and subsequently entombed, Queen Eloana forbade Ascension again and ordered the destruction of all Ascended to protect mortalkind, ushering in disharmony between Solis and Atlantia. The Ascended in Solis revolted, thus starting the War of Two Kings and changing history. As I mentioned, Solis's recorded history is very different from the Atlantians' recorded history, and is full of lies, misleading details, and half-truths.

There are different kinds of *Ascension.*

God and Mortal

If a god Ascends a mortal, especially one who is not a third son or daughter, they do not create another god—a god can only be born—they instead create a demis. Which is why it was always forbidden. Demis are things that should never be: beings with godlike powers who were never meant to carry such gifts and burdens. They are abominations.

God and Godling

If a god Ascends a godling, it results in a godling who lives. Most godlings cannot handle the Culling process because their bodies are still mortal. A godling must drink from a god during their Culling to survive. It's not entirely clear if that is a full act of Ascension or just them drinking as a way to help the healing. If they do not receive the immortal blood, the eather will ultimately kill their mortal bodies—the Culling happens around ages eighteen to twenty-one.

Elemental Atlantian/God not yet through their Culling

This is Poppy's situation—or at least *part* of it. She is an entirely different amalgamation of building blocks.

Atlantian/Mortal
If an Atlantian Ascends a mortal, they become a vampry. It's the same as an Ascended Ascending a mortal, as Atlantian blood is required to facilitate the change.

Vampry/Mortal
If a vampry Ascends a mortal, they become an Ascended—a vampry—as long as they have access to Atlantian blood to complete the change. If they do not have Atlantian blood, the mortal becomes a Craven.

Primal not yet through their Culling/God
This is the case with Sera and Bele. Sera Ascended Bele, but she did not become a Primal. She received the Primal silver eyes and power boost, but she did not register as a full Primal. She could, however, challenge the Primal for authority of the Court, and become a waiting vessel for the Primal power should it need a place to go—which it did when Ash killed Hanan.

As I alluded to above, some one-off creations don't entirely fit the mold of standard history. Still, it merits recording them here for posterity's sake.

I mentioned them earlier, but let's take a look at Revenants…

Revenants:
A Revenant, like a demis, is an abomination and something that should not be. It was Kolis's experiment and crowning achievement, and he used his Primal magic to create them. It then became a pastime of Isbeth's after Callum shared the process with her. For most Revenants—Callum and Millie aside—it takes a third child of two mortals, one who carries a non-dormant ember within them, death, and the blood of a god, King, or someone destined to become King. But not all third children have the trait that allows the transformation, and as we see with Callum and Millie, with the right set of circumstances, a first or second child can become a Revenant, though they are not quite the same as the others.

Kolis says the differences in Callum were due to intent and motivation. I think that may be true, combined with the power and circumstances of the building blocks used to create them. I'm sure we'll find out more at some point.

After the Chosen become Revenants, they are no longer mortal. They have no soul. And they are completely impervious to illness or injury—including things inflicted by god power. They also don't need to eat food or drink blood, nor do they need other comforts. They exist to please their creator.

The only way they can be killed is by the ingestion of draken blood, though it only takes a drop.

Now let's review the Gyrms…

Gyrms:

Gyrms are beings created with Iliseeum soil and eather, which can be found in the blood of a god or the bones of a deity. There are different kinds of Gyrms. The Hunters and Seekers are mortals who summon a god in exchange for receiving their greatest desire. In reciprocity, they offer themselves to the god in eternal servitude. Once they die, they become a Gyrm, and their mouths are stitched shut to keep them loyal to the god or Primal they pledged themselves to. The Priests are considered Gyrms. If a Hunter or Seeker is destroyed and turned to ash, they go to the Abyss.

The Sentinels enter servitude by dying and refusing to pass the Pillars of Asphodel to have their souls judged. In lieu of possibly being sentenced to the Abyss, they become a Gyrm as a way of atoning for their sins. They serve for a set period of time and are more *mortal* than the Hunters or Seekers, retaining the ability to think. If *they* are turned to ash, they can either go back to the god they serve to continue their servitude or choose to go to the Abyss.

There are a few more things I'd like to go over here, but they are sort of out of context, so forgive me.

Dakkais

First, the dakkais. Dakkais were pets of the Court of Dalos. It's unknown if any other Primals used them, but Kolis was fond of deploying them. They are a race of vicious, flesh-eating creatures rumored to have been birthed from some bottomless pit somewhere in Iliseeum. They are the size of horses and heavily muscled and trained like bloodhounds to sense and track eather. A wound to the head can kill them, and when they die, they turn to ash just like the Gyrms do.

Last, but most certainly not least, the *viktors*...

Viktors

Viktors are born with a goal: to guard someone the Fates believe is destined to bring about significant change or serve great purpose—even mortals who are bound to do terrible things can have *viktors*. Some aren't aware of their duty and just come upon their charges in the right place at the right time, the Fates bringing them together. Others *are* aware and become ingrained in the lives of the ones they are sent to protect. It is believed there is only ever one *viktor* per individual to be safeguarded, but we know that's not entirely true as Poppy had both Leopold and Vikter—though at different times. *Viktors* cannot reveal themselves or their reasons for being where they are.

They are mostly mortal because they live and serve like mortals. However, their souls return to Mount Lotho—where the Arae reside—when they die. Upon recycling and returning for their next assignment, they do not remember their past lives. Each time they return to Mount Lotho, though, they do remember. However, some are predestined to figure out what they are and who they were sent to protect even after they return to the mortal realm, and some—like Vikter Ward/ Wardwell—remember everything.

Okay, I think that is a good compilation of data on the evolution of the Land of the Gods and the mortal realm. As I mentioned, this is ever-changing, but I always try to record things as I can to keep a record of what has happened and the consequences. I may not be an official historian, but I am good for more than just a sexy diary entry—though if you ask Poppy, Cas, or anyone else who has read (and enjoyed) them, they may disagree.

BLOOD AND ASH CHARACTERS

In this section, you will find information on individuals of note in the time of Solis and Atlantia following the War of Two Kings. Everything I have witnessed or *seen* is captured for the most part; documented in such a way that one can refer to an individual's dossier and find pertinent details and a timeline of events they were involved in. This is helpful as pulling specific happenings out for each player sometimes brings to light things that didn't make as much sense previously.

It should be noted, however, that I may have eliminated or combined some things I deemed as low priority, or included things the person using these files may not particularly care about. Regardless, the broader happenings are the important historical facts, and none of the additional things I captured—or didn't—will change that.

In addition, some individuals have history in both the time of the gods and after the formation of Solis and Atlantia. Therefore, you may find some of them in the FLESH AND FIRE compilation of files if you are looking for them and unable to locate what you need.

PENELLAPHE BALFOUR OF CASTLE TEERMAN
The Primal of Life and Death / Blood and Bone
Married name: Queen Penellaphe "Poppy" Da'Neer

Oh, what can I say about dear Poppy? Barely an adult, yet poised to change the kingdoms forever. She has featured prominently in my visions for some time, but her future, more than most, is mutable.

Hair: The color of ruby-hued wine and falls to the middle of her back.
Eyes: Green like spring grass—turn molten silver after her Culling.
Body type: Slightly shorter than average height and voluptuously curvy.
Facial features: Oval face with angular cheekbones. Full, bow-shaped lips the color of berries. Strong brow. Nose dips at the bridge and slightly turns up at the tip.
Distinguishing features: Some freckles across her nose to her eyes. Pronounced scar that is a jagged streak of pale pink starting at the hairline and slicing across her temple, narrowly missing her left eye before ending at her nose. She has another, shorter scar running across her forehead and through her eyebrow and a scar on her inner thigh, multiple on her right forearm, and some on her stomach—jagged tears. More scars mar her legs—a prominent one on her inner knee—and there's one on the side of her waist. The healed wound on her thigh is from a Craven bite, not claws.
Other: Her paramour thinks she tastes like honeydew.
Personality: Smart-mouthed, brave. Terrible liar. Kind. Revels in revenge. Not one to wallow in past choices. Impulsive. Reckless with her safety. Stubborn. Competitive. Deflects a lot.
Habits/Mannerisms/Strengths/Weaknesses: Wrinkles her nose when thinking something she doesn't want to share. Regularly sneaks out at night. Wears a wolven-bone and bloodstone dagger strapped to her thigh. Suffers from nightmares but usually unable to sleep once the sun is up. Rarely sick and heals fast. Gets seasick. Hates snakes.
Background: Born on an unknown date in April, she chose the twentieth day as her birthday. Was attacked by Craven when she was six, almost killing her and purportedly killing her parents. The Queen of Solis took her in after the attack and cared for her as if she were her own child, telling her that she survived because she had been touched by the gods. Forced to don the veil of the Maiden at age eight.
Family: Initially raised by Coralena † (a Handmaiden, thought to be a Revenant) and Leopold † (a *viktor*). She is actually the biological daughter of Queen Isbeth † (a demis) and Ires (a god) and descended from Nyktos (a Primal of Death) and his Consort, Seraphena Mierel (the *true* Primal of Life).

What emotions taste/feel like to her:
AMUSEMENT = sugary

ANGER = hot and acidic but can be icy
ANGUISH = tart and tangy, sometimes almost bitter
APPROVAL = buttery cake
ATTRACTION and AROUSAL = spicy and smoky
CONCERN = too-thick cream
CONDESCENSION = scalds throat and stings eyes
CONFLICT = tart and lemony
CONFUSION = tart and lemony
CONTRITION = vanilla
CURIOSITY = spring-fresh lemon
DESIRE = spicy and smoky
DESPERATION = burns
DETERMINATION = salty and nutty, sometimes oaky like whiskey
DISLIKE = sour
DISTRUST = bitter
EMBARRASSMENT = very sweet
EMPATHY = warm
EXCITEMENT = bubbly water or champagne
EXHAUSTION = gritty
FEAR = acrid like bitter melon
FRUSTRATION = prickly
FURY = hot and acidic but can be icy
GUILT = sour
HATRED = hot and acidic but can be icy
HELPLESSNESS = bitter, similar to anguish or like hot, choking smoke
HORROR = bitter
IRRITATION = acidic
LOVE = chocolate and berries
LUST = spicy, smoky, and warm
PAIN = physical feels hot, emotional feels cold
PANIC = bitter
PRIDE = like empathy but richer and warmer cinnamon
RAGE = hot and acidic, can be icy
RELIEF = earthy, woodsy, and refreshing
RESOLVE = salty and nutty
SADNESS = tart and tangy
SHAME = sour and itchy/confining
SHOCK = icy, cool, and slippery
SINCERITY = warm and comforting vanilla
SORROW = heavy and bitter
STRESS = like too-thick, heavy cream
SURPRISE = cool
TERROR = feels similar to pain

UNCERTAINTY/UNEASE = tart and lemony but biting at times
WONDER = bubbly and sugary
WORRY = too-thick cream

This extraordinary woman with a weakness for cheese and strawberries started her life as a sheltered and sequestered Maiden. The title meant she was supposedly Chosen by the gods and was thus hidden behind a veil while merely a child, bound to rules that gave her no say in matters of her life. Until she meets Hawke Flynn, a.k.a Prince Casteel "Cas" Hawkethrone Da'Neer.

Once he enters her life, eventually sparking a love she fears will never be reciprocated, she vows never to hide herself again—even when she's more afraid of herself than anything.

With everything she has ever been taught or believed unraveling as a series of sinister lies, her powers growing, the love between her and Cas getting stronger by the day, and the truths of her heritage coming to light in pieces at every turn, Poppy learns to compartmentalize, process, and accept in record time. But she still struggles with the big truths—that Isbeth, a demis, is her mother, and that she—Poppy—is a god, a Primal born of mortal flesh, the Primal of Blood and Bone, and the *true* Primal of Life *and* Death.

Her journey has been harrowing, to say the least, and I've recorded as much as I can—both things that have come to pass and those I've *seen* via my gift. The bottom line, however? Her future, only some of which was foretold, is still very much hers to write...

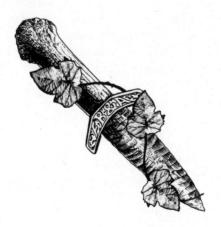

POPPY'S JOURNEY TO DATE:
Born of the demis, Isbeth, and the god, Ires, Penellaphe is raised by Revenant Handmaiden Coralena Balfour and her *viktor* husband, Leopold.

Cora and Leo attempt to flee with Poppy—only age six at the time—and her *brother*, Ian—Cora and Leo's biological son—to remove them from Isbeth's influence, stopping at an inn in Lockswood for the night. While there, a supposed *friend*, a wolven by the name of Alastir Davenwell, believing Poppy to be a threat to Atlantia, betrays them, paving the way for Prince Malik Elian Da'Neer to destroy her. The Dark One considers her the harbinger of death and destruction set to lay waste to both kingdoms as the prophecy foretold. But when Malik sees the Consort—Poppy's ancestor, Seraphena—in her eyes, he hesitates to kill her, already struggling with the idea of taking a child's life. He eventually returns her to Carsodonia, but before then, given the deaths at the inn, the Craven follow the blood trail and eventually attack, causing even more destruction.

Unlike most who suffer a cursed turning or death after being bitten, Poppy survives the Craven attack at the inn, lending credence to the story she is told about being Chosen by the gods. The truth there is that Atlantians cannot be turned if bitten. And she is so much more than that. She is a god. A Primal. Though that is something she does not discover for a while.

For the majority of her life, Poppy believes the Craven killed her parents in Lockswood that night. Which actually isn't true. Isbeth killed Cora sometime later by forcing her to drink draken blood, and Leo was likely sent to Mount Lotho to await his *viktor* rebirth.

However, now orphaned and returned to the capital, the Queen eventually sends Penellaphe to Castle Teerman, where they shroud her under the veil of the Maiden and sequester her, awaiting her nineteenth birthday and the first Ascension since the War of Two Kings—something she is told will heal the Kingdom of Solis. All of that is also a lie. And even more unfortunate, during her time in Masadonia, Poppy is subjected to the tyrannical rule and cruel abuse of Duke Dorian Teerman as his wife, Duchess Jacinda, turns a blind eye.

Afraid of her Ascension and deeply craving freedom and the right to choose, Poppy secretly hopes she'll be found unworthy by the gods.

With her only outlets being honing her fighting skills and sneaking out to help her trainer and friend, Vikter—also a *viktor*—assist in the passing of the cursed by using her gifts and thinking happy memories to ease their suffering, she longs for something more.

Not long before her Ascension, Poppy sneaks out to the Red Pearl—a house of ill-repute—to experience life for a few hours. And, with the help of yours truly in the disguise of a working lady at the pub—I never said I didn't interfere!—finds herself in the rooms of Elemental Atlantian Prince Casteel Hawkethrone Da'Neer, who is posing as "Hawke" at the time. They kiss, and things for the couple are set in motion…both those of the Fates and the plans Prince Casteel has.

Still posing as Hawke, Cas insinuates himself as a guard at the castle and eventually works his way into the inner circle to be one of Poppy's personal guards.

That was something I found incredibly clever. Though when I foresaw it happening, I still wondered about his motives.

Poppy begins to question the natural order of things as time passes and wonders if she can change them, especially as her gifts continue to grow and evolve. Originally, it was only sensing the pain of others, but that quickly morphed into being able to sense all emotions by tasting their unique signatures on her tongue, and an ability to ease others as she does with the cursed. Given that empathy is one of her greatest traits, she hopes to one day use her gifts to help people.

From the moment she entered my radar, I admired that.

When she leaves Masadonia for Carsodonia, accompanied by Hawke, Kieran—whom she discovers is a wolven—and their other allies, an entire world opens to her. She sees and experiences things she's never had a chance to before and decides she won't return to a life with no freedom. She vows not to Ascend, realizing her two choices are to run or to talk to the Queen. But danger surrounds her, and *so* many things are not as they seem.

She soon learns the true history of Solis and the reality regarding the vampry and the Atlantians, and it shakes her, but she's made of stronger stuff. Still, those who see her as the enemy do not relent, and she's eventually wounded to near the point of death. She may have died if not for Hawke's Atlantian blood and its healing properties. But amidst the excitement of the attack and the subsequent fallout, a big secret is revealed: Hawke is really the Prince of Atlantia, whom she has been brought up to believe is the Dark One.

Cue gasps. I mean, I knew this, but can you imagine what it was like for her to discover that little tidbit?

Conflicted and torn between her feelings of betrayal and what she feels for Hawke, whom she now knows is a Prince, Poppy decides to make a run for it. However, she doesn't get far, and her lust ultimately wins out in the end—I mean, doesn't it usually? But even with that and realizing she loves him, she knows she cannot trust him—or at least she shouldn't. And his dark side, while exciting and something that calls to her need for vengeance and meshes with her propensity to kill without hesitation at times, is a bit disturbing.

As I've said before, someone's shadow self is not the be-all, end-all of whether a person is good or not. It's who they are in their hearts and souls that determines whether they can be trusted.

When it's revealed that she's not entirely mortal and Casteel tells her that they are headed to Atlantia to be married, she refuses. She firmly believes that she's not safe with him and his people and has no doubt she'll eventually be ransomed. So, she makes a plan to escape and find her brother. If what she's been told about the Ascended is true, then Ian may be a monster, which means she'll have to kill him. But she won't know until she finds him.

Once again, she doesn't get far. Casteel and Kieran stop her, and Cas gives her an ultimatum: *Fight me and win, and I'll set you free.* Unfortunately, before she can do more than make Casteel bleed, the Craven attack.

With the dastardly creatures taken care of, they settle in for the night, and Casteel reveals more information. The Ascended had no intention of following through with Poppy's Ascension. It would taint her coveted blood, which they need for their nefarious plans. And Ian most likely is not her biological brother. He also tells her what the Ascended did to him, a story that horrifies her, and explains his motivations for wanting to marry her: to prevent war, save *his* brother, Malik, and solve scarcity issues regarding food and land for his people, while allowing her to be free. Win-win. She realizes that his plan has merit and is likely the safest course of action. Plus, there's that little matter of her attraction to him. We must not forget that.

When Alastir—whom she only knows as a trusted wolven ally—shares information about his daughter and assures her he'll help in whatever way he can if she feels she's being forced, her comfort level rises. But when she learns that Casteel is to become King, she wonders if she's really important to him despite everything that's happened or if she's just another pawn in the long game.

Doubts swirling, her gifts and senses continue to grow and heighten. She begins feeling shocks when she touches both Kieran and Casteel. In discussing the different Atlantian bloodlines, Cas reveals that he believes Poppy is descended from the Empath warrior line, and Alastir imparts later that they were sometimes called Soul Eaters.

When the Ascended finally track her down and attack, taking a child hostage, she surrenders herself to save the innocents and asks to be taken to her Queen. Lord Chaney has other plans, however. He confirms that she has Atlantian blood and attacks, full of bloodlust. Luckily, Casteel comes to the rescue and gives her his blood again to help her heal. The closeness and his essence in her help their relationship grow, and Cas finally asks her to pretend. *I'm Hawke, and you're Poppy. No past, no future.*

She does, giving herself to him and reveling in it.

As their journey to Casteel's home continues, despite the danger and hardships, Poppy soaks in all she can about Atlantian culture and the pasts of those she's coming to care about. She learns about Kieran's bond with Casteel and that he once loved and lost, as well as about Casteel's brother Malik, and Shea. And then she finds out about the Joining from Alastir.

When they reach Spessa's End, Poppy meets even more of those close to Casteel and Kieran and displays her burgeoning powers by healing Beckett—a young wolven—after an accident.

While she still wonders if Cas will cast her aside once he's accomplished what he wants, she realizes she's done denying herself and gives herself to Casteel once more without reservation. He's the first thing she has chosen for herself, and she's unwilling to let that go. However, while she loves him, that doesn't mean he loves *her.*

They go through with the wedding and seemingly receive Nyktos's blessing on the union, but Poppy wonders if it's more of an omen.

It's revealed that Poppy is related to the Queen, and that Ileana isn't actually Ascended—something that explains some things Poppy always wondered about. And during another fight, Poppy's gifts morph further, allowing her to project overwhelming fear to assist in victory, somehow also calling to the wolven without meaning to while in distress.

I wouldn't mind a wolven coming to me. But I guarantee there would be no distress involved.

As they deal with continued threats, more signs of the gods' acceptance appear—Nyktos's blessing at the wedding, Aios saving Poppy from walking off a cliff, the voices in her dreams with advice and warnings—Casteel tells her that he thinks they like her. But that doesn't mean everyone does. A bunch of the citizens of Atlantia attack, attempting to stone her, insisting that she's a Soul Eater and has tainted both the Prince and the kingdom. Poppy's gifts flare to life once more in defense, reflecting their hatred back on them threefold, killing them all in the process. And where her blood falls…blood trees appear, a sign of her connection to the gods.

As if there was any doubt.

The attack also strengthens her tether to the wolven, summoning them en masse once more and urging them to protect her. When the Queen and King arrive, Queen Eloana reveals that Poppy is the last descendant of the most ancient ones and carries the blood of Nyktos within her. She then relinquishes her crown and declares that Poppy is Atlantia's new Queen.

With the wolven continuing to act out of character, Poppy is told that she severed their bonds to their Atlantians without meaning to and that they feel her Primal *notam*. She remembers Kieran telling her about the kiyou wolves and how deity blood would usurp any claim to the throne an Atlantian may have. Is she a deity?

The hum in her blood from her magic ramps up, and Cas reveals that she has started to glow when she uses her power. Not a lot, but like spun silver. She then learns about the eather—the Primal essence of the gods.

Additional threats surface, and the Unseen attack, taking her prisoner. During the battle, she hears the voice of who she believes is the silver-haired goddess from her dreams and sees skeletal hands emerging from the earth.

While in the dungeon, she's reunited with an old acquaintance—Commander Jansen—learns about shadowshade and the bones of the Ancients, and sees a rare changeling who can take the form of another person. She also learns that Alastir betrayed her, and that Beckett, the wolven she healed, is dead. It makes her sad. In addition, she's made aware of the gods and deities, the Shadowlands, and Iliseeum as a whole. She also learns that all entombed where she's being kept were deities that became monsters because the Elemental Atlantians rose against them. Those holding her insist that she's dangerous and must be stopped because she has entered her Culling and will start showing the same chaotic tendencies as those before her.

And then she finds out about Malec, and Alastir tells her that O'Meer is her father. She also hears the prophecy for the first time, is told that *she* is the one her namesake warned about, and realizes that Alastir was behind the attack at Lockswood when she was a child.

So much to take in, in such a short time.

When Alastir tells her that he'd rather go to war than have her unleashed on his people and spirits her away to Irelone to be given to the Ascended, she worries it's the end. But Valyn, Casteel, Kieran, Jasper, Delano, Emil, and Naill come to save her.

During the battle following her rescue, she opens her senses and unleashes her power, prepared to end everyone, but stops herself at the last minute, insisting she's not a monster. But she does stop Casteel from delivering the killing blow to Jansen, following through with *her* promise to kill him.

Honestly, I would have done the same.

In the melee, she's shot with a crossbow bolt, and as she lay wounded and bleeding out, a storm rages, deforming the trees around her. Blood trees sprout, starting with gold buds that unfurl to reveal blood-red leaves, and the roots gather around her like a shield. When Kieran rips the bolt free, she realizes she's dying and that Cas plans to Ascend her.

Luckily, Casteel brings her back. During her Ascension, she has another vision of a woman with pale, moonlight-colored hair who looks like her. The female cries a blood-red tear and speaks to Poppy before disappearing.

When Poppy wakes, she's starving and pounces on Kieran but is quickly redirected to Casteel. Her need for blood quickly turns sexual, and things get hot and heavy—yes, I *saw* this in my visions. No, I don't feel guilty for being a voyeur. It was a pivotal moment. Because, afterward, Cas tells her that he loves her, and she says it to him, as well—for the first time.

Needing additional information, Poppy asks many, many questions and finds out that the bond between Kieran and Cas really is broken, that what Alastir said is wrong, and that Cas drained every drop of blood from her to Ascend her because she did, indeed, die. He says she no longer feels mortal to him, nor does she smell that way to Kieran. Instead, they tell her she feels like final and absolute power.

Wondering if Ian might be like her, stronger but not actually Ascended, she sets off, seeing the mist thinning for her and the golden trees of Aios now blood-red.

When they arrive at Saion's Cove, the older citizens bow to Poppy and call her Meyaah *Liessa*—my Queen—and she discovers that she can communicate telepathically with the wolven. She then exacts her revenge on Alastir, vowing never to think about him again.

Everything that has happened in such a short time becomes overwhelming for Poppy—can you blame her?—and she shows the emotion she always tries so hard to hide. Cas is there to comfort her, and they relax by reading some of my steamiest diary entries.

I always hoped someone would come across those journals someday.

Poppy and Cas discuss her claim to the throne, and Cas admits that he will support her if she wants the Crown but says that if she doesn't, they'll have to leave Atlantia. She finds herself torn.

When she's suddenly summoned to help a child, she learns that her powers have evolved even more, allowing her to not only heal but also bring someone back to life. And when she finds out that Nyktos and his Consort had two children, their names and genders unknown, it gets her thinking.

Especially when she's later told that not even the children of deities had abilities that manifested as strongly as hers. Not even the most powerful Elemental can do what she can. When the Queen reveals that Poppy has some of the same powers as Malec, she starts to wonder if the Duchess was right. However, she also learns that Malec cannot be her father since Eloana insists she entombed him before Poppy was conceived. The only thing they *can* deduce for sure is that, somehow, she is Nyktos's descendant. Poppy can't help but worry that her mother was an Atlantian held by the Blood Crown and forced into pregnancy.

It comes to light that Eloana, Valyn, and the Elders—it was not unanimous with us—have already decided on war and plan to burn Carsodonia to the ground, and she knows that only she and Cas can stop it. But only if they're King and Queen. Coming to terms with the fact that not everyone will accept her, Poppy makes her decision.

Suddenly, Ian arrives and summons them to Oak Ambler. She finally sees him and knows she may have to make a tough choice soon: ending him if the brother she knows is gone. In addition, she recognizes that it may be a trap, even though the Queen promised not to harm them if they kept the Atlantian armies at bay.

When the Unseen attack again with no intention of leaving her alive, she unleashes her power once more, remarking that any who try to stop her from taking the crown will fail.

As a Council Elder, I am lucky enough to be in attendance before the crowning and discuss several things with Poppy: her night at the Red Pearl, her lineage, and her need to go to Iliseeum. I also get to announce the happy new couple—the King and Queen who will usher in a whole new era. They are the King of Blood and Ash and the Queen of Flesh and Fire.

Poppy and Cas ask Kieran to be their Advisor, and thinking back on the discussion she had with me and the other facts she knows, she comes to the conclusion that Nyktos's guards are the draken.

She and her most trusted venture through the mists near the Mountains of Nyktos and into Dalos, coming face-to-face with the draken and the King of Gods. She then learns about the Consort and her beginnings, reminded again that gods should not be born in the mortal realm...yet there she stands.

After telling Nyktos about the Revenants, he remarks that they are abominations and apologizes for what Poppy will have to face in the coming days. He then reminds her that she was born of flesh with the fire of the gods in her blood, tells her that she is the bringer of life and death, calls her the Queen of Flesh and Fire, who is due more than one crown and kingdom, and reiterates that she's always had the power within her.

Boarding a ship for their next destination, Poppy and Cas grow closer, exploring more of their desires—with a little help from page two hundred and thirty-eight of my journal. Mmm, yes. That was a good one.

In Oak Ambler, Poppy sees a large cat in a cage and has a flashback to the one she saw as a child. Her power hums in her chest, and it forces the feline to shift into a man. She promises that she will be back for him and wonders if it could be Malec. When she asks about it, she's told that Malec wasn't that kind of deity. Besides, he is supposedly entombed. The cave cat cannot be him.

When brought before Queen Ileana, Poppy vows that the Blood Crown will never lay a hand on her husband again and is finally able to at least see and hug her good friend. Tawny was her companion and confidante for most of her life as the Maiden, and the one person she was able to talk to who knew her without the veil. She's missed her.

In her tête-à-tête with Ileana, many machinations are revealed. The Blood Queen tells them that she always planned for Poppy to become Queen of Atlantia, but that she assumed it would be with Malik as her King. She also says she'd rather see the whole kingdom burn than hand over a single acre of land.

Then she drops the biggest bombshell of all and tells Poppy she's her mother, that her real name is Isbeth, that Cora didn't agree with her plans and thus tried to spirit Poppy away, and that while Coralena survived the attack at Lockswood, she did *not* survive the Queen's wrath.

It's also revealed that Malec is a god. Poppy suddenly remembers what Nyktos said to her. She asks about it, and Isbeth confirms that everything she did, she did for revenge. In a petty snit, she has Ian killed, and Poppy's ancient instincts take over, activating her powers. They fight like gods, and Isbeth ends up killing Lyra, Kieran's friend and lover.

Poppy eventually falls unconscious and later wakes to find that Casteel handed himself over to the Blood Crown. In her rage, she summons another storm. A female Revenant approaches and tells her to quit what she's doing, threatening to stop her if she does not. When Poppy finally stands down, she finds that Tawny has been wounded by shadowstone—something Poppy is unable to heal, even with her newly acquired powers.

Through the process of elimination and some deduction, Poppy realizes that the Consort must be her grandmother, and that Isbeth's vendetta is utterly personal. Eloana took Isbeth's son, so Isbeth took Casteel. And despite Malec being entombed, Isbeth and Malec *must* be her parents.

She decides to summon the draken and do whatever is necessary to bring Casteel home. When she and Kieran arrive in Iliseeum, she finds Nektas, Nyktos's closest draken guard, in his god form. He tells her that Nyktos returned to sleep with his Consort. He then asks Poppy if she is willing to bear the weight of two Crowns and bring back what is theirs to protect and the thing that will allow the Consort to wake. Poppy finds out that is the missing draken—Nektas's daughter, Jadis—and the Consort's son, whom Poppy discovers is not Malec but rather his twin, Ires.

When the realization hits her that the caged cave cat was her father, she summons the draken and sets off for the mortal realm once more, visiting Tawny and reuniting with others. Returning to Oak Ambler, she meets with Jalara. She tells the King that she has a message for the Blood Queen and then beheads him, using *him* as the message. She then destroys the Queen's knights, unleashes the draken, and tells the Revenant to deliver the full message to the Queen, reiterating that she is coming for Isbeth. Her last words ring in the air: "I am the Chosen, The One who is Blessed, and I carry the blood of the King of Gods in me. I am *Liessa* to the wolven, the second daughter, the true heir, owed the crowns for Atlantia *and* Solis. I am the Queen of Flesh and Fire, and the god's guards ride with me. Tell the Blood Queen to prepare for war."

As Poppy readies herself to rescue Cas and get her vengeance, her powers grow even more, making the trees shake and the weather rage. She takes out the Ascended stronghold at Massene and makes some connections.

Unable to eat or sleep, she keeps rehashing what went down at Oak Ambler and wonders if they have a traitor in their midst—someone other than Alastir.

As the days pass, Poppy and Kieran grow closer in their shared grief over Cas's imprisonment, and Poppy uncovers something interesting: There is a record of a Rite at the time of the gods, and second and third children in the history books have no death dates. This leads her to the conclusion that the Rite existed before the Ascended but was eventually lost to time until it was bastardized and taken up again by the vamprys.

In talking with Reaver, one of the draken who answered her summons, she finds out they are bonded to her like the wolven, but it's slightly different. They can't communicate with her like the wolven can, but they *will* answer her call. He says it's always been that way with Primals and tells her she's not wise.

Reaver clearly has no filter, and I'm not sure Poppy caught that nonchalant drop of her true state—that she's a Primal.

Reaver then tells her that a god can kill another, and that she—Poppy—is the first female descendant of the Primal of Life, the most powerful being ever known. He says she will become stronger than even her father, Ires, in time.

When she asks for more information about the Consort, whom she now believes is her grandmother, she is told that speaking the Consort's name is forbidden.

Just as things appear to be coming along, albeit shockingly with all the revelations, Isbeth sends a *gift*. It turns out to be Casteel's ring finger, complete with his wedding band. Poppy absolutely loses it and has to be calmed.

Deciding that she can't—and won't—wait to go after Cas, she makes plans to leave as soon as possible. Kieran insists on going with her, and she tells him that Reaver needs to come, as well.

That night, she dream walks—also called soul walking, where heartmated souls can find each other, even in dreams—and finds Casteel. Once they reunite, sparks fly as usual with the two of them, and he tells her to find him, bolstering her resolve.

Before she can even make another decision, an unnatural storm rolls in, killing all but three of the draken with her. She realizes it has to be Vessa, the strange woman they locked up when she went a little mad. Poppy ultimately kills her, but not before Vessa insists that Poppy will not harness the fire of the gods and bring war, then claims to serve the True Crown of the Realms. Whatever that means.

Sadly, I found out not too long after...

Reaver then explains how Nyktos is not the Primal of Life as everyone assumes. But Kolis *was*. He also explains how Kolis was entombed after the war between the Primals and gods and then subsequently erased from history. Reaver also tells her how the Revenants were Kolis's pet project and explains how mortals were created, going on to further explain why the third sons and daughters are special.

Because Poppy could not bring back the draken who died despite her best efforts, she realizes that she cannot bring back the wolven, either, as they are also of two worlds. This leads to the conclusion that the only way to save Kieran should he be hurt and ensure his continued safety is for Cas, him, and her to complete the Joining, making all of them nearly immortal.

Once they reach Oak Ambler, they encounter a group of citizens trying to leave, most of them grieving lost children who were taken from them. Poppy tells them to go to Massene where it's safe, then calls to the soldiers, telling them that she's not the harbinger but carries the blood of the King of Gods in her. She also asserts that the Ascended are their enemy, *not* her.

Thinking about the storm Vessa conjured and realizing the Blood Crown knows how to use Primal magic, she wonders if the magic Isbeth used was Malec's or Kolis's and whether Malec is the great conspirator from the prophecy.

She inquires about the children and is taken to the tombs, finding seventy-one bodies from the last two Rites. She orders Reaver to burn the Temple to the ground, including the Priests within, and then heals who she can. Unfortunately, they lose five wolven and close to one hundred Atlantian soldiers along the way.

Poppy is suddenly inspired to use magic to locate Cas and find a way to him and gathers what she needs for a locator spell. Before she can set off, Tawny arrives—though Poppy comes to find she is much changed. It's still her friend, but she looks and feels very different. Tawny tells Poppy that she saw Vikter in a dream that wasn't a dream, and he told her that Poppy is a god, and that Isbeth's plan is to remake the realms with Poppy's help.

Wondering about Vikter—she saw him die, after all—Poppy finds out that he is a *viktor,* learns what that means, and figures that he must have determined what he was and possibly who he was supposed to protect and sought out Cora before Poppy was even born.

Going over the prophecy, which they still don't know in its entirety or understand, she wonders who the first daughter is since Poppy is always referred to as the second. She can guess that Malik is likely the once-promised King mentioned.

Poppy learns that the Consort was born in Lasania and was a mortal Princess and the true heir to the throne before coming into her power. But she was born with an ember of pure Primal power—unlike the third sons and daughters. Combined with the knowledge that the Consort's name cannot be spoken by a Primal without making stars fall from the sky and mountains crumble into the sea, she wonders even more about herself and her ancestor.

A large group of soldiers approaches, and a battle ensues. She, Kieran, and Reaver are taken hostage, and she wakes to the Queen's Revenant Handmaiden, who says her name is Millie. She agrees to a deal to save Kieran and Reaver. Two days later, Poppy wakes in her old bedroom at Wayfair with Kieran, learning that Reaver is in a chamber below her.

The two of them discuss the knights in the castle and the extremely odd two people they met—Callum and Millie—and Poppy tries to reach out to Delano telepathically. Seems their plan to come in waves has been thwarted, though she discovers that Whitebridge and New Haven are now under Atlantian control, and Three Rivers is soon to follow.

Brought before the Queen, Poppy wonders how people would feel if they knew the truth about Isbeth and asks how Malik can stand being around her. She then shatters his mental shields and feels the truth of the matter. Isbeth has him removed and lets Poppy name her terms, which she then laughs at.

The Blood Queen allows Poppy to see Cas but won't let anybody else near him. When Poppy finally reaches him, he's in bloodlust and looks to be in really bad shape. She's able to heal him and bring him back from the brink, but he needs more than that. She demands food and water for him, and Isbeth scoffs once again.

Poppy and Isbeth then talk about the lies and the ultimate responsibility for all that has been done. She finally asks how the Queen captured Ires and is told that he came over two hundred years ago, looking for his twin, Malec. She adds that the one who came with him—whom we now know was Jadis—could sense Malec's blood. Isbeth then insinuates the draken was *dealt with.*

When Poppy inquires about her conception, Isbeth says it wasn't forced, but then adds an "either time" and goes on to say she wanted a strong child, and Ires was full of lust and hatred. He even tried to kill her afterward—something Isbeth seems to find perverse pleasure in.

She also reveals that she knew what Poppy would become and that Malec wasn't dead, even though their heartmate bond broke when Eloana entombed him.

With no time to spare, Poppy reaches out to Kieran and says they need to get Cas and leave immediately. She hates the idea of leaving her father behind, but she has no choice.

After a discussion with Malik and thinking back on what she felt when she shattered his shields, Poppy realizes that Millie is the reason he stays. Later, she finds out Malik and Millie are heartmates.

But it's complicated.

Now knowing that Isbeth wants to see the kingdoms burn and blames Nyktos for refusing to answer Malec's call for a heartmate trial, Poppy comes to understand that eradicating all Atlantians is the only justice that will satisfy Isbeth.

After being escorted back to her room, Poppy summons the Primal mist. Using it to escape, she meets up with Kieran and Reaver, and they battle their way through the castle. Kieran is wounded, and she cannot completely heal him. She later discovers that the weapon was cursed. When they reach Cas, they find he's in even worse shape than before and are told that Callum is the cause. She vows to see the bastard dead, and Reaver acknowledges. She's able to bring Cas back to himself somewhat, and they reunite.

In just the way I hoped they would. No voyeur shame, remember?

When Cas relives his time in the dungeon, he tells Poppy about his interactions with Millie and what he came to realize: Millie is Poppy's full-blooded sister. The first daughter. Poppy also learns that Callum showed Isbeth how to make Revenants, and Malik mentions something Reaver said a while back. That Poppy is a Primal. The draken then confirms that she *is* a Primal born of mortal flesh. The first since the Primal God of Life.

Malik goes on to share how Preela, his bonded wolven, was killed. Later, Poppy learns that she was killed in front of Malik and her bones were used to create weapons—one of which Poppy carries on her at all times—the bloodstone and wolven-bone dagger Vikter gave to her on her sixteenth birthday.

Reunited, Poppy and Cas discuss her being the harbinger, her Culling, the prophecy, and the Joining. She then talks through everything she learned with the generals and uncovers information about Malec. As it turns out, he's buried in the northeast corner of the Blood Forest near some ruins and was entombed in a casket covered in deity bones.

She also learns that I helped Eloana entomb Malec.

Yes, I did.

They decide that Malec and Ires will be returned to Nyktos and the Consort once everything is over, and Poppy leaves to spend some time with Tawny and talk to Kieran about the Joining. During their discussion, Poppy feels things from Kieran and discovers there's love there. She then realizes she also loves him. It's not the same as what she feels for Cas, but it's enough for both of them to make the kind of promise the Joining requires.

They set off to find Malec and encounter some hardships along the way—what else is new?—Craven and Gyrms, both of which they thankfully defeat.

When they return, Poppy, Cas, and Kieran partake in the Joining—which did turn sexual…something I wholeheartedly approved of—and end up with synced breaths and heartbeats and shared feelings. Unfortunately, it doesn't remove the curse from Kieran as they hoped it would.

Poppy dreams of the woman with the silver hair again and sees someone she feels could be Vikter. She wakes in Cas's arms with Kieran lying close. After making sure their armies are ready, they set off to meet with the Queen.

It's here where the actual events vary a little from my Seer visions. I was nearly as shocked by the final outcome as those in attendance.

When they reach the Queen, Poppy delivers an ultimatum that they remove the curse from Kieran before she brings Malec out. Callum does, and they deliver the Queen's heartmate to her, despite Millie's warnings to Poppy that something doesn't feel right.

Thinking Isbeth would bring Malec back, everyone watches raptly, ready to act if needed. And this is where it gets weird. Isbeth shocks them all by apologizing and plunging a shadowstone dagger into her lover's heart—the one thing that can kill a god. She rambles on about someone waiting for the sacrifice. The balance the Arae always insist on. The one born of mortal flesh on the verge of becoming a great Primal power. And Callum reveals that as long as both Poppy and Millie share the blood of the Primal and are loved, *he* will be restored. He adds that Isbeth just needed someone of *his* bloodline to set things in motion.

So, Malec *wasn't* the True King of the Realms that everyone was talking about. And Poppy ended up being the bringer of death and destruction anyway since she brought Malec to Isbeth. Putting the prophecy puzzle pieces together, they establish that *Isbeth* is the harbinger, and Millie is the warning. Callum goes on to say that *he* needed to be strong so he could wake, and that Poppy's Ascension freed *him*. He says that when Malec takes his final breath, *he* will be at full strength. When Poppy smells stale lilacs, she realizes who *he* is. It's Kolis. The Primal who stole his twin brother's power and Court and unbalanced the realms.

Millie tells Poppy that Malec is still alive and that things can be stopped. When she summons the draken and starts to use eather, they warn her that it will attract the dakkais. She pulls back but can't sustain it. During her god battle with Isbeth, the dakkais attack, and many die. The Consort comes to her and tells her that it wasn't supposed to be this way, and Poppy remembers what Reaver said about saying the Consort's name.

She realizes the Consort is the true Primal of Life and screams her name, one she didn't even know she knew, and is suddenly struck by lightning, becoming churning light and shadow with eather wings. Fangs appear, and her Culling comes to fruition.

Poppy goes Primal, and a great battle ensues. When she wakes later, she's relieved to see all of her fallen friends alive and whole and learns that Reaver took Malec to Iliseeum, Millie ran off, and Malik followed.

Nektas tells everyone about Eythos and Kolis and relays the story of Sotoria.

He goes on to say that the Consort's Ascension was like a cosmic restart, and only if a female descendant was born and Ascended would the reboot happen again. Malec having a child upset the balance and created a loophole for what was done to Kolis to be *un*done. He says that Callum must be found and dealt with and reveals that Poppy is the Primal of Blood and Bone, the true Primal of Life *and* Death.

When Poppy tells Nektas that she knows where Ires is, he orders them to take him to the god and says they must also find Jadis so they can return to Iliseeum. Nyktos and the Consort no longer sleep, which means the other gods will wake.

The war has only begun.

In the tunnels under Wayfair, Kieran and Casteel are very overprotective, and Nektas makes fun of them for worrying over and safeguarding her, calling them *adorable*.

When the tunnels collapse, Cas and Kieran move to protect her, but they realize that she didn't do it. It wasn't any of them. It's the gods.

Poppy gets excited that it could be Penellaphe, her namesake, and asks if she can meet her. Nektas tells her she'll likely get to meet all of them when the time is right.

I cannot wait to *see* that.

The group finally reaches Ires, and Poppy isn't sure what to say or do. She feels super uncomfortable at first and Cas calms her, as Nektas warns that he will be more animal than man.

Poppy touches her father, and he shifts. She talks to him and asks if he remembers her, telling him she's his daughter. After Kieran gets Ires a banner to wear, the god finds his voice and reaches out to Poppy, telling her he knows who she is.

It was such a touching moment.

They all discuss Jadis, and Ires tells them he believes she's somewhere in the Willow Plains.

All of a sudden, Poppy gets dizzy. When Nektas asks if she's slept, she replies that she rested a little. He clarifies that he meant stasis, but she passes out before more can be said.

Kieran and Cas take her to a spare room in the castle and watch over her, telling her stories of their early time together.

When she finally wakes, she shakes the castle, burns a symbol for life and death into the floor, and opens eyes the pure silver of a Primal.

Poppy's prophecy:

From the desperation of golden crowns and born of mortal flesh, a great primal power rises as the heir to the lands and seas, to the skies and all the realms. A shadow in the ember, a light in the flame, to become a fire in the flesh. When the stars fall from the night, the great mountains crumble into the seas, and old bones raise their swords beside the gods, the false one will be stripped from glory until two born of the same misdeeds, born of the same great and Primal power in the mortal realm. A first daughter, with blood full of fire, fated for the once-promised King. And the second daughter, with blood full of ash and ice, the other half of the future King. Together, they will remake the realms as they usher in the end. And so it will begin with the last Chosen blood spilled, the great conspirator birthed from the flesh and fire of the Primals will awaken as the Harbinger and the Bringer of Death and Destruction to the lands gifted by the gods. Beware, for the end will come from the west to destroy the east and lay waste to all which lies between.

Things of note regarding the prophecy:
- Alastir tells Poppy the prophecy was written in the bones of Poppy's namesake.
- The first glimpse of the prophecy is only this: "With the last chosen blood spilled, the great conspirator birthed from the flesh and the fire of the Primals will awaken as the Harbinger and the Bringer of Death and Destruction to the lands gifted by the gods. Beware, for the end will come from the west to destroy the east and lay waste to all which lies between."
- I introduce Cas as the King of Blood and Ash, and Poppy as the Queen of Flesh & Fire to the people.
- The Priestess called Poppy, "the one whose blood is full of ash and ice."

CORALENA "CORA" BALFOUR †
From all appearances, Coralena was an incredible mother. Despite becoming Poppy's guardian under orders from her Queen, she eventually went against Isbeth to try to save her daughter, likely knowing the punishment would be swift and severe if she were ever discovered.

Eyes: Brown (we later learn that they're very pale like all Revenants but were darkened with magic).
Background: Third daughter. Handmaiden/Revenant.
Family: Husband = Leopold Balfour †. Son = Ian Balfour †.

CORALENA'S JOURNEY TO DATE:
The story goes that being a third daughter, Coralena was a Lady in Wait, given to the Court at the Rite. Before her Ascension, she met Leopold—which they say was an accident, though we know it wasn't since Leo was a *viktor* and knew who his charge was, thus seeking out Cora before Poppy was even born. They fell in love. That much is true, at least. It's said that Coralena requested to forego her Ascension so she could be with Leo—something that had never been done before. It's not one hundred percent clear whether or not *that* part is true. What we do know is that they ended up married and had a son together.
The real history is that Cora was a Revenant, one of the Queen's personal guards, and very close to Ileana—whom we now know is really Isbeth. Coralena

was the Queen's favorite.

After Penellaphe's birth, Isbeth gave her to her most trusted Handmaiden—Cora—so none who sought to gain what the Queen had could use her child against her. But Cora had a change of heart when she discovered Isbeth's plan to marry Poppy to Malik in a bid to bring the kingdoms together. She disapproved, so she and Leo stole away with Poppy and Ian.

Having befriended Alastir before that night, the couple asked for his help. Little did they know that he had ulterior motives for getting close to them, and once he learned the truth about Poppy, he decided to kill her.

Alastir let Malik—the Dark One—in that night, believing the Prince would do what he hadn't accomplished yet. The trail of blood that Malik left in his wake on the way to the inn drew the Craven, thus resulting in Poppy's injuries. Cora tried to save her, pleading with Malik and telling him her daughter would usher in great change and be the end of the Blood Crown, not the end of the realms. She went on to tell him that Leo was Poppy's *viktor*. It did little to sway the Dark One, and Cora ended up stabbing Malik in the chest as Alastir looked on.

It was believed Cora died that night at the inn, overcome by the Craven. However, the Blood Queen later revealed that she did not perish in Lockswood. She lived. But she didn't survive Isbeth's wrath afterward.

She made Cora ingest draken blood, thus killing her.

LEOPOLD "LEO" / "LION" BALFOUR †

Leopold is an interesting subject. As a *viktor*, he was born—or *reborn*, I guess—to guard someone the Fates believed was destined to bring about significant change or serve great purpose. But unlike most *viktors*, Leo figured out what he was, as well as who he was sent to protect and why.

Hair: Coppery red.
Eyes: Pine green.
Body type: Tall.
Facial features: Square jaw with several days' worth of beard growth. Straight nose. Dark brows.
Personality: Caring. Stable.
Habits/Mannerisms/Strengths/Weaknesses: Called Poppy "poppy-flower" and "baby girl."
Background: *Viktor.* Firstborn son. Wealthy but not a Lord—merchant family involved in shipping and friends of the King.
Family: Wife = Coralena †. Son = Ian †.

LEOPOLD'S JOURNEY TO DATE:

Leopold, being reborn with the sole purpose of guarding Poppy on her path of bringing about great change, was one of the rare few who figured out who he was meant to protect and guide and took it upon himself to search out who he knew would eventually become Poppy's guardian—Cora. The two fell in love and ended up having a son. For all intents and purposes, they had a good life, despite knowing the truth about the Ascended and Poppy's fate.

When the Dark One came to claim Poppy, both Leo and Cora fought. Alastir, having betrayed them both, was also present at the Lockswood Inn that fateful night.

Most believed both Cora and Leo died that night. It's later revealed that Cora didn't and was instead killed by Isbeth. Leo's fate, however, still remains unknown.

I surmise that he *was* killed and returned to Mount Lotho and the Arae to await his next life and mission.

IAN BALFOUR †

Ian was the catalyst for so much of Poppy's motivation after Casteel—as Hawke—whisked her away. And while his story came to a tragic end, and despite circumstances, he was a good brother.

Hair: Reddish brown.
Eyes: Hazel—shifting from brown to green. Turned black after Ascension.
Body type: Long and lean.
Facial features: Handsome. Oval face. Smooth jaw. Full lips.
Personality: Gentle. Imaginative. Playful. Kind. Patient. Doting. A bit of a flirt.
Habits/Mannerisms/Strengths/Weaknesses: Voice was as soft as air. Loved to tell stories. A dreamer. Knew the horrors of what lay outside the Rise walls. Called Penellaphe, "Poppy." Wrote his sister monthly letters. Liked coffee. Had nightmares of the Craven attack. Before Ascension, could be found outside on sunny days, scribbling in one of his journals and writing stories. Was a great actor. Liked dancing.
Other: Was older than Poppy by two years. Born in December but didn't know the date and didn't really celebrate.
Background: Looked forward to Ascension. Married Lady Claudeya shortly after Ascending, though he never talked about her. Ascended when Poppy was sixteen as a *favor*. Was the last to Ascend.
Family: Mother = Coralena †. Father = Leopold †. Adoptive sister = Penellaphe.

IAN'S JOURNEY TO DATE:

Ian is an interesting case. He seemed to retain some of his goodness even after his Ascension. Too bad Isbeth had to cut his life short. I wish Poppy could have had more time to see how much was left so she could add that to her memories of playing with him under the willow, making snowballs, and learning how to pick locks.

The night the Craven attacked Lockswood because of the Dark One—i.e., Malik—a woman at the inn pulled Ian into a room to save him.

It's said he always looked forward to his Ascension. I'm sure that changed once he learned the truth…

Three years before Poppy's planned Ascension, one year before Ian Ascended, he beat Lord Mazeen in poker, and the Lord accused him of cheating. That didn't go over well at all and caused some tension.

I've wondered if that's why he ended up separated from Poppy—outside of her being the Maiden and him being slated for Ascension.

Ian Ascended when Poppy was sixteen, even though he wasn't a second son—the ones the vamprys usually made into new Ascended. It was said it was done as a *favor* to Poppy, and that Ileana petitioned the gods to let it be so.

I don't believe any of that.

However, it's worth noting that Ian was the last to *be* Ascended.

He married Lady Claudeya shortly after Ascending, but I think it was more of a political move somehow. He never spoke of her. Maybe he never really married her at all, and it was just a lie. Who knows?

He next appears in my visions right around the time things were getting real with Poppy and her allies.

Vonetta confirms that Ian has Ascended, and then he leads a convoy of about two hundred Royal Knights and soldiers to Spessa's End to request an audience with Cas and Poppy. He says he will only speak to his sister and claims he's come to prevent another war.

He asks about Poppy, wondering how she's doing after her kidnapping. When he finds out she's married, he fakes surprise—I'm quite certain he already knew.

When he meets with them, he asks what Atlantia hopes to gain by taking his sister—not *the Maiden*—and wonders if he's actually supposed to believe she married the monster responsible for their parents' deaths. He makes a comment that he can only imagine the lies the enemy has told her, though he won't hold it against her—nor will the Crown.

At this point, the things he said made me think that while he might have had a spark of goodness left, it wasn't a big one. Either that, or as Poppy said, he was just a really great actor. I honestly don't know. It's really hard to read someone properly in a vision.

Especially since he sort of shifts yet again, saying some additional things before telling the group the villain is always the hero in their own story.

Ian asks if he can speak with Poppy alone, and as they talk, *something* flickers across his face when she talks about how the Ascended feed.

He relays that Tawny is safe but says Poppy can see for herself if she comes. He adds that the *true Queen* has requested a meeting with the Prince and Princess of Atlantia in a fortnight at the Royal Seat in Oak Ambler. He says Ileana promises not to harm either of them so long as they leave the army they've gathered in the north.

As the group mulls it over, Ian flirts with Vonetta and tells her she's more than welcome to join them when they make the trip.

Cas moves to Poppy, and the knights start to advance. Ian halts them and says the Blood Crown has no desire to start another war, then adds that if it comes to that, Atlantia won't win.

He warns them all that if they arrive with any ill will, they will be destroyed, along with Atlantia, starting with Spessa's End. Then he taunts that they could have hundreds of thousands of soldiers and wouldn't beat what the Queen created—alluding to the Revenants.

Here, it felt to me like he was giving them information without it appearing he wasn't loyal to the Blood Crown. And given what happens next, I believe I'm right.

Ian tells Poppy he'll see her in Oak Ambler and then asks to hug her. When they embrace, he tells her he knows the truth and urges her to wake Nyktos, adding that only his guards can stop the Blood Crown.

This shocked me. I wasn't prepared to have it confirmed that he actually *was* acting. Perhaps him being a firstborn son changed his Ascension somehow, just like it did with Millie and Callum when they became Revenants. I'm honestly not sure.

When the group arrives in Oak Ambler, he speaks to Poppy and tells her he hopes she is well and that her travels after they last saw each other went well. This could sound innocuous to those around and mean nothing but her trip to Oak Ambler, but we know he's subtly inquiring if she went to Iliseeum.

The group meets with the Queen, trading barbs, and Ian remains silent all the while.

I saw another flaw in Ian's disguise when Ileana orders Millie to be struck down and he turns away. After the truth comes out about Isbeth—what and who she is—Ian confirms all of it.

After the Blood Queen puts forth her terms for what she wants of Poppy and Cas, Poppy refuses. As punishment, Isbeth has one of her knights behead Ian.

VIKTER WARD/WARDWELL †

Vikter is utterly intriguing—he holds a special place in my heart—and his story is equally heartbreaking and compelling.

Hair: Sandy-blond.
Eyes: Blue.
Body type: Broad shoulders.
Facial features: Weathered, sun-kissed skin.
Personality: Stern. Gruff.
Habits/Mannerisms/Strengths/Weaknesses: Great fighter. Weakness for hot cocoa and chocolate. Prone to migraine headaches. Torn between wanting Poppy to learn and help the Cursed and worrying about her safety because of her recklessness.
Other: Taught Poppy how to fight.
Background: *Viktor.* Has lived many lives.
Family: Wife = Camilia †. Daughter = infant, name unknown †.

VIKTER'S JOURNEY TO DATE:

Vikter, being a *viktor*, has several journeys that are worth exploring. For the sake of this dossier, I'm going to give a high-level overview of what I know about his past and then the notable mentions of his time with Poppy.

Viktors are eternal beings born with a goal: to guard someone the Fates believe is destined to bring about great change or purpose. They are neither mortal nor god. Not all are aware of their duty, but the Fates will always put them with the one they are to safeguard. They are always reincarnated. When they die, their souls return to Mount Lotho, where the Arae give them a new mortal form and purpose with no memory of their previous lives. However, some *viktors* are predestined to figure out what they are and who they were sent to protect. Vikter is one of those.

Vikter had the last name of Ward instead of Wardwell in the time of the gods and was brought before Seraphena to apply a charm to keep her safe and unable to be taken from the Shadowlands. He explains to her that he is a *viktor*—the first.

His lifetimes between Sera's and Poppy's are unknown to me.

The first time I really took notice of Vikter was in the Red Pearl. There's just something about him. He demands attention without even trying.

The night I set up Poppy and Casteel's first meeting. Vikter arrived, and it upped my need to get Penellaphe out of the main area and into *Hawke's* room. Which I did. The rest of that night, well, let's just say I took some time for myself.

But back to Vikter's story…

The following night, Vikter goes to Poppy and summons her to aid a Cursed. They help ease his passing.

When Poppy reveals that she hopes to be found unworthy so she won't Ascend, Vikter tells her that no matter what she does, she *will* Ascend.

Knowing what we know now about Poppy's journey, that statement is very interesting. Because she did, indeed, Ascend—when she died, and Casteel saved her. It just wasn't in the way we all thought—at the hands of the Ascended.

When they find the Lady in Wait, Malessa, murdered, Vikter arrives after Commander Jansen deems the castle safe. He's suffering from one of his migraine headaches, and Poppy eases his pain.

When Poppy's guard, Rylan Keal, is murdered, Vikter arrives with another guard. We know that Jericho killed Rylan, but Vikter did not know that. Everyone was still under the impression that the Atlantians were targeting them. At Rylan's ceremony, Vikter lights his pyre.

He makes his opinion known after the Duke agrees that Hawke can become Poppy's new personal guard and then offers some sage advice to him. He also lays down the law about what Hawke can and cannot do with the Maiden.

As he trains with Poppy, they discuss her adventures coming to an end. When it's time to bring in the new guard who is to take Rylan's place, Vikter escorts her to the Royals to meet Hawke.

Later, after one of her *lessons* with the Duke, Hawke sends for him out of concern, and Vikter escorts Poppy back to her room.

When the Craven attack, he fights with the guards outside the Rise and sees Hawke also outside the Rise. It worries him that she's been left alone, but he knows she can take care of herself. Unfortunately, upon his return, Hawke informs him that Poppy was on the Rise fighting during the attack. The next day, he trains her in hand-to-hand maneuvers.

Sometime later, after assisting with a Cursed and leaving Poppy behind, he escorts her to the Rite and hears Agnes's concerns and warning. Once Hawke arrives, Vikter leaves to tell the commander what he overheard.

Just as Hawke and Poppy are leaving after their rendezvous under the willow, Vikter catches them and knows exactly what was going on. He dons his protective father figure hat and says they'll spend time together over his dead body. After he dismisses Hawke, he lectures Poppy. She gets angry and tries to get him to understand, reminding him of everything she's lost and all she's been denied.

The Descenters attack the Rite, and Vikter tells Poppy to defend herself and not worry about hiding the fact that she can fight. He and Poppy defeat all their foes, but one rises from the floor and mortally wounds Vikter, plunging a sword through his chest, just above the heart.

As he's dying, he tells Poppy she's made him proud and apologizes for not protecting her, saying he failed as a man. He then asks her for forgiveness and passes away.

We know that he didn't actually die. He merely returned to the Arae on Mount Lotho to await his rebirth.

That brings me some comfort.

The rest of these things were revealed *after* Vikter's death:

Poppy recalls him telling her she shouldn't consider the lives of those who hold a sword to her throat.

When he gave her the bloodstone and wolven-bone dagger on her sixteenth birthday, he said, "This weapon is as unique as you are. Take good care of her, and she'll return the favor."

Now that we know the dagger was made of Preela's bones, that statement gives me goose bumps.

He once told Poppy: "I'm not untouched by it. Death is death. Killing is killing, Poppy, no matter how justified it is. Every death leaves a mark behind, but I do not expect anyone to take a risk I would not take. Nor would I ask another to bear a burden I refuse to shoulder or feel a mark I haven't felt myself."

He also said the mist is more than just a shield for the Craven. It fills their lungs since no breath does and seeps from their pores because no sweat can.

Since *viktors* cannot reveal their reasons or identity, Vikter was very deliberate about what he told Tawny in her shadowstone dream and what he asked her to relay for him—like the full prophecy, the fact that Poppy already knew the Consort's name, and what would happen if someone with Primal power spoke it in the mortal realm.

THE HEART DOESN'T CARE

~Poppy~

Drowning in panic and helplessness, I jolted awake with a leashed scream burning my throat.

Heart thundering, my eyes snapped open. My wild gaze darted around the unfamiliar, moonlit chamber. It took me a moment to recognize my surroundings. I started to sit up, but the weight of a warm arm resting against my bare waist stopped me.

Resisting the urge to reach beneath the blanket and touch him, I willed my heartbeat to slow.

It was just a nightmare.

Casteel was beside me, alive and well, and we were at an inn tucked away in the small town of Tadous, halfway to the capital. We weren't in that dark, cold place, trapped and—

Just a nightmare.

The soft bed shifted. A heartbeat later, the scent of pine and rich spice enveloped me, crowding out the faint smell of woodsmoke.

"Poppy?" Casteel's voice, roughened by sleep, reached me a second before his arm tightened around my waist.

Hearing his gruff voice calmed the pounding in my chest. I turned my head, making out the chiseled line of his jaw and the curve of his lush mouth. "I'm sorry," I whispered, clearing my throat. "I didn't mean to wake you."

His chin, slightly roughened by stubble, grazed my shoulder, sending a shiver through me. "It's okay."

No, it wasn't. I couldn't even begin to keep track of the number of times I'd woken him in the middle of the night. "It's official. I have to be the worst person to sleep next to."

"I have to disagree with that. You are officially the best person to go to sleep next to." The short hairs on his leg tickled mine as he drew himself up. "To sleep beside." He kissed my shoulder. "And to wake up with."

The corners of my lips turned up. "You have to say that."

"I only speak the truth." His arm loosened as his hand moved, skimming over the curve of my waist. "Was it another nightmare?" His palm drifted over my hip. "The Dark One?"

I opened my mouth, then closed it. I almost wished it was that nightmare. Those were a product of the past. This one felt like...like a harbinger. I swallowed.

My gaze shifted to the exposed beams of the ceiling awash in streaks of moonlight. A chill entered my skin. "It wasn't that kind of nightmare."

Casteel traced small, idle circles on the top of my thigh. "Tell me about it."

"It's not a big deal," I told him. "Morning will be here soon, and we still have a ways to go, right? We should be asleep—"

"Poppy." The hand on my thigh returned to my hip and then firmed, tilting me so my body was on its side, facing him.

I pressed my hands to his chest. "I don't even remember it." In reality, I wasn't sure how I could forget it: the sight of him, cold and gray, bloodless and immobile.

My heart sped up again. Why would I dream something like that? Now? I pressed my lips together, suddenly hearing Kieran's voice in my mind.

The heart doesn't care how long you have with someone.

Gods, I suddenly understood what had spawned such a nightmare, such feelings of panic and helplessness.

In the moonlight, Cas's gaze found mine. "Tell me about it."

My eyes narrowed. "You're being incredibly bossy."

"And you're being incredibly evasive," he replied. "That worries me."

"It shouldn't."

"And it makes me more curious," he continued, his hand squeezing my hip. "Makes me wonder if you were dreaming of another, and that is why you're being so vague."

"Really?" I stated dryly.

"Yes. My ego got diminished somewhere between Saion's Cove and here," he said. "I am now in need of your assurances."

There wasn't a single part of me that believed Casteel's ego was capable of weakening. Or that he believed I'd dreamt of another. In fact, I doubted his ego would even allow that to enter his mind.

But I'd learned that two could tease. "You're right." I drew a finger down the defined line of his chest. "It was another—"

He gave my rear a light smack, catching me off guard. Surprise caused me to let out a little squeak, but a dart of wicked heat made me jerk.

My eyes narrowed on him. "That was uncalled for."

Casteel's chuckle danced over my lips. "You liked it." Unfortunately, he was right. He palmed the flesh he'd tapped. "And I know you weren't dreaming of another."

"Then why did you suggest such a thing?"

He moved his leg again, nestling his thigh between mine. "Because I wanted to bask in the glory of your assurances."

"You're insufferable," I said, fighting a laugh.

"You meant to say insatiable." Casteel's head lowered, his mouth finding mine with unerring accuracy.

I immediately opened for Casteel. His kisses were compulsory, even these slow, languid ones where he seemed to sip from my lips. Tiny shivers broke out across my skin as his tongue flicked over mine in an intimate, sensual dance.

Using the hand on my rear, Casteel hauled me closer. I gasped as those coarse leg hairs dragged across the most sensitive part of me. The unexpected friction caused my hips to twitch.

"I love how responsive your body is to mine." He pressed his thigh up, causing more friction against me. I shuddered as darts of pleasure radiated out from my core. A deeper, dark chuckle teased my lips. "Have I told you that?"

Before I could think if he had, the hand on my rear tugged me onto his thigh, and he moved his leg up again, hitting that taut bundle of flesh. Tighter, hotter ripples of pleasure skated through me.

Casteel's lips returned to mine. My fingers curled, digging into his chest as he moved me again. The kiss deepened, and he rocked my hips against his hard thigh. Soon, I needed little guidance. His growl of approval rumbled through me as my thighs tightened around his, and I strained against him, feeling my breath picking up and my core clenching. I knew I was damp against his skin. Wet. My cheeks warmed, knowing he could feel my slickness.

His head tilted, and the kiss turned harder, fiercer. Then he broke the contact, his arm clamping down on my hips, stilling me.

"Cas," I cried out, my body vibrating with unspent desire.

Nipping at my lips, he made that deep sound again. "I need to be inside you when you come, and I need you on top, riding me when you do."

I swallowed a moan. "I want that."

He grasped my wrist, drawing it down between us. My fingers brushed his hot, rigid length. He folded my hand around his cock. "Then do it."

Upon his heated demand, a full-body shudder rocked me. I flattened one hand against his chest and urged him onto his back. Both of his hands went to my hips, steadying me as I straddled him. With my hand still encircling the base of his cock, I started to lower myself. My moan got lost in his groan as the head of his cock parted me. Shaking, I planted both palms on his chest and sank onto his length, inch by inch, until our bodies were flush.

Panting, I held myself still, my body adjusting to his size. His thickness seemed to stretch and fill every part of my being. There was a sharp, intense swelling of pleasure that almost bordered on pain as Casteel's fingers pressed into the flesh of my hips. My eyes opened, drifting over the tightly packed muscles of his abdomen, his chest, and then the stark tendons of his throat. He held himself still, his jaw clenched as he gave me time.

He always gave me time.

"I love you," I whispered, tipping forward to kiss him. The position sent a wave of harsh pleasure through me.

Casteel groaned, his fingers spasming on me. "Show me," he rasped. "Show me how much."

And I did.

I began to move. It took a few moments for me to find my rhythm, but he didn't rush me, just allowed me to find the spot that hit just right. Liquid heat flooded my core when I did. I moved faster then, his groans a decadent cacophony as I looked down at us—at me and our bodies.

"Beautiful," he growled. "You're so damn beautiful, Poppy."

I flushed, my breath quickening. My gaze lowered to my swaying breasts, the hardened tips piercing the strands of my hair, to the rounded curve of my lower stomach that no amount of training ever flattened, and the scars there, faint in the moonlight. I saw his hands on my hips, his fingers creating indents in the flesh there. I could see the scars on my thighs, and my legs' thickness and strength from years of training. Unlike Casteel, whose body was hard and defined—every inch of him—I was strong, but under a layer—or two—of softness. I shuddered as I moved up and down his length, watching myself take him into me until I lifted my gaze to his.

His eyes were like heated pools of honey, and the sight of them hit that spot just as well as his cock did.

I rode him then, moving faster and harder. His arms came around me, drawing me down. I shivered as the tips of my breasts grazed his chest, feeling the tension building.

Casteel kissed me and raised his hips to meet mine, both of us moving furiously now. The smoky flavor of his passion heightened what I felt. It was all too much. The tension unfurled. Hot, slick waves of pleasure took me, sweeping Casteel up in the storm, too. He spent himself, each spasm of his cock sending aftershocks of pleasure through me.

"I love you." Casteel's lips brushed mine as I eased my body free of his. He laid me down, so I was on my side, my legs tangled with his. Then stroked my hair as our skin cooled and our hearts slowed. Some time passed before he spoke again. "You going to tell me what woke you up?"

I closed my eyes. Of course, he hadn't forgotten what had awakened him. "You're like a barrat with a bone."

"That creates pleasant imaginary," he remarked. A moment passed. "Remember what we talked about? We share things with each other. Everything."

"I remember. I do. It's just…I don't know." I pressed a kiss to his chest as I stared at the bare, wood-paneled wall. "It's Kieran—"

"So, you *were* dreaming of another," he cut in. "That is…intriguing."

"That's not what I meant." Giving him a wry grin, I shook my head. "I think I had this dream—or nightmare—because of something he said."

Casteel grew very quiet and still then, triggering warning bells.

I rose onto my elbows. "He didn't say anything bad that upset me or anything."

"I know he wouldn't say anything to upset you." His hand smoothed down my back. "He wouldn't do that. But Kieran...he sometimes says things you'd expect to come out of the mouth of a Seer."

"It wasn't like that either." I lowered my chin to his chest. "He was telling me about Elashya."

Casteel's surprise was like a splash of ice water against the back of my throat. "He brought her up?"

I nodded. "That surprises you?"

"Yeah, it does." Casteel lifted his free hand and dragged it through his hair. "He doesn't talk about her much."

"I can understand why." Sorrow pierced my heart as I thought about the love and loss Kieran had felt. "It...it kind of amazes me that he knew he would lose her and still fell in love."

Casteel's gaze found mine in the dim light. "The heart doesn't care, Poppy."

My breath caught. "That's basically what Kieran said. That the heart doesn't care how much time you have with someone." Emotion clogged my throat. "That it only cares that you have that person for as long as you can."

"I didn't always think that." The hand on my back made another sweep. "When everything happened between him and Elashya, I couldn't understand how he'd let himself fall in love. Couldn't wrap my head around it. But then along came you." His fingers tangled in my hair. "Now, I fully understand that the heart doesn't care about plans, duty, or vengeance. It doesn't care about time."

My heart swelled. Kieran had been right. Casteel was right. I knew that, too. I wasn't supposed to fall in love with Casteel, but I did when he was simply Hawke to me, regardless of my duty. And I continued to fall even deeper in love with him, despite the lies and betrayal.

His hand fisted in my hair. "I think I know what you dreamt."

I exhaled a shaky breath. "I dreamt that...that something happened to you. That I lost you."

"Poppy," he rasped.

"It was so real." I squeezed my eyes shut. "I can still feel the hopelessness and desperation."

"It was a bad dream," he said. "You're never going to lose me."

"Promise?" I whispered.

"Promise." He cupped my cheek. "You never need to fear it or even think about it."

I nodded, pulling my lower lip between my teeth.

"Forget the nightmare."

"I will."

"I want you to forget it now."

My lips quirked. "You're being bossy again."

"Only because I don't want you wasting even a second of worry on something that will never happen."

I splayed my fingers on his chest. "It's kind of hard not to think about it, you know? Anything can happen to any of us—"

"That won't happen," he cut in. "But you know what will?"

I tipped my head back. "What?"

"You won't be thinking of anything much longer," he said, shifting and rolling me onto my back.

Casteel's mouth came down on mine, and his weight settled over me. He kissed me until I was breathless, then explored my body first with his hand, then with his mouth. Finally, he delved with his tongue, stealing my ability to think of anything but how he tossed one of my legs over his shoulder, spreading me wide as he laved and licked until I came apart again. Then he started all over again, dipping his tongue, then his fingers in and out of me, slowly and methodically until I squirmed helplessly, pleading for him to stop, begging that he continue. It was only when I thought I may lose all control of my senses that he thrust into me.

Casteel took me hard, first on my back and then on my knees with his skillful fingers playing at the junction of my thighs. Then he guided us onto our sides, face-to-face as he made love to me. He thoroughly exhausted me until I was limp and sated. The nightmare and the fear were nothing but faint memories as I fell back to sleep in his arms, our bodies still joined, knowing the only thing I'd remember about tonight was this.

Us.

Our love.

Our hearts.

PRINCE CASTEEL "CAS" HAWKETHRONE DA'NEER (A.K.A HAWKE FLYNN)

Becomes King Casteel Hawkethrone Da'Neer

To be honest, Casteel didn't feature prominently in my visions until his fate began to align with Poppy's. Once that happened, all sorts of cords started weaving themselves into a gorgeous tapestry of strength and sensitivity.

Hair: Black with a blue hue, brushing the neck and curling over the forehead.
Eyes: The color of cool amber honey.
Body type: Broad shoulders and chest. Long, lean, muscular body. Tall—around six feet, five inches—but not as tall as his brother Malik.
Facial features: High, angular cheekbones. Straight nose. Proud, carved jaw. Fangs.
Distinguishing features: Dimples—right side common, left only shows with genuine and full smiles. Brand of the Solis Royal Crest on his right thigh, just below the hip. Miscellaneous cuts and scars on his body. Deep voice with a slight accent.
Other: His heartmate thinks he smells like pine and dark spice, but his blood smells like citrus in the snow. He's over two centuries old but looks like a mortal of twenty-two. After being stabbed with a dagger made from the bones of the Ancients, he can shift into a silver-eyed, black-and-gold-spotted cave cat, standing five feet at shoulder height.
Personality: Doesn't laugh much. Assertive. No tolerance for threats. A betting man. Takes pleasure in revenge. Persistent when it comes to what he wants. Confident. Progressive.
Habits/Mannerisms/Strengths/Weaknesses: Able to use compulsion. Abhors violence against women. Good judge of character. Knows when someone is lying. Loves to hear himself talk. Driven. Takes pleasure in killing when it's warranted. Loves to read. Feels spousal needs should come before those of the kingdom. Knows how to braid hair. Expert with many weapons. Great tracker. Secretly fascinated with agriculture. Blood has healing properties.
Background: Elemental Atlantian. Second son. Held captive by the Blood Crown. Bonded to a wolven since birth.
Family: Parents = Queen Eloana and King Valyn Da'Neer of Atlantia. Brother = Prince Malik Elian Da'Neer. Uncle = Hawkethrone†. Great-grandfather = King Elian Da'Neer†. Descendant of = Attes, co-ruler of Vathi, Primal of War and Accord. Other ancestral family = Kyn, co-ruler of Vathi, Primal of Peace and Vengeance.

Casteel is an interesting man. Smart, strategic, and savvy, he's not afraid to get his hands dirty to achieve any goal. He also has a bit of a tragic past. Used, betrayed, imprisoned, and abused. Yet still, he prevails.

Poppy brings out the best in him, even his already present loyalty and bravery. Not quick to smile, rare to laugh, and not one for hugs, he softens when she enters his life, creating an interesting dichotomy of fierce protector and sensitive lover and friend.

I feel he's her ultimate match. And given their pairing, it seems the gods and Arae would agree.

I absolutely cannot wait to bear witness to what the future has in store for the new King of Atlantia.

CASTEEL'S JOURNEY TO DATE:

Born to King Valyn and Queen Eloana, Casteel grows up in Atlantia and is close with his older brother, Malik, his bonded wolven, Kieran Contou, and his best friend, Shea Davenwell—who later becomes his intended.

As disturbances between the kingdoms of Solis and Atlantia rise, Casteel becomes convinced he can kill the Blood Crown—Queen Ileana and King Jalara—by himself. Unfortunately, the Ascended capture him and hold him for five decades, torturing him ceaselessly.

Shea and Malik attempt to save him multiple times until the Ascended lay a trap during one attempt and ambush them. Shea and Malik are separated, and Shea tells the Ascended who she's with, making a deal to trade Malik's life for hers and agreeing to leave Casteel.

With the Ascended occupied, Shea reneges on her deal and attempts to flee with Casteel, entering the tunnels with him. Unfortunately, they don't get far and are stopped by a pair of Ascended.

Despite putting up a good fight, the vamprys prevail and tell Casteel that Shea previously traded her life for Malik's, thus turning traitor and allowing the Prince to be taken, which subsequently leads to their current predicament of being ensnared. While he doesn't believe it at first, Shea then tries to save herself *again* by offering to trade Casteel's life for hers.

In a rage, Casteel kills her with his bare hands as well as the Ascended, and then attempts to find and rescue Malik. I feel there is more to the story of Shea's end, and I keep trying to *see* more. Unfortunately, I haven't been able to glean any additional information there. But back to Casteel's escape. He is unsuccessful in rescuing his brother and ultimately ends up on the beach, where he is discovered and returned home.

As I said earlier, I didn't have much interaction with Casteel either personally or via my visions, so my knowledge of the time between that rescue and when he finally meets up with Poppy at the Red Pearl masquerading as Hawke Flynn—with a little help from me—is somewhat sparse. The pieces *after* he meets Poppy are the good bits, though, so let's start there...

Casteel, as Hawke, enters Solis and remains for two years. Posing as a Rise Guard, he watches and waits, following Poppy through her daily routines as the Maiden without being seen, hoping to capture her and whisk her away to Atlantia.

With a plan to use her in Atlantia's plot to save his brother Malik and circumvent war, and working with the Commander of the Royal Guard, Griffith Jansen—who later turns out to be not only a double agent but also a traitor to Atlantia, and a changeling!—Casteel insinuates himself in such a position to become close to Penellaphe Balfour.

While on the Rise, Cas—as Hawke—watches over Radiant Row, thinking about how the entire city is divided into haves and have-nots and visits with his partner guard, Pence.

Hawke sees mist gathering in the distance and knows what it means. The Craven are coming. Pence curses and blames the Atlantians and it takes everything in Hawke not to set the man straight…in a violent way. But he realizes the guard doesn't know any better and lets it go.

Hawke sees a guard unsteady on his feet and knows what's happening. He's been infected. But before he can do anything, Lieutenant Smyth arrives on the Rise and gives Hawke hell. Hawke is flippant with his responses, basically telling the man off. When the lieutenant leaves, Pence asks Hawke how big his balls are because he was so bold and insubordinate.

I'd like to know that, too. *winks*

Hawke asks Pence about Jole Crain, the cursed guard, and the guard tells him that he lives on the third floor of the dorms. He finds him trying to kill himself but can't—the curse won't allow it—and asks him some questions before compelling him and ending his suffering.

Hawke trains in the courtyard and sees the Maiden. While sparring with Vikter, he gets hell for being distracted. While Hawke denies it, Vikter tells him he has some *sage advice*. He says it only takes a heartbeat to lose all that truly matters.

Hawke feels like it's an omen.

He meets with Jansen, Kieran, and Jericho at the Red Pearl. Jansen mentions the guards are good men and says he doesn't like what they have to do.

I'm certain none of them particularly did.

They discuss the Maiden's habits and talk about where best to get to her, and Hawke tells Jericho that no harm should come to the Maiden.

With Hawke as Poppy's personal guard and Kieran still working as a City Guard, the plan is to take the Maiden the night of the Rite. The Descenters are supposed to create a distraction by setting some fires.

After the others leave, Hawke and Kieran talk about the Maiden's ancestry and why the Ascended value her so much. They can't figure it out. Hawke says they'll likely get more out of the Ascended they *befriend*. Kieran agrees and then leaves to check on their other resources.

Meanwhile, Poppy wanders into the Red Pearl downstairs, and I work a little of my matchmaker magic to get her and Casteel in the same room. After that, I knew nature would run its course.

Thinking that Poppy is a maid named Britta, whom Casteel has dallied with in the past, he welcomes the intrusion to his room at the Pearl but is still wary since the woman doesn't smell like Britta, she doesn't feel like Britta, and she makes him feel things Britta never has. But she's a welcome distraction, nonetheless, and he takes her to the bed, kissing her deeply and exploring as much of her as he can with her still cloaked.

When he finally lowers her hood and takes in her face, he's shocked. She may be masked like most are wont to do at the Pearl, but he knows exactly who he has beneath him. It's Penellaphe. The Chosen. The Maiden. They spend an intriguing span of time together before Kieran interrupts with important news, forcing Casteel to leave.

Sometime later, Kieran and Hawke meet Emil and Delano in Wisher's Grove. Cas greets them both, and Emil gives him shit—as usual. Kieran tells the Atlantian he has a death wish.

He really does.

Emil relays that the King and Queen are worried, and Alastir hasn't helped assuage their anxiety. After they talk a bit more, Cas feeds from Emil and sees the Atlantian's memories, which interestingly enough are of Vonetta.

Very interesting, indeed.

Emil offers to stay close in case he's needed, but Cas tells him to go to Evaemon and watch Alastir to run interference.

As they leave the Grove, Cas tells Kieran he doesn't plan to kill the Maiden like his parents do—or would if they got their hands on her. Kieran just takes it in.

When Casteel returns to the room at the Red Pearl, he finds that Poppy didn't wait for him. He trails her through the Grove and finds an Ascended stalking her. He tears the vampry's heart out and leaves him hanging over the branch of a tree. Either he'll be discovered, and it will cause talk, or the sun will take care of him when it rises.

Either way, win-win.

He takes a bath and gets turned on by thoughts of the Maiden, which both confuses him and makes him a little angry. He's conflicted. He pleasures himself to thoughts of her but then thinks about his time in captivity—the assault, his trauma, his healing. Steeling his resolve, he reestablishes his goal in his mind.

Hawke wonders what's going on when Poppy doesn't visit the garden like she usually does. He catches sight of Lord Mazeen with the Duchess and finds out they're looking for a Descenter. He overhears talk about puncture wounds on a body, and then Mazeen mentions Lord Preston—the vampry Hawke strung up for stalking the Maiden.

Good. Then he served as the message intended.

When the Lord walks by, Hawke realizes he smells of jasmine and…something else. When he realizes it's the Maiden's scent, it bothers him more than it probably should.

Britta comes to say hello, and Hawke asks her what happened, indicating what's going on in the castle. She tells him that Malessa Axton, a Lady in Wait, was killed and left in the castle. After some prompting about the Lord, Hawke learns that Mazeen is, indeed, a bit too *friendly.*

His people make things happen to advance their plot and take out Poppy's guard Rylan Keal, thus opening a Royal Guard position at Poppy's side. However, when Jansen comes to Hawke on the Rise to tell him the guard had been taken care of, Hawke finds out Jericho tried to take the Maiden, and she fought back. Even cut him. In retaliation, the wolven hit her.

Hawke heads to the Three Jackals, but Kieran catches up with him before he makes it and says he can't kill Jericho. Hawke says he's not going to. He's going to murder him. Kieran tells him that they're the same, and Cas explains the difference—which is ridiculous.

Hawke and Kieran enter a room at the pub to find Jericho playing cards with some other wolven and Descenters. He tries to calm Hawke, explaining what happened.

Hawke pours him a glass of whiskey as a distraction and then cuts off his left hand. He warns him to do as he's told next time—no more, no less—then leaves, telling Kieran to send Jericho to New Haven.

The day of Rylan's funeral, Hawke watches over the Maiden as Vikter goes to light the pyre.

Sometime later, Kieran and Hawke meet up with Descenter Lev Barron in the warehouse district and find a dead couple and a baby who's turned Craven. It's pure disregard for life and disgusts Hawke. He takes the baby's life and vows to make them all pay.

Summoned to the Duke's office, Hawke goes and meets with the Ascended. The Duke tells Hawke that a guard must not fear death. Hawke disagrees and tells him that if one doesn't fear death, then they don't fear failure. He tells the Duke how he would have handled the situation in the garden and other times watching the Maiden. When the Duke insinuates some things, Hawke says he has no interest in seducing the Maiden or becoming her friend. The Duke warns that her innocence is charming and warns that Hawke will be flayed alive if anything happens to the Maiden.

The Duke and Duchesses address the people about current happenings, and Hawke observes the Maiden. She isn't like others, and it both charms and frustrates him. The Tulis family is outed as Descenters, and Lev is taken prisoner after throwing a Craven hand at the Royals. Hawke orders his people to remove the Tulises so they don't have to give up their only remaining child.

Called back to the Duke's office for the official assignment, Hawke is introduced to Poppy and Tawny and given a rundown of the rules and what's required of him. With each word out of the Duke's mouth, he hates him more and more. When the Maiden is unveiled, he's stunned speechless. She's stunning, and he can see the strength and resilience in her.

Escorting Tawny and the Maiden back to her chambers, Hawke remains outside and eavesdrops on their conversation. Every time Tawny talks him up or tries to convince her friend of something, Hawke thinks how the Lady in Wait has become his favorite person.

Eventually, Vikter brings Hawke his white mantle and warns Hawke to watch himself.

After discussing the Maiden's schedule, Vikter warns Hawke about Penellaphe's nightmares and tells him about her Craven attack when she was six. When Hawke inquires whether he'll know if it's only a nightmare or if it's an attack, Vikter tells him that she will never scream if she's in distress.

After everything is shared, Hawke realizes what an abysmal existence Penellaphe has had. It bothers him more than it probably should, and he can't stop thinking about it.

During his off hours, Cas finds a note from Kieran and goes to the meat packing district. He enters the slaughterhouse building overseen by a Descenter named Mac, then goes downstairs to where Kieran is with Lord Hale Devries. The Ascended is tied up and unconscious.

Kieran wakes him by dumping a bucket of cold water over his head, and Cas asks the Lord where Malik is being kept. The vampry replies that he knows of no *kept* Prince—which is true, since Malik was no longer kept at this point.

Easily sliding into all the things required of him as the Maiden's personal guard, Hawke somehow finds himself torn between his duty and plans, and what he starts feeling for the Maiden.

While guarding her, he starts to wonder why he hasn't seen her in several days after he escorted her to the Duke's office. While thinking about the fires the Descenters set to create chaos, he hears a scream coming from the Maiden's room. He goes in and hides in the shadows, thinking he should probably think of her by name. He looks at the sparseness of her room and once again thinks about the horrible life she's had—not at all like what he and others imagined. He checks on her and catches the scent of arnica.

The mist comes again, and Hawke goes beyond the Rise, seeing Vikter there, as well. He realizes that means nobody is watching the Maiden and goes to check on her. Instead, he finds someone on the parapet firing arrows. He's *very* intrigued when he discovers it's Penellaphe.

Hawke talks to Vikter, and Vikter asks why he hasn't told anyone about Penellaphe being on the Rise. He tries to explain, thinking his respect for her is a complicated mess, then tells Vikter he knows he's the one who trained her.

As time goes on, Hawke and Penellaphe share personal information and get to know each other, stealing intimate moments where they can—which only makes Hawke want things to become *more* intimate.

He realizes how intense things are getting when Britta visits him in his room and basically throws herself at him, and he denies her.

Surly over that knowledge, Cas goes to the Red Pearl and walks in on Kieran and Circe having sex. The couple invites him to join—which wouldn't be a big deal, he's done it before—but he's not in the mood. He sulks, seethes about how he's imagining having sex with Penellaphe, and drinks until they finish.

Kieran gives him shit for sitting with a hard-on and asks him what's going on. He tells him a little and then shifts focus to how he plans to kill the Duke. Kieran tells him he can't. He adds that it'd be revenge and it's selfish.

They discuss Penellaphe being on the Rise and how they really have underestimated her, and Kieran just comes out and says that Cas cares about the Maiden. He denies it and assures his friend that plans haven't changed.

Hawke follows Penellaphe to the Atheneum and finds her hanging outside on a windowsill with my journal tucked against her chest. He teases her about it, reads a bit from it, and embarrasses her before escorting her home. He also calls her *Poppy* for the first time.

This was a real turning point for them. It was clear Hawke was already softening and enthralled, but him using her nickname was a big forward step.

As they walk through the Grove, they talk about her dulling her tongue when she's not with him. She sasses him even more. Then, they talk a bit more about reading.

Cas just can't resist teasing her about my journal, and I love it so much.

When he realizes that his plans will basically just swap one cage for another for her, it bothers him. And the fact that it bothers him bothers him.

Yep. The guy has it bad...

Later, Hawke waits in the Duke's office with his feet on a dead guard. When he sees the canes, his fury rises. He insists that what he's planning isn't revenge and tries to solidify that in his mind.

The Duke comes in and is shocked to find Hawke. Even more so when he sees his dead guard. He threatens Hawke, making him laugh. He reveals himself as the Dark One and the Prince of Atlantia and tells Dorian he has no idea who is in his city.

The Duke insists Hawke will never get the Maiden, and Cas overpowers him. He makes him blink to show him how many times he whipped her and then gives it back.

During, something comes over the Duke and he says that Poppy is and will always be his—I have a feeling he was channeling Kolis there, but that's just my hypothesis.

Incensed, Hawke impales him with a blood tree cane and then puts him behind the banner where the Rite is being held.

When he meets Poppy and the others, he acts like nothing happened.

Cas attends the Rite and spends some quality time under the willow with Poppy. When they emerge, Vikter catches them and has some choice words for them both. Hawke talks back but ultimately lets Poppy go with Vikter.

Kieran gives him hell for not taking Vikter out and taking Penellaphe right then and there. Cas assures him it's only a slight delay. He tells Kieran he'll meet him in the Grove with the Maiden. Kieran says something doesn't feel right to him but tells Cas the Descenters have set things in motion.

When Cas returns to the castle, the Rite battle is already underway. He joins in, looking for the Maiden the entire time. When he finally finds her, it's to see her swallowed in grief and wrath. He watches as she witnesses her friend and guard, someone who was like a father to her, be struck down. Then stands back and watches as she approaches Lord Mazeen with fury in her eyes.

With everything that happened, Casteel knows it's time to make his move. He allows her to take her vengeance but then subdues her. But as he does, he realizes they can't go right away. Jansen sends word to Kieran in the Grove about what happened, and Cas doesn't think delaying for a bit longer will matter much.

Upstairs sometime later, Cas and Tawny talk about how the Maiden just needs time. Tawny tells Hawke she thinks he cares about Poppy. While he admits it to himself, he doesn't out loud.

The Duchess arrives and tells him about the sleeping draft Poppy was taking. She adds that his loyalty is admirable and says the Queen will be pleased.

That makes my skin crawl because we know that's all just a manipulation.

Cas goes to see Kieran at the Red Pearl, and they talk about Valyn. They also discuss how Cas has regrets. They talk about how they still don't know what Poppy's role is with the Ascended. Regardless, Cas can only think about how she deserves a future. He doesn't say that, though. He lies and tells Kieran the plans are the same despite the delay.

Poppy and Hawke set off for the capital with eight men and continue growing closer as the days pass, despite the circumstances. They share things about their pasts and personal things about themselves—vulnerable things. And all along, Kieran continues to remind him to remember his task and stick to the plan.

In New Haven, Cas meets with Elijah, Delano, and Kieran, and they discuss next steps and what's happened so far.

Finally, Poppy and Hawke are no longer able to resist each other and have sex. The next day, he meets with Elijah, Delano and Orion—an Atlantian bearing a missive from the Crown. They find out he's being shady, and when he threatens Poppy's life, Cas rips out his heart and throws it into the fire, telling everyone the messenger died unexpectedly during his journey.

Cas realizes he needs to go to Berkton to meet with his father, but there's a storm on the way. Delano offers to go with him, but Cas tells him he needs him in New Haven. Elijah assures him that Poppy will be okay.

Suddenly, Naill bursts in, saying that Phillips (one of the men they traveled with) is trying to leave with Poppy. They all rush to the stables.

Cas's schemes come to light when he kills one of the guards in front of Poppy and tells her the events that led to where they are now.

Clearly, she doesn't take it well—neither that nor seeing Kieran shift into his wolven form—so he has her confined to the dungeon so she can't escape or hurt anybody.

On his way back from Berkton, he receives word that she was attacked and feels terrible fear. Kieran takes her to his chambers, so he meets them once he arrives and sees how bad things are. He takes her to the floor by the fire and pries the dagger from her hands.

To help her heal, he feeds her his blood and loses himself in her sensual reaction to it.

Finally, he comes clean that he is, in fact, Casteel Da'Neer, Prince of Atlantia—whom she has been taught is and only knows *as* the Dark One. Being—as he calls her now—the absolutely stunning murderous little creature she is, she stabs him in the heart and runs.

When he catches up to her, he explains that he—unlike the wolven or an Ascended—cannot be killed by a blade to the heart. Telling her that everything between them has been real and that nothing has been a lie, he bites her, immediately realizing that she's part Atlantian. He can't control his lust, and they have glorious, unfettered sex in the snowy forest.

It brought back some *very* good memories for me. I should go back and read those journal entries in the volumes I still have in my possession...

Later, Casteel confesses that his feelings got in the way of his plan, and she takes away his pain—both the physical and the emotional—making him realize why the vamprys wanted her so badly. He then tells her he's taking her home to Atlantia, but after some dissent within his ranks, he suddenly realizes that it's imperative for him to show his people that she's under his protection.

After nailing all those who attacked Poppy to the hall walls with bloodstone spikes through their hands and hearts and heads—leaving only Jericho alive, minus a hand—he informs all the others that Poppy is part Atlantian and the two of them are going home to be married. As their journey progresses, they share stolen moments amidst sniping at each other, and Casteel tells her that he has not lied to her since she discovered who he is and explains his reasons for wanting to marry her.

When Poppy tries to escape again, and Casteel realizes she planned to go to the Ascended, hoping they'd take her to the capital where she could find and free her brother, he tells her that he refuses to carve her name in the wall of the tombs like so many of the other dead and returns her bloodstone dagger.

As he watches Poppy's gifts change and grow, Casteel knows there's something special about her—and it's not just her heritage or her blood. When the Ascended finally track her down and attack, he confronts them and says: "I am born of the first kingdom. Created from the blood and ash of all those who fell before me. I have risen to take back what is mine. I'm who you call the Dark One." And then he continues. "Yes, I have the Maiden, and I'm not giving her back."

Something he meant in more ways than one, I'm sure.

After a battle with the Ascended that leaves him afraid she'll be dead when he finally gets to her, he gives her his blood to help her heal and uses a mild compulsion on her to help her sleep, thus skipping the hyperarousal that usually comes from the act of feeding.

Why anyone would want to skip that is beyond me. That's the best part. But I digress...

Casteel's feelings continue to grow, yet she still seems hesitant, so he asks her to pretend and live in the moment with him. To not worry about the past or the future.

As someone all about roleplay and pretending, that was super sexy to me. But it was also ridiculously sweet.

After gifting Poppy with her retribution for Lord Chaney attacking her and taking the child hostage, he sets off to take care of his princely duties, even though he hates leaving her. Being away from her is getting harder and harder as the days pass. Later, when Poppy has a nightmare, he comforts her and *pretends* again. But it's becoming something more than a ruse with him. He can't seem to stop himself from pleasuring her and loves to watch her shatter beneath his touch.

Continuing their journey to Atlantia, Casteel worries about his people. He plans to wait for the first group from New Haven before continuing on to the Skotos Mountains, but he finds that he's not *only* worrying about his people. His protective instincts for Poppy continue to grow—as do his feelings.

When Poppy tells him she's not his and says she only belongs to herself, he asks her if she'd be willing to give him at least a piece, whatever one she chooses, and tells her that it will be his most prized possession.

Could he *be* any sweeter?

They eventually discuss their relationship, what they can expect, and what people will expect of *them*, as well as the changes in Poppy. In passing, Cas mentions her finding someone to love for real after all is said and done, but the way he poses it, it's really still about them—I wonder if maybe he didn't even realize it. When Poppy asks him if he's ever been in love, he confirms that he has, but cuts off any more questions she has by simply saying, "She's gone." He doesn't want to talk about Shea. Who could blame him?

Things are pretty quiet for the next three days until their group comes upon the Dead Bones Clan. Cas gives Poppy a crossbow and shows her how to use it. It's a sign of trust, plus necessary. When the Clan attacks, their group fights valiantly, but Casteel is injured in the battle, shot with multiple arrows—in his left shoulder, just to the right of the center of his back, one in the back, and another in the stomach. The last gets stuck when he tries to pull it out, but he assures Poppy it's not serious.

Once settled in Spessa's End, Casteel rouses with Poppy but wakes up starving. The injuries he sustained took too much out of him, not to mention the blood he gave Poppy to heal. But despite his need for blood, he hungers for *her* and is done waiting. He scares her a bit at first until she realizes his intentions. Then…he devours her. Until Kieran storms in to stop him, worried about Poppy's safety—and Cas's mental state should he accidentally hurt her. Eventually, the Prince comes out of it and apologizes. But he knows he'll never think of honeydew the same.

Despite needing blood, he hesitates when Poppy offers to feed him. When she insists, he ultimately relents and says he'll do it, but only under one condition:

They can't be left alone. They invite Kieran to oversee the act, and when he's fed enough, Casteel lets Kieran leave and offers to ease Poppy's lustful ache—her glorious reaction to having him feed from her. He tells her how brave and generous he thinks she is. How beautiful. And then brings her to climax with skilled hands while finding release himself—something he says has never happened before like that.

Earnestly, he admits that he'll *always* want more when it comes to her and asks to hold her, to pretend once again, even though it hasn't been a ruse to him in quite some time. He doesn't think she'll let him. So, when she does, he tells her that there are no takebacks and pulls her close, reveling in how she melts against him.

My heart is melting again while writing this, just like it did when I *saw* it.

Casteel proposes a field trip to the *real* Spessa's End for Poppy, the one that outsiders don't get to see, but gives her an ultimatum. He'll only do it if they keep pretending to be a couple—his ruse to keep her close. They seal the deal with a kiss, and Poppy laughs. It absolutely undoes him.

Her laugh *is* pretty spectacular.

When a young wolven named Beckett is hurt and Poppy heals him, Casteel witnesses her glowing and wants her so badly it's nearly unfathomable. Being Cas and never afraid to speak his mind, he tells her—both that she glowed and that he wants to do wicked things to her.

Pretty sure I would feel the same.

It's clear that her powers are growing, and it absolutely awes him. However, it concerns him, as well. He discusses her gifts with her and asks her not to use them in front of crowds until they know more and can control the narrative.

They talk about their upcoming nuptials, and Cas tells Poppy that he wants to marry her now in Spessa's End. She agrees, but Alastir is anything but pleased by the news. Casteel isn't happy with the wolven's reaction and reiterates that *Poppy* is what he wants. After the encounter and needing to share some of the beauty of Spessa's End with Poppy, he takes her to the poppy fields and the caves, letting little bits of his truth free and telling her how he feels.

While in the cavern, they agree to stop pretending and have wicked and wondrous sex in the hot springs. When they return to the others, Alastir's ire turns vile, and he blurts out that Casteel is already promised to another—namely, Alastir's niece, Gianna.

Poppy is clearly hurt by the news—who wouldn't be after everything they shared? Casteel can almost see her thoughts on her face and argues with Alastir, saying that what he did was a weak move. He explains his actions once again, reiterating his love for Poppy. He even goes so far as to reveal that she stabbed him in the chest after learning of his original plans in an attempt to smooth things over with those in attendance.

Poppy tells everyone that she knew about his plans to capture and use her, but she fell for him anyway—when he was still Hawke. She goes on to say that he is the first thing she's ever chosen for herself.

Be still my heart.

Later, when Casteel goes to her chambers to wake her, they fight about Gianna. He tells her that he never openly protested the suggestion of the two of them marrying because he didn't want to hurt Alastir's niece but ensures Poppy that he's been completely honest with her about everything—except his need to feed. And he kept that from her for a good reason.

He asks her if what she said at dinner was true—that she's fallen for and chooses him—and admits that he wants everything from her. He shares that his original plan made less sense the more they interacted. And that with her, he can just *be*.

Before he can show her how much he loves her, they're interrupted and told the sky is on fire.

Yeah, that would be an ardor douser.

They wonder if it's an omen and go out to investigate, finding it's not actually the sky but something large in the distance. A bit later, Delano arrives, wounded, with news that the Ascended are on their way with an army.

Casteel sends Alastir and Kieran for reinforcements and asks Poppy to go with them. But, as usual, she's stubborn and resists. He threatens to compel her if she doesn't go but finally relents when she argues that she can be an asset and won't be a liability.

She's a great fighter. I would have believed her.

Kieran is angry about leaving Cas but knows it must be done. They share an emotional goodbye, and Casteel goes to determine who can fight. Once he's assessed, he arranges a strategy meeting and invites Poppy to join. Another sign of trust and love.

In a heartfelt exchange, Casteel admits that the most shame he's ever felt is tied to her and says he actually planned on taking her during the Rite. He even had Kieran and others waiting to move in. He also admits that he wanted...no, he *needed* to be her first everything, and that he still wants everything from her. He adds that he pretends he can have it, even when he knows she'll inevitably leave, leaving *him* still wanting.

Poor guy. I just want to hold him close.

In a moment of vulnerability and honesty, he finally tells Poppy about Shea, revealing that he doesn't talk about her. Not because he loved her but because he hates her and loathes what he was forced to do. He tells Poppy that only Malik and Kieran know the truth. The people of Atlantia think Shea died a hero, and he's okay with that. He goes on to explain that one of the big reasons he couldn't marry Gianna was because she looks like Shea, and it bothered him.

Poppy reciprocates by pouring out her heart to him and telling him how she really feels. He proposes again and asks her to marry him immediately. She accepts and tells him to remember he's worthy.

Casteel and Poppy marry in the traditional Atlantian way, but when they are pronounced husband and wife, the afternoon sky turns as dark as midnight. It's an omen, something that hasn't happened since Casteel's parents married, and is believed to be a blessing from Nyktos, showing his approval of their union.

After the wedding, Casteel takes in his new bride, utterly in awe. Poppy asks him why he stares at her when she laughs or smiles, and he tells her it's like déjà vu, as if he's heard it before, even before meeting her. When she asks about heartmates, he explains that it started at the beginning of recorded time, when one of the ancient deities fell so deeply in love with a mortal that he begged the gods to bestow the gift of long life on the one he chose. The ending of that story is sad, but the beauty behind the thought of having someone who is made for you, to complete you, is beautiful. They also discuss the Joining, which leads to shared blood and bodies.

And let me tell you, a glorious consummation of marriage it was.

When Duchess Teerman arrives with her knights, asking for the Maiden to be returned, Casteel demands that Poppy stay concealed on the Rise so as not to make herself a target. He also tells her that if anything should happen to him, she is to go to the caves. Kieran will find her there. But when the Duchess begins spouting lies about Ileana being Poppy's grandmother and the Queen not being Ascended, his new bride can't stay hidden—or silent. Casteel absolutely loves her spirit, but he hates when she paints a target on herself.

When the Duchess catapults her *gifts*, and Elijah's head lands at Casteel's feet, his fury consumes him. He tells Poppy to kill as many of them as possible and leaps from the Rise.

Once things die down a bit, she suggests she should just go to them so no more of their people die or get hurt, insisting they won't kill her. Casteel tells her they cannot have her because he knows what they will do to her. He says she is what matters now. *They* are.

I absolutely love him.

Before he can get her to safety, she threatens to kill herself if the Solis army doesn't stop, warning them what the Queen would do to them if they allowed that to happen. Cas wants to throttle her and tells her as much—because he knows she would do it. She's that impulsive. And while it shouldn't be something that endears her to him, it does. Luckily, her threat makes the soldiers hesitate—just long enough for the Atlantian Army to arrive.

The new couple greets Kieran and tells him he missed a lot, showing off the marriage imprint. But before Casteel can say more, Poppy's suddenly gone and rushing to the Royal carriage. He catches up, arriving just as Poppy destroys the Duchess. He's absolutely furious with his wife for her stunt earlier *and* for putting herself in danger, yet totally in awe of her—and wickedly turned on. He tells everybody they are not to get near the carriage under any circumstances and then enters with Poppy, closing them both inside. Bursting with emotion, he tells her that he needs her and asks if he can have her, then they show each other with their bodies what words cannot convey.

They spared a single Solis soldier in the battle, a boy barely past the cusp of manhood, and only so he could deliver a message for them. Casteel and a few others set out for the scorched land of Pompay with the boy so he can let the Ascended in Whitebridge know that Spessa's End has been reclaimed, and anyone who comes for it will meet the same fate as those before.

When Cas returns, he tells Poppy the wolven heard her during the battle and veered in her direction. Poppy relays what the Duchess said in the carriage about their brothers being together and Poppy accomplishing what the Queen never could: taking Atlantia.

Setting off again, they travel through the mist in the Skotos Mountains, planning to meet the others at Gold Rock. When they stop for the night, they discuss how the mist seems to be interacting with Poppy. That night, Poppy sleepwalks, but Casteel is able to stop her in time, pulling her back just before she walks off the side of the cliff.

He tells her that he thinks the gods helped him find her and says they seem to like her. Then he tells her he dreamed she was in the same cage he'd been held in and that he couldn't free her. He also tells her about Kieran's dream.

Seems something affected them all. It's my thought that the gods were already restless by this point, and Kolis was already affecting things in the mortal realm a bit.

They finally reach Gold Rock and reunite with the others. As they continue on and pass through the Pillars of Asphodel—not the same pillars as in the gods' times that served as the gateway to the Vale and the Abyss—Cas welcomes Poppy *home.*

With Poppy in awe of everything she's seeing for the first time, he leaves to speak with Alastir, and Beckett offers to take Poppy to the Chambers.

Word of a commotion reaches him, and he takes off to find her, arriving after the attack with Naill, Emil, Alastir, Casteel's parents, and others, only to see nothing but carnage and a mini forest of blood trees that were not there before.

When Jasper growls at him as he approaches, Cas suddenly understands what has happened. Something his mother confirms when she asks him what he has done and what he brought to Atlantia.

Alastir insists there's still time. Casteel drops to one knee, his short swords crossed over his chest as the wolven lower to their bellies or dip into bows, their hindquarters in the air.

Queen Eloana tells Alastir it's too late and removes her crown, placing it at the foot of the Nyktos statue before saying, "Lower your swords and bow before the last descendant of the most ancient ones, she who carries the blood of the King of the Gods within her. Bow before your new Queen."

When Poppy wobbles, Casteel goes to catch her but stops momentarily when all the wolven growl—even Kieran, *his* bonded wolven. He doesn't care. He understands they are just protecting her, something he is all about, and it makes him angry that the Royal Guard and those in the Temple see Poppy and the wolven as a threat. But then what Alastir says penetrates, and he realizes why the wolven are acting the way they are.

All the bonds between the Atlantians and the wolven have been broken. By his wife.

When Poppy explains what happened, Cas is enraged that his people tried to stone Poppy in the Temple and orders Beckett to be found. He also declares for all to hear that a move against his wife is a move against him, and anyone who even tries will die. He then orders that Alastir be seized.

Can you imagine having someone you've known all your life, someone you trusted implicitly, betray you like that? It hurts my heart to think of it.

When Casteel's father declares that Casteel is not the King yet and Poppy is not the Queen and orders Alastir to be put somewhere *safe*, Cas makes it known that if Alastir doesn't go willingly, *he'll* be the first at his throat. But before they can take him away, Alastir instructs the guards to protect their King and Queen— Valyn and Eloana, *not* Casteel and Poppy—and they attack.

Jasper and Kieran are hit with arrows during the skirmish, and Casteel moves to shield Poppy. Unfortunately, he is struck, as well—in the back, the shoulder, and the leg. And the shadowshade-dipped arrows turned his skin to stone.

I once saw someone wounded by shadowshade. It's not something I care to ever see again.

When Cas finally comes out of it a few days later, he and several others set off for Irelone to rescue Poppy, finding her by telling the Crown Guard that if the conspirators don't confess, he will start killing them all—using compulsion to make sure they got the message, and *he* got the information he needed.

He arrives and tears through the enemy, even going so far as to rip out the spine of someone rushing Poppy and Kieran. But when Poppy shouts for him to stop right before he kills a man in a mask, he does so without question, beyond surprised to find Jansen under the mask. Someone he trusted since before the Red Pearl—before things were even really set in motion.

He goes from pride at watching Poppy keep her promise to end Jansen to devastation when one of the Protectors hits her in the chest with a crossbow bolt. He makes promises to Poppy that he'll make it right and ignores his father's warnings and the things Kieran tries to tell him. Instead, he bites into his wrist and tries to get her to drink. When he sees that she's beyond that, he dissolves with grief.

When a blood tree grows around her, he makes his decision and tells those loyal to him to keep everyone else—especially those trying to stop him—away from Poppy and him, threatening to rip their hearts from their chests if they don't. He declares that not even the gods could stop him from doing what he plans to do next.

The one thing his father says he cannot do because he knows what will happen.

Ascend her.

When Poppy awakens, starving, and throws herself at Kieran, Casteel steps in to stop her, urging her to use him instead and marveling at the fact that she is alive but didn't Ascend.

He apologizes for not being there the minute she woke and tells her how in awe he is of her, going on to remind her how brave she is and saying that he's unworthy. When she finally feeds enough to come back to herself, he tells her how much he needs her and loves her, marveling at the fact that she says it in return— for the first time!—and they show each other with bodies and mouths and more just how much.

But even with her back in his arms and still being able to see the beautiful green of her eyes versus the black he so feared, he blames himself for the attack and feels he didn't do enough to ensure her safety.

When Poppy questions what happened when she was out of it, he tells her that she died and that his marriage imprint had even begun to fade, which was when he knew there was no turning back and started the process of Ascending her. They then discuss the things that came after—her trying to eat Kieran, him feeding from Naill, the fact that she didn't, in fact, Ascend.

They talk with Kieran about what happened at the Temple and why she didn't Ascend, thus turning into a vampry. Kieran reminds Poppy that he told her she smelled of Death, not like something dead, and Casteel adds that her blood doesn't just taste old, it tastes *ancient*. Therefore, the blood in her must be old power. They also talk about why she did what she did—or was able to do—in the Chambers, deducing it was her being on Atlantian land combined with the blood she'd taken from Casteel, along with a few other things.

Boy, would they be surprised when they discovered the truth of it.

When Poppy inquires about the wolven bonds, Casteel confirms that his tether to Kieran is indeed broken. Kieran says they just made room for her.

That seriously makes me a puddle of goo. He's just so sweet and sexy.

They discuss Alastir, and Poppy reveals that he was there the night she and her parents were attacked at Lockswood, Casteel tells her that he meant what he said when he promised she could have whatever she wanted. And then he tells her that Alastir is all hers.

Sweet, sweet retribution. There is something utterly erotic about exacting vengeance when punishment is due.

Before they set off for the Skotos Mountains, Casteel tells Poppy how impressed he is with her new strength and asks her to demonstrate by hitting him. When she refuses, he goads her by teasing her about how much she loves my journal—who wouldn't?—and finally gets her to slug him in the stomach, most definitely proving how much stronger she is.

As they ride on, Casteel notes how the mist seems different through the mountains this time. It scatters to let them pass. And when they reach the trees of Aios, they see that they are different, too. Instead of the gold forest they are all used to, they find one full of blood-red trees.

Coming from someone who both saw and enjoyed the beautiful golden trees, seeing them turn the color of blood was indeed a shock. But they were still stunning, and I knew it heralded the changes yet to come.

When they stop to rest for the night, Delano begins howling, sensing Poppy's distress, and Casteel has to wake her from what appears to be a nightmare, marveling at the connection she has to the wolven now.

When they reach the Temple of Saion, Casteel inquires if anyone knows that he's having his father held. He's told that his mother and the Crown Guards think Valyn is with them. He also learns that some Atlantians and mortals attempted to free Alastir and were dealt with, but some are still alive for the couple's... enjoyment.

When they're finally face-to-face with his father, Casteel and Poppy reveal that she's not a vampry. When Valyn still admonishes his son for doing what he did, Casteel tells him that he knew what he was doing the entire time and would do it all over again, even if she *had* Ascended. He then adds that she is his everything and that nothing is greater than she is. They part ways, and the couple heads off to see to Alastir.

With absolutely no mercy, Casteel beheads all those who tried to set Alastir free, leaving only the wolven alive. Cas then tells Alastir that he betrayed both him and Atlantia, but stresses that those weren't the worst of his sins. He then confronts him about that day so long ago when Alastir became the one responsible for Poppy's nightmares and scars. Holding his sword to his neck, Casteel threatens him, ultimately wiping his blade on the man's clothing and turning him over to Poppy so she can have her revenge.

She takes it. Gladly.

They arrive in Saion's Cove to a large crowd heralding the return of their Prince. Cas apologizes to Poppy for overwhelming her but says there is no other way for them to get to Jasper's. When the praise turns to Poppy, and the crowd starts cheering, "Meyaah *Liessa*," calling her their Queen, he once again feels awe.

When they reach the stables and Casteel introduces Poppy as someone very special to him—his wife—the most extraordinary thing happens. All the wolven approach and shift, dropping to one knee with their hands over their hearts, their loyalty directed at Poppy.

Arriving in their chambers, Casteel tells her what's inscribed on their wedding rings—*always and forever*—and reminds her that they are real with each other, always and forever. He then goes on to tell her he knows a lot has happened and that it's okay for her to feel however she feels. When she finally breaks down, he is—as promised—there to pick up the pieces and pulls her close.

Casteel takes the opportunity while Poppy slumbers to peruse my journal. When Poppy wakes and finds him thumbing through the leather-bound volume, he teases her by reading one of my most favorite entries: the night Andre, Torro, and I had a tawdry tryst in a garden, later joined by Lady Celestia, making the evening even more memorable. There was indeed more than one manhood and lots of scandalous lady parts about.

Casteel leaves to speak with his father. When he returns, he's dumped into the middle of an Unseen attack—an extremist group he thought had either disbanded or died out—complete with Gyrms. When they finally prevail, he pulls Poppy to him and congratulates her on her kills.

When they discuss what to do about the Unseen, Poppy tries to convince Casteel that they shouldn't be killed because they don't trust or like her. She believes they should be given a chance to redeem themselves. Casteel agrees to a trial but says he will have the ultimate say on whether they live or die.

They talk about her claim to the throne, and Casteel tells her he will support her in whatever decision she makes. However, they will have to leave Atlantia if she chooses to renounce it. But he reiterates that it's okay. He doesn't want her to take another role she doesn't want and didn't choose, and he loves her more than his people. Though he does add that she would be an amazing Queen and a much better ruler than he would ever be.

A child gets injured in an accident, and Casteel witnesses Poppy healing the girl—someone beyond saving. When she does, he realizes that she is, indeed, a goddess. He's always thought her to be, but this is actual confirmation. When they discuss it later, he surmises that she either willed the girl's soul to remain or brought her back to life.

Casteel introduces Poppy to Kieran's mother, Kirha, and meets his parents at Cove Palace. They all discuss Poppy's heritage, and he learns that Poppy's parents couldn't have been mortal. When he learns more about the past, he's enraged that his parents remained close to Alastir when they *knew* he'd left a child to be murdered by the Craven. His father only replies that Cas will have to learn to stomach things that will haunt his dreams if he is to become King.

When Poppy's brother Ian arrives, they arrange for a convoy to Spessa's End. After they meet with Ian, Cas and Poppy discuss why she didn't kill her brother and whether Poppy should take the crown. But before they can do more than discuss the coronation, the Unseen attack again. This time, Poppy uses her power to defeat them, and Casteel is beyond proud of her—and very turned on.

I saw some of that in a vision and she *was* resplendent.

After the couple claims the thrones of Atlantia, they meet the Council. It's their first time meeting me, and it brings me great pleasure when they realize who I am and that their most scandalous—at least, according to Poppy—and enjoyable reading material is actually my personal journal.

When some of the Council thinks to speak their minds about Poppy, Casteel tells them they will either bow to their Queen or bleed before her.

It made me smile.

After plans are made for their trip to Oak Ambler and Iliseeum, they discuss things they've learned thus far—about me setting them up at the Red Pearl, about the prophecy, about what Poppy has to possibly look forward to regarding her hunger...

Knowing they need someone to act as their right hand, Casteel and Poppy ask Kieran to be their Advisor, assemble the group to make the trip to Iliseeum, and then set off with Kieran, Vonetta, Emil, and Delano.

When they arrive, they do so to many perils: the mist, the Consort's soldiers, and smoke snakes. Casteel urges Poppy to use eather to defeat anything that may harm her and then reminds the group they will not be going into Dalos, and that Nyktos's guards may be near.

When they finally do come face-to-face with the King of Gods, Casteel tries to defend Poppy when she displays a little attitude with Nyktos, and he threatens to kill her. Then he makes Poppy promise that she won't get herself killed when talking to the Primal privately.

After their meeting, Casteel asks Poppy about the woman she's been seeing and surmises that she might be a Primal, too. He also takes Nyktos's final words to Poppy—that she is due more than one crown and kingdom—to mean she'll one day rule both Solis *and* Atlantia.

After they assemble their team to head to Oak Ambler and set off on the ship, Casteel helps Poppy with her seasickness by distracting her in the most deliciously carnal way possible while reading from my journal—it's a particularly wonderful passage.

Casteel admits to Poppy that when the Blood Crown held him as their prisoner, he'd often forget himself and feel like a *thing* as opposed to a person. He tells her that Kieran is the only one who knows the depths of what he went through. He reveals that being called "Cas" or "Hawke" was sometimes all it took for him to remember that he *wasn't* a thing.

No wonder he was so full of wonder the first time she called him that.

As their journey continues, he and Poppy come upon a large cat in a cage, and he marvels at how much it looks like the cave cats of old they believed to be extinct. He hates that he has to tell Poppy that they cannot set him free. Still, he promises to include him in their deal with the Blood Queen. When Poppy inquires whether the cat could be Malec, he tells her that Malec wasn't that kind of deity and couldn't take that form.

When the Queen and her people confront them, Casteel is horrified to find his brother Malik at Ileana's side and asks him what she's done. When Malik reveals that the Queen wanted Poppy to marry *him* and remarks that *he* was to be her Ascension…of the flesh, Kieran has to hold Casteel back.

He further learns that Alastir told Ileana about the ultimatum they planned to give and learns that she would rather see the whole kingdom burn than hand over even a single acre. When he hears Ileana's counteroffer, he tells her that she's out of her mind.

Seems war is inevitable.

As Ileana reveals more, Casteel struggles to accept what he's being told: that Ileana is actually Isbeth, that Isbeth is Poppy's mother, that Malec is a god, that *Isbeth* is a god because Malec Ascended her…

I didn't believe most of it myself.

Then he tells Isbeth they don't agree to her terms, which ultimately results in Isbeth having Poppy's brother killed and causing a skirmish to break out.

During the battle, Cas catches Poppy as she's being choked by Isbeth's magic and orders everyone to stand down. He tells Isbeth that she can have whatever she wants and offers himself up, saying it's the only way for her to control Poppy.

Malik takes him to the dungeon and shackles him with shadowstone around his ankles and throat.

As the days pass, Handmaidens randomly swarm the cell to take blood from him. He's able to take many of them out, resulting in them shortening his chains, but he also learns something invaluable: not all the Queen's Handmaidens are Revenants—one actually *stayed* dead after he took her out.

A few hours after a bloodletting, five Handmaidens enter his cell, followed by Isbitch, as I've come to love to call her after hearing it in a vision. She reveals some things that lead him to realize that Isbeth is a demis, and he learns more about how they're created.

He's enraged when they tell him he hasn't earned the right to see his brother, but it thrills him when he learns what Poppy did to King Jalara and that she knows where Malec is and threatened to kill the god.

Isbeth intuits that Casteel's only interest in Poppy is her power, which doesn't surprise him. But when the Blood Queen keeps talking and reveals that she doesn't want Atlantia, she wants to remake the *realms*, and believes Poppy is destined to help her do it…that *does* shock him.

They leave him alone for a while until Callum comes and stabs Casteel with a shadowstone dagger.

With the captivity, bloodletting, and new blood loss, Casteel realizes he needs to feed and fears becoming the thing he turned into while in captivity before. There are also other similarities between then and now. They bring in a bath, and he refuses to use it, knowing they were always rewards or preludes to punishments, and he hasn't done anything to deserve a reward.

When they remove his index finger, he's more bothered by the fact that they took his wedding ring than by the loss of the digit. And why wouldn't he be? It was a union blessed by the gods and a symbol of their always and forever. At least he knows that Kieran is with her.

When the Queen's Handmaiden, Millicent, comes in to tend to him, something about her seems familiar. He wonders if it's her scent, but he can't quite place it. She proceeds to tell him that she broke the wards in the tunnels when she Ascended into her godhood and that Poppy carries the blood of both the Primal of Life and the Primal of Death within her. Casteel immediately assumes it's Nyktos, but Millicent shuts that down right away by telling him that he knows nothing.

She goes on to inform Cas that while it's true that Isbeth doesn't have the power to remake the realms, she knows how to bring to life something that *does*. The information leaves Cas reeling, thinking about what it could all mean.

That night, Cas dream walks with Poppy at the pool in the cave. He revels in the fact that he's able to touch her. Love her. But he remains cold and hears the clanking of chains, so he knows it's not real. Still, given that it is more than a dream, it confirms one thing: he and Poppy are heartmates.

Later, he regrets not telling Poppy that he is underground and that Isbeth is a demis, but he can't regret what happened in the dream. When more Craven attack, he kills one and takes its shin bone to use as a weapon. It's better than nothing…

When Malik visits, Casteel feels a brief flash of hope that his brother is there to break him out. Sadly, that is quickly quashed. The betrayal stokes his anger, but he does understand some of it. As Malik said, if he fed Cas, the Queen would discover their visit and punish Casteel. Malik does disinfect and bandage Cas's wound, however, leading Cas to believe that Millie must have told his brother about what was going on with him.

They discuss Shea, and Malik admits that he's been thinking about her a lot. When Cas reveals that he killed her, it seems to come as no surprise to his brother. And then they talk about Preela. Malik tells Casteel exactly what happened to his bonded wolven and reveals that Poppy's dagger is made from her bones. It sickens Cas, and he realizes that losing Preela like that was likely the catalyst to what happened to Malik and led to what he became.

Cas then begins to put some things together regarding his brother and the Handmaiden. When Malik asks Casteel not to take revenge on Millie for anything that has been done, Cas asks his brother if he cares about her. Malik tells him he's incapable of that, but she—like Poppy—had no choice in her life. And he owes her. Then he cryptically tells Casteel that everything has to do with Poppy and she likely won't remember him.

Thinking through everything he's learned, all the what-ifs nag Casteel. That night, he dream walks with Poppy again and reveals to her that she's a goddess. He tells her that he knew the minute he learned Malec was a god. But then Poppy tells him that Malec *isn't* her father. His twin, Ires, is. And Ires is the cave cat they saw. It all enrages him, but he's glad Isbeth doesn't know where Malec is entombed.

They talk more, and Poppy tells him they're coming for him and are close. She also tells him that she summoned Nyktos's guards and has Kieran and Reaver—one of the draken—with her.

They share additional information: the fact that he's underground, the fact that Isbeth is a demis and what that means, the fact that the Blood Queen knows how to use Primal energy, and that's what killed the other draken Poppy brought with her…

Recounting this, I can't help but feel relief that Nithe escaped the slaughter. I will always hold the night we shared close.

Callum wakes Cas with a bucket of cold water, and Isbeth confronts him. He taunts her before stabbing her in the chest with the bone. He barely misses her heart and tells her it's payback for what she did to Poppy's brother. Callum comes for him, and he fights, trying to get to Isbeth again—with no luck.

Isbeth then reveals some big and pertinent information. Primals have a weakness. Love can be used as a weapon to weaken and then end them. They can also be born in the mortal realm, and gods pushed Primals into their eternal rest by Ascending. However, the Fates created a loophole, allowing the greatest power to rise again. The rub is that it is only in the females of the Primal of Life's line…suggesting that Isbeth didn't birth a god, she birthed a *Primal*. Poppy is a Primal.

Time passes, and he starts going out of his mind with bloodlust. He barely notices when Poppy comes to him. She uses her gift to bring him out of his haze and heals his wounds. But when he sees Callum instead of Kieran, he knows she isn't there to rescue him. Something happened. She tells him they were caught outside Three Rivers and brought to the Queen. When she offers to feed him, he refuses out of fear of weakening her.

When Cas realizes that Isbeth doesn't know that Poppy brought a draken with her, it pleases him. And when she demands that he be given water and allowed to feed and then displays her power, she utterly awes him. Again. Still, he convinces her to leave. She has plans to make and can't do it down in the dungeon with him.

The next time Millie comes to see him, washing the black color from her hair and clearing her face of paint, he realizes why she seems so familiar. She confirms his suspicions by telling him that she's the first daughter, Poppy's full-blooded sister. She goes on to say that unlike Poppy, she's not a god. She's a failure. The more she reveals, the more answers he gets, but the more questions it raises. She details Isbeth's long-running plan and tells Cas that when Poppy completes her Culling, she'll give her mother exactly what she's wanted since the Queen's son died: revenge against everyone. She doesn't want to remake the realms, she wants to *destroy* them, and Poppy is destined to help with that. She *is* the harbinger foretold. Millie continues by saying that everything prophesied to happen *will* happen. Poppy will bring about the end, and Casteel will fail. He will kill Poppy.

Haunted by his thoughts, he thinks over everything the Handmaiden told him. He knows he will never kill Poppy, but things with the prophecy have been revealing themselves to be true…albeit not as expected.

When Callum returns, he tells Casteel that Poppy stabbed him with his own dagger, and Cas couldn't be prouder. But when Callum reveals that while Casteel's arrogance is impressive, he's seen love bring down the most powerful of beings and has only seen love beat death once—with Nyktos and his Consort, it reveals to Cas just how old Callum is. And then…the Revenant stabs him in the chest, sending him straight into bloodlust.

Kieran, Poppy, and Malik come for him, but he's too far gone to realize what's happening. Kieran distracts him while Malik renders him unconscious, and then Reaver frees him from the bone chains before his brother carries him from the cell. Poppy uses her gifts and tries to heal him, but he's too far gone for it to do much good. He goes for Poppy's throat, but his love for her wins out, and he ends up protecting her instead of hurting her.

I don't think he could have harmed her. I personally believe that he would always know it was her and maintain control, even in the throes of bloodlust.

Casteel meets Reaver and thinks he could like the draken, especially when he helps to remove the shadowstone shackles. Once he's sure they're all safe, Cas asks for some time alone with Poppy. Kieran lingers, and he thanks his friend for helping to free him, but mostly for taking care of Poppy and being there for her when he could not be.

Desperate to prove that she's real and with him again, they show each other how much they love and missed each other and then vow never to be separated again. He assures her that he will eventually be okay.

Poppy tells him what's been going on with her, and he finds out that while she does need to feed, any blood but a draken's will do. He assumes that she fed from Kieran, and it actually makes him happy. She fills him in on everything else that has happened, and as he listens, he struggles with how to tell Poppy that Millie is her sister.

Unable to sleep with that lingering thought in his head as well as the Handmaiden's words about Poppy dying in his arms, he leaves her to sleep and talks with Kieran. They discuss everything Millie told Cas and what it means regarding the prophecy and what they believe to be the truth about Millie and Malik. During their talk, Casteel realizes that Poppy will be a Primal once she completes her Culling and worries about what Isbeth said about love being dangerous for a Primal.

Once Poppy has fed, and they spend some more quality time together, he finally reveals to Poppy that Millie is her sister and that she didn't survive her Culling—Isbeth turned her into a Revenant to save her.

With some time alone with his brother on their journey, Casteel reveals that Millie told him she was Poppy's sister and that he put two and two together about how she ended up the way she did. His brother confirms that Cas's blood wasn't enough to Ascend Millie since he was so weakened from his captivity, and that Callum showed Isbeth how to create Revenants and use Primal magic.

After his discussion with his brother, Casteel tells Poppy that he doesn't think she's a god anymore, and Malik cuts him off, telling Poppy outright that she's a Primal. Casteel then realizes something and turns his ire on Reaver for not telling Poppy she was a Primal right away, and then asks how a Primal can be born of mortal flesh.

As things are brought up that make him realize that Malik was the Dark One from Lockswood and thus responsible for Poppy's scars and trauma, he compels his brother to pick up a dagger and put it to his own throat. Poppy stops Cas and explains that Malik didn't hurt her directly. He actually helped her escape. That doesn't ease Casteel's rage. When Malik contradicts everything Poppy says to try to make Cas understand that he was only protecting his kingdom and family, Cas can't hold himself back. He launches himself at his brother, and Poppy is forced to use her powers to separate the two.

Isbeth shows up where they're staying and kills the Descenter couple who were hosting them. A skirmish ensues, and Cas stops Malik from returning to Isbeth—with some help from Kieran, who knocks him out. But Kieran is wounded in the fight, which leads to Cas stabbing Callum in the chest before bringing Poppy back from the brink.

They head to Padonia and their armies and discuss taking Carsodonia while they meet with Isbeth at the Bone Temple. It's not ideal, but it is something to think about. They also talk about the prophecy, how Poppy's life is hers, the Joining, and everything that was revealed about Malik.

Cas talks to Kieran about the Joining, and the wolven makes it clear that he doesn't want or expect them to do it just to save him from the curse that's now on him from the blade Callum stabbed him with. Cas tells *him* they're more than friends or brothers—they're halves of the same coin. And then he tells Kieran when he plans to do the Joining if Poppy is still willing.

If she's not, can I volunteer?

Just kidding.

Or am I? *wink*

With a cooler head, Casteel confronts his brother, making it clear how he feels about Malik being the Dark One and how it hurt and thus impacted Poppy's life. After further discussions about Alastir, Millie, and Malik's intentions and beliefs regarding Poppy, Cas has a moment of softness where he tells Malik not to get himself killed and asks him to fight *with* them, not against them.

Now, I'm not saying they were close again by any means, but that was a big step for Cas to extend that olive branch, and for Malik to agree—at least in the moment.

Casteel asks Malik about the creepy rhyme that Poppy heard, and Malik tells him he has no idea what he's talking about, confirming that it wasn't his brother. He then orders the bone chains to be removed from Malik. He doesn't want his father or the kingdom to see him again for the first time while in chains.

Seeing the draken for the first time in Padonia leaves Cas speechless, but he feels slightly more sure-footed when Poppy identifies each of them for him. He's taken by surprise once again when he sees Tawny. She no longer feels the same to him, though he can't put a finger on *what* she feels like. It's just something… different.

The group prepares, and Cas tells everyone they will only deliver Malec to Isbeth to have Kieran's curse lifted. After that, they will end the war once and for all. Plans are then put in place to call the generals back, and discussions are had about how to take Carsodonia.

The next few days are full of planning and enjoying his Queen until they set off to get Malec. The journey is full of strife as usual—Craven, Sentry Gyrms, serpents—but it's also rife with information. Cas learns about the different types of Gyrms and how they came to be, how Malec changed after visiting the mortal realm, and that Nyktos and his Consort had their reasons for not intervening when their son was entombed.

With that part of their journey done, he orders everyone to take a day to rest before they leave for the Bone Temple. That night, he leads Poppy to the Wisteria Woods and the bank of the River Rhain, where Kieran waits.

Outside, amongst nature, the three will become one. Could anything be sexier?

The trio begins the ritual: Poppy drinks from them, they drink from each other, and then he and Kieran drink from her, exchanging the words that solidify consent and intent and make tensions rise. I saw the whole exchange in a vision, and let me just say, I had to pay a visit to one of my regular paramours afterward. The three of them, a gorgeous palette of colors blending, sighs filling the air, the trust, love, and respect in the moment...it was truly something beautiful. As were the cords of the Joining that connected them.

When they lay in a tangled, satisfied, bonded heap after, they see that Kieran's wound is healed, but they don't know if the Joining lifted the curse. It's still a worry, but the Joining was about much more than just saving Kieran's life, and all three of them know that. The most astonishing thing to Cas is now sharing a heartbeat with the two most important people in his life. It's a marvel.

The group sets off for the Bone Temple, and Cas, Kieran, and Poppy revel in their newfound closeness. They always had a bond, but it's so much more now. When they reach Isbeth, Cas squares off verbally with Callum and taunts Isbeth about how Malec still sleeps. He also asks why she would ever think that Malec would give her what she wants. Smug as ever, she replies that she *knows* he will.

Once Callum lifts the curse, Cas tells Kieran to let Poppy heal him—for her, not for him—and then stands with them as a unit as they await what Isbeth will do. When she pulls a shadowstone dagger, he comforts Poppy. They can't trust Isbitch, and she's shown she's nothing if not unpredictable, proven once again when she plunges the blade into Malec's chest.

When Callum explains the *real* meaning of the harbinger and bringer of death and destruction bits of the prophecy, Cas reminds Poppy that he never thought she was death and destruction. Still, he's shocked by what Callum reveals and incensed by what he says about the so-called "True King of the Realms." The last straw, however, is when Callum says that *he's* waiting to pick his pretty poppy and watch it bleed. Cas has heard enough and rips the asshole's still-beating heart from his chest with his bare hand...just as Kolis makes his presence known.

The earth cracks open, the wolven run—something Cas has never seen them do—and dakkais spill out of the fissures. They battle with everything they have, but so many fall. Naill. Emil. Delano. He does what he can to avenge them, his attention split between the battle and Poppy's transformation. It absolutely astonishes him, as does Nektas's arrival, and he finds it hard to look away despite the dangers coming at him from all sides. He tries to shield Poppy from the horror of Isbeth's destruction, but she watches—they all do—until Isbitch is no more.

Coaxing Poppy back to consciousness, Cas marvels at everything that happened. Somehow, none of their people are dead, and Poppy completed her Culling. When he informs her that she brought everyone back to life, Nektas corrects him and says that the true Primal of Life, the *Consort*, aided her, and that Nyktos captured their souls before they could enter the Vale or the Abyss.

When Nektas shares the full story of Sotoria and Kolis and Nyktos and his Consort, they're all intrigued—if concerned. As Nektas continues, Cas pieces together that if Kolis hadn't done what he did—killed his brother and stolen the embers—then Nyktos would have become the Primal God of Life, and Malec and Ires would have been born Primals. But they weren't because it took a female descendant.

When Nektas says that Poppy is the Primal of Blood and Bone, the true Primal of Life *and* Death, and that those two essences have never existed in one, Cas reassures her that whether that's good or bad, they already know that *she* is good.

Hoping things will start to look up now that they thwarted the Blood Queen's plans and Malec still lives, Cas feels only anger and frustration when Nektas tells them that they stopped nothing and need to kill Kolis—something Nyktos and the Consort weren't even able to do.

Later in the tunnels, Cas kills a vampry, even though they weren't attacked. He says it was moving toward Poppy and that wasn't okay. He's not sure why she seems to be fading, but it greatly concerns him.

Nektas tells Cas he's too much like the bloodline he's descended from—Attes and Kyn's.

The tunnels collapse, and Cas and Kieran move to protect Poppy. Nektas tells them that it wasn't her, it was *them*. Meaning the gods awakening—primarily Penellaphe, who rests near.

Still worrying about Poppy, Cas's thoughts must be pushed aside for a bit when they come upon Ires in his cat form, caged. He looks absolutely rough. They all see the bars and the wards, and Nektas says that nobody in the mortal realm should have that knowledge.

They tell Ires that Isbeth is dead, that they've come to rescue him, and that all will be okay. Poppy touches her father and he shifts into his god form, telling them about Jadis. Then, he passes out, going into stasis.

Poppy gets dizzy. Nektas asks if she slept, and she says a little. But that's not what he meant. He's inquiring about stasis after her Ascension. Before she can even really answer, she passes out, and Cas and Kieran catch her.

Nektas explains she needs the stasis to complete her transformation and says that the very earth will seek to protect her. He adds that he doesn't know how long she'll sleep but tells them to take her somewhere safe, watch over her, and talk to her. However, he adds that there could be unexpected side effects. She could awaken with no memories of herself, them, or anything that happened.

They take her to a guest room in the castle, and Cas tells Emil to make sure Wayfair is safe. He already planned to make sure they weren't bothered but says the wolven are guarding the premises with Hisa and the Crown Guard.

He asks Cas what they should do with the Ascended and Cas's first instinct is to say, "kill them all." Instead, he orders them to be kept in their homes.

Emil then asks about Valyn and Ires, and Cas realizes he hasn't even thought about those in Padonia. He says to send word to his father but to leave out the bits about Poppy, and tells him Nektas took Ires home to Iliseeum.

Remembering what Nektas said about talking to her, he thinks about the first time he saw her and decides to tell her what it was like in Masadonia before they officially met. Starting with his time on the Rise.

Poppy sleeps for hours. During that time Cas bathes her, washing the dirt and blood of battle away. He tells her that Vikter is part of the Fates in a way and that perhaps being a *viktor*, he sensed Cas's true motives as Hawke. He reminds Poppy that it could have been Vikter who died that night in the garden and not Rylan Keal and admits that he had preconceived notions about her since he hadn't known her yet. But he says that *everything* changed when they met.

Cas holds Poppy to his chest, telling her he had trouble processing everything that happened during his captivity, Shea, what happened after, and admits to using sex, drugs, and drinking to dull the pain. *Then* he started using the pain—literal pain—as a way to escape. The only thing that made him realize how bad things got was when he noticed how much he was taking from Kieran.

Kieran tells him it was okay that he used their bond to gain strength, and it's also okay to forget things, as long as he remembers later. He also asks about Shea and wonders if Cas will ever tell her.

We know that *she* knows that he killed Shea with his bare hands after her betrayal. What more could there be?

His response to Kieran is that Poppy needs to be awake to hear that story and learn all of it.

I want to learn all of it!

Cas talks to Poppy about Malik being kept and what the Lord in the meat packing plant said, realizing that he wasn't wrong given the game Malik was playing, and how Vikter didn't let on what happened during her lessons with the Duke because he didn't want to embarrass her.

Cas really wants to try to find her in dreams but isn't sure it'll work since this isn't normal sleep, it's stasis.

He thinks about the Red Pearl and how brave he thought she was, then mentions the night on the Rise when the Craven attacked. He says that's when everything began to change, and she started to become *Poppy* for him.

Kieran and Cas talk about the day Britta came to *Hawke's* quarters and he hopes Poppy doesn't remember that bit when she wakes. They discuss whether she looks any better and conclude that she does.

Kieran tells Cas that things are calm in the city. A Descenter warned Emil about the tunnels the vamprys use to travel during the day, and Hisa is taking a group down to take care of it. Kieran admits that it's hard not being with them, but

Cas reminds him that he's needed right where he is.

Cas asks about Malik, and Kieran says that Valyn and company were delayed in Padonia but they would arrive soon. He tells Cas to rest, and Cas turns it back on him and asks him if *he's* rested. They determine where they left off in the story they were telling Poppy...

He talks to Poppy about my diary as Delano hangs out at the foot of the bed where he's pretty much camped out since day one, and Kieran takes some time in the bathing chamber. He switches gears to the Duke and tells her he made the asshole suffer.

Bringing up the sense of rightness they both felt under the willow the night of the Rite, he says it was their souls recognizing each other.

Cas asks about Millie, which Kieran finds a strange segue, but they discuss her being different than normal Revs. Then they talk about the Rite and how things got out of hand that night. Casteel says he still feels responsible.

Suddenly, Emil asks someone what they're doing from the hall. Delano wakes and growls, and Kieran takes up a defensive position. Millie blows in and kindly asks them not to kill her. Cas comments that Naill must have found her and Malik just as his brother walks up, looking beat.

The Revenant asks what's going on with Poppy and says she never wanted Poppy dead. Malik insists she won't hurt Poppy, so Casteel asks Millie why she ran. She tells them she got scared when she saw the Consort in Poppy's eyes.

Kieran shifts and says he'll stay if Millie wants to visit with Poppy.

Cas goes into the hall with Malik and asks Emil and Naill to give them a moment. He asks his brother what happened, and Malik tells Cas they were in a fight with some Revenants. He got most of the troublesome ones but there are more out there. When Cas inquires how they were able to kill Revs, he divulges that draken blood can kill Revenants and tells them Millie found a stash.

They talk about trust and the past and their heartmates and come to a bit of a truce.

Back in the room with Poppy, Cas tells her he didn't want her finding out about him the way she did—with him killing the guard in the stables. He also tells her the fear he felt when he received word that she had been attacked after that. Telling her more stories, he says he thought she would stab him after he dropped his engagement bombshell during dinner, but she surprised him yet again by picking the lock and making a run for it.

He admits he fell in love with her well before he realized it. Before they even left Masadonia. By the time they reached Spessa's End, he knew for sure. Then, he tells her there are similarities between her and what Shea did and promises to tell her more when she wakes.

Falling asleep for a bit to get some of the rest he needs, he awakens with a jolt and sees a figure in black with a white dagger in the room. Cas blocks the swing and realizes the man is a Revenant.

He says Cas should have closed the window and goes on to tell him that the blades he carries are made of the bones of the Ancients and able to stop even a primal—he even calls Cas a *false primal*.

I found that very interesting when I saw it, but it became clearer later.

The Rev stabs Cas in the chest, disabling him. He feels helpless as he watches the Revenant go for Poppy again. When he recites the creepy rhyme that Poppy has been hearing—remembering?—for years, something within Cas explodes. A storm rages outside, and he pulls out the bone dagger.

Then...he shifts. Turning into a black-and-gold-spotted cave cat before ripping the Rev apart. Even with his memories altered in his new form, he sees Poppy as his. When Kieran enters, he sees him as his, too.

Emil comes in then, and Cas wants to eat him. Kieran talks him down and says the Atlantian's annoying, but he's also his, just in a different way.

Once Emil's gone, Kieran talks to Cas, reminding him who he is and encouraging him to shift back. When he does, they discuss that he almost killed Emil, collect the two bone daggers, and Kieran remarks that it looks like the one Callum used to curse him.

He then mentions that Cas's shift looked a lot like Ires's and assumes this new development has to do with their Joining bond. He wonders if Poppy can shift, too, and Cas says she'll be excited to hear the news.

They discuss how they could hear each other's thoughts and assume it's another side effect of the Joining. When they decide to put the Rev's pieces in the dungeon so they can interrogate him later, they turn their attention to Poppy.

Suddenly, the walls and floor start to shake and a circle with overlapping pointed crosses appears on the floor. It's the symbol for life and death and blood and bone. When they look back at Poppy, she has silver eather veins under her skin, then shadows coalesce there. She has more color, is warm again, and then...she opens her eyes.

They're the silver of a primal.

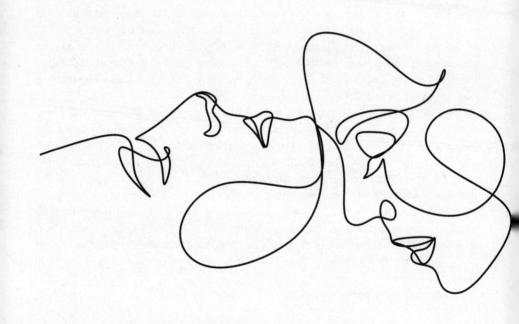

THE KING AND I

Dearest Diary,

I have just arrived back home after some time away, indulging my wandering spirit and restless soul. As you know, I often take off for parts yet unknown in my quest for life. This time was no exception, and I have certainly returned with memories I will carry with me and an encounter I cannot wait to capture within these pages.

As I have done in the past, I rode off with merely a direction in mind, letting the Fates guide my travels and experiences. When I eventually reached the forest outside Oak Ambler, I looked for a place to rest, having been traveling for several days by that time. Lucky for me, I came upon a more than adequate hunting cabin. Even luckier for me, the door was not barred.

Seeing as I didn't know the state of the flue in the fireplace, I decided to forgo setting a blaze in the hearth and instead contented myself with getting heat from the many candles I found situated around the space.

By the flickering light of burning wicks, I settled in with my meager meal of salted and dried meat, some cheese, berries, and bread, jotting notes in you so I may remember all the encounters and experiences I'd relished thus far on my sojourn.

My eyes growing heavy, I rested my head on my folded arms and dozed, dreaming of the dashing, brawny, and ridiculously handsome friends I dallied with two nights back—they were so much fun. But I've already told you about them in a previous entry. Let me get back to my night in the cabin.

I knew I hadn't been resting long, but sounds outside the door suddenly stirred me awake. I didn't know if it was an animal—it was hunting season, and I was sure the wildlife were being driven from their homes in fear for sport—or if it was something or someone else—I was, after all, squatting in someone's residence, even if it appeared to be a temporary abode.

Pulling the dagger from my boot, I remained seated, hiding the blade in the folds of my cloak and waiting to see what might happen. You may wonder if I was frightened, but given how long I have lived, I find that not much scares me. Concerns me? Absolutely. And so I was, concerned how things might play out.

When I heard and saw the knob on the door turn, I knew my supposition of it being an animal was incorrect. I was definitely about to be confronted by someone on two legs. I only hoped they were benevolent.

As the wooden slab swung in, the light of the full moon outside haloed and silhouetted a tall and broad form. From what I could see in the shadows, they were otherwise occupied with retrieving something from a bag slung across their chest and hadn't yet realized they weren't alone. I remained silent and still, simply observing as the figure took two steps through the doorway, the light of the candles finally reaching the fine features of his handsome face.

The candlelight must have registered then, for he looked up, an expression of shock and alert rising. He dropped the bundle he had retrieved from his pack and immediately drew his sword from its scabbard. When he did, the pommel and blade glinted in the fire's light, and I saw the design, the craftsmanship that had been captured in countless artistic renderings and on the pages of books spread across the kingdom. I was sitting in front of none other than Elian Da'Neer, current King of Atlantia.

Even in the low light of the room, his black hair glinted blue, and despite the look on his gorgeous face—now shifting a bit to anger—his straight nose, high cheekbones, and proud jaw that appeared carved from granite lit something within me.

He still had yet to speak, so I gently and quietly laid my blade on the table and stood slowly, raising my hands in front of me, palms out in a placating gesture.

I bowed my head and addressed him, calling him Your Majesty. That seemed to disarm him a bit, and I saw his rigid stance in his long, lean, and toned body relax a fraction. I went on to say that I meant no harm or disrespect and that I was merely a weary traveler looking for a place to rest for the night. I added that I had every intention of compensating whoever owned the cabin for my time spent. I pointed to the bag of coins I'd left on the mantel.

The King sheathed his sword and took a few more steps into the room, shutting the door behind him and closing out the chill from the autumn night beyond. While that should have put me at ease, the room seemed somehow smaller with the two of us now closed within it. He had a strange pull about him that drew you in and held you captive, though most enjoyably. I swallowed hard and met his golden-amber gaze.

He asked me my name, and I replied, putting as much respect into my tone as I could muster. Surprisingly, what I saw cross his features next wasn't what I expected. It wasn't confusion or uncertainty, it was recognition. He asked if I was the Seer, one of the newly created Council Elders, and I confirmed. That seemed to disarm him entirely for some reason. He picked up what he'd dropped earlier, set his pack aside and pulled out the chair opposite me, settling into it with a weary sigh and gesturing for me to sit across from him in the spot I'd vacated earlier.

He joked and asked if I planned to use the blade on the table, gracing me with a devastating smile that had my insides quivering as he flashed a set of dimples that made my heart skip a beat. He was clearly a descendant of the Court of Vathi with features so fine. I returned his grin and dropped the dagger into the bag I had hung over the back of the chair.

I asked the King if he wanted some wine. When he agreed gratefully, I pulled out my skin and extra cup and poured him a generous helping, topping off my serving, as well.

He asked what I was doing in his hunting cabin. So, I told him about my wandering soul and thirst for adventure and how I regularly used out-of-the-way shelters to rest during my journeys, making sure to compensate my unknowing hosts generously.

As the night wore on, and the wine continued to flow, Elian became more comfortable—he even told his guards to set up camp farther into the forest. I felt myself relaxing, as well. I had seen him, of course, knew of his legacy, how he'd summoned a god and singlehandedly smoothed things over between the wolven and the Atlantians after the war. Still, I'd never had the pleasure of being in his company except from a distance and for a very short time.

As is my way, even without libations, my comments turned flirty, and my innocent touches became more numerous and intentional. I could tell that Elian was not unaffected. I caught him swallowing thickly on more than one occasion, his Adam's apple bobbing and casting shadows on his graceful neck.

With the wine working its way through my insides and the candle flames and body heat warming my skin, I found myself shedding layers of clothing as the night progressed. He had done the same, simply making himself more comfortable, and I suddenly realized how comfortable we were becoming.

It is well known throughout the kingdom that the King and Queen have an open marriage. They have children, of course, and I truly believe they love each other in their way, but it's no secret that the Queen prefers women and has no issues with the King taking lovers.

With that knowledge firmly affixed to the forefront of my mind, I bolstered my courage and stood, approaching Elian where he sat slumped in his chair, a bit away from the table, legs spread in ease. I situated myself between his thighs and looked down at him, attempting to convey with a look alone what I desired, testing the temperature of the waters and hoping he'd take the plunge with me. He stared up at me earnestly, his gorgeous, glittering eyes going a bit heavy-lidded, his chest rising just a bit faster with his breaths.

I slowly, oh, so slowly, reached out a hand, moving toward his face in increments, waiting to see if he'd stop me. Instead, he grabbed my fingers and put my palm flat against his cheek, turning into it and kissing the inside of my wrist. My belly fluttered, and heat suffused me at the touch of those soft, pillowy lips to the sensitive flesh there.

He breathed in deeply, and I knew he could scent my arousal. I wasn't the least bit ashamed. Quite the contrary. I hiked up my skirts with my free hand and settled myself firmly on his thigh, letting him feel what the night had done to me, the heat and dampness that had settled at my core.

He groaned when I rocked myself on his leg and let my head drop back in bliss, our still-linked hands falling to the base of my neck right above the ruffled bodice of my gown.

Before I could even take a breath, he had freed my breasts from the confines of their trappings, the air caressing my nipples and making them bead. It wasn't exactly comfortable seeing as I was still clothed, but all thoughts of discomfort fled when he lapped at first one rosy bud and then the other, massaging one with a thumb as he took the other into the wet, hot cavern of his mouth. He licked and laved, making me nearly pant with want.

I ran a hand up his free thigh, twisting my wrist so I could palm the steely length of him where it struggled to be free of its soft leather cage. Elian groaned again and renewed his fervor at my chest when I applied just a bit of pressure and squeezed, dipping an index finger behind the flap of his breeches to gently scrape along his length with a blunt nail. That made him hiss and raise his head to look at me.

The look in his eyes was nearly indescribable. The closest I can come is to say he looked as if he were starving.

I deftly undid the ties at his waist and groin with one hand and tugged at the hem of his shirt with the other. He ripped the tunic over his head and then attacked my clothing with such haste and intensity I feared I'd be down to one gown for the remainder of my journey.

He pushed me back and off just enough that we could both rid ourselves of what remained of our clothes, and then he picked me up, swinging me into his powerful arms with no more than a thought before carrying me through to the bedroom area of the cabin.

He laid me on the soft covers, and I unabashedly slid back, dropped to my elbows, and bared myself to him, flashing him a sultry smile. He didn't miss a beat, he simply dove, devouring me so masterfully and thoroughly that I saw stars when I crested that peak and fell over the other side. He didn't stop at just one, though. He circled that tight bundle of nerves and nipped at its hood. He thrust his wicked tongue into me as a prelude of things to come. He inserted one and then two fingers inside me, twisting and turning and hitting that spot deep inside that had me gasping for breath and soaking his digits.

When he kissed and nipped his way up my body and took my mouth in a fiery and passionate kiss, I knew I wanted to taste him as he had done with me. I flipped us, taking him a bit by surprise if the startled gasp was any indication, then kissed and licked my way to his impressive length, caressing from the root up and swirling my thumb over his tip as I looked into his eyes and showed him with my expression how much I wanted him.

When I took him into my mouth, his hips bucked off the bed, and he reached to grasp my hair—not roughly but none too gently either, the slight bite of pain blending with the pleasure and the power I felt pleasing him thus. I used my hand to caress as I alternated between steady suction and pressure with swirling loops of my tongue. I felt him stiffen further, felt his body tense, and readied myself to indulge in him when he suddenly stopped and pulled from me.

I pouted and told him that we were just getting to the good part. He laughed, flashing those incomparable dimples again, and then pulled me up onto the bed with him, kissing me intensely and seductively. He moved his tongue across mine in a way that reminded me of what he had done earlier, and I almost came again from that alone. When he lowered a hand and inserted three fingers this time, I almost combusted from the sudden intrusion, and all before he had even moved. At the first gentle glide and thrust, I did shatter once more, the cry rising from within and breaking our connection as my muscles locked.

I was so entranced I didn't register his movements and could only gasp when he entered me to the hilt in one smooth motion. The bite of being filled was only compounded by his length hitting that spot inside once more in a way that was so pleasurable it almost hurt. I shook and craved to move my hips, rotating them just slightly, needing to feel that surge and retreat, but he only chastised me with a chuckle and held me in place, prolonging the pleasure.

He teased, kissing and licking my neck, nipping my shoulder, then retaking my mouth with leisurely conquest. Then, he finally moved. I could only call to the gods as he elicited a firestorm of feelings and sensations inside me, across me, within me. Could only hold on as he took me relentlessly, as I dreamed he would. As he punished me with pleasure and nearly killed me with desire. I felt as if I were floating above myself.

Thinking I couldn't possibly take any more, he struck, his fangs burying deep in my throat, sending me careening into the abyss again. He hummed a little, took one more deep draw, and then stiffened, his back bowing as he emptied himself within me.

Elian surprised me after. Seemed he was a cuddler. We lay entwined on the bed, talking for hours until the sun rose. And when he returned from his hunting excursion, I was waiting for him as he'd asked me to be. He told me he let his guards know to keep their distance, and we spent another night as we had the one before. And another after that. He actually had to send one of the wolven into town to buy me a new gown because it didn't survive his insatiable hunger on that second day.

Now, every time I see him at a formal kingdom function or run across a piece of artwork or book with his likeness, it sends me back in my memory to those days I spent with him in our very own woodland oasis.

And I have to say, it brings me a perverse kind of pleasure knowing that if anyone finds my journals, this one in particular, they will know that I once had a brief fling with a King.

Willa

PRINCE MALIK ELIAN DA'NEER

Malik is…complicated. As the heir to the throne, his life started fine, spending time with his brother and friends, exploring as teenagers will. But then tragedy struck, and things were never the same.

Hair: Nearly shoulder-length, light brown with blond hints.

Eyes: Bright gold.

Body type: Tall—a couple of inches taller than his brother. Thin since captivity.

Facial features: Golden-bronze skin. Sharp cheekbones. Straight nose. Proud jawline. Full mouth.

Distinguishing features: Dimples.

Personality: Kind. Generous. Prankster. Was the life and soul of the family until the Blood Crown took him. Not nearly as serious as his brother. Abhors violence of any kind.

Habits/Mannerisms/Strengths/Weaknesses: Loved to *experiment* with food and drink. Shields his emotions. Not skilled at compulsion—or resisting it. Generally, he thinks he knows everything, but he didn't know the true history of the realms until his imprisonment.

Background: Elemental Atlantian. Was bonded to a wolven—Preela. Posed as the Dark One and passed himself off as *Elian* instead of Malik.

Family: Mother = Eloana Da'Neer. Father = Valyn Da'Neer. Brother = Casteel Da'Neer. Uncle = Hawkethrone†. Great-grandfather = King Elian Da'Neer†. Ancestors = Attes and Kyn, co-rulers of Vathi, Primals of War and Accord and Peace and Vengeance.

MALIK'S JOURNEY TO DATE:

Born to King Valyn and Queen Eloana, Malik grows up in Atlantia and is close with his younger brother, Casteel, his bonded wolven, Preela, and his friends, Kieran and Shea. The group often spends time exploring, getting into mischief, and going to the beach—Malik loves to feel the sand between his toes. He also spends time training to fight alongside his brother until it comes time for him to learn to rule the kingdom.

When Casteel takes it upon himself to confront the Blood Crown and ultimately gets captured, Malik assumes the responsibility of finding and freeing him. He and Shea—Casteel's fiancée—mount a rescue attempt, accessing Carsodonia through the mines in the Elysium Peaks. They fail many times until the one time they don't.

Sort of. Nothing is as it seems.

During the rescue attempt, Shea and Malik get separated, and Shea tells the Ascended who she's with, making a deal for a trade: both brothers for her life. So, having been tipped off regarding the details of their plan, the Ascended set upon them as she and Malik carry Cas through the dungeon tunnels. With the vamprys occupied with Malik, Shea reneges on part of her deal and attempts to flee with Casteel, thus allowing them to take Malik into custody—where he remains for a century.

While in Solis, Malik's bonded wolven, Preela, attempts to rescue him. She even makes it all the way into Carsodonia before they capture her. King Jalara then kills her in front of Malik, but not before he and others assault her. After her death, they make seven bloodstone and wolven-bone daggers from her remains. The Queen gifts one to her Handmaiden, Coralena, who then gives it to her husband Leopold. Eventually, it makes its way to Poppy.

Broken from Preela's murder and his time in captivity, Malik begins doing as he's told—enough that he convinces the Blood Crown that he's turned on his kingdom and family. He uses some of the leeway the Queen has granted him and assumes the persona of the Dark One, infiltrating Solis and cultivating a network of Descenters therein. Eventually, he discovers that Coralena and Leopold Balfour are taking Isbeth's daughter, Penellaphe, away from the capital, and Malik is well aware of the prophecy surrounding the child and how the Queen plans to use her. So, when she sends him to bring Poppy back to the capital, he does as he's told, albeit with ulterior motives. Leaving a trail of blood in his wake as he makes his way to Lockswood, it causes a horde of Craven to follow and attack the town. In the confusion, Malik makes his move. Cora tries to convince him that Poppy's not the harbinger—she might very well be their savior. She even stabs him in the chest to stop him. But he overcomes her and resumes his personal mission to kill the child. He never thought to do something like that, but safeguarding the kingdom and stopping Isbeth's plans is more important than a single life. However, when he sees the Consort in Poppy's eyes, he can't go through with it. Instead, he saves her and returns her to Carsodonia.

The Queen's first daughter enters the scene during his time in captivity—before Poppy was even born. And Isbeth makes Malik do unspeakable things to Millicent—the depths and specifics of which we do not yet know. Somewhere along the line, Malik realizes that Millie is his heartmate. While he feels he isn't capable of caring about anyone anymore, he owes Millie and refuses to leave without her.

When Cas and the rest of the group answer the summons the Queen issued via Poppy's brother, Ian, Malik stands beside the Queen, dressed in clothes of wealth and privilege. He tells his brother that *Ileana* has opened his eyes to the truth.

It may have sounded like he was taking the Queen's side there, but I like to think he was just making his brother aware that he knew the truth about the Ascended and everything that went along with that.

When the secrets start to unfold, Malik confirms that Isbeth intended to use him, marrying him to Poppy to unite the kingdoms and having him be Poppy's Ascension…of the flesh.

Isbeth shocks everyone by giving her Revenant demonstration and having

Millicent struck down, and Malik can't help his reaction. He jerks and almost takes a step forward before stopping himself. However, unable to look away, he stares until she finally rises once more—something that doesn't go unnoticed by the others in the room.

When Isbeth reveals more of her ultimate plan and sadly states that she no longer has the blood of an intended King—since Cas is now the King of Atlantia—Malik smiles apologetically, but he's anything but sorry.

Poppy and Isbeth end up in a fight, and Poppy is incapacitated. In order to save her and the others he loves, Casteel surrenders himself to Isbeth, and the Queen orders Malik to retrieve him.

After Isbeth removes Cas's finger and sends it to Poppy, Millie makes Malik aware that his brother is suffering from an infection. He goes down to see Casteel, and the reception isn't exactly a family reunion. He tells his younger sibling not to be a brat and then disinfects his finger.

As they talk, Malik reveals that he was furious to learn Isbeth's truth and that their parents lied to them both. He wonders if either of them would be where they are now if they *had* been told the truth centuries ago.

Seeing how his brother is suffering, he's genuinely sorry he can't feed him and help ease his misery. But he says that if he does, Cas will be punished. Knowing what they did to his brother the last time, he doesn't want that to happen.

Malik mentions that he's been thinking of Shea lately and tells Cas that he knows what she did—that she turned them over to the Ascended. He's sorry to hear that Casteel was the one to kill her and says he remembers how much she loved Cas. He also guesses that Casteel never told anyone about her betrayal.

Casteel mentions Millicent and, once again, Malik can't control his response. As his brother tells him more, he becomes very interested in what things the Handmaiden told Cas. Come to find out, it's about the Revenants. Malik agrees that Millie is odd but asks that Cas not take it out on her. He says that, like Poppy, she's had very few choices in life.

As they talk more, Malik tells Cas *everything* has to do with Poppy. When Casteel reveals that Poppy was entirely on board with coming to rescue him, not even *knowing* him, Malik says that she doesn't know him—or at least doesn't remember him. When Cas questions that, Malik doesn't answer except to say that he'll find out soon enough.

Upon the Queen's next meeting with Poppy and her two guards—Kieran and one other he doesn't know—Malik remains stoic when Kieran tries to bait him. Then, when the Queen asks her daughter if she's been able to resist the men's ample charms, Malik can't help but grin.

Poppy insinuates that all the lies will soon be revealed, and Malik asks what she expects: for Solis's people to turn their backs on all they've ever known? He then goes on to say that they will fear Poppy.

Not long after, Poppy breaks through Malik's mental shields and shocks him, sending him reeling, even giving him a nosebleed. When he's unable to compose himself completely after, the Queen orders her Handmaidens to remove him. He waves her off.

Isbeth soon tells Malik to take her *guests* to their rooms—separately. He takes Kieran to one and Reaver to another below as Callum takes Poppy to see Cas.

Later, when Poppy questions why the Queen summoned her to the Great Hall, Malik tells her it's so she can see how much she's loved. He goes on to relay that Isbeth has been warning everyone about her, reinforcing their fears that she's the harbinger. As they discuss the lies that were told about the Atlantian-captured cities, and Poppy tells Malik that his kingdom/father would never do the things that Isbeth claims, he shows no emotion.

Poppy notices his attention on Millie and taunts that she'll tell the Queen that Millicent is the reason Malik stays. He threatens her, and not long after, the Queen orders him to leave.

Isbeth goads Poppy and tells her to unleash her power but not to forget that she's not sitting in front of an Ascended. She crushes a Solis couple with her power to prove her point.

Poppy, Kieran, and Reaver leave Wayfair—and a huge mess in their wake. Malik follows and offers to take them to Cas if they get out immediately. When Kieran tells him it's suspect, he tells *him* it's a significant risk and reminds them that he helped Cas when he had the infection. He simply says he doesn't want his brother anywhere near the Queen.

They still don't believe him, so he answers a question that Poppy asked him some time back, confirming that he stays for Millie. He then explains that they're heartmates. When Kieran calls her crazy, Malik warns him and then tells him that while he still loves the wolven like a brother, he won't hesitate to rip out his throat if he doesn't lay off the Handmaiden. He reveals that he's done many unimaginable things for Millie—stuff she will never learn about.

Making their way to the dungeon, Malik urges them to hurry. He details how he ran into Callum earlier and felt he needed to check on his brother—to see what Callum might have done. When they all see what he did—wounding Casteel gravely enough to kick start his bloodlust—they realize they can't get him out, at least not while conscious. So, Malik has Kieran distract Casteel while he puts him in a sleeper hold.

Kieran suggests they will need the deity bone chains for when Casteel wakes, and Malik agrees. When Reaver uses his fire to free Cas, Malik is shocked to find that he is a draken. Once they get Casteel free, he carries his brother through a series of tunnels and out of the castle. He then leads them to a friend's house—Blaz, and his wife Clariza. Both Descenters.

When Clariza greets them with skepticism and a dagger, calling him *Elian*, Poppy tries to calm her by reinforcing what Malik told her and Blaz: that the unconscious man in their friend's arms is the King of Atlantia, and she is the Queen. When they bow, Poppy shocks Malik by telling them not to because she's not *their* Queen.

Once they get Casteel into a bed, Malik tells Poppy that his blood won't do much for Cas. It has to be hers. Though when they try to secure him, he fights, the bloodlust taking control. Stunned, Malik watches as Poppy heals and soothes his brother. They finally settle him, and Malik tells Poppy that Cas needs motivation, like the scent of her blood, then explains that if he doesn't take enough, things will be even worse for him.

With Cas still not entirely with it but calmer, Malik goes to get Reaver so he can remove the bone chains. When he returns, Cas acts as if he wants to attack the draken, and Poppy tries to remind him who it is, telling him that he probably doesn't want to take him on. Malik remarks that it looks like he *does.*

Once things are settled there, Malik leaves, presumably to fill Blaz and Clariza in on what's going on. He ends up on the settee in the living room to rest. Before he goes to sleep, however, he tells them all that he will secure a ship to smuggle them out of Solis and away from Carsodonia.

Talking later, he tells everyone that Blaz and Clariza are good people. When Poppy asks him if Millie is her sister, he wonders how she knows. Cas remarks that Millie both told *and* showed him, and Malik says how much she and Poppy look alike and adds that they both ramble.

As an answer to some of Casteel's questions, Malik confirms that Millie would have been a god had she survived her Culling. When Reaver enters and reiterates what he heard, only referring to Millie as *the Handmaiden,* Malik gets upset and tells him that she has a name, thus letting everyone know there's more to their relationship than meets the eye.

The conversation continues, and Malik explains that Casteel's blood wasn't strong enough to Ascend Millicent—he was too weak from the captivity, and Isbeth didn't consider that. When they ask about Ires, he explains that bone chains and the deity bone cage nullify the god's eather. He then mentions how Callum showed Isbeth how to make Revenants and says he wishes Millie would have kept her mouth shut about…everything. Everybody who knows those secrets is dead, and he doesn't understand why she took such a risk.

His final bit of knowledge is that while she isn't powerful enough *yet,* Poppy's purpose is to destroy the realms. And she will be strong enough to do just that after she completes her Culling.

He shares with Poppy that Isbeth named her after the goddess who warned of the prophecy, then goes on to say how Poppy has already taken part in Isbeth's plan by being born. But then he adds that perhaps her free will is greater than the prophecy and what Isbeth wants—after all, Coralena believed she would usher in change and not destruction.

When Poppy displays her shock at Malik having known Cora, and he can see that she remembers that fateful night in Lockswood, he tells Casteel that what they did to Preela broke him. He said he was never loyal to Isbeth—not after what she did to Cas and what Jalara did to Preela. Not after what Isbeth made him do to Millie. He wanted to kill the Blood Queen and actually tried before realizing what she was. And he likely would have *kept* trying if it weren't for the prophecy. But when he learned of that, he couldn't let Isbeth destroy the realms or Millie. He had to do *something*.

He says that killing a child was a line he simply couldn't cross. Even when he tried again, thinking it was the only option, he saw the Consort looking at him through Poppy's eyes. He didn't know that was possible, and it stayed his hand. When additional questions arise about the events of that night, he explains that the Craven followed the trail of blood he left—the distraction was the only way he knew he could get past Leo and Cora.

Cas doesn't take kindly to learning that his brother was the source of Poppy's pain—both physical and psychological—and compels him to pick up a dagger and put it to his throat. When Malik says even more, insinuating that he would have tried to kill her even if he *had* known she was his brother's heartmate, Casteel launches himself at Malik, taking him down and beating him until Poppy uses her power to separate the two.

When cooler heads prevail—a bit—Clariza warns them a group of guards is approaching, and Malik tells everyone they need to get out and make their way to the docks. Unfortunately, that doesn't happen, and Isbeth, Callum, and her guards burst in.

Isbeth tells Malik that he belongs to her and accuses him of betraying her— which he did. She then tells him to get over what was done to him and Cas. He'll never get over it. He finally speaks up, telling her to fuck off, and she insinuates they haven't engaged in that in many years.

As much as I adore sex, I simply cannot imagine *anyone* with Isbeth, let alone Malik. But I digress.

Callum wounds Kieran, and Malik moves to grab him, but the shadows throw him back first. When Isbeth tells them they can all go except for him, he tells the group that it's okay and heads for Isbeth. Cas tries to stop him, and Malik demands he let him pass. Poppy attempts to convince him to stay with them by reminding him that he's no good to anyone dead, implying Millie. Kieran knocks him out to make sure he doesn't go with the Queen.

When Malik awakens, they are already on their way to Padonia, and he is bound by bone chains with his hands behind his back, riding astride a horse led by Reaver. He explains how the white banners above the doors signify that those places are havens for Descenters.

The group reveals the details of their plan, and Malik makes it very clear that he is appalled they're even thinking of doing what Isbeth wants and giving her Malec. As they talk more and discuss the curse that Callum put on Kieran, he tells the wolven that he doesn't want anything bad to happen to him and that he still cares. When Reaver mentions the curse not working if Kieran, Cas, and Poppy are Joined, Malik feels relief. He assumes they are and hadn't even thought of that— unfortunately, they're not. Yet.

As they camp, the brothers have a bit of a heart-to-heart. He imagines that

Casteel hates him, and Malik doesn't blame him. He knows that Cas looked for him for the entire century he was gone and wished and prayed that he would give up. When he heard that the Descenters were calling Cas the Dark One, he hoped his brother would hear of the man they called Elian and think Malik had betrayed Atlantia, forcing him to give up his search. Things get heated, as sibling discussions can, and Cas tells him that he lied to and betrayed Poppy for Malik's benefit, making it clear that doing so is something he can't easily forgive. He then asks how someone who abhorred violence of any kind could even *consider* harming a child. Malik explains that when all was said and done, he couldn't leave Poppy there to die. He took her back to Carsodonia and the Queen. He goes on to say that he got a glimpse of Poppy before they put the veil of the Maiden on her and saw what his actions had done. And while it's a small comfort, Cas is lucky he didn't see the wounds when they were fresh.

As more details of that night in Lockswood come to light, Malik reveals that Alastir saw and recognized him. He also says that when he saw the Consort in Poppy's eyes, he believed what Cora did: that Poppy would end the Blood Crown. Over the years, however, he realized that it didn't matter who Poppy was at heart. All that mattered was whether Isbeth found a way to exploit Poppy's power: Isbeth will stoke her anger, Poppy will respond with rage, and after her Culling, she'll reply with death. Cas takes offense to the insinuation and grabs Malik by the throat, telling him she'll never do what he says she will.

Malik wants to believe that Poppy can control her actions and tells Cas he won't hurt her like he would have done when she was younger. He also reminds him that Millie hasn't tried to hurt her either. When Cas mentions what Millie said about him ultimately killing Poppy after her Culling, Malik replies that it couldn't have been easy for her to tell him that. While the Handmaiden doesn't know her sister, she wouldn't wish that kind of end for her. Still, he hates that his brother had to hear that he would be the only one who could stop Poppy and that it would mean his brother killing his heartmate.

When Malik asks Cas about the Joining, he's stunned to learn they haven't completed it. When Cas asks him why he didn't try to kill Poppy again—or why Millie didn't—Malik explains that Poppy is still her sister, even if she wasn't supposed to know about her. As for him, by the time Poppy was old enough that he didn't see her as a child, he figured Cas would kill her to get back at the Blood Crown. When Cas asks him if he *wants* to defeat the Blood Crown and if Millie does, as well, he answers in the affirmative. Malik then agrees to join them in finding Malec, killing Isbeth, and ending the fight once and for all.

Just before Casteel removes the bone chains, he asks Malik about the rhyme he said while in Lockswood. Malik listens to Cas recite it and says it's disturbing, but he has never heard it before.

They reach the others, and when Malik sees Delano, he kneels. Delano, in wolven form, nudges his hand with his head, making Malik shudder. He places a palm on Delano and closes his eyes, unable to stop the tears. Preela was Delano's sister, and that pain is still as fresh as it was when the Blood Crown took her from him.

In Padonia, the reunion with his father is tense. And even though he's no longer chained, it's clear he isn't completely free. Naill and Email watch his every move. During dinner, he's shocked when Valyn reveals the Blood Queen's true identity, making it known that he and Eloana knew all along.

The distrust remains clear as they set out to find Malec. They won't even give him a weapon, despite the threat of the Craven. He insists they give him something to fight with when they are attacked, trying to reason with them that he can't help them take down the Blood Crown without something to fight with. He's told to use his charming personality and to shut his mouth.

Poppy casts the Primal magic locator spell, and he can tell it worked and says as much. As they follow the trail, he assumes it will lead them to the coast. He asks Poppy why she hasn't asked about that night in Lockswood. She doesn't reply, so he nudges her, insinuating that she must have lots of questions. Poppy asks him how Coralena died, and he explains that Isbeth made her drink draken blood, but that she favored the Handmaiden, so it was one of the few times the Blood Queen didn't draw out a death.

When they reach the tunnel and are set upon by Gyrms, Malik once again asks for a weapon and then suggests that Poppy just go all Primal on them.

After retrieving Malec, Malik rides next to the wagon. In Padonia again, they put him in a chamber under guard once more. He's always been good at being where he's not supposed to be, however, so he sneaks out and surprises Poppy in the stables, where she's with Malec's casket. He touches it and remarks that it doesn't feel like anything special to him. He asks her if she senses anything, and she shrugs, clearly lying.

Later, as they're discussing sabotage and sacrifice, Malik reveals that all manner of things crossed his mind regarding thwarting what they were about to do but that he prefers not to be burned alive. When he reminds Poppy that she sacrificed her father to save Cas, at least in a way, he adds that he's relieved to know she did. He explains how he's done all manner of things for Millie. When asked if she would do the same for him, he replies that Millicent would be more apt to set him on fire. Poppy seems stunned, and he explains that while they're heartmates, she doesn't actually know that.

Malik hopes Millie won't be at the Bone Temple but assumes that Isbeth will likely demand her presence. When Poppy asks why Millie hasn't tried to stop Isbeth, Malik explains that while she is strong and fierce, she's not a demis like the Queen. And that while she is Isbeth's daughter, she's not evil. She'd never kill a child or her sister—unlike him. He then tells Poppy how Jalara killed Preela in front of him, and that Poppy carries a piece of his bonded wolven with her in the form of her dagger's hilt.

Once they reach the Bone Temple, they finally entrust him with a sword, and he helps Emil and Naill unload Malec and carry him to the Temple. Without looking at her, he asks Millie if she's okay.

As events unfold and Poppy pieces together her part in the prophecy—that she was the bringer of death and destruction by bringing Malec to Isbeth—he swears when it all comes together. As the earth cracks open and the dakkais spill forth, he fights and tries to safeguard Millie. Delano saves him at one point, but Malik ends up fighting Callum. When Isbeth lashes out at Millie, he protects her as best he can but dies—until Poppy, with the Consort inside her, brings them all back to life.

Awakened, he sees that Millie is gone and goes after her.

She's always his first thought.

His first priority.

Later, he returns to Wayfair with Millie to talk with Poppy and Cas, only to find Poppy in stasis. He makes sure Millie can sit with her and then talks with his brother for a while. They air a lot of stuff, and once everything is said, they come to a bit of a truce. While talking to Cas, though, he brought up he and Millie being heartmates while she was just in the other room. He's not sure if she heard or not.

But does it really matter? She hates him—or so he says. And he believes she should.

MILLICENT "MILLIE" MIEREL

There is still so much we do not yet know about Millicent, but I am utterly intrigued by what we *do* know and anxious to uncover more.

Hair: Nearly white-blond and waist-length with tight curls.

Eyes: An incredibly pale silver-blue—almost colorless.

Body type: Round hips. Several inches shorter than Poppy and shorter than the other Handmaidens.

Facial features: Olive skin. Oval face. Full, wide mouth. Strong brow. Stubborn jaw.

Distinguishing features: Fangless teeth. Some freckles on nose and cheeks. Wears a mask in a reddish black that extends from her hairline to below her eyes and stretches to nearly her jaw on both sides—looks like the wings of a bird of prey.

Personality: Kind. Cheery and chipper. Polite. A bit odd. Keeps emotions behind tight walls.

Other: Possibly close to two hundred years old—the war ended four hundred years ago, and Ires came to Isbeth two hundred years later.

Habits/Mannerisms/Strengths/Weaknesses: Not susceptible to compulsion. Carries crescent-shaped shadowstone blades. Claims to excel at behaving but has a habit of shedding blood needlessly. When she uses arrows, she tips each with shadowstone. Loves to hum but is terrible at it. Has a habit of rambling. Forced loyalty is to Isbeth, but she still tries to protect people.

Background: Revenant Handmaiden. Didn't survive her Culling, so Isbeth turned her into a Revenant. However, most think she's *like* a Revenant yet…not, which is somewhat true given that she's not a third daughter and her origins were slightly different.

Family: Mother = Isbeth †. Father = Ires. Sister = Penellaphe Da'Neer. Ancestors = Nyktos and Seraphena.

MILLIE'S JOURNEY TO DATE:

Born to Queen Ileana (a.k.a Isbeth) and Ires Mierel, Millicent's life started as a bit of a lie and something not hers to command. The *first daughter* referenced in the prophecy, she was always meant to be a tool. That became even truer when she didn't survive her Culling, and Isbeth, unwilling to let her die, used Primal magic to turn Millie into a Revenant—or at least something having Revenant traits. I'm still wondering if there's more to that story that has yet to be uncovered. Anyway, it resulted in her becoming one of the Queen's personal guards—a Handmaiden— and being trained in every manner of death known.

She and Malik Da'Neer are heartmates, but as far as I know, she remains in the dark about that fact. Though maybe she does know and just chooses to ignore it. It's also been said that Isbeth forced Malik to do many unspeakable things to her, and it forever changed their relationship. We do not, however, know what those things are yet.

Millie's history comes to me in flashes and bits. I haven't been able to piece it all together quite yet, but most of what happened when she finally met Casteel and then her sister is fairly clear.

When Poppy, Casteel, and their group infiltrate the castle and come across Ires as a cat, Millie cuts them off in the hallway. Delano sees her as a threat and immediately attacks, but she bests him in seconds, shocking the others. Casteel attempts to use compulsion on her to make her let Delano go, and it has no effect. When the wolven asks her what she is, she tells them all she's a Handmaiden…and many other things.

Millie politely asks Delano to behave himself and reveals that she has a nasty habit of shedding blood unnecessarily. She also insinuates that she excels at behaving and makes a point to emphasize that *they* have not behaved by going where they should not have gone—the underground tunnels—and seeing what they should not have seen—Ires.

She offers to keep it from the Queen if they promise to do as they're told, but adds that if they don't, it won't be them who pays the price, it'll be their cohorts who approach the eastern gates. This lets the group know that their plan has been foiled.

While they're all before the Queen, Isbeth uses Millie to demonstrate what a Revenant is and what they can do by having a guard stab her in the heart. She dies and then resurrects as she always does, once again moving to stand at the Queen's side and listening to them discuss a Revenant's strengths.

When the Queen has Ian beheaded, Millie can't hide her shock. To me, that indicates she's not as icy as she tries to portray.

As Poppy raises the furious storm outside of Oak Ambler after Casteel gives himself up, Millie appears before her and tells her to stop, hinting that Poppy will hurt innocents if she continues. When she orders the others of the group to intervene, and nobody moves, she tacks on a threat that if they don't stop her, *she* will. Poppy throws a net of power at her, and Millie tells her it won't work, also making Poppy aware that a shadowstone arrow is pointed at her head.

After Poppy finally calms a bit, Millie tells her she's sorry about Ian. She then makes sure the group understands that all the vampyrs have left and only innocents remain, so they shouldn't be so hasty to wipe out the entire place. When Poppy threatens her further, Millie laughs and says she would welcome the final death.

They talk a bit more, and Millie finally reveals that the Ascended will take Cas to the capital, but she doesn't know where. She goes on to say that Isbeth will have the Revenants and Malik watching him, and that the only way Poppy can save him is if she brings the fire of the gods.

This may seem like an innocuous statement, that Poppy should bring everything she has, but in my interpretation, she's actually telling Poppy that she needs to secure Nyktos's guards. I love that she revealed that Poppy needed to get the draken without coming right out and saying it.

About thirty days into Casteel's imprisonment, Millie goes to see him. After looking him over, she informs him that she thinks his finger is infected. When Cas asks her why she's there, she admits that she made a promise to someone—which we later find out was Malik. She tries to get him to bathe, and he sasses her at every turn. Finally, she quips that he must be cranky because he's hungry and tells him that Malik gets that way, too.

Interesting that she knows that and would bring it up.

Cas asks her where his brother is, and she replies that he's probably here, there...everywhere he's not supposed to be. When he states that she must be around Malik a lot to know what he's like when he needs to feed, she says she's really not. She's just observant.

I don't believe that for a second. Knowing what we know about Malik's extracurricular activities beyond the Queen's notice, that statement about him being in places he shouldn't takes on a bit of a new meaning, though I'm not saying that because I have proof. It is merely conjecture.

As Millie scrubs the symbols from her skin using Cas's bath water, they talk about the tunnels and wards. She tells Cas how Poppy broke the wards when she Ascended into her godhood, allowing things to get in and out, though not even Callum knows when and where. When Cas asks more about the golden one, Millie tells him that Callum's really old.

Millicent reveals that she would have killed Isbeth, but the Queen is a god— we know she's really not, but... Then she says that she believes Poppy will eventually kill her, telling Casteel that she saw Poppy after Cas gave himself up and realized how powerful she is. Cas tells her his wife is unlike anybody else, and Millie agrees. However, when he mentions that Nyktos is the reason for Poppy's uniqueness, she corrects him by saying that he knows nothing if he thinks Nyktos is the *true* Primal of Life and Death. She then details how Isbeth needed a tool/weapon to destroy the realms and lets it slip that Isbeth figured out how to bring to life something that can.

Millie is there to head off Poppy, Kieran, and Reaver while they're on their way to Carsodonia to save Casteel. A fight breaks out, and they eventually have a discussion where Millie calls Poppy the Queen of Flesh and Fire. Ultimately, they all end up at Wayfair.

Later, Millie tells Poppy the Queen wishes to speak with her about the future of the kingdoms and the True King of the Realms and informs Poppy that New Haven and Whitebridge have fallen under Atlantian control—the Blood Crown received a missive. She adds that everyone's been on edge since. Poppy refuses to wear the outfit Millie brings her because it's white and says she won't be forced to look like the Maiden again. She tells Millie to either get her something else or she'll go naked. Millie jokes that it would almost be worth letting Poppy go like that just to witness the outcome.

As they talk more, Poppy warns Millie not to refer to Isbeth as her mother. When Poppy pushes with her powers, Millie blocks her attempts to read her. As she leaves Poppy, she tells her she'll keep Kieran and Reaver company and comments on how handsome Reaver is.

Everybody has a crush on Reaver, it seems. I can't stop seeing him as a youngling, though. He will always be that for me since I *saw* him in my visions during the time of the gods.

Later, while escorting Poppy and the others to the Great Hall, she confirms that Reaver is right when he says the statue in the Hall isn't Nyktos. Once inside, Millie reminds Poppy to calm herself lest everyone think the harbinger is among them. When the Queen says that Cas, unlike Malik, never learned to make his stay easier, Millie can't control her anger. She may not particularly like Malik—or at least she *pretends* not to—but it's clear she can't help but be concerned about him.

It greatly amuses Millie when Poppy stabs Callum in the heart. The Queen, however, is *not* amused and punishes Millie's impudence by making her clean up the mess.

Once again in the cell with Casteel, he states that Isbeth won't hurt Poppy; she'll hurt others to *get to* Poppy. Millie confirms. Then, pretending to have blood in her hair, she washes it in Cas's tub, revealing that its natural color is nearly white, not flat black. She then scrubs her face, making her true appearance known and highlighting her likeness to Poppy. When Cas only looks on, she tells him that she has something important to tell him and then informs him that she's the first daughter. She adds that she was never meant to be, but neither was the second. When he questions that, she confirms that she and Poppy are full-blooded sisters and that Ires sired them both. She explains to Casteel that she is not a god like her father, though. She's a failure. He tries to argue, and she tells him that, like his brother, he has no idea what is and isn't possible—like the real history of the realms, for example.

Millie details how everything Isbeth has done has been for a reason: When she took Cas the first time, why she kept Malik…it was all so she'd have someone from a strong Atlantian bloodline to Ascend Poppy and make sure she didn't fail like Millie did. Once Poppy completes her Culling, she'll give Isbeth what she's wanted since her son died: revenge against everyone. And she doesn't want to remake the realms. She wants to destroy them.

Poppy is destined to do that—to be the harbinger foretold…she won't have a choice. Millie then reminds Casteel that while Isbeth isn't strong enough to remake the realms, she created something that *is*. Thinking about that makes her a bit sad, and she lets some of her emotions slip and show. This is another indicator that Millie is different from other Revenants. It's clear she has emotions; therefore, she has a soul. Other Revs do not.

Millie knows the Queen will succeed, no matter what anyone does. First, Poppy will complete her Culling, and then her love for Cas will become one of her very, very few weaknesses. He will be the only thing that can stop her. Either way, Millie's sister won't survive; she'll either die by Casteel's hand or drown the realms in blood.

Adorned with paint at the Bone Temple, Millie is very uneasy and concerned about Malec being brought to Isbeth. She tries to warn Poppy and asks where Reaver is, telling Poppy she should be worried because Isbeth didn't ask about the draken. She feels that something is very wrong with all of what's going on and says as much.

After Callum heals Kieran, it buoys Millie when the wolven stabs Callum in the chest. She remarks how seeing him taken down never gets old but makes sure to tell Kieran to go for the head next time if he wants it to last longer.

Millie watches Isbeth kiss Malec in his casket and remarks how it looks like she's about to climb inside. When she hears her mother say, "It cannot be any other way," she jerks her head, only to see Isbeth plunge a dagger into Malec's chest.

Confused and not understanding what exactly is going on, she can only listen as Callum gloats, calling her a failure. She suddenly realizes that it was supposed to be Poppy on the altar, which makes better sense when Callum explains the prophecy to them.

Millie asks who the harbinger is, and Callum tells her that *she* is—*she* was the warning. Callum inquires if she really thought Poppy would destroy the realms and says that it would take her eons to be that powerful.

After Casteel rips out Callum's heart, Millie tells Poppy they still have a chance to stop what's been set in motion because Malec still breathes. Chaos ensues, and Millie is hit on the head with a rock as the stone explodes. Malik catches her before she hits the ground, and then Delano saves them both from a dakkai.

Millie engages with the other Revenants and screams at Poppy to get the dagger out of Malec's chest and get to Isbeth. When she can't, Millie goes. Just as she finally reaches Malec and gets her hand around the dagger's hilt, Isbeth blasts her with eather and she dies.

She gets up after Poppy calls to the Consort and then watches Poppy take out the dakkais and Isbeth. In the confusion afterward, Millie sneaks away.

We know that Malik went after her.

Eventually, she finds that out, too, because she shows up at Wayfair with him. When she discovers that Poppy is in stasis, she's concerned. She visits with her for a while but ultimately leaves.

Wait until she discovers what Poppy has turned into…

QUEEN ELOANA DA'NEER
Becomes Queen Mother Eloana Da'Neer

Hair: Onyx-colored.
Eyes: The color of cool amber honey.
Facial features: Proud jaw.
Personality: Frenetic. Cautious. Strong.
Habits/Mannerisms/Strengths/Weaknesses: Always has what's best for the kingdom in mind. Finds it hard to talk about her missing son. Calls Casteel "Hawke." Worries greatly for her people—to the point it sometimes overshadows hope. Doesn't talk about Malec much. Prone to stabbing Valyn. Has killed to keep Iliseeum's location a secret. Poisoned Isbeth with belladonna. Entombed Malec.
Background: Elemental Atlantian. Was young when she became Queen. Her bonded wolven died during the war. Was married to Malec.
Family: Ex-husband = Malec. Husband = Valyn. Sons = Malik and Casteel. Brother = Hawkethrone †.

Eloana is not only the Queen Mother of Atlantia's current King, she is also a pivotal piece of the gears that were set in motion where Isbeth is concerned. Malec had an affair with Isbeth when he was married to Eloana. Eloana thought he hung the moon but soon realized that Isbeth wasn't like his other mistresses—she was his heartmate.

ELOANA'S JOURNEY TO DATE:
After Poppy is attacked at the Chambers of Nyktos, Eloana walks into the Temple and sees what Poppy has done. She asks what Hawke has brought back to Atlantia with him and then tells the onlookers to bow to their new Queen.

When Poppy insists that none of what's going on is her, Eloana tells her that she may not have realized she summoned the wolven, but she did. Many shifted without warning. She then turns her attention to Cas and tells him that he needs to care why the wolven are acting as they are, declaring that the bonds between the wolven and their Elemental Atlantians have been broken. She goes on to tell Poppy that the godly blood in her supersedes any oaths between the wolven and their bonded Elemental Atlantians, and that's why the bonds broke.

The attack on Poppy shocks Eloana, and she tells Poppy that she's not a Soul

Eater and that her attackers should have known exactly what she was when they saw the eather in her blood become visible.

As discussions of Malik arise, Eloana wonders aloud if the marriage between Hawke and Poppy is a ploy—she knew her son's original plan.

When Alastir attacks, Eloana is stunned once again when Cas is hit with arrows. She commands the Crown Guards to stand down. She doesn't understand why they would go after her child—their Prince and now-destined King.

Alastir and his cohorts abscond with Poppy. I imagine Eloana assisted with those who were poisoned by the shadowshade.

After Poppy and Cas go through their harrowing ordeal and return to Atlantia, Eloana welcomes Hawke at Cove Palace but then sees the differences in Poppy. She knows she was Ascended and stares in disbelief because she's not a vampry. Everything brings up a slurry of emotions for Eloana, things I felt in my vision: relief, joy, love, and sorrow.

Having had time to think about what happened with Alastir, Eloana explains that she thinks he believed the Royals would support his plan to be rid of Poppy, which was what he meant when he cried "It's not too late" at the Chambers. Eloana can't help but keep bringing up Poppy's Ascension, and Poppy gives her a piece of her mind for disrespecting her. Eloana apologizes and is surprised by Poppy's understanding.

Eloana and Poppy discuss Poppy's heritage. Eloana confirms that Poppy does share abilities with Malec and remarks that she even looks like him. She assumes that Malec must be her father, though there are some things about that hypothesis that don't add up.

She tries to soften the blow of the news to Poppy by telling her that Cora could still be her mother, just not mortal. However, she realizes that Alastir would have known, therefore making that untrue.

She reveals that she knew Alastir had found someone he believed to be Malec's descendant but didn't know anything about her and had no idea that Poppy was the one he'd spoken of.

After additional thought, Eloana later reveals that it's impossible for Malec to be Poppy's father because she found him after the war and entombed him in bone chains under the Blood Forest, which was four hundred years ago. It would have only taken two hundred for him to become weak enough to die, so he would have been dead long before Poppy was born. However, she theorizes that maybe the Blood Crown discovered where Malec was entombed and helped him rise. They then hypothesize that Poppy must be Nyktos's great-granddaughter.

When the golden trees of Aios turn blood red, Eloana tells Poppy that the trees represent the blood of the gods, and the changing color signifies that a deity is in line for the throne. They were red when the deities ruled and turned gold after Malec was dethroned. She also refers to Ileana as the Queen of Blood and Ash and tells Poppy the root of that story.

Despite everything, Eloana continues to defend Malec, telling Poppy he wasn't a bad man or a bad ruler, he was just someone who became lost.

When plans are made for their next moves, Eloana asks Poppy what they're going to do about Malik and inquires what Poppy will do if Ian is not as she remembers. After Poppy answers, she worries about the state Malik will be in and almost thinks it would be better for him if he were dead. The thought of that makes her dissolve into tears, and Poppy comforts her as she cries. She also calls Poppy logical, brave, and strong.

Eloana later reveals that she, Valyn, and the Elders already decided that war is inevitable. They plan to burn Carsodonia to the ground and cut off the head of the snake, so to speak. She then goes on to say that only Poppy and Cas, Atlantia's new King and Queen, can stop what's in motion.

However, Eloana also reveals that a different battle is brewing in Atlantia between those who can trust a stranger and see Poppy as the rightful Queen, and those who can't. She adds that even if Poppy abdicates, the divisiveness will be as destructive as war. She then admits that she thinks Cas and Poppy are the best things for Atlantia and explains to Poppy why she thinks she's fit to rule. Eloana informs her that she has days—maybe a week—to decide, but if she chooses to wear the crown, she needs to do it for the right reasons.

Valyn, Cas, and Vonetta appear and tell everyone there is a convoy of Ascended at Spessa's End. When Ian requests a meeting with Poppy and her allies, Eloana fears it's a trap to grab Poppy, Cas, or both of them.

After returning to the capital, Eloana's crown of bleached bone becomes shiny and gilded. She tells Poppy that the coronation can be whenever they'd like it to be but that the Elders are eager to hear their news.

We definitely were.

She offers to send word regarding the changing of the crowns while Cas and Poppy meet with the Council.

During the coronation ceremony, Eloana crowns Poppy and then introduces her to Rose, the palace manager. She's surprised when Poppy not only asks her to call her Penellaphe and not *Your Majesty*, but also changes the Atlantian Crest to show equality between her and Casteel. The crest initially had unweighted weapons, the sword being much greater than the arrow. In the new version, the sword and arrow are the same size and perfectly crossed at the middle.

When they talk more about what needs to be done—a trip to Oak Ambler and a trip into Iliseeum to recruit Nyktos's guards—Eloana theorizes that waking Nyktos could be what forces the Blood Crown's hand, though she and Valyn plan to stay at the palace while Poppy and Cas go to Iliseeum. They'll serve as Crown surrogates while the new King and Queen are gone.

Following the events at Oak Ambler that lead to Casteel being taken prisoner by the Blood Crown again, Poppy seeks Eloana out upon her return. Eloana instantly sees that Cas isn't with Poppy and reaches for her husband—who isn't there—when she realizes *why* her Hawke didn't return. When Poppy admonishes her, saying that Eloana knew what Isbeth was and wasn't, and by keeping that from them, it led to current events, it makes her stomach drop.

Poppy relays to Eloana that the Blood Queen killed her brother, Hawkethrone, and now they have her son. Again. Poppy knows exactly why the Blood Queen wanted her sons—because it's personal.

She accuses Eloana of knowing that Ileana was Isbeth and that she *wasn't* the first Ascended—she's not an Ascended at all. Eloana swears she didn't know until she found Malec after the war and entombed him. Poppy tells her it doesn't matter *when* she learned the truth, just that she didn't reveal it.

When Eloana asks if her son is alive, Poppy asks her *which one* and relays that Malik is cozied up with Isbeth, and then shows her the marriage imprint, proving that Cas is alive. Though she adds that it means very little given what has happened.

Eloana explains that it was all ego and tells Poppy why she did what she did. Then she admits that she didn't want to go to war with Solis, partly because Isbeth's identity and story would come out. Poppy relays that Malec lied to her about being a deity and that Isbeth knew all along. Eloana then humbles herself and admits that Malec will always hold a piece of her heart.

Poppy tells Eloana about her parentage and reveals that the Queen planned to have her marry Malik and retake Atlantia. Eloana doesn't see how Isbeth's plan *wasn't* a success since Poppy *is* the current Queen. Poppy then asserts that she's been used her whole life and won't let it happen again. She tells Eloana that she plans to wake the draken and states there will be no preventing the war now.

Poppy asks Eloana to look after Tawny, her first friend, and Eloana summons me to help the poor girl after her shadowstone stabbing.

I'm unsure what Eloana did after that, but when the plan is put in motion to return Malec to Isbeth, Valyn contacts her about where and how she entombed the god.

The Queen Mother is in for a shock when she hears about everything *else* they uncovered while they were away.

KING VALYN DA'NEER
Becomes King Father Valyn Da'Neer

Hair: Blond.
Eyes: Gold.
Body Type: Tall. Broad-shouldered.
Facial features: Cut jaw. Straight nose. High cheekbones.
Distinguishing features: Dimples, though they rarely show.
Personality: Direct. Sometimes aggressive when it comes to a goal. Not the jealous type. Very reserved with his emotions.
Habits/Mannerisms/Strengths/Weaknesses: Fights with graceful brute force. Will do anything to protect his wife. Always has what's best for Atlantia in

mind. Likes wine.

Background: Elemental Atlantian. Bonded wolven died during the war. Was newly crowned when he fought Jalara in Pompay. Eloana has stabbed him many times, but he insists he probably deserved it.

Family: Wife = Eloana. Sons = Malik and Casteel. Grandfather = King Elian Da'Neer †. Descendant of = Attes, co-ruler of Vathi, Primal of War and Accord. Other ancestral family = Kyn, co-ruler of Vathi, Primal of Peace and Vengeance.

Valyn is not only the King Father of Atlantia's current King, he also played a significant role in the power shift within the kingdoms.

VALYN'S JOURNEY TO DATE:

Following Poppy's display of power after the attack in the Chambers of Nyktos, Valyn reaffirms Alastir's statement that Poppy called the wolven. He tells Cas to think about why his bonded wolven—Kieran—is ready to attack him.

Later, during discussions, Valyn comforts Eloana when the conversation turns to Malik. He also reminds Cas that he and Poppy are not the King and Queen yet. After Alastir's display of treason, he tells the wolven that he will be held somewhere safe and will accept the decision without argument. He adds that if he doesn't, Cas or the other wolven will likely attack, and Valyn won't intervene.

Once plans are made, Valyn joins the group that goes to Irelone to rescue Poppy. When she's mortally wounded with a crossbow bolt, Valyn panics when he realizes Casteel plans to Ascend her. He tells the guards to seize his son, but the wolven encircle them, making him unable to do anything but watch.

After the events at Spessa's End, he admits that he's impressed by what was done but doesn't believe it was enough. He still wants retribution and war.

Casteel secrets him away for *safekeeping*, and Emil and the others escort him back to Atlantia. He later meets Cas and Poppy in the Temple of Saion. When he sees Poppy for the first time since her near death, he's shocked to see that she hasn't Ascended. He remarks that he was present when Cas came out of his shadowshade poisoning and realized that Poppy was gone. He adds that he's never seen him like that, and it's something he will never forget.

In a moment of truth, Valyn tells Poppy that if she *had* Ascended, he would have been obligated to kill her and would have tried without hesitation, even knowing the wolven would not have let him make it to her. Her becoming an Ascended would have meant a war that would have weakened them to Solis.

Valyn agrees that Poppy is no longer mortal and remarks that it must have to do with her heritage, though he is unwilling to discuss it more without Eloana present—he's protecting her from a history that has haunted them for centuries. Though he does advise that everyone keep Poppy's changes a secret from those who aren't in their inner circle or were there when Cas saved her.

When the time comes for them to mete out justice against Alastir, Valyn asks for assurance that the wolven will not survive the night. He adds that if he does,

Valyn will see to it that he dies at dawn—something he will personally ensure, so long as a crown still sits upon his head.

Poppy thanks Valyn for his hand in rescuing her, and he tells her that she doesn't need to thank him. She's family now.

The fact that he switched his way of thinking so quickly was at first suspect to me, but the more I meditated on it, the more I realized that it's just the way things are with Poppy. It doesn't take people long to see her and realize she's special—Primal powers aside.

After the attack at the Contou residence, Valyn tells everybody that the attackers were the Unseen and shares more information about the group.

In discussing the recent treason, he says he believes the Crown Guards involved in the attack spoke openly to those who weren't, thus infecting them with their nonsense.

Upon their return to Atlantia, they see that the trees of Aios have turned from gold to red, and Valyn tells Cas that the people will see the shift as a sign of great change.

Valyn meets with Cas and Poppy at Cove Palace. When Eloana asks if Hawke's grown taller, Valyn remarks that Cas stopped growing ages ago—right around when he stopped listening to his parents.

At one point, Valyn slips and calls Poppy *Maiden*. Cas threatens him and says to *never* call her that again.

After Poppy saves Marji, the young child who was run over by the carriage, they discuss Poppy's abilities. Valyn knows of no other Ascended mortal with Atlantian blood who went through the Culling and didn't become a vampry. Nor does he know of any living half-Atlantian descended from the gods. He then tells Poppy that it's impossible for Cora and Leo to be her parents.

When they discuss Alastir's part in all of what's happened and what Valyn and Eloana knew and didn't, Valyn says he knew that Alastir had found someone he believed to be Malec's descendant but didn't know anything about them.

It's known that Valyn and Eloana have killed to protect the secret of Iliseeum. So, when pushed about what happened to Poppy and those they killed while protecting the realm of the gods, Valyn tells Cas that if he is to become King, he needs to learn to handle doing things that will turn his stomach and haunt his dreams.

They discuss Poppy's heritage some more, and Valyn tells Poppy that no other deities could be her parents because Malec killed them all. Then he adds that, to him, her powers are too strong to be several generations removed. He goes on to say that the changes in the trees of Aios signify that a deity is in line to take the throne. He adds that Poppy's mother would have to be nearly as old as Malec and either an Elemental Atlantian or of another important bloodline—possibly one they believe died out.

Talk turns to the prophecy, and Valyn admits his curiosity.

Poppy says she wants to destroy the Ascended, and Valyn believes he has a supporter in his war efforts. However, he tries to convince them not to rush to Spessa's End to meet with the Ascended convoy and says that Cas is speaking like a man in love, not a King.

Valyn and Eloana return to the capital and relinquish their crowns. During discussions, Valyn knows Cas and Poppy want to talk about more than just what happened during their meeting with those in Solis. He refers to Ian as an Ascended and irritates Poppy. When he suggests that her claim to the throne might be contested, he is quickly put in his place.

During the meeting with the Council, Eloana tells him it's time, making him allude to the fact that they don't take the traditional route with anything. He sternly corrects Lord Gregori about Poppy's heritage and is pleased by her show-of-force response.

Once Poppy and Cas are officially crowned, Valyn advises them that they will need to choose an Advisor. When Cas mentions he already knows who he will ask to be the Advisor to the Crown, Valyn agrees that Kieran is a good choice.

After the group decides to go to Iliseeum, Valyn remarks how waking Nyktos could be an unnecessary risk but says that he and Eloana will stay at the palace to serve as Crown surrogates while they are away.

After Casteel gives himself up to the Blood Crown, Valyn briefly sees Poppy after she returns to Evaemon without her husband and immediately leaves for the north.

With the army, he greets Poppy at the northernmost point of the kingdom and tells her that he knows she'll get his son back. He adds that Cas is a very lucky man to have found her and made himself hers. Then he says that he and Eloana are even more fortunate to have her as their daughter-in-law.

With sadness, Valyn asks Poppy a favor. He requests that she make Malik's death as quick and painless as possible if she should see him. She agrees to his request.

Valyn arrives in Massene, and Vonetta tells him what happened with the draken in Vessa's storm. He gives Reaver his condolences for the loss of his brethren and sistren and vows to make the Blood Crown pay tenfold.

During discussions with the generals and others about Oak Ambler, Valyn challenges Gayla La'Sere when she says their methods before may have been brutal, but they were effective. He argues that given where they are now, they weren't effective at all. They retreated. They didn't win.

Poppy decides to warn the mortals about the impending city seizures, and Valyn isn't sure that's wise. As he hears more of the plan, he struggles to agree. He's not worried about leadership; he's concerned about his daughter-in-law. Her. He reminds Poppy that none of his family members have entered the capital and returned as they were before they left—*if* they came back at all. Poppy refuses when Valyn offers to go with her and reminds him what Isbeth would do to him if he were captured.

After Poppy dresses in her white outfit, Valyn goes to see her and makes a remark about how many weapons she has. He tells her that she's the most powerful one and without outright saying it, asks her to remember that. She replies that she doesn't want to be a weapon, she wants to be a healer, and he comments on how honest she is. Taking her in, he remarks that she looks like his favorite painting in the palace, the one of the goddess Lailah in her white armor.

Poppy mentions what she saw while asleep, and Valyn corrects her when she tells him about her shared dreams with Casteel. He calls it dream walking and tells her it's actually soul walking because they're heartmates.

With some shame, Valyn reveals that Alastir knew who Ileana really was before he did; he didn't know until Cas was taken the first time, and only because Eloana told him. He then says that he would never have retreated before had he known.

As the discussion turns to Malec, Valyn says that Eloana never talked about him. He knew that part of her still loved him and always would—even though he didn't deserve it and she loves Valyn. Poppy scolds him again for not telling the truth sooner, insinuates that they wouldn't have had to negotiate with Isbeth if he had, and says that Atlantia is built on lies as much as Solis is.

Valyn asserts that they truly believed she was a deity, a descendant of one of the mortals Malec had an affair with. They didn't know that Malec was a god until Poppy revealed that to them. He also says that Eloana told him about Malec and Isbeth's son, but he still believes she didn't know the full truth until Alastir told her.

When the group takes Castle Redrock, he searches the keep with some other soldiers. They find and fight the Craven and the dozens of bodies—veiled women with their bodies mauled. He wishes Poppy didn't have to see it.

After Lin tells Valyn about the tunnels under the Temple, Valyn sends all the generals to secure them.

As more secrets come to light, Valyn wonders how a Priest of Solis knows a prophecy spoken by the gods eons ago. He's also disgusted that they think the True King is Malec.

When Poppy asks Valyn where and how Malec was entombed, he tells Poppy that Eloana used old magic and bone chains to secure him. He adds that Malec wouldn't be conscious and likely wouldn't remember himself, let alone seek retribution. However, he agrees they need confirmation and says he'll send word to Eloana.

After discovering the Ascended Priests and Priestesses, Valyn is shocked that Poppy didn't know the vamprys served in the Temples, too. When she and the others go to find the children, Valyn stays with the Priests and Priestesses. Later, he asks Poppy what she wants to do about the Priests and Priestesses and reminds her that she doesn't have to be the one to do everything.

Valyn wonders if the conspirator in the prophecy refers to Isbeth—the remaking of the realms could just mean taking Atlantia.

Poppy addresses the townsfolk, and Valyn and she talk about her need to delegate. She insists she should be the one to talk to the families, and he tells her that Cas is lucky to have found her. She tells *him* that they're both lucky.

They make a plan for their route and how they will accomplish their goals, and Valyn promises Poppy that Vonetta will have no issues with the generals in her absence, that they will take down no Rises, no innocents will be killed, and Poppy's wishes will be carried out.

Later, in Padonia after Casteel's rescue, Valyn greets his son and shakes as they embrace. He tells his son that he told Poppy not to go and get him and is put in his place fast. Despite having a lot to discuss, it will have to wait.

When Valyn finally comes face-to-face with Malik again, it's uncomfortable—he goes pale, his voice cracks, and he stiffens when Malik greets him impassively. All he can do is tell him that he looks good with a vacant tone.

Sven asks what the Blood Queen would want with Malec, and Valyn reveals who she really is, saying that she was Malec's mistress and informing them that she was never a vampry because a god cannot create a vampry. They create something else.

Talk turns to how Isbeth thinks Malec can help her destroy Atlantia and remake the realms, and Valyn is shocked. The god won't be in a good state and will need to feed—a lot. He'll eventually recover but there's no telling what mental state he'll be in or what he might do.

Eloana gets back to him about Malec's whereabouts, and Valyn shares the information: he's in the northeast corner of the Blood Forest near some ruins, entombed in a casket and covered in deity bones. He then reveals that I helped Eloana entomb Malec, though he has no idea what Primal essence Eloana and I used to do it.

As the group readies to leave for the Bone Temple, Cas tells Valyn that he's to remain in Padonia with Vonetta, saying that she will need his support to rule. It's an order, so he'll obey but bidding the others goodbye is difficult.

He is certainly in for a shock when he finds out everything that happened...

ALASTIR DAVENWELL †
Ex-Advisor to the Crown

Oh, Alastir. While the root of his beliefs and the reason for his actions may have come from a somewhat noble place—wanting to protect the kingdom above anything—he certainly didn't think things through when it came to what his actions would do to those he purported to love. Not only did he betray those he was quick to say were family, it ultimately cost him his life.

Hair: Long, sandy-blond.
Eyes: Pale blue.
Body type: Broad-shouldered.

Facial features: Ruggedly handsome.

Distinguishing features: Deep groove scar in the center of his forehead.

Other: Raspy voice. At least eight hundred years old but looks in his forties.

Personality: Not prone to violence. A bit of an alarmist.

Habits/Mannerisms/Strengths/Weaknesses: Incredibly loyal to his kingdom.

Background: Was King Malec's bonded wolven but has been unable to shift since their bond broke. King Valyn and Queen Eloana's Advisor to the Crown. Part of the secret Protector brotherhood. After he betrays Cas by kidnapping Poppy, Poppy kills him by slitting his throat.

Family: Daughter = Shea †. Niece = Gianna. Great-nephew = Beckett †.

ALASTIR'S JOURNEY TO DATE:

To me, Alastir has always been a little shady. As a prominent wolven, Malec's bonded, uncle-like figure to both Princes and Kieran, and the Advisor to the Atlantian Crown, he featured in my visions, of course. Still, there was always...something there that made it slightly unclear and a bit too mutable. After recent events, that reason became clearer. I only wish I had *seen* it beforehand. But, then again, I don't mettle in the affairs of the Fates—at least not much.

Let's pick up the wolven's timeline when he enters Poppy and Cas's story, shall we?

As the group is traveling, Alastir arrives at New Haven just ahead of the storm.

After seeing Poppy for the first time and noticing the bite mark on her neck, he comments that he's missed a lot and goes on to talk with her. Later, during their formal introduction, he mentions that he's surprised by her last name and says *Balfour* goes back hundreds of years in Solis. I can only imagine it's because he knows about the last oracle or something about Leopold. He also mentions that he's surprised to hear of her Atlantian descent, given how close her parents were to the Blood Crown.

When Poppy mentions the night the Craven attacked her family, Alastir responds with a bit of curiosity. Poppy thinks it's because he's wondering if that's how she ended up scarred. But now that we know he was there, I wonder...

In the banquet hall later, Poppy politely greets Alastir, and he speaks with Kieran briefly in another language. He then mentions his shock at hearing about her proposal to Casteel and refers to her as the Maiden. When Cas chastises him, he acquiesces but not before stating that no one can change the past, regardless of current circumstances. During dinner, when talk turns to how Poppy tried to murder Cas, it takes Alastir aback. I can guess what was going through his mind there. He was already scheming to ensure the prophecy didn't come to be. And then to learn that she'd tried to murder his Prince...

They discuss the skewed history and what the people of Solis believe, and Alastir mentions that not all in the kingdom are loyal to Queen Ileana and King

Jalara. He is, of course, speaking about the Descenters—particularly those faithful to Atlantia and those who think as he does: The *Protectors*. As talk shifts to the plans, Alastir clarifies that his allegiance is to the Kingdom of Atlantia. To those at the table, it would have sounded like he was talking about Cas and his plans, but we know that's not true. Alastir was loyal to the kingdom first and foremost until the very end, and that meant he couldn't be okay with Casteel's new plans pertaining to Poppy. He also warns about unrest among the wolven.

Alastir asks to speak to Poppy privately, and they take a walk. They discuss the fact that she can fight, and then Alastir reveals how his daughter, Shea, was Casteel's intended. He puts Poppy at ease and promises he'll help her get out of her current situation if she feels it's not what she wants. This may have seemed altruistic to Poppy, but there were much deeper machinations at hand. He also says he'll ask around to see if any of his people know about her parents, but we now know that he already knew them both.

After leaving to check the roads with a small group, Alastir returns following the Ascended attack. He and his men take care of several of the Queen's knights, and then he witnesses Poppy healing the injured. He asks her if she's sure that her brother, Ian, Ascended since he doubts they would have let a half-Atlantian Ascend. He also tells her about the Empath Warrior bloodline and how they could siphon the energy behind emotions, feed on others in that way, and how they were called Soul Eaters.

Alastir leaves for Spessa's End before the rest of the group. When he speaks with Poppy later, he tells her about the Joining and the wolven's bond to the Elemental Atlantians, indirectly revealing that he was Malec's bonded wolven.

Becket gets injured, and Alastir rushes him to Vonetta's. He's absolutely stunned when Poppy heals the young wolven—it's much more than what she did after the Ascended attack, complete with a glow. He apologizes to her for those looking at her suspiciously and treating her strangely and advises her to ignore the looks, saying if she won't remove herself from the situation, she can't show that it bothers her.

This all seemed very counterproductive to what he planned. But maybe, despite knowing that he would be betraying her, he did have some fondness for her and a softness in him somewhere. And perhaps he really thought that he could just get her to leave if he overwhelmed her thoughts and triggered her self-doubt.

Alastir admits that he doesn't understand how love sprang up between Poppy and Casteel given the Prince's original plans for her as the Maiden. Then, he goes on to say how he's seen Cas in love before and that the people expected someone else to become their Queen because Cas was promised to another.

Now *that* seems more in line with Alastir's end goal. It was a grand opportunity to make Poppy doubt herself and her relationship with Casteel—and incredibly manipulative.

When Casteel chastises him for bringing that up, calling him weak for doing it, Alastir claims that Cas marrying his niece Gianna would have strengthened the relationship between the wolven and the Atlantians. Jasper warns Alastir that he's overstepping, but the wolven still accuses Cas of refusing his duties to his people.

I honestly think that this was where the switch was completely flipped for Alastir. He had been plotting already but seeing that it was beyond hope and that he couldn't talk Cas out of his plans or get Poppy to leave on her own just reinforced that he'd have to take matters into his hands.

As the others disperse, Alastir stays in Atlantia. When he meets back up with the group in Saion's Cove, he's shocked to see that Casteel and Poppy got married and even more surprised to hear that Nyktos blessed the union. He requests to speak with Casteel privately, likely hoping to talk some sense into him and bring him around to Alastir's way of thinking.

I'm not sure what he got up to between that point and when Beckett led Poppy to her ambush at the Chambers of Nyktos, but, like most, he arrives after the attack, witnessing the end of the display of what she can do. He tries to reason with the Queen, telling Eloana that it's not too late and knowing what it will mean for the Crown.

He makes it known that Poppy is calling the wolven at the Temple and says that he can feel the broken bonds because he can sense Poppy's Primal *notam*. When Cas orders the guards to seize Alastir, he's shocked and states that Cas has no authority over the guards or him since he is not yet King. They still secure him. When Valyn orders him to be put somewhere... *safe*, he's incensed.

Shouting, "Protect your King and Queen," Alastir signals those loyal to him to act, and they infect everyone trying to protect Poppy with shadowshade. He tells Poppy that *she* is the threat to Atlantia, not him, then knocks her out and whisks her away.

While Poppy is in the crypt, Alastir visits and apologizes for Jansen's behavior. He then tells her about the gods, deities, Shadowlands, and Iliseeum. He goes on to explain how Poppy is dangerous. Says she's entered her Culling and will start showing the same chaotic tendencies as those who came before her—the deities that became monsters, thus causing the Elementals to rise against them. He explains about Malec and reveals that Eloana and Valyn knew about Malec's powers. Then, he implies that Malec is Poppy's father and adds that the King had many mistresses, and there were others like her—children born of the deity—who never reached their Culling.

I've never been able to pin down whether or not Alastir knew that Malec was actually a god and not merely a deity or if he knew about Ires and Millicent.

Alastir tells Poppy about the prophecy and reveals that they've met before— the night her parents were killed. He thought she looked familiar when he met her in New Haven—something in the eyes—and had a nagging feeling but didn't know for certain she was the one until she told him her parents' names. He admits that he was there to help them flee Solis and claims that he didn't strike her parents down but that he *would* have killed them both *and* her if given the chance. He goes on to say that the Dark One killed her parents, and that darkness outside his influence was there that night. When Cora and Leo told him about Poppy and who she descended from—the Blood Queen—he knew he had to do something, so...he let that darkness in, in the form of Malik.

Then, Alastir reveals all sorts of secrets: that he can no longer shift, that he plans to give Poppy to the Ascended, and that while he doesn't want to harm Casteel, he will if he gets in his way. He adds that he doesn't think that Cas's plan is enough. Alastir and Valyn want the Ascended to pay, and so long as Poppy is alive, the throne is hers by birthright. He says he would rather go to war than have the likes of her unleashed on his people.

When Cas and the others come to rescue Poppy, they take Alastir into custody from the crypts, as well. Cas uses compulsion on him to learn the names of everyone involved and to find where they passed her off to the Ascended. While tucked away, a handful of Atlantians and mortals try to free Alastir but are also captured. Later, Casteel retrieves Alastir from the crypts under the Temple. Believing that Poppy is dead, Alastir is at first relieved when Casteel reveals that he won't kill him, and then shocked to see Poppy. He tells her that what he started won't end with his death. She tells *him* that she'll never think of him again, cuts his throat, and then lets the wolven cannibalize him.

After his death, we learn that Alastir knew that Ileana was Isbeth and that *he* was the one who killed Isbeth and Malec's child.

KIERAN CONTOU

I have had my eye on Kieran for some time, but then again, he's pretty easy on the eyes. I even dallied with his aunt and her bonded Elemental Atlantian once upon a blue moon…

Hair: Dark and trimmed close to the skull.

Eyes: Striking pale blue like a winter sky.

Body type: Lean.

Facial features: Warm beige skin. Sharply angled face. Goes from coldly handsome to strikingly attractive when he smiles.

Distinguishing features: Slight accent. Faded claw marks across his chest. A healed puncture wound near his waist.

Other: Fine dusting of hair on his chest. Over two hundred years old.

Personality: Snarky and sarcastic. A bit anal. Not the hugging type. Not modest. About as transparent as a brick wall. Go-to expression is bored with a hint of amusement.

Habits/Mannerisms/Strengths/Weaknesses: Moves with the grace of a dancer when he fights. Often sleeps in wolven form and kicks but rests easiest as the sun rises. Loves biscuits…well, food in all forms. Doesn't like crowded cities. Excellent at making alcoholic drinks. His loyalty to his family and those he loves goes beyond any bond, including the Primal *notam*.

Preternatural traits: Fawn/sand/tawny-colored in his wolven form. Slight foresight—has feelings that tend to come true. Nearly as tall as a man, even on all fours. Imprint is like cedar: rich, earthy, and woodsy. Blood smells like the woods, earthy and rich.

Background: Bonded to Casteel since birth. Lost a great love—Elashya—who was born with a wasting disease.

Family: Mother = Kirha Contou. Father = Jasper Contou. Sisters = Vonetta, and a new baby sister, name still unknown. Aunt = Beryn.

This loyal, protective, funny, and fierce wolven is the perfect balance for Casteel and Poppy. He would do anything for them, and they for him.

KIERAN'S JOURNEY TO DATE:

Born as the first child to Jasper and Kirha Contou, Kieran was bonded to Prince Casteel at birth. The two shared a crib more often than not, took their first steps together, and sat at the same table most nights, even refusing to eat the same vegetables. They were inseparable. As they grew older, they were rarely apart, even though they sometimes appeared to hate each other, often coming to blows over minor things—as siblings are wont to do.

Kieran once had a great love, Elashya, who was born with the same wasting disease her grandmother had. It didn't reveal itself for more than a hundred years, but when it did manifest, it was virulent, shut the body down, and killed her within days. He will always harbor sadness for the loss.

Adventurers at heart, Kieran spent considerable time exploring with Casteel, Cas's brother, Prince Malik; and their friend, Shea. When they went into the tunnels, they ensured they wouldn't get lost by marking the stone walls with their initials. I'm sure some can even be seen today. Kieran and Casteel even tried to sail past the Mountains of Nyktos once to see if any of the land beyond was habitable and almost drowned in the process.

Now, on to when things really start to pick up...

When Casteel tries to take down the Blood Crown, Kieran doesn't know the plan and is expressly forbidden from going to the capital. He immediately knows that Casteel is injured when he suddenly feels sick and realizes it's serious when it robs him of all his strength. Kieran discovers that Cas has been captured when he doesn't return, Kieran can no longer walk, and no amount of food or water sates him. He quickly loses weight and remains in that weakened state for the entire five decades Casteel is held by the Blood Crown.

Kieran is the only one who knows what Cas went through during his imprisonment and often had to help the Prince remember who he was back in those days after he returned, reminding him that he wasn't a *thing*. It's a terrible link to solidify a tether to someone, but it's there for the men, nonetheless. The two have a bond that goes beyond friendship and family. They are two sides of the same coin.

When Casteel devises the scheme to become *Hawke Flynn*—a name that Kieran actually picked—to capture the Maiden and use her as a bargaining tool to free his brother, Kieran is all-in. Despite hating most of Solis because of its many Ascended and crowds, he knows he will go wherever Casteel does without question.

And this is where the Fate lines of Kieran, Poppy, and Casteel converge for me in my visions...

Kieran starts out in Masadonia as a City Guard, traveling with Casteel into enemy territory to begin their ruse. He keeps Setti with him there, and he and Casteel meet secretly when they can. They use the Red Pearl a lot, but they also communicate via notes left in Wisher's Grove.

He and Cas meet at the Red Pearl with another wolven, Jericho, and Descenter Griffith Jansen, a commander of the Royal Guard—a changeling who later reveals himself as a traitor to the Crown and is swiftly dealt with. After leaving to take care of some business, Kieran returns to let Hawke know that the envoy has arrived, not yet realizing the Maiden is in the room. If he had, I wonder if he would have delayed his interruption.

Later, Kieran and Cas meet with Emil and Delano in the Grove so that Cas can feed. When Emil is...well, Emil, Kieran tells him he has a death wish.

For real, though. He just can't keep his mouth shut. And once Kieran finds out about Vonetta...he's probably going to be ready to hunt him, too.

When Cas finds out that Jericho tried to take Poppy the night he killed Rylan

Keal and ended up hitting her, Kieran tries to head him off, telling him he already knocked the wolven on his ass for his insubordination and telling Cas he can't kill Jericho. He thinks maybe he's gotten through to Hawke—and he did—but when they get to the Three Jackals, he can only stand by and watch as Cas cuts off Jericho's left hand.

Later, he goes with Cas to the warehouse district, summoned by one of their Descenters. When they arrive, Lev tells them there's something they need to see. When he sees, he thinks he never needed to see that. Nobody does. The Ascended turned a baby into a Craven. He can barely watch as Cas does what needs to be done.

Kieran leaves a note for Casteel, telling him that he's in the meat packing district with a new friend. When Casteel arrives, Kieran tells him he's been freezing his balls off and then takes great pleasure in scaring and tormenting Lord Devries, until he brings up stuff that it took Kieran much too long to talk Casteel through.

Kieran spends some quality time with Circe at the Red Pearl, but Cas interrupts. Kieran invites him to join, but Cas declines. After, they discuss the Duke and what Casteel wants to do to him, and Kieran tells him it's revenge. And selfish. Cas tells him again that he wishes Kieran hadn't come, and Kieran basically tells him to shut up.

He would never leave Cas.

The night of the Rite, he and Cas meet and discuss the plan. Cas tells Kieran he'll meet him in the Grove later with the Maiden, and Kieran once again tells him he doesn't like it. It doesn't feel right. He does say that the Descenters are doing their part and creating the distraction, though.

Little does he know that's not all they're doing.

After the Descenters attack the Rite, Hawke takes the opportunity to spirit Penellaphe away under the guise of escorting her to the capital and the Queen. Kieran joins him, along with Royal Guards Phillips Rathi, Bryant, and Airrick, and Huntsmen Luddie and Noah. Leading the convoy with Phillips, Kieran takes notice of Hawke and Penellaphe's interaction, noting how their relationship has already progressed. When he hears Penellaphe laughing loudly over Hawke disclosing that he brought along my diary, he sees something in Casteel that he hasn't seen in quite some time—life.

I love that my journal made the journey with them.

On their first night of travel, the convoy sets up camp in the Blood Forest. While four of the guards rest, Kieran and three others keep watch several yards from where the Maiden attempts to sleep. Kieran and Hawke have a talk about the dangers and worries, and Kieran tells Cas that he surprised him—he hasn't heard the Atlantian laugh like he's done with Poppy in a long time. He teases Cas about going to keep Poppy company and is close enough to notice Hawke giving Penellaphe pleasure later.

After she falls asleep, Kieran teases him some more, telling him that Poppy likes him. He indicates that although they will reach Three Rivers prior to nightfall, they can't stay there. The Prince suggests that if they break off halfway to Three Rivers and ride through the night, they could possibly make it to New Haven by the morning. Kieran asks him if he is ready for that and mentions the growing relationship between him and Penellaphe, reminding Hawke to remember the task at hand.

Farther into the Blood Forest, they're ambushed by a group of Craven. Kieran moves with the grace of a dancer, fighting with a sword in each hand. After Airrick dies in the attack, Kieran takes the guard's place, riding alongside Hawke and Penellaphe.

When they stop, Kieran and Cas talk about what the Maiden did with the dying guard. During the discussion, Cas calls her *Poppy*, and Kieran questions it. Cas pushes back, acting like it's no big deal. Kieran warns him about getting too familiar and outright asks if she's still a maiden. It upsets Cas, but Kieran reminds him of what she's dealt with and that doing more will only fuck with her.

After resting near Three Rivers, Kieran shares his cheese with Poppy on the road while teasing her and answering her questions. They finally reach New Haven and reunite with the others of their group, meeting to discuss plans. During one of those meetings, Kieran watches as Cas rips out Orion's heart and then tosses it into the fire.

Later, Kieran discovers Phillips trying to escape with Penellaphe, and a fight breaks out. Phillips cuts him on the stomach and leg during the skirmish. Unable to do much else, Kieran shifts into his wolven form and gives chase, punching through the barn door in pursuit.

When Bryant attempts to flee the stables, Kieran kills him. Once all threats have been neutralized, he changes back and joins Penellaphe and Hawke in their discussion of what's been going on, scoffing at the things the Maiden *thinks* she knows.

Once they move Penellaphe to the dungeon, Kieran comes upon Jericho and his cohorts attacking her. He subdues them and brings the Maiden to Hawke's chambers. Once in front of his friend, he tells him not to let her drink his blood and accidentally calls him *Casteel*—which does not go unnoticed by Poppy.

Later, after Poppy tries to escape and Cas catches her in the snow, Kieran talks with him. Cas tells him that she's half-Atlantian and they talk about why the Ascended really wanted her. Cas finally admits he cares about Poppy, and Kieran is thrilled. They talk about how everything has changed and Kieran insinuates that Cas is in love. He tries to deny it and changes the subject.

While Hawke deals with the traitors who attacked Penellaphe, Kieran asks her if she's going to bathe and tells her she smells of Hawke. A bit embarrassed, she agrees. When she's in the tub for longer than anticipated, he goes to check on her, utterly shocking and scandalizing her. Trying to soothe her, he tells her that scars are revered among his people and never hidden.

I personally agree. Some of the most fascinating and deep people I have ever met and had the pleasure of being with had scars that were like roadmaps of their lives on their bodies. Tracing them was like taking in the personal braille of their history etched on their flesh.

Escorting Penellaphe and Hawke to the common area, Kieran steadies the Maiden when she stumbles, shocked by the sight of the traitors spiked to the wall. As they make their way to the dining hall, Kieran assures Penellaphe that they deserved what Casteel did to them. When they discuss how Penellaphe isn't mortal and that she's at least part Atlantian—something they recently discovered after Casteel fed from her—he tells her that every so often, a child of both kingdoms is born.

When Landell—another wolven—speaks up about his objection to the Prince's announcement that he's taking Penellaphe home to marry her, Kieran urges him to shut his mouth. He doesn't, and Hawke kills him by ripping out his heart. Seeing the shock on Penellaphe's face, Kieran asks her if she'd like to return to her room.

While he might have been making sure she understood that she wouldn't be allowed to retire to her chambers alone, it was becoming clear that Kieran was developing a fondness for Poppy right along with Hawke.

As they walk, she asks him about the older man who came to dinner, and he tells her that it was Alastir Davenwell. Kieran goes on to explain that he is like an uncle to both Princes and him. As they walk more, he realizes her scent is different and tells her as much, saying that she smells of death.

Discussing the truth about the Ascended, Kieran tells Penellaphe that while the Prince earned his Dark One nickname, he is the only thing in both kingdoms she doesn't have to fear.

Later, when Penellaphe attempts her escape, Kieran shifts and accompanies Casteel into the woods to retrieve her. Cas tells her that if she fights him and wins, she'll earn her freedom, then orders Kieran back to the keep. When the Prince returns, Kieran heads out with him to deal with the dead Craven Cas and Poppy encountered, and Kieran reveals to Penellaphe that it is a great honor to guard that which the Prince values so greatly.

There was no use denying Casteel's feelings for Poppy any longer, and anyone could see Kieran's softening for her, as well.

At dinner, Kieran steals food from Penellaphe—as is common for him—and they further discuss bloodlines. They've talked about them before, but there's a lot she doesn't know. Kieran tries to educate her a bit but also teases her. When she asks why he calls her *Penellaphe*, he tells her that nicknames are reserved for friends. He then asks her if she always has so many questions—something he does for the entirety of their budding relationship and likely will for many, many years to come, I'm sure. It's just something unique to them and their bond, and I find it utterly endearing.

The following day, Kieran goes to escort Penellaphe to breakfast and confesses that he knew Cas's plans. He further says that he knew they had changed before Casteel did—before he knew she was Atlantian. He then adds that he just knows things sometimes.

Jasper has the same gift, and I wonder if they have Seer blood somewhere in their line. But that's just my assumption. I have no proof to substantiate those thoughts.

When Casteel arrives for the meal, Kieran moves to Cas's left in a position of power and protection and reminds him that if they can't convince Alastir of his and Penellaphe's *fake* engagement, there is no way they'll be able to persuade the King and Queen. After they talk about Penellaphe's murderous tendencies and shock most of those at the table, they continue with the meal, and Kieran tells Penellaphe about the gods and their rest.

After dinner, despite my diary likely being the most interesting book in her chambers—something Kieran is quick to point out—Penellaphe goes looking for something to read and finds a nearly hidden volume that mentions the wivern, ceeren, and other things. She asks Kieran about it. He reveals that it's a book of Atlantian records and moves in to take a closer look. As he does, his arm brushes hers, and he feels a shock like being struck by lightning, making him jerk away and jump back.

When the Ascended arrive, Kieran shifts. As Casteel is talking to Lord Chaney, he slinks around the keep, coming out near the stables. As a fight breaks out, Kieran jumps on a knight's back as the Ascended is doing his best to kill Elijah. Later, he tears out Lord Chaney's tongue for annoying him and leaves the rest to Penellaphe.

Am I wrong for thinking that's sexy? For Mrs. Tulis, her son, the man the knight slaughtered at Chaney's command, the others who died during the fight, and those who perished later, I would have done the same as Poppy—and probably worse.

In the library later, Kieran tells Penellaphe the story of Casteel's imprisonment and explains his bond with the Atlantian. He also reveals that the wolven Malik was bonded to died while trying to rescue him. They talk about Alastir and him being Malec's bonded wolven, the war, and how the bonds changed afterward.

Everything changed after that war.

They ready themselves to leave for Atlantia, and Kieran and Casteel discuss strategy. They anticipate making it to Spessa's End by the end of the week and talk about those they hope to join them in the battle with the scouts and knights the Blood Crown will inevitably send.

When they come upon tree hangings with unique shapes during their journey, Kieran warns Casteel. They know exactly what they are—the mark of the vicious, cannibalistic people of the land who live outside the Rise. The Dead Bones Clan attacks, and they fight.

Luckily, Kieran isn't hurt. I would have hated to see that fine skin marred...and there was plenty on display after he shifted. Poppy certainly noticed.

Kieran sees the damage Casteel took during the skirmish and worries about the Prince's control. He makes it clear that he doesn't believe Cas when the Prince insists that he's fine. The arrows did quite a number on him.

Resting in Pompay, Kieran hears Poppy scream and bursts into the room she's sharing with Casteel. He realizes immediately that he misread the situation and that it was a scream of pleasure, not one of distress. He apologizes and moves to leave until Casteel turns to him, and Kieran sees that the Atlantian is starving. He urges Penellaphe to run and moves to make Casteel lunge for him. As usual, she doesn't listen and tries to talk Casteel down. Luckily, the minute she calls him *Hawke*, he snaps out of it, apologizes, and walks past Kieran and out the door.

Once Casteel is gone, Kieran checks on Penellaphe, ensuring the Prince didn't hurt her or force himself on her. When she assures him that she's fine and asks what happened, Kieran explains that Cas saw him as a threat to her in that moment. He goes on to say that Cas needs to feed, and that he warned him about walking the razor's edge of control and what would inevitably happen.

Penellaphe and Kieran share many things: that Cas told her about his nightmares, why Kieran believes Cas hasn't fed, and stories about his and Cas's shared childhood. When she mentions Shea, intuiting that the *friend* in Kieran's story is her, he warns her not to bring Shea up around Cas.

Discussing Casteel later, Kieran tells Penellaphe that he's happy she finally acknowledged that she cares for Casteel. When she asks him if Cas would have really let her go if she refused to marry him, Kieran tells her that, yes, she could have left, and Casteel would have let her leave, but she wouldn't have been free of him—because he knows the depth of their connection, even if *she* hasn't realized it yet.

With Cas finally agreeing to feed, Kieran referees, monitoring Penellaphe's heartbeat and making sure Casteel takes enough but not too much. Knowing what will inevitably happen between the two of them after the feeding, he leaves.

I, for one, wish he had stayed. All three of them knew about the Joining by that point; they could have had a practice run, at least. And I know for a fact that Poppy and Casteel knew all sorts of tips and tricks about adding a third to their play from reading my diary. Heck, both Casteel and Kieran had practical knowledge, and I'd bet Poppy would have been totally receptive, if a little shy.

Talking with Alastir after Beckett's injury, Kieran confirms that Penellaphe did, indeed, intend to kill Casteel when she stabbed him, shocking him and everyone else in the room.

Honestly, if they knew her, they likely wouldn't have been so surprised.

When word comes that the sky is on fire, Kieran is one of the first to head to the parapets to investigate the claim and is there when Penellaphe arrives. They discuss what it could be and what to do and ultimately decide to wait. Unfortunately, that wait isn't long. They're attacked, and Delano is wounded in the skirmish. Kieran stands by as Penellaphe heals him. Later, in a strategy session, Kieran suggests alternate routes the New Haven refugees could take to avoid the Ascended.

To Kieran's chagrin, Casteel orders him to accompany Alastir over the Skotos

Mountains. When he argues and says he should stay with Cas, that his bond and duty necessitate him defending Casteel with his life, the Prince tells him that he's fast, strong, and will not fail, then tells him that he wants him guarding what is most precious to him—Poppy. When all is said and done, Penellaphe doesn't end up going, but Kieran knows why Cas wants *him* to go. He doesn't want Kieran to sacrifice himself, and he wants to ensure that Alastir can't thwart what he has planned by going to the King and Queen about the marriage before Casteel has a chance to tell them. They exchange a heartfelt and affectionate goodbye. As he leaves, Kieran turns to Penellaphe and tells her to protect her Prince, calling her *Poppy* for the first time, thus solidifying that they are friends and that he cares.

Kieran and other reinforcements arrive right in the middle of Poppy's standoff with Duchess Teerman. As the army moves in to attack, Kieran, in wolven form, nudges Poppy's hand where the wedding imprint resides. Poppy and Casteel tell him that he missed a lot while he was gone—which he did. The wedding was just one of *many* things.

He stands guard outside the carriage when Poppy and Cas have their hot and heavy celebration of life after dispatching the Duchess. Later, Kieran reveals that he and the other wolven heard Poppy calling to them for help and veered toward her. He also tells her that he believes he and the reinforcements were able to make it through the mountains and the mist so easily because the gods allowed it.

As they set out once more, Kieran rides with Poppy and Cas while the others go a different way. They are to meet back up at Gold Rock. During their journey, Kieran teases Poppy about their sleeping arrangements and insinuates that it will either become uncomfortable or *interesting*.

I'd go with the latter.

Poppy sleepwalks and nearly kills herself, and Kieran tells her that he believes the earth shaking was a god returning to their resting place, and that the goddess Aios stopped Poppy from walking off the cliff's edge. He then shares that he dreamed about being chased by his own ghosts during her episode.

After Poppy's attack at the Chambers of Nyktos, Kieran arrives in wolven form with many others and makes eye contact with her as the dozens of wolven move in, circling her and scenting the air. Protecting her.

Pupils shining a silvery-white, Kieran growls when others get too close to Poppy after her display of power. He even snaps at Casteel when he says he will destroy anything or anyone who dares to stand between him and his wife. Bunching to attack, he only stops when Poppy commands it. Still on alert and ready to pounce, he finally backs down when Poppy reminds him that *he* told *her* that Casteel was the only person in both kingdoms she was safe with.

Alastir turns on them and orders the guards to attack Poppy. Kieran leaps to protect her and is hit with an arrow dipped in shadowshade, freezing him in place and turning his skin as hard as stone and as cold as ice. Just like it did with Jasper, Casteel, and others.

I've seen what shadowshade can do, and it is not for the faint of heart. It is a terrifying sight to behold, indeed.

Finally out of his paralysis and part of a larger group, Kieran rushes in to rescue Poppy in Irelone. He sees that they bound her with deity bones and carefully removes them. When Casteel arrives and rips a Protector's spine from his body, Kieran quips that he's just a little bit angry.

And let me tell you, Casteel Da'Neer is *incredibly* alluring when enraged.

After Poppy deals with Jansen, a Protector shoots her in the chest with a crossbow bolt. Kieran frantically tries to pull it from her, hurriedly telling Cas that it missed her heart but got an artery and lung, reinforcing that the wound is mortal but that there's still time. When he sees that Cas won't be deterred from Ascending her, Kieran assures him that they will deal with whatever comes... Together.

Sometime later, Kieran is present when Poppy wakes and realizes he can still feel her Primal *notam*. When she pounces on him in hunger, he warns Cas that she's much faster and stronger now, but then realizes she didn't Ascend.

Overseeing Poppy's first feeding with Cas, Kieran forces her to stop when she starts to take too much. When bloodlust turns to another type of lust, he leaves the couple to their devices.

When Poppy reveals more about what she was told while being held, Kieran confirms that the bond between him and Cas *is* broken and tells her he thinks the wolven instinctually knew what she was all along but didn't quite put the pieces together. When she goes on to tell them about the bits she heard regarding the prophecy, Kieran informs her that Atlantians don't believe in them.

As she worries about the bond shifting to her and what it means for him and Cas, Kieran reassures Poppy that their bond goes well beyond power and that it just means they've made room for her.

I absolutely adore these three!

They then discuss Poppy's gifts, the deities, and immortality, and Kieran reveals that Poppy smells like final, absolute power to him now.

When they talk about Alastir again, Kieran says he believes the wolven still cares about Cas and his family but is loyal to the kingdom above all else. He then goes on to say that he assumes Alastir realized what Poppy was before anyone else and knew what it would mean for the kingdom and the Crown.

It doesn't excuse his actions, but I also see the reasoning there.

Kieran—in wolven form—and Poppy wait as Casteel retrieves Alastir. When Poppy wonders if Alastir's plan failed, Kieran telepathically answers, surprising her. After she slits Alastir's throat, Kieran calls to the wolven, and they converge en masse to devour the disgraced wolven.

The next evening at the Contou residence, Kieran brings food and word that Valyn wants to meet with Casteel. He, Cas, and Poppy talk about the evening prior and how Casteel read parts of my journal about wicked kisses in secret places and foursomes—oh, those passages are *good*! But let me tell you, the real thing was even better... And Kieran laments that he wasn't there for the foursome talk. Occasionally, I imagine sitting down with them and relaying some of the stories firsthand. It would be a delightful experiment to be sure.

Cas heads off to speak with his father, and Kieran stays with Poppy, explaining things about Nyktos and the wolven and their history, then telling Poppy that his people will respect her differently than they do the King and Queen because she is proof that they come from the gods. When she goes on to tell him what the Duchess told her about the Blood Queen being happy about Poppy taking both Atlantia and Solis, Kieran says that her actions determine whether she'll become a threat to Atlantia, not her bloodline.

When she brings up hearing him in her mind at the Temple, Kieran asks about his imprint. She reaches out to test it and tells him that it's like cedar, woodsy and rich. He assures her that he can't read her thoughts all the time—only that one time at the Temple so far—and that if he could, he imagines her mind would be a cyclone of questions. When they attempt to communicate telepathically, they succeed—both ways. Kieran theorizes that the *notam* allows the communication.

After a battle with the Unseen, Kieran, Cas, and Poppy discuss the fight. Kieran explains how he tried to keep her out of it, and Cas tells him that his wife can take care of herself. When Kieran reminds them that things are different now, Poppy compromises by telling *him* they'll handle whatever comes…together. When discussions turn to the attack that killed Poppy's parents, Kieran tells her that everything she's been told about Cora and Leo is most likely a lie.

Kieran returns from checking on Sage after she's injured and brings a textbook and his father with him. From the book, they learn about Gyrms and that Iliseeum is real. They also discover where it is purportedly located. Discussing it more and veering onto the subject of how the Gyrms came to be in their realm, Jasper reveals that most things about the Land of the Gods were kept secret, especially the magic. He goes on to say that *I* am one of the few people who knows about it, taking all of them by surprise. They then tell Jasper about my journal, and he reveals that I'm one of the oldest changelings alive *and* one of Atlantia's Elders. And while I wish he wouldn't have—because a woman's age should be kept secret and sacred—he tells the group that I am over two thousand years old.

When news comes that a child has been injured in an accident, Kieran sets off with Casteel and Poppy. As they approach the little girl named Marji pinned under the carriage, Kieran realizes the girl is dead. When Poppy resurrects her, seemingly without consequence, Kieran kneels, paying homage.

After Cas and Poppy's sexy little tryst in the garden, they and Kieran take in the sights of the city and end up in a museum. They discuss Nyktos and his connection to wolves, viewing paintings of the King of Gods with a dark gray wolf, sculptures of him with a wolf, and a drawing where a white wolf stands behind him. They also discuss how Malec Ascending Isbeth is what led them to where they are today, the cave cat Poppy saw when she was younger, and the fact that godlines and their hierarchy have been greatly skewed by incorrectly reported history spearheaded by the Ascended.

Later, they come upon a wolven wedding, and Casteel dismisses the guards. Kieran spends some time with his friend, Lyra, and they all dance and have fun. Kieran tells Poppy that she honors them by joining in on the dances. After, Lyra pleasures Kieran in the shadows of the bluff, and he catches Poppy watching.

When the time comes to meet with the King and Queen, Kieran stands guard and helps Poppy assert her and Casteel's position, speaking for the entirety of the wolven and stating that it doesn't matter if Poppy *is* Malec's daughter or not.

They discuss how Leopold could not have been Malec using an assumed identity or a changeling in disguise, and Kieran questions how Malec can be Poppy's father at all, given he's been presumed dead for centuries. Then he wonders if they're wrong. Perhaps her father is actually someone else. He suggests that the only way to know if Malec has risen is for them to go to the Blood Forest and check, which is nearly impossible with all the Craven about and how deeply it lies within Solis.

Poppy's brother extends an invitation for them to meet. Informing his parents of their journey to Spessa's End to meet with Ian, Kieran begins gathering wolven to join them on the trip. When they arrive in the city, utterly exhausted, Kieran communicates with Poppy telepathically, and she orders them all to rest.

Later, in their wolven forms, Kieran and Delano, along with Netta and Nova, accompany Cas and Poppy to their meeting. When they come face-to-face with Ian, Kieran makes his distaste clear, and Poppy orders him to stand down.

During dinner, Kieran and Poppy talk about Iliseeum, Fate, and relationships. They chat about Lyra, and he teases Poppy about watching them at the wolven wedding. He then tells her about his lost love, Elashya.

In Evaemon, Kieran accompanies Poppy and Cas through the palace. When her nerves get the best of her, he reminds her that she is a descendant of the gods and runs from no one and nothing. As the Queen relinquishes her crown to Poppy, Kieran and the others kneel out of respect.

Kieran accompanies Cas and Poppy to the hall for the Council meeting, and I finally meet Poppy and Casteel in person. When it's time for the big announcement to the people, Kieran remains in his mortal form, and I delightfully announce the new King of Blood and Ash and Queen of Flesh and Fire to their people.

Later, Poppy and Cas summon Kieran. He believes it's to discuss the Joining, but utterly shocking him, they reveal that they want him to be their Advisor to the Crown. He initially protests, insisting that it should be someone older—like his father—but Cas makes it very clear that they never even considered anyone else. That chokes him up a bit.

Poppy asks some questions about the draken, and Kieran tells her that she shouldn't be so excited about them. He goes on to say that the draken were notoriously unfriendly and temperamental—not to mention they breathe fire—then adds that he hopes none of their group pisses them off.

Little does he know *he'll* be at the center of one of those draken's ire.

As the group sets out for Iliseeum, they make their way through the tunnels.

Just as Netta is talking about wanting to read my journal—who wouldn't?—she falls through the floor, taking years off Kieran's life. He attempts to save her and pull her up, but he's not quite able to reach her to get a good enough grasp. Luckily, Poppy is able to use her power to save his sister.

Once in Iliseeum, and after battling some skeletal soldiers, they approach the Temple, and Kieran realizes what the *statues* are—draken. When Poppy touches one, causing the stone to crack, revealing an eye, Kieran warns the rest of the group.

The girl simply cannot help herself. Her curiosity gets the best of her much too often.

Back in the mortal realm after nearly dying of anxiety when Poppy dared to antagonize the King of Gods, she, Kieran, and Cas spend late dinners trying to come up with a way to get past the Rise around Castle Redrock without being seen.

Over dinner one night, Kieran and others discuss going to Oak Ambler, and he lays out the plan. They will travel by sea, coming in where the Ascended don't expect, and another group will approach by land on the other side, diverting their attention.

In disguise, Kieran and the others enter the city. The state of things there is shocking to them, as is finding a caged cave cat that turns into a man at Poppy's touch—she really does need to stop touching random things. Before they can go much farther, a Handmaiden and some Royal Guards and knights stop them, and they realize they've been thwarted. Brought before the Queen, Kieran is shocked to find Malik there—and looking hale and hearty to boot. When Malik talks about how he was meant to be Poppy's Ascension of the flesh, Kieran has to hold Casteel back, warning him that his loss of control is precisely what they want.

After the Blood Queen reveals all her secrets and sets her terms, killing Ian as a punctuation mark, Kieran fears for Poppy's state of mind. A battle begins, and Lyra dies, enraging Kieran even more.

In the woods of Oak Ambler after the melee, Poppy regains consciousness, and Kieran is forced to tell her that Cas handed himself over to Isbeth in order to save them. He tries to explain that there was nothing they could do, and that the Queen gave them Tawny as a gesture of *goodwill*. In her fury, Poppy conjures a storm. Kieran tries to calm her and begs her to stop, but she throws him with her power.

After a period of calming and taking care of Tawny, they return to Evaemon and Vonetta and Kieran go with Poppy in wolven form to inform Eloana what has happened and to reveal the truths of what Poppy was told about her being a god and more. Once everything is laid out, Poppy announces that she's going to summon Nyktos's guards.

When I saw that proclamation in my visions, I cheered her on. Poppy can be a bit naïve at times—all of this is new to her, after all. But when push comes to shove, she is one of the bravest people I have ever had the pleasure of viewing or meeting.

Kieran accompanies Poppy to Iliseeum once more to summon the draken and almost gets his arm bitten off. Nektas reveals that Ires is Poppy's father, and they all learn about Jadis.

Back in the mortal realm, the back and forth between Reaver and Kieran continues—they bicker like adolescent siblings, I swear. When Jalara appears and tries to rile Poppy, she counters with her statement that *he* is the message to the Blood Queen. Kieran launches from the shadows and grabs hold of the King's arm with his teeth as Poppy beheads him.

On their way to Massene, one of the wolven—Arden—becomes visibly agitated, and Kieran rides ahead to see what upset him so much. He's unable to hide his horror at what he sees on the walls surrounding Massene, and it bleeds over to Poppy. When *she* sees the bodies on the wall, Kieran calms her as best he can.

Once they breach the Rise, they dispatch most of the Rise Guards before dawn arrives and the Ascended return. When the rest surrender, they question them, asking what was done to those on the Rise. The one who answers states that he wasn't sure he saw what he did—that the Ascended were monsters—and Kieran confirms that it was all real before ordering them to be taken to the barracks and guarded but not harmed.

None of the guards outside Cauldra Manor surrender, and death reigns. On the hunt for the Ascended, Kieran finds the manor's underground chambers, which are similar to those in New Haven. Once inside, they see that the cells are full of Craven. They surmise that the vamprys let them out from time to time just to terrorize the locals and keep up their ruse of the *gods' displeasure* when edicts are not followed.

Twenty-eight days after Cas's surrender, everyone is exhausted from barely sleeping, and Poppy is having trouble controlling her power. Kieran has been able to bring her back from the brink but getting her to take care of herself in general has been a challenge. When she fights him on things, he reminds her that he's doing what she and Cas asked him to do—he's advising.

Kieran chooses to sleep next to Poppy in his wolven form, as much as a comfort to him as it is to her. They're both missing a vital piece of themselves, and they may be the only other people in the realm who can understand the pain of that. But he would never sleep next to her in his human form without Cas present. It's a sign of respect.

Vessa, a crone referred to as *the widow*, is allowed to remain in the manor. The creepy woman who speaks in rhymes tries to stab Poppy, and Kieran comes into the library just after it happens. He refuses to go near her, though, believing her to be a spirit. A *laruea*. When it becomes obvious that Vessa's madness stems from her belief in the prophecy, he warns Poppy that she should not be walking around alone. They don't know who else might believe it or how far their fanaticism could go.

Kieran arrives with Emil, Perry, and a package meant for Poppy. He shields his emotions as much as he can—he knows nothing good can come of whatever's in the box—and informs her that only her blood can open it. When Poppy goes to bleed for it, he reminds her to be careful and states that anything could be in a locked *gift* sent by the Queen.

Once they all see what's inside—Casteel's pointer finger with his wedding ring—Kieran slams the box closed, attempting to shield Poppy as much as possible. When she threatens the Queen, he says he would love nothing more than to do everything Poppy stated she wants to do, but they can't. He fights the Primal *notam*, attempting to disobey her order for them to help her exact her revenge, and tries to reason with her. He explains that if she does what she wants in the heat of the moment, she will kill innocents—something she won't be able to live with later—and nobody will ever see her as more than a thing of rage and pure, uncontrollable power.

Once she's calm again, Kieran gives her Cas's wedding ring. She orders that the finger be burned, but *not* by him. He then tells her about the note that was inside: an apology from the Queen for the pain she knew she'd cause Poppy.

Isbeth really is a piece of work.

When they discuss going to Carsodonia, Kieran tells her there's no way she's going alone and that she can appoint someone as Crown Regent to look after things while they are both gone. He also reminds her that Cas is a part of him and will need him there just as much as he needs her. She agrees but tells Kieran that she wants Reaver to come, too. Nektas wants Ires back, and Reaver can help that happen.

It becomes clear that Poppy needs to feed, and Kieran offers himself, reminding her that Cas would want that.

Poppy shares her choice for regent, and Kieran approves—his sister will make a great Crown Regent.

They talk strategy, and Kieran reminds her that Cas will be in bad shape when they find him. And her father, Ires, will be even worse. He gently tells her there's no way they can get them both out safely. He makes sure she understands and then stresses that they *will* get Ires out. That much is not in question—just the when.

When Poppy dream walks with Cas, and Kieran wakes after sensing it, he tells Poppy how Jasper once told him that heartmates could walk in each other's dreams—fortifying his belief that she and Casteel are heartmates.

A freak storm surges, shaking the manor, and Kieran tells Poppy he doesn't think they should be inside. He urges her to leave before the whole building comes down. Unfortunately, once they're outside, they witness the draken falling. Poppy tries to bring one back to life, and Kieran tells her that while she can heal, once a soul departs a being of two worlds, they're gone. Reaver confirms by telling her that only the Primal of Life could restore the spark to a dual-natured.

Kieran trails Poppy when she realizes that Vessa had to be the one to call the storm. They come upon her using dark magic, and Kieran warns Poppy to be careful. She kills Vessa. Later, Reaver tells Kieran that he's wrong if he thinks

Nyktos was the Primal of Life and Death and stresses the difference between surviving any injury and coming back to life when talking about the Revenants. Kieran realizes that only Malec could have shared the knowledge of how to use such magic with Isbeth, who then shared it with Vessa to create the storm—however, we later learn that he wasn't the only one who could have shared such things. Callum could have, as well.

Kieran tells Poppy *they* lost the draken and that it isn't only her burden to bear. He adds that there was no way she could have known that Vessa was capable of something like that. Nobody could have. When talk turns to the fact that Poppy cannot heal the wolven, Kieran reassures her that it's okay. Everybody dies eventually.

During the Council meeting reception, Kieran points out the generals to Poppy and then joins her during the briefing. Gayla La'Sere asks how they can expect people to fight back, and Kieran replies that they *can't* until the mortals know they have support from the Atlantians. He insists the mortals will find the strength to fight once they're assured that Atlantia is not the enemy, and they reinforce that they mean to help disband the Blood Crown and stop the Rite.

They journey through the Pinelands to Oak Ambler, and Kieran sees a group leaving the city. They stop to talk to some, and several reveal that their children were taken. When Poppy makes promises to some of the parents, Kieran warns her that it wasn't a good idea.

Poppy tries to gain entrance to assist the residents attempting to leave, but the Rise Guards don't believe she is who she claims to be. Once she neutralizes them, Kieran comforts her by telling her they will save thousands. They enter the battle, and Kieran shields Poppy from a volley of arrows. When only a small number of soldiers remain, Kieran attempts to get them to surrender.

Once inside the chambers under Castle Redrock, they battle the Craven. Kieran is furious that the Ascended turned the stronghold's servants. Poppy's fury matches his, and she orders him and the others to find the vamprys and bring them to her.

Outside the chamber of drained Chosen, Kieran doesn't stop Poppy from seeing it. He understands that she needs to grasp the gravity of the situation—until some of the bodies start to twitch. He urges her out, and she doesn't stop him. When he tells her they'll turn, she acknowledges it, but he can see the sorrow in her. Emil leaves them to take care of it.

They finally receive word that some chambers full of white-robed figures were found, and know it's the Priests and Priestesses. Priest Framont tells Poppy it's time for her to fulfill her *purpose*, and Kieran orders their people to guard the Temple tunnels immediately.

When Vonetta joins them with a Priestess, Kieran is shocked to discover that she's an Ascended. But not as surprised as he is when they enter a room filled with stalactites created from blood, and a floor littered with bones. When Poppy goes to kill the Priestess, Kieran stops her, telling her that it's not worth the depletion of her energy and power. Ultimately, they find seventy-one bodies from the last two Rites in the room, and countless other remains from previous Rites.

It breaks my heart to think of so many children being slaughtered. And for what? The god complexes of a group of people who never would have come into existence if not for the greed and selfishness of a single moment in time? It's nearly unfathomable.

Kieran retrieves Poppy to help heal Perry after he takes an arrow to the shoulder in Massene, and Reaver informs him of Poppy's dizzy spell. Concerned, he suggests that she sit out the healing and let it happen naturally, and then asks her if she needs to feed. When she insists that she's fine and they go to Perry, it's to find Delano reading my journal that he took from Poppy's cabin on the ship—much to Kieran's amusement. Again, I say everyone should read it. Delano may even discover some new ways to please his partner, given the things I reveal in there about some of my most sensual and incredible threesomes and foursomes. But I digress…

Curled up with Poppy in his wolven form as he has taken to doing of late, Kieran wakes to Poppy's silent screams through the *notam* and unconsciously shifts to comfort her. He wraps her in his arms, and when she asks him to promise to kill her if she becomes a monster because she knows that Cas will never be able to do it, it both angers and saddens him. He tells her she doesn't give herself enough credit and would never let things get that far. Eventually, however, he agrees to her demands.

When Poppy has an idea about possibly using Primal magic to help locate Cas, they talk to Perry about what his father may have divulged. One of the items needed for the spell is a cherished possession of the one they wish to find. Kieran immediately thinks of Poppy but then quickly adds that he doesn't consider her a *thing*. He knows that distinction is important to her, just as it is with Cas, and he feels bad for even saying it like he did. When Poppy reveals the carved horse she's been carrying around, it brings back memories, as Malik made one for Kieran, too.

When Gianna and Tawny approach Poppy at the encampment later, Tawny tells them about her dream of Vikter and what she learned about the *viktors*. When she gets to the bit about the Arae and Mount Lotho, Kieran reveals that it's been written that Lotho is in Iliseeum. As Tawny reveals more, Kieran wonders why Vikter didn't tell anyone about his role or motivations, but then learns that *viktors* can't. While protecting their charges, they cannot reveal their reasons.

As Tawny reveals the longer prophecy, Kieran assumes the *once-promised King* mentioned is Malik. They discuss more about what each of the lines could mean. Tawny reveals that Vikter had one other thing he wanted her to pass along, but she was to tell only Poppy. Kieran doesn't like it and makes his unease known but ultimately lets the women speak.

Pseudo plan made, Kieran, Reaver, and Poppy head out for the capital. After Poppy dream walks with Cas again, she discusses what he told her with Kieran and Reaver. They talk about demis—amidst the usual bickering between Reaver and

Kieran—and try to unravel what the legend about the demis means and how it could work in their favor if Isbeth is, indeed, a demis.

Later that night, after a Craven attack and Kieran discovering that Poppy needs to feed, discussions lead to them talking about Cas and whether his captors would allow *him* to feed. Kieran reveals that they let him the last time they held him and comments that it's been forty days at most since he last fed. When he finally goes to feed her, cutting his wrist with a two-inch slice, he orders her to drink and not sip and tells her not to feel ashamed. When she drinks, he lets some spicy memories slip to tease her, utterly embarrassing Poppy yet taking her mind off the act. Poppy heals his cut when she's finished, and Kieran is amused that she won't acknowledge what he revealed—that he knows she watched him and Lyra at the wolven wedding, and that he watched her and Cas in return.

On their journey later, they discuss the differences in class and things between Atlantia and Solis and then talk about Lasania. He wonders where he's heard the name before. They then talk about the differences between the mortal realm now versus when Reaver was last in it, and the draken tells them that the Consort was born there as the true heir and Princess. Kieran is shocked to learn that the Consort was partly mortal.

They come upon over two dozen soldiers and talk about how they might be able to make it past them. Kieran decides to use mud to disguise his and Poppy's faces, and a story about how they were on their way to the Willow Plains and ran across some Craven. Things don't go as planned, and they're soon overcome by both Royal Guards and Revenants and captured.

When Poppy tries to negotiate and says they can have her if they let Kieran and Reaver go, he refuses to be separated from her. The Revenant reveals that they're not prisoners, and it takes Kieran by surprise, only to be cut short by Poppy succumbing to a shadowstone wound. He barely catches her before she falls unconscious.

Two days later, Poppy finally wakes, and he reveals that he tried to give her blood while she was out. He also informs her that Reaver is in the chamber below them and that the *golden fuck* as he calls Callum, tried to separate him from her. Once she's more coherent, Poppy reveals they are in her old rooms at Wayfair. He tells her they've brought Reaver to him whenever he demanded it, that the draken is actually behaving himself, and that they've been taken care of but never left without guards. He mentions that the Royal Knights are *everywhere*, but they're the only Ascended he's seen so far. Only Millie—the Revenant Handmaiden—and Callum have interacted with him and Reaver.

He brings Poppy up to speed by telling her that their armies should be at New Haven or even Whitebridge by now—approximately three to four days out—and that if they don't return to Three Rivers as planned, Valyn will come looking for them. He also inquires as to how far away Poppy can communicate telepathically with Delano. She thinks if she can access the Rise, she might be able to reach him. Since he was stripped of his weapons when they arrived, Poppy offers Kieran her dagger, but he refuses.

Millie escorts Kieran and Poppy to the Great Hall, flanked by four Handmaidens and six Royal Knights. Isbeth enters the hall on a litter, which utterly disgusts Kieran. But what really takes him aback is when he sees Malik with her.

Seeing and sensing Poppy's reaction to everything the Queen babbles on about, Kieran warns her not to do anything rash and tells her to remain calm no matter what happens. The Blood Queen has a frail young woman brought in for the *Royal Blessing*, and it horrifies Kieran. He knows what the spectacle really means. They use Atlantian blood to make it appear as if the Blood Crown has the gods' blessing and that their touch can heal. But he knows it's not a cure at all. It's only a reprieve from whatever ails the one being *blessed*.

When the Blood Queen approaches, Kieran refuses to bow to her but stiffens as Malik accompanies Isbeth. He tries to bait him by calling him *Prince,* and the Queen stymies him by telling him that he looks as scrumptious as the last time she saw him.

I agree with dear Isbeth, but she did not mean it the way I would if speaking with our handsome wolven.

Callum arrives to take Poppy to Cas as requested, but they won't let Kieran go with her. As they lead her away, Kieran tells her that he'll be *listening* for her, insinuating that he will be in wolven form so he can hear her via the *notam*. Later, she lets him know that both she and Cas are okay. However, he isn't so sure about Cas. He can't imagine how he *could* be all right. Not long after, Poppy reaches out again and tells him they need to get Cas out immediately, relaying that he's underground and somewhere near the Temple before suggesting they go through the mines.

During their escape, Kieran runs into Poppy on the third-floor landing of the turret's spiral staircase and asks if she conjured the mist. They intuit that the screams they hear are Reaver's doing, and Kieran tells her they'll discuss the mist more later—it's not the time now as they have less than a minute before they end up getting locked inside.

Reaver joins them, covered in blood, and Kieran leads them both out onto the breezeway after a fight with some knights and guards. He warns Poppy to conserve her energy and tells her that Cas will need her to be strong. As they watch Reaver dispatch some knights, he asks Poppy to remind him to stop antagonizing the draken.

As the mist keeps everyone busy, they make a plan to enter the tunnels. When they get to the Temple's cella and the candles roar to life, Reaver tells them it's because of Poppy and the blood she carries within her. Kieran turns and tells her she's "so very special."

Malik comes up behind them, and Kieran is immediately ready to fight the Prince, even commenting that he's only a little conflicted about handling the *inconvenience* Malik poses. Kieran laughs when Malik insinuates that he's taking a huge risk and then tells them to trust him. The Prince then goes on to say that what he's done has all been for Millicent because she is his heartmate. It stuns Kieran. His distrust of Malik is as strong as his reluctant need to believe that his one-time friend hasn't entirely forsaken his family and kingdom for the Blood Crown. He goes through a significant internal struggle, toggling between anger, hope, disappointment, and uncertainty.

When he finally asks Malik why he didn't get Cas out, Malik says that he refuses to leave Millie. Finally reaching Cas, Kieran tries to stop Poppy from rushing into the cell and is devastated at seeing Cas almost Craven-like in his bloodlust. He remarks that Casteel is too far gone and doesn't like Malik's suggestion for getting him out to give him time to come back to himself. Eventually, he tells Poppy they must knock Cas out to safely remove him from the cell, and then hope he *stays* unconscious.

Kieran distracts Cas while Malik knocks him out and then tells Poppy they need to bind him for everyone's safety. He soothes her when she cries over the thought. After he's secured, he offers to carry Casteel, but Malik refuses. Instead, Kieran just covers Cas and the chains with his cloak.

Malik takes them to some of his friends, Descenters Blaz and Clariza, and they learn that Malik befriended them while posing as Elian—his middle name and the moniker of his ancestor. Working together as a unit, Poppy and Kieran deal with bringing Cas out of his bloodlust and feeding him. When Casteel is more himself, Kieran leaves the couple alone and goes to talk with Malik.

Once they're all settled and rested a bit, Cas comes to chat with Kieran and assures him the Blood Crown only took blood this time. Kieran reminds Casteel that he has him and Poppy, always and forever, and then assures Cas that he'll feed Poppy as soon as she wakes.

They discuss needing to leave by nightfall and talk about Reaver and Malik. Kieran relays that Malik can secure a ship and have them smuggled out, but remarks that he trusts few with Poppy's safety—and Malik definitely isn't one of them... Still, he hasn't left or betrayed them yet, and Kieran acknowledges that he's risking a lot to help them.

Discussions turn to Millie and how she is only leverage if Isbeth knows that she and Malik are heartmates. Cas reveals everything he learned about Millie being Poppy's sister and tells Kieran that she's like a Revenant, yet...not. They talk about the prophecy, and Kieran wonders how Millie was a failure. He assumes that Isbeth turned her into a Revenant to save her after she didn't survive her Culling.

When Kieran asks if Millie was Isbeth's first attempt to create something to remake the realms and Poppy was the second, Cas agrees, and Kieran says there's no way Poppy would ever help Isbeth. Casteel goes on to tell him that Millie said that only Cas can stop Poppy, and only by killing her. At the thought, Kieran suggests they have Reaver torch the Revenant. They talk about Poppy some more and realize that once she completes her Culling, she'll be a Primal. They then conclude that she did, indeed, create the mist.

Kieran follows Cas to wake Poppy and tells her she needs to feed. Casteel bites Kieran's wrist, and he jerks a bit when she closes her mouth around him. Still, he shows her inappropriate memories and gets way too much satisfaction out of it.

Kieran is definitely a man after my heart. If I had the power to transfer memories and visions, nobody would ever be thinking of war.

Later, he hugs Cas, and Poppy asks him if he believes that Millie is her sister. He tells her that he didn't at first, but he does now. When Reaver seems surprised by the news, Kieran can't pass up the opportunity to rib him a little. As they discuss how things went so wrong with Millie's Culling, Kieran asks why they didn't use Ires's blood, and Malik explains that the cage nullifies his eather.

Malik mentions Preela in conversation, and Kieran tells Poppy that she was Malik's bonded wolven. As Malik continues the story, Kieran is outraged when he realizes Malik was the Dark One from Poppy's memories and planned to kill Poppy as a child. Cas attacks Malik, and Kieran lets it play out. He refuses to step between them and thinks Malik deserves whatever hell Cas rains down upon him. When Poppy uses her power to separate the brothers, Kieran catches Cas before he falls.

The Queen arrives with her guards and Callum, and the group readies themselves to fight until they realize they can't. Callum tells Kieran he's always wanted a pet wolf, and Kieran tells him to fuck off. Later, in the melee, Callum cuts Kieran with a shadowstone blade and whispers a spell. Reddish black smoke billows from and then soaks into the wound. Shadows ripple over Kieran's body and throw Malik back before Cas stabs Callum in the heart.

The Queen gives them an ultimatum: return with Malec or Kieran dies. After they depart, Malik goes to follow the Queen, and Cas tells him not to. In order to keep him with them, Kieran knocks him out and tries to reassure Poppy that he'll be fine, saying she shouldn't worry about the curse Callum put on him.

Kieran stays mostly in wolven form on their journey to Padonia but does his best to reassure Poppy and the others when he can. He also does his damndest to protect Poppy, and that includes saving her from herself at times.

Later, when Cas comes to him, Kieran tells him that he doesn't want them to feel obligated to do the Joining just to save him from the curse, and Cas reminds him that they're not just brothers or friends, they're part of a greater whole.

I adore their connection so much. And it only got better when things ramped up and Poppy entered the mix.

They meet up with the others, and Kieran watches Malik carefully as Delano approaches. He's unsure how things will play out as Preela, Malik's bonded wolven, was Delano's sister. Later, discussing their plan and strategy, Kieran realizes that the Blood Forest is where it is because Malec is entombed there.

Once things settle down, Kieran goes to talk to Poppy about the Joining. He first jokes that no one would turn down joining with a King and a Primal. When she goes to reassure him, he tells her not to make it weird but is unable to stop his feelings from showing. He tells her that he's not doing it because of their titles or lineage but because he loves them both. When Poppy asks him what kind of love, he tells her it's the kind that allowed him to promise he'd kill her if needed.

After a journey fraught with hurdles, Kieran waits for Poppy and Cas in the Wisteria Woods and jokes that he thought they'd fallen asleep. When Poppy asks about the other wolven surrounding them, he tells her that it's a great honor for them to oversee such a tradition. Before they begin the Joining, he reminds Poppy that he and Cas expect nothing of her but he is unable to control his body's natural responses. Moving behind Poppy, he apologizes and says that he's trying to behave but it's hard because she's beautiful.

It was such a beautiful, pure moment, it almost brought tears to my eyes. But him controlling his behavior wasn't the only thing that was hard. Talk about manhoods worth journaling about…

During the exchange, Kieran tries to keep it light by teasing Poppy as he always does. Afterward, they cuddle together, and he notices that the mark on his arm is gone, though none of them are sure if the curse went with it. Things after the Joining change, but all for the better. They share a bond that cannot be broken. Kieran also feels his attraction for Poppy growing, but he knows it's different than what Cas feels for her, and is tied up with what he feels for Cas, as well.

Once they reach the Bone Temple, Kieran remarks that the armies have never come this far west before. After Cas teases him about thinking about having sex with Poppy in her armor just like he is, they give Poppy the same pep talk they did in Evaemon.

Once they deliver Malec to Isbeth, Callum uses a milky-white blade to lift the curse from Kieran's arm, and then Kieran stabs him in the heart with bloodstone. Millie tells him to cut off his head next time if he wants him to stay down longer. After Poppy heals Kieran's cut, he assures her that he's fine and turns his attention to Isbeth, shocked when she plunges her dagger into her heartmate's chest.

Poppy screams at Kieran and Cas to get the dagger out of Malec, but chaos ensues. Many are killed, and Cas and Kieran take down the Revenant who killed Emil. In the midst of everything, he can't help but be awed at the changes Poppy undergoes, but the awe soon turns to something else as the shockwave she lets loose almost takes him and everyone else out. Luckily, Cas shields him.

Once everything dies down, he coaxes Poppy back to consciousness and confirms that she has fangs, telling her that Cas will have to help her through that bit since it's not something in his wheelhouse.

He comforts her when she sees that all their friends are once again alive and whole, and he and Cas tell her that she brought everyone back to life. Nektas is quick to correct them, saying that it was actually the Consort working through Poppy that did it. As more is said, Kieran inquires what Nyktos *is*, if he's not the Primal of Life and Death. And wonders aloud why he would honor the Consort remaining unknown.

Despite what's ahead of them, finding and dealing with Callum is at the top of Kieran's priority list. But they have much more important things to worry about. Kolis is free, and who knows what that means for the realms…

I shudder to think what might come for all of us next.

In the tunnels below Wayfair, Kieran and Cas worry about Poppy. She's cold and doesn't feel right to them. He and Cas are super overprotective of her—something she doesn't need in the slightest—and Nektas calls them adorable. Kieran says he doesn't think he's ever been called that.

I would call him that all day if he wanted.

They find Ires and help him become himself again, finding out that Jadis is likely being kept in the Willow Plains.

When Poppy passes out and goes into stasis, he and Cas take her to a spare room, and he goes in search of some clothes. He spends most of his time with them and Delano in the chambers, watching her and waiting for her to wake up.

As Cas tells stories to Poppy, talking to her as Nektas said to do, Kieran listens in and interjects in a few places, telling Cas that what happened to him wasn't his fault, asking if he's going to tell Poppy the full story about Shea, and reinforcing their bond.

He's out of the room when the Revenant attacks Casteel and comes in to find his bonded Atlantian not as he left him but as a spotted cave cat. He talks to him, tells him to remember, and can suddenly hear him in his mind. He stops him from eating Emil, sends the Atlantian on his way, and then helps Cas shift back.

They gather the bone daggers and talk about those for a bit, until the walls and floor start to crack, a symbol appears, and Poppy opens her silver eyes.

The Primal of Blood and Bone and Life and Death.

Interview with Kieran Contou, Advisor to the Queen and King of Atlantia

by JLA

Good morning readers of The HighGrove Annual Herald Mail, this is JLA coming to you today with a truly extraordinary interview with the one and only Kieran Contou, Advisor to the Queen and King of Atlantia. In the Advisor's first-ever interview, he will answer questions submitted by the, ahem, most curious members of our esteemed community.

I want to start by apologizing to our more reserved readers and, once more, to the Advisor, for the intimate nature of most of these questions. I had hoped that they would be more interested in what the role of an Advisor entailed and what we can expect from our new Queen and King, but I've been advised that a rather large percentage of HighGrove Annual Herald Mail readers have recently become members of Miss Willa Colyns' Book Club, which has left them quite thirsty for intimate details of the Advisor's life.

That being said, please join the Advisor and me as we unravel some of the mysteries surrounding our new Advisor.

JLA: Thank you so much for agreeing to this interview. I know you're not a fan of questions.

THE NEW QUEEN HAS ARRIVED

THE NEW CREST

FESTIVAL OF THE KIYOU

Kieran: I love being asked questions.

JLA: I think I detect a hint of sarcasm there.

Kieran: Never.

JLA: Then let's get started. Were you surprised to be anointed as the Advisor to the Queen and King?

Kieran: I was.

JLA: Who did you think they'd choose?

Kieran: My father. Or anyone with more experience. But once I thought about it, I understood that not only do they value my thoughts, but anyone else would likely find themselves on the verge of insanity dealing with them.

JLA: So, are our new Queen and King difficult to work with?

Kieran: I wouldn't say difficult.

JLA: What would you say, then?

Kieran: More like...unpredictable. And inquisitive. One often prefers to handle insults by ripping out the heart of the offender, and the other has a tendency to stab first and ask questions later.

JLA: Oh.

Kieran: Only if you get on their bad side, though. I would suggest not doing that.

JLA: I don't believe I or the Highgrove community have any intention of doing such a thing.

Kieran: Relieved to hear that, as I, too, have certain tendencies.

JLA: For example?

Kieran: Ripping out the throats of those who would harm either of them.

JLA: All right, then. I'd expect nothing less from the Advisor. Moving on. Let's get to some of the questions asked by the community, shall we?

Kieran: Can't wait.

JLA: If you could change one thing about your past, would you? If so, what?

Kieran: I try not to think about what I would change. It's in the past. Dwelling there only leads to more things you wish you had chosen differently.

JLA: I would have to agree with that. I, too, try not to dwell in the past, but there are still things I can't help but wish I could change when I think about them. There must be something that comes to mind.

Kieran: I suppose if I had to give an answer, I would say it was allowing Cas to go after the Ascended by himself.

JLA: You wish you hadn't listened to him?

Kieran: Yes. I wish I had listened to my gut and either stopped or followed him.

JLA: Sometimes, we have to learn the hard way when it comes to listening to our instincts.

Kieran: Sadly, some never do.

JLA: Very true. Now, I have a question regarding your sister. What was it like growing up with her?

Kieran: Difficult.

JLA: Oh. Well, I was not expecting that answer. I've met your sister. She is quite lovely.

Kieran: You haven't had to live with her. Play dolls with her. Keep her from falling off a cliff or drowning before she learned how to swim. Chase off any wannabe suitors or—

JLA: Speaking of suitors. Are you aware of anyone your sister is romantically involved with?

Kieran: No.

JLA: Truly?

Kieran: Truly.

JLA: Are you certain? I was under the impression there is a certain someone in your sister's life.

Kieran: I am certain if I allow myself to acknowledge that there is a certain someone in my sister's life, that someone would no longer be in possession of said life.

JLA: *stares*

Kieran: *stares back*

JLA: Okay, then. So, another member wants to know if you like to be touched in your wolven form?

Kieran: If I like the person, then yes.

JLA: If not?

Kieran: They would no longer have a hand.

JLA: Makes sense. One asked if your father went through the Joining.

Kieran: He has not.

JLA: What does he think of you completing the Joining with the Queen and King?

Kieran: He is thrilled. It is an honor to uphold the tradition of the Joining.

JLA: There were many questions about the Joining.

Kieran: I'm sure there were.

JLA: A main one kept coming up. Readers of the Herald are quite curious to know exactly where your...appendages were?

Kieran: Does that matter?

JLA: Apparently, it does.

Kieran: It doesn't.

JLA: Well—

Kieran: The Joining was a very emotional experience for the three of us, first and foremost. Such a bond, in and of itself, is an act of love and commitment. Yes, it became physical, which I am sure was not a shock to those paying attention. All I will say here is that the three of us were equal participants in all things.

JLA: You spoke of love. Do you love our Queen and King?

Kieran: Of course. Next question.

JLA: Um, someone wants to know your shoe size.

Kieran: What an absurd question.

JLA: You see, I believe they are trying to determine what your—

Kieran: I know what they're trying to determine. Next question.

JLA: Do you secretly wish Reaver was attracted to you?

Reaver: *walks past chamber* He does!

Kieran: No.

JLA: Not at all?

Kieran: Not even remotely.

JLA: He is quite handsome.

Kieran: He also stepped on my paw.

JLA: I'm sure it was an accident.

Kieran: I am positive it was not.

JLA: Do you prefer to sleep in your mortal or wolven form?

Kieran: I prefer to sleep in my wolven form if I believe that either I or another could come under threat. Otherwise, either is fine.

JLA: It is noted that when our King was held captive, you mostly slept in your wolven form while with our Queen. Was that the reason?

Kieran: Yes. I wanted to be able to react instantaneously to any threat other than when she had a nightmare. I would *only* sleep in my wolven form if Cas is not present.

JLA: Is there a reason for that?

Kieran: Yes.

JLA: What is it?

Kieran: It was my way of respecting boundaries.

JLA: That was before the Joining. Have those boundaries now changed?

Kieran: If they have, I wouldn't share them with an entire populace of people interested in my shoe size and whether or not I harbor secret feelings for an oversized draken.

JLA: Point taken. Will you possibly share what was on your mind when Poppy first fed from you? You thought something that made her blush.

Kieran: I most definitely did. She was prying into my thoughts and memories without asking. So, I showed her something that, at the time, made her think twice about doing that.

JLA: You sound very amused by that.

Kieran: I am.

JLA: And what was this thing that you showed her?

Kieran: What she already knew but pretended she didn't—her and Cas watching me on the beach while in Saion's Cove.

JLA: Ah, yes. Our Queen was quite...curious then.

Kieran: Very curious.

JLA: Is she still...curious?

Kieran: What do you think?

JLA: I think I should ask another question.

Kieran: *chuckles*

JLA: Someone has asked who...cuddles better? The Queen or the King?

Kieran: I would have to say me. I'm a wolven. We are the best at cuddling.

JLA: The, uh, the rest of the questions are quite...personal.

Kieran: More personal than asking where my appendages were during the Joining?

JLA: Shockingly, yes.

Kieran: Then I believe this interview is over.

JLA: Yeah, I think that's for the best. Thank you.

Kieran: My pleasure.

JASPER AND KIRHA CONTOU

As the leader of the wolven plus a Council Elder, Jasper holds positions of esteem not only within their group but also with the Atlantians as a whole. And as his wife, Kirha, is revered in her own right. Here is what I know about Jasper…

Hair: Shaggy and silver.
Eyes: Pale blue.
Body type: Tall.
Facial features: Stubble on chin. Tan skin.
Distinguishing features: Black ink on both arms swirling all the way to his shoulders.
Preternatural appearance: Impossibly large. Silver fur.
Other: Has foresight. Imprint is like rich soil and cut grass. Earthy and minty feeling.
Personality: Family-oriented.
Background: Head of the wolven. Member of the Council of Elders.
Family: Wife = Kirha. Son = Kieran. Daughters = Vonetta and new infant.

And his wife, Kirha…

Hair: Cornrows – narrow rows of small, tight braids.
Eyes: Wintery blue.
Facial features: Skin the color of dark, night-blooming roses. Broad cheekbones. Full mouth.
Other: Sometimes has a way of knowing things like her husband and son.
Personality: Warm and maternal.
Habits/Mannerisms/Strengths/Weaknesses: Likes to knit. Has a green thumb. Really hard sleeper.
Background: Wolven.
Family: Husband = Jasper. Son = Kieran. Daughters = Vonetta and new infant. Sister = Beryn.

JASPER AND KIRHA'S JOURNEY TO DATE:

JASPER

Jasper and Kirha are always somewhat lumped into my visions and knowledge of Kieran and Vonetta, but I'll try to separate some of their more prominent appearances.

Jasper arrives in Spessa's End during dinner two days after the rest of the group. When he meets Poppy for the first time, he has a visceral response. I can only assume it's because of the static lightning charge most wolven get from her. When Alastir makes his thoughts known regarding his feelings about Poppy and Casteel's engagement, and the elder wolven implies that Cas marrying Gianna

172/Jennifer L. Armentrout with Rayvn Salvador

would have strengthened the wolven/Atlantian relationship, Jasper warns him about overstepping.

As the group eats, and Casteel shares stories about his time with Poppy, Jasper finds it amusing that Poppy stabbed Cas after learning about his original plans for her. It prompts him to remark that Casteel clearly takes after his father regarding women and sharp objects. He then makes his stance clear by saying that if Cas chose Poppy, the rest of them can—and should—too.

In his time with Poppy, Jasper notices that she doesn't register as others. He mentions it to her, saying she has a different but familiar scent he can't place. When it's noted that Poppy might be descended from the Empath Warrior bloodline, he disagrees since very few could heal with their touch.

Jasper officiates at Cas and Poppy's wedding and remarks that Nyktos approves of it when the day turns to night. He mentions that nobody has seen anything like that since Valyn and Eloana's wedding, and it wasn't that overt.

When the group splits off in the Skotos, Jasper goes with Emil and Quentyn. Their group is the first to arrive at Gold Rock for their rendezvous.

Jasper arrives at the Chambers of Nyktos with the other wolven after Poppy is attacked. He's compelled to protect her, as well, and lets out a rumble of warning when Casteel gets too close to her. When things settle a bit, Jasper shifts and offers Cas his old room at the palace to care for Poppy. When Poppy worries about the wolven's reaction, he tells her that as long as Cas doesn't give them a reason to act differently, the wolven will protect Cas as fiercely as they do her.

Someone brings up Poppy's claim to the throne being contestable, and it makes Jasper laugh. When Alastir makes his move against Poppy, Jasper shifts and lunges for him, but a shadowshade-dipped arrow finds its mark, which forces him to shift back to his mortal form before his skin hardens and turns icy.

Jasper joins the group that rescues Poppy in Irelone. He kills the Descenter who shoots Poppy with a crossbow and snaps and snarls at Valyn when he tries to intervene and stop Cas from doing what he needs to do.

Once Poppy is better, he goes with Kieran to her and Cas's chambers to discuss the Gyrms and the Unseen. He's very irritated that Valyn didn't tell him about them. They flip through the book he brought to learn more, and Jasper remarks that they aren't living creatures.

He later reveals the location of Iliseeum and tells Poppy that she's the only one who can get there alive. The mist there is said to be deadly to anyone it doesn't recognize as a god. He also tells them that Valyn and Eloana have killed to keep Iliseeum's location a secret.

When they're talking about Primal magic, Jasper mentions that Dominik and I are likely the only ones who know about Iliseeum or how to use the magic needed to conjure Gyrms. I don't think that's entirely true, but I was happy to share what I knew when they asked.

When Poppy's brother comes and requests an audience, Jasper joins the group that goes to Spessa's End. After meeting the Ascended, he remarks that Ian is one hell of an actor and talks about Alastir having lots of beliefs that don't make any sense.

After Poppy returns from Oak Ambler, Jasper is en route to Evaemon with Kirha and their new daughter.

KIRHA:

Pregnant and almost ready to give birth, Kirha sleeps through the Unseen/Gyrm attack.

The following day, Cas asks her about Gianna's whereabouts, and she tells him that she's likely in Evaemon or close, somewhere in Aegea.

When Kirha meets Poppy for the first time, she's sorting through some yarn with Kieran. They talk about her pregnancy, and she reveals that she's only a month from giving birth and that the Healers think it's a girl. She also mentions her hope that this is their last baby.

Before the group heads out, she tells Poppy that their house is always open to her and Cas and hugs her. She also tells her that Cas's parents are good people, and once they get over the shock of all that's happened, they will welcome her with open arms.

After it's announced that the wolven will accompany Cas and Poppy to the Spessa's End meeting, she tells them not to worry about her—she isn't going to have the baby in the next week.

Just after giving birth, she and Jasper make their way to Evaemon to meet with everyone.

THE PORTRAIT OF DESIRE

Oh, Diary, do I have a story to tell you.

I may have mentioned my desire to have my portrait done. I try to have my likeness captured every so often, just to remind myself of the passing of time. It can become a blur occasionally to one who has been around as long as I.

Anyway, I attended a party a few weeks ago where the Lord and Lady had some delightful art on the walls of their keep. I inquired about the talent, and the master of the manor told me about a highly sought-after husband and wife in Spessa's End. Given their gifts, I could see why people coveted their work.

As I bathed that night, a vision came to me of a stunning couple. As events unfolded, the knowledge of who they were came to me. The wife was Kieran and Vonetta Contou's aunt, Kirha's sister, tying them not only to the head of the wolven but also the Atlantian Prince and the Crown.

With that information in mind, and anticipation running high, I made the journey and asked at the local tavern where I might find the couple. The innkeeper pointed me toward the outskirts of town and gave me the general direction of the artists' abode.

As I rode up, the sights immediately struck me. The cottage sat near the coast of Stygian Bay, the glistening waters casting crystalline shards over the clay and sandstone façade of the dwelling. The Skotos Mountains rose like silent sentinels beyond, framing the area perfectly. It seemed the ideal place for artists to reside, as even one such as I, with no artistic talent to speak of beyond my ability to put words to paper, could see how inspiring it was.

As I dismounted and straightened my gown and cloak, I felt a little shiver run down my spine. My lips tipped in a small smile. I knew that feeling. It was my gift. And while it may not have thrown images into my mind's eye just yet, my intuition knew that this meeting would be fortuitous indeed—and likely in more ways than one.

Even now, as I write, I remember the feelings coursing through my body. The sense of excitement. The wanton rush of things not yet experienced that I, as a Seer, knew would be memorable.

When I knocked on the door and heard footfalls from within, the hairs on the back of my neck stood on end, and goose bumps peppered my arms. While the chill may have played a part, it was more the exhilaration of what I simply knew would be, combined with the mystery of what I had not yet seen.

As the viewing panel in the door slid to the side, revealing an ice-blue eye surrounded by dark smoky topaz skin, that excitement grew.

In a voice like bells in a cavern, both delicate and resonant, she asked if she could help me.

Already feeling a pull to this gorgeous creature from just the sound of her voice and the view of that glacial eye, I gave her my name and explained how I had learned about them and then subsequently found them.

And then...she smiled. It was like the sun coming out on the dreariest of days and immediately warmed me. It also made me want.

When she opened the door, I beheld more than an eye and a smile in a nearly perfect face. She was like a goddess—and I would know—with curves in all the right places, dips and valleys creating a road map that anyone would want to explore, and hair the color of rich, deep autumn leaves—a deep, burnished brown.

She told me her name was Beryn Moxley and introduced me to her husband, Vanian. The man was at least six and a half feet tall with broad shoulders and powerful thighs. In contrast to his wife's dark tresses, his hair was a burnished gold, a lock falling across his forehead to partially obscure one flashing gold eye. What struck me the most, however, were his hands. In contrast to his powerful almost warrior-like physique, his hands were almost graceful. The only thing marring their perfection were the splotches of color staining his skin and the dark crescents under his nails. But to me, that only made him more captivating.

When he shook my hand, a spark of electricity made its way through my synapses, sparking a vision of entangled limbs and licentious sighs. I shivered again.

Over a meal, we discussed my commission, talking about setting and light, wardrobe and tone. Both artists were incredibly gifted and knowledgeable, and I knew I was in good hands. I would be in good hands in more ways than one... I simply had to let nature run its course.

The couple offered to let me stay in the loft of their studio, which they had outfitted with comfortable furnishings to accommodate those, like I, who had traveled some distance to have their portraits done.

Over the days as I posed, bedecked in only a chemise, one ruffled strap falling off a delicate shoulder, and reclined seductively on a chaise, the couple and I got to know one another. We spoke of both the mundane, such as history and philosophy, as well as hopes and dreams, connecting

178/Jennifer L. Armentrout with Rayvn Salvador

us on an intellectual level that I found utterly sexy.

As the days passed, and Beryn adjusted this or that on my person, her silken hands caressing skin, her heated breaths brushing my flesh as she leaned to move me to and fro, I saw—and felt—the changes occurring. Her touches lingered. Her lips got closer. Her breaths became just a bit more labored as she crouched before me to adjust the hem of my chemise or right the neckline.

And as I sat, looking at Vanian as he painted, I saw that he wasn't unaffected either. I watched his chest rising and falling just a bit more rapidly, his gold eyes darkening as his pupils dilated. I noticed the shift in our dinner conversations as the time wore on.

Even here at my desk, I can feel the weighted heat of his stare and the tremble Beryn's nearness induced.

On our last full day of work, I realized I was done waiting. If one of them didn't initiate, I decided that I would. It was clear there was attraction, and the sexual tension over the last fortnight was keeping me awake at night. I needed to feel their hands on my skin. Their breaths in my hair and on my body. I needed to watch as they ran seasoned fingertips over each other. Elicited wanton sighs and cries of pleasure. I needed to taste their individual and mingled essences. I just...needed.

When next Beryn approached to adjust me, I reached up and brushed a luscious lock of her burnished hair back, lightly skimming my fingers over the swell of her breast and bare shoulder as I did. Her breaths immediately ramped up, pushing her impressive bosom into the bodice of her gown and straining the stays.

Her ice-blue eyes locked with mine, and I saw the widening of her pupils, the black nearly eating the glacial hue.

And then I did what I'd wanted to do from the moment I saw just half her face in the portal of the door. I reached up, slipped my hands under that gorgeous fall of hair to frame her beautiful face, and kissed her.

Her lips were pillowy soft and smooth as silk. She hesitated only a beat before melting into the embrace, giving as good as she got and loosing a sigh into my mouth. At the opening, I slipped in with my tongue and swirled, capturing her taste and recording it to memory. She was like vanilla and ice and I wanted to devour her.

Absently, I heard what sounded like a paintbrush falling to the floor and paused in my delving to glance at Vanian.

He stood near his easel, his stance rigid and eyes rapt, taking in the scene before him. Without hesitation, I caressed the side of Beryn's face with my left thumb and freed my right to beckon him forth.

He stumbled a bit at first but then stepped from behind the canvas, slipping the neck ties of his apron over his head and dropping it on his stool before continuing our way.

When he reached us, Beryn had taken a seat on the chaise next to me, her hand still on my thigh, her thumb caressing the skin there and making me shiver. But what really made me burn was the look in her husband's eyes as he took in the sight of the two of us.

I lowered my gaze to find the obvious—and impressive—evidence of how much he enjoyed what he saw, and reached out again to grasp his hand, shifting on the chaise to a more seated position and pulling Vanian down beside me so the three of us rested on the chaise side by side with me in the middle.

I leaned back a bit and placed a hand on both of their shoulders, exerting gentle pressure and urging them to meet in the middle over where I sat. Their mouths met hungrily, tongues lashing and teeth gnashing as they played out their desires, showing without words that there was consent between the two. Showing me that I was welcome.

The couple still drinking from each other's mouths, I ran a hand from the hollow of each of their throats and down the fronts of their bodies, taking in the differences and recording them in my mind. I felt myself becoming more aroused and couldn't wait to see where this night took us.

They paused in their embrace, and both turned their gazes to me, blue and gold orbs searing me where I sat, dark smoky topaz and alabaster skin filling my senses and making me want only one thing.

More.

I removed my hands from their waists and reached to the already loosened ties of my chemise, undoing them completely and wiggling until the top fell to my waist. I watched both their gazes fall to my heaving bosom and ran my hands up my midsection to cup my breasts, my head falling back in pleasure.

I heard a low growl from my right and then felt a grip ripping my hand free before hot lips attached themselves to my aching breast. A scorching tongue swirled around my pebbled nub, and the throbbing at my core intensified.

And then I felt equally hot yet delicate lips on my neck and let out a low moan, moving my hands to the backs of both their heads, my hips rising of their own volition at the insurgence of pleasure.

They licked and laved, tasted and nipped, and I reveled in the attention. Exalted in the decadence. But I needed to sample, as well.

I gently stood, my chemise falling to the floor in a puddle around my feet and leaving me completely naked. Once again, I heard a low growl from Vanian, this time followed by a gasp from Beryn, and a smile split my lips.

I turned and glanced into Vanian's eyes with a knowing look before pivoting to his wife and seeing the same desire I felt mirrored there. Reaching out a hand to each of them, I tugged them to stand with me, then turned to Beryn. I pulled her closer as I backed into Vanian, feeling the heat of their bodies on my naked and needy flesh.

With deft movements I removed every stitch of Beryn's clothing, caressing and kneading areas as I revealed them, all the while enjoying Vanian's hands roaming over my naked body, learning its curves, finding both the soft areas and the firm. When I finished disrobing Beryn, I grasped the nape of her neck with sure fingers and gave her a scorching kiss, her breaths becoming mine as we breathed for each other. And then I turned to her husband.

As I had done with Beryn, I removed all his clothing with measured sureness, gliding my fingers and palms over his flesh and taking in the smattering of hair on his chest, the chiseled V of muscle at his waist, and the long, proud jut of his erection. And as he had done with me earlier, all the while, Beryn ran her delicate hands over my flesh, learning me. It was an erotic feast for the senses.

Looking into Vanian's eyes, I gave him a long and lingering kiss and then reached behind me and grasped both of Beryn's hands, bringing one to my breast and the other to her husband's manhood. He hissed and pumped his hips, and I took in the erotic sight of her darker hand against the porcelain tone of his flesh, the slight give of the skin as she caressed him from root to tip, swirling her thumb over the pearly bead there and using it to ease her way down the shaft.

My nipple beaded and pressed into Beryn's palm, and she rubbed her hand over me, creating a delicious friction that had me temporarily closing my eyes.

Gods, I'm soaking wet just sitting here penning this. Can you imagine how I felt in the moment, so overcome with desire?

When we'd each played a bit, I lowered myself to the floor, propping myself on my elbows with bent and splayed knees. Vanian immediately grasped onto the invitation and moved to settle himself between my thighs, looking at his wife first for approval. When she sucked in a breath and nodded, he dove, and I cried out at the pleasure. I shifted slightly, trying hard not to disrupt the fervor of Vanian's sensual assault as I urged Beryn to her knees, pulling her lower until her delectable pink pearl was within easy reach. I mimicked what Vanian did to me on his glorious wife until each of us cried out, shouting to gods who likely weren't listening.

When Beryn and I had come to our senses again a bit, we turned to Vanian. Urging him onto his back, I moved to the side of his head as Beryn prowled up his body. When she was poised above him, I leaned down to take his mouth in a glorious kiss, just as she lowered herself onto him. He let out a grunt, and I swirled my tongue, matching the swiveling movements of Beryn's hips and her tempo.

I felt the tension in Vanian's body as his pleasure ramped and watched a beautiful flush spreading across Beryn's silky smooth skin. Needing to touch her, I moved behind her, lowering myself and using Vanian's leg to create delicious friction at my center as I palmed Beryn's buxom breast with one hand and swirled a finger over her clit with the other.

In a heartbeat, she cried out, and the pleasure I felt ignited my own orgasm, spiraling me into the heavens. I latched my mouth to the salty skin of Beryn's shoulder to muffle my cry, and then moved back to give her some room.

But it seemed Vanian wasn't yet finished.

He bent his knees and scooted back, never losing contact with Beryn as she continued to come, then flipped her over and drove into her, making her eyes fly open and her mouth drop in a gasp.

I needed to watch, so I moved to the head of them, feeling no guilt at my voyeurism as I watched Vanian pleasure himself and his wife, driving into her over and over as he reached a hand under her bottom to pull her tighter to him. She orgasmed again, her face a delightful thing to see, and I couldn't stop myself from reaching down to test my own receptiveness to another round.

Biting my lip, I met Vanian's gaze, and he uttered something unintelligible before driving into Beryn one last time and then bowing his back, the movement causing the small table of paints to topple to the floor, splattering all of us in a rainbow of colors and making me erupt once more.

It was all absolutely glorious, and something I will not soon forget.

When all was done, we simply lay together on that drop cloth amidst the paint, the colors making our flesh into the canvas. Beryn and I rested our heads on each of Vanian's pectorals, the three of us still petting and scraping and kneading.

The portrait Vanian completed of me now hangs above my mantel, and every time I look at it, I remember that night.

And what a night it was.

Willa

EMIL DA'LAHR

A core part of Poppy and Cas's group, Emil features almost as prominently in my visions as Kieran, but always on the periphery and admittedly not very clearly.

Hair: Auburn waves.
Eyes: Amber.
Body type: Reedy.
Facial features: Strikingly handsome.
Personality: Easygoing. An enormous flirt. Snarky and sarcastic.
Habits/Mannerisms/Strengths/Weaknesses: Very good with a crossbow. Likes to flirt with Poppy to get a rise out of Casteel. Always seems to be where Vonetta is.
Background: Like Kieran, helped Cas remember who he was and remind him that he wasn't merely a *thing* after his captivity.
Family: Quentyn = unknown relation but share last name.

EMIL'S JOURNEY TO DATE:

Emil journeys to Masadonia to feed Cas while he's undercover as Hawke and offers to stay, but Cas tells him that he needs him in Evaemon, keeping an eye on Alastir and running interference.

Emil arrives in New Haven with Alastir just ahead of the storm. The minute he's introduced to Poppy, he's greatly amused by her—and especially her mouthiness.

I kind of love her for that, too.

When Alastir tells her that he knew about her before, that she was the Maiden Chosen by the gods, Poppy replies that it must have come as a shock since their gods are asleep and can't choose anyone. Emil agrees.

When Alastir questions how an Atlantian spent so much time near the Blood Crown without being discovered—they were all still under the impression that Poppy was only part Atlantian due to either Cora or Leo being of Atlantian descent at this time—and Poppy makes a comment about them being a blood bag, Emil agrees with her but sends a questioning look at Kieran when she reveals that she doesn't know which of her parents was Atlantian.

Before dinner, Poppy greets Alastir politely, and he comments on it, alluding to the fact that none of the others in the room have manners. Emil grins.

While sitting down to dinner, Cas reveals that his fiancée is upset with him, and Emil quips that it's not a very good sign if he's already upsetting her when they're not even married yet. As they make conversation about how Poppy and Cas met, Poppy tells them that he was her guard, and Cas corrects her and says that they actually met in a brothel—thanks to yours truly, thank you very much. Emil chokes on his food.

Alastir asks Poppy additional questions about her time as the Maiden and says that he assumed she was *kept*, given they were awaiting her Ascension. She confirms and takes it further, saying she was essentially caged. Emil is stunned to learn she was virtually imprisoned in her room all day, every day.

Poor Poppy. She really was nothing but a prisoner until Casteel, in essence, kidnapped her. Ironic, isn't it?

Emil sets off for Spessa's End with Alastir after he and Casteel discuss that it would be better to travel in multiple groups.

When Beckett gets hurt, Emil calls for a Healer. Poppy heals the young wolven instead, and he is gobsmacked to see the glow emanating from between Poppy's palms.

Later, when Alastir and Casteel argue over obligations, Emil tries to defuse the situation.

Cas reveals that Poppy stabbed him in the chest with a bloodstone dagger, and Kieran adds that she meant to kill him. Emil wonders how many times Poppy has made Cas bleed.

Plenty, let me assure you. But it's just another reason they are so entertaining.

Emil interrupts Cas and Poppy's sexy time to alert them that the sky is on fire. When the couple reaches the terrace, he fills them in on what they've seen and what has happened, telling them Delano ran ahead to scout. They venture to the Rise and take in the sight, knowing that it doesn't mean anything good. Emil then relays what the scouts said about the Ascended army and weaponry headed their way.

He addresses Poppy as *Your Highness,* and she balks. He and Naill explain that she's engaged to a Prince; therefore, she is a Princess, and it's simply how things are done. Emil then congratulates her on her engagement, but as always with Emil, it's offered with just a bit of snark. He then goes further to say that after the wedding, they'll have to call her *Your Majesty* instead and winks at Poppy.

If looks could kill the poor boy, he would be a pile of smoking ash. Cas does not take too kindly to his flirtatious ways.

Emil travels with the group through the Skotos Mountains. When Poppy wonders about the dangers of an ambush, he offers that there hasn't been a Craven attack that far east since the war. With Jasper, Emil breaches the mist.

When they get to the trees of Aios and Jasper mentions the Chambers of Nyktos, Emil supplies that it's a Temple just beyond the Pillars and tells Poppy she should visit and see the beauty.

The group splits and agrees to reconvene at Gold Rock. Emil goes with Jasper and Quentyn, and when they meet up again, he tells Poppy that he's glad she made it and bows jauntily, further irritating Cas. They trade stories of how their nights went, and Emil mentions the mountains shaking. Cas acknowledges that they felt it but doesn't elaborate—something Emil notices.

After Poppy's attack at the Chambers, Emil is there to witness the wolven surrounding her and the Queen relinquishing her crown and looks on in fear. As the wolven yip and howl and cry, he remarks that they're likely summoning the entire city. Eloana explains that the Atlantian-wolven bonds have been broken and the wolven are responding to Poppy. Emil backs up even farther in trepidation, causing one of the wolven to stalk him. As they poise to attack, Poppy commands them to stop, and they stand down. Emil thanks her for her timely interference.

Casteel asks Emil to get clothes for Delano and Kieran, and he does as his Prince asks. When they conclude that Beckett was the one who brought Poppy to the Chambers and is therefore responsible, Emil sets off with Naill and Delano to find him. What they don't yet know is that it wasn't Beckett; it was the changeling, Jansen, masquerading as Beckett. The poor young wolven had already been killed.

After Alastir takes Poppy, Emil is part of the group that rescues her from Irelone. He and others then escort Valyn back to Atlantia.

When Cas and Poppy reach the Temple of Saion, Emil is relieved to see them and tells Poppy as much, addressing her as *Your Highness* again.

He fills them in on the group who tried to free Alastir and says it got a bit bloody when they were dealt with. Emil then returns Poppy's dagger to her, explaining that he found it under a blood tree when he and some others went to look for evidence.

After Cas retrieves Alastir, Emil goes to get Kieran and Poppy, telling them that Alastir thinks Poppy is dead and sharing that they didn't correct his assumption.

On their way to wait for Cas to call for them, Emil notices Poppy acting strangely and asks her if she's okay. She tells him that she is. We later learn that this was when she heard Kieran's voice in her head for the first time.

Emil, Naill, and Quentyn leave the Temple of Saion early before the rest of the group does. Later that night, Emil shares dinner with the group at the Contou residence as they talk about Iliseeum.

On the way to the capital, Emil and Naill bicker about everything from whiskey to weapons. They are always picking at each other, but it's clear it's all done in love. The two of them are incredibly close, and it's evident for anyone to see.

When Poppy mentions that she would like her own horse, Emil sets off to get her one and says that he'll find one that's worthy of her beauty and strength, flirting with her as he always does and raising Casteel's ire. Emil soon returns with Storm.

The Unseen and Gyrms attack and Emil throws a dagger. Once they're able to take a breath, Emil wonders what the Unseen thought to accomplish. He then postulates who tipped them off as to where they would be and suggests it was probably an individual from the inn at Tadous or someone who saw Arden on his way to Evaemon.

When the group gets closer to the palace, Emil rides ahead to announce the group's arrival and then waits for them just inside the Temple entryway with at least ten guards. When Cas and Poppy approach Queen Eloana, Emil bows like everyone else. He witnesses the transfer of crowns and then accompanies the couple through the palace until it's time for the Council meeting. I don't actually remember Emil being there when we all were, but I suppose that's a sign of a good guard.

Emil joins Poppy, Casteel, Kieran, Vonetta, and Delano for their trip through the tunnels to Iliseeum. He comments that he didn't even know there *were* tunnels under Evaemon and goes on to say that they're only going to Iliseeum because none of them has any sense. He adds that he'd love to avoid being suffocated to death by the mist if at all possible.

In the tunnels, the floor crumbles beneath Vonetta, and Emil catches her as she falls. On his stomach, barely holding her, he tells everyone that he *sort of* has her and urges her to try to grab Kieran's hand. She can't reach. Then, Emil being Emil, he tells her that he'll throw himself in after her if she falls, and they can find out what's really under the tunnels. When she points out that they'd both be dead, he tells her it's just semantics. The tunnel under Emil starts to crack, and Poppy finally uses her eather to save them.

Once again on the move, the path ahead narrows, and they can't tell what's on the other side of the mist. Emil voices his hope that it's not a draken ready to flame-broil them. Once in Iliseeum, geysers of dirt start erupting all around them, and Emil remarks that it's rude before he peers into one of the holes. He swears but doesn't say anything more. When they see the skeletal hands and bodies emerging, Vonetta chastises him for not warning them, and he apologizes. As they fight the Consort's soldiers, Emil remarks that cutting off their heads doesn't work—something already obvious to most. Vonetta remarks that he's a mess, and he tells her that she's beautiful—a flirt, even in the midst of battle. Hundreds more skeletons appear, and Emil fights back-to-back with Vonetta. When the smoke snakes billow from the soldiers' mouths, he voices his regret for coming on the trip.

When Poppy uses her eather to defeat the skeletons and then tells them they should get moving before more arrive, Emil shares his hope that they don't. Gazing at the beautiful city of Dalos, he remarks that he believes the Vale probably looks just like it. Luckily, they heed my warning and don't venture in. Those who do, don't return.

As they continue toward the Temple and see the large draken statues, Emil remarks that if it comes to life, he is out of there; they will have never seen an Atlantian run faster. When Poppy touches one of the statues and the stone cracks, revealing a bright blue eye with a vertical pupil, Emil screams for everyone to run.

Back in the mortal realm, they have a dinner meeting to discuss their trip to Oak Ambler. The plan is to split into two groups, with Emil and Lyra posing as Poppy and Cas in the other group, accessing Castle Redrock's eastern gates via land while Poppy and Cas and the others arrive by sea.

Unfortunately, the plan falls short for everyone, and Emil, Naill, Hisa, Vonetta, and Lyra are captured by the Ascended. When they all come together again, Emil tells Poppy that it's okay to hug Tawny.

When the Queen gives her Revenant demonstration by killing Millie and having everyone watch her rise again, Emil disgustingly remarks that it's an abomination to the gods.

He then watches in horror as Ian is murdered and witnesses Poppy's Primal fury. Later, in the woods outside Oak Ambler, he tells her that Tawny is hurt but alive and that the bleeding has stopped. Attempting to deal with everything, he and Vonetta share a drink from a flask, and he asks what the plan is. When Poppy reveals that she's a god and has confirmation, Emil reaches for the flask again.

Emil, Delano, Naill, and Vonetta accompany Poppy back to Oak Ambler to meet with Jalara. When they split off, Poppy tells Emil to be safe. Later, he tells Delano that he's confident he can take out the twenty guards on the north wall. When he meets back up with the group, he openly shares his disgust and fury over what they found on the Rise. Naill drags his sword across the side of the barracks to get the guards' attention, and Emil says, "Well, that's one way to do it."

Kieran asks when the mortals will stop referring to the wolven as overgrown dogs, and Emil replies that they don't know the difference and then spits on a guard who was about to stab Netta.

The group encounters a bunch of Craven, and Emil asks why the Ascended would keep a stable of them. Poppy tells him what the mortals of Solis were led to believe and guesses that they probably let the Cursed out from time to time to terrorize the locals. Emil is shocked to hear that people would actually believe those kinds of lies.

When they eventually return from Oak Ambler, Emil escorts Vonetta to see Poppy and doesn't miss his chance to tease her by bowing low and calling her *Your Highness*. When she asks if he's going to keep doing that, his only reply is, "Probably."

After her mission to spread the word about Poppy and the Atlantians, Vonetta relays that it went well. She tells them they told scores of people about Poppy and Casteel's marriage and Poppy's godhood, and Emil states how he wishes he could have been there to see their reactions. Poppy says that she doesn't deserve any credit for the way things went because it was Casteel's idea to reveal the Ascended's lies, but Emil reminds her that it was her idea to put out the word that she was a god and thus deserves credit, as well.

As they talk more about what it means now that the truth is out, Vonetta goes to grab a piece of bacon, and Emil swipes it up first. She is utterly affronted—I would be, too. Bacon is the answer for everything, and that answer is always yes—but he offers to share it with her. When she asks him why he's there at all, he tells her it's because he missed her. She clearly doesn't believe him, and he tells them all that he came because they received a missive from Duke and Duchess Ravarel. The only words: *We agree to nothing* (in response to Poppy's hope for negotiation).

Emil walks in on a screaming woman he calls *the widow*, and Poppy tells him that her name is Vessa, but the crone just tried to stab her. She then asks for the woman to be put somewhere safe. Emil wonders why she isn't being put in a *cell*, and Poppy tells him that she's worried about Vessa's advanced age and wants to make sure she doesn't get hurt.

Sadly, it's something she will later come to regret.

Emil joins Kieran and Perry to deliver the locked box from the Blood Queen. He explains that a Royal Guard delivered it, said it was for the Queen of Atlantia from the Queen of Solis, and then slit his own throat the minute he stopped speaking.

As Poppy adds her blood to the lock, a shadow leaks from the box, and Emil curses and then says a little prayer when he sees what's inside—Casteel's finger and his wedding ring. He, Naill, and Vonetta later go out into the pines to respectfully take care of the box's contents.

As I pen these details, I'm noticing a trend with Emil. He seems to be the one to take on the tough tasks in order to spare those he cares about. He may hide behind a mask of sarcasm and a flippant mien, but he has a big heart.

After the tragedy of Vessa's storm, and Poppy's subsequent enactment of punishment, Emil mentions the god of death—who he calls out as Rhain—during their discussion. Reaver corrects him and says there was never a god of death, only a Primal of Death. As we know, Rhain is the God of Common Men and Endings.

When they begin talking about Revenants and Kolis, Emil confirms for Reaver that the Chosen were the third sons and daughters.

Emil is present for the briefing with the generals and pours wine and water for those who want it. When Lizeth calls Poppy *Liessa*, they all bow, including Emil. Later, when Valyn asks what will happen at Oak Ambler, Emil tells him they may as well get back on their knees because he won't like it, and Poppy will likely go full god on them again.

As they leave for Oak Ambler, Emil and a small horde of guards flank Poppy. They encounter a group of people leaving the city, and Emil is on alert as Poppy stops to talk with them. When one reaches into their bag, Emil goes to draw his sword to protect her, and Poppy stops him. As more details are revealed, Emil comments that two Rites back-to-back isn't normal—and is concerning.

At the Oak Ambler gates, the Rise Guards don't believe that Poppy is who she says she is despite her assertion and the copious Royal banners. When they openly disrespect her, Emil makes it very clear that he hopes he gets a chance to kill the mouthiest one. When Forsyth alludes to the fact that the Atlantians are from a godless kingdom, Emil remarks on the painful irony of the Ascended calling them godless.

After Nithe unleashes his fire, and the mortals clear the Rise, Emil lets Poppy know when the last of them is clear. They fight their way inside, Emil and Kieran striking out with swords, and Emil warning everyone about the castle's archers.

Once things calm, Poppy tells the draken to find a safe place to rest, and Reaver chooses the top of Castle Redrock. Emil is aghast when he sees where the draken decided to roost.

Later, in the chambers under Castle Redrock, Emil leads the guard, Tasos, as he moves to where the Ascended sequester themselves during the day. They see a ton of dead servants and eventually come upon a horde of Craven. They fight, trying to get to Arden. Unfortunately, when they finally reach the wolven, he's dead. After discovering the additional chambers with all the bodies of the Chosen on the verge of turning, Emil offers to take care of them, saying he'll cover them and make it quick.

Once again taking on the tough tasks.

Reaching the room with the stalactites, Emil bickers with Naill about it being a real word. The two would argue about whether the sky is blue, I swear.

When General Cyr tells them that a group of residents wish to leave, Emil agrees with Poppy and Vonetta that they should be allowed. While planning Cas's rescue, Emil suggests that Poppy, Kieran, and Reaver take whiskey with them as a distraction and a way to make sure anyone who stops won't look too closely at them. As they go to leave, and Poppy tells Vonetta she trusts her to rule in her stead, Emil asks why not him. Vonetta calls him a mess again, and he teases Netta, telling her she likes his kind of mess—which means she likes *him*. He then bows to Poppy and tells her to go and get their King.

After they rescue Cas, Emil meets up with them in Padonia. When Cas embraces Delano and Netta, Emil asks if Cas missed him, to which Cas replies that he didn't think about him once—don't worry, he later gets a big hug from the King. Emil then turns his attention to Poppy, telling her that he knew she would get him—Cas—and placing her hand against his armor-adorned chest as he looks upon her with respect. When they discuss Malik, Emil remarks that he doesn't look anything like what he expected—meaning the Prince looks healthy and not like a captive—and asks if it's true that Malik didn't want to return with them. Cas tells him it's complicated.

As the Padonia Rise comes into view, and Poppy remarks how beautiful the wisteria trees are, Cas says they should be pulled out. Emil agrees and adds that they're weakening the Rise and have even breached the eastern wall in some areas. When Poppy asks about the Ascended who ruled there, Emil tells her that they were gone before their people arrived, just as they were in Whitebridge and Three Rivers. Cas asks more about that, and Emil tells him that the Ascended fled Three Rivers but thankfully left the mortals alive.

As they cover more of what happened while the groups were apart, Emil tells Poppy that her plan worked, and the people heard about what happened in Massene and Oak Ambler before they even reached Three Rivers. Poppy corrects him and says it was *their* plan, all of them, and Emil blushes at the recognition.

He isn't quite so humble when Poppy praises Vonetta for how she handled the armies, and she replies that she had help. Emil suggests that *he* was the best of that help.

Just before Valyn and Malik reunite, Casteel asks Emil and Naill to keep an eye on his brother. Taking that to heart, Emil and Naill strategically place Malik between them at dinner. When Sven and General Aylard chastise Valyn for keeping the truth about the Blood Crown a secret, Emil remarks that things are getting awkward. Cas then threatens Aylard, and Kieran quips that things are about to get even *more* awkward, making Emil laugh. After dinner and a nod from Casteel, Naill and Emil escort Malik from the room.

Following a fight with the Craven in the Blood Forest, Emil remarks that the trees are leaking and asks what it is. Perry taunts him by telling him that it's in the name—*blood* trees—which utterly grosses Emil out and causes him to hurriedly wipe his hand on his pants. Reaver joins them, and Emil tells him it's nice that he finally showed up...until the draken snaps at him. *Then*, he tells him it's nice to see him.

The boy has a death wish, I swear. His mouth is going to get him into serious trouble one of these days. The more I learn, the more I love him, but...

Poppy executes the locator spell and all watch with rapt curiosity. When the flames shoot up, Vonetta backs into Emil and says she thinks it's kind of beautiful. Emil simply gives her a look and shakes his head.

Now, these two are a couple to watch. Their relationship—whatever it may be—isn't widely known as yet, but it isn't exactly a secret, either. And I have a funny feeling it's going to evolve beautifully. That's not anything Seer-related. It's pure woman's intuition.

Emil is more than put out when the group encounters a bunch of Gyrms again. Talk turns to why their mouths are stitched shut, and Poppy says it's a good thing, alluding to the fact that if they were open, the serpents inside them would slither out—which they soon encounter up close and personally. When one of the Gyrms lets out a low moan, Emil is utterly disturbed and says as much, but he's not as bothered as when the snakes come out to play.

Emil spends the night of the Joining with Vonetta. Gods, I wish I could have been a fly on the wall for *that* evening of pleasure.

On the trip to the Bone Temple, Emil remarks that those of Solis are probably shocked that the Atlantians don't look like the Craven as they were led to believe. When they reach the Temple, Emil and Naill unload Malec, and then Malik comes to help them carry the casket. As they look on, and Isbeth leans in to kiss Malec, Emil can't hold his tongue and remarks how disgusting it is.

When Isbeth stabs Malec, a shockwave bursts free, and the ground starts to shake and cave in. Emil remarks that he's never seen wolven run from anything before and notices something emerging from one of the holes in the ground. He alerts the others, and they all start fighting the dakkais, Emil utilizing his quick reflexes to narrowly avoid being injured. As events unfold, he warns them that even more are coming. One rips open Naill's chest, and Emil throws the creature free, devastated by what he sees. But there's no time to mourn. The battle continues. While fighting a Revenant, Emil is speared through the chest and dies.

Not knowing what happened in between, Emil suddenly finds himself alive and healed and standing next to Hisa—the only evidence of what happened his bloodied and torn clothing and destroyed armor, which he quickly removes. As Nektas tells the story of the realms to Poppy, Emil and the others move in closer.

It's only the beginning. And knowledge is power, after all.

Casteel tasks Emil with settling and securing Wayfair as Poppy goes into stasis, something that's easy for him. What's not quite so easy is reconciling that the gods have awakened.

When Kieran and Cas return with Poppy in stasis, Emil tells them that the wolven are guarding the premises with Hisa and the Crown Guard, and he's made sure no staff will interrupt them.

He asks Cas what he wants to do about the Ascended and acknowledges when Cas says to keep them under house arrest.

Emil asks about Valyn and Cas tells him to send word to Padonia but to leave out the parts about Poppy.

Before he leaves, Emil tells Casteel to let Poppy know she has his everlasting devotion and utter adoration when she wakes. Cas calls him a fucker and he laughs and leaves.

When he returns later with Kieran, it's to find that Cas has shifted into a spotted cave cat and seems about ready to eat him. He takes the hint and leaves when Kieran urges him to go.

Dearest Netta,

Let me start by acknowledging I risk both life and limb by writing you if a certain overprotective brother of yours intercepts this message. May we both pray to the slumbering gods that doesn't occur, as I do prefer my heart and other—far more exciting—parts remain intact and fully functioning.

But what I have to say is worth the risk.

I know you enjoy my company. Or, more notably, what you once called, and I quote, my profanely wicked and talented tongue. And I also know you believe that my interest in you is nothing more than physical. While it is definitely on the physical side, I've come to the realization that it is about more than not spending the night alone or getting off.

It started when I discovered that, as soon as I left your presence, all I could think about was how you tasted and your sighs. Your kisses. Your slick heat. Your laugh. Gods help me, I'm starting to sound like Cas, but it's true. I can taste your laughter. It's soft and sweet with a hint of spice, and while that sounds utterly ridiculous, nothing about the way I felt when the floor gave way beneath you in the tunnels could be described as such.

My heart stopped.
It fucking stopped, Netta.

I've never felt such fear before—not in my entire life. And trust me, I have partaken in many things that have caused me a great deal of fear. But nothing could compare to the thought of never hearing your laugh again, seeing you smile, or even being on the receiving end of one of your clever, cutting insults. There's nothing passing about that.

I care about you, Netta. Deeply. And because of that, I feel that I must be honest before we find ourselves seeking pleasure from each other either while home or on the road. I want more than just a few passing hours. I want you. Today. Tonight. Tomorrow. I want to see what the future has in store for us.

Admittedly, I am a bit afraid of sharing this with you. Doing so could bring an end to us before there is even an us. But I cannot continue as we have been if you don't find yourself also wishing to see what a future could look like.

If not, I will respect and honor your wishes. But as much as my libido is cursing me for admitting this, I don't think I can continue on as we have been. I believe that my feelings for you would only increase, and that would not be fair to either of us.

So, where do we go from here, Netta? It is up to you. I figured it would be best to avoid any unnecessary awkwardness. If you do not visit with me in the near future, I will safely assume that I have your answer.

Yours,

Emil

P.S. You looked absolutely ravishing this morning, dressed in the blue tunic.

VONETTA CONTOU

Admittedly, Vonetta didn't feature as more than Kieran's sister for me for the longest time. However, when she started accompanying Casteel and Poppy on their missions and ultimately became Crown Regent, I started seeing more and more of her, and suspect that will continue.

Hair: Black cornrows—tight, narrow braids—that reach her waist.
Eyes: Wintery blue.
Body type: Tall.
Facial features: Skin the color of night-blooming roses. Sharply angled face. Broad cheekbones. Full mouth.
Distinguishing features: Throaty feminine laugh.
Other: Sixty years younger than her brother, so about one hundred and forty.
Personality: Easygoing. Kind. Suffers no fools when it comes to men.
Habits/Mannerisms/Strengths/Weaknesses: Loves candied fruit and demands it from Kieran when he annoys her. Terrible cook. Quick with a blade. Found it hard to believe that *anyone* in Solis was innocent until she met more Descenters.
Preternatural traits: Fawn/sand/tawny-colored in her wolven form but smaller than Kieran. Imprint is woodsy, like white oak and vanilla.
Background: Spessa's End Rise Guard. Helped Casteel remember who he was and remind him that he wasn't a thing after his imprisonment.
Family: Mother = Kirha Contou. Father = Jasper Contou. Brother = Kieran. Sister = new infant not yet named. Aunt = Beryn.

VONETTA'S JOURNEY TO DATE:

I first noticed Vonetta in my visions and research when she met Poppy at the Contou residence.

The first time she meets Poppy, she tells her that she can call her Netta and admonishes her brother for not telling the soon-to-be Queen that he has a sister. As they shake hands, Vonetta feels the same lightning-like static charge the other wolven have. And, like her brother, she tells Poppy that she smells old, though not of death like Kieran did.

Netta watches while Poppy heals Beckett, and like others, believes she may be from the Empath Warrior bloodline.

The wolven indulges Poppy in a training session and brings her a gown to wear for her wedding the following day. Poppy asks about the Joining as they talk, and Vonetta tells her what she knows, explaining that it strengthens the bond. She adds that it doesn't always have to happen at the wedding—it can occur before or after—that it's not always sexual, and it is never weird. She also says that no one *expects* Poppy to do it.

As Vonetta helps Poppy get ready, Poppy laments how she's the reason everything they've built in Spessa's End is now at risk and apologizes for bringing trouble. Vonetta reassures her that it's not her fault, nor is the inevitable battle.

When Vonetta adds jewelry to Poppy's ensemble, she explains that diamonds are traditional and are the joyous tears of the gods given form. Wearing them signifies that the gods are with someone, even as they slumber.

Poppy asks questions about what will happen next after the wedding, and Vonetta tells her that once she and Cas reach Evaemon, the King and Queen will demand a celebration in her honor—one that will last days—so they can introduce her.

When Duchess Teerman and her knights arrive and a fight breaks out, Vonetta's hind leg is injured in the battle. Once things settle, and the others set out, Vonetta remains behind in Spessa's End but plans to return to Atlantia soon for her mother's birthday and the birth of her new sibling.

Vonetta arrives at Cove Palace to inform the Royals, Cas, and Poppy that a convoy of Ascended are in Spessa's End, requesting an audience with Casteel and Poppy. She says that Ian is leading the group and informs Poppy that her brother has, indeed, Ascended. Both she and her brother feel Poppy's grief at hearing the news.

The siblings inform their parents that they are again heading to Spessa's End. It's an arduous trip, and Vonetta is exhausted once they arrive. She's also still reeling over the fact that she can hear Poppy in her head.

After their discussions with Ian, Vonetta wonders if he told Poppy to wake Nyktos, hoping that the King of Gods would kill his sister. Though she realizes that Cas and Poppy are considering it regardless, so she'll have to deal with whatever happens.

In Evaemon, Vonetta displays some hostility toward Perry. Given the happenings of late, she's a bit overprotective since Cas's friends have betrayed him. She also takes it upon herself to become Poppy's shadow on her first day in the palace as they await the transfer of crowns.

Vonetta, in wolven form, joins the group of guards during the Council meeting. I remember seeing her and her brother in wolven form that day. They're absolutely beautiful and majestic. When Ambrose refuses to bow to Poppy, and Cas tells him to either bow before his Queen or bleed before her, Vonetta makes her agreement known with a deep growl.

Unwilling to miss a chance to see Iliseeum, Vonetta joins the group that travels to the Land of the Gods. During the trip, she asks about my journal, saying she might be interested in reading it—as one should be. Just as she does, the floor collapses, and she falls. Luckily, Emil catches her, and Poppy is able to use her eather to lift Netta to safety.

When they pass through the mists, and skeletal soldiers erupt from the ground, she berates Emil for not warning them about what he saw in the hole and then tells him he's a mess after he calls her beautiful amidst the chaos. As the group battles the skeletons, she fights back-to-back with Emil until Poppy finally finishes them with her power.

As she gazes upon Dalos, she wonders if any gods are awake. Then, realizing what covers the ground, she remarks that they're walking on diamonds.

Back in the mortal realm, they plan to go to Oak Ambler, and Vonetta agrees to go with the group approaching by land. Unfortunately, the Ascended capture them before they make too much progress.

During the Blood Queen's demonstration with the Revenant, Vonetta verifies that Millicent is dead after the knight stabs her in the chest. She tells the group that there's no pulse and she smells of death.

In the forest outside Oak Ambler, after Cas is taken prisoner, Vonetta shows Poppy Tawny's injury and reassures her they'll get Cas back. Despite her assurances, Poppy loses control of her power and throws Vonetta back reflexively. When Poppy feels bad later, Netta tells her not to be sorry.

Back in the capital, she follows Poppy in wolven form to meet with the Queen Mother and plans to stay until her parents and her new baby sister arrive.

Vonetta spends the night with Emil (and is seen leaving him, utterly sated).

Netta accompanies Poppy when she heads back to Oak Ambler to deliver her message in the form of King Jalara's head.

During the seizure of Massene, Vonetta attacks from the Pinelands after Poppy opens the eastern gate, then happily attacks and kills a guard who taunted Poppy about raping her. Inside Cauldra Manor, Vonetta, Delano, and Sage head into the underground chambers and lead the way for Poppy.

After delivering the Atlantians' message to the mortals regarding what is coming and looking for additional Descenters to add to their cause, Vonetta returns and tells Poppy that it seemed like people were ready for someone to do something about the Ascended. She also relays that she told the people the Maiden not only married the Atlantian Prince but is also a god.

Poppy asks her to become the Crown Regent, and she accepts, but she's not happy about staying behind when they go to rescue Cas.

When the locked box containing Casteel's finger arrives from the Blood Queen, she, Naill, and Emil take care of the contents. Later, when she checks in with Poppy, they discuss Ian and Isbeth. She remarks that Ian was polite and warm—nothing like she expected. She then relays the stories Ian told her.

During a moment with Reaver later, Vonetta asks who the god of death was before Rhain. He tells her there was never a god of death, only a Primal of Death. She then remarks on how similar Kolis and Solis sound and asks Reaver why Kolis's magic only worked on the thirdborn sons and daughters. What she doesn't know is that it didn't. It worked on others, but it was…different.

When the Atlantian armies arrive—two hundred thousand strong—Vonetta lets Poppy know and suggests that she wear her crown while addressing her people. She then leaves to lead the wolven into the city and helps to secure the Temple.

After they encounter the Ascended Priests and Priestesses in Castle Redrock's underground chambers, she briefly shoves one of the Ascended into a stream of sunlight after the vampry repeatedly tries to bite her. Once they discover the chamber full of murdered children, she asks Poppy what they're going to do about the Temple and agrees that they should just burn it to the ground.

Later, she tells General Cyr that if people want to leave the city, they should be allowed. Poppy agrees with her and then bolsters the new Queen's confidence before speaking to the crowd.

As they make plans to separate, Vonetta promises to look after Tawny for Poppy, and they plan to meet in Three Rivers.

Vonetta and the armies take New Haven and Whitebridge while Poppy is away.

After Casteel's rescue, Vonetta meets the group outside of Padonia and greets Cas in wolven form. He tells her he missed her, and then she goes to greet Poppy before returning to the city ahead of everyone else.

Vonetta brings Tawny to see Poppy once everyone's settled and explains that she and Gianna have been teaching Tawny to fight, remarking that the woman is a quick learner.

When Poppy asks for a hug from Vonetta on two legs instead of four, she laughs and obliges. Poppy commends her on leading the armies spectacularly, and Vonetta replies that she didn't do it alone.

Later, during discussions, Vonetta remarks that Malec would eventually recover from his entombment and ends up in the Blood Forest as they're looking for the god. Poppy remarks that she isn't even supposed to be there, but they're both happy to see each other. When Poppy does the spell to locate Malec, Vonetta asks if the ruins are the right place and remarks how beautiful the magic trail is.

Once they retrieve Malec, Netta rides in front of the procession on the way back to Padonia. Then, the night of Poppy, Cas, and Kieran's Joining, she spends the night with Emil.

Before going to confront Isbeth, Poppy and Cas decide that if neither of them can rule, then she is to take the throne and order her to stay in Padonia with fifty thousand soldiers. She agrees until the realization of what would have to happen for her to be next in line to rule hits her. Before the couple greets their people, Vonetta hands them their crowns and says they only reveal their true natures when a god sits on the throne.

Just wait until she realizes that Poppy isn't just a god, she's a Primal.

Emil,

I expect to see you in my tent tonight.

Yours,
Netta

P.S. Please never bring up my brother in the same letter you speak of how I taste again.

P.S.S. I know I looked good this morning, you couldn't stop staring at me.

TAWNY LYON

Tawny was Poppy's only friend when she was still the Maiden—so much more than just her maid. Tawny was her confidante and her conspirator in getting up to no good. She was the one thing that Poppy held on to while trying to keep a grasp of the normal in an otherwise abnormal existence.

Hair: Brown and gold curls that turn snowy white after shadowstone poisoning.

Eyes: Brown that turn nearly white except for the pupils after shadowstone poisoning.

Facial features: Rich brown skin.

Body type: Tall. Lithe.

Personality: Sarcastic and flippant.

Habits/Mannerisms/Strengths/Weaknesses: Randomly jumps from topic to topic in conversation. Has a weakness for sweet cake. Excels in idleness. Not good at shielding her emotions. Twists hair around her finger when anxious. Can be insistent when it comes to what she wants. Never believed in the Fates. Memory is notoriously subjective.

Background: One of the few allowed to speak with the Maiden and see her unveiled. Second daughter of a successful merchant. Given to the Court at age thirteen. Was assigned to the Maiden shortly after her Rite.

Family: Older brother and sister.

TAWNY'S JOURNEY TO DATE:

After Tawny helps Poppy sneak out to head to the Red Pearl where she eventually meets Hawke for the first time, Tawny discusses what happened and their upcoming Ascension with the Maiden.

When Poppy is almost abducted, Tawny helps to tend to her wounds and secure the necessary medicine. She also learns the Duchess's theory about the intruder being an Atlantian.

The night Poppy's guard Rylan Keal is murdered—by Jericho—Tawny sleeps in Poppy's bed with her, comforting her friend and easing her worries, as well.

Despite the Rite preparation taking much of her time, she finds a few moments to spend with Poppy and learns that she and Hawke kissed. She eventually gets the full Red Pearl story out of her friend.

Like usual, Tawny accompanies Poppy to the atrium, even grabbing some of her favorite sandwiches beforehand. She watches, amused, as Poppy speaks up to the Ladies in Wait after they make fools of themselves with Hawke. But she feels bad after, when the Duke makes his displeasure known. Following Poppy's punishment for speaking to the other Ladies in Wait, Tawny again helps her with her wounds.

The night of the Rite, she joins her friend until Poppy tells her to go and have fun. Later, when all hell breaks loose, her attempts to keep Poppy from entering the fray during the Rise attempt are futile. And after everything, she can only help Poppy bathe and change, unsure what else to do to help her friend.

Poppy's ordered to go to the capital, and Tawny reveals she can't go with her—it's too dangerous, and she could become a liability. Before they part ways, the two share a touching goodbye in the Maiden's quarters the morning Poppy sets out for the capital with Hawke and the other guards.

In the time that Poppy is gone, Queen Ileana keeps Tawny with her at the capital but doesn't Ascend her. I wonder if she knew she could use Tawny as leverage. When Poppy comes to Castle Redrock, Tawny attempts to warn her by telling her friend that the Queen isn't what she seems. She tries to tell her more, but Ian cuts her off.

The Queen gives her Revenant demonstration, and Tawny is horrified when the knight stabs and kills Millicent. She's even more traumatized when another beheads Ian. When all hell breaks loose—again—Tawny is wounded in the shoulder in the melee. After Casteel surrenders, the Queen gives Tawny to the Atlantians as a sign of *goodwill*. Her gash is bad, the veins standing out, thick and black. Poppy heals her outward physical wound, but they discover it was delivered with shadowstone, and the poison starts to spread, inching up her throat like black vines.

Once they return to the keep, Delano takes her to a room to recover, and the Healers and Elders are summoned. The Healers and I are able to help her, but it changes her irrevocably. Her hair turns white, her eyes turn nearly colorless, and she doesn't register as mortal any longer—nor can Poppy read her emotions. We're not sure exactly *what* she is just yet.

Tawny doesn't give a straight answer when asked if someone told her about Primal magic. She merely says: "Yes, and no." She then reveals she knew she was dying until she saw Vikter, and thinks the Fates did something to save her. It changed everything she originally believed in—or rather the things she *didn't*.

She says everything played out like a dream that wasn't a dream. She remembers getting stabbed, then there was nothing for a long while, then a silver light. She thought she was entering the Vale, but then she saw Vikter. He told her that Poppy was a god. Isbeth had let it slip before, but Tawny didn't believe her. Ian did, though. At the mention of Poppy's brother, Tawny apologizes for what happened to him.

She goes on to say that all she knows is that Isbeth plans to remake the realms and believes Poppy can help her do it. She admits that she wasn't around Isbeth all that much and had no idea why they summoned her to the capital. They told her they feared she'd be taken, too, after the threat on Poppy's life. When she got to Wayfair, she saw the Handmaidens—the Revenants—and knew that nothing was right about that place. When the Queen revealed that Poppy was her daughter, Tawny just assumed she was addled.

In the dream that wasn't a dream, Vikter told her things he nor she could have known, like Aios stopping Poppy from walking off the cliff in the Skotos

Mountains, that Nyktos *and* the Consort approved of Poppy and Casteel's marriage, that Cas had been taken, and that Poppy would eventually free him. He also told her about being a *viktor*, and she relays all of that to Poppy.

She and Kieran bicker over how *un*helpful her information was, and Tawny says that Vikter didn't think they knew the whole prophecy. She shares the complete version (see Prophecy section).

They ask if she ever saw or met anyone named Malik, and she tells them she doesn't know anyone by that name.

She doesn't, because he went by Elian.

When Poppy worries about her destiny, especially given the harbinger bits in the prophecy, Tawny tells her that she didn't get the impression from Vikter that Poppy was destined for evil. She then relays to Poppy alone what Vikter told her about the Consort.

She also mentions how she didn't want to believe what Ian said about what happens to third sons and daughters. Despite being a second daughter, she worries that she is like a Revenant now—dead but not—and Poppy promises to find out what happened to her.

After telling Poppy she has always known how much she is loved, she promises to see her friend again in Three Rivers.

They actually see each other next in Padonia, and Tawny tells Poppy how Netta and Gianna are teaching her how to fight.

When Casteel returns, she greets him, and he tells her that he's happy to see her alive and well. She tells him that she's glad he loves Poppy as fiercely as her friend loves him and that she doesn't have to punch him for lying to her and kidnapping Poppy.

I'm sure this was another moment where Cas thinks she's his favorite person. Anyone that fiercely loyal to his Queen deserves respect.

When Poppy leaves to confront the Queen and take Malec to the Bone Temple, Tawny sees her off.

THE LAKE

~Poppy~

"You're going to get us into so much trouble." In the dappled silver light of the moon, Tawny's cloaked figure dipped beneath a low-hanging branch. Even though no one entered this part of the Grove, neither of us removed our hoods yet out of caution. "You know that, right?"

"This was your idea," I reminded her. "I was about to go to bed when you came to my chamber with this grand plan."

Her cloaked head turned toward me. I couldn't see her face, but I could hear the smile in her voice. "How dare you accuse me of such tomfoolery?"

"Tomfoolery?" I wrinkled my nose. "That is such a silly word."

"A silly word for silly behaviors," she remarked. "I heard Rylan saying it the other day. He told Vikter that he suspected you were up to some tomfoolery when you were supposed to be in your chambers."

Rylan was likely correct. I grinned as I stepped around a large boulder tangled in some exposed roots. Tawny and I had walked this path so many times at night. The scant moonlight breaking up the shadows was no hindrance. "If I was, I was likely doing something else you suggested we do."

Tawny's quiet giggle reached me. "Just so we're clear, tonight may have been my idea, but you started it."

"And how did I start this?"

"Was it not originally your idea?" She walked under a pine that must've fallen against another during one of the late-summer storms. Its fallen, dried-out branches crunched with her footsteps. "To go swimming in the lake?"

"Possibly." Truth be told, I couldn't remember who'd suggested the first late-night swim.

I glanced behind me, unable to see anything more than the dark outline of the sweeping pines. We were far enough inside the Grove that no one could see us. Anyone within the large swath of woods that separated the haves from the have-nots of Masadonia wouldn't be able to see the inner walls around the castle, either—even in broad daylight. We also weren't near the section they'd cleared to use as a park of sorts.

"Are you worried someone will discover us?"

"Not at all." Tawny's steps slowed. "No one but fools like us travels this deep into the Grove. I'm just being overly dramatic so I won't be able to hear a spirit if one *is* following us."

My grin turned wry. "As often as I've walked the Grove, I've yet to see a single ghost."

She snorted. "You sound disappointed."

"I kind of am."

"Well, there's always a first time," she remarked. "I'm not sure what would be more frightening, though. The spirit of a guard? Or an animal, like a wolf."

My brows knitted. "I'd have to go with the spirit of a guard. But I thought the ghosts here were those who died within the Grove."

"Who knows? Honestly, a rabbit's spirit might be the scariest thing."

"What?" I laughed. "I cannot wait to hear the justification for that."

"There's nothing more frightening than something cute and fluffy that happens to be dead and reanimated."

"Oh, my gods." I shook my head. "I don't think spirits are the dead reanimated, Tawny."

"How would you know?"

"Because I've seen the Craven," I said, the smile fading from my lips. I'd seen *cursed* mortals die and then come back. I knew what the reanimated dead looked like.

"True," Tawny murmured, stopping as the tang of sorrow reached me. She waited until I was beside her and then folded her arm around mine. "By the way, do you know what I've heard?" She lowered her voice, even though the only other things in the Grove besides us were likely small, fluffy critters and large birds. Well, the only *living* things, I supposed. "About the new guard?

"The new guard?" I questioned, even though I knew exactly who she spoke of. Only one name was on everyone's lips these last several weeks. *Hawke Flynn*. My stomach dipped, tangling much like the bare roots around that bolder earlier. There was so much wrong with that, I wasn't even sure where to begin.

"Yes, the new, extraordinarily handsome guard you seem to have completely forgotten about," she replied dryly. "Despite the fact that you've spent quite a few mornings of late engrossed in the guards' daily training."

My cheeks warmed, and a pair of golden eyes shone brightly in my mind...as did well-formed arms honed from wielding a sword, slick with sweat. "I have no idea what you're speaking of."

Tawny's laugh was light. "Sure."

I said nothing to that because Tawny knew I lied. Everyone was aware of who Hawke Flynn was. I imagined even Duke Teerman found himself a bit engrossed in watching the guard. It was the way he moved, the fluid gracefulness when he trained. Or how, when he entered the Great Hall for the City Council sessions, he didn't just walk. He *prowled*.

I cleared my throat. "What have you heard?"

"That he's found someone new to occupy his spare time with," she shared as the scent of damp soil thickened around us. "Britta."

"Oh? I'm sure they make a lovely couple," I heard myself say as a pang of envy lanced my chest. Britta was one of the many maids who worked within the castle, and I wasn't at all surprised to hear that she was one of a string of many—at least according to the gossips—who'd caught Hawke's eye. Not only because she was one of the prettiest maids but because Britta enjoyed life and all it had to offer. She was bold with her affection. She was experienced. The only time I'd ever seen her appear scandalized was when she spoke of the dancing she'd seen behind the curtains at the Red Pearl.

Which made me very curious about what type of dancing she'd seen.

But I wasn't sure if the envy curdling low in my stomach was directed at her or purely because I…well, I had no idea what it was like to catch another's attention in that way. To be…wanted. To become experienced. To truly live.

And I likely never would.

Spying the glistening water through the trees, I pulled myself out of my thoughts. There was no point in dwelling on that, was there? The future was inevitable, and I didn't want to spoil these moments I had with Tawny.

Sooner rather than later, we wouldn't have any of these.

The quiet lake appeared ahead of us, its still waters reflecting the moonlight and catching the shadows of the long tree branches still flush with leaves. That would change soon, too. The late-season heat would end in a blink, and I would wake up one morning to see that all the leaves had fallen. Another winter would be upon us.

Slipping free of Tawny's hold, I walked ahead. Once I reached the water's edge, I reached up and lowered my hood, baring my face to the night sky. There was nothing better than feeling the air on my cheeks and brow.

"You look like you're going to turn into a statue," Tawny commented.

Grinning, I glanced over at her. She'd already dropped her cloak onto one of the nearby flat rocks and now stood in just a shift as she kicked off her ankle boots. She had her mass of caramel-hued curls piled high atop her head, making her cheekbones appear sharper and higher. I eyed the smooth skin of her brow and cheek and felt another unwanted twist of envy.

I looked away, annoyed with myself as I unlatched my cloak. I folded it neatly before laying it beside Tawny's since it didn't belong to me. I wasn't even sure whose it was, but it must've been worn by a man. There was still the distinctive spice of some cologne lingering on it. I'd sort of helped myself to it when I saw it lying in one of the many first-floor chambers. Now, I took care of it. I wasn't even sure why. It wasn't like I planned to return it to where I'd found it. I hoarded clothing of color like others collected books or knickknacks.

Tawny tossed a grin in my direction as she padded barefoot into the water. A soft squeak left her. "Oh, it's cold. Definitely cold."

The water was always chilled, which was odd, considering the floor of the lake was made of some sort of dark rock. One would think it would absorb the sunlight and warm the waters, but that wasn't the case.

Tawny waded out several feet, her arms folded across her chest as she muttered to herself about what a bad idea this was.

"The other lake?" Tawny asked from where she was now up to her waist in the water. "The one by Wayfair? Was it always this cold?"

I nodded. "Yep. Even on the hottest days." I didn't have a lot of clear memories of walking the elms outside Wayfair with Ian when I was a child, but I did remember the lake there. This one reminded me so much of that one, except it was larger and had a waterfall. But there was something else the lakes had in common. Something I hadn't remembered until now. "You know what's strange?"

"Besides the fact that I'm the only one in the lake?" she asked, splashing water at me.

"Besides that." I began toeing off my boots. "The woods surrounding the other lake in Carsodonia are also rumored to be haunted. At least, that is what Ian claimed."

"Ian claims many things."

I laughed as I unhooked my sheath with the bloodstone and wolven-bone dagger, placing it on the cloak. I inched closer to the water's edge, the grass cool beneath my feet. "He said the woods were..." I squinted. "He said they were haunted by the spirits of those afraid to face judgment."

"That's kind of sad," she said, slipping down so her shoulders were just barely visible. "But why would they haunt those woods?"

"He said it was because the lake was a doorway to where Rhain ruled," I told her. "One of many."

"Your brother has a very active imagination."

"That he does," I murmured.

"Did he say the same thing about this lake—wait, don't answer that. I don't want to know."

Laughing, I inched closer to the water. "I don't recall if he..." I trailed off, the back of my neck tightening suddenly. My skin prickled. Stopping, I turned and scanned the trees. The Grove was quiet except for the breeze rustling the branches and the distant calls of birds.

"Poppy?" Tawny called. "Did you hear something?"

I gave the expanse of trees another look. "No. I just..." My brows knitted. I wasn't even sure what had stopped me. I hadn't heard anything. I'd just...*felt* something. But what? I had no idea.

Shaking my head, I walked into the water. The coldness stole my breath, but I powered through it, knowing it was best to just go for it. The pale shift I wore trailed behind me as I reached Tawny's side, finding that she was still staring at the bank of the lake.

I followed her gaze, seeing nothing. I looked back at her. "Did *you* hear something?"

"No." The warm breeze tossed a loose curl over her face. "But I expect a spirit to wander out of the trees at any moment in an attempt to get a peek at our unmentionables."

"I don't know if you're being serious or not," I said, letting myself sink. The moment the water rose above my chest, I thought my heart stopped for a moment. But after a few seconds, the shock of the cold faded. I waded farther out, my feet gliding over the smooth rock at the bottom of the lake. I then swam and made it to the deepest part of the lake, where the water crested my chin.

Tawny was still staring at the woods.

I let my senses open just a tiny bit. Not a lot. Tart, almost lemony unease gathered in my throat. "Are you okay?"

"Yeah. Yes." She backed up in the water.

"I swear I didn't see or hear anything, but if you'd rather head back, we can." I pushed off the lake floor.

"No. I'm fine. I'm just being weird." Tucking the wayward curl back, she faced me. A moment passed. "You don't believe in spirits, do you? I mean, the kind that remain here. With us."

I opened my mouth, unsure how to answer. "I don't know. I've never seen one, at least that I know of." I shrugged. "Do you believe?"

She swam closer, biting her lip. "I didn't."

My curiosity piqued. "But?"

"But I saw one once."

"Really?" I narrowed my eyes. "Are you being honest?"

"Yes. I am." She splashed me, creating a ripple that cascaded across half the lake. "And it wasn't when I was a young child. It was only a few years ago."

I stared at her. "You saw a spirit here? Was it at the castle?"

Tawny nodded. "I was in the atrium with Loren. The Mistress had just left, and Loren had dozed off. I was supposed to be reading. And I was. Sort of." She drew her teeth over her lower lip and looked back at the bank. "I felt this…I don't know. A cold draft? Suddenly. Like a burst of wind. Then I looked up and saw it standing in the corner."

"It?" I whispered.

"Her. It was a woman. I thought she was a guest at first. She was solid. Or at least she *appeared* that way initially," Tawny said as tiny bumps appeared along my skin. "I started to smile at her, but I realized that she didn't…well, she didn't look right."

"What do you mean?"

"Her gown was old." Her brow creased. "Like something I'd seen ladies wearing in paintings from hundreds of years ago. And she was pale. Not white. *Pale.* She stood so still, and I realized she looked almost…fuzzy, you know? Like her features weren't clear. At first, I thought it was because of the sunlight coming in from the windows, but then I realized I could see through her lower half."

My eyes went wide.

"I know." Tawny let out a nervous laugh. "For a moment, I couldn't move or think. I was just frozen. Time stopped. We just sort of stared at each other."

"You weren't afraid?"

"No." She drew her fingers through the water. "But that wasn't the strangest thing. I wasn't afraid at that moment, but afterward, I was terrified. I wouldn't stay in the atrium alone for months. But at that moment, I wasn't scared. And she..."

I drifted closer to her. "What?"

"She..." Tawny looked away, shaking her head. "She just faded away. Disappeared."

"And that was it?"

Tawny nodded. "Yeah."

I had no doubt in my mind that she spoke the truth about what she'd seen, but as she floated away, I thought maybe that wasn't all. "Why didn't you tell me this before?"

"I don't know. I haven't told anyone." She spun in the water. "It's not that I thought you'd think I was out of my mind or something."

"Well..." I teased.

She laughed. "It's just that I really don't know what I saw."

"It sounds like you do." I glanced around the lake, thinking of the weird feeling I'd had. "Maybe there is something to what Ian said about the woods."

"You think—?"

The branches of one of the trees rattled loudly above us, jerking our heads back to peer up. Something large was up there. On reflex, my hand went to my thigh, but then I remembered I'd left my dagger with the cloak. Damn it. Several limbs shook again, this time hard enough to send leaves falling.

"My gods," Tawny whispered as a bird took flight.

A *huge* bird with a silvery-white body and wings. Stunned silent, we watched it circle overhead. The bird's wingspan had to be four feet or more. It must have been some sort of hawk or maybe an eagle, but I knew of none *that* size—at least not in these parts of Solis.

My heart thrummed as the bird silently moved out of view, disappearing over the Grove. I slowly lowered my chin and looked over at Tawny.

"I would like to change my earlier statement about the spirits of bunnies being the scariest," she began. "A spirit of *that* thing would be."

I laughed as I turned my gaze back to the sky. There was no hint of the silver hawk—at least I thought it was a hawk—and I couldn't help but feel like Tawny had upon seeing that spirit in the castle. I had that distinct feeling of not knowing what I saw but knowing I'd definitely seen *something*.

NAILL LA'CROX

Another core part of Poppy and Cas's group, like Emil, Naill shows up nearly everywhere the Elemental Atlantian does in my visions and research.

Hair: Dark, close-cropped.
Eyes: Dark gold.
Body type: Tall.
Facial features: Rich, dark skin. High, sharp cheekbones. Striking smile.
Personality: Quiet and obedient.
Habits/Mannerisms/Strengths/Weaknesses: Rather skilled with a needle and thread. Seems to appear out of nowhere at times. Incredibly fast.
Background: Elemental Atlantian. Like Emil, has helped Casteel remember who he is and that he's not a thing in the past when feelings grabbed him. Has known him longer than anyone but Kieran and the Contous.
Family: Father runs the mills that create electricity; he keeps the ancient wheels working.

NAILL'S JOURNEY TO DATE:

During the trip to the capital, when the guards are killed in the stables, and Poppy is placed in a cell for her safety—and their peace of mind—Naill goes with Delano to remove her and take her to more comfortable quarters. He immediately goes on alert when Jericho arrives in the dungeon. Six others come up behind him, and Naill tells them they're all being incredibly foolish. When Mr. Tulis spews his vitriol, Naill reminds him that the Maiden didn't take his son; the Ascended did. A fight inevitably breaks out, and Naill rips out a Descenter's throat. Eventually, he gets knocked out.

When Poppy greets Alastir, Naill is lumped into the group the elder wolven says aren't very well-mannered—I actually think Naill is incredibly polite. As Cas relays the story of how he didn't plan the proposal and subsequently how Poppy said no at first, Naill fearlessly chimes in that she also told the Prince he was out of his mind and several other things.

Right after Cas and Poppy discuss the Empath line and almost kiss, Naill interrupts with news that the Ascended are coming from the western roads. When the vamprys enter the yard, Casteel tells Naill to be smart, and the Atlantian takes off.

Following the Ascended attack, he goes to scout the western roads to make sure they're clear so they can leave as soon as possible. As they're riding for Atlantia, he witnesses Poppy hitting Cas. When Casteel shrugs it off, Naill remarks that it didn't look like a love tap to him.

As they ride past the tree hangings, Naill is the first to spot the Dead Bones Clan, shouting to the group that they're in the trees to the left. He takes an arrow to the leg in the skirmish and is nearly shot again until Poppy takes out his attacker with a crossbow. After the attack, Naill rides ahead to scout and ensure they don't run into any more clansmen. As they continue on, and Poppy asks questions about the Dead Bones Clan, Naill explains that they aren't just anti-Craven in protecting their territory. They're anti-*everyone*.

When they reach Pompay, Casteel relays the story of its tragic history, and Poppy wonders why she's shocked after everything she's already heard. Naill replies that it's not something anyone ever gets used to and he wouldn't want to. He says he needs to be shocked so the line between him and the vamprys doesn't thin.

Poppy comes upon Naill and Delano sitting on the wall facing the bay in Spessa's End. Delano says she looks like she could use a drink and offers her the bottle. Naill warns her that it tastes like horse piss. He's likely not wrong. I have had my fair share of rot-gut whiskey and other assorted steel-tub liquor throughout the years. And while it does the job, it's not always palate-pleasing.

Emil calls Poppy *Your Highness*, and she seems bothered by it. Naill informs her that even before her crowning, it's customary and would be a great dishonor if they didn't address her as such.

On the way through the Skotos Mountains, Naill splits off with Beckett and Delano to head through the mist, and their group is the last to reconvene at Gold Rock.

Despite always being calm and collected, witnessing Poppy's display of power at the Chambers of Nyktos is shocking and scary to him. Like several others there, Naill is tracked by a wolven, even as he softly tries to reason with it. Once things calm, Casteel orders him to join Emil and Delano in finding and bringing Beckett to him. Unfortunately, poor Beckett is already dead.

Naill is part of the group that rescues Poppy in Irelone and happily vents his anger by tearing through the Ascended. As they make their way back through the Skotos, he feeds Cas in a hunting cabin in the foothills. Once Poppy wakes, even her earliest transformations—namely her strength and agility—awe him.

When Cas teases Poppy about finding her perched outside a window with a certain book in her hand—my diary, if you couldn't guess—Naill is super intrigued by the story and even more so by the book. I hope they shared it with him later.

Poppy thanks him for helping Casteel after Irelone, and by extension, her. She then tells him to call her *Poppy* instead of Penellaphe, which makes him smile. After Kieran shifts, Naill retrieves his clothes but gives the wolven grief and says he should have let him return to the kingdom buck-ass naked.

Naill wonders about the storm that could have twisted and bent the trees and is even more shocked when they ride past the trees of Aios, and he sees that the leaves are no longer golden but blood-red. At the Temple of Saion, Naill leads Alastir from the crypts and forces him to his knees in front of Cas and Poppy. After the traitors are dealt with, Naill leaves with Emil and Quentyn before dawn.

Once they arrive at the Contou residence, Naill dines with everybody, and they talk about Iliseeum. He then joins the group headed to the capital, engaging in his usual banter and bickering with Emil and mentioning that he hasn't had a green bean casserole in years when talk of food arises. As Emil continually flirts with

Poppy, Naill wonders aloud if the Atlantian has a death wish—I wonder the same!

The Unseen attack, and Naill is hit in the arm with an arrow yet still fights with everyone to battle back the Unseen and the Gyrms. Later, Poppy inquires about some buildings and is told they house machinery that converts water to electricity. Naill says that it's all incredibly boring and complicated but that he could probably recite each piece and state its purpose since his father oversees the mills.

During the transfer of the Crown from Eloana and Valyn to Poppy and Cas, he stands guard and then walks with the group through the palace. He's also present for the Council meeting and my announcement of the new rulers to the people of Atlantia.

Instead of joining the group that heads to Iliseeum, Naill chooses to stay in the capital to spend some time with his father. He is, however, present for the dinner meeting afterward where they make a plan for Oak Ambler. He's put in the group with the King and Queen decoys and is eventually captured by the Ascended.

When Poppy wakes in the woods outside of Oak Ambler after Cas sacrifices himself, Naill bows over a prone Tawny. When they return to speak with Eloana, he stands guard at the door with Hisa and is happy to be part of the group to accompany Poppy back to Oak Ambler to meet with King Jalara.

As they ride to Massene, Naill speaks with Poppy when she feels Arden's anxiety. He rides ahead with Kieran to investigate and is horrified by what they find on the Rise—all the murdered mortals. Because of that and more, he happily joins in on the fight with the guards. Once some surrender, Poppy orders him to take Arden and stay with the prisoners in the barracks.

Naill leaves with Vonetta and Wren to deliver the ultimatum to Duke and Duchess Ravarel, look for Descenters, and warn the mortals about what will happen if their demands are refused. Once done, they all return to camp.

Poppy sends Naill to secure Vessa in a bedchamber that locks from the outside so she can't hurt herself or anyone else after the crone attacks her. He does as instructed. Sadly, it doesn't stop Vessa from using Primal magic and killing many of the draken later.

After the Blood Queen sends her horrific message—Casteel's ring finger—Naill joins Emil and Vonetta in respectfully dealing with the box's contents.

Naill rushes to check on Poppy when the storm appears and remarks that it's the same type of tempest that happened when she Ascended to her godhood. When they go out and witness what is happening with the draken, Naill steadies Poppy and then eventually trails her as she goes to take care of *the widow.*

When Reaver is talking about Nyktos, Naill remarks that he's never heard the name Kolis before. Talk shifts to the Rite, and Naill asks if the Chosen had a choice in being Ascended, and Reaver tells him they did—Eythos always let them choose.

Naill makes Poppy something to wear—a white outfit to send a message—

and vigilance ramps up as Naill helps to keep an eye on the generals, aware that the Unseen are very much still a threat.

In the Temple, Naill finds another pair of holy people and is the first to reveal that the Priests and Priestesses had Ascended among them, something they hadn't known before. When Vonetta brings in another Priestess, Naill joins the group that follows her. They come upon a chamber with blood stalactites and bones. After having a ridiculous argument with Emil about the word *stalactite*, he points out that the hole in the floor is actually a deep well.

Sage is injured, and Naill helps Poppy heal her. When Reaver shifts, it takes Naill by surprise, but not as much as when Sage replies with a "yum" in response to what she sees. Naill reminds her that the draken can breathe fire, but it doesn't seem to faze her. I get it. I had an absolutely incredible experience with a draken myself, and they are quite delicious.

When Cas returns, Naill waits until all the wolven greet the King before stepping in for a hug. He tells Cas that it hasn't been right without him and not to leave again. His elation soon turns to shock when he sees Malik.

Everybody fills Poppy and Cas in on what's been happening with the seizure of the cities, and Naill informs them that the Ascended left a graveyard in Whitebridge and Padonia, just like they did in Pompay. They discuss the Duke of Three Rivers, and Malik mentions knowing him. Naill can't hold back his ire and sneers at him, asking him how complicated things have gotten and using his princely title. Later, Cas asks him and Emil to keep an eye on Malik, and Naill happily agrees.

In the Blood Forest, while looking for Malec, Naill battles a large group of Craven with the others. When Reaver arrives, he alerts the group to the draken's appearance. That dealt with, Poppy casts the spell to find Malec, and Naill is surprised by the reaction.

Later, despite being tasked with guarding him, Naill doesn't realize that Malik isn't in his chambers but rather speaking with Poppy in the stables.

When they finally get to the Bone Temple, Naill remarks that the Blood Queen brought along some friends. He helps Emil unload Malec and then carries the casket with the other two, commenting on how heavy the god is.

Callum lifts the curse from Kieran with a white blade of some sort, and Naill's shocked to see the inky mist seeping from the wolven's wound. I imagine anything having to do with Primal magic is shocking, especially when it's all so new to them.

After Isbeth stabs Malec and the resulting fight ensues, Naill tries to save a Royal Guard from a dakkai but isn't fast enough. He does scruff and save Rune as the draken fire rains down on the Temple, however. Eventually, he's taken down by a dakkai and dies with his chest ripped open. When he revives, it's to find everyone alive and healed but with evidence of the fight still very much present.

As they're told the story of the realms, Naill knows it's only the beginning.

We all do.

Naill then leaves to try to find Malik and Millie.

DELANO AMICU

Delano is one of my favorites to see in my visions. He's not only adorable in his mortal form, he's also resplendent in his wolven form. A caretaker at the core, he's incredibly loyal and always there for whoever needs him.

Hair: White-blond.
Eyes: Pale, wintery blue.
Body type: Tall. Heavy and strong as an ox.
Facial features: Pale skin. Boyish appearance.
Distinguishing features: Near-constant crease in his brow.
Preternatural appearance: White fur.
Other: Imprint is springy and featherlight.
Personality: Reserved.
Habits/Mannerisms/Strengths/Weaknesses: Very fast. Loyal to a fault.
Background: Not bonded to an Elemental Atlantian. Whole den was killed by the Ascended, including his mother, father, and sisters. In a relationship with Perry.
Family: Mother †, father †, and unknown number of sisters †. Sister = Preela †. Partner = Perry.

DELANO'S JOURNEY TO DATE:

When he was young, the Ascended murdered Delano's entire den, including his parents and sisters—though the vamprys waited a while before killing them. His other sister, Preela, was later killed by King Jalara in front of her bonded Elemental Atlantian, Malik.

After the Blood Crown captured Casteel and he later escaped, Delano helped him remember who he was and reminded him that he wasn't a *thing*. He became part of Cas's inner circle and isn't very far from him at any given moment if he can help it.

Delano accompanies Emil to Masadonia when the Atlantian goes to feed Cas, but the next time he sees the Prince and Kieran isn't until they reach New Haven with the Maiden. They conduct several meetings to discuss plans and strategy and Elijah calls Delano a marshmallow. When he gets riled later, the Descenter says the marshmallow is getting crispy. Delano threatens him—as he should.

I absolutely love Delano being a marshmallow, though. It makes me smile.

A guard tries to leave Haven Keep with Poppy, and Delano ends up killing one of the Huntsmen in the stables during the escape attempt. Even though he doesn't know everything that happened in Masadonia—Kieran is supposed to update him later—he escorts Poppy to the dungeon.

While she's down there, he brings her cheese and bread and remarks that he'd bring her stew if he thought she wouldn't throw it at him. He also tells her that she would be dead if she were meant to be or they intended her to be.

Delano stays with her until Hawke arrives and then leaves to get some first-aid supplies, but a bit later, Jericho and his cohorts attack. Delano and Naill were about to take Poppy somewhere more comfortable, so they witnessed it all. Delano protects Poppy, even going so far as to throw her his sword so she can fight.

After her escape attempt and Cas chasing her to the woods, Casteel reveals that Poppy is part Atlantian, and it shocks Delano to the core. He wonders how the Prince knows but then sees the bite mark on Poppy's neck.

After switching locations and Poppy's most recent escape attempt, Delano stands guard outside her room and replies with the most snark he can muster every time she demands to be released. At one point, he rushes into her chambers, swearing he heard her screaming for help and calling his name. When she swears she was only screaming internally, Delano is confused.

He would find out later that it was the Primal *notam*.

The Ascended arrive, and Delano remains in wolven form, lurking in case he's needed. Then, he and Naill go to check the western roads, returning to tell everyone they are safe enough to travel.

During their journey, the Dead Bones Clan attacks the group. Delano leads the horses into the woods and then rejoins the fight. One of the clan members remarks that his fur would make a great cloak, and Delano bites him extra hard for the comment. After the battle, he retrieves the horses so they can be on their way again.

In Spessa's End, Delano offers Poppy some whiskey after dinner and asks her not to stab Casteel, telling her it makes him anxious.

The sky is suddenly ablaze, and Delano leaves to see why. When he returns, he's injured—shot with arrows. He collapses and passes out. Poppy heals him as she did with Beckett.

After Cas and Poppy's wedding, Delano travels with Naill and Beckett through the mist in the Skotos Mountains and plans to meet the others at Gold Rock. His group is the last to arrive, but it all worked out fine.

Following Poppy's attack at the Chambers of Nyktos, Delano arrives with the other wolven. They all encircle and protect Poppy, growling when anyone gets too close.

It soon becomes clear that Poppy is way more than she seems, and Delano joins the others in bowing to her and letting out a howl. Discovering that Beckett was the one who led Poppy to the Chambers, thus leading to her attack, Delano, Emil, and Naill go to find the youngster.

When Poppy is captured and taken to Irelone, Delano joins the group that sets out to rescue her. On their journey later, he discovers that he can feel what Poppy dreams. In response to her thinking she's a monster in sleep, he tells her that she's not, she's meyaah *Liessa*. Then he orders her to wake up—but not aloud; he tells her telepathically.

Poppy heals Quentyn's pain when they deliver the news that Beckett was murdered, and Delano's eyes glow with silvery wisps of light in his irises, just like hers, solidifying that the wolven are bonded to her.

And he will become one of the most closely bonded.

A carriage strikes down a child named Marji in town, and Delano runs to retrieve Cas and Poppy. He shifts and leads them to the little girl, but it's too late. He can't help but let out a whimper when she passes but is both relieved and awed when Poppy brings her back to life.

Delano extends an invitation to his King and *Liessa* to join in on some wolven wedding festivities. He asks his Queen to dance, and she tells him to call her *Poppy*, not something more formal.

After meeting with Poppy's brother Ian, Delano joins the group headed to the capital. Once they arrive, he witnesses the transfer of crowns and guards the couple during the Council meeting.

On the journey to Iliseeum, Delano wears double swords on his hips. When Cas starts teasing Poppy about my diary, Delano asks her not to stab his King.

But he likes that book just as much.

Vonetta falls through the tunnel floor on their trip to Iliseeum, and Delano uses a torch to illuminate the situation. His concern triples when he surveys the floor and sees that it won't hold much longer for any of them.

In the Land of the Gods, skeletons burst from the ground, and Delano asks how they're supposed to kill already-dead soldiers. After Poppy uses her power to end the fight and she and Cas embrace, while everyone is a bit uncomfortable, Delano remarks that Poppy and Cas kissing is better than them fighting.

Delano takes part in the large planning meeting to discuss Oak Ambler. When they reach the city, he leaves his cloak behind for someone who needs it, absolutely disturbed by the state of the citizens. Dressed as a Solis guard, he's wary as they enter the underground walkway in Castle Redrock, somehow sensing the Ascended know they've arrived. There are no guards at the tunnel entrances, and he imagines there would be, especially since it'd been breached in the past.

When they come across the caged cave cat, he suggests that the Ascended brought it with them to Castle Redrock and remarks that it looks underfed. When Poppy touches it, and it shifts forms to become a man, Delano tells her to stop touching things. He then wonders aloud if it's a wivern.

Headed off by Millie and her guards, Delano attacks and is taken down in record time, pinned by blades at his stomach and under his chin. When the taunts come about Isbeth, Delano states that it doesn't matter what the Blood Queen is because Poppy is a god.

After Cas surrenders, and the Blood Crown returns Tawny, Delano takes her to a room in Evaemon and summons the Healers and me.

Delano, Naill, Emil, and Vonetta accompany Poppy back to Oak Ambler to meet with King Jalara and deliver Poppy's *message*. Just before she kills the King, Poppy tells him that Delano comes from a line of those given mortal form by Nyktos himself. After she separates the King's head from his body, Delano drops Jalara's head at the Revenant's feet and then takes the dead King's crown to Poppy.

During their trip to Massene, Delano and Poppy communicate via the Primal *notam.* He tells her there are twenty Rise Guards at the northern gate and two dozen mortals on the wall. He relays that Emil can take out those on the Rise. Once given the signal and they deal with the guards, he follows Emil to the gate.

Traversing the underground chambers of Cauldra Manor, Delano leads the way with Vonetta and Sage to ensure Poppy's safety. As Poppy later wanders the ruins outside the manor, he accompanies her as a guard.

Like Poppy, Delano wonders about what Reaver said would happen if someone spoke the Consort's name in the mortal realm. He says it sounds like she's just as powerful as Nyktos.

When Poppy goes all Primal after receiving Casteel's finger from the Blood Queen, Delano protects Perry but then tries to comfort Poppy once she calms down.

During the meeting with the generals, Delano keeps an eye on things in wolven form and growls when Aylard insinuates that Poppy is more concerned about the people of Solis than those of Atlantia—her people.

On their return to Oak Ambler, Poppy alerts Delano that they're approaching the gate, and he telepathically assures her that she has their support. Then he, Vonetta, Sage, and Arden lead the wolven into the city.

When Perry is injured, Delano sits with him, reading from my journal—good reading material, indeed, and a great way to pass the time. However, I can't imagine it would lead to much relaxation. Quite the opposite, actually. Poppy checks on them and heals Perry, and Delano thanks her and then kisses his partner.

Later, as they're discussing the Primal magic they plan to use to locate Malec, Delano reminds everyone they still need a cherished item once they figure out the blood situation.

The group splits and plans to meet in Three Rivers. Delano and his group are forced to go to Padonia first, and Poppy reaches him via the *notam* there after she, Reaver, Kieran, and Malik leave Carsodonia with Casteel.

Poppy, Cas, and the others reach Padonia, and Delano launches himself at his King. Cas tells Delano that he missed him.

Malik hesitantly approaches and kneels by Delano, speaking softly. He nudges Malik's hand with his head, and Malik starts to cry and places a hand on him. They both miss Preela, and this is the first time they've had a chance to grieve together.

They narrow down that Malec is entombed near Masadonia, and Delano realizes that the Blood Forest grows where it does, partly because Malec is interred there. Three days later, they're near the Blood Forest, fighting a group of Craven and then casting the spell to locate Malec's entombment spot.

When they find the tunnel, Delano agrees with Sage when she indicates that the wolven should enter the tunnel first. As the Gyrms attack, Delano notices they aren't attacking Poppy, and he tells her that maybe they recognize her somehow.

At the Bone Temple, Delano makes his dislike of Callum very clear. When all hell breaks loose, Delano saves Malik from a dakkai while he's helping Millie and then knocks Poppy out of the way of draken fire. She tells him they need to get to

Malec and stop him from dying, and he tells her she has his support.

With her power, Isbeth sends Poppy's dagger back at her, and Delano jumps in front of Poppy to save her. The blade hits him in the chest, and he dies.

After Poppy merges with the Consort and brings everybody back to life, he nudges her with his nose, and she hugs him. He gets as close to her as possible, grateful to be alive and that those they love are also okay.

Delano accompanies Cas, Poppy, Kieran, and Nektas into the tunnels under Wayfair. They retrieve Ires, and Poppy goes into stasis. He returns with them and stays with Poppy in wolven form, watching out for her the entire time she's asleep.

When Malik and Millie arrive, Delano moves to protect Poppy but ends up letting them have some time with Kieran watching.

I'm very interested to see how Delano handles the news of Cas's shifting and Poppy awakening as a Primal.

PERRY

Hair: Dark and cropped.
Eyes: Amber.
Facial features: Rich brown skin. Handsome, broad, warm features.
Personality: Quick to smile. Generous.
Background: Not bonded to a wolven. In a relationship with Delano. Is a Lord; even has quarters at the palace. Likes cigars. Father wanted him to focus more on the land they owned and other business ventures instead of joining the army—Perry agreed.
Family: Father = Sven.

PERRY'S JOURNEY TO DATE:

When Perry meets Poppy and greets the rest of the group at the palace, Vonetta moves in to protect her from him. He takes that as confirmation that the rumors he's heard about the new Queen of Atlantia are true. He helps Poppy off her horse and then asks if Delano is with them since he hasn't seen his lover yet.

On the ship to Oak Ambler, Perry tells Poppy she'll get her sea legs in no time. It's clear she's not so sure. Once they arrive, he offers to keep a ship nearby for them to use to return to Atlantia. He's told to go back immediately—it's just too risky.

He pulls Casteel aside and asks him to keep an eye on Delano for him while they're apart, saying that sometimes the wolven is too brave. Cas promises that Delano will return to Perry.

Perry and the crew plan to take everything the group brought back to Atlantia—including my journal.

It's good to see that everyone is keeping it so safe.

Perry plays the part of taskmaster perfectly as they load and unload crates of wine bottles for Oak Ambler. The ruse allows Casteel to compel the guards and then slip with the others past the Rise.

Later, Perry arrives with Kieran and Emil to deliver the Blood Queen's *gift* to Poppy. He tells her the box has Primal magic and explains that those who know how to use it can create wards and spells that only respond to certain bloodlines. He relays that it should only require a drop or two of her blood. When asked how he knows all that, he explains that he learned about Primal magic from his father.

When Poppy loses control over seeing Casteel's dismembered finger, Delano—in wolven form—nudges him away.

As the storm kicks up, and the draken start falling from the sky, Perry arrives at Vessa's room to see that she's using Primal magic.

As Reaver tells them how the eather is stronger in thirdborn sons and daughters, Perry pays special attention and listens as the draken explains that Kolis's essence made the Revenants what they are—neither alive nor dead.

Perry takes his medallion off the gold chain he wears and gives it to Poppy to carry Casteel's wedding ring. He then sews the medallion into his armor—it's clearly special.

He also offers up his cigar box to store Poppy's and Casteel's crowns and joins the others to guard the couple as they brief the generals.

Later, Kieran retrieves Poppy to heal Perry after he's shot in the shoulder with an arrow. He argues that she doesn't need to worry about him when she has so much other stuff she needs to do.

As they talk about the book Delano is reading, Perry remarks that I have led an interesting life—boy, have I ever—and then says that Casteel must have been overjoyed to read the journal and then meet me at the Council meeting.

The feeling was—and still is—entirely mutual.

Poppy heals him, and then he and Delano share a sweet kiss.

Perry joins Poppy and Sven in discussing Primal magic. When his father seems a little scattered, he gives him some whiskey to help him think. Once he's settled, Perry asks why he keeps returning to the locator spell. As they get into more detail, Perry suggests that my journal may be the cherished item needed for the spell.

I mean, it's definitely prized by many, but given what I know of Primal magic, I don't think it would work as they intend.

When Poppy and the group return to Padonia with Cas, he gives the King a one-armed hug and tells him he looks good and that he's been keeping an eye on Delano—a twenty-four-hour assignment. (I'm sure it's one he doesn't mind.) He adds that he never doubted that Kieran and their Queen would get Casteel back.

He catches sight of Malik and stiffens, his jaw tensing when he sees that the Prince looks good and not like he's been a prisoner for a century.

As they discuss what happened while they were away, Perry tells them that no one was left alive in Whitebridge. Thousands were killed and turned into Craven—so many, they actually lost soldiers and wolven during the fight.

Once they discover that Eloana and I buried Malec in the Blood Forest, Perry realizes they never knew the blood trees grew where they did because it was the place of Malec's interment.

Three days later, Perry joins the group in fighting a large group of Craven while looking for the god. He wields a bloodstone axe like an extension of his arm.

When Emil complains about the trees *leaking* and asks what it is, Perry quips that it's in the name, insinuating that it's blood.

Noticing that the Gyrms protecting Malec didn't attack Poppy, he points it out to the others and says that he can't be the only one who notices.

I lost track of him after that. I'm not sure if he was there when they went to the Bone Temple or if he stayed behind, but I know it's not the last we'll see of this fascinating Elemental Atlantian.

HISA FA'MAR

Hair: Jet-black. She wears it in a single braid.
Eyes: Amber.
Body type: Tall. Muscular.
Facial features: Skin is light brown with golden undertones.
Personality: No-nonsense.
Habits/Mannerisms/Strengths/Weaknesses: Knows the magic that can create Gyrms.
Background: Elemental Atlantian. Commander of the Crown Guard.
Family: Unknown. Her family of choice is wolven Lizeth Damron, whom she is in a relationship with.

HISA'S JOURNEY TO DATE:

I do not know much about Hisa's beginnings, but I hope to fill in those details as soon as possible. However, I can recount how she fits into the story once Poppy and Casteel enter the picture.

After the Unseen attack at the Contou residence, Hisa orders the guards to search the grounds. She mentions the Descenter mask found at the arson site and surmises that between that, the courtyard attack, and the ruins, they must all be connected and the work of the Unseen.

She's present when Poppy and Casteel meet with Valyn and Eloana at Cove Palace. She's also in attendance for the couple's crowning and immediately begins shadowing her new charges.

Joining Kieran, Vonetta, Delano, Emil, and Naill, Hisa stands guard for the Council meeting. I remember seeing her there—she's beautiful, has a presence, and is hard to miss.

When the group goes to Iliseeum for the first time, Hisa leads them through the crypts to the access tunnels and uses her keys to unlock the entrance. When they go to leave, she asks them to be safe and says the kingdom wants to get to know their new rulers.

Attending the planning meeting with Casteel's parents, she realizes the land party will be spotted before the by-sea group even arrives in Oak Ambler—all attention will be on them. She then becomes part of that group, arriving by land with Lyra and Emil posing as Poppy and Cas. Unfortunately, the Ascended capture them almost immediately.

After Tawny gets injured, Hisa remarks that she's never seen a mortal wounded by shadowstone before and wonders if/hopes one of the Elders might know how to help. I did, thankfully.

When she's ready to send her *message,* Poppy asks Hisa to send word to the Blood Crown that she wants to meet with them at the end of the following week and says to let them know she'll only speak with the King or the Queen.

Once the group makes it to Massene, Hisa undertakes the task of creating a map of Oak Ambler. Later, she encourages Poppy to share the plans and makes sure to be present for the briefing with the generals. When they discuss warning the mortals before they converge on the cities, Hisa agrees that it's a good idea. They then go over battle strategy, and she states they should kill any Ascended who attack, but only capture those who surrender. As planning drags on, she voices her concerns about the timing of rescuing Casteel and says she disagrees with that part of the scheme.

As the others go off, Hisa stays with Valyn to ensure the plans are followed. When her girlfriend, General Lizeth Damron, goes to leave to take care of her duties, she tells her to be careful. Lizeth responds: "But be brave." And Hisa says, "Always," before kissing her.

I love that so much.

Hisa and Valyn lead the army inside the city. Once there, she searches Castle Redrock with him and the other soldiers. They find and fight the Craven inside. When they encounter the Priests and Priestesses, Poppy has Hisa watch Framont and the others as she speaks with Valyn. After, they follow the Ascended Priestess to the room where the bodies of all the murdered children are.

As they settle in later, discussions turn to using magic to help locate Casteel. Not long after, Atlantian visitors arrive—Tawny and Gianna—and Hisa is unhappy that Lin didn't get their names. When she sees Tawny and the evident changes in the mortal, she's understandably leery of her.

In Padonia, Hisa joins the generals at the entrance to the manor. Later, over dinner, she and Lizeth share a quiet moment, and she insinuates that she knows why Isbeth wants Malec. Wondering about the *after,* Hisa asks what's to become of the god after they defeat the Blood Crown. Do they put him back in the ground? She's told someone will return him to his parents, Nyktos and his Consort—likely Reaver.

The night of Poppy, Cas, and Kieran's Joining, Hisa spends time with Jasper and Valyn.

Once they retrieve Malec, Hisa rides next to the wagon, guarding their prize. When Poppy replies to Sven's order to, "Be careful" with, "But be brave," it makes Hisa smile.

During the big battle with Isbeth at the Bone Temple, a Revenant with shadowstone kills Hisa. Later, she revives and ends up sitting on a wall, staring at Poppy—likely in awe.

LIZETH DAMRON

Hair: Chin-length and icy-blond.
Eyes: Wintery blue.
Facial features: Fair skin.
Background: Wolven. A general of the Atlantian Army.
Family: Unknown. Her family of choice is Elemental Atlantia Hisa Fa'Mar, Commander of the Crown Guard.

LIZETH'S JOURNEY TO DATE:
Like Hisa, I do not know much about Lizeth. Therefore, I can only tell you what I saw as it pertains to others.

Lizeth enters my field of view after Poppy and Casteel are crowned the new King and Queen of Atlantia.

Just before the meeting with the generals, Lizeth arrives with General Aylard and is curious about what's going on. When the generals and others discuss strategy, Lizeth approves of the assessment that controlling the supplies to other ports is good—it will prevent the Blood Crown's forces from entering that way, too. Seeing the map of Oak Ambler for the first time, she instantly knows it's Hisa's work.

When Poppy displays her power, Lizeth drops to a knee and addresses her as meyaah *Liessa*.

Before setting out for Oak Ambler, she and her girlfriend, Hisa, share a tender goodbye.

Later in Padonia, she welcomes the group's arrival with Sven.

Over dinner, when she and Hisa are talking quietly, and Hisa mentions knowing why Isbeth wants Malec, she surmises that it's because the Blood Queen thinks he will give her Atlantia.

Despite being a general, Lizeth looks forward to nothing more than an end to the war once and for all.

LABYRINTHINE ESCAPADES

Dearest Diary,

This evening's rendezvous deserves an entry. I knew the minute I walked away, sated and smiling, that I wanted to capture the event in glorious detail.

The air felt charged tonight during my time out, though whether from an encroaching storm or my excitement, I knew not. Regardless, it kissed me as it passed, billowing my gown and caressing my bared skin, making goose bumps rise deliciously. I can feel them in this moment as I write, a frisson of anticipation skittering down my spine.

I can almost taste the whiskey I sipped as I walked, the scents of jasmine and night-blooming roses surrounding me like a fine perfume, reminding me of the buxom blonde I dallied with some moons prior. She'd smelled of forbidden nights and wicked fantasies—something we'd made a reality. Mmm. I'm shivering now just remembering it.

But back to tonight's adventure...

As I walked to join my paramour for our scandalous tryst, an agreement made on the dance floor of a Lord and Lady's pre-Rite ball, the maze rose on either side of me, its lush, leafy walls silvery-green in the moonlight. I reached out and touched the shrubs, the scrape of the sheared branches and leaves on my palm and fingertips reminding me of whiskers on delicate flesh.

Making my way to the center of the labyrinth, I recall thinking of what awaited me there. Not a mystical beast of lore, but a virile male of exquisite masculine beauty—though if I'm being honest (and I am always honest with myself) I'd hoped he would devour me in much more pleasurable ways.

Even now, here in my chambers, my face stretches as I remember the thought—and the ways in which those hopes were fulfilled.

But I'm getting ahead of myself.

I made my way through the twisting and turning hedgerows until I reached the center of the maze, finishing my last sip of liquor as I cleared the leafy wall, the delicate burn of the spirits like a warm hug. It lit me from within, but not as much as the scene spread out before me.

The gracious hosts of this evening's activities—well, the ones inside the manor, anyway—had bedecked their labyrinthian garden with an ornate wrought iron table and chairs and tall sconce torches with flickering firelight.

The circular clearing was filled with flowering trees that I knew would be a vibrant fuchsia in the daylight but were the color of mulled wine in the incandescent glow of the moon.

But even that wasn't what caught my attention. No, what had me stopped in my tracks, my gaze riveted, was the man sprawled on a cushioned chaise lounge, his taut, toned skin on display, nothing but the gossamer tail of one of the curtains affixed to the arch under which he sat covering his manhood.

His features were as I remembered yet made almost more ethereal by the moonlight. Chiseled cheeks and square jaw, a scar running along his cheekbone to his right temple. The healed wound only heightened his attractiveness and lent credence to his strength. He had an intelligence about him that you couldn't escape, even from one look into his gorgeous green eyes, slightly hooded and highlighted by the slash of dark brows. His tawny hair was just above shoulder-length and wavy, giving him a roguish air and blatant sex appeal that had first drawn me to him across the ballroom.

I continued taking him in, my wandering gaze traveling leisurely from head to toe. Even from the distance, I could see that he was primed and ready for me, eagerly awaiting my arrival.

I clearly remember now the thrill that ran through me, the sense of power and pride. Just the anticipation of meeting me here had done these things to a man who had seemed so very much in control earlier in the eve. I also remember thinking—and hoping—that he'd exert some of that control over me.

He did not disappoint.

I walked toward him, putting an extra sway in my step, and running my tongue over the rim of the crystal glass I held, holding his gaze the entire way.

I set the tumbler on the table as I passed, watching, attention rapt, as General Ximien palmed himself through the gauzy curtain, the muscles in his bent leg bunching, the moonlight glinting off sweat already dotting his tempting skin the captivating color of amber.

When I reached him, I started disrobing, slowly, pieces and accoutrements of my festival attire falling to the dewy grass beneath my slippered feet, my gaze never leaving his.

He peered up at me all the while, the light in his eyes flashing, his teeth gripping the plump flesh of his lower lip, impressive chest heaving with breaths.

I asked him if he liked what he saw, and his only response was a deep groan as he gripped himself harder.

When I shed the last vestiges of my attire, I let my hair down, watching as a blue-black curl fell forward to flirt with a nipple. The silky feel of it added to the intense pleasure I felt starting to spiral up my spine, making the already tight buds bead almost painfully in the humid night air.

And still, he merely stared—the appreciation in his gaze ratcheting my desire. Something about the distance between us was even more erotic than if he'd reached for me, that charge in the air creating an invisible tether that turned into a buzz in my blood. Yet despite the excitement, I felt empty, bereft. In need of touch.

And so, I touched myself. I gripped my breasts, palming the heavy globes and pinching the tingling tips between my fingers, my eyes closing and head falling back on a sigh.

In a heartbeat, I felt the air stir and heard movement as General Ximien, one of Queen Heana's Royal Guards, jerked me against his hard body, his pulsing cock trapped between us, leaving a cooling trail of wetness behind as he shifted for better access. I suddenly wanted to know what he would taste like. Would he be smoky? Sweet? Tart?

But before I could voice those desires, he had my hair wrapped around a fist and his mouth on mine, a finger sliding into the crevice of my backside as he pulled me tighter against him.

It was no tentative kiss. It was one of claiming—unleashed passion and pent-up desire, coalescing into a firestorm of need. I remember thinking that if our first kiss was such, the rest of the night should be *glorious, indeed.*

I reached between us and palmed his impressive erection, the silky feel of his skin over the steel beneath wringing a groan from me. The Arae had blessed him. My fingers barely touched around the thickness of his shaft, and when I opened my hand, my fingertips finding the coarse curls of his groin, the time it took in my slide until the heel of my hand reached his tip was a bit shocking—in the most captivating and exciting way.

I recall thinking that I couldn't wait to feel the stretch and burn of him. To see if his curve hit me in that spot inside that made galaxies burst to life behind my eyes.

He released my hair and hoisted me into his powerful arms. I wrapped my legs around him, the ridges of his abdomen creating a delicious friction that had me tightening my thighs and rotating my hips in his hold.

He raised an eyebrow and flashed me a devastating smile, whispering something about me being greedy before nipping my lip. I can't remember if I said anything in return.

When he deposited me on the chaise, I wondered if we'd go straight to the fucking—I was certainly primed and ready—or if he'd have other ideas. Turned out, he had a great many other ideas.

He urged me back on the cushion and then jerked me down, his fingers indenting on my thighs in a way that had me wondering if I'd have bruises on the morrow. They'd be badges of honor if they did manifest.

He urged my thighs apart, moving closer to drape first one and then the other leg over his broad shoulders as he flashed me a lascivious grin.

And then he descended.

He ran his turgid tongue along the length of me several times, then delved deeply, swirling and twisting that wonderful muscle in ways no other lover had (and I have been with a great many and varied bedpartners over my long life). Just as he had me panting, he retreated, but not far, just up a bit to lap at that bundle of nerves already throbbing for him. For more.

He repeated the process several times, always keeping me guessing as to what he would do next. All I could do was try to breathe and grip his sandy hair in my fists, urging him on as my body came alive.

When I finally crested that peak and cried out my pleasure to the night, my muscles locked tight and core convulsing in a seemingly never-ending wave, he drank of me as if I were the finest wine.

With one final scandalous lick, he raised his head, a knowing smirk on his face, and then told me I was delicious as he took my lips in a searing kiss so I could taste for myself.

In that moment, I wanted to return the favor. I wanted to see how he tasted and thought back to my initial thoughts as I'd felt the evidence of his desire on my stomach. When I told him as much, he actually declined. I wasn't sure that a man before him had ever said no to having my lips wrapped around their cock. But this one, he said that he wanted to be deep inside me when he found his release. That he wanted to feel me squeezing him so tightly it was almost painful before I shattered and screamed his name to the heavens.

And that's exactly what he did.

With barely a warning, he sheathed himself in me, to the hilt, and the wanton invasion startled a gasp out of me. As expected, he stretched me delightfully and hit me so deeply, the combination of sensations was just shy of pain. But that fever-bright edge of pleasure-pain only coiled my need tighter.

He set a beautiful rhythm, not too fast and not too slow, and I swiveled and lifted my hips to meet each thrust, holding on for the ride, my arms barely able to wrap around his broad chest and shoulders, my nails digging in.

He hissed at one point and asked for more, and I obliged, scoring his back with evidence of the pleasure he wrought.

When he shifted positions and found that spot deep inside me, I did indeed see stars. And he was punishing in his single-minded tenacity to wring every last ounce of pleasure from me until I did—as he'd wanted—scream his name to the moon, the night birds taking flight from the trees, their cries in harmony with mine.

Even now, in the quiet of my room, I remember the ecstasy. I felt that orgasm from the top of my head to the tips of my toes and everywhere in between. The tingling rush and tightening release as I simply let go and gave myself over to the pleasure. It was extraordinary.

I had assumed that he would follow me, but he surprised me yet again by picking me up in one deft move and moving us both to the cool dampness of the lawn, the chilled dew a striking contrast to my heated flesh.

He positioned me on my hands and knees, running a calloused palm down my spine and eliciting a shiver before caressing and grasping one round globe of my ass.

He gently lowered my head with a hand on my hair, and I felt his broad tip at my entrance. I braced myself for another invasion, but he eased himself in this time with aching slowness, tiny advances and delightful retreats, the friction of the slide making my body come alive again in ways I didn't think possible.

When the teasing almost became too much, I pushed back into him, and he moved his hands to hold me still, gently admonishing me before leaning over to nip my earlobe and swirl that incomparable tongue around the shell of my ear.

He continued his erotic torment until I found myself doing something I didn't remember ever doing before. I begged. I pleaded. I whimpered for release. I wanted to feel bad about that, but I didn't. And even now as I write this, I don't. I loved that he had given me something I hadn't experienced before.

But those words, the sounds I let free, seemed to make something snap in him. Suddenly, he was thrusting with such an intensity, I worried it might break me, but...what a way to go. When he reached around and down and pressed against my clit, I erupted in another intense orgasm, the force of it locking the air in my lungs.

With two final thrusts, his thighs connecting with mine, he roared his release to the night.

I still couldn't catch my breath, much less hold myself up any longer, but before I could extricate myself or fall flat on my face, he rose and urged me up with him, the two of us still connected, still throbbing. He loosely wrapped a gentle hand around my throat, his thumb caressing my pulse point, and kissed my shoulder, then my neck, causing a new flurry of goose bumps to rise.

I tipped my head to the side to give him better access, and he didn't disappoint. Just as I felt him starting to slip free of me, he kissed the spot behind my ear, gently, sweetly, making me sigh. And then he whispered something I will never forget.

He said, "You are a remarkable and extraordinary creature, Wilhelmina Colyns. You have beauty to rival the gods, and cunning to put any cave cat to shame. You have utterly bewitched me, and I shall never forget you for as long as I live. I will take these memories with me into battle when next I am called."

I turned in his arms and kissed him then, showing him without words how much I appreciated the evening, as well. We had given each other things that I didn't think either of us realized were missing.

We dressed in silence, simply stealing appreciative glances at each other. He helped me with the last bits of my corset and gown, even though I didn't need the help, and I assisted in straightening the lapels of his vest and the cuffs of his shirt.

We shared one last dance under the stars, no music but the sounds nature provided, and then kissed sweetly one last time, an intimate goodbye.

I turned as I was leaving the clearing, wanting a mental portrait of the setting to take with me. General Ximien was fastening his sword belt around his waist and tucking a wicked-looking dagger into his boot but looked up at me with such a look of reverence it made my body flush.

He called to me that he'd find me again, and I gave him a saucy wink and told him he could try, then made my way through the intricate hedgerow maze once more, so dazed from pleasure that I took a couple of wrong turns and had to double back.

When I reached my carriage and headed home, the events of the night continued to play in my mind, just as they do now.

I have always said that life is for living and I have never been one to waste a day, but I think if anyone were to ask me, I might give up one of those days for another hour in that man's arms. The pleasure he brought me was incredible—and as you know, diary, I am no stranger to seduction and pleasure. Plus, I was able to take one of the Blood Queen's guards away from his Royal duty for a while. Just long enough for what I saw in my vision to manifest—or at least I hope.

I guess we'll see.

Still, tonight was definitely an encounter fit for these pages.

Willa

QUEEN ILEANA (A.K.A ISBETH) †

Isbeth is a complex ruler. She started out as merely a woman in love, but circumstances embittered her and caused her to become something cold—and all of that was before she had time to let the circumstances of her unusual Ascension affect her. I could give her a pass; she did, after all, lose her child and have her love stolen from her, and all after being denied the one thing she wanted most. However, we all have a choice in how we behave and whether we use the things that happen to us in our lives to make us better, transmuting that negative energy so we vibrate at an even higher frequency and then using it to help others. Or if we fall into the despair and let it turn us dark. Isbeth embraced her need for revenge and let go of all her light to reach her ultimate goals.

Hair: Dark auburn in loose, waist-length curls.

Eyes: Nearly black.

Body type: Slender. Almost impossibly narrow waist.

Facial features: Pale skin. Lush, red lips. High, arched brows. High cheekbones.

Distinguishing features: Nose pierced with ruby gem. Faint glimmer of silver in her pupils.

Other: Also known as Queen Ileana. Laugh like tinkling bells. Smells like roses and vanilla.

Personality: Cruel. Conniving. Vindictive. Strategic. Dramatic. Narcissistic.

Habits/Mannerisms/Strengths/Weaknesses: Still loves Malec. Has a thing for cleanliness. Incredibly detail oriented. Wears Malec's ring on her index finger—Atlantian gold with a pink diamond.

Background: Demis—was Ascended by a god. Malec's heartmate. Queen of Solis.

Family: Son = name unknown † (killed by Alastir). Daughters = Millicent and Penellaphe.

ISBETH'S JOURNEY TO DATE:

As the Queen of Solis, Ileana was always on my radar. As an Atlantian, I simply couldn't abide what she and her people were doing. But when I started getting glimpses of overlapping items for her—layered images, even—it was *then* that I realized there was much more than meets the eye when it came to the Blood Queen.

When I saw the meeting between Poppy and Ileana, whereupon she revealed her true identity, I knew that nothing would ever be the same. It answered so many questions yet created a multitude of others at the same time.

From the minute Poppy, Cas, and their people come face-to-face with Ileana/Isbeth following Ian's invitation, the Blood Queen employs the snark. There is seemingly no end to her narcissism. When Poppy gives as good as she gets, Isbeth remarks that Ian didn't tell her that Poppy had found and sharpened her tongue.

She asks Poppy if she's bonded to Kieran. When she responds that she's bonded to all the wolven, the Queen taunts Malik and tells him he missed out. She then adds that she knows Poppy became Queen of Atlantia—just as she hoped—but that she married the wrong brother. Malik chimes in and confirms that, yes, Poppy was to be Ascended, and that *he* was to be her Ascension of the flesh.

Cas lashes out at his brother, and Ileana chimes in that she's curious about which of the brothers would win in a fight. She says she'd bet on Casteel as he was always a fighter, even when on the verge of being broken.

She makes it clear that she invited them so they could come to an agreement regarding the future. She says she is fond of Poppy but warns her against thinking that the care is a weakness because she is *the* Queen and demands respect.

Ileana reveals that Alastir told her about the ultimatum Poppy and Cas came to give and doesn't hide her joy when she finds out that he's dead. As they talk about the deal some more, Ileana vehemently states that she will see the entire kingdom burn before she offers even a single acre of land. She then counteroffers: claim Atlantia in her name and swear fealty to her. She tells them they can keep their Prince and Princess titles but that she will send several of her Dukes and Duchesses over to establish Royal Seats in Atlantia. Once they make the citizens believe it's what's best for the kingdom and dismantle the armies, they are then to bring Queen Eloana and King Valyn to Carsodonia to be tried for treason.

As talk of war surfaces once more, Ileana tells them she has over one hundred thousand mortal soldiers and several thousand Royal Knights if it comes to that. Still, they should really be worrying about the Revenants...because they're not mortal. She demonstrates this by having Millicent killed so they can all watch her resurrect. She explains more about the Revenants and says she has enough to make an army.

She states that the War of Two Kings never ended; there has merely been a strained truce. She then adds that she wants the Atlantian people's respect, which is why she hasn't yet attacked. Poppy argues as Poppy is wont to do, and then Ileana reveals that the people likely won't be so accepting once they discover their new leader is the Queen of Solis's daughter.

Poppy tells her that Duchess Teerman said that Ileana was her grandmother. In response, Ileana calls her loyal but stupid. She tells Poppy that she is her mother and explains why she had Cora raise her. She then claims that she had no idea about the abuse Duke Teerman inflicted upon Poppy and says she would have flayed the skin from his bones and left him to be eaten by buzzards had she known. She also reveals that Cora was a Revenant and that she survived the Craven attack at Lockswood but not Ileana's wrath for absconding with Poppy.

After that big revelation, she adds that she isn't actually Ascended and wasn't the first vampry. She then details her poisoning at the hands of Eloana, as well as her Ascension by Malec, whom she insists Eloana ruined.

Seeing the doubt, Isbeth proves she's not Ascended by ripping off the curtains and remaining unharmed in the sunlight. It shocks those gathered, but not as much as her next tidbit. She tells them that Malec is a god, and that Eloana didn't know. She shares Malec's plan and what happened and says that the former King and Queen of Atlantia took everything from her when all she did wrong was love. She says she'll never feel again what she felt for Malec and vows to take everything from them—from Atlantia—in retribution.

When Poppy tells her that the blame lies with her and nobody else, Isbeth orders Ian to be killed, claiming that she loved him as if he were her child and flipping everything around on Poppy, telling her Ian's death was *her* fault.

Manipulative sociopath, much?

In her rage, Poppy's power flares and takes Isbeth by surprise, though she easily redirects the eather with a single flick of her nails. She then tells her daughter that Poppy's greatest weakness is that she doubts what she sees with her eyes and knows with her heart. She tells her that they're gods and should fight like gods. She follows the proclamation with a show of power that grips Poppy by the throat to teach her a valuable lesson.

Lyra attacks to save Poppy, and Isbeth kills her without hesitation. When others move to attack in response, she warns that if anyone else even thinks it, she will snap Poppy's neck. Turning her attention back to her daughter, she says that Poppy needs to learn that she never had a choice, even though she still believes she does.

As Isbeth tightens her hold on Poppy, Casteel pleads with her to stop and offers to give himself up, stating it's how the Queen can best control Poppy—by taking what she values most. She remarks that he was always her favorite pet and says that when Poppy wakes, she'll know exactly what needs to be done to keep her husband alive.

She orders Malik to retrieve his brother and allows the others to leave, giving them Tawny as a sign of *goodwill*, though with a shadowstone wound.

They leave and head back to Carsodonia, where she has Malik and all the Revenants watching Casteel.

Visiting her new prisoner, she tries to get Cas on her side and to *open his eyes*. When Cas accuses her of being the reason Poppy has her scars and states she was abused, Isbeth is clearly bothered and asks if the Duke's death was painful. Cas tells her yes, that he made it so, and she tells him she's glad.

As talk turns to Casteel's parents, Isbeth says that she pitied his mother. She didn't hate her at first, but she certainly does now. Isbeth then tells him that she's a demis and asks what Cas knows about Malec.

After Poppy beheads Jalara, Isbeth tells Casteel what happened, and he laughs. She also tells him that Poppy claimed Malec is alive, knows where he is, and threatened to kill him. When she says that she believes Poppy could actually do it, she asks Cas if it's true that the god is still alive and where he is. He tells her he doesn't know, and she believes him.

Talking more, Isbeth says she never wanted to be at war with her daughter.

She fully expected Poppy to go along with the plans and let Malik Ascend her. She then adds that she doesn't just want Atlantia, she wants more, and things have already begun—Poppy was destined to help her accomplish her goals.

Casteel taunts her about seeing a cave cat in Oak Ambler and asks if it's the same one Poppy saw as a child. Isbeth tells him the cat is fine and in the same place Poppy saw it, then threatens to feed it the next finger she takes from Casteel—the first being the one she sent to Poppy with the note of *apology* and his wedding ring.

Taking her unawares, Cas stabs her in the chest with a sharpened bone, barely missing her heart by an inch.

Remarking on how strong Cas is, she says it's to be expected; he's Elemental and also has Poppy's blood in him. She tells him about the Primals' weakness and how love can be used as weapons to impair and then end them, that a Primal can be born in the mortal realm—something she learned from Malec—and that the gods rushed the Primals into their eternity by Ascending. However, she says the Fates created a loophole that allowed the greatest power to rise again, but only in a female of the Primal of Life's lineage, thus suggesting that Isbeth didn't birth a god, she birthed a *Primal*: Poppy.

When Poppy and the group come to rescue Casteel, her subjects carry Isbeth into the Great Hall on a litter that looks like a gilded bird cage. Basking in the thunderous reception she receives, Isbeth remarks that she won't waver in the face of a godless kingdom and then tells the crowd that the harbinger has awakened, and that Atlantia is laying waste to cities while raping and brutalizing the people of Solis. She follows that with a promise the people will be spared, before asking them to avenge their King.

Isbeth gives a subject a *Royal Blessing*, gloating because the truth is out, and those with Poppy know what's actually happening. Later, she tells Poppy she can easily reclaim the lost cities, earning some name-calling from her daughter. Poppy then breaks Malik's mental shields, and Callum gets stabbed. Isbeth tells Poppy that what she did wasn't nice and orders the *mess* and Malik to be removed.

Flexing her power some more, she grabs Poppy by the chin and reminds her that she carried her in her womb and cared for her until it wasn't safe to do so. She says that's why she tolerates from her what she wouldn't take from anyone else, and why she'll give Poppy what she hasn't earned. She tells her that she can see Casteel or her father—the cave cat, Ires—but not both, and then adds that she must choose now or see neither.

Isbeth separates Kieran, Reaver, and Poppy and has Malik escort the men to individual rooms. As she leads Poppy through Wayfair, she reminds her that Reaver's and Kieran's safety depends on her behavior and brings up watching Poppy and Ian running through the halls they now walk, once again rehashing the painful memory of Ian's death.

When Poppy sees the state Casteel is in, she lashes out, and Isbeth tells her that threats aren't necessary and are actually pointless since her Revenants can't be killed, and any draken who remain are with the Atlantian armies.

Isbeth taunts Poppy that Cas would be in better condition if he just behaved, and Poppy reacts with a show of power. Isbeth warns her that she'll only tolerate so much disrespect, which causes Poppy to pull back. The Queen remarks that Poppy is powerful and has grown, but she'd better learn to control her temper, and fast.

While talking about Coralena, Isbeth insinuates that the Handmaiden hid her actual eye color—the nearly colorless hue—from Poppy with magic that Isbeth *lent to* her.

Sometime later, Callum gets stabbed again, and it annoys Isbeth. Because Millie laughed, she orders her other daughter to remove the Revenant. Poppy asks Isbeth how she's been able to hide her identity from the Ascended for so long, and she says that they don't look too closely and would rather be oblivious than see what's right in front of them. Not to mention, they see her as being godlike. She adds that those who *do* question are swiftly dealt with.

Looking at her daughter, Isbeth tells Poppy that her eyes are like her father's and says the essence would get stronger and swirl in them when he got angry. Poppy asks Isbeth how she captured Ires, and the Blood Queen says that he came to her two hundred years after the war ended, looking for his brother. She then adds that the *one with him*—presumably, Jadis—could sense Malec's blood and led Ires right to her. Isbeth also reveals that the draken had been *dealt with*.

She relays that while she knew Malec had a twin, she thought it was Malec when she first saw Ires—until he spoke. She even entertained the idea that maybe she could *pretend* it was Malec and fall in love with Ires. When Poppy inquires, Isbeth tells her that she didn't force herself on Ires. He chose to stay. She said he'd become intrigued by the world and curious about the Ascended and what his brother had been doing, but when he wanted to return to Iliseeum, she couldn't let him. He was angry, but when they came together, both times, it wasn't against his will. It wasn't an act of love, but she wanted a strong child and knew what Poppy would be with Ires as her father. For him, it was just about lust and hatred. He even tried to kill her afterward.

When Poppy asks her where Ires is, Isbeth tells her that he's not at Wayfair, silently confirming that the Blood Queen wouldn't have let her see him even if Poppy *had* chosen him over Casteel. She says she couldn't let Ires leave because she needs him to make Revenants. She also lets it slip that the etchings in the stone and the *borrowed* magic are safeguards to keep things in—and out.

The two continue to bicker: about Poppy not bowing, about the Rite and the Craven, about Poppy being the harbinger. And Isbeth tells Poppy if the Atlantian armies show up at the capital, she will line the Rise with infants. To which Poppy says she won't negotiate.

Isbeth admits that vengeance has kept her going all this time and states she doesn't actually want Atlantia; she wants to see it burn, and every Atlantian dead. But she doesn't blame Eloana, even though she has something very *special* in store for her. She blames Nyktos for not answering Malec's call for the heartmate trial. That was the catalyst and why Malec Ascended her in the first place. The Primal could have prevented all of what happened.

She goes on to say that Malec said Nyktos was particularly fond of the Atlantians and saw them as his children. Their creation was the result of the first heartmate trial and a product of love. By eliminating them, Isbeth feels she would get the justice she seeks.

As they continue talking, she tells Poppy that she'll do what she was born to do: deliver death to her enemies. She says that Poppy's just like her, and Isbeth will force her hand if necessary to prove how alike they are.

Then, as an act of power, she kills a mortal couple by crushing them with her will. When Poppy lashes out, she has her escorted to her room and kept under guard, telling her they'll talk more later.

After Poppy and the others escape, Isbeth catches up to them and tries to take Malik back. In the melee, Callum wounds and curses Kieran. Isbeth orders Poppy to find Malec and bring him to her and warns them all that there's no escape—they're surrounded by Revenants. She adds that if Poppy refuses her command, she'll regret it until her last breath. She gives Poppy a week to retrieve Malec. Poppy demands three, and Isbeth agrees to two. When Poppy says she needs something of Malec's, Isbeth hands over the pink diamond ring that used to belong to her heartmate, saying it's all she has of him.

Before she leaves, Isbeth kills Blaz and Clariza, making them nothing but dry husks and saying that the only good Descenter is a dead one.

Isbeth arrives at the Bone Temple with a sizable force. When Poppy and the others arrive, she asks where Malec is and refuses to have the curse lifted from Kieran until she sees the god. Once the casket is open, she tells them that he won't rise unless given blood and that nothing can wake him. She speaks old Atlantian to Malec and then gives the okay for Callum to lift the curse on Kieran when Cas reminds her to live up to her end of the bargain. She once again states that if Nyktos had only granted them the heartmates trial, they'd be together, though not ruling over Atlantia. They'd have traveled the realm, found a place where they felt at peace, and would have lived out their days with their son and any other children they may have had. She then tells Malec how much she loves him and insists that he has to know that, even in sleep. She kisses him and reiterates how much he and their son mean to her, then pleads with him to understand as she screams and stabs him in the heart with a shadowstone dagger. Sobbing, she apologizes some more and shouts for her army to protect their King—meaning Kolis.

Isbeth continues to taunt Poppy, and a fight breaks out. When Delano dies, the battle turns godlike. Isbeth is eventually wounded: a cut curving across her temple, narrowly missing her left eye, another on her forehead, and her nose and mouth bleeding. But when Millie tries to remove the dagger from Malec's chest to stop the events in motion, Isbeth has enough in her to take out her first daughter with eather, remarking that she's been betrayed by *both* daughters.

When Poppy gets the upper hand, she rips the crown from Isbeth's head and backhands her with it, knocking out some teeth. Then, when Poppy screams the Consort's name, Isbeth can only watch in stunned amazement. The awe soon turns to terror.

Poppy tells her that the Consort knew what Isbeth plotted and saw it all in her sleep. Isbeth argues that the Consort must know that she did it all for Malec and her child—the Consort's son and grandson. Poppy returns that it was all for nothing. The Consort likely would have forgiven Malec for Ascending Isbeth, but her grief, hatred, and thirst for vengeance rotted her. What she became and brought upon the realm will not save her, heal her, or take away her pain. It will not bring her glory, love, or peace.

Then the Consort, through Poppy, tells Isbeth that what she's done to those of her blood will not be erased. Nothing of Isbeth will be recorded in history yet to be written. She will not be known or worthy of remembrance. Then, Poppy—with the Consort—strikes out with power, breaking Isbeth's arms, legs, and spine. She speaks in the Consort's voice and tells Isbeth that her death won't be honorable or quick, and that Nyktos awaits, ready to start her eternity in the Abyss. Isbeth bleeds from her pores. Her flesh cracks and peels as muscles and ligaments tear, and bones splinter. Her hair falls out, no longer rooted.

And then, she is no more.

KING JALARA †

While a vital piece of the puzzle, I must admit that King Jalara is somewhat gray-washed to me. Alas, he did play a role in history and thus must be recorded.

Hair: Golden, brushing the tops of his ears.
Facial features: Heavy brow. Straight nose. Square jaw. Thin lips.
Distinguishing features: Good-looking.
Personality: Smug.
Habits/Mannerisms/Strengths/Weaknesses: Always wears his crown. Rarely smiles.
Background: King of Solis. Originally from the Vodina Isles. By the time he fought in Pompay at the Battle of Broken Bones, Malec was no longer on the throne. It's said that he was close to Leopold's father. Was alive during the Atlantian's rule. Killed Preela.

JALARA'S JOURNEY TO DATE:

Honestly, Jalara seemed to blend into the background more often than not during my research. Until Isbeth makes her move. *Then*, Jalara starts to flex the muscles of his position a bit more.

When Poppy arrives in Oak Ambler, Jalara doesn't meet with her immediately. When he finally does, he disrespectfully calls her *Maiden*, but is visibly shocked to see that she wears the crown of gilded bones.

Not holding back, he makes it very clear how he feels about the wolven, calling them disgusting heathens and overgrown dogs. He also threatens to take every rude word that Poppy says out on her husband, taunting that Casteel has found his stay with them less than pleasant. He then relays how Ileana almost convinced him that Poppy had been captured despite his sacrifice and revels in the remembrance of his screams of rage, calling them a serenade for the ages.

When Poppy calls the Blood Queen *Isbeth*, Jalara gets annoyed and says Ileana is no longer Isbeth. I can only imagine it hurts his pride a little since, as Isbeth, she was Malec's heartmate and not Jalara's wife and he knows that she never got over him. He then taunts Poppy that she can't defeat Ileana and outright laughs at her, saying that while she may be of Nyktos's blood, she really is—and will always be— only the Maiden who is part beauty and part disaster.

After expressing his irritation that they called upon him to receive a message that isn't submission or surrender, Poppy tells him that *he* is the message.

Kieran, in wolven form, attacks and holds him in place as Poppy beheads him.

REFERENCE

PAGES

NYKTOS
KING OF THE GODS

RHAIN
GOD OF
COMMON MEN
AND ENDINGS

RHAHAR
THE
ETERNAL GOD

IONE
GODDESS OF
REBIRTH

AIOS
GODDESS OF
LOVE, FERTILITY,
AND BEAUTY

HEARTMATE
SOULMATE BOND BETWEEN A DEITY AND MORTAL,
TYING THEIR LIVES TOGETHER

ATLANTIAN
RESULT OF A HEARTMATE TRIAL UNION

ATLANTIAN OF ELEMENTAL BLOODLINE
DIRECT GENERATIONAL OFFSPRING OF THE
FIRST ATLANTIANS WHO WERE GIFTED LIFE BY THE GODS

DRAKEN
DRAGONS GIVEN MORTAL FORM
TO BE GUARDIANS AND PROTECTORS

OTHER BLOODLINES
CHANGELINGS, CEEREN, SENTURION, ETC.

ASCENDED
THE ASCENDED CHOSEN

SERAPHENA

QUEEN OF THE GODS

PENELLAPHE

GODDESS OF
WISDOM, LOYALTY,
AND DUTY

SAION

GOD OF
SKY AND SOIL /
EARTH, WIND,
AND SKY

LAILAH

GODDESS OF
PEACE
AND VENGEANCE

THEON

GOD OF
ACCORD
AND WAR

BELE

GODDESS OF
THE HUNT

DEITY

CHILDREN OF
THE GODS

WOLVEN

KIYOU WOLVES GIVEN MORTAL FORM
TO GUIDE AND PROTECT THE DEITIES

The other bloodlines are descendants of a deity and
the first Atlantian. Their abilities are tied to the Court
of the Primal they descend from.

ATLANTIAN BLOODLINES

Wolven: Kiyou wolves given mortal form by a god—thought to be Nyktos—to guard and protect the children of the gods and guide them in the mortal world.

Elemental Atlantians: Atlantians with the purest bloodline—one that can be traced to the very first and, therefore, to the gods. They are descendants of the first mortal who underwent the heartmate trial with a deity and were thus granted a longer life.

Some of the older bloodlines are the descendants of deities and the first Atlantians. Their abilities to shift are directly related to the deity they descend from, and thus the god or Primal. Some of the newer generations are descended from Elemental Atlantians and wolven. Changelings are often said to be products of a deity and wolven pairing, though I'm not sure that's true in every case.

Cecren: Can shift into waterfolk.

Wivern: Can shift into large cats.

Changelings: Most can only shift into varied animal forms, but a select few can take on the appearance and mannerisms of another person. Some have other skills, as well, such as Seer visions.

THE SENTURION WARRIOR BLOODLINES

The Warrior bloodlines—warriors born and not trained—differ from the other Atlantian bloodlines. There were dozens of unique lines at one time, each marked by special talents that made them dangerous to face in battle. Many Warrior lines died out hundreds of years before the Ascended, and their abilities changed as mortal blood was introduced to the lines.

Empath: Sometimes called Soul Eaters. Able to read the emotions of others and turn them into weapons, amplifying negative feelings. They could also heal. The closest Warrior bloodline to the deities. They were skilled in battle and thought to be the boldest and bravest of the Warrior lines.

Primordial: Able to summon the elements during battle—mostly earth, wind, or rain.

Cimmerian: Able to call upon the night, blocking out the sun and blinding their foes to movement.

Pryo: Able to summon flames to their blades.

Unknown: Able to call upon the souls of the ones who were slain by those they fought.

COUNCIL OF ELDERS

Being part of the Council, I never really considered documenting the Elders and any notable items about each of us. But then I realized why I was creating these files to begin with, and it suddenly seemed important. So, without further ado, I give you…the Council.

Before Malec O'Meer's [Mierel's] rule, when deities still reigned but the other bloodlines had started to outnumber them, the Council of Elders was formed to prevent anyone from making a choice or decision that could jeopardize the people of Atlantia.

The Crown retains ultimate authority, but the Council has a say, and our opinions are heard.

We were only ignored twice, and both times had grave consequences. The first was before Malec's rule when we thought the crown should be worn by one of the bloodlines and not the deities. The second was when Malec Ascended Isbeth, and we advised him to apologize and make it right.

He did not.

We help rule alongside the King and Queen of Atlantia when needed. Typically, we're not called upon unless a significant decision needs to be made. Before the transference of crowns recently, the last time the Council gathered was when Malik became the Blood Crown's prisoner.

The Council is made up of a mix of representatives, nine in total at any given time:

JASPER CONTOU

See Jasper's file for more information. As the head of the wolven, Jasper represents them on the Council.

However, there are alternates for when he cannot attend a meeting or vote (see below).

LADY CAMBRIA

Hair: Blond with silver strands.
Bloodline: Wolven.
Personality: Finds humor in others' ridiculousness. Somewhat cautious, but more strategic.
Background: Assists with the security of the kingdom and holds a position in the Atlantian Army.

WILHELMINA COLYNS (it's strange writing about myself in the third person)

Hair: Thick, curly, raven-black.

Eyes: Golden-brown.

Facial features: Deep, rich brown skin. Full lips.

Distinguishing features: Impish smile. Throaty, smoky voice.

Bloodline: Changeling. Seer.

Personality: Headstrong. Also finds humor in others' ridiculousness. Deep thinker. Matchmaker.

Habits/Mannerisms/Strengths/Weaknesses: Knows a face whether half-hidden or not. Likes whiskey. Sensual.

Background: Oldest member of the Council—two thousand years old. Author of *Miss Willa's Diary*.

SVEN

Hair: Dark.

Eyes: Amber.

Facial features: Rich brown skin, broad and warm features.

Bloodline: Elemental Atlantian.

Personality: Easily bored.

Habits/Mannerisms/Strengths/Weaknesses: Has always been fascinated with Primal magic—collecting things having to do with it, talking about it…

Background: Assists with the security of the kingdom and holds a position in the Atlantian Army.

LORD GREGORI

Hair: Dark, turning silver at the temples.

Eyes: Bright yellow.

Bloodline: Elemental Atlantian.

Other: Very old—one of the oldest Elders—but at least one thousand years younger than Wilhelmina.

Personality: Set in his ways. Anxious. Somewhat bigoted and closeminded.

LORD AMBROSE

Hair: Icy-blond.

Eyes: Golden.

Facial features: Pale skin.

Bloodline: Elemental Atlantian.

Personality: Worrier. Dismissive.

JOSHALYNN

Hair: Dark brown.

Facial features: Sand-colored skin.

Bloodline: Atlantian.
Personality: Kind-hearted.
Background: Husband and son died in the war.

There are two other males on the Council. One mortal and one unknown bloodline. I do not know much about them and have never paid them much heed, thus I am leaving them off this record for now.

AS THE FATES COMMAND

Dearest Diary,

Even as I sit here in my night rail, my sleeveless and gloriously low-cut gown of red silk resting next to me on the ottoman, I can feel the path my paramour's hands took, can taste his smoky-sweet flavor on my tongue. Can imagine what I'd like to do with him next.

The Red Pearl is not a new place for me, as you are well aware. I haunt it regularly, like a crimson ghost with unfinished business. The reason for that is simple: The energy in the place is unparalleled. It is an establishment of vice and pleasure, and at the root of it all...life. People come to the Pearl to live. And that, my dearest and oldest friend, is my goal for each day I am in this realm—as you know. But tonight's series of events deserves an entry. I believe I may have written about this lover before, but tonight was special. He is special. Everything about what happened is extraordinary.

For a Seer of some power, it is not easy to catch me unawares, yet I found myself surprised more than once this night. First by the appearance of someone I never thought to see in the Red Pearl—a girl in a robin's egg blue cloak and lace mask—then by a waking vision of the room upstairs and knowledge of exactly what I had to do, not to mention the surprises of the rest of the night, which I cannot wait to capture in great detail on these pages.

The Maiden came into the Pearl tonight, dear one. The Maiden! I knew it was her the minute she walked through the door, and I couldn't take my eyes off her as she played cards with a few guards, drank some champagne, and took in the environment like a starving beggar taking in sustenance for the first time in much too long. And as I watched her, I felt myself falling into that misty abyss of vision, where everything seems both surreal and much too real. In brilliant multicolored detail, I saw exactly what I needed to do. And so, when the opportunity arose, I directed sweet Penellaphe upstairs to the door I knew would change her life forever.

Once she was away, I shifted my attention to the reason for the Maiden's acute distress. A captivating man of some years, sandy hair a halo around his head, sun-weathered skin begging to be touched, and eyes so clear a blue it was like looking into the sea—one you wouldn't mind drowning in. And then I saw something I had never seen before with him. Something I never thought to see. My second sight flared to life, and I caught the unmistakable aura of a being of unfathomable age. Something I hadn't seen since I'd crossed paths with none other than Penellaphe's previous guardian, Leopold. The man was a viktor. But there was also something...more about this mortal. Something utterly unique.

I was so shocked by the discovery that I found myself immediately taking steps toward him. We were known to each other—quite intimately, in fact—but I had no previous designs on spending time with him this eve. Yet what I'd just seen made the lure to go to him almost unbearable. And not just because of his magnetic draw, which he had in spades. It was power. The gifts bestowed upon me by the Fates called to those given to him.

Now that my eyes had been opened, I could only imagine what a night with him would be like. Unfortunately, Sariah still knelt by his side, her hand running up and down his strong and muscular thigh, her adoring gaze taking in the handsome, almost gruff veneer of his visage—one I knew could soften into something akin to art. And I noticed that he rubbed at his temple, likely beginning to suffer from one of the migraines that often plagued him. I wished I could take away his pain.

With a sigh, I decided to leave him to Sariah's adoring attentions and took my leave, excusing myself up the stairs to the middle of the hall, where a table rested below a dormer window that opened to the roof. The moon shone brightly through the glass, beckoning me like a siren's song. I flipped the latch and pushed it out, the opening just large enough to permit a person to pass through. Scaling the table and stepping out onto the Red Pearl's roof, I took in the sights, sounds, and smells of the night, closing my eyes and basking in the wonder for a moment before settling myself on the tiles, situating my red gown around me.

Head back, soaking in the night and ruminating on what I'd just seen, I started when someone pushed aside my long fall of hair and gently kissed my neck. I kept my eyes closed, imbibing the feel of firm lips with just a hint of stubble and the smell of leather and musk. My aura tingled, and I knew exactly who stood behind me. It was as if I'd conjured him with my thoughts.

He nipped my earlobe and then settled himself beside me on the roof. I met his clear blue eyes and smiled. When he returned the expression, such a beautiful look on that brutally handsome face, it made my heart skip a beat. It somehow felt like the greatest gift. Still, I saw some pain in the lines at the corners of his eyes.

I hitched up my skirts and settled myself facing him on his lap, looking into his eyes as I moved to massage his head and temples, scratching my nails across his scalp before kneading the tight muscles of his neck. He dropped his head back, a moan of pleasure escaping that went straight to my core.

Still rubbing the base of his neck with my fingers and his temple with the thumb on one hand, I brought the hand at his nape around and ran my fingertips down his throat, reveling in the way his Adam's apple bobbed as he swallowed thickly. He raised his head and opened his eyes, his gaze meeting mine. The look in those blue orbs was so intense it took my breath. I saw need there—a desire that matched mine.

His hands firmly on my hips, I undid the ties of his long vest and tunic so I could reach more skin, my fingers tracing and charting and putting to memory every scar. He had a body honed for battle, and the strength I felt in not only his physical presence but also his character had turned me on from the first moment I saw him in the Pearl years ago. With him at my mercy now, thighs tensing, rod thickening, fingers clenching, I felt powerful. And despite his leadership with his men and brutality with his foes, I knew him to be open to submission and oftentimes tender in his dominance.

He slid one hand to better cup my bottom and raised the other to slide beneath the bodice of my gown, his large, calloused hand cupping my breast and making my nipple pebble. My head fell back on a moan, and I pushed myself into his touch, the movement bringing me into more direct contact with his impressive cock between us, clearly on board with whatever happened next.

The jolt of wanton electricity the movement shot through me pulled a gasp from me, making me snap my attention to his face once more. His gaze was on my chest, on the breast he'd freed, and I watched as he licked his lips. A rush of heat flooded me, making me clench with desire. I lifted some on my knees, ignoring the way the roof tiles dug into my skin, and moved to give him better access. He didn't disappoint.

In the next heartbeat, he had his firm lips and hot mouth pressed to my chest, his talented tongue laving and licking and flicking across my sensitive peak. I felt its twin tighten with jealous need, the friction of it rubbing against the silk of its confines ramping my desire. Both breasts felt heavy—swollen with want. It made me groan, and I both felt and heard Vikter chuckle.

More frustrated than amused, I pulled the halter of my gown over my head and let the crimson material pool at my waist, baring myself fully to him. Then I placed a fingertip under his chin and tipped his head up so his gaze met mine. With an eyebrow raise and a sly smile, I told him without words what I needed. And he didn't disappoint. He pressed my breasts together, alternating between nipples with long licks and swirls of his tongue and nips of his teeth before kissing away the sting. I was positively drenched from just that attention and found myself panting for more.

I moved back just a bit and smiled at the sound of protest he made—he was most definitely a breast man. His sounds of disapproval didn't last long as I reached between us and palmed the rigid length of his cock through his breeches. He groaned and raised his hips, seeking more of my touch. I wanted the same, so I didn't hesitate to undo the fasteners at his waist and delve my hand into the opening.

He throbbed in my palm, silken skin over steely heat. As I pumped my hand up and down his length. I watched the expressions cross his face, relished the way his mouth dropped open to emit short pants of heated breath, each of which caressed my aching nipples and fanned the flames of my desire.

Swirling my thumb over the head of his cock, I spread the liquid there, imagining the pleasure we were both about to experience. When I hitched up my skirts and moved so his crown rested at my pulsing, drenched opening, he lifted his lids and said something to me about the people below and anyone walking by in the hall being able to see. I remember emphatically stating, "Let them. We'll teach them something," before placing my hands on his shoulders and impaling myself fully on him.

We both let out shocked puffs of breath at the invasion, which soon turned to groans and moans of pleasure as feelings bombarded us. He stretched me deliciously, his length immediately hitting that spot deep inside me that made me even wetter—and neither of us had even moved yet. He lifted his hands to my breasts once more, fondling and caressing, his eyes focused on his ministrations. Every swipe of his thumbs over my nipples made my core tingle and convulse around him, causing him to involuntarily lift his hips in response, sending him trailing over that hidden treasure deep within.

Before I could even catch up to the sensations, I came around him with a shocked cry, the convulsions so intense it was almost painful. I felt him throb and jump inside me in response as he uttered a rough oath to the gods. And then his hands were on my hips, lifting me and slamming me down on his length, the brutality of the claiming ramping up my desire once again and stealing my breath. As he lifted me, I rotated my hips, swirling myself around his length before he pulled me back to him, the movement coaxing another curse from him and a breathy exclamation from me.

I was ramping up again so fast I hadn't even had a chance to catch my breath from the first orgasm before another blasted free, drenching us both in my pleasure. He didn't let up, didn't let me regather myself as the aftershocks continued, making every nerve ending in my body tingle.

Before I could even track what he was doing, he'd lifted me from him and reclined, pulling me up so I straddled his head instead of his waist. And then his mouth was on me, wrenching a rough cry from me that quickly turned into my oath to the gods as he feasted. He sucked on my nectar, making sounds of appreciation and delight that made me pulse. He swirled his tongue around my swollen clit, following its length like few men knew to do. He delved in deeply and twirled within, the sensations just as good as when he'd been buried in me balls-deep. He nipped at my nether lips, then licked away the sting, making me ache. I needed more. And I told him as much.

With a skill few would possess, he somehow managed to get up and switch our positions, moving me closer to the window. His heat surrounded me despite the chill in the air. I felt him rip off his vest and tunic and then saw it land beside me on the tiles before the skin of his chest touched my back, his heat soothing yet frustrating. He cupped one breast and pushed up the skirts of my gown with his other hand, his fingers slipping through my folds.

Making sure to anchor us both, he deeply plunged two fingers into me. It wrenched another gasp from my throat as he curled his middle digit to stroke that spot deep inside again, then slightly scissored those wicked invaders to stretch me, and swirled his thumb over my clit maddeningly. I felt like I would combust. I literally panted at the sensations, never coming down from what he'd done to me before.

In a daze, I vaguely realized that he'd withdrawn and was pushing me closer to the window. When he placed a gentle hand between my shoulder blades and applied pressure, I realized what he wanted and felt my inner muscles clench at the thought. A smile graced my lips as I leaned over the sill of the dormer window and rested my hands on the table below, wiggling my derriere in invitation.

I heard a chuckle followed by a sound of protest from behind me and then felt a sudden chill, only to next find myself being pulled back so Vikter could place his clothing on the sill to protect my stomach. I flushed with gratitude and endearment at his thoughtfulness. When he gently guided me back down, I went willingly, anchoring myself and preparing for the carnal onslaught about to ensue.

And he didn't disappoint. He flipped my skirts up my back and plunged, wrenching a cry from me that I was sure those down the hall could hear distinctly—not that it would be differentiated from the other sounds rising from within the Pearl. He set a furious rhythm with his thrusts, withdrawing almost to the point of separation before shoving back in. It was exactly what I needed, what I craved, I only wanted...more. And so, I told him as much. And he delivered.

He moved one hand to the base of my throat in a proprietary hold that only fanned the flames of my desire. I never felt threatened or in danger with him. What I did feel was conquered—and for someone as independent and old as me, that was a rarity. Never faltering in his indefatigable pace, my cries turned to screams until I shattered in one of the most intense orgasms I'd had in ages, the pleasure locking every muscle in my body and pulling all my connective tissue tight until it snapped like a rubber band, making me sag against the sill and catch myself on the table.

As I did, I felt his thighs tighten against the backs of mine, and his length grow inside me before he finally tumbled over the cliffs of pleasure and released himself deep inside me, the hot jets setting off aftershocks of orgasm within me and bringing a huge smile and a contented sigh to my lips.

As I looked up, I caught sight of someone coming down the hall, beige-brown skin almost glowing in the light of the sconces, blue eyes flashing with mirth as he looked at me and gave me a crooked smile and a tip of his head before continuing on and knocking on the sixth door on the left.

Vikter slid from me and placed a kiss in the center of my back before I felt him use something to clean me and then set my skirts to rights. He turned me to face him. When I looked up into his roughly handsome visage, I saw satisfaction there. Relaxation. I asked him how his headache was, and he just laughed, the rumbly sound settling somewhere deep in my belly, causing sensations I didn't know how I could still feel.

He helped me right the top half of my gown, and I helped him clean up, do up his breeches, and re-don his tunic. He kept the vest in his hand—that would definitely need to be laundered, and I almost chuckled aloud at what those who took care of it would think.

When we were both put back together, I peered over the end of the roof and found a group of smiling people staring up. They waved and hooted, smiling goofily, one couple clearly needing to come in and get a room before guards seized them for public indecency—something I should have probably been more worried about.

Vikter went through the window and then helped me through,

picking me up from the table as if I weighed nothing and setting me before him. He simply stared into my eyes for a beat before pinching my chin in his thumb and forefinger and tipping my head so he could take my lips in a languorous kiss. He placed one last peck on my mouth, caressed my cheek with the backs of his knuckles, and then backed away before turning on his heel and heading down the stairs without a word.

I took a deep breath and leaned against the table behind me, listening to his footfalls, my gaze tracking his departure and reliving what had just happened and what I'd uncovered tonight.

Vikter Wardwell, a Royal Guard, was also a viktor, an eternal being born with a goal: to guard someone the Fates believe is destined to bring about great change or purpose. But from what I saw, he was also...different. And I couldn't wait to find out more.

That's right, dear diary... Vikter is a viktor, the very first, in fact, chosen and commanded by the Fates. But here's the kicker. Most viktors don't know anything about their previous lives or exactly why they are where they are in this one. But given what I saw this night, Vikter is different. He remembers. And he knows. And there seems to be even more to that story besides.

Which makes me wonder what is to come for our dear Penellaphe Balfour. I'm sure it's even greater than what I've seen.

KNOWN WOLVEN

Much before my time, the kiyou wolves were given mortal form to serve as guides and protectors to the children of the gods. Strong and loyal, they hold a high place in society because they were chosen by the gods themselves. Several wolven have played a role in the story that has unfolded, particularly as it pertains to the tale of Poppy and Casteel. I wanted to record them in one place in case the information was ever needed.

Alastir Davenwell †
[see Alastir's file for additional information]
Hair: Long, sandy-blond.
Eyes: Pale blue.
Body type: Broad-shouldered.
Facial features: Ruggedly handsome.
Distinguishing features: Deep groove scar in the center of his forehead.
Other: Raspy voice. At least eight hundred years old but looks in his forties.
Personality: Not prone to violence. A bit of an alarmist.
Habits/Mannerisms/Strengths/Weaknesses: Incredibly loyal to his kingdom.
Background: Was King Malec's bonded wolven but has been unable to shift since their bond broke. King Valyn and Queen Eloana's Advisor to the Crown. After he betrays Cas by kidnapping Poppy, Poppy kills him by slitting his throat.
Family: Daughter = Shea †. Niece = Gianna. Great-nephew = Beckett †.

Arden †
Eyes: Vibrant blue.
Preternatural appearance: Silver and white fur.
Other: Imprint is like the salty sea.
Background: Was one of Poppy's main guards. Dies in an underground chamber full of Craven.

Beckett Davenwell †
Hair: Black.
Eyes: Winter-blue.
Body type: Body of a thirteen-year-old boy.
Facial features: Tan skin.
Preternatural appearance: Black fur.
Personality: Energetic. Excitable.
Habits/Mannerisms/Strengths/Weaknesses: Has a habit of not watching where he's going. Loves to chase leaves and butterflies while in wolven form.
Background: Killed by Jansen so the changeling could take his place.
Family: Alastir is his great-uncle. Shea and Gianna are his cousins.

Coulton
Hair: Bald.
Eyes: Winter-blue.
Facial features: Olive skin tone.
Other: Older.
Background: Works at the stables in Spessa's End.

Delano Amicu
[See Delano's file for additional information]
Hair: White-blond.
Eyes: Pale, wintery blue.
Body type: Tall. Heavy and strong as an ox.
Facial features: Pale skin. Boyish features.
Distinguishing features: Near-constant crease in his brow.
Preternatural appearance: White fur.
Other: Imprint is springy and featherlight.
Personality: Reserved. A bit of a softie.
Habits/Mannerisms/Strengths/Weaknesses: Not bonded to an Elemental Atlantian.
Background: Whole den killed by the Ascended, including his family. In a relationship with Perry.
Family: Mother, father, unknown number of sisters †. Sister = Preela †.

Effie †
Background: Dies by a spear to the chest in Oak Ambler.

Gianna Davenwell
[See Alastir's file for additional information]
Hair: Warm blond and wavy.
Eyes: Pale wintry blue and wideset.
Body type: Buxom and voluptuous. Several inches shorter than Poppy.
Facial features: Thick brows. Sharply angled cheekbones and nose. Small mouth but full lips.
Background: Casteel's second intended after Shea.
Family: Uncle = Alastir †. Cousin = Shea †. Second Cousin = Beckett †.

Ivan †
Preternatural appearance: Brindle fur.
Background: Jericho's cohort. Staked to the wall by Casteel.

Jasper Contou
[See Jasper and Kirha's file for additional information]
Hair: Shaggy and silver, waving around his ears and at the neck.

Eyes: Pale blue.
Body type: Tall.
Facial features: Tan skin. Stubble on chin.
Distinguishing features: Black ink on both arms swirling all the way to shoulders.
Preternatural appearance: Impossibly large. Silver fur.
Other: Has foresight. Imprint is like rich soil and cut grass. Earthy and minty feeling.
Personality: Family-oriented.
Background: Head of the wolven. Member of the Council of Elders.
Family: Wife = Kirha. Son = Kieran. Daughters = Vonetta and new infant.

Jericho †
Hair: Dark and shaggy.
Eyes: Pale blue.
Body type: Large.
Facial features: Hint of a beard.
Personality: Blood-thirsty.
Background: Was part of Cas's original crew from the time at the Red Pearl. Killed Rylan and tried to grab Poppy in the process. Loses his left hand to Cas's ire. Tries to take out Poppy in the dungeon. Staked to the wall by Casteel but left alive. Eventually killed by Cas when he removes the bodies from the wall.

Keev †
Facial features: Onyx-hued skin.
Other: Appears a decade older than Poppy.
Personality: Stoic and slightly distrustful.
Background: Injured during Ascended attack and lets Poppy take his pain so he can heal. Lost someone a long time ago. Killed by the Ascended—one of the heads slung in Spessa's End.

Kieran Contou
[See Kieran's file for additional information]
Hair: Dark and trimmed close to the skull.
Eyes: Striking pale blue like a winter sky.
Body type: Lean.
Facial features: Warm beige skin. Sharply angled face. Goes from coldly handsome to strikingly attractive when he smiles.
Distinguishing features: Slight accent. Faded claw marks across his chest. A healed puncture wound near his waist.
Preternatural appearance: Fawn/sand/tawny-colored fur. Slight foresight—has feelings that tend to come true. Nearly as tall as a man, even on all fours.
Other: Fine dusting of hair on his chest. Over two hundred years old. Imprint

is like cedar: rich, earthy, and woodsy. Blood smells like the woods, earthy and rich.

Personality: Snarky and sarcastic. A bit anal. Not the hugging type. Not modest. About as transparent as a brick wall. Go-to expression is bored with a hint of amusement.

Habits/Mannerisms/Strengths/Weaknesses: Moves with the grace of a dancer when he fights. Often sleeps in wolven form and kicks in his sleep but sleeps deepest as the sun rises. Loves biscuits…well, food of all types. Doesn't like crowded cities. Excellent at making alcoholic drinks. His loyalty to his family and those he loves goes beyond any bond, including the Primal *notam*.

Background: Bonded to Casteel since birth. Lost a great love—Elashya—who was born with a wasting disease.

Family: Mother = Kirha Contou. Fater = Jasper Contou. Sisters = Vonetta, and a new baby sister, name unknown as yet. Aunt = Beryn.

Kirha Contou
[See Jasper and Kirha's file for additional information]
Hair: Cornrows – narrow rows of small, tight braids.
Eyes: Wintery blue.
Facial features: Skin the color of night-blooming roses. Broad cheekbones. Full mouth.
Other: Sometimes has a way of knowing things like her husband and son.
Personality: Warm and maternal.
Habits/Mannerisms/Strengths/Weaknesses: Likes to knit. Has a green thumb. Really hard sleeper.
Family: Husband = Jasper. Son = Kieran. Daughters = Vonetta and new infant. Sister = Beryn.

Krieg †
Background: Died in the Massene battle. Head left on a spike near the Pompay border.

Kyley †
Background: Died in the Massene battle. Head left on a spike near the Pompay border.

Lady Cambria
Hair: Blond with silver strands.
Bloodline: Wolven.
Personality: Finds humor in others' ridiculousness.
Background: Assists with the security of the kingdom and holds a position in the Atlantian Army.

Lizeth Damron
[See Hisa Fa'Mar's file for additional information]
Hair: Chin-length and icy-blond.
Eyes: Wintery blue.
Facial features: Fair skin.
Personality: Brave.
Background: Wolven general. Hisa Fa'Mar's girlfriend.

Lyra †
Hair: Pin-straight and dark brown.
Eyes: Pale blue.
Facial features: Golden-brown skin.
Preternatural appearance: Smaller-sized. Deep brown fur.
Other: Imprint is like warm, rolling waters. A bit younger than Kieran.
Personality: Brave. Sweet.
Background: Is Kieran's friend with benefits. Killed by Isbeth.

Preela †
Background: Malik's bonded wolven. Was captured and tortured by the Blood Crown before King Jalara killed her. Bones made into seven daggers.
Family: Brother = Delano.

Roald †
Background: Died in the Massene battle. Head left on a spike near the Pompay border.

Rolf †
Preternatural appearance: Brown fur.
Background: One of Jericho's cohorts. Attacks Poppy in the dungeon and is killed by Poppy with the sickle sword then nailed to the wall with bloodstone by Cas as a warning.

Rune
Preternatural appearance: Brown and black fur.
Background: With group at the Bone Temple. Saved by Naill and then killed by a dakkai but then brought back to life by Poppy when she's merged with Sera.

Sage
Hair: Short, dark, and spiky.
Preternatural appearance: Blackish gray fur.
Other: Imprint is like fresh rain.
Habits/Mannerisms/Strengths/Weaknesses: Appreciates the male form—especially Reaver's.

Shea Davenwell †
[See Alastir's file for additional information]
Personality: Wild. Brave. Smart. Never backed down from anything. Outspoken.
Habits/Mannerisms/Strengths/Weaknesses: Capable of defending herself. Never asked for help and often refused the offer.
Background: Casteel's intended. Turned traitor while trying to rescue Casteel and ended up being killed by him.
Family: Father = Alastir †. Cousin = Gianna. Second Cousin = Beckett †.

Vonetta Contou
[See Vonetta's file for additional information]
Hair: Black cornrows—tight, narrow braids—that reach her waist.
Eyes: Wintery blue.
Body type: Tall.
Facial features: Skin the color of night-blooming roses. Sharply angled face. Broad cheekbones. Full mouth.
Distinguishing features: Throaty feminine laugh.
Other: Sixty years younger than her brother, so about one hundred and forty.
Personality: Easygoing. Kind. Suffers no fools when it comes to men.
Habits/Mannerisms/Strengths/Weaknesses: Loves candied fruit and demands it from Kieran when he annoys her. Terrible cook. Quick with a blade. Found it hard to believe that *anyone* in Solis was innocent until she met more Descenters.
Preternatural traits: Fawn/sand/tawny-colored in her wolven form but smaller than Kieran. Imprint is woodsy like white oak and vanilla.
Background: Spessa's End Rise Guard. Helped Casteel remember who he was and remind him that he wasn't a thing after his imprisonment.
Family: Mother = Kirha Contou. Father = Jasper Contou. Brother = Kieran. Sister = new infant not yet named. Aunt = Beryn.

ATLANTIA CHARACTERS

Alastir Davenwell †
Wolven
Advisor to the Crown (King Valyn and Queen Eloana)
Malec's bonded wolven
Betrayed Casteel and was murdered by Poppy

Arden †
Wolven
Died in a Craven attack in underground chambers

Aurelia
Draken
Only one of three draken awakened

Beckett Davenwell †
Young wolven
Poppy heals him
Killed by Jansen so he could take his place

Carriage Driver
From Saion's Cove

Casteel Da'Neer
Elemental Atlantian
New King of Atlantia
Poppy's heartmate
Joined with Poppy and Kieran

Coulton
Wolven
Works in the Stables at Spessa's End

Dante †
Atlantian

Killed while scouting with Delano near Spessa's End

<u>Delano Amicu</u>
Wolven
One of Cas and Poppy's inner circle

<u>Dominik</u>
Atlantian
A commander of the Crown Guard

<u>Effie</u> †
Wolven
Killed in Oak Ambler battle

<u>Elian Da'Neer</u> †
Da'Neer ancestor who summoned a god

<u>Elijah Payne</u> †
Atlantian
New Haven resident
Killed by Ascended and head thrown at Spessa's End

<u>Eloana Da'Neer</u>
Elemental Atlantian
Previous Queen of Atlantia
Helped to entomb Malec

<u>Emil Da'Lahr</u>
Elemental Atlantian
Part of Cas and Poppy's inner circle
Has a casual relationship with Vonetta

<u>Gayla La'Sere</u>
Atlantian
General in the Atlantian Army

<u>General Aylard</u>
Atlantian
General in the Atlantian Army

<u>Gianna Davenwell</u>
Wolven
Casteel's second intended after Shea

Griffith Jansen †
Atlantian
Changeling
Rare changeling that can take another's form
Killed by Poppy

Harlan
Mortal or changeling
Works the stables in Saion's Cove

Hisa Fa'Mar
Atlantian
Commander of the Crown Guard
Lizeth's girlfriend

Ivan †
Wolven
Part of the group that tried to kill Poppy in the dungeon
Staked to the wall by Casteel

Jasper Contou
Leader of the Wolven
Kieran and Vonetta's father

Jericho †
Wolven
Left hand removed as punishment for trying to take Poppy w/o orders and then staked alive to the wall by Casteel—later killed

Joshalynn
Atlantian
Council Elder

Keev †
Wolven
Killed in New Haven

Kieran Contou
Wolven
Bonded to Casteel
New Advisor to the Crown
Joined with Poppy and Cas

Kirha Contou
Wolven
Kieran and Vonetta's mother

Lady Cambria
Wolven
Council Elder Alternate

Landell
Atlantian
Resident of New Haven
Very against Poppy becoming Queen
Casteel rips his heart out of his chest

Lin
Atlantian
Soldier in Aylard's regiment

Lizeth Damron
Wolven
General in the Atlantian Army
Hisa's girlfriend

Lord Gregori
Atlantian
Council Elder

Lord Murin
Atlantian
Changeling
General in the Atlantian Army

Lyra †
Wolven
Was Kieran's friend with benefits
Killed by Isbeth

Magda †
Atlantian
New Haven resident
Killed by Ascended
Elijah's niece

Malec O'Meer [Mierel]
God
Nyktos and Sera's son
Has been entombed for eons
First to Ascend another—Isbeth (thus turning her into a demis)

Malik Da'Neer
Elemental Atlantian
Prince of Atlantia
Was held by the Blood Crown for ages
Millicent's heartmate

Marji
Atlantian
Young
Was brought back to life by Poppy

Marji's Father
Atlantian
Saion's Cove resident

Marji's Mother
Atlantian
Saion's Cove resident

Miss Seleana
Mortal
Seamstress in Saion's Cove

Naill La'Crox
Elemental Atlantian
Part of Poppy and Casteel's inner circle

Naill's Father
Elemental Atlantian
Runs the mills in Evaemon

Nektas
Draken
First draken
Bonded to Nyktos
Daughter Jadis was taken by the Blood Crown

Nithe
Draken
One of the draken Poppy summons

Nova
Atlantian
Guardian

Odell Cyr
Atlantian
General in the Atlantian Army

Penellaphe Balfour
Primal of Blood and Bone and the *true* Primal of Life and Death
Previous Maiden
Nyktos and Sera's granddaughter
Ires and Isbeth's daughter
Casteel's heartmate
Joined with Cas and Kieran

Perry
Elemental Atlantian
Casteel's friend
In a relationship with Delano

Preela †
Wolven
Malik's bonded wolven
Killed by King Jalara
Bones made into seven bloodstone daggers

Quentyn Da'Lahr
Elemental Atlantian
Young

Raul
Mortal
Resident of Evaemon
Stable hand

Reaver
Draken
First to rise when Poppy summons Nyktos's guards

Renfern Octis †
Mortal
Young
Killed by Lord Chaney

Roald †
Wolven
Killed near the border of Pompay

Rolf †
Wolven
Part of the group that tried to kill Poppy in the dungeon
Beheaded by Poppy with the sickle sword
Staked to the wall by Casteel

Rose
Mortal
Palace manager at Evaemon

Rune
Wolven
Present for the Bone Temple battle

Sage
Wolven
Has a thing for Reaver

Shea Davenwell †
Wolven
Alastir's daughter
Casteel's intended
Betrayed the Da'Neers
Casteel killed her with his bare hands

Sven
Elemental Atlantian
Council Elder
Perry's father
Fascinated with and knowledgeable about Primal magic

Talia
Atlantian
Healer

Thad
Draken
Part of the group that Poppy summoned
Sera brought him back to life in the god times

Valyn Da'Neer
Previous King of Atlantia
Casteel's father

Vonetta Contou
Wolven
Kieran's sister
Has a casual relationship with Emil

Wilhelmina Colyns
Atlantian
Changeling
Seer
Oldest Council Elder
Has a fondness for recording her carnal encounters in red journals

Wren
Mortal
Descenter

SOLIS CHARACTERS

<u>Agnes</u>
Mortal
Masadonia resident
Marlowe's (Cursed) wife

<u>Blaz</u> †
Mortal
Descenter
Clariza's husband
Working with Malik when he was posing as Elian
Killed by Isbeth

<u>Britta</u>
Mortal
Maid
Used to dally with Casteel

<u>Bryant</u> †
Mortal
Huntsman/Guard
Died during Hawke's ruse

<u>Callum</u>
The first Revenant
Was around in the time of the gods
Sotoria's brother

<u>Clariza</u> †
Mortal
Descenter
Blaz's wife
Working with Malik when he was posing as Elian
Killed by Isbeth

Commander Forsyth †
Command of the Rise Guard in Oak Ambler
Killed during Oak Ambler takeover

Commander Jansen
Atlantian
Changeling
Was posing as a guard as part of Casteel's ruse to capture the Maiden
Killed by Poppy when he reveals his true colors

Coralena †
Revenant
Handmaiden
Poppy's foster mother
Killed when Isbeth made her ingest draken blood

Dafina †
Mortal
Lady in Wait
Dies during the Rite massacre

Diana †
Mortal
A second daughter – ten years old
Killed by the Ascended

Duchess Jacinda Teerman †
Ascended
Poppy's guardian
Leader in Masadonia
Killed by Poppy

Duchess Ravarel
Ascended
Leader of Oak Ambler
Disappeared

Duke Dorian Teerman †
Ascended
Poppy's guardian
Leader in Masadonia
Killed by Hawke

Duke Ravarel
Ascended
Leader of Oak Ambler
Disappeared

Duke Silvan †
Ascended
Leader in Massene
Killed by Poppy

Framont †
Ascended
Priest
Killed by Poppy

Hannes †
Mortal
A member of the Maiden's Royal Guard
Died in his sleep

Hawke Flynn
Elemental Atlantian
Casteel's alter ego
Royal Guard for the Maiden

Ian Balfour †
Ascended
Poppy's brother
Cora and Leo's son
Isbeth has him killed

King Jalara †
Former King of Solis
Ileana/Isbeth's husband
Killed Preela
Poppy beheads him as a message to Isbeth

Leopold †
Viktor
Poppy's foster father
Nobody knows exactly what happened to him, though it's assumed he returned to Mount Lotho to await rebirth

Ley Barron †
Mortal
Descenter
Lost a brother to the fever and another to the Rite
Presumably killed by Duke Teerman

Lieutenant Smyth
Mortal
Royal Guard
Loves to get on Hawke's case

Lord Brandole Mazeen †
Ascended
Duke Teerman's friend
Used to torture Poppy
Poppy cut off his arm and then head

Lord Chaney †
Ascended
Poppy kills him

Lord Haverton †
Ascended
Leader at New Haven
Secretly deceased

Loren †
Mortal
Lady in Wait
Dies during the Rite massacre

Luddie †
Mortal
Huntsman
Casteel kills him with a crossbow bolt to the neck

Mac
Descenter
Works the meat packing district

Magnus
Mortal
Duke Teerman's steward

Malessa Axton †
Mortal
Lady in Wait
Presumably killed by Lord Mazeen, died drained of blood

Millicent
Revenant
Isbeth and Ires's daughter
Malik's heartmate
Poppy's sister

Miss Willa Colyns
Atlantian
Changeling
Council Elder
Seer
Lived in Solis for quite some time
Likes to masquerade as a Lady at the Red Pearl
Author of diary found in the Atheneum

Mr. Tulis †
Mortal
Descenter
Killed after trying to kill Poppy—staked to the wall by Cas

Mrs. Tulis †
Mortal
Killed by Lord Chaney

Murphy †
Mortal
Taken and killed during the Rite

Noah †
Mortal
Huntsman
Died while escorting Poppy to the capital

Pence
Mortal
Rise Guard

Peter †
Mortal
Taken and killed during the Rite

Priestess Analia
Ascended
Priestess
Poppy's tutor

Queen Ileana/Isbeth †
Demis
Queen of Solis
Malec's heartmate
Poppy and Millicent's mother
King Jalara's wife

Ramon
Mortal
Ascended took his son Abel

Ramsey
Mortal
One of the Duke's stewards

Rylan Keal †
Mortal
Royal Guard
Killed by Jericho during Hawke's ruse

Sir Terrlynn †
Ascended
Royal Knight
Cas cuts off his head

Tasos
Mortal
Rise Guard in Oak Ambler
Showed the group to the underground chambers full of Craven and dead Rite children

Tawny
Mortal
Lady in Wait

Poppy's handmaiden and friend
Stabbed with shadowstone and turned into something as yet unknown

<u>Tobias Tulis</u> †
Mortal
Child given over to the Rite

<u>Vikter Wardwell</u> †
Viktor
Poppy's guard, friend, and trainer
The only *viktor* known to remember all his lifetimes

<u>Wren</u>
Mortal
Descenter

KNOWN DESCENTERS and AIDS

Descenters are mortals or Atlantians who follow the Dark One and wish to see Atlantia rise from the ashes. They are believed to be responsible for the disappearance of a number of Ascended and are known to start riots. Some, but not all, Descenters have Atlantian blood. If they do not have Atlantian blood, they are usually kin to those who fought alongside the Atlantians during the war and therefore know the truth.

While Descenters follow the Dark One, they are not ruled by him. They do their own thing, and their love for their kingdom rises above and beyond any other loyalties.

Alastir Davenwell †
Wolven
Advisor to the Crown (King Valyn and Queen Eloana)
Malec's bonded wolven
Betrayed Casteel and was murdered by Poppy

Blaz †
Mortal
Clariza's husband
Working with Malik when he was posing as Elian
Killed by Isbeth

Clariza †
Mortal
Blaz's wife
Working with Malik when he was posing as Elian
Killed by Isbeth

Elijah Payne †
Atlantian
New Haven resident
Killed by Ascended and head thrown at Spessa's End

Ivan †
Wolven

Part of the group that tried to kill Poppy in the dungeon
Staked to the wall by Casteel

Jericho †
Wolven
Hand removed and then staked alive to the wall by Casteel—later killed

Keev †
Wolven
Killed in New Haven

Landell
Atlantian
Resident of New Haven
Very against Poppy becoming Queen
Casteel rips his heart out of his chest

Lev Barron †
Mortal
Blond
Presumably killed by Duke Teerman

Mac
Mortal
Bald
Leader of the Descenter group at the slaughterhouse

Magda †
Atlantian
New Haven resident
Killed by Ascended
Elijah's niece

Mr. Tulis †
Mortal
Killed after trying to kill Poppy—staked to the wall by Cas

Rolf †
Wolven
Part of the group that tried to kill Poppy in the dungeon
Beheaded by Poppy with the sickle sword
Staked to the wall by Casteel

<u>The Unseen</u>
All-male secret brotherhood/organization
Wear masks that resemble wolven

<u>Wren</u>
Mortal

THE GUARDIANS

Atlantia's elite soldiers. The Guardians are an all-female battalion of strong and powerful warriors birthed of the ancient Warrior bloodlines.

Physical Attributes:
All-female fighting force.
Leader is tall and blond [Nova].
Wear all black.

Preternatural Abilities:
Only females of the bloodline have unique abilities due to their bloodline.
In terms of strength and mortality, they are like Elemental Atlantians.
They need blood to survive.

Habits and Mannerisms:
Guardians always train the armies of Atlantia.
One Guardian is equal to twenty trained soldiers.
Long, warbling war cry.
Use stone swords that ignite when/if struck together.

History and Lore:
The last of their bloodline, they are born in a long succession of Guardians who will defend Atlantia to their dying breath.

Guardians are the only Warrior bloodline left.

Only about two hundred Guardians remain.

294/Jennifer L. Armentrout with Rayvn Salvador

KNOWN DRAKEN

A very, very long time ago, even before Primals and gods and certainly before my time, dragons existed in both the mortal realm and the Land of the Gods. When the gods came to be, Eythos, the Primal God of Life, befriended the dragons. He wanted to learn their stories and histories, so he offered to give them mortal form. Those who agreed became known as the draken.

Aurelia

Preternatural appearance: Greenish brown scales. Long neck. Wings the length of her body. Larger than Nithe and Thad but smaller than Reaver. Rows of horns and frills around neck.

Background: One of only three females of the awakened twenty-three draken. Pointed out each of the draken to Poppy so she knew which was which.

Basilia

Background: Attes's draken

Crolee

Preternatural appearance: Black and brown scales.

Family: Distant cousins = Ehthawn and Orphine †

Davina †

Hair: Long and honey-brown.

Eyes: Vibrant blue.

Facial features: Reddish brown skin.

Preternatural appearance: Small. Reddish brown scales.

Other: Most call her "Dav."

Personality: No one knows if she likes them or is seconds away from setting them on fire.

Habits/Mannerisms/Strengths/Weaknesses: Wears a slender, black-bladed dagger on her forearm and another on her thigh.

Background: Brought Sera meals. Killed when Kolis sent his draken.

Family: Older sister who died long ago.

Diaval

Hair: Long, wavy, and blond.

Eyes: Ruby-red.

Facial features: Handsome but smug.

Background: Kolis's draken.

Ehthawn

Preternatural appearance: Large. Onyx-hued scales.

Family: Twin = Orphine †.

Iason
Hair: Dark.
Background: Kolis's draken.

Jadis
Hair: Dark.
Preternatural appearance: Greenish brown scales. Long neck. Oval-shaped head.
Personality: Fearless. Inquisitive.
Background: Taken prisoner by the Blood Crown.
Family: Father = Nektas. Mother = Halayna †.

Naberius
Preternatural appearance: Black with red-tipped scales. Wide jaw and broad, flat nose. Horns sprout from head and curve back—as long as a mortal leg. Wide wingspan and spiked tail.
Background: Kolis's draken.

Nektas
Hair: Long, black hair streaked with red (becomes streaked with silver).
Eyes: Blood-red with vertical pupil (become sapphire blue with vertical pupil).
Body type: Tall. Long legs.
Facial features: Copper skin. Broad, proud features.
Distinguishing features: Ridges on skin that resemble scales.
Preternatural features: Black and dark gray scales. Spiked tail. The size of three large horses. Long, graceful neck. Head is half the size of a horse's body. Flat, broad nose. Wide jaw. Pointed horns on head like a crown. Body is at least twenty feet.
Personality: Quiet. Reserved. Sage-like.
Habits/Mannerisms/Strengths/Weaknesses: Extraordinary hearing. Can manifest clothing.
Background: Was Eythos's bonded draken, the very first—was close to him even before he was given his dual nature. Created the first mortal with Eythos. When Eythos died, it severed the bond, and he ended up bonded to Nyktos by choice.
Family: Daughter = Jadis. Mate = Halayna †. Distant relative = Thad. Bonded Primal = Eythos and then Nyktos.

Nithe
Hair: Soft, blue-black waves to just below his jawline.
Eyes: Sapphire blue with vertical pupil.
Body type: A few inches over six feet. Broad shoulders. Thick thighs. Toned waist and hips.

Facial features: High cheekbones. Chiseled, square jaw. Plush lips.
Distinguishing features: Chin divot. Ridges on skin that resemble scales.
Preternatural appearance: Scales the color of ash. A little larger than a horse (smaller than Reaver and Aurelia but larger than Thad). Wings the color of midnight. Rows of horns and frills around neck.
Personality: Strong, silent type.

Orphine †
Hair: Long and dark.
Eyes: Crimson with a vertical pupil in the time of the gods.
Body type: Tall. Rounded hips. Looks soft.
Facial features: Pale skin.
Preternatural appearance: Large. Onyx/Midnight-hued scales.
Other: Looks to be in her twenties.
Habits/Mannerisms/Strengths/Weaknesses: Likes to read.
Family: Twin = Ehthawn. Distant cousin = Crolee.

Reaver
Hair: Blond. Shoulder-length.
Eyes: Crimson with vertical pupil in the time of the gods. Blue with vertical pupil in recent times.
Body type: Long legs.
Facial features: Sand-colored flesh. Sharp, strong, chiseled jaw. Wide-set eyes tilted down at the inner corners. Full, bow-shaped lips. Not classically handsome but interesting and striking.
Distinguishing features: Faint but distinct scale pattern on skin.
Preternatural appearance: Purplish black scales. Large but not as big as Nektas. Smooth, black horns starting in the middle of the flattened bridge of his nose and rising up the center of his diamond-shaped head. The ones around his eyes are smaller but lengthen into sharp points that jut out from his frills as they travel up his head.
Other: Gruff voice. Can change his teeth and breathe fire while in his god form.
Personality: Aloof. Sarcastic. Easily irritated.
Background: Was young when what Kolis did came out. Was hidden away with the other younglings. First draken to emerge after Poppy summons Nyktos's guards.

Sax
Background: Kolis's draken.

Thad
Hair: Fair.

Eyes: Crimson with vertical pupils.

Facial features: Pale. Soft features.

Preternatural appearance: Brownish black scales. Long neck with rows of horns and frills.

Other: Appears a few years younger than Sera.

Personality: Accepting.

Background: Sera is forced to kill him and then brings him back to life.

Family: Nektas = Distant relative.

NOTE: Seventeen of the twenty-three draken Poppy summoned were killed in the Primal storm that Vessa conjured.

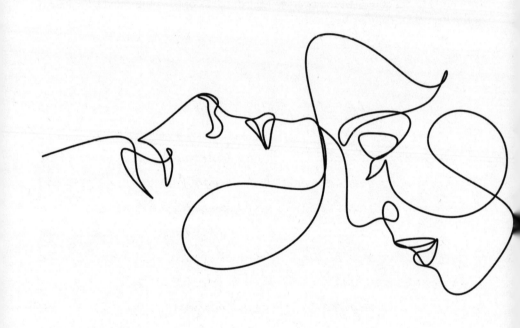

FIRSTS OF FLESH AND FIRE

Dearest Diary,

Tonight was a night for firsts, and you know I don't have many of those anymore—though not for lack of trying.

This entry is dedicated to the new Queen of Atlantia, for without her, this never would have happened. Though I do feel a little bit bad reveling in the moment here when the reason it did happen stems from some pretty harrowing and quite unbearable circumstances. Alas, it was a splash in the pond of time, a moment of pleasure stolen amidst a multitude of chaos, and thus deserves to be celebrated.

I was traveling for some Council business, which took me just outside of Spessa's End. That night, I had a vivid vision of leaping flames and flashing scales and knew that Penellaphe had summoned the King of Gods' guards to help rescue her husband and bring an end to the Blood Crown. I had seen some of those future events in flashes, as well, and knew a bit of what would be ahead in the days to come.

But back to my vision of fire...because fire it did become.

Please forgive me, I'm getting ahead of myself. Blame it on the lingering awe and continued satiation. A smile graces my lips even now...

Instead of leaving the area, I requested an additional night's stay at the establishment where I had rented a top-floor room and decided to wait and see what might unfold. Something in my vision, though incredibly vague and not at all targeted, urged me to stay. And so, I did. One must follow their instincts. Life would be ever so dull if we did not.

As the day grew to smoky darkness, I visited a local pub just down the street from my lodgings and settled in with a tumbler of whiskey and some stew. Just as I was about to give up and return to my rooms, the door opened, and one of the most beautiful men I had ever seen walked in.

He was a good few inches over six feet with broad shoulders and thick thighs, his upper body a delicious triangle as it tapered to a toned waist and hips. His hair hung in soft waves to just below his jawline, and I watched slack-jawed as he raised a hand to run his fingers through it.

He wore casual clothing in varying shades of gray with a few black accents and positively exuded an air of primal power with a hint of danger.

As he got a little bit closer and within the light thrown about the room from the fire, I took in his face. He had high cheekbones and a chiseled square jaw, a divot in the middle that I wanted to lick. His lips were plush and inviting. Even his Adam's apple was sexy as he swallowed.

He looked around the space, presumably attempting to find a place to sit. When his gaze reached the table where I supped, I took in his eyes. They were silken sapphire fire—a color not seen much. The wolven had ice-blue eyes, a sign of their dual natures. This blue signified the same, but the vertical pupils in that sea of cerulean solidified my assumption from when he entered the pub. Before me stood a draken in his god form.

I gestured to the empty seat at my little table and inclined my head as I crossed my legs, letting the split in my skirts give an inviting view of a toned, rich brown thigh and calf. The draken followed the movement and then took me in again, looking quickly at the chair across from me before finally heading my way.

My heartbeat stirred in my chest, excitement ramping. When he sat across from me, never taking his captivating gaze from mine, his aura nearly knocked me out of my seat. This was power. Ancient power. The power of the gods made flesh. And it turned me on.

I finally found my voice and greeted him, giving him my name and asking his. He didn't say anything for so long that I feared I had scared him away, but then he finally spoke, his deep timbre rumbling and stirring things in my chest and lower.

He told me that his name was Nithe and asked me if I knew what he was. I assumed he could sense the changeling blood in me, perhaps even know somehow that I was a Seer. I told him I did, and we struck up a conversation. He was quite funny, something I didn't expect. He was also incredibly polite and made me feel appreciated, seen, and heard. We drank whiskey and enjoyed the fire and each other until the barkeep signaled last call.

Never taking my eyes from his, I bolstered my courage and asked him if he'd like to return to my rooms with me. He hesitated for only a second before agreeing, then rising and taking my hand. I led the way, just down the street, and climbed the stairs to my rooms, putting a little extra sway in my step.

As the door snicked shut, Nithe pulled me to him, the hard ridges of his body cradling the softer planes of mine. He kissed me as if he were starving, tangling the fingers of one hand in my hair as his other took an adventurous journey down the dips and valleys of my backside.

I felt the impressive ridge of his manhood behind the flap of his trousers and my body responded in kind with a rush of heat and desire.

He stepped back just enough to bring his hands to the laces on my dress, and I mirrored him, untying the ties at his neck and waist and loosening the fly enough to see the crown of him. My mouth watered, and I couldn't help but wonder if his scales presented anywhere while he was in his mortal form.

Shaking those thoughts for the moment, I continued divesting him of his clothing, turning him to help rid him of his shirt and noticing the fine line of ridges on his back that resembled scales. Then I helped him peel away mine until we stood before each other, gloriously naked—and I do mean gloriously. Nithe was a work of art with sculpted pectorals and biceps, bulging triceps and shoulders. He was long and hard and shifted just to the left, something I knew from my vast experience meant very good things for me.

As he ran his lapis gaze down my body, my nipples pebbled in response, and I felt a quiver in my thighs. My breath caught, and I stood frozen to the spot, utterly captured by his attention. His power. I reveled in it, letting my head fall back and releasing a soft sigh.

Nithe took that as an invitation and moved in, licking and laving my neck and breasts. I could do naught but grasp the silky strands of his blue-black hair and give myself over to the sensations.

When he hoisted me into his arms, I happily wrapped my legs around him, clasping my ankles behind his back and bringing us together as I shamelessly rubbed myself against his erection. He let out a low rumbling growl that I felt in my chest and at my core, and I took his mouth with abandon.

I only released my grasp on him when he lowered me to the bed, bracing himself on his arms above me and taking me in once again from head to toe, his perusal like a physical caress. He made a comment about how I looked like a goddess spread out before him with my hair splayed around my head, and I blushed a little. It was possible that he knew firsthand—at least more than I.

I reversed our positions and he let me, lowering himself to the mattress with his delectable upper body propped on his elbows. He watched me raptly, those vertical pupils expanding in the sea of blue, as I took him in hand and then lowered my mouth to him. I took as much as I could, using my hand to bring him additional pleasure, and smiled a little when a small hum made him groan and drop back onto the bed. The more I worked him, the more I relished his bliss, the more aroused I became.

As if he could sense—or scent—the change, he took control, moving in a fluid motion to position me on my hands and knees facing the balcony doors. He ran calloused fingertips down my spine, lingering on the globes of my ass for a beat before I felt him at my entrance.

He eased in at first, and the stretch was magnificent. As he worked inside more and more, the fullness was almost more than I could bear. When he finally seated himself fully, hitting that spot inside me that made flashes of color burst behind my eyelids, I lost myself to the rapture.

Begging for more, he delivered, thrusting harder and faster, bringing me higher and higher. I felt as if I were at the highest peak of the Skotos Mountains, about to leap. But there would be no fall. No, I was sure I would fly.

One hand still on my hip to keep me steady, he brought the other around to cup a breast, my nipple beading against his palm. He squeezed, just this side of pain, and I felt the rush where we were joined. He clearly felt it, too, as he groaned and rotated his hips as he thrust, hitting both my pleasure pearl and that magical spot deep inside.

I honestly wasn't sure how I was still conscious, the pleasure was almost unbearable, yet I still hadn't come. When he slid that hand on my breast down the front of my body and circled his index finger over my clit, I shattered with a scream, my body spasming around his and pulling him in deeper, squeezing the silk over steel.

He pulled out while I was still trembling both inside and out, and I almost screamed my frustration until he flipped me over and immediately took me again, staring into my eyes as he thrust and lifted my hips to meet his, sweat dripping from his brow and glistening on his chest.

I scratched my nails down his flesh, hard enough to mark but not to draw blood, and he hissed, his eyes closing. When he swirled his hips again, and I felt myself tightening once more, I reached around and gently played with that tight knot of muscle, causing him to lose control of his tempo a bit. On the next thrust, I came with another shout.

He pushed inside one more time. Hard. Deep. Then he bowed his back and roared, his essence bathing me in warmth unlike anything I had experienced before. The aftershocks of my orgasm pulled all I could out of him until he collapsed atop me, breathing heavily and seeming to take in my scent.

I petted his back, swirling my finger in the perspiration there, fingering the ridges that were a sensory dream, and marveling at how every muscle on his body seemed carved from stone.

At some point, I must have fallen asleep, because the next thing I knew, a gentle kiss on my temple roused me. Nithe stood at the side of the bed, still breathtakingly naked. He brushed some hair back from my face and then leaned down to kiss my lips. When he rose, he told me that he had to go but assured me that thoughts of our encounter would not be far from his mind for quite some time. I told him the same and then watched as he walked to the balcony, his tight backside flexing with every step.

He opened the doors wide, glanced over his shoulder at me with a smile, and then jumped.

I gasped and flew off the bed to the railing, looking down. When I saw nothing, I lifted my gaze, taking in the magnificent creature in the sky. His scales were the color of ash, and his wings were huge and darker than midnight. He had jutting black horns starting in the middle of his snout to run up over the center of his massive head. The farther back on his head they went, the longer and sharper they became, eventually jutting out from thick frills. He looped a circle and then dove, banking at the last moment to come as close as he dared to the building.

I felt the brush of air on my face and body and put a hand to my chest, in absolute and utter awe. It was like a wave, and it wasn't something I would soon forget.

I watched until I could no longer see him as he flew toward Spessa's End and then returned to the room, closing and locking the balcony doors behind me.

Picking up his discarded shirt from the floor, I slipped it over my head and pulled it to my nose, inhaling and taking in the woodsy, earthy smell.

Surrounded by his scent and still tingling from our encounter, I fell asleep to sweet, sweet dreams.

Willa

THE LAST ORACLE
Not a lot has been revealed about the last oracle to be birthed, but what we *do* know is significant.

Prophecies are dreams of the Ancients. They are then shared with the oracles—rare mortals able to communicate directly with the gods without having to summon them—and then passed on to the Gods of Divination.

The prophecy we know today was the last dreamt by the Ancients. It is a *promise* known by only a few, dared to be spoken by even fewer, and only repeated by a descendant of the Gods of Divination—like Penellaphe, Goddess of Wisdom, Loyalty, and Duty—and the last oracle.

That oracle had the last name of Balfour. She was kind and a great conversationalist, and it is said that Princess Kayleigh Balfour of Irelone resembled her.

We know that Poppy received the last name of Balfour from her foster parents Leopold and Coralena, so it makes you wonder what else is hidden within that little bit of knowledge, doesn't it?

THE DEAD BONES CLAN
The Dead Bones Clan is a group of vicious, cannibalistic mortals of the land outside the Rise. They used to live all across Solis, mainly where the Blood Forest now grows. Most assumed they were eradicated when the Ascended burned everything between New Haven and Pompay. But at some point over the past several hundred years, they ended up near Spessa's End.

Physical Description: Wear masks made of human skin.

Habits/Mannerisms/Strengths/Weaknesses: Hang symbols from trees—brown rope fashioned into a circle or noose with a bone crossing through the center. Like the Royal Crest but instead of a straight line or arrow slanting in toward the center, it's a bone slanting out. Also create the symbol out of rocks on the forest floor. Supposedly kill and eat anything/one they perceive as a threat. They aren't just anti-Craven with keeping people out of their territory; they're anti-everything and everyone. Usually, only attack when hungry. Cannibals—but nobody knows why that is.

THE PROPHECY
Gods, what can I say about the prophecy? It has changed more than I take new bed partners. But then again…has it? What *has* changed is the interpretation of what was prophesied in the bones of Penellaphe Balfour's namesake, a God of Divination. And that is still changing even now.

Let's take a peek at what we know so far, shall we?

From the desperation of golden crowns and born of mortal flesh, a great primal power rises as the heir to the lands and seas, to the skies and all the realms. A shadow in the ember, a light in the flame, to become a fire in the flesh. For the one born of the blood and the ash, the bearer of two crowns, and the bringer of life to mortal, god, and draken. A silver beast with blood seeping from its jaws of fire, bathed in the flames of the brightest moon to ever be birthed, will become one.

When the stars fall from the night, the great mountains crumble into the seas, and old bones raise their swords beside the gods, the false one will be stripped from glory as (NOT UNTIL) the great powers will stumble and fall, some all at once, and they will fall through the fires into a void of nothing. Those left standing will tremble as they kneel, will weaken as they become small, as they become forgotten. For finally, the Primal rises, the giver of blood and the bringer of bone, the Primal of Blood and Ash.

Two born of the same misdeeds, born of the same great and Primal power in the mortal realm. A first daughter, with blood full of fire, fated for the once-promised King. And the second daughter, with blood full of ash and ice, the other half of the future King. Together, they will remake the realms as they usher in the end. And so it will begin with the last Chosen blood spilled, the great conspirator birthed from the flesh and fire of the Primals will awaken as the Harbinger and the Bringer of Death and Destruction to the lands gifted by the gods. Beware, for the end will come from the west to destroy the east and lay waste to all which lies between.

I know, I know, it is a lot. Even I, with some inside knowledge, have not been able to decipher it all. I can tell you what I *do* quote-unquote know, however. I shall break it down incrementally and tell you what I have deciphered. Please note that while I'm a Seer, I am not a God of Divination. And as events unfold; so, too, does the interpretation and the possible double meanings of some of the prophecy's stanzas.

From the desperation of golden crowns [**the Golden King**, **King Roderick, to stop the Rot**] *and born of mortal flesh* [**King Lamont** and **Queen Calliphe**]*, a great primal power rises as the heir to the lands and seas, to the skies and all the realms* [**Seraphena Mierel, the true Primal of Life, the Queen of Gods, carrying the only ember of life, thus the only reason anything still lives/exists**]*. A shadow in the ember* [**Nyktos**]*, a light in the flame* [**Sera**]*, to become a fire in the flesh* [**the union to eventually become Poppy**]*. For the one born of the blood and the ash, the bearer of two crowns* [**Sera**]*, and the bringer of life to mortal, god, and draken* [**the Primal**]*. A silver beast with blood seeping from its jaws of fire* [**Ash**]*, bathed in the flames of the brightest moon to ever be birthed* [**Sera again**]*, will become one.*

When the stars fall from the night [**the War of the Primals**]*, the great mountains crumble into the seas, and old bones raise their swords beside the gods* [**The Consort's soldiers and draken**]*, the false one will be stripped from glory as* [**not until!**] *the great powers will stumble and fall, some all at once, and they will fall through the fires into a void of* *nothing. Those left standing will tremble as they kneel, will weaken as they become small, as they become forgotten. For finally, the Primal rises, the giver* [**Sera**] *of blood and the bringer* [**Nyktos**] *of bone, the Primal of Blood and Ash.*

Two born of the same misdeeds [**the capture of Ires and Jadis—how Isbeth got pregnant**]*, born of the same great and Primal power in the mortal realm* [**Millicent and Poppy, born of Ires, son of the true Primal of Life and a Primal of Death**]*. A first daughter* [**Millicent**]*, with blood full of fire* [**Revenant with embers in her blood**]*, fated for the once-promised King* [**Malik's heartmate**]*. And the second daughter* [**Poppy**]*, with blood full of ash and ice* [**granddaughter of the Asher and…Death—like Ash**]*, the other half of the future King* [**Casteel's heartmate**]*. Together, they will remake the realms as they usher in the end* [**the Awakening**]*. And so it will begin with the last Chosen blood spilled* [**Poppy was the last Chosen, and her blood was spilled—her birth**]*, the great conspirator* [**Kolis**] *birthed from the flesh and fire of the Primals will awaken as the Harbinger and the Bringer of Death and Destruction to the lands gifted by the gods. Beware, for the end will come from the west* [**the mortal realm**] *to destroy the east* [**Iliseeum**]*.*

**Note to self. Make sure to update these records as pieces become clear or visions manifest.

POTENT NOTABLES

You know how someone can say something to you, and it strikes you in such a way that you automatically make a mental note? Well, there have been a plethora of those moments as I got glimpses of Poppy, Cas, Sera, and Nyktos over the years—not to mention others. Here are just some that I made sure to notate for my records.

FROM BLOOD AND ASH

"'You're an absolutely stunning, murderous little creature.'"

"'Fear and bravery are often one and the same. It either makes you a warrior or a coward. The only difference is the person it resides inside.'"

"'Death is like an old friend who pays a visit, sometimes when it's least expected and other times when you're waiting for her. It's neither the first nor the last time she'll pay a visit, but that doesn't make any death less harsh or unforgiving.'"

"'With my sword and with my life, I vow to keep you safe, Penellaphe. From this moment until the last moment, I am yours.'"

"'Promise me you won't forget this, Poppy. That no matter what happens tomorrow, the next day, next week, you won't forget this, forget that this was real.'"

"'Nothing is ever simple. And when it is, it's rarely ever worth it.'"

"Some truths do nothing but destroy and decay what they do not obliterate. Truths do not always set one free. Only a fool who has spent their entire life being fed lies believes that."

"'The next time you go out, wear better shoes and thicker clothing. Those slippers are likely to be the death of you, and that dress...the death of me.'"

"'You're such a bad influence.'"…"'Only the bad can be influenced,

Princess.'"

"'Bravery and strength do not equal goodness.'"

"'I'll say it again. I don't care what you are. I care about who you are.'"

"Some things, once spoken, were given a life of their own."

"There was always someone whose pain cut so deeply, was so raw, that their anguish became a palpable entity."

"Loneliness often brought with it a heavy, coarse blanket of shame, and a cloak constructed of embarrassment."

"'You're important to me, Poppy. Not because you're the Maiden, but because you're...you.'"

"Hawke wasn't the catalyst. He was the reward."

A KINGDOM OF FLESH AND FIRE

"'Your heart, Poppy? It is a gift I do not deserve. But it is one I will protect until my dying breath.'"

"'The world, no matter how big, is often smaller than we realize.'"

"'You don't deserve everything that I've laid at your feet, and you sure as hell don't deserve the fact that I'm still trying to hold onto you. That when it comes time for you to leave, I'm still going to want you. Even when you inevitably do leave, I'll still want you.'"

"'I don't want to pretend. I'm Poppy and you're Casteel, and this is real.'"

"He was the first thing I'd ever truly chosen for myself."

"'Let's make a deal that we don't borrow tomorrow's problems today.'"

"'Always. Your heart was always safe with me. It always will be. There is nothing I will protect more fiercely or with more devotion, Poppy. Trust in that—in what you feel from me.'"

"'You can't spell dysfunctional without fun, now can you?'"

"'I fell for you when you were Hawke, and I kept falling for you when you became Casteel.'"

"'But even so, sometimes, the heartbreak that comes with loving someone is worth it, even if loving that person means eventually saying goodbye to them.'"

"He was both the villain and the hero, the monster and the monster-slayer."

"'I need to feel your lips on mine. I need to feel your breath in my lungs. I need to feel your life inside me. I just need you. It's an ache. This need. Can I have you? All of you?'"

"'You're beautiful when you're quiet and somber, but when you laugh? You rival the sunrise over the Skotos Mountains.'"

"'Dear gods, you have her on her own horse? Soon, she'll be running one of us over instead of stabbing us.'"

"'There is no side of you that is not as beautiful as the other half. Not a single inch isn't stunning. That was true the first time I said it to you, and it is still the truth today and tomorrow.'"

"He had my whole heart, and he had from the moment he allowed me to protect myself, from the moment he stood beside me instead of in front of me."

"'A cell is a cell, no matter how comfortable it is.'"

"Feelings were not stagnant. Neither were opinions or beliefs, and if we stopped believing people were capable of change, then the world might as well be left to burn."

"'I don't know what you want from me.'"…"'Everything. I want everything.'"

"'When it comes to bacon, the answer is always yes.'"

"'But I was once told that the best relationships are the ones where passions run high.'"

"'Beauty, my sweet child, is often broken and barbed, and always unexpected.'"

"'Change can be good just as much as it can be bad.'"

"'Thank you.'"…"'For what?'"…"'For choosing me.'"

"And kissing Casteel was like daring to kiss the sun."

A CROWN OF GILDED BONES

"'You will bow before your Queen. Or you will bleed before her. It is your choice.'"

"'You need to understand that I will do anything and everything for *my* wife. No risk is too great, nor is anything too sacred. Because she is my *everything*. There is nothing greater than her, and I do mean *nothing*.'"

"'You are the foundation that helps me stand. You are my walls and my roof. My shelter. *You* are my home.'"

"'Bravery is a fleeting beast, isn't it? Always there to get you into trouble, but quick to disappear once you're where you want to be.'"

"'I love you, Penellaphe. You. Your fierce heart, your intelligence and strength. I love your endless capacity for kindness. I love your acceptance of me. Your understanding. I'm in love with you, and I will be in love with you when I take my last breath and then beyond in the Vale.'"

"'The heart doesn't care how long you may have with someone. It just cares that you have the person for as long as you can.'"

"'You. All I ever need is you. Now. Always.'"

"'Life doesn't wait to hand you a new puzzle until you've figured out the last one.'"

"'There cannot be equality in power if there is no choice.'"

THE WAR OF TWO QUEENS

"'You people and your concern for nudity is tiresome.'"

"'Whether she ruled over all the lands and seas or was the Queen of nothing but a pile of ashes and bones she would—*will*—always be *my* Queen. Love is too weak an emotion to describe how she consumes me and what I feel for her. She is my everything.'"

"'We're two hearts…one soul. We'll find each other again. We always will.'"

"'Be careful but be brave.'"

"'I love you…with my heart and my soul, today and tomorrow. I will never get enough of you.'"

"'I'm never *not* in awe of you. I'm always utterly mesmerized. I'll never stop being that. Always and forever.'"

"'From blood and ash...we have risen!'"

"'To speak her name is to bring the stars from the skies and topple the mountains into the sea.'"

"This cold, aching hollowness that had woken in the last twenty-three days. It tasted like the promise of retribution. Of wrath.'"

"'You're more than a Queen. More than a goddess on the verge of becoming a Primal. You're Penellaphe Da'Neer, and you're fearless.'"

A SHADOW IN THE EMBER

"'I know what I am. I've always known. I am one of the worst sort. A monster … But don't you *ever* tell me how I feel.'"

"'It is far easier to be lied to than to acknowledge that you have been lied to.'"

"'I want to kiss you, even though there is no reason for me to other than I want it.'"

"'You are the heir to the lands and seas, skies and realms. A Queen instead of a King. You are the Primal of Life.'"

"I wasn't sure how one could seduce another into falling in love with them after stabbing them in the chest.'"

"'One of the bravest things to do is to accept the aid of others.'"

"He was like the brightest star and the deepest night sky given mortal form. And he was utterly beautiful in this form, wholly terrifying.'"

"'Where's all that bravery?'"…"'My bravery ends when I'm faced with something that can swallow me whole.'"

"'I believe he slipped and fell upon my blade.'"…"'Was it his throat that fell upon your blade?'"…"'Odd, right?'"…"'Odd, indeed.'"

"'In case you're wondering, this is me intentionally staring.'"…"'Pervert.'"

"'Don't. Not a single word.'"…"'Excuse me?'"…"'In case you have trouble counting, that is two words.'"

"'You are trouble.'"

"'A monster wouldn't care if they were one.'"

"'You interest me because there seems to be little time between what occurs in your head and what comes out of your mouth. And there seems to be little regard for the consequences.'"

"'That life for any being is as fragile as the flame of a candle—easily extinguished and stamped out.'"

"'Love is the one thing that not even fate can contend with.'"

"'You're a blessing, Sera. No matter what anyone says or believes, you are a blessing. You always have been. You need to know that.'"

A LIGHT IN THE FLAME

"'I never wanted to love. Not until you, *liessa*.'"

"'I would have loved you if I could have. There would've been no stopping me.'"

"'I can sense your need. Feel it. Taste it. You're drowning in it.'"…"'I'm fucking drowning in it.'"…"'Then drown with me.'"

"'Needing me or anyone to look out for you doesn't mean you're weak, that you can't defend yourself, or that you're afraid. We all need someone to watch over us.'"

"For the first time in my life, I felt like I was more than a destiny I'd never agreed to. More than the embers I carried within me. I felt like…*more*."

"'Because you just tore apart a god with your hands, and I found that…kind of hot.'"

"'Just because someone shares the same bloodline as you doesn't mean they deserve your time or thoughts.'"

"'Daddy Nyktos is not happy.'"

"'You're a *viktor* named Vikter?'"

"'I will gladly suffer anything Kolis dishes out as long as my blood is spilled instead of yours.'"

"'Just don't forget how to be so exquisitely reckless later.'"

"'You never know how much you can take until you can't take more.'"

"'Forgiveness benefits the forgiver, and it's easy. Understanding is acceptance, and that is far harder.'"

"'Fate just sees all the possible outcomes of free will.'"

A SOUL OF ASH AND BLOOD

"'You can call me that. Or you can call me death, whichever you prefer.'"

"I wasn't a good man. I was just hers."

"When I was around her, I didn't think of the past or the future. I simply lived."

"I would come back. I would look for her. And if she wasn't here? I would find her again. Sooner rather than later. She would be mine."

"Again, I couldn't help but think…that in a different life, I would've been built for this."

"Poppy…she was worth the risk. To give her a chance to actually live."

"'Are you going to put some clothing on?'...'Do I need to?' 'I mean, it's your dick hanging out, not mine.'"

"It was too damn easy to...to live right alongside Poppy. And, gods, I wanted that. Badly."

"I knew this was real. What was between us. What she felt for me. What I felt for her. This. It was real."

A FIRE IN THE FLESH

"I knew nothing bad could reach, scare, or disturb me here. Because I wasn't alone. A wolf sat on the bank of my lake, one more silver than white. He watched. And I knew I was safe."

"Because I loved him. I was *in* love with him. And right or wrong, I would do anything for him."

"'I'm nothing without you, *liessa*,' he whispered as he started to slip away, and the embers hummed in my chest. 'And there will be nothing without you.'"

"'I will *always* find you, Sera.'"

"'Even if I'm not looking at you, you are still all I see.'"

"'I never wanted until you.'"

"'I've lived because of you.'"

"I knew I was not a part of the cycle of life. I *was* the cycle. The beginning. Middle. The last breath before the end. Death's steadfast companion. I was Life."

"He was the nightmare that had become my dream. The calm in my storm. My strength when I was weak. The breath when I couldn't breathe. He was more than my King. My husband. Ash was the other half of my heart and soul."

"'But I still fell, Sera. Hard and fast. Irrevocably. Even without my *kardia*, I fell in love with you.'"

"'You're simply my first, Sera, and you will be my last.'"

PLAYLISTS

Have you ever had moments of your life that just seem as if they should be set to music? Sometimes, I feel that way about my visions. Occasionally, I even hear notes floating on the breeze while the scene plays out in my mind. Poppy and Casteel's and Sera and Nyktos's journeys are like symphonies in themselves, but the beat and tempo and cadence of each milestone in their lives is a perfect complement to some actual musical scores out there.

Here are some that I think you should check out and tie back to what happened in the stories of their lives.

FROM BLOOD AND ASH:

Mr. Brightside by The Killers
The Hand That Feeds by Nine Inch Nails
Coming Undone by Korn
Heavy in your Arms by Florence and the Machine
Stand By Me by Ki: Theory
Freak On a Leash by Korn
Story of My Life by One Direction
I Am the Storm by Ramin Djawadi
Hunger of the Pine by alt-J
Carrion Flowers by Chelsea Wolfe
Everybody Knows by Sigrid
If I Had a Heart by Fever Ray
Castle (The Huntsman, Winter's War Version) by Halsey
Running Up That Hill by Placebo

Spoils of War, Pt. 1 by Ramin Djawadi
Hunter (featuring John Mark McMillan) by RIAYA

A KINGDOM OF FLESH AND FIRE:

Hunger of the Pine by alt-J
If I Had a Heart by Fever Ray
Legend Has It by Run the Jewels
Heathens by Twenty One Pilots
You Don't Own Me by Grace
Something in the Shadows by Amy Stroup
Animals by Maroon 5
Hunter (featuring John Mark McMillan) by RIAYA
Deadcrush by alt-J
Sympathy for the Devil by The Rolling Stones
Spark by Tori Amos
Precious Things by Tori Amos
Shut Up and Dance by Walk the Moon
In Every Dream Home by Roxy Music
What I've Done by Linkin Park
Running Up That Hill by Placebo
No Light, No Light by Florence + the Machine
Everybody Knows by Sigrid
Take it All by Ruelle
I'm Afraid of Americans by David Bowie
Castle by Halsey
The Outsider by A Perfect Circle
Young Forever by Jay-Z ft. Mr. Hudson
Freak on a Leash by Korn
Suga Suga by Baby Bash
Elastic Heart by Sia ft. The Weeknd and Diplo
Flesh Blood by Eels
Wrong by Max ft. Lil Uzi Vert
Grey Blue Eyes by Dave Matthews
Bottom of the River by Delta Rae
Hurt by Johnny Cash
Cry Little Sister by Gerard McMann
Keep Hope Alive by The Crystal Method
Welcome to the Party by Diplo
Scars to Your Beautiful by Alessia Cara
Castle on the Hill by Ed Sheeran
Say You Won't Let Go by James Arthur

Titanium by David Guetta ft. Sia
Set the Fire to the Third Bar by Snow Patrol
OTEP by Head
The Hanging Tree by James Newton Howard ft. Jennifer Lawrence
Just Say Yes by Snow Patrol
Cosmic Love by Florence + The Machine
The Bells by Ramin Djawadi
The Last War by Ramin Djawdi
Heroes by Peter Gabriel
Closer by Nine Inch Nails
The Perfect Drug by Nine Inch Nails
Human by Rag'n'Bone Man
Khalessi by Ramin Djawadi
Guardians at the Gate by Audiomachine
O'Death by Jen Titus
Requiem for a Tower by London Music Works
Seven Devils by Florence + the Machine
Crown by Camila Cabello and Grey
Gold Dust Woman by Hole

THE CROWN OF GILDED BONES:

All Your Rage, All Your Pain by Secession Studios
Hallelujah by Jeff Buckley
Arcade by Duncan Laurence
What a Wonderful World by Alala
Heart of Courage by Two Steps From Hell
Mythical and Mighty by Secession Studios
Dracarys by Ramin Djawadi
Wicked Game (ft. Annaca) by Ursine Vulpine
Get Your Freak On by Missy Elliot
The River by Blues Saraceno
Woke Up This Morning by Alabama 3
Wildest Dreams by Duomo
#1 Crush by Garbage
Bomb Intro by Missy Elliot
Cold Wind Blowin' by The Barrows
Killing Machine by Tony Crown
Heathens by Twenty One Pilots
Heart of Darkness by Secession Studios
My Songs Know What You Did in the Dark by Fall Out Boy
Power by Kanye West

The Night King by Ramin Djawadi
WAP by Cardi By ft. Megan Thee Stallion
Immigrant Song by Led Zeppelin
Why Can't We Be Friends by War
Wrong by Max ft. Lil Uzi Vert
The Army of the Dead by Ramin Djawadi
Guardians at the Gate by Audiomachine

THE WAR OF TWO QUEENS:

Hurt by Nine Inch Nails
Deadwood by Really Slow Motion
My Body is a Cage by Peter Gabriel
Stand by Me by Ki Theory (VIP Mix)
The Rains of Castamere by The National
Coming Undone by Korn
Desperado by Love Shayla (Rihanna Remix)
Wildest Dreams by Duomo
Cold Wind Blowing by The Barrows
Red Warrior by Audiomachine
Heathens by Twenty One Pilots
Find My Baby by Moby
Seven Nation Army by The White Stripes
I Am the Storm by Ramin Djawadi
The Storm by Secession Studios
Human by Rag'n'Bone Man
If I Had a Heart by Fever Ray
Raspberry Swirl by Tori Amos
Precious Things by Tori Amos
Arcade by Duncan Laurence
Elastic Heart by Diplo, Sia, The Weeknd
Monster by Bon Iver, JAY-Z, Kanye West, Nicki Minaj, Rick Ross
Make Me Bad by Korn
Warrior by Atreyu, Travis Barker
Take it All by Ruelle
Running Up That Hill by Placebo
Counting Bodies by The Perfect Circle
Castle (Winter's War) by Halsey
Tokyo by Tomandandy
Warriors to the End by Epic Score
Closer by Nine Inch Nails
Don't Let Me Down by The Chainsmokers

Earned It by The Weeknd
Head by Step
In the Air Tonight by Phil Collins
All Your Rage by Secession Studios
Industry Baby by Lil Nas X
No Light, No Light by Florence + The Machine
Centuries by Fall out Boy
Cosmic Love by Florence + The Machine
Collapsing Universe by Really Slow Motion
Change by the Deftness
Castle on the Hill by Ed Sheeran
WAP by Cardi B, Megan Thee Stallion
Love Me Like You Do by Ellie Goulding
Winds of Winter by Ramin Djawadi
The Bells by Ramin Djawadi
The Night King by Ramin Djawadi
Mythical and Mighty by Secession Studios
Hunger of the Pine by alt-J

A SHADOW IN THE EMBER:

Venom by Eminem
Freak On a Leash - Korn
Heathens by Twenty One Pilots
Not Meant for Me by Wayne Static
Change (In the House of Flies) by Deftones
Bodies by Drowning Pool
Slept so Long by Jay Gordon
Down with the Sickness by Disturbed
Cold by Static X
Excess by Tricky
No One Quite Like You by Trentemoller/Tricky
Running Up That Hill by Placebo
Wicked Games by Ursine Vulpine
Arrival to Earth by Steve Jablonsky
Desperado Slowed (Remix) by Rihanna
Power by Kayne West
Hurt by Johnny Cash
Legend Has It by Run the Jewels
The Last War by Ramin Djawadi
My Body is a Cage by Peter Gabriel

A LIGHT IN THE FLAME:

Venom by Eminem
Darkness by Eminem
My Little Box by John Frizzell
Money Power Glory by Lana Del Ray
I Did Something Bad by Taylor Swift
Requiem for a Tower by London Music Works
Mythical and Mighty by Secession Studios
Seven Devils by Florence + the Machine
The Bells by Ramin Djawadi
Heavy In Your Arms by Florence + the Machine
Radioactive by Imagine Dragons
Let it Rock by Kevin Rudolf, ft. Lil Wayne
Paint It, Black by The Rolling Stones
Say Something by Christina Aguilera
The Monster by Eminem ft. Rihanna
Sucker for Pain by Lil Wayne, Logic, Imagine Dragons, Wiz Khalifa, and Ty Dolla $ign
Free Bird by Lynyrd Skynyrd
Heathens by Twenty One Pilots
Running Up That Hill by Placebo
Fallout by Neoni
Figured You Out by Nickelback
Cry Little Sister by Gerald McMann
Out of My Mind by Reuben and the Dark
Red Right Hand by Nick Cave
Wrong by MAX, ft. Lil Uzi Vert
Alone and Forsaken by Epic Geek (The Last of Us)
Darkside by Neoni
When It's Cold I'd like to Die by Moby
Glitter and Gold by Barns Courtney
Can't Hold Us by Macklemore ft. Ryan Lewis
Otherside by Macklemore ft. Fences
Protector of the Earth by Two Steps from Hell
All Your Rage, All Your Pain by Secession Studios
Day Ones by Baauer ft. Novelist, Leikeli47
Tokyo Drift by Teriyaki Boyz
New Blood by Zayde Wolf
I Am the Storm by Ramin Djawadi
Jenny of Oldstones by Florence + the Machine
Warriors to the End by Epic Score
In the Air Tonight by Phil Collins
Ligeti Requiem: ll. Kyrie by Gyorgy Ligeti, Jonathan Knott

Every Other Freckle by alt-J
Gold Dust Woman by Fleetwood Mac

A SOUL OF ASH AND BLOOD

Save Yourself by Stabbing Westward
Happy by NF
What Do I Have to Do by Stabbing Westward
Welcome to the Party by Diplo, French Montana, et al.
Tear Down the Bridges by IMAscore
Let You Down by NF
Sick Boi by Ren
Out Of My Mind by Reuben and the Dark
Keep Hope Alive by The Crystal Method
Andrew's Song by IMAscore
NF – The Search by Sound Audits
Interests of the Realm by Ramin Djawadi
Hi Ren by Ren
Homeland by Jenna Carlie et al.
Illest Of Our Time by Ren
The Outsider by A Perfect Circle
Human by Rag'n'Bone Man
Fate of the Kingdoms by Ramin Djawadi
Unholy (Ft. Kim Petras) by Sam Smith
Fading Memories by IMAscore
Castle of Ice by IMAscore
Where We Rise by Neoni
Darkside by Neoni
Fallout by UNSECRET and Neoni
Money Power Glory by Lana Del Rey
House of the Rising Sun by Five Finger Death Punch
When It's Cold I'd Like To... by Moby
Let It Rock by Kevin Rudolf, Lil Wayne
Last to Fall by Will Van De Crommert
Seven Nation Army by The White Stripes
Wildest Dreams by Taylor Swift
Warriors to the End by Epic Score
I Am the Storm by Ramin Djawadi
Godzilla (Ft. Juice WRLD) by Eminem
Animal Flow by Ren

A FIRE IN THE FLESH

Start a Riot by BANNERS
A Dangerous Thing by AURORA
Hollowed Kings by Ursine Vulpine and Annaca
Shady by Birdy
For This You Were Born by UNSECRET and Fleurie
We Have It All by Pim Stones
Faint by Oliver Riot
Ultraviolet by Freya Ridings
Risk It All (Ft. Ruth) by Christian Reindl
After Night by MXMS
Fangs by Little Red Lung
Tears of Gold by Faouzia
Lost Without You by Freya Ridings
Wolves by Freya Ridings
Something Sweeter by LUME
Handmade Heaven by MARINA
Slip Away by UNSECRET and Ruelle
Waking Up Slowly – Piano Version by Gabrielle Aplin
If the World by Josh Levi
Love and War by Fleurie
Believe by Tales of the Forgotten et al.
Walking on Fire by Skylar Grey and Th3rdstream
One Last Time by Jaymes Young
Down by Simon and Trella
Hypnotic – Vanic Remix by Zella Day
Exit for Love by AURORA
Cold by Oliver Riot
The Enemy by Andrew Belle
Comply by Llynks
Fallout by UNSECRET and Neoni
Heartbeat (Acoustic) by Ghostly Kisses
I am not a woman, I'm a god by Halsey
I Feel Love by Freya Ridings
Play With Fire by Sam tinnesz, Ruelle, and Violents

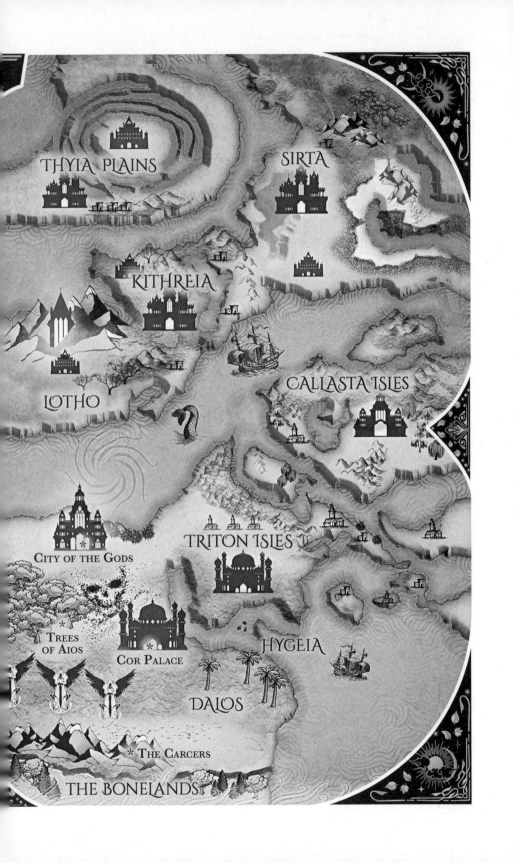

THYIA PLAINS

SIRTA

KITHREIA

LOTHO

CALLASTA ISLES

CITY OF THE GODS

TRITON ISLES

TREES
OF AIOS

COR PALACE

HYGEIA

DALOS

* THE CARCERS

THE BONELANDS

FLESH AND FIRE HISTORY TIMELINE

This is a look at how things shook out before Sera entered Iliseeum. Some details were gathered via research and speaking with others; therefore, could be slightly inaccurate due to knowledge not yet known or available. Other bits are things I have *seen*.

CLOSE TO 1000 YEARS BEFORE SERA IS BORN:

Kolis sees Sotoria picking flowers and instantly falls in love with her.
She sees him, gets scared, and falls from the Cliffs of Sorrow.
Callum tries to take his life but Kolis makes him a Revenant.
Kolis begs Eythos to bring her back to life, and he refuses.
Eythos believes his twin accepted his decision.
Eythos meets Mycella, and she becomes his Consort.

SEVERAL DECADES LATER:

Kolis discovers a way to bring Sotoria back to life, by becoming the Primal God of Life.
Kolis destroys all record of the truth in both realms.
He switches fates with his brother.
Thousands of gods and several Primals die as a result of what Kolis does.
Kolis brings Sotoria back to life.
She's horrified by what's been done.
Kolis doesn't understand why she's so morose.
Sotoria possibly starves herself.
Nothing Kolis does gets her to love him.
Sotoria possibly fights back against him.
She dies again.
Eythos and Keella mark her for rebirth.
Sotoria's soul will never enter the Vale, it will continuously be reborn.
Kolis murders Mycella while she's pregnant and destroys her soul.
Somehow, Nyktos miraculously survives.

TWO HUNDRED YEARS BEFORE SERA'S BIRTH:

King Roderick promises that the firstborn Mierel daughter will become the Consort of the Primal of Death.
Nyktos is about nineteen years old when the deal is made.
Eythos takes embers from himself and Nyktos and hides them in the Mierel bloodline.
He believes he's hiding the embers in the one being able to stop Kolis—Sotoria's reincarnation.
Eythos dies—killed while weakened by a shadowstone stab to the heart.
Kolis retains his soul and puts it in the Star diamond.

THE START OF SERA'S LIFE:
Sera is born—an en caul birth.
Rot begins in the mortal realm—possibly Iliseeum, as well.
The mortals believe it's a countdown to the expiration of the deal that King Roderick made.

TEN YEARS LATER:
An oil spill happens in the Stroud Sea, and an enraged Phanos erupts from the water in a hurricane and destroys every ship in port, killing hundreds. His roar of fury sends shockwaves across the land and makes ears bleed. After, the waters were free of pollutants.
It seems to me that Phanos is channeling the Ancients a bit there.

SEVENTEEN YEARS AFTER SERA'S BIRTH (BIRTHDAY):
Sera is presented to the Primal God of Death to become his Consort.
Nyktos rejects her.

TWENTY YEARS AFTER SERA'S BIRTH (ANOTHER BIRTHDAY):
The Primal God of Death claims Sera.

TWENTY-ONE YEARS AFTER SERA'S BIRTH:
Sera is fated to die at age twenty-one unless she's Ascended by Nyktos. But the catch is…he has to love her. And he's incapable of love with his *kardia* removed.
It's unclear if she'll die due to the Culling/Nyktos's blood, by Kolis's hand, or another way.
If Sera dies, both realms die with her.
Thankfully, the fact that they're heartmates means that Nyktos *can* love her. So, when he decides to be selfish and Ascend her instead of taking the embers and letting her die, she becomes the true Primal of Life.

FLESH AND FIRE CHARACTERS

As with the earlier part, this section contains information on individuals of note in the time of the gods. Here, too, I have recorded things I've found via research or *saw*, documenting them to be used for reference. If something happens to be missing, it's likely because nobody recorded it—which is entirely possible since, for example, any and all mention of the Consort was erased—or I never saw it in my visions. If things come to light later, either through unearthed references or my sight, I will update the records as needed. But for now, this is a fairly comprehensive detailing of what happened when Seraphena Mierel entered Iliseeum, and those involved in the subsequent impactful and multi-realm-changing events.

SERAPHENA "SERA" MIEREL
Consort to the Primal of Death / *The* Primal of Life
Court: The Shadowlands

Oh, dear Sera. She has a fire I envy and a past I condole. Promised to another over two hundred years before she was even born, her future was never hers. Used as a tool, a pawn in a bid to right a wrong, she was stripped of her rightful honors and forced to commit unspeakable acts. Thankfully, things worked out for her—at least mostly—but it certainly wasn't an easy road.

Because I have no firsthand knowledge of the Consort, my files on her are extensive. I wasn't sure what someone would find important, so I detailed most everything I *saw*. She and Ash also fascinate me, so I found I *wanted* to record as much as possible.

Hair: Pale blond. Curly. Down to her waist/hips.
Eyes: Deep forest-green that become silver with Ascension. Tilted at the corners.
Body Type: Tall. Voluptuous.
Facial features: Stubborn chin.
Distinguishing features: Crescent moon birthmark above left shoulder blade—unseen by mortals but sometimes felt. Thirty-six freckles on her face. Twelve on her back. A constellation of birthmarks on her thigh. Golden Consort imprint on her right hand. Right-handed—wears her dagger on her right hip.
Preternatural features/abilities: Can sense emotions. Can sense death. While healing/reviving, glow erupts under the skin and seeps from hands. Power sometimes comes with the scent of fresh lilacs. Can use compulsion on Primals. Can turn into a silvery-white cave cat with green eyes spliced with silver.
Personality: Impetuous. Brave. Stubborn. Contrary. Curious. Impulsive. Reckless.
Habits/Mannerisms/Strengths/Weaknesses: Afraid of snakes. Suffers

from severe anxiety. Trained with weapons. Trained as an escort. Not good at remembering voices. Can't swim. Walks when she can't sleep. Rambles when she's nervous. Likes to read. Extraordinarily good at not remaining unseen. Can hold breath underwater for ~two minutes. Holds breath to get anxiety under control.

Other: Twenty years old. Winter birthday. Full Consort title = The One who is born of Blood and Ash, *the* Light and the Fire, and *the* Brightest Moon. Before Kolis kidnapped her, she had killed twenty-two individuals with her hands.

Background: Promised as a Consort two hundred years before she was born. Attempted to take her life.

Family: Mother = Queen Calliphe. Father = Lamont †. Ancestor = Roderick Miercl †. Stepsister = Ezmeria "Ezra." Stepbrother = Tavius †. Stepfather = Ernald †. Shared soul = Sotoria †.

SERAPHENA'S JOURNEY TO DATE:

At six summers, Sera discovered her gift. A beloved barn cat, Butters, died, and Sera and Ezra found him. Sera brought him back to life without even trying. Unfortunately, her stepbrother Tavius saw and reported it to the Queen, making Sera's life even more difficult.

At age seven, her family left her behind when they went on holiday to their country estate, and she was never allowed to have dinner with them. She wasn't even allowed a lady's maid, for fear they'd be a bad influence on her. I find this so very sad, and my heart breaks for her.

At a much too early age, she began training in weapons and hand-to-hand combat, becoming even more skilled than most of the Royal Guard.

At age eleven, she sprained her ankle, and Sir Holland, the knight in charge of her training, bandaged her and gave her more affection than anyone in her family.

Her father died by suicide when she was young—I'm not sure at exactly what age...young enough for her to not really know him at all. It changed her.

In the months leading up to her seventeenth birthday, she trained with the Mistresses of the Jade in sensual warfare, being told that the most dangerous weapon isn't a violent one.

They are absolutely correct. I've been known to use my wiles to get my way, but I was never forced to, and certainly not as a teenager. And especially not for a task I was told I could not fail at like Sera: becoming the Primal of Death's Consort, making him fall in love with her thus weakening him, only to…end him.

Despite being the daughter of the current Queen and the deceased King of Lasania, Sera has only been recognized as a Royal and a Princess three times in her life. Still, being the Maiden made her a target. There were at least two kidnapping attempts.

At age seventeen, Sera was made to feel naked, exposed, and helpless as she was trussed up and readied to be presented to the Primal of Death. Unfortunately, he rejected her in a very public manner, making her life even harder for the years to come—something he would come to regret deeply later.

Despite the increased hardships and her miserable living situation, Sera found ways to fill her time and feel useful. Ezra started helping the less fortunate in Lasania, and Sera helped her stepsister, stealing excess food from the kitchens and getting her hands on anything else that could potentially help. She also helped the less fortunate in other ways and protected the lost.

At the age of nineteen, Sera started having severe, troublesome, and worrisome headaches. At about that same time, she became sexually active and used it as a way to feel less hollow inside.

Gods, I feel for the poor girl so much. What a dear. Sex should be a celebration of life, not a substitute for the things one needs to survive and thrive. But Sera makes the most of everything that has gone wrong, taking comfort in the ironic twist that failing to become the Primal's Consort means she's no longer hidden away and doesn't have to remain pure.

As you can see, she did not have an easy upbringing, and her teenage years were even more fraught with unease as Queen Calliphe sent Sera out to commit unspeakable acts of violence for even the most minor perceived slights.

But let's get back to when things all changed. Leading up to her seventeenth birthday, she was already undergoing training with the Mistresses of the Jade, was better in combat than a lot of the guards, and kept at arm's length because of her Chosen Maiden status. All of this contributed to her growing anxiety, which she desperately tried to control with breathing exercises.

As I mentioned before, on her seventeenth birthday, she was readied for presentation to be offered to the Primal of Death as his Consort as a way to honor the deal struck between the Primal and King Roderick Mierel some two hundred years before Sera's birth.

Lady Kala leads Sera to three Shadow Priests, who take her to a circular chamber to be presented to the Primal. They summon him, and Sera feels real terror when he arrives. However, as she's been trained to do, she smiles shyly and goes to kneel in supplication, only he suddenly comes before her. He feels cold to her, and that coldness only grows as he leans in and tells her that he has no need of a Consort. Just as quickly as he arrived, he's gone. At first, she feels relief at being left behind, but then panic flares—and rightfully so. The next three years would be ever so dreadful for dear Sera.

Despite it not being her fault at all, she's blamed by all—her mother one of the worst—and it shatters and shrivels something inside her, changing her irrevocably.

The Priests present her on each of her next three birthdays, but the Primal of Death never shows himself again. I later discovered they never actually summoned Nyktos.

In her twentieth year, Sera's mother orders her to show some Lords of the Vodina Isles what a hot piece she is—something crude they said to her—and kill them all.

Every year the Primal of Death didn't claim her made things harder for Sera, but the six months following her twentieth birthday were some of the worst. Food was no longer sent to her chambers, making it necessary for her to raid the kitchens. She no longer received clothing. And she was always left alone. The only time she even saw her mother was when she was ordered to *send a message*.

Now, I know that Calliphe had trouble looking at Sera, even from a very young age because she looks so much like her father and the Queen missed him like a limb, but to neglect and abuse your child like that? It makes me furious.

But back to her ordered assassination. Going after the Lords of the Vodina Isles, Sera heads to the docks and kills all four of them, setting their ship free to be found later by whomever. She then heads to the Luxe, hears a shrill cry, and follows the sound, only to see a woman killing a man with eather. She feels warmth in her chest and sees a man tossing a dead child aside. She realizes that both the man and the woman are gods and vows to kill at least one of them—the male for sure. She knows she'll likely die in the process and makes peace with that knowledge.

Just as she's about to launch her attack, someone grabs her and carries her away. Something about his voice is strangely familiar. She pulls a dagger on him and ends up pinned against an outdoor wall. Meeting his gaze, she realizes that he's *also* a god. She wonders if he's from the Shadowlands, the Court of the Primal of Death, and therefore knows who she is.

Oh, he knew all right.

When the three murderous gods return, she and the god she's with hide in plain sight by making out against the wall. Once the coast is clear, he orders her to go home. In true Seraphena fashion, she simply walks away, ignoring him.

Meeting up again, Sera realizes he's been following the other gods, too. They decide to investigate the Kazin house together, and she finds it odd that the gods would kill and want it to remain unknown. She learns that this isn't the first time these gods have done something like this and hears about the other victims.

Sera feels jolts of static whenever she and the god touch, and the eather in the god's eyes makes her think of the Primal of Death. Despite what she feels and the confusion it raises within her, she doesn't hesitate to pull her shadowstone dagger and put it to his throat. He comments on the weapon and asks her where she got it. She lies and says she took it from her stepbrother.

Easily disarmed, she has to answer why she so eagerly rushes toward death. She tells him to just get on with killing her but finds herself wanting to relax into him. Before she can unravel that thought more, he tells her to be careful and leaves.

The next time Sera trains with Sir Holland, he tells her she's been off lately, and she realizes she's been trying to come to terms with the fact that she threatened and kissed a *god*. And the more she thinks about it, the more she realizes how right it felt to be around him.

When Holland calls her *Princess*, it annoys Sera, and she corrects him, saying she's an assassin and bait. He corrects *her*, but she once again insists she's merely a weapon and nothing more…except for maybe a martyr. She was prepared to die killing the murderous gods, but she knows she won't survive killing the Primal of Death.

Sera goes to see Odetta and asks her what it means to be touched by life and death—something she's been told before. Odetta says that only the Fates know.

That's a loaded answer if I ever heard one. It makes me wonder if Odetta knew more than she let on.

After visiting her father's painting in her mother's room and getting into it with the Queen, Sera heads to Stonehill and feels warmth in her chest, indicating that someone close has died. She sees the god, Madis, again and enters Joanis Designs, only to find the seamstress dead. The smells of charred flesh and something fresher permeate the air. Lilacs, perhaps?

She feels someone sneaking up on her and whirls, stabbing out with her dagger and getting…the god—her sexy god—right in the chest. Stunned, she watches as he pulls the blade free and destroys it. She threatens him and says she's unimpressed by his show of force, not surprising given her usual lack of self-preservation. He asks her if anything scares her and calls her *liessa*. Once again, she feels a sense of…rightness being with him. Even more so when he tells her that she feels terror but isn't afraid.

Nobody has ever seen her like that.

As they discuss what keeps bringing them together, he confesses that he's watched out for her, but more than that, he's *wanted* to.

Now *that* is a comment that means so much more than it sounds on the surface, especially since we know he's watched her since she was a child.

Sera suddenly gets an odd feeling in the center of her chest, right in the spot where she normally feels her gifts responding to death. The heaviness unfurls within her, and she turns back to the seamstress's body for no discernible reason, suddenly catching the scent of stale lilacs in the air.

The dead seamstress stirs, rises, and attacks. The god steps in and stabs Andreia with his shadowstone sword. Once she's dead, Sera asks the god what *liessa* means—the word he's been calling her. He explains that it has many meanings, but it always means something beautiful and powerful.

If that didn't give her a boost, I'm not sure what would.

While training later with Sir Holland, Ezra comes for her—stirring the knight's ire—and asks for her help, telling her about an abusive guy named Nor and his children. Sera agrees.

After donning the appropriate attire, she goes to see Nor. On the way, she and Ezra discuss the Rot overtaking the land. Near the Temple of Keella, Sera hears protestors speaking about the Rot and the Crown. While their rants are true, the words spoken bother her. Despite that, she has a job to do and does it, killing Nor, taking care of a battered woman, and rescuing the man's abused son.

While walking through the elms to her lake, Sera sees a reddish brown kiyou wolf that's been shot in the chest with an arrow. She approaches and tries to help, ultimately bringing it back to life. It licks her hand, and she feels the same warmth in her chest that she usually does around death or when she uses her healing gift, only it's stronger this time. She wonders if it's because of the wolf's size.

She makes it to the lake and is filled with wonder at how it feels like home. Heading in, she enjoys herself until she realizes she's not alone. She calls out for whoever is there to show themselves and is stunned when the god walks out from behind the waterfall. She tries to scold him for being there. When he tells her he was there before her, and she realizes that he watched her undress, she's shocked—more so when he says she's like a goddess made of silver and moonbeams. Regardless, she demands that he leave.

Once again, his voice—like a smoky, shadowy caress—feels familiar to her, and she grows inexplicably warm.

She asks him about his ink, and he hedges. As their talk progresses, she threatens him again—shocker, right?—and then reveals she's a Princess. She asks him his name and sees his tattoo in its entirety. He says that some call him Ash, and tacks on that it's short for many things.

Sera exits the lake and gets dressed but only dons her slip before he warns her that they're not alone. Sera sees Gyrms for the first time, and their scent reminds her of something. She's worried they will kill the god but can't help but bicker with him as they fight the creatures.

Eventually, she ends up unconscious from the battle. When she wakes, she calls Ash beautiful and realizes that she's on the grass with her head on his thigh. Surprised he stayed, she engages in more conversation with him, and he fills her in on some stuff she questions. Many of the things Ash says utterly surprise—and delight—Sera, and she finds herself a little awed.

She realizes she's been smiling, and he teases her that she's gifted him with three. When she asks if the other gods are kind, he corrects her that *he's* not kind but then says he maybe has one kind and decent bone in his body—for her.

Unable to stop herself, she asks him why, and he tells her that he wants and needs to kiss her. She realizes that she is attracted to him on a visceral level, as well, and tells him to go ahead.

He smiles, and she sees his fangs for the first time before sharing a kiss to end all kisses. When Ash tells her to show him what she wants, she doesn't hesitate. She demonstrates what ramps her up and controls his movements as he pleasures her with his hand. When she crests that peak, he sucks her flavor from his fingers and tells her that she tastes like the sun.

Sera moves to reciprocate, and he confesses that it'll become more than kissing and touching if she does that, admitting how badly he wants her. She tells him that she feels the same before they kiss, cuddle, and chat a bit more, and then part ways.

Back at the castle, she learns about the riot the night before and talks to Ezra about the ruler Lasania needs. Despite the gravity of their conversation, she finds she can't stop thinking about Ash.

Sera raids the kitchens and takes what she finds to check on some of the farmers on the outskirts of town. Unfortunately, she discovers the Coupers have succumbed to the hardships of the Rot. Distraught, she heads to see the King and talks to him about the Coupers and what's going on in the kingdom. Tavius is there, and they argue as usual. During the exchange, she feels something dark in the center of her chest where her gift generally springs to life, but this time, it's slick and cold.

On her way to training, Sera hears a servant calling for help and goes to investigate, only to find it's a trap. During the attack, she tells her assailants that killing her won't stop the Rot and learns that the Royal Guards were paid to take her out. She defends herself and ups her body count to seventeen. When discovered later, she lies and says she found the guards dead. She also sees the golden god we eventually find out is Callum—and not a god at all.

Later, Sera overhears Ezra giving instructions to a carriage driver and follows her. She ends up helping Healer Dirks with some injured townsfolk. She and Ezra discuss her attack and the role the servant girl played, and Sera finds out that Tavius is broke—an insinuation that he couldn't have been the one who paid off the guards. She's not sure she believes that.

Ector arrives in the mortal realm and confronts Sera. She knows he's a god, but he tells her not to kneel to him, making her realize that she's never knelt for Ash. Ector tells her that he was ordered to give her something and presents her with a narrow birch box. Inside, she's stunned to find a gorgeous new shadowstone dagger and feels a flush of emotion. She's never been given a gift before.

That is just so very sad. Everyone should be given a gift at some point in their life, especially when they're young.

Sera's nursemaid passes away, and Sera starts feeling more and more ill after the funeral. She tells Sir Holland about her symptoms, and he instructs her to rest and says he'll bring her something to help her feel better. When he returns, he tells her the story of Sotoria and says that Sera reminds him of her. He also assures her that everything will be okay regarding her becoming Consort and the fate of the realm.

As an Arae, he would know… But Sera doesn't know that yet.

The Rite arrives, and Sera attends, posing as the Queen's handmaiden. In the Sun Temple, Sera feels the energy of the place coating the air and crackling across her skin. It reminds her of the jolt she got when Ash touched her.

As she watches her stepsister, she realizes that she's jealous of Ezra and wishes she was worthy of her family. A Chosen is presented to the King of Gods, and Sera is shaken when Kolis looks directly at *her*. She wonders if she only imagined the Primal's attention, but thinking about it only makes her head hurt worse.

Later, Ezra comes to Sera, clearly shaken and asking for her help. When she sees why, Sera realizes that Mari—Ezra's friend—is dead. Her sister begs her to save Marisol, and Sera realizes that Ezra loves the other woman. Sera brings her back from the dead and worries for a moment that she'll come back like the seamstress did—not mortal any longer. Her fears are assuaged when she realizes that Mari doesn't have fangs. Ezra thanks her and tells her she is and has always been a blessing, not a failure. They hug, and her stepsister says she loves her. Despite the positive outcome, Sera worries about the feeling of dread overtaking her. She fears she's playing like a Primal and will be punished for it.

After a night full of nightmares of chasing a dark-haired man and having wolves and serpents chasing *her*, Sera wakes late the next morning, thinking—and hoping—the Primal of Death doesn't know what she did. Unfortunately, she rouses to find Tavius in her room. She immediately reaches for her dagger, only to find it gone. Sera accuses Tavius of being behind the attack the other day, and he tells her that he wouldn't waste his coin on her.

Seeing that Tavius has her dagger, she lunges for it, and he pins her to the bed. He tells her the King is dead, and he is now the ruler of Lasania. She also finds out that Sir Holland has been reassigned and sent to the Vodina Isles to work on a so-called peace treaty. She knows that's not true. He was sent there to die, as the people of the Isles no doubt want revenge for what she did to their Lords.

Sera asks her stepbrother why he hates her and realizes that he sees her, the last rightful Mierel heir, as a threat. She hadn't considered that… Still, she tells him that he is not and will never *be* her King. He calls in the guards, and they take her to the Great Hall.

Tavius secures Sera to the statue of the Primal and whips her. As she feels something dark and oily spark within her, icy fire pours out of her body, her blood hums, and the center of her chest throbs. She feels as if she can taste shadows and death in the back of her throat. She vows she'll kill Tavius—slice his hands from his body and carve his heart from his chest before setting him on fire. When laughter erupts from her, it's an ancient, endless, dark sound that isn't hers.

Suddenly, the Primal of Death appears, and she's stunned to see that it's Ash.

He shatters one guard, making her laugh darkly. When Ash claims her as his Consort, she laughs again.

She had to be in shock, and her injuries certainly didn't help.

Ash confronts Tavius, and the icy fire in Sera's veins returns as she watches her mother beg for her stepbrother's life. Instead of killing him, Ash leaves Tavius to Sera, and *she* kills him. Still riding on the high of taking care of that menace, she realizes the familiarity she's felt with Ash makes sense now, and it enrages her. Furious, she attacks him.

He tells her that if he leaves her in the mortal realm, she'll become a target, even if she escapes punishment for killing the new King. So, he claims her. He tells her she no longer has a choice and apologizes, promising that her family will be safe.

They leave the castle, and she asks Ash why he didn't tell her who he was. He asks *her* if she would have still been interested in him if she'd known he was the Primal of Death. She has no real answer for that.

When they reach her lake, Sera discovers why she's felt so at home there all these years—it was a way for her to get to him. They pass through to Iliseeum, and Sera is stunned to find that one of the hills she sees is actually a dragon. Well...a *draken*. She meets Nektas and Ash tells her to pet him. She hesitates, afraid to be swallowed whole, but does it anyway. Three other draken emerge.

Sera sees the palace and assumes that Ash impaled those she sees hanging on the wall. It makes her wary. Rhain approaches, and they meet. Ash confesses that he'd hoped there would be some time before the others realized he'd arrived with a guest. He tells her that very few know about her but asks if he can introduce her as his Consort. She agrees.

After she meets Aios, the goddess takes her to her room and has food and bath water prepared for her. Ash arrives sometime later when Sera's in the tub and tells her that Tavius was sent to the Abyss. He offers to help her wash her hair, and she accepts. As he goes about the task, they talk, and Ash asks about her training. She lies and inquires why he never returned. He tells her that the Priests never resummoned him. He admits what he felt from her that day he came and explains why he did what he did, stunning Sera with the knowledge that he can feel and taste emotions.

Sera asks Ash why he made the deal and is told the answer is complicated. He says he'll tell her when she's dressed. The sexual tension ramps up between them again, and Ash tells her he knows she enjoys and wants his touch, which has nothing to do with the deal. Both of them are very interested in certain aspects of their union. He pleasures her again with his hand and admits to thinking about their time at the lake every time he takes care of himself.

He applies healing ointment to her back and reminds her that he's the same person he was before, despite her knowing that he's the Primal of Death. He then goes on to say that she knows more about him than most.

More than most? She knows him completely. They are heartmates, after all.

Sera wonders about the deal with King Roderick and learns that Ash didn't make it; his father did. He goes on to explain that the deal transferred to him when his father died, along with all the power and responsibilities of the Primal of Death. Sera suddenly realizes that what he said when he brought her to Iliseeum, about her choice ending, pertains to him, as well. He didn't choose any of this either.

She learns more about his parents. He also reveals that he's had others watching her. When talk turns to Madis, Cressa, and Taric, Ash tells her that he doesn't think the murders are connected to her, though he says he waited so long to come to her again out of fear of exposing her.

Sera realizes that everything she believed about the Primal of Death is wrong. He's a good man, but it doesn't matter because she has a duty. She returns to the subject of Lathan—the friend he had watching her that he was forced to kill—and asks why Ash had him watching over her. He explains that his enemies will now become hers. As the reality of her situation sinks in, she laments the unfairness of it and considers everything that will happen after she kills him.

Aios arrives and fills Sera in on several things she's been wondering about. The goddess tells her how she came to be in the Shadowlands and how she and the others feel safe in Nyktos's Court. After she leaves, Sera finds that Ector is guarding her room and realizes she isn't allowed to leave. The god tells her that he's there for her safety. When she calls Nyktos *Ash*, it stuns Ector, and he tells her that he doubts even the Primal of Death knows what to do with her.

Not many would. Sera is truly unique and wonderful.

Davina takes over maid duties and calls Sera meyaah *Liessa*. Sera learns that it means: my Queen. The draken tells her about the dangers surrounding the House of Haides.

Saion escorts her downstairs, and Ash returns the dagger he gifted her, now with a sheath. She immediately secures it to her right thigh before asking him some questions.

Sera learns he can't read her mind, and that he doesn't feed anymore. When she inquires about him being a prisoner, he tells her he has been many things and hesitates to answer. She wonders if he'd rather them get to know each other or be strangers and is stunned when he confesses that he wants them to be as close as they were at the lake once again, but that talk of his imprisonment isn't up for discussion.

Sera meets Jadis and learns more about the draken, which she finds utterly fascinating.

When next she sees Ash, she runs into him, and he jerks and hisses. It concerns her. Even more when he urges her not to touch him. She insinuates she doubts his interest in her and says he's all talk. He backs her against a wall and tells—plus demonstrates—how real and potent his interest is. He explains how badly he wants to be inside her and knows she wants it too without even having to read her emotions. She tells him that she doesn't like him—a lie—and he responds that it's better that way.

They can resist it all they want, but it's futile. Don't you sometimes wish you could just tell people that so they would stop wasting their time and appreciate what's right in front of them?

Sera tours the House of Haides and learns that her coronation will happen in a fortnight. When she asks if she'll be Ascended, she's surprised by Ash's response. He tells her that this was never her choice, and he won't force an eternity of it on her. She also learns that he views love as an unnecessary risk.

With some thought, Sera realizes that Ash's mother was likely murdered by another Primal and considers that Ash may actually be incapable of love given what happened to his parents. She also wonders how he'll respond to her unusual gift.

Some days later, another Primal arrives, and Ector escorts Sera to safety. She chooses to be sequestered in the library instead of her chambers and ends up spying on the interaction between Veses and Ash. The feelings it rouses in her are confusing, but she chooses to push them aside for the time being.

Later, she wanders the grounds and winds up in the Red Woods. She finds a wounded silver hawk—that she later discovers was one of Attes's *chora*, an extension of him in his *nota* form—and heals the animal, compelled by an old, powerful instinct. After, she sees the similarities between the Rot back in Lasania and what is happening to the Dying and Red Woods.

Hunters and entombed gods attack Sera, and she realizes she can't kill them all. Ash suddenly appears and saves her, and she learns about the entombed gods and the blood trees. After the attack, Saion escorts her back to the House of Haides and realizes she's been injured. She falls unconscious and wakes to find Nektas with her in his god form. He tells her the only reason she isn't dead is because Ash used a rare antidote on her.

She believes that all of Ash's decisions and actions are because of the deal. She has no idea that he already loves her, though even he doesn't realize it yet because of his lack of *kardia*.

Ash arrives and asks Sera how she got so strong as she seems truly unfazed by almost dying. She says she *had* to be strong. Talk turns to the attack in the woods and how the gods got free, and Sera learns that the Shadowlands dying has nothing to do with the deal.

Ash tells her that he's asked everyone to give her space and admits he's been avoiding her too because spending more than a few minutes in her presence has his desire overwhelming his common sense. She scoffs. He kisses her and admits that he doesn't know why he fights it since she'd let him have her. He pleasures her once more.

Randomly, he tells her that he counted her freckles and reveals that she has thirty-six, telling her there should be no doubt in her mind about his interest in her. She realizes that he found release this time, too, even though he wasn't touched. He asks if he can lie with her, and she agrees, confessing to him that she's had sex before and learning that Ash is a virgin. It shocks her, and she wonders aloud why.

She realizes that his life is as lonely as hers, and that he's risking everything with her because he can't help himself—even though he thinks they'll both end up hating him for it. He falls asleep beside her but is gone when she wakes.

Aios brings Sera breakfast and eats with her in her chambers before they go for a walk and help Reaver with his flying. The goddess tells her that Ash has never had any sexual or romantic interest in anyone before Sera. She then meets Bele and Rhahar. Bele is the first to bow to her and tells her why it's so important that everyone does it. She also shares that the other Courts are taking bets on how long she'll live.

Later, a seamstress arrives to do a fitting and talk revolves around the coronation, the Chosen, and the Ascension. Ash checks on her and reveals that no mortal has Ascended for several hundred years, then tells Sera the truth about the fate of the Chosen and that Kolis knows and doesn't care. He also explains how some Chosen are simply disappearing. She demands they find a way to stop the Rites and learns that Ash has been hiding the Chosen away, though he prefers it appear as if he's doing nothing. She has to steel herself. Lasania is all that matters. She can't worry about the mortals. The Chosen aren't her problem.

That night, unable to sleep, she goes out onto the balcony and finds Ash. She tells him she's dealing with what she learned, and they discuss the difficulties of their positions, and the way death has affected them both. He says she's not a monster and touches her, causing another jolt of energy to pass between them. He then goes on to say that a monster wouldn't care if they were one. She kisses him.

Seeing that he's struggling, too, she tells him that he isn't responsible for the actions of others and moves to explore. Enjoying the playfulness she has with Ash—something she's never had with another—she pleasures him, delighting in making the Primal of Death shake. After, they spoon, and she falls asleep, thinking over all the new things she's experienced in the short time she's been with Ash.

The next morning, she realizes she felt something shift the night before when they fell asleep, like something growing between them that was more than mutual lust. She feels connected to him in a way that goes beyond the deal, and it warms her chest. She's shocked to find Nektas with her, and even more surprised when he tells her he's never seen Ash sleep so peacefully before and claims her as one of his.

Denied going to court because of the risk and with nothing to do but think about things, she's happy to be able to walk with Ector, despite her thoughts spiraling about how Ash lifts the darkness from her and the growing feelings between them. She learns more about the god and finds out he knew Ash's parents and knows about the deal.

She and the draken follow him to see what's going on at the southern gate, and she feels warmth in her chest when she sees Gemma, realizing the mortal is dead. The heat in her chest vibrates, striking against an instinct she's never felt so powerfully before. She wonders if the draken can sense what's building inside her.

She starts to glow a faint, silvery-white, and the scent of freshly bloomed lilacs rises. Humming grows in her ears, awakening a calling in her that overrides all thought. Eather swirls around her fingertips, her throat goes dry, and her pulse races as light flares along Gemma's skin, and the girl revives. Ash remarks with astonishment that Sera carries an ember of life.

Sera's thoughts flash back to Sir Holland telling her that she carries an ember of life, hope, and the possibility of a future. As she thinks on that, she's told the gods and draken in attendance felt the power ripple, and it's likely that everyone in Iliseeum felt it. She learns that many will come looking for the source and that could be a very bad thing.

And it is. A *very* bad thing. Even though most who were the real threats already knew.

Ash tells her that he's felt it before and asks her how many other times she's used her gift. He reveals that the Hunters and the murderous gods were likely looking for her, and if he'd been closer, it would have drawn him out, too. She reveals how she healed the hawk in the woods and brought back Marisol before she left the mortal realm. He tells her that her gift is from the Primal of Life, but not Kolis. The real one: Ash's father. She learns that Eythos was the true Primal of Life, and that the ember was his—and Ash's once upon a time—until Kolis, Eythos's twin, stole it.

Sera learns the story of Eythos, Kolis, and Sotoria. She admits that she'd never used her gift on a mortal before Mari because she didn't want the power or the ability to decide someone's fate or use the power anytime the choice was presented. She thinks that makes her weak, but Nektas tells her otherwise. She wonders—with some horror—if she and Ash are related and is happy to find out they are not, but she still questions how her gift can help. She then learns that Kolis has Eythos's soul. And given the poppies started blooming once she arrived after being dormant for hundreds of years, Nektas insists her mere presence is bringing life back to the realm.

The Rot in Iliseeum is from Kolis losing his powers, and while she argues that it's the deal expiring, she's told it has nothing to do with that. She's shocked to find out that what's happening in Lasania would have happened regardless of the bargain, and suddenly realizes the clock ticking down wasn't for her kingdom, it was for *her.*

Sudden relief sweeps through her at not having to manipulate and kill Ash as she was trained to do. It lightens her load yet overwhelms her with guilt. Bele outs Sera's motives, and she confirms when asked outright. She explains that was why she kept going back to the Temple. Sera believes she'll die now and can no longer think of Ash as…well, Ash. He's Nyktos. He tells her that she would have died the second she pulled the shadowstone blade from his chest after killing him. She attempts to apologize but is told they're under siege.

She offers to help and reminds them that she's trained, saying the danger is there because of her and she will not just stand by and do nothing. She's not a danger to their people and means them no harm, even though Ash believes she's a danger to him. Still, she rides with Ash, Rhahar, Saion, and Rhain to the gates at the bay, revealing that she can feel death—the souls leaving their bodies. Ash tells her to stay with Ector and Rhain, and she takes up a post firing arrows at the dakkais.

After the fight, Sera learns the rules for attacking another Primal's Court. Suddenly, she realizes that if Kolis wants her dead, she will be. He knows *something* is in the Shadowlands, though doesn't know the source. Nyktos insists he'll keep it that way, no matter what.

With a divide between them, they trade barbs and Sera screams at Nyktos to stop reading her emotions, especially if he isn't going to believe what he feels. She goes on to say that she never wanted to fulfill her duty and nothing she did with him was an act.

Feeling like a monster, she offers to heal Nyktos's wounds, and he lets it be known that he doesn't trust her enough to let her try. That stings. She's concerned about him and doesn't want anything to happen, so she asks Nektas how she can get him to take sustenance. He says he thinks they can probably get Ash to feed from her because he's mad enough to do it.

Well, alrighty, then.

The draken asks Sera if she would have killed Ash if she'd never learned it wouldn't save her people. She can't say yes. Nektas says that Ash knows that, too, and that's why he'll feed. So, she goes to him and tells him to take from her. She admits that she always knew she'd die young. He tells her to leave and says if she doesn't, he'll feed from and fuck her. She taunts him, asking if that's a promise. He admits that he might kill her. Still, he calls her *liessa*.

They engage in a little hate sex, though it's anything but, it's more frustration, and he starts to heal.

After asking if he took enough blood, she goes to leave. He tells her to rest, and she says he can go fuck himself. When he grabs for her, Sera notices that he feels warm for the first time. He tells her that she's no real threat to him because he'd never love her, and she asks him if he's sure about that. Sera submits as he takes her again, biting his thumb and drawing blood. He spanks her, and she knows that neither of them will ever be the same.

Later, she wakes alone with a headache, wondering if Nyktos's body was warm because he fed. She doesn't think she can repair things with him, but she wants friendship if nothing else. If she can. She thinks on whether there's another way for her to save her people. Maybe the ember was put in her for another reason. She suddenly feels sickened at the thought of Kolis going after Nyktos before and admits, even if only to herself, that she cares about him and his people. She knows that getting caught by Kolis means she'll die, and that will hasten the death of both realms.

Paxton brings water for a bath and Sera feels like crying at the thoughtfulness of the gesture. She learns the boy's story, and he tells her that they can't wait for her coronation and are proud to have her as their Consort.

While in the bath, Sera is attacked. Hamid strangles her. She fights, breaks a stool in the process, and stabs him with a jagged leg. He falls and cracks his head on the tub. When the others arrive, they discuss the mortal and his motives, and she remembers that Hamid visited Gemma.

Suddenly, Sera becomes unsteady on her feet, her face and head hurting terribly. She gets dizzy and tells them she gets migraines like her mother but adds in the bit about her teeth bleeding lately. Nyktos brings her some healing tea—the same she had with Sir Holland—and they recount when things started. They tell her she's going through the Culling and why.

Nyktos keeps her at arm's length and tells her she'll be his Consort, though in name only. He adds that she's merely a vessel for the ember she carries—no friendship or love will be involved.

Low blow, Nyktos. But given what I saw sometime after this, I understand what you're trying to do here…

After breakfast, Sera sees Gemma and finds that her touch removes all wounds. She tells the girl that Nyktos won't hold her accountable for Hamid's actions because she didn't tell him to attack Sera. Then things get complicated. She learns that *she* is who Kolis is looking for. His *graeca*—his love or life. She also learns what Kolis is doing with the missing Chosen—turning them into Revenants.

We know he's actually turning them into Ascended *and* Revenants.

Compelled to do so, Sera apologizes to Gemma for bringing her back to life and then tells Bele and Aios what Odetta said about her being touched by life and death. She asks them if they can seek out the Fates, then insists they find Nyktos immediately and tell him what Gemma and Odetta said.

Cressa, Madis, and Taric show up. Sera gets knocked around, and Taric takes her blood, doing something else that Sera can't pin down. She stabs him in the chest with the butter knife she hid from her morning meal. In the skirmish, he attempts to use compulsion on her, but it doesn't work.

Saion checks on Sera, and she tells him to go to Bele, who got injured in the fight. She feels a flare in her chest that chills her to the bone, knowing it's the goddess. She watches the murderous gods die, and then Nyktos appears. She explains that Taric did something to her.

He tells her to remember that she may feel fear but she's never afraid and gives her back her dagger. She asks if she can try to save Bele and is told the ember in her isn't strong enough to bring back a god. When she insists that the goddess died because of her and again asks to be allowed to try, Nyktos tells her not to take on that guilt but allows her to go to Bele anyway. She brings the goddess back to life and finds that isn't all she did. She also Ascended her.

Afterward, she waits with Saion and Ector in Nyktos's office and asks them if they're afraid of her. She doesn't know what Ascension means for a god, so Ector and Saion tell her. Nyktos walks in and thanks her for saving Bele. He takes care of her wounds and tells her he summoned the Fates, saying that Kolis will back off until he figures out what exactly he's dealing with. She's also told that not every god she brings back will Ascend—they have to be fated to do so.

This made me wonder about the history. If the Primals took to ground because the gods were Ascending so rapidly, *how* and *why* did that happen? Hopefully, I'll be able to fill in that puzzle piece at some point.

After dozing for a bit, Sera wakes and is told the Fates have answered. Nektas is waiting for her and Nyktos in the throne room. Nyktos seems concerned about Sera's wellbeing, and she tells him that if she lost too much blood, it's on Taric, not him. He kisses her, and his lips are warm. After, he tells her that the kiss changes nothing. Still, she feels hopeful.

And she should. It changes nothing because he already knows she's it for him.

When Sera walks into the throne room, she's shocked to find Sir Holland. She's instantly relieved to see that he wasn't sent to the Vodina Isles, but then realizes why he never seemed to age in all the years she knew him. She learns that the Arae cannot affect her fate anymore and learns from Holland what Eythos did—she has the essence of his power in her.

Sera also learns that she and Nyktos are soulmates. It explains why they feel so right together. She confesses to feeling that and says she's had a hard time walking away from him. It makes her wonder if that's why he seems to find her so interesting. The soulmates thing isn't the only reason. She's drawn to *who* he is.

Sera and Nyktos try to tease out the prophecy and imagine it means that Kolis will destroy all the lands. Holland tells her she has many possible paths, but they all end the same. She says she wants to know more and learns that she is fated to die before the age of twenty-one. It'll either be at the hands of a god, a misinformed mortal, Kolis, or even Nyktos himself—though one could possibly be an accident.

She learns that Nyktos's blood will force her to go through the Culling, and because she's mortal, she will not survive it. There's also no way to stop it. Nyktos is horrified, and she assures him it's not his fault.

Holland stresses that her recklessness and impulsivity may give whatever Eythos believed upon hearing the prophecy a chance to come to fruition and then shows her the broken thread of fate. He explains that the only thing the Fates can't control is love. He goes on to say how she won't survive the Culling, not without the sheer will of what is more powerful than fate or even death—not without the love of the one who would aid in her Ascension.

Sera asks if she needs the blood of a god who loves her to survive and finds out it needs to be the love of a Primal. And not just any Primal. The one the ember belonged to. Nyktos.

That is so very unfair to both of them.

She then learns something that shakes her even more. She's had many lives and is the reincarnation of Sotoria, Kolis's obsession. She denies it, and then things get worse. She finds out that life has only continued because of the ember in her bloodline, the one she now carries that is the only ember of life in both realms. And what that means is…if she dies, everything and everyone in both realms goes with her.

She is the Primal of Life.

Nyktos bows to her, and she asks him not to, then starts to have a panic attack. Nyktos calms her. Once she has her breath again, she remarks that the prophecies are pointless and learns more about them, the oracles, and the Gods of Divination.

They discuss Bele's Ascension, if she looks like Sotoria, the Craven, and whether she'll run to Kolis versus running *away* from *him*.

Sera asks what Kolis will do to Nyktos if he finds that he's hiding her from him and learns that Kolis cannot kill his nephew. Life cannot exist without death. Which leads her to wonder about a Primal of Life *and* Death.

Nyktos admits to having his *kardia* removed. When she appears confused, Penellaphe tells Sera what that is and what it means—he's truly *unable* to love. It stuns her.

Then she gets pissed that Holland didn't tell her there was no point in her duty when they were in the mortal realm and worries about how long the realms have.

Talk turns to how to safeguard her as much as they can, and Vikter Ward, a *viktor*, arrives to place a charm on her arms, explaining what it will do. Holland sees her distress and tells her not to give up, reminding her of the broken thread and saying that fate is never written in bone and blood. It can be as ever-changing as one's thoughts and heart. She reminds him that Nyktos can't love, and he tells her that love is more powerful than the Arae can even imagine.

Before he leaves, Sera asks Holland if she'll ever see him again, and he can't answer. Still, he reminds her of something she already knows: All that she trained for wasn't a waste. She *is* his weakness. Only the *him* isn't Nyktos, it's Kolis. She realizes that her true destiny is to be a weapon against the false Primal of Life, though she doesn't want to seduce Kolis. The thought makes her ill.

Nyktos leads her back to his office and asks what she's thinking. They discuss when he had his *kardia* removed and who knows about it, and she wonders if it hurt and *why* he did it. He tells her, though we find out that was only part of the truth. They decide to continue with the plan and keep her hidden.

Sera doesn't see the point of the coronation if she's just going to die in five months, and Nyktos asks if the idea of her death even bothers her. In answer, she lists all the things she's currently dealing with—including death. *Dealing* has nothing to do with how she feels about it. When he says it's unfair, it surprises her, and she tells him that it's not fair to him either.

Sera tells Nyktos that whatever safety the coronation would provide isn't worth it, and he tells her that her safety is worth everything, even the Shadowlands. However, he ruins the moment when he says that the embers are important. He doesn't say *she* is.

The next time Saion escorts her to her chambers, they have a very serious discussion about where she stands now that the truth is out.

Sera meets Orphine, who also wants to kill her for even *thinking* about hurting

Nyktos. However, she adds that Sera is special to them, too, because she's life.

Later, Sera wakes to a deafening crack, covered in a blanket she didn't get. Orphine rushes into the room and tells her not to go out onto the balcony. She does it anyway and sees the battle underway.

Orphine and Sera argue over Sera helping, and she learns all sorts of things about the draken. During the battle, Orphine stops her from reviving a fallen guard, and Ector keeps her from bringing Davina back to life.

A blast of eather almost hits her but gets Orphine instead. A pale-haired and light-skinned god comes to Sera, clearly looking for her. He doesn't stop an entombed god from attacking her. In the melee, Sera is wounded in her shoulder and on her forearm.

Sera sees Nyktos take on his true Primal form and wipe out the rest of the entombed gods, ripping the last one in half. She admits to him after that she found it kind of hot.

I mean…there is something sexy about that kind of savage beauty and control.

Nyktos carries her inside, and she tries to tell him that she's not hurt. He says he can feel and taste her pain, adding that she needs blood, especially since she won't be able to heal while in the Culling. He refuses to let her stay in pain and asks her to let him help her.

Sera takes his blood and thinks it tastes like honey. It makes her feel tingly all over, and she can feel his power vibrating in her chest. Her pain fades, and she feels at peace. She also feels his touch more than ever. Her skin humming and blood hot, she realizes it's a side effect. He tells her that he can feel and taste her need. That he's practically drowning in it. She tells him to drown *with* her.

They have sex, and Sera doesn't hold back. She wants him to hear, see, and know what he does to her.

Later, with the guards, Sera reassures Bele that she's not to blame for anything. The goddess thanks Sera for saving her life. When Sera tells the group about the god who was ready to let her die, Nyktos gets visibly upset. They come to the conclusion that the attack had to be led by another Primal since they are the only ones who can control the draken.

Knowing the embers and Sotoria's soul make her the perfect weapon to be used against Kolis, she scales the palace wall and makes it to the Black Bay, hoping to stow away on a ship and head to Dalos and Kolis in a bid to save the Shadowlands.

A silver hawk—which is actually Attes in his *nota* form—saves her from some Shades in the woods, and she somehow almost brings one back to life. When Nyktos appears, Sera runs from him, determined to fulfill her destiny. She can't stop the Rot nor can she protect him. She has no other purpose but this. Furious, he tackles her but absorbs the blow, demanding to know why she was running from him. She tells him that she was trying to *save* him.

Sera confesses what she believes is her true destiny. She's Kolis's weakness, and whatever happens to her will be worth it. The mortal realm can be saved, *he* can be saved, and no one else needs to get hurt. Nyktos tells her that he will gladly suffer anything Kolis dishes out so long as she's spared, though he doesn't stop from mentioning the embers yet again. Sera gets angry and screams. Power explodes from her, throwing Nyktos into the air.

In seconds, Nektas is crouching in front of Sera, protecting her from any reflexive retaliation the Primal of Death may deliver. Almost in tears, she apologizes and says she doesn't even know what happened but worries it will happen again.

She realizes that Nyktos will never let her go, and he confirms as much. She argues that she's no better than a prisoner, and he tells her that's her choice. He says her destiny is not to die by Kolis's hand and insists there may be another way for them to go about things.

Back at the palace, Nyktos tells her the next time she puts a dagger to someone's throat—even his—she'd better mean it, and then orders her to her room. He follows her into her chambers and informs her that she'll sleep within arm's reach from now on, then carries her to his room and throws her onto the bed. Stubborn, she refuses to undress, making him do it for her before they fall asleep.

The next morning, Sera wakes alone, and Baines brings her water for a bath. Orphine says she'll escort her to Nyktos once she's ready. As they walk, Sera notices the design on the throne room door for the first time—the wolf. Once inside, Nyktos tells everyone that Sera tried to go after Kolis to protect the Shadowlands and says her bravery is unmatched among them. He then whispers that none shall harbor ill will toward her now and should see her as she is: brave and daring. If not, the negative thoughts will be their last. He vows to destroy them, no matter how loyal they are to the Shadowlands. He tells Sera that she's brave and strong and more than worthy of them.

She feels like he's saying *more*.

Nyktos suggests they try to remove the embers from her and she's stunned. She didn't think that was even possible. Nektas tells her the embers aren't fully hers until she Ascends, so they *should* be able to remove them. Nyktos's blood would ensure she'd survive the Ascension then, though she learns she might Ascend into an actual god.

After they discuss when to go to the Pools of Divanash, talk turns to other things, and Sera learns how Nektas's mate Halayna died, and that he was the first draken and the one who helped Eythos create the mortals.

They talk more about removing the embers, and she finds out that only the *usual suspects* in the Shadowlands know of the plan—and they only know she has one ember. They also support it, even the bit about Ascending her. Only Nektas knows about Sotoria's soul, though, and it needs to stay that way. It would be too risky for the others to know.

Sera asks Nyktos if he will continue the Rite after becoming the Primal of Life and then learns why it was started in the first place. She explains what life is like for a Chosen in the mortal realm and finds out the mortals started that, not the gods. Sera wonders if all the missing Chosen have been turned into Craven like the seamstress—though she knows about the Revenants, too. She then asks what will happen to Kolis and the Rot if they succeed in removing the embers. They tell her they may never be able to kill the false Primal of Life because of the necessary balance, but they can weaken him enough to entomb him. She tries to tell them there is a way to kill him and it's right in front of them—her—but Nyktos refuses to hear it.

The sound of chaos outside interrupts them, and Sera finds out about the Cimmerian and how they fight. She decides to push her luck and goes outside to join the battle. She kills a Cimmerian primed to attack Rhain and is reminded that she can be killed; the enemy doesn't know what's inside her.

During the fight, Sera gets injured on the left side of her waist, and Nyktos comes to her. They flirt a bit, even as fighters die around them. Her gift flares to life at the deaths, and Nektas growls at her in warning, telling her to control herself.

Once the fight is over, Rhain reluctantly thanks her for her aid and verbally roasts her a bit. He casually mentions that Nyktos has endured and sacrificed things for her, which piques her interest. Ector tries to cover and quickly chimes in that Rhain is merely being dramatic.

Nyktos reappears, and Sera yells at him, telling him that she won't be ordered around as if she has no control over her life anymore, especially when she can help—no matter the risks. Then she reminds him that she's never really been allowed to value her life or think for herself.

He asks her what kind of life she's lived, and she won't answer. And he won't tell her what he's sacrificed when she asks.

Sera wonders if Taric could taste the embers in her blood when he drank from her. Nyktos tells her that no one else will feed from her—he won't allow it—but…yes, the god would have tasted the embers. He then goes on to tell her that her blood tastes like a summer storm and the sun. Like heat, power, and life. Soft and airy like sponge cake.

The Primal is a poet. Seriously.

Nyktos explains about shadowstepping, and Sera asks if she'll be able to do it once she Ascends. He tells her that she will, reconfirming his faith in their plan. They also talk about Tavius, and he calls her brave and strong.

It chokes her up.

He says she needs to rest—she's going through the Culling and got cut with shadowstone. Then he adds that he wonders how else the embers are protecting her since a mortal or godling would have died. Not even his blood in her would have been enough.

Later, back in her room, she notices that her wound looks several days old instead of hours. Which makes her wonder just how strong her embers are. Settling in, she thinks about Ash as she masturbates, somehow *knowing* he's in the room watching her, even if she can't see him. She does see dark tendrils and intuitively knows it's him. She can *feel* his touch. She climaxes and calls to him as she does but gets no answer. Just as she dozes off, she swears she feels the bed shift as if someone lowered themselves to the mattress.

The next day, Nektas asks her what she thinks of the plan to remove the embers, and she says she's tentatively hopeful. As they talk about their journey to the Vale, she finds out that it isn't dangerous, but the road to get there is.

Nyktos arrives not long after, just after Jadis manages to set a chair on fire. He makes a flippant comment about Sera's dress that annoys her and then talk turns to more important matters. She discovers that the army in wait is because Nyktos plans to go to war with Kolis. Unfortunately, she realizes that he doesn't trust her enough to speak plainly or truthfully around her, and that bothers her greatly.

Nyktos dismisses her, but she tells him she chooses to stay with him. As he works, she asks him about the Books of the Dead. She tries to goad him, referencing others she should or could be spending time with, and he warns her that she should be selective of how she spends her time with others. They discuss the night before and their needs, and she offers him a deal: pleasure for the sake of pleasure.

Nyktos calls her reckless, but then suddenly asks if she has her dagger, saying they're about to have company. He apologizes for what's about to transpire, and Sera meets Attes for the first time. The Primal refers to Sera as an accessory, and she threatens him without hesitation. Nyktos tells her to behave, but Attes asks if she knows not to repeat what she hears, and she can't hold her tongue, snapping at him again. She learns that Kolis is denying her coronation.

After hearing that Nyktos must be granted permission to take a Consort, she curses. Attes tells them that Kolis will summon them when he's ready. After the Primal leaves, Nyktos tells her to argue with him to distract him from his anger. She kisses him instead.

Sera assumes that Kolis must think the embers are in Nyktos and that he's the one who Ascended Bele, but she's told the false Primal of Life knows they aren't in his nephew. He already tested Nyktos. When she realizes what those *tests* likely were, she discovers that Nyktos has had to convince Kolis of a great many things.

He tells Sera that Attes was provoking her by trying to influence her with his Primal essence. When she had no reaction to it, Attes knew and realized that she's more than what they said. Ector tells her about who is and isn't affected by a Primal's presence, and she realizes that Attes could know that she is the one who carries the embers.

Sera learns that Kolis could have outright forbidden Nyktos from taking a Consort, and while he can still claim her, she'd have no protection.

Thinking about how that meeting with Kolis will go, she fears she looks like Sotoria and worries. Nyktos vows not to let the Primal touch her. She argues, saying that she won't be the reason for any more death, and he tells her she never was. She's not so sure. However, she won't hide, and he won't put her in danger—even though she's always *been* in danger.

Nektas follows Sera back to her chambers and calls her meyaah *Liessa*. She calls him meyaah draken in return, saying she's as much his Queen as he is her draken. He asks if Ash was wrong to doubt her motivations, and she confesses that getting to Kolis never crossed her mind—at least not recently. She then learns what Nyktos has had to convince his uncle of and what Kolis will do if he learns the truth. It hits deep.

Sera argues that it isn't personal for her like it is for Nyktos. She's not Sotoria. Nektas asks her why she no longer calls Nyktos *Ash* and proceeds to tell her that his father called him that. He says it means something that he introduced himself to her as that right off, saying that he is as she wishes him to be.

She spends the remainder of the afternoon training and realizes she doesn't want Nyktos to have to choose between the Shadowlands and her. Later, in his room to sleep, he apologizes for questioning her motives, saying he won't hide the summons from her when it comes. Talk turns to why she holds her breath and how she manages her anxiety, and she suddenly realizes that she left her dagger in her bedchamber. She's unprotected for the first time in her life...

The trust has been solidified.

Sera wakes on what should be her coronation day and once again thinks about fading away. Shaking herself out of it, she goes to have breakfast with Saion and Reaver and asks Saion where he's from. He tells her the story of how Nyktos saved both him and his cousin, Rhahar.

Later, she sees others training and learns they do so every day in the morning for a few hours. She's shocked when Saion refuses to train with her. Undeterred, she squares off with Nyktos. She ends up cutting off a lock of his hair. As they spar, Sera makes a list of demands.

After besting him just a little bit—I'm sure he probably let her—he says he'll train her, totally shocking her. Needing to get in the last *word*, she curtsies to him and leaves.

Nyktos draws a bath for her in his chambers, and she eventually falls asleep in the tub. She wakes, and he reheats the water for her. Driven by her desire, she tells him that her want of him is a choice; one she's at least brave enough to admit. Then, she tries to leave.

Before she can go, he admits to wanting her, too, and tells her how badly. He admits that he thinks about her all the time. She taunts him about the blowjob she gave him and asks if he wants that again or is back to just more talk.

And then it's not just talk...

They share how each of them felt in their early lives, and Sera tells him she was basically a ghost in Lasania. He tells her to sleep and says she was never a ghost to him.

She wakes with only Nektas in the room and they talk a little. Sera remarks that there's no way Ash has forgiven her, even if he understands and accepts *why* she planned what she did. He tells her that if Ash didn't understand or accept, she wouldn't be where she is, smelling of the Primal, and he wouldn't have detected peace from Ash when he found them together.

Ash and Sera share dinner, and he tells her they'll go see Ezra tomorrow in the mortal realm but makes sure she understands they can't stay long. And they can't say anything about Kolis.

They talk about their plans for going to the Pools of Divanash and more. She tells Nyktos she hopes his plan works because he's good, and he should be the Primal of Life. He tells her not to mistake his handling of her as him being *good*. She explains that she isn't good either. Nyktos reminds her that she's been willing to sacrifice herself for others and thus *is* good, but then goes on to say that there's no such thing as a good Primal, telling her their history. He adds that she's neither good nor bad because of the embers.

Sera feels a shift between them and notices that his skin is warmer again. He remarks on her freckles once more, and she feels even more of a shift. It's not desire fueled by the need for blood or sustenance, nor is it spurred on by anger. This is real. She kisses him because it's different now, and he calls her *liessa*.

They head to the mortal realm, and Sera takes in how the mortals act in Ash's presence. They meet with Ezra, and Sera tells her stepsister that killing the Primal wouldn't have stopped the Rot. When Ezra confesses that she doubted Sera could make the Primal of Death fall for her, Sera is surprised. Ezra adds that she figured she'd end up getting killed after becoming impatient and just stabbing him, which makes Sera laugh.

On the way out, Sera and Ash run into Calliphe. Sera tries to leave, but her mom stops her, telling her she didn't know what Tavius had planned. Ash tells her that she should count her blessings and thank her daughter, because it's the only reason she still breathes.

Back in Iliseeum, after training with Bele and spending some pleasurable time with Ash, Sera goes to his office to see him. He takes her belowground to show her something, and she sees the cells. She realizes that she can't tell the difference between the embers and her heart being excited around him and believes that he had his *kardia* removed to protect others, not himself. He tells her about the bone chains and those with dual lives and then takes her to the pool room. She's amazed and asks him why he went to the lake if he had this. He tells her it's because it was *her* lake.

Be still my heart.

Sera learns that Ash checked on her before her seventeenth birthday because he was curious—I now know it was much, much before that. Him wanting to know more about her makes her happy.

Wanting to test things, he says he plans to draw the eather out of her by goading her into using it on him, then tells her if she behaves, she can go for a swim or be fucked. She doesn't want to do it, doesn't want to accidentally hurt him, but he asks nicely, and she confesses to hating when he says "please."

They fight hand-to-hand, and eather ramps up in her as she thinks about losing the fight with Taric. When Ash grabs hold of her, she distracts him with talk of sex to break away. He pins her, and she confesses that she likes to submit to him—then does. He takes her on the stone and tells her that she's always safe with him, calling her *liessa*.

They spend some time in the pool, and Ash tells her more about Lathan. He admits that Sera's one of the strongest people he knows, both mentally and physically—mortal or otherwise. Then he adds that his assertion has nothing to do with the embers. They play a bit more in the pool, and once again, Sera feels as if he and she have become...more.

She spends the rest of the day with Aios and the younglings, realizing that she's not only been calling Nyktos Ash, she's also started seeing him as such. Calling him Nyktos doesn't feel right anymore. She wants to stop Kolis and the Rot and restore Ash's rightful destiny, but she doesn't want to do what's needed to weaken Kolis. She wants a future of her own, and she wants it with Ash. She *wants* to be his Consort.

Sera decides to deal with her epiphany that she cares about Ash like she does everything else—by *not* dealing with it at all.

Talking to Ash later, she tells him about Nektas's eyes flashing blue earlier, and finds out that all the draken had blue eyes until Kolis did what he did. After, they turned red. However, Nektas's changing color may mean that Sera is closer to her Ascension than they realize.

Sera decides that Ash doesn't need to know how she feels about him. She knows he cares about her, though she thinks the way she feels might be more. Could it be love?

They leave for the Pools of Divanash, and Nyktos shows her the poppies growing in the Red Woods. As they near the Pillars, Sera's embers vibrate, and she sees the souls of the departed. Ash tells her about Eythos's struggles being near the Pillars as the Primal of Death and asks if she feels the need to use the embers or if it wears on her. She lies and tells him no.

He reminds her that she's stronger than she thinks—*her*, not the embers—and tells her to see if she can glean anything about the souls. She tries but then stops, deciding she doesn't need to since the embers will be back in Nyktos soon. Still, they throb within her.

They come upon the riders, and the three bow to her. When they finally reach their destination, Ash tells Nektas to watch out for her because she's important to him. Again, *her*, not the embers. Unable to help herself, she blurts out to Ash that she wants to be his Consort. He kisses her knuckles and palm and tells her he'll be waiting for her when she returns.

Nektas and Sera enter the Vale. She confirms to the draken that she meant what she said at the crossroads: she cares about Ash. She also tells him that if she'd been able to kill Nyktos, Nektas wouldn't have had to kill her because she would have done it herself. He says that if that's true, he's even more right than he thought. He expounds by saying how Ash could have messed him up in the Dying Woods after she blasted him, but he stopped himself because he cares for her. She admits that she knows he does.

The draken tells Sera that Ash had his *kardia* removed not so he didn't become like his father but so he didn't become like his uncle. Nektas implies that he thinks she loves Nyktos, and she quickly says she doesn't, insisting she doesn't even know what love feels like.

After encountering the Shroud and resisting the sirens' song, they finally reach the Pools. Nektas explains what to do—she needs to reveal a deep secret. Her truth is to confess that she tried to take her life. The Pools accept her sacrifice, and she sees Delfai with Kayleigh Balfour in Irelone.

Once they're out of the Vale, Nektas insists she can talk to him if she's ever *not* okay. If she does, he'll make sure she *is*.

That draken can be surly, but he, like his bonded Primal, has a heart of gold.

He halts her on their journey and says they're about to have company, warning her not to strike first. He tells her about the nymphs, and they end up fighting them. Fury explodes from Sera, and she winds up killing them with her eather—the kind that only the Primal of Life can wield. The type that can kill another Primal.

I can only imagine hearing that made Sera wish she *could* kill Kolis instead of entombing him.

When they return to the House of Haides, Sera sees Veses straddling Ash and feeding from him. She flees to the pool room underground, her anger shaking the palace. Roots wrap around her in a protective gesture. Ash tries to calm her, reminding her of her breathing exercises, but he's finally forced to compel her into falling asleep.

Sera wakes naked in Ash's room with Bele and Rhain, shocking Rhain a bit. He tells her she's powerful and says he's never seen anything like what she did—not even from a Primal in their Culling. She finds out she was in stasis for three days and that it *could* have been weeks. She could have even died. When she asks about the roots, she finds out they were trying to protect her. Rhain goes on to tell her that if she loses it like that again, she might not wake up. They explain what she needs to do to keep herself strong.

She learns where Ash is, and the gods tell her he was worried about her. She goes to her room and decides there will be no more physical contact with Ash. She'll stay in her quarters and use her bathing chamber despite the bad memories there. Somehow, she needs to create distance between them, and she wants her own future.

Sera requests bath water and actually bathes in her tub. After, Bele wants to know what happened before the events in the pool chamber and reveals that she knew Veses was in the palace. She goes on to say that she thought the Primal's visits would stop and tells Sera that Nyktos has never acted the way he does with Sera before—and it's not just because of the embers.

Bele tells Sera that he verbally slayed them after his bravery speech and adds that she's seen Veses feed from Nyktos before but has never seen them having sex. She explains that sex doesn't always happen with feeding and tries to reassure Sera that Nyktos doesn't trust or even *like* Veses.

Sera's not quite so sure. Seeing is believing, after all.

Ash comes to see Sera and apologizes for what she thinks she saw. She reminds him that it happened only hours after she told him she wanted to be his Consort but refuses to admit that she's hurt. She does lash out and snap that his claim of virginity was a lie, though. Trying to get to the bottom of it, she asks him what she saw, and he tells her it's complicated. She finally admits that it hurt her feelings and breaks off their pleasure deal, stating she wants to be free of him completely once the embers are out of her.

Later, she goes to talk to him about Irelone and is super polite—not like herself at all. She figures Nektas can go to see Delfai with her, but Ash says he will go so he can hear what is said about removing the embers. She states that she wants to leave immediately, and he asks her to wait because there have been sightings of Kyn's draken near.

Finally, he comments that he doesn't like how she's become: how she was trained to be—empty and blank. He tells her to be herself and accepts the blame for what happened, pleading with her not to change. She admits that she doesn't want to be like she is now, but she won't allow herself to feel like that again.

Self-preservation is a slippery slope.

The summons comes, and Sera realizes she could be kept in Dalos. She worries that Kolis will be able to sense the embers in her and is told how him sensing anything can be explained away—she *has* taken a lot of Ash's blood. When she asks how nice they'll have to be to the false Primal, Rhain tells her to do anything and everything Kolis orders her to do, adding that Nyktos can only refuse a few things on her behalf.

Sera refuses to be a part of whatever Kolis does in retaliation for Ash not answering the summons in a timely manner and insists they should go soon. He tries to say she's more important, and she cuts him off. Reaver sticks up for her with Nyktos, and it delights Sera. Though she is surprised to hear that he's protecting her *from* Ash.

Once again, she refuses to do anything until they answer the summons. He capitulates, and they make plans to leave for Dalos in an hour. Sera changes, and Aios asks her if she'll go after Kolis. Sera opens up to the goddess about Sotoria and her being Kolis's *graeca*. She explains that killing Kolis is her destiny. Being Nyktos's Consort never was.

Aios asks her why it can't be both, then tells Sera about her time in Dalos as one of Kolis's *favorites*. Sera can't believe what she's hearing and apologizes, telling Aios how strong she is. The goddess tells her that Kolis is incapable of love, even for his *graeca*. Which means…he has no weakness.

Sera doesn't believe that can be true of anyone. When she meets up with Ash, he tells her she's beautiful, and she tells him not to say that. He explains that they'll have to act as they did with Attes while in Dalos—as if they can't get enough of each other. All that manages to do is irritate Sera because she can't believe he doesn't get that she was *never* pretending. She tells him it's too late for that, and he asks why she even wanted that from him to begin with.

She confesses that she wants a life and a future and won't try anything with Kolis. Though she does worry that he will recognize her and try to claim her. She's reminded that she doesn't belong to anyone. Nyktos says he will protect her, but Kolis *could* try to keep her. Ash says he'll level Dalos and leave it in ruins before he lets that happen. She begs him not to intervene if Kolis recognizes her as Sotoria, and he snarls that the embers aren't the only important thing. She is.

Sera asks Ash what she should expect and learns that the ink on his skin is a collection of one hundred and ten tattooed drops of blood signifying the things Kolis demanded of Ash. He reminds her again that she's good, no matter what happens, saying she's not a monster now nor will she be when they return. He holds her close and kisses her forehead as they shadowstep.

Sera barely fades, and Ash tells her they need to get the embers out of her soon—it's clear they're getting even stronger. As they make their way, he tells her not to let anyone lure her away and warns her not to trust anyone. He tells her that Dalos is also called the City of the Dead, which she believes when she sees the gods strung up outside the palace. Her primal essence flares.

She begs Ash to stop her from attempting to resurrect them and tells him to use compulsion. Instead, he kisses her, using his shadows to block her sight. He calls her strong and brave.

In the presence of Attes and Dyses, Sera goes to bow, and Nyktos stops her. She learns that Dyses was testing her. Ash kills him, but she swears she sees his hand twitch. And she didn't feel her embers respond to his death.

After talking with Attes, she remarks that the Primal finds perverse pleasure in provoking Ash and that it almost seems as if Attes is looking out for her. She wonders if he might be a friend—or at least an ally.

Nyktos helps her breathe and bow, and she slips on her veil of nothingness again. Sera is relieved when Kolis doesn't recognize her as Sotoria. The relief is short-lived, however, when Dyses—whom she witnessed Ash kill—walks into the room. She wonders then if he's a Revenant.

When Kolis chastises them for their faux pas of not asking for permission, she blurts that their failure to seek approval was her fault and says she feared Kolis would find her unworthy. Kolis decrees what her punishment should be, and she's sickened when she realizes he expects her to kill a draken youngling. She asks what the boy did to deserve it and what will happen if she refuses. The young draken answers her, saying that Kolis will still kill him, then her, and then end with summoning a draken from the Shadowlands to be killed.

Sera asks Kolis why he'd use this as punishment. She wants to know what he gains from it. His reply? "Everything. It will tell me everything I need to know."

Before she goes through with it, she asks the draken his name. He tells her it doesn't matter and that he's not worth remembering. Suddenly, she feels something shift within her. She senses the twisted and evil bits in Kolis's essence and feels an ancient power come to life inside her. It's rage, pure and primal. She realizes that the power in him was hers, stolen from the Primal of Life. Then she feels Sotoria and thinks that his pain, retribution, vengeance, and blood will be hers. Sotoria, through Sera, pays the price Kolis demanded.

Sera knows the draken's death will mark her and she'll leave some of her goodness in the atrium. Still, she feels Sotoria and knows the woman is settling in to wait for what she's owed.

Later, after they leave, Sera asks Ash to take her to Vathi. She even goes so far as to beg him. He tells her they should survive to honor the sacrifice the draken made, but she tells him it's not enough. He caves and takes her, and she urges Attes to bring the youngling's body to her. She thanks Ash for doing as she asked and explains that she has to do this. She refuses his touch and instead asks why Kolis would do something like this. He says the false Primal of Life was making Kyn their enemy.

And boy did he ever. Not that the Primal needed much help...

When Attes returns, Sera wonders if they can trust him. Ash tells her it's too late for that now. When she brings the young draken back to life, he calls her meyaah *Liessa*. They exchange names—his name is Thad. After, Attes bows to Sera and vows not to betray her confidence and tell anyone what she did. He *also* calls her meyaah *Liessa*. Sera tells him not to and insists she's not anything.

Ash asks her why she spoke out and says she doesn't deserve what she was made to do. She argues that he doesn't either and then goes on to say that she did it for him.

Sera asks about Dyses being what Gemma mentioned—a Revenant. Perhaps a demis. She also asks why Kolis didn't act on the fact that he knows his nephew knows who has the power to Ascend and that it's *not* Kolis. Ash tells her it's so Kolis doesn't expose himself as a fraud.

She reminds Ash that they now have permission to go forward with the coronation, and he tells her that's not all they have. They also discovered that Kolis didn't recognize her. He asks her what happened back in Dalos, saying she felt different to him. She tells him that the rage wasn't only hers, it was also Sotoria's. Ash says he thinks Holland was wrong. It's clear Sera has two souls: hers *and* Sotoria's.

The plan is to have the coronation the following day and then leave for Irelone to talk with Delfai. Sera walks around the halls and courtyards with Reaver and cries, noticing that she's crying blood. Later, she has supper with Aios, Bele, and Reaver in her receiving room before returning to her bedchambers.

Not much later, she feels something similar to what she feels with Ash just before Ector comes flying into the room, followed by Veses. Sera realizes that the Primal likely unleashed the Shades as a distraction like Taric did. When Veses tells

Rhain she hasn't come for Nyktos, Sera sees fear in the god's eyes.

The Primal insults Sera and wants to know how she became the Consort, stating she knows it's in title only. Sera tells Veses that Ash called her *the worst sort* and continues to taunt the Primal, telling Veses that her future with Nyktos has nothing to do with her. To top it off, she calls her pathetic.

Reaver moves to protect Sera, and she tries to hold him back. Unfortunately, she isn't able to stop Veses from hurting Reaver. In her rage, Sera plunges her dagger into Veses' eye and gets hit by eather. She learns that Veses sent the draken into the Shadowlands, thinking she was *helping* Nyktos.

Veses insinuates that either Sera has a lot of Nyktos's blood in her, or he found a Primal in their Culling. Sera tells her she's had *all* of Nyktos, not just his blood, and punches Veses in the throat. She then scrambles toward Reaver but is thrown across the room and into the couch.

When Bele arrives, the goddess tells Sera the draken is hurt badly. Sera senses that death is imminent. Luckily, she is able to save him, and it somehow feels like a homecoming this time. She throws a dagger at Veses, but the Primal stops it in mid-air.

Sera freaks out about Veses knowing her secret, but Ash tells her she won't get a chance to tell Kolis about it because she'll never get out of the cell they're about to put her in. Sera tells him that Veses didn't want to tell Kolis about her, she wanted to *kill* her. But the Primal was afraid to go through with it once she saw what Sera could do.

Sera apologizes to Ash for him having to kill the Shades—she knows he doesn't like doing it, thus giving them their ultimate end—and tells him that Veses sent the enemy draken that attacked them *and* released the entombed gods.

She thanks Bele for her aid with Veses and learns from Saion that Ector will be okay despite what the Primal did to him. She knows she'll need Ash's blood to recover from the skirmish—she can't risk another stasis—then takes what she needs from Ash and feels peace, seeing a memory of her fighting him in the courtyard during her training request.

Sera asks him about it and learns why she saw that. She then tells Ash that she doesn't hate him at all. He orders her to fuck him, and she gladly accepts. Once again, it feels like *more* to her. After, she tells him that he can feed from her if he needs to. He declines, saying he doesn't deserve to.

Later, Sera feels the embers vibrating in her chest but not with the kind of energy that restores life. It's the kind that ends it. Ash explains why Veses could feel Sera but Kolis couldn't, and she learns that Veses never let on that she felt her.

Resting with Reaver, Sera doesn't want to leave the youngling or risk waking him by moving but asks why Ash told Veses she was his Consort in name only. He tells her that Veses is different, and it's complicated. Sera asks him point-blank if he cares for Veses, and Ash says he pities and loathes the other Primal. She then asks him what he feels for *her*, and he tells her he feels curiosity, excitement, amusement, yearning, need, want, anger, always awe, and…peace.

Erlina arrives, and Sera discusses the coronation with her and Bele. The seamstress addresses Sera formally, and she goes to tell the woman not to. Bele merely glares at her. Sera's thoughts then turn to Veses, and she worries that the Primal goddess will be missed. She learns that she won't—most will be happy she's gone.

Sera asks to see Rhain to learn what's going on with Veses and Nyktos and discovers the price Nyktos had to pay for Veses' silence, which was done solely to protect Sera from Kolis. She then realizes that Ash wasn't protecting the embers at all, he was protecting *her*.

When she discovers that Ash is always cold because of how Veses feeds, it makes her furious. Her emotions explode, and she starts shaking the palace again. Rhain does his best to calm her. She's able to quiet herself, but vows to Rhain that she'll kill Veses, making a move to do just that.

The god blocks her and promises Veses will be dealt with. Sera suddenly realizes that once Nyktos Ascends, he will be able to Ascend a god to replace Veses in the Callasta Isles. Rhain calls her *Your Highness*, stupefying her. He goes on to say that she will be and *has been* his Queen.

Sera learns that only Rhain, Ector, and Nektas really knew about what was going on with Veses and Nyktos. After thinking about it, Sera says that Ash shouldn't feel shame over the blackmail, though she would feel the same.

Rhain asks her if she loves Nyktos, and Sera can't answer. He tells her the hesitation is all the answer he needs, and says he was wrong about her. Sera suddenly realizes she *does* love Ash, and it makes her a little sick to her stomach.

Acknowledging one's truth will sometimes do that.

Without thought, she blurts to Ector that she *wants* to be Nyktos's Consort, stunning both him and her.

Rhahar, Rhain, Ector, Saion, and the twins escort Sera to the coronation. Aios and Kars—a guard—take her the rest of the way. Sera asks Aios if she's ever been in love, and the goddess tells her that it doesn't feel the same for everyone. She adds that, to her, it was like feeling at home in an unfamiliar place. As if you're finally seen, heard, and understood. And when you think of what you would do for the person and realize it's anything, that means it's love.

That's actually a wonderful way to put it.

Sera comes to realize why she paid the price for Ash in Dalos and why sex with him has felt like *more*—because it is. He's always been Ash to her. Despite her wanting that to change given everything going on and all that happened, it never has. She's most definitely in love with him.

Ash comes to her and takes her hand from Aios, telling Sera to breathe. He uses shadows to block them from view as she calms.

She notices Ash's crown, and he tells her she won't have to wear hers until after tonight. He reads her a bit, and she politely asks him not to. But she does open up to him, telling him that she still wants the coronation, calling him Ash to his face.

He confesses that counting her freckles has become a habit and relays that she has twelve on her back. It makes her feel warm, and she notices the embers buzzing in her chest. There was a feeling of rightness before with him, but this is different. Once again, more.

Sera sees her crown for the first time, and it's beautiful. When Ash bows to her, she and the crowd are stunned. He's the Primal of Death, after all. Ash crowns her and bestows her new title upon her: the One who is born of Blood and Ash, *the* Light and the Fire, and *the* Brightest Moon. A golden imprint suddenly appears on her right hand, and she asks Ash if he did it. He explains that the Arae must be acknowledging their union.

He tells her about the imprint and blessings, and she wonders if it's because of the embers. He explains that the imprint only fades upon death. He also tells her about Keella and the other Primals. Sera asks if Keella knows about Sotoria's soul, given she's the Primal of Rebirth. He says he isn't sure. After all, it wasn't a rebirth. However, it is possible.

Sera realizes that her new title contains bits from the goddess, Penellaphe's, prophecy. She asks Ash about it, and he tells her that his mind kept returning to thoughts of her hair and how it was like moonlight. He also tells her the different symbolism of blood and ash.

She discovers that nothing has happened in Vathi since she was last there and is relieved to hear that the Court didn't come under siege after what she did with the young draken—bringing Thad back to life.

Ash insinuates that she'll be involved in discussions to come, and it satisfies her, projecting it for him to feel. She explains that it's nice to be included. Still, she wonders what Attes wants to talk to them about. Ash apologizes for contributing to her feeling of unimportance before. He says that she matters. Always. And kisses her temple.

Keella approaches the couple, and Sera feels a charge of energy skitter up her arm as the Primal holds her imprinted hand. She intuits that Sera's title may be another blessing, just like the mark. The embers inside Sera hum in response to their exchange, and Sera notices Keella's clever, knowing smile as she says things without really saying anything at all.

They go through the procession of Primal greetings and Ash keeps her grounded with a hand on her. Finally, their crowns are removed, and Ash tells her that he has soldiers making sure the road is safe. He asks her to sit with him and rubs her neck. She calls him Ash again when she thanks him, and then inquires if it bothers him. He admits that he missed it.

Ash comes clean about some things that have been on his mind. 1—Her calling him Ash in her coronation dress. 2—Seeing her out of the dress. 3—Seeing her naked on her new throne. And 4—Seeing her bare, with nothing *but* the crown. He then wonders if he's worthy of exploring the above things that have quickly become obsessions. Running his hands over her body he finds her dagger and revises his list. He says that seeing her in nothing but the dagger has taken second place, and that thoughts of hearing her call him Ash when she comes have become the first. She replies that she'll call him whatever he wants.

Sera gives in to the desire and tells him that she needs him inside her when she calls him Ash. Then, in a vulnerable moment, she admits that she doesn't want to sleep alone—she wants to be with him. To talk or…whatever. He calls her beautiful, coaxing a smile.

He asks her what she thought of the coronation, and she goes on to ask him about the dakkais and Vathi. She reveals that she believes Keella knows Sera has Sotoria's soul, and Ash says that the Primal of Rebirth is one of the few he somewhat trusts, though he doesn't trust anybody completely when it comes to her.

Sera is both nervous and excited about going to Irelone and happy that Ash will finally be the Primal of Life he should have always been. He tells her that saving her life is the most important part of their plan. He then asks her what changed with her wanting to become his Consort. She sasses that she should be allowed to change her mind, and he tells her that she's entitled to the *realm*, making her feel warm all over.

She goes on to explain that her emotions didn't change, only how she wanted to proceed. She projects her feelings, but she can tell he doesn't understand what he feels. And she knows why. It saddens her. She confesses to knowing about his deal with Veses and thanks him for his sacrifice. Still, she makes it clear that she'll kill the Primal if he doesn't.

Ash finally opens up about things with Veses, and Sera is furious to find out that she's forced pleasure on him, too. The fact that the Primal actually wants Kolis and not Ash at all makes things even worse. When she discovers that the deal has been going on for three years, it incenses her. Ash calms her and says that he doesn't regret keeping her out of Kolis's hands, then thanks her for being her. He begins to tell her what he wishes but stops himself mid-sentence and simply kisses her instead.

Sera tells Ash to feed when he confesses that he's hungry and realizes his reluctance is tied to his past and being forced to take blood. It makes her sad.

It makes me sad, too.

He indulges, and she wants to move beneath him but remembers how Veses used to push the limits, so she lets him have all the control. He takes her as he feeds, and his body warms. It's something that's beginning to bring a sense of pride to Sera. Once more, he starts telling her what he wishes but stops himself again.

They go to Irelone to meet with Delfai. This time, Sera doesn't black out at all during the trip. She realizes the embers are getting even stronger. Projecting anxiety, Ash comments, and she finds out what the emotion tastes and feels like to him.

When they reach their destination, Sera sees how the guards react to Ash and his display of power and realizes how Kolis would have been greeted in the mortal realm—how *Sotoria* likely reacted to him.

She and Ash meet up with Kayleigh, and Sera asks about Delfai, telling the Princess what she knows about him. Kayleigh seems perplexed at the situation given the last time she saw Sera, but Sera decides she won't tell her how she's come to be with Nyktos. She fears that her true mortal identity—Kayleigh never knew she was a Princess—and her new title will cause problems.

Sera finds out that Kayleigh has been waiting to hear if she'd be forced back to Tavius and Sera feels bad. She wishes she had sent word about his death so Kayleigh could move on. As they chat, Kayleigh insinuates that Sera was no handmaiden to the Queen, and Sera refuses to acknowledge. Then, Ash tells the Princess the truth, utterly stunning Sera.

During the meeting with Delfai, Sera learns about the Star diamond and realizes that Holland lied about not knowing how Kolis took the embers. She remarks that a Fate giving The Star to Kolis should be considered interference. She's told that Kolis still has The Star, but it isn't needed to take the embers out of her. Her process is a bit different.

Delfai refers to her as a vessel and it makes Ash furious, stunning Sera. She then learns that taking the embers from her will have little effect on the realms, making her feel both relief and dread. Until she discovers *how* it's done and what it means: she'll die.

She can't hold back a sardonic laugh, given she had assumed she would die all along. Delfai tells her there are only three options. Either Nyktos becomes the true Primal of Life and restores balance to the realms. Someone else takes the embers on. Or Sera completes her Ascension, and…Sera snaps at him not to finish that sentence, knowing exactly what it means.

Ash can't hold back his anger and moves to attack Delfai. Sera pleads with him not to kill the God of Divination because it isn't his fault. And Ash doesn't deserve another mark for another death. Delfai is shocked when Ash calms since he foresaw his end. Then he spouts some nonsense about a silver beast, the brightest moon, and two becoming one.

Oddly, Sera feels a little freer at knowing the end is truly coming for her. She tells Ash he has to do it; that he needs to take the embers and kill her. Suddenly, she realizes that he knew how to remove them from her the entire time and could have done it already but didn't want to because he knew he'd have to end her life. She reminds him that getting the embers out of her will kill her no matter what and then confesses that she doesn't want to die. She says she wants to live but needs a future where Kolis is defeated, and the Rot is no more. She needs the realms to be safe. That's all that matters. Ash argues that *she* matters. Not the realms. Her.

She tells him he did nothing wrong and apologizes for everything. She says there was never any guarantee he would have loved her, even with his *kardia*. He insists he would have, that nothing would have stopped him, and that he could have saved her. Once the words are out, he lets the despondency take him.

She instructs him to kiss her, and he lets out a soul-torn groan.

They have sex, and he confesses that he wishes he'd never had his *kardia* removed, saying he never wanted to know love before her. She sees his eyes turn red, full of Primal tears of grief, and it breaks her heart. Still, she has to accept what needs to happen. She asks Ash to take her to her lake when the time comes, and he promises he will.

That lake is such a catalyst for change in Sera and Ash's love story.

As they shadowstep back into Iliseeum, they find the Shadowlands under attack. Saion comes to tell them what's going on and explains how bad it is and who is involved. When Sera goes to look at what Saion is hesitating to say, he tries to stop her. She shakes off his hold and sees, then wishes she could stop Ash from seeing what she just did—so many of his people dead.

Sera has Saion help her get Aios down from where she's been hung on a spike. He hesitates, but she demands it as his Consort. When they finally get her down, Saion warns her what using her power will mean for the dakkais. She says, "Fuck the dakkais," and Saion tells her he likes her. She returns the sentiment.

After helping Aios, she goes to save Ector, but Saion stops her, physically holding her back this time. He reiterates that using the eather will draw in more dakkais and she'll be swamped and killed. The dakkais attack anyway, and all that's left of the god is a mess. Seeing Ector like that tears something open within Sera. She screams in rage and unleashes a pulse of power that vaporizes the dakkais. Her nose bleeds, and she feels bone-deep exhaustion. She can't even feel Rhain's touch when he catches her, and she tries to stop herself from losing consciousness.

Sera sees Ash drawing the dakkais to him with Primal mist and feels tendrils of it on her skin. Suddenly, she hears his voice in her head telling her to run. Instead, she runs toward him, and the shadows swallow her.

If you could see me, you wouldn't see a shocked face at Sera not following orders. She'll likely never change. And, honestly, I hope she doesn't.

Sera loses the sword she found and hits a wall, falling and seeing only glimpses of gold hair and clothing. She realizes she needs to find Ash and have him take the embers from her now before any more innocents die.

Feeling someone behind her, Sera swings, finding Attes. Believing he's come to her aid, she thanks him, but he tells her not to do that quite yet. Confusing her, Attes tells her that what he's about to do is the only way. He disarms her and hauls her against him, and she hears Ash shouting for her. Attes tells her that all they want is her and orders her to remove the charm that keeps her in the Shadowlands. He promises that if she does as he asks, no more lives will be lost.

Sera once more hears Ash roaring her name and hesitates. Attes tells her that if she refuses to come with him, Kyn will leave none but the Primal—Ash—standing. Sera sees Ash then and hears him roaring for her. She locks eyes with him for a moment and then makes Attes promise again that no one else will be harmed. He gives his word, and she agrees to leave. At those words, she feels a similar sensation to what she felt when Vikter placed the charm. Attes tells her she made the right choice, though Sera knows it was never a choice.

It wasn't. But the reasons behind that will only become clear much later. As much as I adore Attes, I absolutely hated him in this moment when I *saw* these things.

Unconscious, Sera dreams of her lake and a wolf more silver than white in moonlight watching her as she swims. She feels safe, submerges herself, and then surfaces to see Ash where the wolf was. She remembers the smell of smoke and charred flesh and death from the battle. The musty smell of the ship Attes shadowstepped them to. She recalls the explosion of pain in the back of her head when Attes finally released her.

She wonders how long the Primal of War and Accord has been working with Kolis and if he kept his word to stop the attack on the Shadowlands. She worries whether their people are all right. With all her might, she wishes she could see Ash one last time and tell him she loves him.

She wakes to the scent of stale lilacs and feels a shackle around her throat— effectively chained. Someone comments that she's awake, and she recognizes the voice. She's told she's been out for two days and that Attes wasn't supposed to hit her quite so hard.

When she looks, she sees the imprint on her hand, so she knows Ash is alive. Looking around, she finds she's in a gold cage, and the voice—Callum—reveals that they know she's a mortal with embers in her. Sera realizes that said embers are unnervingly quiet for once.

The person speaking comes into view then, and she recognizes the Revenant. He greets her using her full name and tells her that Attes kept his promise. Kyn pulled back on the attack. That news should have brought her relief. Instead, it only makes her more aware of her current circumstances. She sees that she's been dressed in sheer gold gossamer. Callum tells her she was covered in filth and stank of the Shadowlands and the Primal there, which had to be rectified. She tells *him* that the only stench on her is from where she is now. Callum warns her not to let Kolis hear her say things like that.

Sera learns that Callum told Calliphe how to kill a Primal, and that Kolis has known everything since Sera was born. Apparently, her father summoned him to try to make a new deal to replace the one King Roderick made, trying to spare Sera. The more she hears, the more she realizes that *graeca*, which she was told meant both love and life, has always meant life to Kolis—the embers of life. Kolis knew they were inside her the day she was born.

With sickening clarity, she realizes that everything Ash did and sacrificed was for nothing. She notices, however, that Callum never mentions Sotoria and assumes that Kolis still doesn't know that bit. She asks why the false Primal of Life didn't just take the embers early. Why did he wait until she was in the Shadowlands? She's reminded of the blood and ash.

Sera sees Kolis and thinks about her true duty. All of a sudden, she feels a wash of terror and fury rush through her, but realizes the emotions are only partly hers. She knows Sotoria was in a cage like the one she's in when Kolis brought the mortal back to life. Suddenly filled with numbness, Sera dons her veil of nothingness and refuses to kneel before the false King.

Talk of the last oracle ensues, and Sera learns that the goddess Penellaphe's vision wasn't quite complete, and those who know the whole thing haven't lived to tell the tale. She learns prophecies often come in threes and seem unrelated until they're pieced together. Callum and Kolis tell her more of the prophecy, and Sera remarks that Kolis is the great conspirator. He tells her that her attitude amuses him. They finish telling her the prophecy, and she recognizes her new title in it. Sera assumes that Delfai, Keella, and Veses likely knew the whole prophecy, just as Kolis does.

The Primal tells her she's the bearer of two crowns, and she realizes he needed her to be coronated and to restore the draken's life to fulfill those bits of the prophecy. He reveals that he needed to be sure the embers had reached a certain point of power for the rest of the prophecy to take place.

They finish relaying the rest of it, and Sera realizes it references a Primal of both Life *and* Death. When she learns more about Kolis's plans, she laughs at him and says the prophecy will bring his death.

As more details come to light, Sera is shocked to discover that Kolis wants to kill all the Primals. She asks him why he needs more power and tells him he's selfish. In response, he grabs her by the neck, telling her that Nyktos would have taken the embers the moment he felt he was ready. Eythos was setting up his son to become *the* Primal so that Nyktos could raise his father from the dead once he assumed the role. Kolis then tells her he's going to drain her, take the embers, and complete his final Ascension, then taunts her that she knows what that means for his nephew.

He gloats that nothing will be forbidden or impossible once he Ascends and bites her above the shackle around her neck. She wonders if Ash can sense and feel her pain and realizes he'll know she's dead when his imprint vanishes.

Suddenly, she feels the embers flare and hears Sotoria in her head yelling, "No!" She speaks aloud, using Sotoria's voice and saying, "You're killing me again, after all these years." Despite his best efforts, Sera feels no pain anymore, only rage. She laughs and tells Kolis she's Sotoria and then explains everything Eythos did.

Kolis releases her and hugs her to him. She sees the horror on his face as he realizes who he has to kill—again—in order to get what he wants.

Fading, Sera's gaze drifts to the open doors where she sees a silver-white wolf crouched by the trees and bathed in moonlight.

She knows it's Ash.

Sera awakens chained in a cage in a circular chamber. Kolis tightens his hold and asks her if she's really Sotoria. Crying, Sera wonders if the tears are hers alone. She's scared—even of just Kolis's voice.

Attes tells Kolis that Sera isn't well and urges him to see. Callum takes another tack and tells Kolis to take the embers. Says if she dies, they die right along with her. He tells Kolis he needs to take them and Ascend. Attes chimes back in that if

Sera dies, Kolis's *graeca* will be lost.

Hearing the word again, Sera thinks it has a third meaning outside of love and life. Obsession. It's clear that's the root of what Kolis feels for Sotoria. With that thought, Sera loses consciousness again.

She senses a storm of gathering power, and the wolf comes—mist and shadows everywhere. Sera watches as the throne crumbles and a shockwave tosses Attes aside and lifts Callum, slamming him into the cage's bars.

Ash shifts into his Primal form and challenges Kolis. Suddenly, Hanan appears, and Sera watches as Ash destroys the Primal's spear and then kills him. For some reason, she finds his display of power disturbingly hot.

An earthquake shakes the building, and Hanan's crown disappears. Sera knows everyone, everywhere likely felt it and realizes that Bele probably just rose as the new Primal of the Hunt.

Kolis lowers Sera gently, but before he can let go, Ash tells his uncle to get his hands off his wife. She watches the exchange and realizes that Kolis can't kill Ash. Balance is required.

Ash gathers Sera into his arms but is ripped away. The two Primals argue about war, treason, custom, and faith. Then, they battle.

As they fight, Attes grabs Sera. She calls him a traitor. Attes says he knows what he's done, but there's no time for that. He warns her that Kolis will kill Ash. Begrudgingly, Sera asks Attes to help her stand, then takes one of his shadowstone daggers. When he rages, she uses the little strength she has to tell him to calm down, saying he's not worth the effort.

She taps into the embers, compels Ash and Kolis to stop fighting, then lifts the dagger to her throat. She threatens to end herself, and they plead for her to stand down.

When Kolis stabs Ash in the chest, Nyktos tells Sera to run. Attes reminds her that Ash is still alive and then yells at Kolis that *Sotoria* needs his help, hoping to stop the false King from wounding Ash worse. He finally lets up and comes to Sera, lifting her.

Inside Sera, Sotoria whispers that it isn't fair, speaking of dying again.

Sera comes to in Kolis's arms, thinking about Ash. The false King tells her that she'll live as long as she is who she claims to be. He takes her into the water, and Sera sees ceeren swimming all around her.

Kolis calls to Phanos. When the Primal arrives, he says he thought Sera was Nyktos's Consort. Kolis brushes that off and orders him to help her.

Phanos takes Sera and mentions how Nyktos took Saion and Rhahar from him as he walks. He says that he should be amused by what's happening, but he finds no joy in it. He tells her they're in the water off the Triton Isles near the coast of Hygeia, adding that water is the source of all life and healing.

Sera suddenly hears singing. Phanos says that what is about to happen would cure most, but with the embers inside her, that's impossible for Sera—it's merely a temporary solution. He mentions a steep price and tells her to remember the gifts she's about to be given.

He breathes into her mouth and then sends her into the water, where the ceeren do the same, dying as they give their lives for hers.

It's utterly tragic, and nearly broke my heart when I saw it.

Sera asks Kolis why he did what he did, and he tells her that he won't allow her to die. Sera tells him she doesn't want anyone dying for her, and he tells *her* she has no choice, then taunts her that if she were Sotoria, she'd know that.

He says that if he looks and listens hard enough, he can see Sotoria in her.

She runs for the guards and grabs a sword. Kolis orders her not to be touched and tells the guards to leave, remarking that he *expected* her to run. He demands she put down the weapon, and she tells him to make her, then stabs him in the chest. He says he's not amused and tells her how she could have done better.

She starts to run, and he stops her by her hair, saying he's more accustomed to this—her running. They fight. Kolis hits Sera, then feels bad about it. She mouths off, and Kolis says he never wanted to be a villain, blaming Eythos for that.

Sera asks him if there's anything he *doesn't* blame his brother for. Kolis tells her not to push him and calls her *so'lis*.

The false King threatens Ash, and Sera threatens *him*. He grabs her by the throat, and she gasps that he's killing her again.

When he says they're going *home*, she tells him off. That really angers him, and he shifts into his deathly form, scaring her, then compels her.

Once the compulsion lifts, Sera finds herself wet and in another grander gilded cage. She thinks about Aios and her captivity and falls into despair. Eather cracks the cell. She tries to calm herself and looks the space over, seeing what appears to be a cluster of diamonds at the top of the cage, the throne, and the layout of the sitting areas. Her rage flares again, and it cracks the shadowstone.

She knows she needs to calm and taps into a memory of Ash's voice telling her to breathe. As she does, she weeps, noticing she's crying the blood tears of a Primal.

Sera thinks about how Eythos's plan was not well thought out at all. Sotoria has woken up, and Sera doesn't like the idea of her being trapped. She laments everything that's happened so far.

Knowing she needs a weapon, she begins looking around. She searches through some chests in the cage and finds one full of glass cocks. Taking one, she breaks it, turning it into a fairly decent—albeit unusual—weapon.

When she touches the bars of the cage, she feels pain and realizes it won't be easy to get out of her predicament.

Needing to shed her wet clothes, she searches for something else to wear and finds herself disgusted by the choices. Without options, she picks a gown and changes, then feigns sleep when Callum enters the room.

As he nears her, she repeatedly stabs him with the makeshift dagger, then takes his key. She's about to take off with it, then decides it'd be smarter to leave it in case she's captured and returned. She tosses it far under the bed and runs. On her way out, she encounters a guard and stabs him, then sees some Chosen. She tells them she won't hurt them, but one calls the guards.

Making her way farther, she encounters an orgy in progress, then smells blood. When she comes upon a woman feeding from a man, it doesn't look like the feedings she's seen. With pitch-black eyes, the woman says that Sera smells of Revenant and god. Like life. She comes at Sera, and Sera stabs her, watching her crumble into nothing and shocking her. She checks on the male and finds him dead.

The guards enter, and Sera grabs one, only to find out it's a draken. He's amused, and that just pisses Sera off, so she nails him with eather.

The previously dead male rushes out and attacks, having turned Craven.

Sera falls unconscious and dreams of her lake. When she wakes, she's back in the cage, and Kolis is with her. She mentions being kept as a prisoner, and he tells her she's a *guest*. Sera asks him how long he's been watching her, and he wonders if it bothers her. She swears, and he tells her that her language is far more uncivilized than he remembers.

He smells her, mentions what he scents, and she realizes that he's picking up on her lake. Somehow. He tells her he's irked and reminds her what happens when she displeases him.

Sera brings up his *favorites*, and he tells her they were all ungrateful, then says he can sense the embers in her. When he calls her *so'lis* again, she asks him what it means. He explains how the old Primal words break down and says that Kolis means "our soul;" therefore, *so'lis* is "my soul." It disgusts Sera.

She remembers some things Holland told her and considers what she needs to do, weighing her options. She brings to mind all those she knows and thinks about how they matter. All of them. With those thoughts, she realizes she needs to become the blank canvas and do what's required.

She takes the key from under the bed and hides it with the menstruation rags—somewhere a male would never look.

Callum enters the room and asks how he should refer to her, clarifying that he doesn't believe she's Sotoria. She asks him about Ash, and he ignores her questions, continuing with giving her instructions.

He mentions being familiar with her mother, Calliphe, and brings up the wards Nyktos put on her family. When he says something about being invited inside, Sera realizes that Revenants must need to be invited into places.

Callum tells her that he's been watching her for years. She taunts him and threatens to tell Kolis that Callum was the one who shared how a Primal could be killed.

He brings the Chosen in and tells her that if she doesn't follow his directions, he'll kill them. She's stubborn, and he doesn't hesitate to break a Chosen's neck. Before he can kill another, she behaves. He tells her to bathe, and she threatens to kill him. However, she begrudgingly does as he says, stuffing down her post-traumatic stress at having to use the tub.

When she looks in the mirror, she sees eather in her eyes. Hearing a sound, she looks up at the window near the ceiling and sees a shadow blocking out the light. An enormous silver hawk flies in a second later, locking its blue eyes with hers. Sera swears she feels a Primal. As she thinks that, the bird shifts and becomes Attes.

Sera lashes out, and Attes says he deserved the blow, though he reminds her that he saved her, calling her a hellion. When she scoffs, he explains that he stopped what could have happened by taking her.

Attes conjures some clothes, making Sera jealous of his ability. Once dressed, Attes tells her this wasn't the first time he saved her. She's skeptical, but he reminds her about when the hawk saved her in the woods. It was him. When she asks about Primals shifting and then brings up Eythos, he tells her that he shifted into a wolf, not a hawk, but that Kolis *does* take his hawk *nota* form.

She wonders why she didn't feel him, and he explains that they're not detectable in their *nota* forms. It's them, yet…not. He tells her that the other silver hawks she saw were Attes's *chora*—an extension of him and very much alive.

Attes explains that he's known about her longer than even Kolis or Nyktos. When she asks why he was surprised about Thad if he knew she had the embers, he says it had been a long time since he'd seen real life restored, then says he assumes she can do what she can because the embers are bonding with her.

As they talk about the events that led to the present, he tells her that the Fates prohibited Eythos from telling Nyktos what his father did. It was their way of trying to reestablish balance.

Sera tells him to get Ash out of Dalos. He says he would if he could, then tells her about the bones of the Ancients and what they can do. When she mentions that the bones can be destroyed, given what Ash did to Hanan's spear, he tells her that only the Primal of Life and the Primal of Death can destroy them.

She asks him how Ash is, and he tells her he's not conscious, then explains how he's being kept in the Carcers, saying the prison is terrible. He establishes that he can't help. When she tells him he's only saying that because he's worried about himself, he corrects her and says he's more concerned about what Kolis will do to her or Nyktos. He adds that he's loyal only to the true Primal of Life, and that's her now.

He points out the scar on his face and tells her that Kolis gave it to him. He also reveals that Kolis took and killed Attes's children, saying he's never really stood with the false Primal of Life.

He explains how things are different now because of her but not because of the embers. It's because of the one who can kill Kolis. Sotoria. He outright asks her if she's Sotoria but then says himself that she's not, adding that if she were, she'd look just like her, and she wouldn't have spoken *through* Sera earlier.

Sera asks about the differences between rebirth and being reborn, and Attes explains. Then he wonders why the Arae told Kolis how to take the embers.

He insinuates that Sotoria's soul is trapped within Sera, and it bothers her. She asks if anyone knows what will happen to Sotoria if Sera dies, and Attes tells her no.

Their discussion ends with him asserting that she's not the weapon Eythos thought he created.

When she insists she can still fulfill her duty, he says she might be right, but she can't kill Kolis.

She hopes he's wrong.

Sera tells Attes that she stabbed Kolis, and it shocks him. He says the false King must be weaker than he thought.

Attes mentions Sotoria's soul being lost again, and it angers Sera. She snaps that she knows Sotoria's soul is the most important thing, and he tells her that *she* matters, too.

Sera mentions having a plan, and Attes is shocked—she hasn't been there long. As she thinks about it, she asks what will happen if she manages to free Ash. He won't return to the Shadowlands quietly. Attes tells her he will if he's smart. He then explains how word of what he's done will have spread, and he's powerful, the second Primal most wouldn't want to piss off. Sera assumes Attes is the third, and he calls her clever.

She tells him he's incredibly stab-worthy, and he says he's heard that before. Assuming her role as the Primal of Life, she orders Attes to back Nyktos, and Attes swears—an unbreakable bond. Then he bows and pledges his sword and his life—even though he doesn't actually *have* a sword at present.

Sera asks about Sotoria again, and Attes says he's been searching for a way to safeguard her soul. When Sera asks if Sotoria's name means something like Kolis and *so'lis* do, he tells her it means "my pretty poppy."

She asks Attes to get her a weapon made from the bones of the Ancients, and he tells her all the reasons it's a bad idea. She capitulates. He then asks Sera if she can feel Sotoria. When she says she can, he says he hopes she hears what he's about to say and says he will save her this time. Then, he leaves.

With nothing else to do, Sera trains, wondering what exactly she was trained *for* and if Holland knew all along that she wasn't a weapon.

She remembers the wolf she saw while gathering rocks as a child and gives in to her feelings of missing Ash like a limb. She thinks about making Ash swear to live before she dies and getting him to see that he's not to blame.

Sera wakes later, but she really doesn't. She's at her lake, and the colors of the landscape remind her of the Shadowlands.

Ash arrives.

He asks her to look at him. She does, and each of them thinks they're the one dreaming. In reality, it's a shared dream. Not caring what it is, they give in to their desire to touch each other and have sex. She tells him that she loves him, and he calls her beautiful.

Suddenly, he sees her bruises and gets upset. Sera starts to wake, telling him she can no longer feel him. Then, she's back in the cell, but can still feel where they touched and what they did.

The Chosen come to take care of their chores, and Sera behaves. Callum stares, and she asks him if he wants something, then tells him she doesn't think he's right in the head—what with dying all the time and all.

She asks him about the Chosen she saw during her escape attempt. Before he can answer, Kolis enters the room and asks what they are discussing. Callum explains that they were talking about Antonis—the one who turned Craven.

Kolis tells her they're an unfortunate side effect of creating the Ascended. When Sera points out the differences between Eythos Ascending the Chosen and what Kolis does, it angers him. He tells Callum to leave and then asks if she's been resting. She reminds herself to stick to the plan and plays nice.

He orders her to have some fruity water, and Sera asks where Nyktos is. Kolis wants to know why. She tells him it's merely a curiosity, then asks about the army. He tells her they haven't left the borders of Dalos and explains they're in the Bonelands to the south along the coast beyond the Carcers. He tells her it's full of forgotten Temples and bones of dragons.

Sera asks him why he hasn't forced them out since he wants to be all-powerful, and his answer makes her realize that he needs things to rule over. He says the mortals have become complacent, and says he plans to take a more active role.

She asks if her abduction will heighten tensions, and he says his taking her will only be a problem if the other Primals think that she's worth going to war over. He says a little more, and she realizes he basically admitted that, in his current state, he thinks he'd be defeated if things escalated.

He asks again why she inquired about Nyktos, and she gives him the same answer. He tells her that she never screamed in terror for *him*, then warns her not to say anything unwise. She admits that she's fond of Ash, tempering what she *really* wants to say, then tells Kolis that he scared her.

He tells her it wasn't his intention, and she goes on to explain her *fondness* for Ash. Kolis shatters the glass he holds. She tries to calm him by saying that Nyktos only wanted the embers, not her, and tells Kolis Ash didn't know what Eythos did. He tells her not to lie, and she says she's not.

Kolis then asks her if she's fucked Nyktos, and Sera carefully answers that they're attracted to each other. Kolis tells her that someone wouldn't kill another for a person they don't love, and she says people kill for any and all and no reason. He argues that Primals don't and then says that every life he's ever taken has been for love. Sera tells him that she's sorry love has only ever inspired death for him.

She reveals that Ash removed his *kardia*, and Kolis tells her Nyktos is currently in stasis. She confirms that he's gone to ground, and Kolis acknowledges. She asks why it didn't happen sooner, and he explains that the chamber is made of shadowstone, which is dragon fire and anything dead. Not much can penetrate it, and the earth isn't one of the few. He explains how shadowstone absorbs eather like it does light.

As they talk more, Sera insists she's telling the truth about Ash and his *kardia*, and Kolis says he can believe it. It sounds like something his nephew would do. He would think it would stop Kolis from striking out at someone Nyktos loves. He admits that Nyktos fears becoming him and says he made sure he felt that way.

Sera's embers flare, and Kolis tells her to calm herself. She starts glowing. Once he orders her to sit and calls her good like a pet dakkai, he tells her he doesn't believe what she said earlier about her feelings for Nyktos. He says the marriage imprint proves there's love and mulls over what to do. She says it just appeared and then explains the difference between loving someone and being *in* love with them. After, she shuts it all down again and becomes the empty vessel she needs to be.

Kolis says he's in love with Sotoria, and Sera asks him how he can know. Then tells him to prove it by releasing Nyktos. He grumbles that her demand proves she loves his nephew. She doesn't deny it—she already told him she loved Ash—but says it would show her that he's willing to do anything for her. He lists what he's already done, and she tells him that it's the bare minimum required to show love, adding that releasing Nyktos would matter because he doesn't want to do it but knows it would please her.

When he asks her why, she tells him and adds that Kolis has only endangered her. He asks why she would be interested in falling in love, and she says it's because she's never known it. She reasons that commonality could bring them closer, and he asks if she thinks he's a fool. Her reply is that love makes you idiotic. He counters that she tried to kill him, but she says she also stabbed Nyktos.

Kolis asks her what will change if he releases Nyktos, and she tells him she won't fight him. He thinks that means she'll submit… Kolis tells her that if she's lying about Sotoria, he will take her soul in both life *and* death.

Later, Callum reads a book as Sera nibbles on her meal. She asks him if Revenants eat, and he tells her they don't need food or blood—they need nothing. She assumes it's because they're dead, and he tells her that assumption is rude but won't correct her with the real reason.

They discuss that Revenants must die, and Sera asks Callum if he was Chosen. He says he wasn't, and she points out that he's not like the other Ascended Chosen. He tells her there are no others like him.

Well…not *yet*. We know that changes. Sort of.

Sera peppers him with questions, and he eventually talks about how painful her death will be when Kolis discovers she's not Sotoria.

She asks about the painted masks they all wear, and he says they're symbolic. They show who the Chosen, Revenants, and gods serve.

When she says she's seen Kolis go full Primal, it shocks Callum. He tells her that means she's seen the true Death.

The next day, the Chosen prepare Sera. Kolis walks in wearing his crown and tells her not to engage with anyone.

She's not sure what to expect, so she simply watches Kolis sit on the throne. Elias escorts the gods into the chamber, and Sera doesn't like the looks and expressions on their faces. In thinking about things, she realizes she wasn't clever enough in clarifying what state Ash should be in when he's released. With that thought in mind, she behaves as Kolis gets progressively edgier.

The false King suddenly asks a god if he finds her distracting. The god apologizes and says she's interesting to look upon. Pleasing to the eye. Kolis makes him detail which bits are *pleasing*. As the god details the parts, Sera can't hold back and finally asks: what the fuck?

Kolis tells Uros—the god—that he may have offended Sera, then asks her if she is. She says she's just unimpressed. Kolis turns back to the god, says that Uros offended *him*, then implodes him. Sera can only stare and gape when he turns to her and asks if she finds Uros more impressive now.

He tells her he's impressed by her calmness, then calls Elias in and tells him to get Callum to find the Sun Temple Uros was from a replacement. The god asks if he should get someone to clean up the mess, Kolis waves his hand, and it all disappears.

A goddess walks in and states her business. Kolis cuts Dametria off, clearly tense, and suddenly excuses himself.

The goddess prowls to the bars of Sera's cage. As Sera watches, Dametria asks if Sera likes what she sees because she likes what she sees beneath Sera's gown. Sera asks the goddess what kingdom the Sun Temple she represents is in, and Dametria is shocked that Sera spoke. She says no others before her have—meaning the *favorites*. She then tells Sera she's heard rumors she is the Shadowlands' Consort.

She reveals that the Temple is in Terra. Based on what Dametria says about people from Lasania coming, too, asking for blessings on their work with Terra, Sera surmises that Ezra succeeded in strengthening the relationship between the kingdoms.

The goddess insinuates that Kolis is off pleasuring himself, disgusting Sera. Elias swears, and Dametria tells Sera she was at the coronation, so she knows she's the Consort.

Sera uses the bathing chambers while Kolis is gone. When he returns, he looks more relaxed, lending credence to what Dametria insinuated.

Kyn shows up, and Kolis asks if he's brought news. The Primal answers that he has but suggests they speak privately. Kolis says talking in front of Sera is fine since she's not going anywhere.

She watches and listens as they discuss the armies and what should be done next.

Kyn suggests that a clear message can still be sent and is likely needed because of Sera, calling her *that*. The discussion continues, and Kyn says he's not worried about retribution, including Nektas, and Sera laughs. He asks her if he made a joke.

Sera reminds Kolis that he said he didn't want to go to war, and he tells Kyn he's brave and loyal and has his gratitude. Kyn tells Kolis he has more than bravery and loyalty from him. He says Kolis has his army and his command, then adds that their plans have changed. He reasserts that Kolis needs the embers.

They talk about balance, provocation, and need, then discuss that Nyktos will be a problem if he's released.

When Kolis notices Kyn looking at Sera, he asserts that she draws the eye. Sera doesn't want a repeat of what happened with Uros. Instead, Kolis asks her to come closer. She becomes blank once more and moves. He then asks Kyn what he thinks. Kyn eye fucks her and again says she draws the eye.

Kolis agrees and then adds that you don't want to think it but do. He then asks the Primal what he would do if Sera weren't in a cage and his. He insinuates that Kyn would be between her thighs or in her ass in a heartbeat.

Kyn asks what happens if she's not Kolis's *graeca*, and Kolis says Kyn can have her when he's done if she's not. The Primal seems pleased and agrees.

Sera knows she won't survive if it comes to that.

The Primals make the deal, and Kyn tells Kolis he's honored. Says the King's potential gift moves him. Then mentions he's glad he brought a gift for Kolis, as well.

He calls to Kolis's draken, Diaval, and the male brings in someone bound with a hood over their head. Diaval shoves whoever it is to their knees, and Kyn says the gift is a bit battered and bloody, but it required some convincing.

He rips off the hood, and Sera sees that it's Rhain.

He's been bitten and beaten. If he weren't a god, he'd likely be dead. Kyn confirms his name for Kolis and then says he's originally from the Callasta Isles. It shocks Sera to find out that he's from Veses' Court.

Kolis confirms that he's the son of Daniil and says Rhain resembles his father the last time he saw him, alluding to the fact that he was beaten, too.

Rhain lashes out, then they discuss Rhain's father and brother. Sera realizes she knows very little about Rhain.

As they trade banter and insults, Sera thinks about the key and has an almost prophetic vision. Because she knows why Kyn brought Rhain alive. So Kolis could kill him.

Sera listens as they talk about the gifts that Rhain's father and brother had and the assumption that he has them, as well. Suddenly, Sera hears Rhain's voice in her head saying her name.

As Kolis drones on, Rhain tells Sera to listen to him, urging her to use the essence and bring down the palace.

When Kolis finds the necklace Rhain is carrying in a pouch around his neck, Sera's shocked to see it, knowing it's Aios's. She lies and tells Kolis it's hers but insists she didn't know what Rhain could do.

All lies are at least partial truths…

She then reveals that Rhain doesn't even like her. When Kolis asks why, she says it's probably because she stabbed Nyktos, then adds the personality traits the god probably dislikes.

Sera tries to talk around the assumption that Rhain is there as a spy, saying that everyone already knows she's at Cor Palace. But then Kolis tells her she's not.

Kyn and Sera bicker, and Kolis warns her. He then turns to Rhain and says he believes Sera, so he'll make the god's death quick.

Sera cries out and urges that Kolis doesn't have to kill him, adding that he's only loyal to Nyktos. Kolis snaps that he should be loyal to *him*. Sera amends and says he's worried about Nyktos, and Kolis should be thrilled.

Kolis is clearly confused, so Sera says that the gods in the Courts should care about their Primals. If they don't, how can they care about their King? She says loyalty shouldn't be punished by death or torture.

Rhain tells Sera telepathically that it's okay. He's prepared to die.

Sera's not having that.

She tells Kolis there's another option. He can release Rhain. It would show that he's a benevolent ruler. That if the god were to be released in his current condition, it would prove that Kolis can be both fierce and giving. She tells him she'll do whatever he wants as long as he lets the god go. Kolis renders Rhain unconscious and asks Sera why she wants to save the god. She tells him she's trying to prevent a war and says she'll do anything if Kolis promises that Rhain will return to the Shadowlands no more hurt than he is now. Another deal.

Kolis dismisses Kyn, but the Primal gloats in his last look at Sera. After Rhain is removed from the chamber, Kolis tells Sera they'll share a bed tonight.

After dinner, Sera bathes and sees the gold nightgown set out for her. Kolis appears and tells her she's far bolder than before—meaning as Sotoria. He asks if what he requested of her was a surprise, and she tells him it only surprised her because he offered her to Kyn just moments before. He tells her that her advice was wise and that releasing Rhain shows he's reasonable and fair—and worthy of loyalty. He tells her Rhain is back home, and Sera thanks him. She assures him of things that are a lie and fears she's *all* lies now.

They go to bed.

And Sera remains awake.

The next day, Callum tosses a dagger into the air and asks her if she slept. She lies and says she got tons of rest. Callum tells her she's being quiet and insinuates that she learned she could whore herself to get her way. She gets pissed and uses eather to redirect the Revenant's dagger, almost stabbing him. Unfortunately, he moves quickly enough to avoid it.

She calls him *Cal*, and he gets pissy. Then she tells him she realizes she's not in Cor Palace. He reveals she's in the Vita, a sanctuary in the City of the Gods.

Kolis comes in wearing his crown, leading a timid-looking goddess. He introduces her as Ione and says she's from Keella's Court. He then adds that the goddess is unique. She can see into others' thoughts and uncover truths, lies, and all that is needed.

Uh-oh.

Kolis tells Sera it won't take long, that Ione will be quick and efficient. He orders Sera to sit, and she feels Sotoria rise, filling her with anger and fear. Kolis says she seems nervous, and she says it's because a god did this to her before, and it hurt.

Callum fills Kolis in about Taric. Kolis asks Sera if Taric found her, and she says it was him, Cressa, and Madis, then asks him why he had Taric searching for the embers if he already knew where they were. He tells her that he ordered Taric to look for his *graeca*.

Kolis asks Sera if the other gods fed from her, and she says only Taric did. He then asks if the god told her what he saw, and Sera says he didn't have a chance to say anything before he died.

Ione tells Sera that what she's about to do doesn't have to hurt. She adds that it will be uncomfortable and likely make her tired and headachy. Sera says she can't do it, and Kolis compels her, telling Ione to be quick.

Ione kneels and explains that she needs to take Sera's blood. When the goddess realizes Sera can't respond, she lifts Sera's hand, sees the imprint, then looks into her eyes. Kolis asks what's wrong, and Ione tells him it's nothing before lowering that hand and picking up Sera's other one. She bites her wrist, and Sera feels a sting travel through her until she feels scratching at her mind.

Visions flash, and Sera shakes on the inside. Tears threaten. She is in terrible pain and worries that Ash can feel it, even in stasis. The embers inside her swell, and Sera pushes with her mind, snapping Ione's head back and sliding her across the shadowstone floor.

Callum calls what she did inappropriate, and Kolis demands to know what Ione saw. The goddess says the embers in Sera are strong, and he says he already knows that much. He asks if Sera is his *graeca*, and Ione tells him she carries the one called Sotoria. That she is her.

Sera freezes, realizing the goddess lied. Kolis asks her more questions, and she gives more half-truths. Sera realizes that Ione is lying about basically everything and wonders why.

Kolis gets all emotional, and Callum says it has to be a lie. Ione tells him she doesn't lie and has no reason to. Sera realizes what a huge risk this is for the goddess.

They discuss how Sera doesn't look like Sotoria, and Ione tries to explain it away. She then tells Kolis she's glad he found his *graeca*, and Sera almost chokes on her water.

The goddess asks Kolis if he requires anything more of her, and he thanks her for her assistance. When she turns to leave, she addresses Sera as *Consort*. Kolis interjects, saying the coronation was neither recognized nor approved.

Sickened, Sera realizes that nobody can contest Kolis's claim. Callum continues to argue, but Kolis brushes him off. When Sera snaps that she was always telling the truth, Kolis says he sees that now and dismisses Callum. He approaches her, telling her she looks more like Sotoria when she smiles. When Sera asks about Nyktos and Kolis honoring their deal, he gets angry and bites her.

Agony seizes Sera, and Sotoria screams within her. The embers swell, and Sera fights for control. She tries to employ her breathing techniques to regain calm and pictures Ash in her mind, distancing herself from the present.

Kolis finally loosens his hold, and Sera jumps to her feet. She realizes he found his release while feeding and is disgusted. He apologizes, saying he shamed both himself and her. He lost control. Sera can't help her fight or flight response, and he insists it'll never happen again. He begs her to say something, and all she can say is that she needs a bath.

As she bathes, she thinks over everything that happened. The violation. And hates that she feels weak over what happened.

After breakfast the next day, the silver hawk flies in again and becomes Attes. He calls her his Queen, then manifests clothes again. Sera tells him how jealous she is. He apologizes for not returning sooner but says he has news. Then he notices her bite wound. It clearly upsets him, but she tells him she's okay. He doesn't believe her, but she insists.

Attes tells Sera that Nyktos is being awakened from stasis and assumes she's made progress with her plans. She tells him Kolis promised to release Nyktos and says she needs to make sure he doesn't have a reason to go back on that word and find a loophole.

Attes confirms that he knows about the deal she made to free Rhain and asks if she made a similar deal to free Nyktos.

Sera calls Kyn a dick. Attes agrees but says he wasn't always like that. He tells her about how the Primals deal with their long lives and what happens if they don't rest or go to Arcadia.

Sera asks how Kyn will respond to Nyktos taking his rightful place as the King of Gods, and Attes says he hopes he will respond wisely. Then he asks if she's okay, shocking her.

She says she is, and he begrudgingly accepts and then turns into his hawk to leave.

Later, Callum waits in the chamber wearing black, which almost disturbs Sera more than his white does. She realizes it's been at least a day since Attes visited, and Sera worries Kolis has changed his mind. However, she reminds herself that he can't because he made a deal.

Callum tells Sera he doesn't believe her, and she asks him about what. He says he doesn't believe she's open to loving Kolis as she said and thinks she will try to escape the first chance she gets.

She tells him she doesn't care what he thinks and calls him insignificant. He says she *should* care because Kolis will find out. He insists again that she's not Sotoria, and she asks him why he's so sure. He tells her it's partly her appearance, and Sera realizes he must be old if he knew Sotoria before. She asks him. He says he's old but didn't know her.

What he really means is that he didn't know *Sera*...

Callum points out that Kolis cares about her, and she insinuates Callum is worried she will replace him in Kolis's life. He says he's concerned about the destruction of the realms due to a charlatan.

He insists Kolis is trying to save the realms, and Sera can only stare. He amends that he was, but is now more concerned if his great love is returning to him.

Sera clarifies what's going on and asks at what point between becoming a Primal who's never existed and killing all who refuse to bow to him would he save the realms. Callum says that life must be created. No matter what.

Sera asks if that's what Kolis is doing with the Chosen, and Callum waves her off, saying it doesn't matter.

She disagrees.

He says she's trying to change the subject—she is. He then says that Kolis has personal reasons for wanting to be the Primal of Life and Death/Blood and Bone. He tells her it'll be bad when Kolis discovers the truth, and she shrugs it off, saying she's been validated, and has had her truth confirmed.

Callum says Ione lied.

Sera worries about Ione if Kolis ever discovers she lied. Sera tells Callum he must be delusional if he thinks a god would risk Kolis's wrath.

He basically calls her a whore again, and she has to hold herself back. Still, she asks him if he remembers what she promised him. He sasses, and she details how his death will be the thing of nightmares.

The embers take control and conjure a storm. It takes Callum by surprise, but he remains composed. Kolis walks in and asks them why they always look like they're about to go at each other's throats. Sera tells Kolis that Callum still doesn't believe that she's Sotoria. Kolis tells her the Rev is in denial, then drops a bomb.

Callum is Sotoria's younger brother.

The news makes Sera choke, and she can barely get her words of disbelief out. It sinks in that he's telling the truth, and she wonders about the overabundance of terrible brothers in the realms. She bickers with the Revenant, and Kolis comments on their fighting reminding him of how he used to quarrel with his brother, then going on to tell her how she had two siblings: an older sister and Callum, the younger brother.

Kolis tells Sera how he went to Sotoria's family when she left him—he means when she *died* while running from him—and apologized. He tells her the parents were frightened and cowered. Only Callum remained unafraid. He tells her that they talked, and Callum shared details about Sotoria, saying she was strong and fierce and always looked out for him.

Kolis continues, saying he—Callum—grieved her death and felt responsible. When Sera asks why he would feel that way, Kolis tells her that Callum was supposed to be with Sotoria but was instead screwing the baker's daughter.

Sera asks how Callum became a Revenant, and Kolis tells her how Callum used a small knife to cut his throat. He tells Sera how he held them both as they died, adding that he couldn't allow him to perish, so Death gave life.

She asks for clarification, wondering if Revenants are demis. Kolis tells her they're not and then adds that they'll discuss it more when there aren't more pressing matters to attend to. Kolis tells Callum to go on ahead.

He calls Sera *so'lis* and wants to talk about the deal they made. He tells her that Nyktos has not been released, adding that he's not reneging, but Nyktos is in stasis, and that needs to be resolved first.

She asks what that means, and he tells her Ash is young but powerful. So, when he woke, Kolis had to ensure he behaved himself.

Sera asks how he is, and Kolis says telling her would likely upset her. She argues that not knowing will only make her worry more. Kolis says he had Nyktos incapacitated, and he will need time to recover. When Sera reacts, he says it's not easy seeing her affected so by news of another. He adds that worry practically seeps from her pores.

Warning bells sound for Sera, and she reminds him that she told him she cared about Nyktos. Kolis gripes that it's all he can think about and mentions watching him in stasis. Sera assumes he was probably seething.

He wonders what inspires her care for Nyktos and her fear for *him*. He says she wasn't afraid of him at first, but that's changed. He then mentions Eythos having heightened intuition and foresight. He says he gets why she seemed frightened after he threatened someone she cares about and saw him as Death, but he doesn't get the timing of the changes in her.

She is shocked that he doesn't understand why she's frightened, and he reasserts that he apologized and said it would never happen again. She realizes she should probably lie but can't, telling him that his apology and promise don't make what he did okay. She comes right out and says that he forced himself on her.

He rewords and says that he realizes his *display of love* was intense. The word disgusts her. He then adds that he realizes he lost control. She says it was much more than that, and it's not all right. He asks what will make it okay.

She tells him she needs some time.

He argues that his word should be sufficient to make her trust him, and she tells him she doesn't know him. He gets upset and booms that he's the King of Gods.

She asserts that his display isn't helping her fear. He pulls back and then orders her to say something. She begrudgingly utters a thank you.

Sera once again wonders what kind of state Ash is in.

Kolis turns to her and apologizes once more. It almost sounds sincere, but then he shifts to scolding her for using the embers. She argues that Callum provoked her, and he says the essence does not belong to her and is not hers to use. The embers throb in response before he gives her a final warning. Sera vows that as soon as Ash is free, she will become Kolis's worst nightmare.

When alone, Sera checks for the key and finds it still in place. After dinner, she trains to burn off her excess energy and combat boredom. As she does, she worries about Ash. Rhain. Aios. Orphine. Bele. And the rest. She starts going over and over the should've, would've, could'ves and vows not to be powerless again.

When she sleeps, she arrives at her lake. Ash joins her again, and they talk about how it doesn't feel like a dream to either of them. Ash asks her if Kolis has hurt her and says he knows he has—he remembers the last time they were together and the bruises. She tells him she doesn't want to discuss that. She's Sera here at the lake, and someone else back in the cage.

He reminds her she's brave and never afraid, even when she feels fear. He then asks if she can access any weapons, and she tells him about the glass cock. He asks if she told Kolis about what will happen once she begins the Ascension—that only he—Ash—can Ascend her. He urges her to tell Kolis that she'll die without Ash, saying Kolis will do whatever's necessary to keep Sotoria alive because she's his weakness.

He mentions that only the Primal of Life can summon the Fates and makes Sera promise that she'll tell Kolis and call on the Arae. She does but then asks how she'll know he's been released. He tells her that Kolis will make it into a spectacle. She'll know.

He says he'll fight for and free her even if it means Dalos's ruin, then tells her he's nothing without her, and there will *be* nothing without her.

She wakes, only to find Kolis watching her sleep. Again. He asks who she was dreaming of and tells her she was smiling. He then says she smells of mountain air and citrus, which shocks her, as that's how Ash smells to her.

She says she doesn't remember her dreams, and he instructs that they'll start fresh. He asks how he can make that easier, saying there's no limit to what he'll do for her. He offers her frivolous things, and she tells him she wants out of the cage.

He thinks that means she wants to spend time with him, so it makes him happy. She asks him what he plans to do about the embers, and he tells her he'll take them and Ascend her, not knowing she is already on her way. She asks what Ascension will mean for her, and he says she'll become an Ascended. Sera can only think about the woman she killed.

She then asks what will happen when *he* Ascends, and he tells her he will ensure loyalty in both realms.

After breakfast, Kolis frees her. They walk, and Elias joins them. Sera asks if it'll be night anytime soon, and Kolis says it will be in about a week. He explains that it's only night once per month, which is the equivalent of three days in the mortal realm. Sera's shocked that she's been there for three weeks already. Kolis tells her that she slept for several days after her escape attempt.

Looking at the city, Sera remembers telling Ash that it was beautiful and him telling her that it is on the surface and from a distance. She asks Kolis how many live within the City of the Gods, and he says there aren't many. When she asks what happened, he tells her they're dead. She thought he killed them, but he tells her it was the Fates. She then asks about the current scent of death, and he tells her *that* was him. Some gods disappointed him.

Kolis walks away, and Elias reminds Sera to be careful how she speaks to

Kolis, warning her that he's easy to rile. She thanks him.

The false King returns, and they continue their walk. Sera sees all the alcoves, and Kolis tells her she looks perplexed. She replies that it's just a lot of sex. He asks if it bothers her, and she says it doesn't; it's just a lot. He explains that being near Death makes the living want to *live*. And what better way to capture that feeling?

They get to the Council Hall, and the embers hum within her, making her nervous. He asks her why, and she says it's the crowd. He tells her she needn't worry. When she says she knows, he takes it as her thinking she's safe with him.

It's so not.

When they enter, Sera sees a napping draken and the throne. She locks gazes with Kyn and wonders if he knows Kolis's gift is no longer on the table for him. Then she sees Attes. And Keella. The Primal goddess has sadness in her eyes. Sera wonders if she knows her plans went awry.

Phanos and Embris aren't there, nor are Maia or Veses—though that one is to be expected since she's still a prisoner at the House of Haides.

Callum brings in a floor pillow, and she's made to sit at Kolis's feet like a hound. She watches as the servants enter and listens as Kolis addresses the gathering. Sera notices Diaval, another beautiful god next to him, and more draken. She also sees the Revenant, Dyses.

Kolis orders her to drink when a server brings around a tray, then shifts his focus to Keella. The Primal goddess says she's come because of Sera and knows who she is. Kolis says she should, insinuating that Keella knows whose soul Sera has. He then asks her if she knew before the coronation.

Keella addresses Sera using her Shadowlands title and asks about Nyktos. Kolis snaps and says he is where he should be, given he killed Hanan. Keella then asks if he did it to protect his Consort, referencing the law. Kolis says his nephew's actions could have had lasting consequences. Keella counters that another has risen, and it should be a blessing, then asks if he's going to stop what he's doing since it goes against tradition and honor.

He asks her since when, then adds that he didn't sanction the coronation. Turning to Kyn, he asks if he gave permission, and Kyn lies and says he didn't.

Keella asks if Sera will be released when Nyktos is, and Kolis tells her that she's not going back to him. When the Primal asks if she is there of her own free will, Kolis tells her to ask Sera herself. Sera wants to yell that she's not there of her own accord, but she knows better. She says she's in Dalos by choice. It makes her feel ill.

Sera watches as a god grabs a passing servant and bites her. It makes her see red. She asks if the Chosen have choices, and Kolis says they've had nearly all their choices made for them all their lives. He looks at the couple and says it appears as if the servant is enjoying herself. Sera disagrees. He tells her that where they couldn't be touched or spoken to in the mortal realm, they can in Dalos. He says Sera views them as victims, whereas he sees those starved for what's been forbidden. He tells her that the Chosen have opportunities in Dalos. They can shed their veils or Ascend.

He reveals that the couple's names are Orval and Malka, and they are known to each other. She asks what would happen if they weren't, and Kolis wonders if it matters. She emphatically says that it does, and he points out another couple. He mentions the servant's name is Jacinta and the god is Evander. He then tells her that pain is what turns Evander on. Looking at Sera, he asks her what she would do if she could. She says she'd kill him and then asks what Kolis would do to her. He says he wouldn't do anything.

When Sera sees tears on Jacinta's face, she stands and asks for a weapon. Kolis calls for Elias, and he hands her one of his daggers. Sera looks at Callum and sees him smiling.

That should have been a red flag.

She walks up to Jacinta and Evander, grabs the god by the hair, and tells the woman to leave. Then, she strikes.

And the screaming starts.

Sera starts to tell Jacinta that she's okay now, and the woman freaks. She tries to rouse the god, calling him, "Evan." Naberius—the sleeping draken—rouses, and Sera sees that Keella has a hand pressed to her chest.

Kolis orders Jacinta and Evander's body to be removed, and Naberius moves toward Sera. Kolis tells him to stand down.

Attes calls to Sera and tells her to return to the dais. She panics and asks why Jacinta would act like that if she were being abused and traumatized. Kolis asks her how she knew that was going on. She starts to say that he told her, and he interrupts, saying he asked her what she would do, not that Evander was forcing Jacinta.

Sera argues that she saw the tears on Jacinta's face, and Kolis asks her if they were tears of pain or pleasure. He goes on to say that she only hears what she wants to hear and thinks about herself. She argues some more and then asks whose Court Evander belonged to. Kolis tells her he was from the Thyia Plains. Sera gets it then. Kolis wasn't proving some twisted version of reality. He was getting back at Keella and using Sera as the weapon.

When Kolis smiles, Sera can only think how vile and corrupt he is. The embers start to hum, and she feels Sotoria. The ancient power swamps her and riles her primal rage.

Attes calls to Kolis, telling him it's time to start court. Kolis orders Sera to sit, and she watches a dakkai eating a leg bone, then watches as Kolis just kills a god. When he tells her she appears displeased, she asks if this is really how he wants them to spend time together. He says he's multitasking. She adds that she never expected *this* when she asked for time out of the cage, and he asks what she means. She tells him that he's only shown her death. He questions more, and she mentions Evander. He says that's on her, and she breaks down the errors in that statement, then adds that he killed a god for calling another a cheat.

He says it's about maintaining control and balance. She questions that, and he says every action has a reaction. Disrespect is met with a response: death. She asks if *she* is to be sentenced to death, and he says she's different. He won't punish her.

He tells her to stand and come to him, ordering her to sit on his lap. He continues with what he was saying, repeating that he won't punish her but *will* rethink their deals. He asks if she understands. When Sera says yes, he tells her he's capable of more than just death.

Sera scans the crowd and finds Kyn with a woman on his lap, drinking from and fondling her. And he's looking right at Sera.

She suddenly sees a flash of red and gold and follows it, her breath leaving her when she sees a crown and then a familiar lithe figure and golden hair.

Veses.

The Primal goddess is free and looks pretty good. Veses smiles, and fury rises within Sera. She feels the embers rise with it. Sotoria stirs, and Sera senses her nervousness. She worries what Kolis will do about the surge of power. Sera remembers what he said about punishment and can only imagine what he did to Sotoria.

Veses addresses Kolis, and he beckons her forward. As she and Kolis talk, Sera ruminates on Veses and Ash and her true feelings.

Kolis asks Veses if she recognizes Sera. The Primal says she isn't sure, and Sera calls her out as a liar. She tells Kolis they met in the House of Haides.

Veses and Kolis talk some more, and as Kolis goads Veses, Sera realizes that he's enjoying himself. As things turn crass and Kolis insinuates that Veses would do *anything* he asked of her—and she agrees—it turns Sera's stomach.

Veses asks Sera why she's there, saying she thought she was the Shadowlands' Consort. Kolis tells her she's wrong and says he never gave permission. Veses then assumes that Sera's presence must be punishment, and he corrects her. Veses snipes and says she could find something less crushing for Kolis to use to warm his lap if that's what's going on. He orders the Primal goddess to apologize, and she's taken aback. He tells Veses that she's speaking to his *graeca*. Veses says it's impossible and must be a lie, but Kolis insists he had it confirmed.

When Kolis orders her to apologize again, Veses does, but with scathing venom. Then she grits out that she's happy for Kolis. Before she leaves, Kolis summons her back and says that she still disappointed him and must be punished. He calls Kyn over, and Sera knows what's about to happen. She watches in horror as the events start to play out, and just as it's about to get really bad, she cries out. Veses tells her she doesn't need her to interfere, and the embers within Sera start to hum.

Kolis asks her what she's doing, and Sera says what he's doing isn't right and asks him to stop. He pushes back, and she tells him it's the right thing to do. Seething, he rises and says they're returning to her quarters. Before they leave, Phanos tells Kolis he needs to talk to him. Kolis says he'll be back shortly.

They return to the cage, and Kolis chastises Sera, reminding her that he told her not to question him or use the embers, yet she did both. He details what he's done for her and says she isn't appreciative. He tells her that he wanted to show her what he's risking for her, confusing Sera. He calls her his soul again but tells her he's her King and will be obeyed.

He chains her, stretching her painfully, then says he wants to hate her for making him do this to her, but he can only love her. She scoffs. He tells her that she still lives. Nobody else would. That's proof of his love. Then he weeps.

After Kolis leaves, Callum gloats, thinking aloud how much pain she must be in. He says he almost feels sorry for her. She doesn't give him the satisfaction of responding. He goes on about her not really being his sister, and she tells him the fact that he thinks what is being done is wrong only if she's his sister makes her feel justified in her disdain.

He admits that the Hall punishment was wrong and below Kolis, then insists he's better than that. She asks *when* he was better. Callum says he was before Eythos died. He tells her that Kolis loved his brother.

She thinks things over and knows the display was all about Kolis exerting power. Callum says everything changed after Eythos's death and asks if Sera believes she's better than everyone after she gives details that she was the only one willing to step in at the Hall. She agrees with him and says she is better—anyone who would at least try is.

She calls Callum a loyal lapdog, and he says he'll always be loyal. Kolis forgave him for not keeping Sotoria safe and gave him eternal life. Plus, he's keeping the realms together.

It irks Sera. She wonders if Callum was ever good but calls him delusional. Like Kolis. Callum says he'll be happy to share that with the King. In response, she threatens to tell Kolis how his *firstborn* shared how to kill a Primal with Calliphe. They bicker about Kolis's motives and whether Sera is who she claims to be. She slips up and calls Sotoria *her*, and Callum catches it. Sera backtracks, only for Callum to reveal that Eythos was the one who killed Sotoria the second time. Sera can't believe it. She goes over all the questions and her plight.

Finally, Kolis enters and releases the shackles. Sera cries out and can't do much but sag into his arms. Kolis apologizes repeatedly.

The Chosen bring in stuff for a bath, and Kolis tells her to bathe, rest, and all will be well. She barely keeps herself from laughing. Before he leaves, he mentions that he stopped Veses' punishment. She does laugh then.

And can't stop.

This time when she sleeps, Sera doesn't dream. Callum is in the room on the sofa again when she wakes, and she feels a Culling headache coming on. Kolis enters, and she realizes she needs to act like nothing has happened. He tells her she looks lovely, and she plays her part and apologizes, shocking both Kolis and Callum. Kolis says he understands, and she lays it on even thicker.

Callum seethes, and Sera tries to contain her glee.

Kolis tells her to come for a walk with him, Callum and Elias trailing along after them. He takes her somewhere, then calls for Iason and Dyses. The Revenant and draken walk in with a Chosen. Suddenly, Sera knows exactly what's going on.

She tells him he doesn't have to prove anything, and he insists he must show her what he can do. She tries to talk him out of it, and he simply instructs the Chosen to unveil himself. Kolis asks the Chosen—who she finds out is named Jove—how he is and says he'll be blessed.

Jove says it's an honor, and Sera tries again to stop Kolis, knowing it's anything but. When she moves to stop him, he tells her she's always had a kind heart, making both her and Sotoria shudder.

He tells her she needs to know why it's so important and leaves how it's done up to her—Jove can be remade or used as sustenance. Balance is necessary.

She asks if he can at least make it so it doesn't hurt. He does, and then Sera realizes she may have turned pain into forced pleasure. She's not sure which is worse. It makes her sick.

Kolis explains the process of what he's doing and calls Elias over to give Jove his blood. Sera realizes Kolis can't use his blood because he's the true Primal of Death. He tells her that without the embers of life, the Chosen become the Ascended. Then says he's been working on the drawbacks, like their sun intolerance and bloodlust.

Sera wonders what happens if they can't control their hunger, and he says they're put down. He tells her that gluttonous gods were killed under Eythos's rule, as well, and he was used as the weapon to do it.

Kolis appears to truly believe that he's creating life and cares about it besides. She asks about the difference between the Ascended and the Craven, and he tells her that the Craven are dead, revealing more about them. Sera thinks about Andreia.

He tells her that newly made Ascended are watched, and the one she encountered would have been too if she hadn't tried to escape and pulled the guards from their posts.

She asks what happens if an Ascended chooses not to feed, and he tells her they will weaken, and their bodies will eventually give out. She asks why an Ascended would decide that, then guesses it's maybe so they don't become an indiscriminate killer. Kolis says that everything created or born has the potential to be a murderer.

Sera gets frustrated when Kolis just isn't getting her points about choice and consent, and he brings up balance again. He goes on to say that the Primal of Death is supposed to remain distant from anyone they may have to judge—all but the other Primals and the draken. He complains that it isn't the same for the Primal of Life. He goes on to say that it made sense to the Arae, and all comes back to the balance established when the Ancients created the realms.

Sera chimes in that she thought Eythos created the realms, and Kolis tells her that he created some but not *the* realms. The Ancients were not the first Primals, nor can any Primal become an Ancient. He tells her there must always be a true

Primal of Life and a true Primal of Death.

Sera realizes that means Kolis can never be killed.

She feels disheartened and wonders about Holland, Eythos, and Keella. Why did they do what they did if he can't be killed?

Later in the cage, she thinks about The Star and wonders if it could hold embers *and* a soul simultaneously. Callum asks her what she's doing, and she tells him she's praying. When the embers respond to a Primal nearing, Callum says it's strange because Kolis is occupied.

Veses blows in, nailing Callum in the face with the door. He tells her Kolis isn't around, and she says she's not there for him. Callum says it's unwise to go against His Majesty's edicts, and Veses says she doesn't intend for him to find out she came.

Sera calls Callum an ever-faithful servant and insinuates that he will tell. Veses tells Sera that she and Callum have something in common: loyalty. Callum warns her, and Veses tells him she isn't going to hurt Sera and manipulates him by saying she wants to talk to her about what happened in the Hall.

Frustrated, Callum tells her she has ten minutes and leaves. The moment he's out of the room, Veses reveals her true colors. She tells Sera she enjoyed what Kyn did, going into way too much detail.

Sera tells her that while she may have gotten off, it was still without consent. She asks Veses how she got free of the House of Haides dungeon, and Veses outlines chewing off her arms. She says Hanan's death woke her from stasis, and she knew that Nyktos had killed him.

She then details all her shocks after and says she was *devastated*. But she wasn't all that torn up about Hanan.

Veses tells Sera she's excited that the Shadowlands are about to invade Dalos and says she knows about the deal Sera made for Nyktos's freedom. She goes on to reveal there's doubt about who she claims to be and says the Primals alive when Kolis became the Primal of Life remember what Sotoria looked like.

Sera reiterates what she keeps hearing: wrong hair color, too many freckles, more curves...

She tells Veses she doesn't get her. She's beautiful—at least on the outside—and could have anyone. Why would she waste her time pursuing the two most ineligible beings in both realms? She warns Veses she'll likely tell Kolis about Veses' visit, and the Primal goddess says she won't because she knows how he would react, and she's too *good* to put Veses in that position.

Sera says she'd rather see her dead than punished, then goes on to tell her she knows about her deal with Nyktos. The Primal tries to goad Sera, but Sera isn't having it. She tells her she doesn't get how she could do that to someone, clearly knowing what it's like to be forced.

Veses insists she's tried to protect Nyktos, and Sera calls her a mess. Veses reacts by telling Sera she's a whore. They reveal how much they each know about the other, and Veses says their violent reactions when it comes to those they love are the same.

She goes on that when the truth comes out about Sotoria, Sera will get to see just how sadistic Kyn can be. Sera calls her a sick bitch, but Veses says she's not. She's just tired. Then she adds that she won't lose Kolis to Sotoria again. She'd rather see him dead.

She says she's worried about Nyktos and suggests that maybe Sera should just sacrifice herself.

Before Veses leaves, Sera apologizes about what happened in the Hall but mentions she still plans to watch the Primal goddess burn.

When Sera emerges later, Kolis is on the bed, waiting for her. She tells him that she's tired, and he says that's good. They can sleep together again.

Sera asks about Nyktos, and Kolis says he's being prepared for release—unless he gives a reason for that not to happen.

She hesitates to go to him and covers by saying she doesn't know what he expects of her. He points out that he waited for her, while she didn't wait for him. Her virtue is safe.

Later, Sera's gums start bleeding, and she realizes that whatever the ceeren did must be wearing off. She's barreling toward her Ascension.

Kolis suggests a walk, and Sera asks him where Callum is. He tells her that he sent the Revenant away to handle something important. Sera asks about the Revs. She wants to know if they need things like friendship, love, and sex. He says they don't. They are only driven by their desire to serve their creator.

She says she can't imagine not wanting anything, and he counters that he thinks it's probably freeing. She thinks it's a poor imitation of life.

She goes back to the subject of Callum and says he's different. Kolis acknowledges and reveals he's *full* of wants and needs. He then tells Elias to stay back and moves with Sera to a staircase. He says he was told that motivation plays a role—the magic in creation. Feeling = becoming. He says he's not so sure because he tried with others, and it never worked. Sera thinks it's because the feelings were real with Callum. With the others, he was only pretending.

He takes her high to look over the City of the Gods. She sees the glimmering buildings and the Carcers, noticing the shadowstone deposits within. She realizes that's where Ash is. She asks Kolis about the Fates clearing the city, and he tells her they do whatever they like. Especially when the balance is upset.

He explains that when he became the Primal of Life, he gave the gods in Dalos a choice. They could serve him or die. He killed half. It displeased the Fates, so they wiped out the rest. Kolis admits he could have acted less rashly.

He looks at Sera and says he sometimes sees Sotoria how she was in her, but everything is amplified. He says he wishes she looked how she used to. It offends Sera, and he doesn't get it. Once again, he asks what she wants or needs in order to forgive him. She immediately thinks of The Star when he says "jewels," and decides to try.

She makes up a story about her mother and an irregular silver diamond. He offers to get it for her, and she thinks fast and says she doesn't think Calliphe even has it anymore. He tells her he has one, and she asks to see it. He takes her back to the cage, and it confuses her until he summons down the cluster at the top, and it transforms before her very eyes into a silvery diamond shaped like a star.

He tells her that it's called The Star and says it was created by dragon fire long before the Primals could shed tears of joy. He adds that he came upon it by chance, which she knows is not true at all.

She asks why he keeps it hidden, and he says he keeps it with what he cherishes the most. The comment makes her sick. She asks to hold the stone. When he lets her, she feels a jolt and sees the streaks of milky white inside the diamond. Images form in her mind, and she sees an Ancient, a dragon, and the destruction of a mountain creating the Star diamond. She watches as it buries itself. Then the visions shift to Eythos and Kolis and the events that played out for Eythos's last moments.

Sera suddenly blurts, "You cried," and Kolis freaks out. He asks what she saw and rips the diamond away. He turns Primal, and she becomes nothing but rage. She uses the embers, and he reminds her what he warned, saying what happens next is on her.

He traps her, and she panics, then has a moment of clarity. The bars can be destroyed by her since, for all intents and purposes, she is the Primal of Life. She takes control, letting out the rage and dismantling the cage and chamber. Then she attacks him. He tells her to stop, but she throws the words from her vision back at him.

He realizes she saw Eythos's last moments, and she stabs him with a bone. After, she gets in close and tells him she wants him to remember that she wants nothing more than to kill him. Then, she stabs him repeatedly, leaving the bone buried somewhere sensitive.

She astral projects and finds Ash, seeing him coming. She watches as he annihilates all in his path while looking for her. She fills with eather but doesn't feel right, then collapses. He gets to her and lifts her, telling her to open her eyes and assuring that he's got her.

She sees flashes outside and tenses, but Ash tells her it's just Nektas. She can barely talk but manages to ask if she's dreaming. He tells her it's real. When she asks if he's okay, he laughs, given the circumstances. She reminds him that he was imprisoned, but he says she was imprisoned, too, just in a different way.

They discuss Veses a bit and what to do about Kolis. They also talk about what happened, and Sera has to soothe Ash's anger. She tells him he needs to take her somewhere safe and remove the embers.

Elias comes in, and they discuss where his loyalties lie. Ash keeps from killing him—barely—and Elias swears his fealty to Sera. He says he sent word to Attes and insists he can take Kolis somewhere that will buy them some time.

Attes arrives and urges them to get a move on. When Ash moves to attack him, Attes pleads his case, and Sera tells Ash the other Primal can be trusted. Says he saved her life.

She gets dizzy, and Attes says she was shifting into her Primal self. When Elias once again says he can get Kolis away, Sera asks if it's safe for him, and he's honored she's worried about him.

Attes conjures Setti, and they get Kolis onto the horse. As they're about to leave, Sera remembers The Star. She tells them they need to get it and they discuss how. She reveals to Ash that his father's soul is in the diamond, and he asks if she's sure. She says she is.

After she summons the diamond, Ash says he can't feel the soul. Sera wonders how they can put Sotoria's soul in the stone, and Ash says Keella should know how to get a soul out and in.

Ash shadowsteps them to a beautiful cavern of hot springs in the mortal realm, and she tells him the story of Kolis and Eythos, leaving out the part about his mother. When he asks to hold The Star, she doesn't let him, explaining that she doesn't want him to see what she did.

As they clean up, one thing leads to another, and they have sex. Losing themselves in each other for a bit.

As they spend time together, they talk about everything that's happened and catch one another up, talking about what things mean and what's next. They discuss his *nota* and Primal forms, then Ash leaves to get her some clothes.

When he returns, he tells her that he went to the Bonelands, and Sera asks about Bele and Aios. They talk more about freeing Eythos's soul, and Sera wonders if Ash will be able to interact with it.

As talk turns to Attes, and Ash makes it clear that he still doesn't trust him, Sera tries to make him understand why Attes could never be loyal to Kolis. Then, she tells him what Phanos did. When she sees the wheels of his mind turning, she has to stop that train of thought and insist that nobody else will give their life to save hers.

They go to the Bonelands, and Ash tells her how the Ancients became displeased with advancement and were connected to all living things. So, when they realized that mortals and the land could not coexist, they chose to cleanse the land. They then created the Primals, splitting their essence between them and creating a shared balance. The Primals and gods eventually joined the mortals to battle the Ancients.

Ash asks Sera how she's feeling, and she admits that she's tired and achy. Bele arrives and hugs Sera, something she's never done, then thanks her for saving Aios. She asks about Kolis, and Sera tells her she gave him a beat down.

They discuss Bele's new status and what was done with Elias, and Bele tells Sera that Veses is free. She tells the new Primal that she knows.

Sera sees Elias tied to a pillar and watches as a draken knocks a rock onto him. When Ehthawn moves in for pets, Sera asks about Orphine, finding out that she didn't make it. Sorrow fills her and she apologizes.

Sera struggles to ascend the steps. Ash finally helps her, and Saion and Rhahar come, both embracing Ash. Then Lailah joins with Rhain. Sera is filled with gratitude that Ash won't be alone after she's gone.

She sees Crolee, and Saion and Rhahar greet her. Ash says that Sera saved him, and Rhain says many of them wouldn't be there if it weren't for her.

Attes arrives with his draken, and Sera watches the draken interact. There's some aggressive flirting going on between Aurelia and Nektas, and Sera remembers Reaver saying he thought Nek was sweet on the female. When she turns her attention to the Primal, she witnesses some aggressive flirting between him and Lailah, as well, and finds out that Lailah is originally from Attes's Court.

They discuss The Star, and Keella comes forward, telling them what they need to do. Sera pulls Eythos free and then falls unconscious.

When she wakes, she finds herself in Keella's Court. She asks about what happened and Ash tells her all is well. She apologizes to him for cutting his time with his father short and he tells her he was ready to go. He tells her what Eythos said to him before leaving.

Sera realizes that Ash gave her blood and chastises him, saying she doesn't want him weakened. They bicker as usual, and Nektas arrives, laughing that they're arguing. He tells her that the time gained by Ash giving her his blood is never time wasted. He then goes on to say that he can scent her death, and the two share a sweet moment.

Attes, Ash, and Sera argue about Sotoria's soul, and Sera makes them understand that the soul is alive. Attes mentions how he met her after Kolis brought her back. Then they all discuss what happens if the embers die with Sera. They talk about The Star being able to hold both the embers and a soul, and what needs to happen in order to end Kolis.

Sera says there will be war, and Ash insists he only cares about her. Attes says it's way bigger than that, and Ash says she matters. She finally realizes that it's time. She tells him she loves him. Attes chimes in and asks if Nyktos's *kardia* was removed properly.

Keella explains that a soul cannot be brought back twice. Without the Arae intervening, at least—which never ends the way one intends. She wonders if the Fates are the reason she was born with Sotoria's soul and not *as* Sotoria.

Keella asks if Ash has sensed dual souls. He says he only ever feels Sera's. Keella tells him he needs to anchor himself to his Consort's soul. She calls forth the soul and Sotoria worries about Sera, making *Sera* worry. Finally, they get her out and transfer her to the diamond. As she leaves, she tells Sera in her mind that they'll meet again.

In the Bonelands, Attes promises Sera he will support Ash. Elias wakes up and asks how things went with the diamond. They tell the god it went well. They talk a little more until Rhain arrives. He says that even when the rest of them didn't really see her to her core, Ash always did. Ash walks up, and Sera thinks how he'll make a great father someday. He reads her emotions, and she tells him to stop.

Saion comes then and jokes that they're fighting again. Rhahar joins, and they settle a bet. Saion said they couldn't go more than an hour without arguing. She turns to Ash and jokes that they're his friends. He says they *were*. It melts Sera's heart to hear him acknowledge them as his friends.

Sera looks around and wishes she had more time. She thinks of everyone and looks for each of them. Then, she tells Ash to take her to the lake, reminding him that he promised.

Saion tells her to have safe travels, and Rhain moves forward. He kneels and holds his sword out. The others follow suit. The draken bow their heads. Rhain says the oath, ending with "forevermore," and they all destroy their swords.

Seems with the right intention, not all eather is blocked by shadowstone, and it *can* be affected by more than itself.

Sera tells Ash there's something she wants to talk about, and he won't look at her. He tells her that even if he's not looking at her, she is all he sees. She tells him she loves him and says it's not his fault, making him understand. He lists all the things he'd rather be doing, and she almost gets sidetracked because several of them are super sexy. She continues, telling him she wants him to live. Be King. He argues that it's her place, and she tells him she doesn't want him to be alone. She wants him to love.

He gets angry, and she makes him promise. He does. Then, they have beautiful, heartbreaking sex.

He tells her all the things he adores about her and says he never wanted until her. Thunder booms, and Ash says Kolis has been found. She laments being out of time but tells him everything she wanted and says that he gave her all of it. She tells him that she loves him again and then says it's time.

He takes her into the water and feeds as she reminisces, swearing she'll remember. She begins to fade, and Ash says fuck the embers and tells her to take his blood. He says he won't let her go. He'll Ascend her.

She asks what she'll become, and he says he isn't sure. She begs him to take the embers but he tells her to shut the fuck up and says if he loses her, the realms and everything in them are gone—he'll destroy it all. He tells her not to die. Tells her to say fuck the greater good. She says he's good, but he insists he isn't.

Finally, she drinks. She sees memories of her and her mother. Holland. Ezra. Jadis. The gods. More. Ash begs her not to leave and says he loves her, even if he can't. He says he's *in* love with her.

Sera sees Odetta. The woman tells her to open her eyes. She does, and Sera sees creation. All of it. She sees the explosion, the Primal of Life, the creation of the draken, the mortals. She sees it all and understands. The Ancients must never rise. They are the end that will shake all realms. They'd be blood and bone and ruin and wrath of the once-great beginning. Sera realizes she's the beginning, middle, and the last breath before the end. She's life. Death's steadfast companion.

Pure power fills her, and she wakes in Ash's arms. A shockwave bursts free and knocks him back. She *becomes* the essence.

While in stasis, Sera can hear talking. She hears the stories Ash relays. Listens to him tell her how unprepared he was for how alive he felt with her. He admits he could still feel after his *kardia* was removed, but not strongly. Not until her. He says he should have known from their first kiss what they were to each other.

He reminisces about their first few meetings, her bravery in going to Kolis alone, her misplaced loyalties. Ash talks about his father. Sera sees it all and feels Jadis on her feet.

When Ash says he wanted to be strong like Eythos, Nektas says it had nothing to do with strength. He talks about how Eythos was after Mycella's death, and Ash says he would have destroyed the realms and everything in them if he'd lost Sera.

Nektas reminds Ash that he saved her, and Ash tells Sera he'll be waiting for her.

Sera finds herself on the bank of her lake, but this time she sees a silvery-white cave cat with two gray younglings. When they lock eyes, she sees herself.

She starts to wake, and Ash tells her not to rush it. She's hungry and thirsty and restless. Suddenly, she gets all sorts of information downloaded. She becomes power, and Ash reminds her of how they are together. How they like to be. He tells her she needs him. His blood. Says he's hers.

She says the Primal of Life has never fed from the Primal of Death before. They're meant to be two halves of a cycle but separate. He says that all of him is hers, and she feeds.

After, he asks if she knows him, and she says she always will.

Ash tells her he was terrified he'd lose her. She says he didn't; he saved her. He then says he was afraid she wouldn't remember and that he'd still lose her. She insists he won't. Ever. He tenses and tells her that when he releases her, she needs to run. She's confused. He then tells her that he needs her too much and won't be able to control himself. He'll shift. She says she trusts him. Tells him she's his. Tells him to take her. However.

He does, using his shadow tendrils to heighten her pleasure. He tells her that he loves her and says he's not sure when it started. She shakes and says she thought she'd die without ever knowing what his love felt like. He says he couldn't and wouldn't allow that. He tells her he'll spend eternity making sure she knows how he feels.

Nektas asks if they're okay, and Ash threatens him. Sera realizes that she somehow Ascended without dying. The embers are her. She's the Primal of Life. The Queen of the Gods.

She says as much, and Ash says he's her Consort. She says he's the King.

The King fucks his Queen.

And it was glorious.

She asks if she'll ever get used to her fangs, and he assures her that she will. She wonders if any Primals Ascended without getting their memories back and he tells her about those who had trouble and mentions that Kyn never did.

As they begin to have sex again, Sera finds herself tensing when he goes to feed. He tells her it's okay, and says he sensed her unease, even though it's harder to read her now. Plus, he says they need to behave because they have to talk. She says they should discuss Kolis, and Ash agrees but says not now. He tells her that every Primal felt her Ascension and says they'll deal with whatever comes. Together.

He comes clean about why he didn't take her as his Consort initially. Part of it was to keep her unknown to Kolis, but also he had a dream the night she was born. It was her at her lake, smiling at him. Then, he saw her dying, and him… He chalked it up to imagination until he saw the lake for real. He kept track of her. The vision terrified him so much he had his *kardia* removed right before he brought her to the Shadowlands.

He laments what her life was like because of him. Insists he was a coward. She denies it, but he tells her what the vision showed him of after she died. He destroyed everything. It showed he'd fallen in love. So, he tried to stop it. He tells her he fell in love anyway, and she tells him she felt more than love when he held her in the lake. Ash says there's only one reason for that. They're heartmates.

He talks about how when the Arae see threads of fate joining, they cannot intervene. He says their joined souls created the first-ever Queen of the Gods. Sera remembers Holland telling her that love is more powerful than the Fates. They talk about the Arae toeing the line of what's allowed and what's considered interference, and she goes out onto the balcony, seeing life returning to the realm. She stopped the Rot.

As she rests, she sees a box by Ash's bed and opens it, finding all the hair ties he took from her when he undid her braids. It makes her heart swell.

When Ash returns, they share sweet nothings of love, and he tells her that he wants them to trust each other, telling her he'll always see her as strong no matter what. He hints that he thinks he knows what happened to her in Dalos, and they talk more about Rhain. She urges Ash not to do or say anything about what happened when her plans were first revealed.

She assumes that Holland knew everything and tells Ash what the Arae really said to her. That love is more powerful than the Fates. They think and talk about how powerful life is, and Sera figures she should be concerned about things and be thinking about the future, but only one thing is on her mind.

She asks Ash to tell her again that he loves her, and he does. Repeatedly. And then…

They make love.

PRINCESS/QUEEN EZMERIA "EZRA"

Hair: Light brown.
Eyes: Brown.
Facial features: Stubborn, hard jaw.

Personality: Kind. Compassionate. Smart. Clever.

Habits/Mannerisms/Strengths/Weaknesses: Seems immune to heat and humidity. Spends a lot of time doing charitable work. Doesn't know how to defend herself. Doesn't like talking about the deal King Roderick made with the gods. Wears jewelry often. Rambles when she gets nervous. Believes you can't hate someone you've never met. Loves chocolate scones. Likes iced tea. Likes to read, but not misery fiction.

Other: Is at least nineteen years old.

Background: Princess of Lasania who later becomes Queen.

Family: Father = King Ernald †. Brother = Tavius †. Stepsister = Seraphena. Stepmother = Queen Calliphe. Consort = Marisol Faber.

EZMERIA'S JOURNEY TO DATE:

Ezmeria was one of the few who did not treat Sera like a bargaining chip or something to be used. She treated her like a person instead of a cure. For this, I appreciated her.

Ezra is present when Seraphena comes before the Primal God of Death to honor King Roderick's deal—something Ezra hates. Nyktos denies her, creating all sorts of uproar amidst those in the know.

Later, Ezra comes to get Sera, begging for her aid. She says she needs Sera's ability to borrow food from the kitchens for the orphans and then tells her about Nor—a terrible abuser—and his children. Ezra offers Sera a gown for the excursion, and they discuss the Rot. When Sera returns from her outing and tells Ezra that Nor "tripped and fell upon her blade, neck first," Ezra tells Sera she's a little scary.

Sera and Ezra discuss the state of things in Lasania and the riot in Croft's Cross. As talk once again shifts to the Rot, they go over who would be the best ruler for Lasania. Ezra tells Sera that *she's* the Queen Lasania needs.

When the Healers get overwhelmed after an attack, Ezra and Sera help Healer Dirks. Ezra states that she doesn't think Tavius is stupid enough to try to kill Sera since she's the one thing that can stop the Rot—at least as far as they know.

Ezra sees Sera's injured arm and learns that Tavius is responsible. She tells Sera that she believes her brother is evil. She also divulges information about the god she saw—someone we now know wasn't actually a god at all.

Callum is an enigma wrapped in a mystery, and uncovering more about him is both intriguing and a bit terrifying. But I digress...

When Odetta passes, Ezra attends her funeral and then the Rite. However, disaster strikes the evening of the ceremony, and Ezra rushes to get Sera to save her love. Sera doesn't think she can, given Marisol's state, but Ezra begs her, saying she should try using her abilities on someone deserving. Ezra goes on to say that she loves Mari and can't be without her.

Sera heals the woman. When she comes to, Ezra asks her how she feels and then interrupts her answer with a passionate kiss. She thanks Sera and tells her she is a blessing and always has been—that she's not and never was a failure. She then reveals that she hasn't told the King and Queen about Mari because, if she did, they'd plan a wedding before there was even an engagement. She admits things are still new but she believes Marisol loves her as she does her, and they're meant for each other.

Ezra catches Tavius whipping Sera and asks him if he's lost his senses. Later, when Nyktos appears, she and the Queen are the first to kneel before the Primal. When the god's attention turns to Tavius, and Calliphe begs for his life, Ezra speaks up, saying that he's a monster and always has been. She then agrees with Nyktos, saying that Tavius is of little significance. After, Ezra dispassionately watches Sera kill Tavius before being led out of the Great Hall.

When Sera and Ash return to the mortal realm, Ezra is in the middle of holding a town hall. The minute she learns that Sera has arrived, she has the guards clear the Great Hall, leaving only two inside the closed doors. As they talk, Ezra confesses that she was never a fan of the deal, mainly because it was unfair to Sera.

Sera reveals the truth, and Ezra believes her instantly, even though she doesn't—and can't—divulge what caused the Rot, only that fulfilling the deal wouldn't have stopped it. Ezra knows how important it was and *is* for Sera to save Lasania and even calls it her kingdom, believing that Sera should be able to acknowledge that she should have been Queen.

As acting ruler, Ezra implements as many things as she can to help the kingdom. She immediately begins building pantries for the people, not just the Royals, and starts a bit of a food bank so people can come on certain days at certain times if they are in need. She is also in talks with the Queen of Terra, trying to strengthen their faith in Lasania and proving that an alliance would be beneficial. She tells the Queen that Terra has fertile fields primed for crops and Lasania has labor workers. Those who want to relocate to Terra for at least part of the year could work in those fields.

She adds that several more farms have been lost, but the Rot's progression hasn't sped up. Then she confesses that she didn't believe that Sera could make the Primal God of Death fall for her. She honestly thought she'd get herself killed by being too impatient and just stabbing him.

When Sera asks about Marisol, Ezra says she's perfect and with her father. She also says that she sent a missive to the Vodina Isles to inquire about Sir Holland but hasn't received a response as of yet.

As the two say goodbye, Ezra tells Sera that she hopes she sees her again and soon—she misses her. She then says that many of Sera's plans have already been set in motion, like building homes in Croft's Cross.

That's as much as I've *seen* for dear Ezra, though I imagine there is a lot more. We know that she brought about significant positive change during her rule.

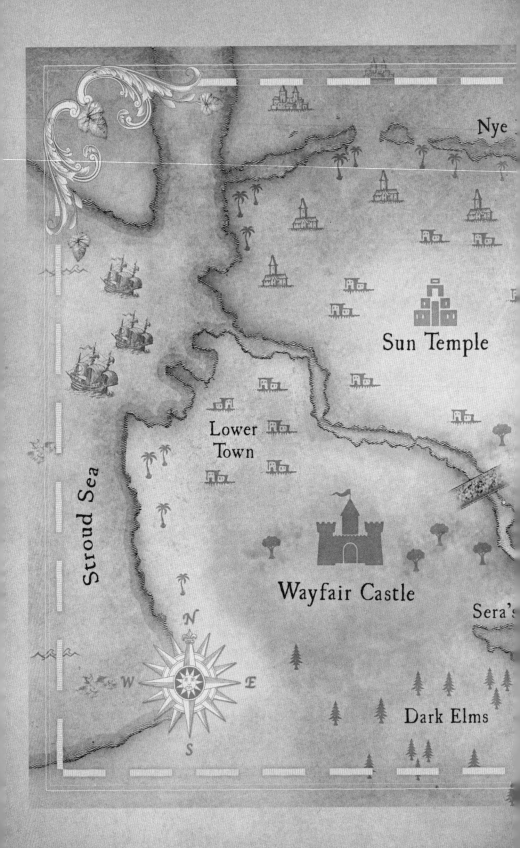

Nye

Sun Temple

Lower
Town

Stroud Sea

Wayfair Castle

Sera's

Dark Elms

N
W   E
S

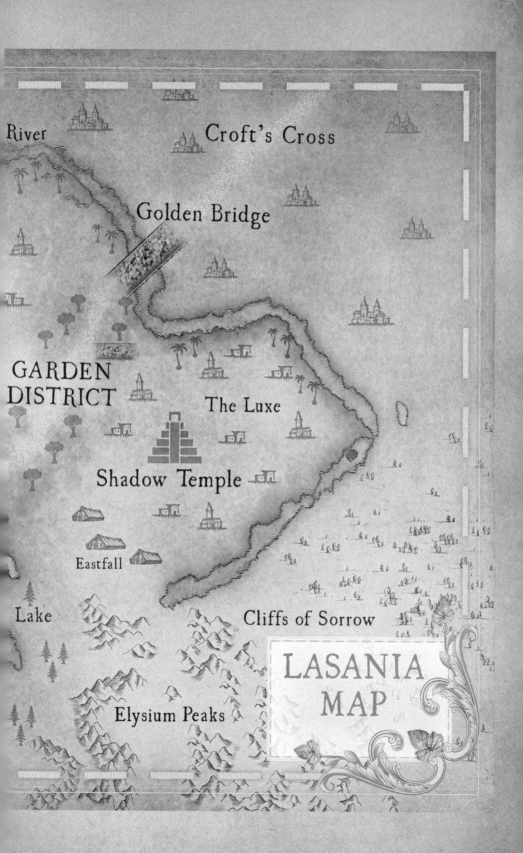

MARISOL "MARI" FABER

Eyes: Black.
Facial features: Rich brown skin.
Background: Becomes Queen Consort of Lasania.
Family: Father = Lord Faber.

MARISOL'S JOURNEY TO DATE:

Marisol, like her father, is brilliant and tries to find natural ways to stop the Rot.

When Sera heads out to save an abused boy, Marisol says she'll drive around so Ezra doesn't do anything idiotic.

After Nyktos's refusal of Sera as Consort, Marisol doesn't treat Sera any differently.

On the night of the Rite, after attending, she is injured while helping a child in Lowertown at Three Stones. The outing wasn't supposed to be dangerous, but when some men started fighting, Mari got caught up in it and was knocked down, thus hitting her head.

When Ezra brings Sera to her, she's dead. Sera brings her back to life, and she doesn't even remember getting hurt. She passionately kisses Ezra, confirming to Sera the bond between the two women.

Marisol later becomes Queen Ezmeria's Consort and goes on to have a fruitful rule.

QUEEN CALLIPHE

Okay, I'm just going to say it. Calliphe is a doormat. She's also utterly ignorant. I get grief. I do. But for a mother to utterly ignore her child because she looks like the husband she lost? That's unforgivable. Even worse to use her as a pawn and a tool and never treat her like a person. And to speak out for those who *hurt* your child so dreadfully? It's unforgiveable. I am absolutely in Ash's corner, saying "hear, hear" to sending Calliphe to the Abyss.

Hair: A few shades darker than Sera's pale blond.
Eyes: Dark brown.
Facial features: Beautiful smile.
Distinguishing features: A few wrinkles and shadows under her eyes.
Personality: Cold—at least to Sera. Hard.
Habits/Mannerisms/Strengths/Weaknesses: Hard to read. Never smiles at Sera, though she will with others. Often gets migraines that require healing draughts. Keeps a portrait of King Lamont close and spends hours with it. Wears lots of jewelry.
Background: Married Ernald shortly after Lamont's death but never stopped

loving her first husband. After learning about Sera's gift, she feared her daughter would use it on the Primal God of Death.

Family: First husband = Lamont Mierel †. Second husband = King Ernald †. Stepson = Tavius †. Stepdaughter = Ezmeria. Daughter = Seraphena.

CALLIPHE'S JOURNEY TO DATE:

Queen Calliphe is a hard woman, and I can say without guilt that I don't like her all that much.

When Seraphena is about to go before the Primal of Death to offer herself as his Consort, Queen Calliphe tells her daughter that she won't and can't fail them. When Nyktos refuses Sera, Calliphe yells at her, asking her what happened. Before Sera can even answer, she slaps her daughter, asking her what she did and telling her that she's failed Lasania, and that everything is now lost.

Calliphe often puts on airs of superiority, like when addressing the Lords, whose presence she often feels is an insult. She proposes an allegiance with the Vodina Isles in exchange for aid. The deal: two years of crops. Referring to Sera as her *handmaiden*, she offers to show Lord Claus and the other Lords of the Vodina Isles just what a "hot piece" her daughter is after some crude remarks, knowing she can easily order Sera to murder them.

After the meeting, Calliphe catches Sera in her chambers and argues with and insults her—like usual. She says she has to keep up appearances but wouldn't have to if Sera hadn't failed. She mentions that kingdoms that once prayed for an alliance with Lasania are now calling her the Beggar Queen.

Calliphe, Callum, and several guards find Sera after she's attacked. The Queen doesn't believe Sera's *lie* about finding the guards dead but won't say anything in front of a *god*. She then spends the night bemoaning the ruination of her utterly irreplaceable, expensive carpet.

Seriously?

The night of the Rite, Calliphe is angry to find Sera there. Later, she walks in on Tavius whipping Sera and asks him what in the gods' names he's doing, acting shocked. Personally, I think she knew about the abuse all along—after all, she had a hand in it herself—but that's just my humble opinion.

When Nyktos appears, she is one of the first to kneel before the Primal. As Nyktos pins Tavius to the Primal statue with a whip around his throat, Calliphe screams, rushes forward, and begs for her stepson's life. She tells Nyktos that Tavius is the heir to the throne and promises he'll never do anything like he did to Sera again. When Nyktos backs off, she thanks him. He tells her to shut up, and surprisingly, she does. Then, she watches Sera kill Tavius.

At that point, she looks at Sera, *really* looks at her, and sees what she has molded her daughter into by training her to become her personal assassin. Ector and Saion lead her out of the Great Hall.

Sometime later, after Sera leaves for Iliseeum, a guard tells Calliphe that Sera has returned to the mortal realm with the Primal. She doesn't think it's true but goes to investigate anyway. She ends up seeing Sera as she and Ash exit the Great Hall and stops Sera as she's leaving, saying she didn't know that Tavius planned to do what he did. Nyktos cuts her off, telling her she owed her death that day, and the only reason she still breathes is because of grace she doesn't deserve. Calliphe thanks him, and Ash tells her that Sera is the one who requested she be spared—he wanted to take her to the Abyss with Tavius, where she belongs. He then tells her to spend the rest of her undeserving life thanking her daughter.

PRINCE TAVIUS †

Hair: Light brown.
Eyes: Blue.
Facial features: Handsome.
Personality: Cruel. Classist. Short-tempered. Arrogant. Abusive.
Habits/Mannerisms/Strengths/Weaknesses: Drinks too much. Womanizer. Holds little respect for those who put food on his table.
Other: Just turned twenty-two.
Background: Having a torrid affair with recently widowed Miss Anneka, a merchant's wife. Betrothed to Princess Kayleigh of Irelone.
Family: Mother = unknown. Father = King Ernald †. Stepmother = Queen Calliphe. Sister = Ezmeria. Stepsister = Seraphena.

TAVIUS'S JOURNEY TO DATE:

Tavius enters my radar taunting Sera, something which seems to be a favored pastime of the spoiled Prince. He mentions that his intended, Princess Kayleigh of Irelone, is nervous about their wedding night, to which he replies that he'll be gentle—just the thought of that gives me shivers. He goes on to tell Sera that the Primal God of Death is monstrous, and that's why he's not depicted in any artwork, adding that he has fangs and scales like the beasts that protect him. He taunts his stepsister about the *blood kiss* and says he knows she was under the tutelage of the Mistresses of the Jade; therefore, she probably can't wait to *serve* the Primal.

Tavius stands next to his father when Lord Claus returns with Lasania's Lord, who is now only a head, something that truly shocks the rotten Prince. It doesn't last long, though. He quickly remarks that Sera should have been given to the Lord.

Sera found Tavius whipping a horse the previous week and gave him a black eye, threatening to use the whip on *him*. So, he decides to use it on *her* the next chance he gets.

When Sera arrives after checking on the farms, Tavius blames her for the Coupers' deaths. He argues with her and tells her he can't wait to take the throne.

When Ernald orders him to leave, Tavius throws a bowl of dates at Sera, hitting her in the arm. After, his father tells him that he doesn't want to see him for the rest of the day and threatens him before once more telling him to leave.

The fact that the King still treated Tavius, at twenty-two summers, like a child who needs to be put in a corner amuses me. But what else can we expect from the pissant.

Tavius attends the Rite and alerts his stepmother to Sera's presence. After Sera is attacked, Tavius situates himself in her chambers as she wakes. When Sera brings up her attack, he claims he had nothing to do with it and says he wouldn't waste a single coin on her. Sera says that being called his sister is an insult, and it incenses him. He then reveals that he has her dagger—the one she usually keeps close. He pins her to the bed, telling her that the King died last night in his sleep—an ailment of the heart. He then adds that *he* is now the King.

I personally believe he helped that along. The timing of the King's death was a bit too coincidental for me, even *if* it was a result of Sera using her gift to restore life. I'm just not so sure that's the only reason the King died. But, again, just thinking aloud—or on paper, at any rate.

Sera insults him, and he spits on her, telling her he doesn't believe for even a second that the Primal of Death will come for her. He adds that he's always seen her, the last heir of the Mierel line, as a threat to him taking the throne. When he demands that she acknowledge his title and she refuses, he's thrilled because he can punish her for treason—which he does graphically as he whips her.

When the Primal of Death reappears, he threatens Tavius but ultimately spares him, only to allow Sera to kill him instead. Ash sentences him to the Pits of Endless Flames, where he will burn until he's freed, whereupon Nyktos will do much worse to him than Sera did. Unimaginable things.

Is it wicked of me to smile at the thought of what exactly Nyktos does to Tavius when he *visits* him in the Abyss?

PRINCESS KAYLEIGH BALFOUR

Once Tavius's intended—a political marriage to be sure—Kayleigh becomes Queen of Lasania's neighboring kingdom. But she also keeps company with some interesting friends, like Delfai, a God of Divination, which many thought had died out.

There's something very intriguing about Kayleigh. Maybe it's because I see the tie between her, Coralena, Leopold, and Poppy. It could be because she's descended from the last oracle. But perhaps not. It could be even more I do not yet know.

Hair: Long, thick, brownish blond.
Eyes: Green.
Body type: Straight shoulders.
Facial features: Pink, sun-kissed skin. Heart-shaped face.

Personality: Kind. Good listener.

Habits/Mannerisms/Strengths/Weaknesses: Prefers Cauldra Manor to Castle Redrock.

Other: Has a black-and-white cat.

Background: Was betrothed to Prince Tavius of Lasania. Conspired with Sera to make herself sick to avoid the wedding. Has seen enough Primals to know their eyes are silver.

Family: Father = King Saegar. Mother = Queen Geneva. Descendant of the last oracle.

KAYLEIGH'S JOURNEY TO DATE:

Let me start out by just saying that I am *so* happy that the Princess was able to get out of marrying Prince Tavius.

Sera once found her crying in the gardens after Tavius hurt her, and Kayleigh wasn't surprised when Sera warned her about her stepbrother. Afterward, she and Sera concocted a plan to make her *unavailable* for the Royal engagement announcement. Sera gained a potion from a Healer that would make Kayleigh appear very ill, thus necessitating a postponement of the engagement. Kayleigh convinced her parents that it was the warmer, more humid climate that made her sick.

When Sera searches for Delfai, she uncovers his location when using the Pools of Divanash, seeing that he's at Cauldra Manor with the Princess. After Sera and Nyktos arrive in Irelone, Kayleigh recognizes Sera immediately and knows that her companion is a Primal. She's fearful because she knows that Primals are easily offended if not given the proper respect.

When Sera asks about Delfai and describes him, Kayleigh calls him *the scholar* and confirms that he is, indeed, at Cauldra. She goes on to say that he's been there for a few years and is teaching her how to read the old language.

Confronted with the opportunity, Kayleigh thanks Sera for her help with Tavius and the engagement. As they talk more, Nyktos apologizes for how other Primals have been. When Kayleigh asks about his Court, she's shocked to discover that he's from the Shadowlands. She asks Sera how she came to be with him, and Sera tells her it's a long story.

The couple asks her to take them to Delfai. She reveals that Irelone learned Ezmeria had taken the throne of Lasania, and Nyktos tells her that Tavius is in the Abyss. She's relieved and laughs before revealing that she worried about being forced to return to him and kept waiting for word that he'd become betrothed to another. The news that she is now free brings tears to her eyes.

Kayleigh realizes that Sera was never the Queen's handmaiden. When Nyktos tells her who Sera really is and was meant to be, Kayleigh doesn't seem surprised.

ALWAYS SAFE WITH ME

~Ash~

"Godsdamn it," Sera growled, the essence of the Primals swelling inside her and spilling into the air around us.

Her rising frustration called forth a rough chuckle as I pulled her back against my chest. Her vanilla and lavender scent surrounded me. "Now, how would you get free from me?" I asked, staring down at all her glorious, silvery-blond hair. My fingers itched to sink into those soft strands. Unfortunately, that wouldn't help her gain control of the essence thrumming through her body. "You can't reach that dagger or any other weapon, even if you had one. What would you do?"

She struggled against me, not accomplishing much but making me fully aware of all her lush curves. "Scream loudly?"

My lips twisted as my gaze flipped to the gray stone walls of the underground chamber deep beneath the House of Haides. "No."

"Beg?"

Smiling then, I tilted my head toward the graceful length of her throat. "There are very few things I would be interested in hearing you beg for," I told her, feeling her tense against me. "And your life is not one of them."

My touch? My bite? My cock? I wouldn't mind hearing her beg for those things using that pretty mouth of hers. My jaw clenched.

I needed to fucking focus.

What we were doing down here was important. It had nothing to do with her begging or my cock. "I can feel the essence in you ramping up. It's there. Charging the air. You can summon the eather. Will it to manifest into energy that can break my hold. You won't hurt me."

She turned her head slightly toward mine. "I'm not worried about hurting you."

"Then what's stopping you?"

"Those few things you're interested in hearing me beg for."

I went rigid. Immediately, my mind flashed to what I'd thought of seconds earlier.

My touch.

My bite.

My cock.

Three things I'd never wanted to hear anyone beg for—not before her. Then again, she wouldn't have to beg. That should concern me. Greatly. Instead, it sent a bolt of lust arcing through me. Fast and hard.

Sera tipped her head back against my chest, and I saw her lips curve slightly. "I bet I can guess at least one of those things."

"And what would that be?"

She turned her head toward mine. "I don't know if I should speak it. It may be too bold."

What an interesting thing for her—of all people—to say. "There is not a single part of me that believes you're worried about being too bold."

"But you may find me speaking it to be...distracting."

Find her distracting? There hadn't been a moment since I came upon her in that sweetly scented passageway when she *wasn't* distracting.

I should be used to it by now.

Which also meant I should be able to overcome it. Focus. Behave.

But it was like I was a different person when I was around her. Someone with no past. Someone not tethered to the present or a future and all the shit that came with it. I wasn't even a Primal. I was just a man who...

Wanted.

I moved my arm before realizing what I was doing—or maybe I knew exactly what I was doing. I drew her onto the toes of her boots and brought that plump ass of hers against my cock. I knew the moment she felt me. I immediately sensed her spicy, smoky passion. "I'm already distracted."

She drew her lower lip between her teeth. "You may be *more* distracted."

Knowing I could block out her rising arousal and *should*, I still didn't. That someone else I became around Sera wanted to drown in her. "Tell me what you think I'd like to hear you beg for." I paused, enjoying the slight wiggle she gave her hips. "Or is it you who has become nothing more than talk?"

Her laugh was pure music, a sound not heard enough, and even more distracting as she stretched farther up, dragging her ass against my cock.

Godsdamn.

Her mouth was less than an inch from mine. "Your *cock*," she whispered.

Godsdamn.

Dull pain suddenly erupted in my foot as Sera brought her boot down on mine. Hard. Surprise rippled through me, quickly followed by a burst of amusement. It was just a second, but long enough for her to take advantage.

Breaking free of my hold, she spun toward me. A look of pure, unfiltered smugness settled into the tilt of her full lips as she walked across the hard soil and stone. "That's how I'll get free."

Eather pulsed through me as the beast inside me stirred, awakened by the smugness in her smile. "Is that your grand battle plan when you have no access to weapons? Speak of cocks?"

"If it works, why not?" Her gaze lowered, and a faint pink stain spread across her freckled cheeks. "And it most definitely worked."

Understatement of the century. "Perhaps a little too well."

Her breathing pattern picked up as her gaze finally returned to mine. The emerald green was heated. "Is that so?"

I stalked toward her, feeling more like the wolf inside me than the god. Duty and responsibility fell to the wayside as I saw the challenge in her stare. The *want*.

Sera stayed still as I neared her, but I knew better than to trust she wouldn't try anything. She, too, was distracted. But she was alert.

Sera liked to win.

Maybe the only thing she liked more than my touch, my bite, or my cock.

As expected, Sera made her move when I was about a foot from her.

She darted to the left, stroking my wolf's need to catch her—and mine. Anticipation burned through me as I spun, snagging her with an arm across her chest.

I tugged her back against me, keeping my arm folded over her upper chest. "That was far too easy, Sera." I flattened my other hand against her lower stomach, smiling tightly as she jumped. "I don't think you're seriously trying to evade me."

"What…?" Her breath hitched as I drew my hand down and over the delicate laces running along the front of her leggings. "Do you think?"

"I'd say it's obvious." Feeling her stance widen, I knew what she wanted. I slipped my hand between her thighs and the taste of her desire sharpened in the back of my throat. She gasped as my fingers pressed against her center. "You wanted to be caught."

"I don't like being caught." Her hips twitched as I began moving my finger in slow, small circles. "Ever."

I laughed. "Liar."

A shiver went through her, and she clutched the forearm I had over her upper chest. "Though being caught this way isn't all that bad." A quiet, breathy sound escaped her as my fingers found that sensitive little jewel of hers through her thin pants. "Do all Primals fight this way?"

My fingers halted. The mere idea of another touching her this way brought a brutal growl from deep within me.

Sera's amusement sweetened the taste of her desire. Yanking on my arm, she kicked back as she twisted, curling her leg around mine.

Or she attempted to.

Done with the training, I wasn't having it.

I had other things in mind now.

"Wrong move." Lifting her off her feet, I turned us toward the old stone table, where her dagger was still embedded in its surface. "But I don't think you tried very hard then, either."

She really hadn't.

I was stronger and faster than her, but she was far more skilled in fighting than what she now displayed.

Sera made a sweet sound as I carefully forced her upper body onto the table. Her feet barely reached the floor, causing her heart-shaped ass to rise into the air. That was also a sweet sight. She started to flip on me, but I was faster. Pressing down on her, I worked my leg between hers to prevent her from using them against me.

She could do some real damage with those muscles.

Her legs were powerful, whether she was kicking the shit out of an enemy or using that strength to clamp down on my hips.

Not wanting her far-too-delicate skin against the rough slab of the table, I worked my right arm beneath her cheek and leaned over her, trapping her between the table and me.

I breathed in her exquisite scent, letting it invade every part of my being. A low, vibrating hum emanated from my chest. The feel of her beneath me, soft, warm, and yielding, was like a miracle, filling me with sensation. One of homecoming? Of belonging? I wasn't sure, but whatever it was, I couldn't get enough of it—of her.

Sera may taste like sunlight, but she was more like the moon and compelled like the tides, time, and light.

I would never get enough of this feeling. Ever.

My jaw tightened with need. A throbbing pulse of lust raced to the tip of my cock. Titling my head, my breath stirred the faint wisps of hair at her temple.

I fought through the fog of rising desire and the pounding need to take control—to take *her*. I knew she didn't like it when I read her emotions, but what she felt, what she could possibly be thinking, was too important for me not to. Opening my senses to her as her fingers curled against the rough stone, I searched for any signs of panic or fear, but all I found was the sharp, sultry spice of her passion. The need I felt was amplified in her, increasing with each moment I had her pinned beneath my body.

I sucked in a breath, sudden understanding hitting me as I closed off my senses to her. "You like it," I rasped, stunned by the realization. Sera, my brave, beautiful *fighter* wasn't just excited. She was highly aroused by being dominated. Surprise gave way to wonderment as I slid my hand to her hip. I'd sensed the same from her the night I'd first fed from her. I'd chalked it up to her reaction to my feeding. "You like it like *this*."

Sera didn't say anything, but I felt a faint shiver coursing through her body. There was no escaping what she felt—that spike in her arousal was so potent it broke through my shields. I knew I was right.

"I can *taste* your desire." My lips brushed against her cheek. "Spicy. Smoky." I growled as I rocked my hips against her ass. Sera shuddered. "I don't even have to try to read you."

Dragging my palm across her lower body, I dipped my hand between her thighs. She pushed her body against my questing fingers. "I...I do."

Even through the pants, her heat was scorching—fucking divine—as I tried to reconcile the two vastly different sides of her that I'd only seen once before. "Why? Tell me."

"I..." Sera moaned as I stroked her. "I don't know."

Little liar.

"I think you do know." I shifted my arm, lifting my hand to the laces of her pants. I found the knot and easily loosened it. Her sigh brought a smile to my face. "Or maybe I'm wrong, and you don't know." I slipped my hand beneath the gap between her pants and waist, eager to get between her thighs, but I made sure to give myself time to feel her—to marvel at the warm softness of her skin, belly, and then finally lower, where she was the softest. Where she was so wet. "But I am not wrong about you liking it like this."

Sera tipped her ass up just a little bit, a silent request I would do everything in my power to answer. I knew what she wanted. Dragging in her sweet scent, I eased a finger inside her tight heat.

"I like..." Sera made a breathy sound as I let more weight settle on her back.

"Like what?" I asked as her thighs clamped down. "Being dominated?"

Her entire body shook as she gripped the hand I'd placed near her. "I like...*submitting* to *you*."

"*Fuck.*" I jerked against her, eyes briefly closing. I'd already known what her answer would be. I wouldn't have continued like this if I hadn't. But hearing her say it drove home how much more this was—it was more than lust and sex. More than getting off. I let out a ragged breath. "You never submit to me."

Sera turned her head, and those beautiful eyes locked with mine. "I'm submitting now."

A strange, intense sensation swept through me, seizing my gut as I felt eather bleed to the surface of my flesh. Blood pounded through me, muting the soft sounds of rushing water in the pool. "Is that what you want? Now?" I knew it was, but I needed to hear her say it. "Like this?"

A flush hit her cheeks. "I think you can feel that it is."

Oh, I could feel it. And I'd heard it when I curled my finger inside. "I can."

Her throat worked on a swallow. A moment passed, and then she whispered, "I know I can let this happen."

I went completely still. What I'd felt earlier was right. This was so much bigger. It was about trust.

And she trusted me.

Me.

I wasn't sure what I'd done to deserve it. Not when I could still see her flinch—could still taste the shame I'd made her feel when it was quiet.

"I think I understand," I said, feeling a little unsteady on my feet.

Her lips parted as I held her gaze. I thrust my finger into her once and then twice before slipping my hand free. I didn't look away. Neither did she. Heart pounding, I gripped her pants and shoved them down to her knees before doing the same with mine. Her breathing picked up as I grasped my cock, dragging the head over the curve of her ass. Neither of us spoke as I pushed between her thighs, entering her tight, damp heat.

Fates.

The feel of her clamping down on my cock caused every muscle in my body to tighten. Pure, raw pleasure coursed through me, stroking the beast in me once more. It wanted me to fuck. *I* wanted to fuck, hard and fast. But I could feel my god form beginning to slip. I could see it in the hand she held so tightly. The flesh was starting to thin, revealing the shadows beneath.

Fuck.

If I let go and took her in my Primal form? A shudder of fear went through me. She was mortal, and I was the furthest thing from that.

She was…she was too important to me.

I couldn't lose control. I wouldn't. Because I could be as strong as she was. Sera deserved that.

Holding on to that, I let out a harsh breath. Seconds ticked by, moving both too fast and yet too slow. In control, I pulled back, feeling every damn inch. My nerve endings fired off bursts of pleasure as I nestled just the tip at Sera's entrance and then plunged back into her. Her moan got lost in my groan.

Her nails scraped across the stone and dug into my flesh as I picked up my pace. Each thrust felt like a thousand tiny explosions, jolting our bodies. My hips moved faster and faster, pushing us ever closer to the edge of what felt like insanity.

"Harder," she gasped, fingers pressing into my fist. "Take me."

I shuddered, plunging into her.

Sera strained against my hold, and her voice was fevered as she whispered, "Fuck me."

My breath was ragged against her cheek as I held her in place just as she wanted—as she needed from me.

And I gave it to her.

I drove my cock into her slickness, over and over. Thrust *harder* as I turned my hand beneath hers. *I took her* as I threaded our fingers together. *Fucked her* as I took her hand in mine, holding it.

Her moans brought forth a rush of savage satisfaction. I drove my cock into her, each stroke going deeper as I felt her tightening around me.

Dragging the bridge of my nose over her jaw, my lips coasted over her throat as I pounded into her. My mouth opened when I ground against her, and I scraped my fangs along the skin of her neck.

Sera began to tremble as her release took hold, and she let go of all the pleasure that had been building in her core. Ecstasy powered down my spine. When she came, she took me with her over that cliff. I sealed our bodies together, leaving no space between us. Our moans mingled. I wanted to feel every tiny contraction of her muscles. I needed her to feel each pump of my cock as my body found the same pleasure as hers.

We rode the aftershocks, and I slowed my movements against her as she went utterly limp beneath me. As the tension left her body, a sweet taste gathered in the back of my throat, reminding me of chocolate—chocolate and berries.

Unsure what I was picking up from her, I lifted my mouth and made sure I hadn't pierced her skin.

I hadn't.

"You are always safe with me, *liessa*," I promised.

That was an oath I'd never break.

Because she trusted me.

And that was a gift. One I would cherish and protect.

NYKTOS

Also known as Ash

The Primal of Death / King of the Gods in the Blood and Ash timeline

Court: The Shadowlands

Hair: Thick. Reddish brown. Wavy. Falls against his cheeks.

Eyes: Silver.

Body Type: Unbelievably tall. Broad shoulders. Lean stomach. Defined chest.

Facial features: Skin a luscious golden-brown like wheat. High and broad cheekbones. Straight nose. Full, wide mouth. Thick lashes. Looks to be in his early to mid-twenties.

Distinguishing features: Wears a silver band around right biceps. Scar on chin. Black lines on the insides of hips that curve downward, creeping along the sides of his body—blood drops; one hundred and ten. Ink also stretches across his entire back. At the center of his spine, the ink is a circular, twisted swirl that grows larger and lashes out in thick tendrils that wrap around the front to his waist and connect to the ones down his hips. The drops represent the lives he's had to take. His marriage imprint is on his left hand.

Preternatural features: Swirling eather in his eyes. When using power, he sometimes glows. When he becomes full Primal: shadows bloom under his skin and swirl, glowing white veins appear. Eather-laced midnight pours out of him. Air thickens and sparks as eather wings spread out behind him. Skin becomes the color of midnight streaked with pure eather and gets hard as stone. Wings can turn solid like a draken's—a seething mass of silver and black. Eyes spark with so much power the pupils disappear.

Personality: Stoic. Private. Doesn't like attention from the other gods.

Habits/Mannerisms/Strengths/Weaknesses: Deep, husky laugh. Can sense and taste emotions. One of the strongest Primals. Young for a Primal. Able to call his horse Odin to him at will, the equine turning into shadow and sinking into the skin around his silver band when not needed—a part of him. Can see the souls of the departed. Can shadowstep anywhere, no matter the distance. Can summon a soul with a touch. Can use compulsion. Can shift into a silvery-white wolf. Doesn't make a habit of punishing mortals for speaking their minds. Fights gracefully. Bites his lip when attraction flares. Used to like to read. Doesn't particularly like to be touched—except by Sera. A quick learner when it comes to sex. Views love as a weapon—an unnecessary risk. Loves to swim; spent plenty of time at the lake when he was young. Has beautiful penmanship.

Other: Two hundred and twenty years old. Smells citrusy and fresh. Tastes woodsy and smoky—like whiskey. Blood tastes like honey but smokier. Had *kardia* removed, so is incapable of love. Also called: The Asher. The One Who is Blessed. The Guardian of Souls. *The* Primal God of Common Men and Endings.

Background: Was forced to kill his friend Lathan—something that haunts him still. Made a deal with Veses many years before meeting Sera to keep her safe. Mother was killed while Nyktos was still in her womb. Initially rejected Sera because of what he felt from her on that day—determination, anguish, and hopelessness. Had just finished his Culling when the deal was made with the Mierel family. All of Eythos's power and responsibilities transferred to Nyktos upon his father's death. Was once forced to feed until he killed. Knows what it's like to be a prisoner. (See below for additional background information.)

Family: Mother = Mycella †. Father = Eythos †. Uncle = Kolis. Second Cousin = Aios.

NYKTOS'S JOURNEY TO DATE:

My, oh my. What do I say about dear Nyktos? Beautifully tortured. Unbelievably caring. Dealt a bad hand literally from birth yet prevailed and even persevered. What I know of the Primal of Death is only what I was able to cobble together from research and my sparse visions. I wish I had seen him and Sera as clearly as I have Casteel and Poppy, but alas that was not to be. Still, what I have learned and seen of Nyktos has made me fall quite in love with him—generally speaking, of course. Seraphena is one lucky Primal.

To start with, some history…

In a vengeful rage, determined to punish his twin for causing him to lose his love (Sotoria), Kolis murders his sister-in-law, Mycella, while she's pregnant with Nyktos. Somehow, Nyktos survives. It is unknown *how*, exactly, but it earned him the "*One Who is Blessed*" part of his title. Nyktos grew up seeing constant sadness on his father's face at the loss of his Consort. Later, after seeing that and realizing that love could become a weapon and was a dangerous and unnecessary risk, he asks the goddess Maia to remove his *kardia*, thus making it impossible for him to love.

We find out later that that *later* was right before Sera came to the Shadowlands, and it's because of a vision he had of what would happen if he fell in love with Sera and then lost her.

Nyktos had barely finished his Culling when his father made the deal that affected the Mierel bloodline—which Eythos told Nyktos about before he died, though he never explained *why* he did it. It didn't impact Nyktos then because he was not yet the Primal of Death. But when Kolis murdered Eythos after switching roles with him, all his father's power and responsibilities transferred to Nyktos.

When Phanos, the Primal of the Sky, Sea, Earth, and Wind destroys Phythe over a perceived snub, Saion and Rhahar flee the Triton Isles. Unfortunately, defection from one's Court is considered an offense often punishable by death. Nyktos intervenes on their behalf, meeting with them while in captivity and touching each of their shoulders. The next day during court, he informs Phanos that the Primal cannot punish gods who no longer belong to him and tells Phanos they belong to *him* now. You see, he took possession of their souls when he touched them, making them his and no longer a part of the Triton Isles, thus allowing them to leave as they both wished. After, they become incredibly loyal to Nyktos and part of his inner circle.

Acting as the Primal of Death and knowing that he is now responsible for the deal made with Roderick Mierel, Nyktos checks on Seraphena occasionally, curious about her. He witnesses her at her lake and finds it soothing.

He actually started checking on her as a child. He saw her collecting rocks, swimming in her lake, doing other things. And all of that started because of a dream he had on the day she was born, showing him what could happen in the future.

During his earlier days as the Primal of Death, Kolis used to make him come to him in Dalos, whereupon Nyktos would have to pretend that he didn't hate his uncle with every fiber of his being and convince Kolis that he was loyal to him. In reality, Nyktos never accepted his way of life and had been looking for a way to destroy his uncle or entomb him since he Ascended. Seeing how Kolis treated his *favorites* only reinforced the loathing Nyktos felt for his kin. And being forced to do things like rip out a godling's heart for daring not to bow properly to Kolis, or feed until he killed, only increased his hatred.

Before the mortals started losing faith, he used to be summoned to the mortal realm often. He would sometimes grant the petitioner's request to take the life of another if they were evil and deserved it. Other times, he killed the summoner if the request was for profit or a petty slight. As time went on, he visited the mortal realm less and less.

Until he was summoned to accept Sera as his Consort.

He'd already had Ector and Lathan watching her once she turned seventeen—before he was forced to take Lathan's life. But when the Priests summon him to Lasania to claim Seraphena and honor the deal her ancestor made, he arrives at the castle with a rumble, extinguishing all candles before sending the flames surging toward the ceiling. As the air splits, eather pours out, and he appears, surrounded by churning shadows. He senses Seraphena's feelings and whispers to her that he has no need of a Consort before extinguishing the candles again with a whoosh and disappearing with another rumble. When the candles flame anew, he's gone. He says he was never summoned again, even though Sera was led to believe he had been.

The next time Nyktos sees Sera in person, she's older, and he is in the mortal realm—something he still doesn't do often. Posing as Ash, he sees her trailing the same gods he has been keeping an eye on and grabs her before she rushes in. She fights and rails at him, which does little but greatly amuse him. He questions her about what she was planning and tells her that him jumping in to save her interfered with his plans. He also makes her aware that he doesn't have a single decent bone in his body.

Sera attacks him, and he pins her between him and the wall, realizing who she is in the process. He promises her that the three gods will pay for what they've done. When he senses Taric, Madis, and Cressa returning, he tells Sera to wrap her legs around him and kiss him as a way to hide in plain sight. She gets feisty and bites him. He kisses the hell out of her and bites her back, sucking blood from her finger. After, he clarifies that he wasn't pretending to enjoy the kiss and admits that maybe he has *one* decent bone in his body.

If you ask me, Nyktos is made of good. While no Primal can be *good* per se, Nyktos is the best of the best. And while he may not like to admit it, I am sure I'm not the only one who sees it.

Taking stock, Ash doesn't believe the other gods sensed him and tells Sera to go home. When she challenges him and asks if he's leaving, he informs her that he's not.

Later, he startles her outside the Kazin home they're both investigating and confirms he was following the gods, too. Once again amused by her spunk, he suggests they look around together since they seem to have common goals. He informs her that the gods have done this before and confesses that he planned to try to capture one of them and *chat*. While he has every intention of getting to the bottom of things, he warns her that she should let it go.

Sera, not afraid of much—apparently even a god, as she thinks Ash is—brings her shadowstone dagger to his throat. He questions her about the weapon given shadowstone is rare in the mortal realm. After they discuss it, she tells him she stole it from her stepbrother—a lie. When he asks her if she knows what would happen to her if she tried to use it on him, and she says she does, he confesses that knowing she'd still try makes him think of their kiss earlier and her tongue in his mouth.

Cheeky devil.

Ash disarms her and tells her she's too brave, calling her *liessa* for the first time. He asks her what drowns out her fear and pushes her so eagerly toward death. She says she doesn't know. After a little more discourse, she tells him to get on with it: killing her. He's both surprised and amused that she thinks he would.

He tells her to be careful but warns that he'll be watching.

Following the gods later, Ash enters Joanis Designs. Acting on instinct, Sera stabs him in the chest. He chastises her for being reckless, pulls out the dagger, and destroys it. Not having learned her lesson about self-preservation, she threatens him and seems utterly unimpressed by his show of force and energy. It only makes him laugh.

He asks her what scares her and calls her *liessa* again, realizing she's only scared on a superficial level. Unable to stop himself from touching her, he caresses her cheek and tells her that while she may feel terror, she's not terrified. She snarkily asks him if he's the God of Thoughts and Emotions, making him laugh again.

She's clearly trouble, but he can't keep away.

Ash confesses to Sera that he was alerted to the gods entering the mortal realm. He tells her that he's kept an eye on her to keep her from getting into any more mischief. When she tells him it isn't necessary, he replies that he *wanted* to—something that surprises even him. They share information, and he says he hasn't discovered anything about the Kazin family murders nor found any evidence explaining why Madis did what he did, though he insinuates the god was lazy this last time.

He explains that the gods' victims' souls just cease to exist, which is a fate crueler than being sent to the Abyss, where you're at least *something*. When she asks, he confirms that he's indeed from the Shadowlands and tells her what happens to a soul after someone passes.

As they talk more, Andreia Joanis—who they thought quite dead when they arrived—begins to stir, then rises and attacks them. He kills the seamstress with his shadowstone sword and tells Sera that he's never seen or heard of anything like what they just witnessed. He knows that Madis didn't just kill her. He did something else to her—something disturbing.

When Ash tells Sera he has to go, he urges her to do the same, calling her *liessa* again. When she asks him what it means, he tells her that it has different meanings to different people but that it always means something beautiful and powerful.

I saw this exchange in a vision of the past, and let me tell you, I swooned.

Sometime later, Ash hides and watches Sera as she spends some time in her lake. When she demands that he reveal himself, he comes out from behind the waterfall and tells her she's like a goddess made of silver and moonbeams—she really is. Seraphena is absolutely stunning. She gives him hell as she always does, and he calls her a liar when she tells him she doesn't want him to stay. Their discourse continues, and he admits that he's aroused but a little afraid of her, and is being careful around her despite the lure he feels to be bad.

When she finally asks his name, he tells her it's Ash. She inquires if it's short for something, and he tells her it's short for many things. She asks about his tattoos, and he hedges, instead telling her to get dressed and promising not to look as she does. Not long after, he realizes they aren't alone and instructs her to unsheathe her blade, saying that what comes isn't from the mortal realm.

He explains to her that the nightmare creatures she's seeing are called Gyrms, Hunters more specifically, out looking for something. Once again, he tells her to go home, and they bicker as they fight the Gyrms. Despite her distracting outfit—a very flimsy scrap of clothing—which he makes sure to point out to her, he says he's impressed that she can fight and explains how best to kill a Gyrm.

Sera reveals her revulsion for snakes as she discovers what's inside the Hunters, and Ash teases her about it—naturally. But in her defense, I'm not particularly fond of serpents either. Ash clarifies that what the seamstress turned into is not a Gyrm. He still doesn't know *what* happened at Joanis Designs. He explains the different kinds of Gyrms to Sera, and when she asks if the Priests are Gyrms given their stitched mouths and creepiness, he tells her they are.

He suggests perhaps the Hunters were looking for him since he has plenty of enemies. When she implies that he did something to deserve them, he calls her on it and says she's being awfully judgmental.

Ash then tells Sera a secret: mortal knowledge of the gods, Primals, and Iliseeum isn't always accurate. Boy, is that true. I swear things change every time I make a note in these files. He goes on to say that some Primals are extremely young, and many gods have been around longer than they have.

Many Gyrms dispatched around them, Ash tells Sera that taking a life should always leave a mark. Lightening the mood, he ribs her about openly staring at his body. She denies it, and he tells her that she lies prettily and calls her *liessa* again.

Ash insists they interest each other, which is why they've both stayed at the lake. He goes on to say that he feels that way about her because she speaks her mind and has little regard for the consequences of doing so.

A woman after my own heart.

Ash admits to Sera that he's only killed when he's had to and never enjoyed it. She says she's sorry, and it surprises him. He tells her about Lathan and how he was forced to take his life. His surprise soon turns to shock as she shows compassion that he had to kill his friend.

I wasn't sure anybody had ever done that for him before.

Ash asks her why she's by the lake. When she says it's calming, he completely understands. It intrigues him that she comes often and is never followed or escorted. As they talk more, and Sera's self-deprecating side comes out, it annoys him that she would ever question her beauty. He tells her he was impressed by her fighting skills and then teases her that she likes him.

Sera asks about Iliseeum and the Shadowlands, and he tells her what they're like, asking if he can touch and play with her hair as they chat. He explains how death has made the Shadowlands less magnificent than it used to be.

He's able to make her smile a few times as they talk, and he remarks that she's graced him with those expressions. When she tells him he's kind, it surprises him, and he quickly denies it. But then he admits that maybe he has *one* decent bone in his body. At least, when it comes to her.

As I said, Nyktos has plenty of decent bones in his body, he just needs those around him like Sera to make him see that.

Overwhelmed by desire, Ash confesses that he wants and needs to kiss her. She tells him to do it. Admitting that he's never wanted to hear the word *yes* more, he tugs at her lip with his fangs. She gasps, and he tells her how much he likes it. He then urges her body down onto the ground and teases her about the kiss being…satisfactory. After the second one, he pauses, a bit overcome, but then kisses her again and drags his fangs down her neck. When she says his name, he stills and admits that he's never heard it said quite like that before, then adds that she can call him whatever she wants.

That one kind and decent bone was most definitely being ruled by his wicked and indecent bones. I couldn't love it more.

He implores her to show him what she likes so he can give it to her, and she demonstrates how he can pleasure her. When he touches her, he tells her she feels like silk and sunshine—be still my heart. Taking control of the movements as she clutches his wrist, he calls her *liessa* and tells her to fuck his hand. She gladly does. Smart girl. Afterward, he samples her pleasure from his fingers and tells her she tastes like the sun.

The *sun*… Oh, my gods. The words that come out of this Primal's mouth… He's one of a kind for sure.

Sera touches him, but he hesitates. He confesses how badly he wants her—*not* her hand—around him but doesn't want to debauch her on the ground—he shouldn't knock a good ground shag—or have her regret anything. He admits that he doesn't have much experience and then distracts her with more kisses.

As they lie together, he admits how he wants to count her freckles and plays with her hair. When they finally get up and finish getting dressed, he advises her to go home quickly and to be careful.

Ash sends Ector to the mortal realm with a new shadowstone dagger for Sera to replace the one he destroyed so she can keep herself safe. I love that he worries for her but realizes that she can take care of herself, as well.

Days later, Nyktos feels Sera's emotions across the realms as Tavius tortures and whips her. He intervenes, his fury on full display. Pronouncing that he is the Asher, the One Who is Blessed, the Guardian of Souls, *the* Primal God of Common Men and Endings, and the Primal of Death, he seems to terrify everyone in attendance—all but Sera.

He demands to know who took part in what was done to her and kills four guards for the transgression. He then turns to Tavius and claims Sera as his Consort. As punishment for what the boy-King did, Ash pins him to the Primal statue with the whip around his throat. The Queen begs for Tavius's life, further enraging Ash.

Sera asks him to let Tavius go, and he does as she wishes, calling her *liessa* again when he realizes that *she* wants to murder the bastard. She carries out her promise to cut off his arms, stab him in the chest, and shove the whip down her stepbrother's throat. After some quite normal conversation, something snaps within Sera, and she attacks Nyktos. I can only imagine it's because of everything he put her through by not claiming her before and not telling her who he was when she met him again. He reminds her that even as a Primal, he feels pain. Once again, he admits that he's a little afraid of her.

Sera calls him Nyktos in a fit of ire, now knowing his real identity and hating that she can't take her frustrations out on him. He tells her not to call him that; says he's not that to her.

Ash informs her what will happen now that he's claimed her and realizes that she honestly thought he'd leave her to the consequences of her actions regarding Tavius. He tells her he refuses to let her be executed and promises that her family will be safe, even though he doesn't feel they deserve it.

He explains to her how he knew to come when he did, touching her, unable to stop. She remarks that his touch is cold, and he asks her what she thinks Death feels like. When she wonders why he didn't tell her who he was before, he questions if she would still have been interested in him if she knew he was the Primal of Death. He stresses that he never lied to her. She assumed.

Heading to the lake to gain entrance to Iliseeum, Ash is amused that she feels such ownership of the body of water and remarks that there's a reason she's found it so calming all this time: it is how she can get to him. He admits that he could have—and probably *should* have—told her who he was earlier, but she was fearless, he was interested, and though he hadn't wanted or expected everything that'd happened with them thus far, he liked that they were themselves...no deal and no obligations. She *wanted* him to touch her and didn't feel she *had* to let him. He explains that he enjoyed it all and didn't want it to end.

Once in the realm of the gods, Ash points out that all the hills she sees are draken and explains the difference between a dragon and a draken.

After passing a Rise full of impaled dead, people begin noticing their arrival. He tells her he'd hoped they would have some time before anyone knew she'd arrived, especially since very few know about her yet. He asks if he can introduce her as his Consort, and she agrees.

As they start meeting the gods in the Shadowlands, he gets a little miffed that Lailah brings up the so-called family tradition of kidnapping mortal girls, alluding to Kolis's obsession with Sotoria.

Ash calls to Aios to take Sera to her room and have food sent to her. The goddess is startled when she feels a jolt from Sera as they touch and looks at Ash. He only responds with, "I know." He tells Sera to trust Aios and promises he'll return soon.

Later, he finds Sera bathing. When he takes in her wounds, he confesses he can't wait to visit Tavius in the Abyss to make him suffer. He brings her something to help with the pain and healing and offers to wash her hair—a first for him. But he can't resist her moonlit locks.

Ash wonders what her life was like after he rejected her and learns that a knight trained her in weaponry and hand-to-hand combat so she could defend herself. He'd hoped she would just carry on with her life after his rejection. When she asks why he didn't return, he tells her that the Priests would never summon him again and tries to get her to understand that what happened wasn't personal.

Oh, it was personal, all right, but not at all what she thought. It was so much more. And so much sweeter yet heartbreaking.

Ash tells her that she didn't do anything wrong when he rejected her and explains what he felt from her that day—that she was afraid and felt she had no choice—thus revealing that he can sense and taste her emotions. He tells her that he saw her as brave but still felt anguish and hopelessness—someone forced to fulfill a promise they didn't make. He had no need of a Consort forced to marry him, and so he told her as much.

She emerges from the bath, and he dries her and tells her he knows what she feels when he touches her—the sounds she makes aren't forced; she lets him touch her because she likes it. He explains that he reads her body language, though; he doesn't delve into her emotions.

Being more than interested in certain parts of their union and agreement, he pleasures her again, telling her that he thinks about her and their time at the lake every time he takes himself in hand. He then applies ointment to her back and insists he's still the same man she met, despite her knowing more about him now and who he really is. He tells her that he revealed things to her he's never told others, and he never lied to her.

When Sera asks about those she saw impaled on the Rise as they entered, he's stunned that she thinks *he* did it. He explains about the politics of Iliseeum, which leads to him revealing that he didn't make the deal with her ancestor. His father did.

Ash goes into how all powers, responsibilities, and deals transferred to him when his father died, Ascending him into his Primal status. He relays that his parents loved each other very much, and his father was a widower when he made the deal with Roderick. Eythos died loving his wife, so Ash was always confused why he made the deal at all.

Neither he nor Sera consented to the agreement, which is something they have in common. He tells her that he considered coming to her and telling her everything well before now and the events that played out, but felt it was better if he limited contact. He didn't want to expose her.

The discussion turns once again to the murders, and Ash tells Sera that he doesn't think they're connected to her. He explains things about Lathan better, and when she asks why he kept an eye on her given there were no consequences for him regarding the deal, he tells her he isn't sure and insinuates that perhaps he should have left her be. While she may have been killed by Madis and his crew, dying may have actually been a better fate for her. At least then his enemies wouldn't also become hers.

Word comes in that Shades are loose in the Dying Woods, so Ash leaves Sera to go and deal with them. When he gets back, he has breakfast with her.

As they discuss the dynamics in the House of Haides, he explains that keeping her in her chambers is a necessary evil, but if she thinks that's what being held against her will feels like, she has no idea. He admits that he's unfortunately well-acquainted with the feeling, referring to his time in Dalos.

I hate that she will experience that for herself soon enough.

Ash returns the dagger he gifted her, now with a sheath, and apologizes for upsetting her and keeping her sequestered.

Talk turns to feeding, and he explains how it works and why being weakened comes into play, admitting that he doesn't feed anymore. Ever. He just makes sure to never get that weak. When she asks if he was a prisoner before, referring to what he'd said about being well-acquainted with the feeling of being a captive, he tells her that he's been many things, leaving it at that and not elaborating. She tries to get him to say more by offering up that they should learn more about each other. Ash admits that he doesn't want them to be strangers and would very much like them to be as close as they were at the lake. However, he isn't willing to discuss his imprisonment.

He quickly changes the subject, and they talk about the draken. Ash explains that he's been around them long enough that he can understand them, even while they're in their draken forms. He feeds little Jadis some bacon and admits that Nektas will likely burn him alive if he finds out Ash is giving it to her.

He teases Sera about stabbing him in the chest in the mortal realm, letting her know he's hopeful she won't do it again. Then he explains that Nektas knew Ash wasn't seriously injured that day because of their bond. If he were, the draken would have come for him. Sera remarks that she really needs to get a better handle on her anger, and he confesses that he finds it...interesting.

Later, Nyktos returns from a duty and talks to Sera about her future in the Shadowlands. When she accidentally bumps into him, he jerks and hisses, telling her not to touch him, afraid to reveal his weakness. When Sera alludes to the fact that she doubts his attraction, it stuns him, and he tells her he's *very* interested. He goes on to say that it's becoming real and potent—like its own entity.

She tells him he's a lot of talk and no action, so he backs her against the wall, needing to make things clear. He explains that the last thing he wants to be is in control or decent when he's around her. He wants to be so deep inside her he forgets his name—and knows she wants it, too. He licks and nips at her. Sera, ever the contrarian, insists she doesn't like him, and he tells her it's probably better that way.

He gives Sera a tour of the House of Haides and then heads to the library to discuss more rules. While there, he reveals that he injured his back during his skirmish with the Shades—which explains the flinching. Though poor Sera doesn't know that until much, much later and thinks he's put off by her for some reason.

As he relays more about the rules and how things work in Iliseeum, he tells her that the do-not-harm-the-Consort rule was broken only once, and because he wants to make sure she's safe, her coronation will be in a fortnight.

When she asks about the Ascension, Ash gets uncomfortable and tells her what it entails, explaining that she won't Ascend. None of this was ever her choice, and he refuses to force someone into a near eternity of what he's gone through. *See? What did I tell you? Considerate—even if he doesn't like to admit it.*

Sera calls him *Your Highness* for the first time, and it arouses him, even though it was said with a hefty dose of smartassery. Not long after talking about his mother's death and her father, he tells her that love is a dangerous and unnecessary risk.

A few days later, Ash holds court and looks directly at Sera where she hides in an alcove, thinking how it's the longest she's been in his presence in days, even though she thinks he doesn't know she's there. Not long after, Theon announces that Veses has arrived, and Ash has Ector escort Sera to safety as he leads the Primal goddess into his office.

Sera sneaks away and enters the Red Woods. Ash goes after her, appearing just as a group of entombed gods rise and attack. He tells her to be silent and explains about the gods and the blood trees. He then asks Saion to escort Sera back to the palace and to grab Rhahar to join Ash in checking the tombs. Unfortunately, Sera succumbs to her wounds from the fight.

After he and Rhahar square things away in the woods, Ash returns and admits to Sera that he used compulsion to get her to drink the antidote, calling her *liessa* again as they discuss the attack. He divulges that the gods were carefully set free, likely by another god to see what might happen. He says they would have swarmed whoever opened the tomb.

He explains that the Shadowlands are dying and is surprised when she tells him she believes it has to do with the deal her family member made. It's not that at all.

As talk turns to Veses, Ash realizes that Sera is jealous. He tells her that he hates every moment of being in the Primal's presence and calls her a pit viper.

Ash admits that he told everyone to give Sera space after her ordeal, and that he's been actively avoiding her. He tells her that being around her for more than a handful of minutes makes desire overcome his common sense. Not able to stop himself, he kisses her, then gives in to his other desires and tells her to be still as he pleasures her with his hand. Once again, he laps her essence from his fingers and then kisses her once more, letting her experience her delectable taste.

Ash tells Sera he hopes there's no doubt when it comes to his interest in her and relays that he's counted her freckles—she has thirty-six. He then asks if he can lie with her and admits he's a virgin, explaining that he's never let it get that far with anyone because it's too much of a risk. When she asks him why he's risking it with her, he confesses that he can't help himself, even though he knows they'll both end up regretting it. They wind up sleeping beside each other, but he rises and leaves before she wakes.

Ash takes care of some things at the Pillars and then goes to see Sera after her seamstress fitting. He's surprised to learn that mortals still think the Chosen are Ascended. He tells her the true fate of the Chosen under Kolis's rule and admits that he doesn't know why the Rite is still held. He explains that he hides the Chosen away in an effort to protect them, even though he prefers for people to think he sits back and does nothing. He then tells Sera how some Chosen have simply disappeared. They're just…gone.

Out on the balcony that night, Ash confesses that he always thinks about the Chosen and asks her to join him. When she does, he tells her that part of the reason he couldn't sleep was because he was staring at the adjoining door in their chambers and thinking about her.

As talk turns to his role, Ash tells Sera that he finds it difficult to judge souls and explains that he used to answer summonses but stopped when the deaths quit leaving a mark—something he feels should always happen. Though he enjoyed the justice when mortals realized who he was and that he could kill them and have their souls for eternity.

He learns that Sera has killed, too, mostly bad people but also others when her mother commanded her to do so. He reassures her that he doesn't think she's a monster and feels a jolt when they touch, going on to say that a monster wouldn't know—or at least think—they are one.

Kissing his scar, Sera asks about his ink. When he explains, she tells him that he isn't responsible for others' actions. She smiles at him, and he tells her not to, saying there's nothing he wouldn't let her do when she does. She takes that as an invitation and pleasures him with her mouth.

The next day, he is required to hold court again and tells Sera she can't be there—it's too risky. After her arguments, he once again questions her recklessness, saying that most mortals don't live as if their lives are forfeit.

Gemma is attacked while Ash is away, and he arrives just as she dies. Sera starts to glow, and he calls out to her, stunned. He watches as she brings Gemma back to life and remarks that Sera carries an ember of life.

Once he realizes what's going on and what his father did, awe gives way to wonder, which turns to hope. Shadows swirl under his skin as he demands that no one speak of what they witnessed. He then tells Sera that her doing what she did likely created a big ripple of power that would be felt throughout Iliseeum and detected by many gods and Primals. He warns her that others will come searching for the source of that surge. Suddenly, he realizes that he's felt it before but couldn't pinpoint the location at the time. He knows this wasn't the first time she brought someone or something back. He tells her that the Hunter Gyrms and murderous gods in the mortal realm were searching for *her*.

As his emotions heighten, the shadows behind him coalesce into the shape of wings. He asks why she didn't tell him about her gift. When he learns that she has indeed brought someone back before, he laughs—Marisol, the wolf, what happened in the Red Woods…

Ash explains that his father was the true Primal of Life and assumes the ember she now carries was his—and Ash's once upon a time before Eythos's twin stole it.

He relays the story of Eythos, Kolis, and Sotoria and then explains why Primals haven't intervened. He says the ember in her is a chance for life and details how the poppies have started growing again after being gone for hundreds of years. He also shares that Kolis has Eythos's soul.

When she brings up the deal, he tells her the Rot is a byproduct of Kolis losing the powers he stole and has nothing to do with what Roderick did.

Sera starts acting strangely, and Ash becomes concerned, thinking she's feeling too much for it to be just shock or confusion. Then she reveals her motivations—her true plan. How she was trained with one purpose in mind: to end the deal in favor of the summoner by making him fall in love and then ending him. When she tries to apologize, he snarls at her and tells her not to.

A horn sounds, interrupting them, warning that the Shadowlands are under siege. After he warns anyone within earshot to never speak of what they've learned—the embers or the deception—he sends Saion, Bele, and Rhahar to find out what's going on.

After arming himself, he's told about the ship capsizing. When Sera mentions feeling strangely, he is surprised to find that she can feel death and tells her what she's experiencing. He bids her to remain with Ector and Rhain and tells the gods to make sure she stays alive. Then Ash, Saion, Rhahar, and Theon ride out of the gate.

They head down the bluffs, engaging the dakkais as the creatures advance on the homes in Lethe. He, Bele, Saion, Rhahar, and Theon crouch on horseback, firing arrows at the enemy. When he gets next to the bay, he recalls Odin to his arm and fights hand-to-hand.

Suddenly, several dakkais about to attack him from behind drop dead, and Ash finds Sera firing arrows at them.

The draken incinerate the dakkais, and Ash looks up to check on Sera. Nektas takes the enemy draken down, and Ash orders Rhain and Ector to return Sera to the palace. He arrives later with Saion and Nektas and asks her if she got injured. He confirms that Kolis was behind the attack and likely knows *something* is in the Shadowlands but doesn't know the source.

Ash tells Sera that his father wouldn't have put the ember in a mortal body without a reason, and until they figure out what that was, Kolis absolutely cannot get his hands on her.

When Sera feels shame for what she's done, he laughs, thinking she's a very good actress. He adds it to the list of her many talents and decides to shame her more by discarding her pain. It made me sad to see that, because it was so very clear that he was lashing out because *he* was hurt.

Sera tells him off for reading her emotions and promises that none of her actions or feelings have been fake. She then adds that she's glad he didn't take her three years ago because it means she doesn't have to do what's been expected of her.

Nektas whispers something to Ash, and he tries to send the draken to the wall, telling him he's fine. Finally, he admits that most of the blood on him *is* his.

Despite the pain he's in and his increasingly weakening state, he doesn't believe that Sera's ember is powerful enough to work on a god or a Primal—which we find out later he's quite wrong about. Regardless, he doesn't trust her enough to let her try to heal him.

Ash orders Nektas to put her somewhere safe, even from herself since she clearly doesn't value her life. When Nektas eventually brings her to *him*, he gets irritated. Nektas says he thought he was following orders—matchmaking draken!

When Sera suggests that he needs to feed, it raises Ash's ire, and he sends her away. But before she leaves, he asks if she truly has no fear of dying.

She still doesn't leave, and he roars at her to go, warning her that if she doesn't get out, he'll feed from and then fuck her. She taunts him, and he calls her reckless, admitting that he might kill her if he takes from her—he hasn't fed in decades.

Giving in, he feeds and tears off her gown, unable to stop the flood of emotions bombarding him. When she suggests he hasn't taken enough, he tells her it *has* to be enough. As the feelings from the bite ramp up, Sera begins pleasuring herself. One thing leads to another, and he feeds more as he takes her, watching where they're joined, the dark, hazy outline of his eather wings forming behind him as he fights his true nature.

He tells her he's never felt anything like what he's experiencing. When she echoes his sentiment, he asks her not to lie, then warns her that her faith in him is reckless.

What else is new? She's always reckless.

In the afterglow, he can't stop himself from asking her how she can be so convincing. She takes offense and tells him off again.

Ash insists he's had more than enough blood and admits that ripping off her dress will be his favorite memory for years to come.

Coming from someone who's been lost to the throes of passion and experiencing another lose control, it *is* quite titillating and something not easily forgotten.

After telling her to rest—which she doesn't appreciate—he tells her that she'll never get him to fall for her and reinforces that she'll never be able to weaken him to the point where she'd be an actual threat. She challenges that assumption—as she challenges just about everything.

Ash spends some time away from Sera. The next time he sees her, he arrives just after Sera fights off Hamid's attack in the bath. He reveals that he tasted her fear and came running. When she shows ire that he read her emotions again, it both amuses and arouses him.

As he gets the details of what happened, he's floored to discover that her attacker attempted to strangle her. When Sera states she'll never take a bath again, it greatly upsets him. He is about to question Hamid when Ector kills him, further irritating Ash.

He takes Sera to her bedchambers and admits that he hadn't gotten around to assigning a guard to her today. He asks her about the attack and inquires whether Hamid said anything during. He orders Rhain and Aios to sit with Gemma and instructs them to reconnoiter Hamid's house for clues.

Despite the circumstances and not trusting her, Ash grows concerned when Sera is suddenly in pain and weak. He worries that he took too much blood and wonders if it could be her Culling—which is impossible since she's mortal. Still, he asks a guard to stay with her and goes to fetch some healing tea.

After Ash returns, Sera mentions that the tea is the same as the one her knight, Sir Holland, used to give her. He's stunned to find out the teas are the same and wonders how a mortal knew about it. He explains that Sera's headaches and bleeding gums are symptoms of a god's Culling and says he thinks the ember inside her is giving her similar side effects. He figures she'll have a few more weeks or months of symptoms before they subside, but she will not Ascend.

Ash tells her not to wait if the symptoms return and to instead ask for the tea right away. He then asserts that sex between them will not happen again. She'll be safe in the Shadowlands and become his Consort as planned, but neither of them wanted this, and love was never on the table.

He states that he would never think of her even if he considered friendship and lashes out, telling her she's merely a vessel for the ember. He can't help responding to her flare of hurt, but still tells her there's nothing else to discuss.

Ash is called away to Lethe to deal with an incident: Cressa and Madis led Shades into the city, so he goes to clean up the mess.

When the gods attack, he roars at them for daring to enter his Court and touch what is his. He explodes Cressa and tells Madis to join his sister.

Taric tries to use eather against Ash and it annoys him. Advancing on the god, he grabs Taric's wrist, shattering the god's sword into nothing. Taric taunts him, telling Ash to kill him and calling him the Blessed One. But then says it won't matter and warns that *he* won't stop—*he* being the false Primal of Life. He says Kolis will tear apart both realms, but it will be nothing compared to what he'll do to Nyktos. He tells Ash that he can't stop his uncle, neither could Eythos, and promises that Kolis *will* have Sera. In answer, Nyktos rips out his heart.

Ash figures out that Taric went through Sera's memories when he bit her and reminds her not to forget that while she feels fear, she's never afraid. To punctuate his point, he returns her dagger.

As things start to settle somewhat, he realizes that Bele was taken down in the siege. When Sera goes to her, he tells her that the ember inside her isn't strong enough to bring back a god. Aios begs him to let her try anyway. When Sera says it's her fault that Bele died, it angers Nyktos—because it's *not* her fault.

Just before he gives the go-ahead, Ash tells Nektas to be sure the guards are ready for anything and then tells Sera to do what she does. He watches, stunned when it works and Bele revives.

Nyktos tells Sera that what she did is impossible—the ember shouldn't be strong enough. However, despite that, she just Ascended Bele.

As they discuss what that means, Nyktos tells Sera that Bele can now challenge Hanan for control of their Court.

They talk more about what she did and discuss what happens now. He thanks her again for saving his friend and is shocked that his gratitude surprises her. He helps clean her up because he wants to, not because he feels he has to, and tells her that he summoned the Fates.

Nyktos warns Sera that Kolis will back off momentarily until he figures out what he's dealing with. They talk more about the Ascension, and Nyktos agrees with Saion that not all gods Sera brings back will Ascend—they must be *fated* to. He then explains how the lives and deaths of gods differ from mortals.

Asking her if Taric said anything to her, she reveals that they were looking for her in Lasania. The *viktors* were protecting her. He goes on to say that it's been a long time since he's heard anything about them.

When he asks her if she wants to take a bath or rest, he's uncomfortable when he realizes that she doesn't want to go back to her room because of what happened with Hamid. He takes her to his chamber instead and falls asleep, waking to Reaver, who tells him that Nektas has returned and is in the throne room. Nyktos tells Sera that means the Fates answered.

Overcome, Nyktos kisses Sera but quickly tells her it changes nothing. The poor Primal just can't fight what he feels for her, even though he thinks he should.

When they get downstairs, he's surprised to see the goddess, Penellaphe. He's told she's come about Sera and that she brought an Arae with her.

Sera is shocked by the Arae's appearance, and Nyktos discovers that Holland was the knight who trained Sera in the mortal realm. He accuses Holland of tampering with destiny while masquerading as a mortal and finally understands how *Sir* Holland knew about the healing tea.

As Holland and Sera reunite, Nyktos accuses the Arae of learning about the deal and taking the place of someone who was meant to train Sera to kill him. Holland corrects him and says it was just to *kill*, not to murder him specifically. Nyktos asks why Holland never informed Sera of the pointlessness of her endeavor and displays his annoyance that the Arae intervened at all.

He then asks Holland if he knew what would happen to Eythos. Holland says he didn't, but if he had, he would have stepped in, the consequences be damned.

Nyktos asks why his father did what he did and is told the better question is *what* he did. Nyktos learns that Eythos took the ember he passed onto Ash to keep him safe. He also learns that he and Sera are soulmates. After Sera talks about the sense of rightness she's felt with him since day one, he confesses he's felt the same.

He asks what his father's motivations could have been and learns about Penellaphe's vision and the prophecy. He thinks the great conspirator and the bringer of death must be Kolis and reveals that he and Eythos were both in the west—in what is roughly present-day Carsodonia.

They discuss timing, and Nyktos vows he won't let Sera die before she turns twenty-one. When he's told he can't stop fate, he says it can go fuck itself.

Holland reveals the threads of destiny, and Nyktos is shocked and furious to find that some of them indicate that he'll kill Sera. There are many ways he can, but one is unintentional. He's then floored to learn that his blood will make Sera go through her Culling, which horrifies him because he knows she won't survive it. Sera tells him it's not his fault.

Holland shows him the one thread that can disrupt fate—unexpected love—and tells him that he's right, Sera will not survive the Culling without the sheer will of that which is more powerful than the Fates or even death. She needs the love of the one who aids in her Ascension.

He further learns that the only way for Sera to survive is with the blood and love of the Primal her ember belonged to. The revelation horrifies him because of things he set in motion many, many years ago.

Many more than Sera knows at this point.

Sera tells him it's unfair, and he tells her it's more unfair to *her*. Then the bomb really drops. He finds out that Sera is the reincarnation of Sotoria, Kolis's long-lost obsession, and they find out *exactly* what his father did and why. No god has risen since Eythos hid the ember in the Mierel bloodline—until Sera Ascended Bele, anyway. The last bit of information they receive isn't much better. He's told that life has only continued because the ember is still in Sera. If she dies, everyone and everything will die right along with her.

Which can only mean one thing.

Seraphena is the Primal of Life.

Nyktos bows to Sera and relays the conclusion he just reached. She says she doesn't deserve to be the Primal of Life, snapping at him. When she starts having a panic attack, Nyktos calms her and then asks Holland and Penellaphe if they're positive no one else knows what Sera is. They tell him that Eythos, Embris, and Kolis knew about the prophecy, but the last two didn't know anything more than that as far as they're aware.

Sera makes her feelings on prophecies clear, and Nyktos agrees with her. He then tells her that Kolis's actions killed hundreds of gods, and that the Gods of Divination were hit the hardest. No mortal has been born an oracle since.

Nyktos reminds Sera that only those present at the time it happened know that she Ascended Bele. Neither Hanan nor anyone else knows the full extent of what Eythos did when he put the ember in her bloodline.

Sera reveals that she recently saw Kolis in the mortal realm, and the news stuns Nyktos. He remarks that Sotoria didn't belong to Kolis then, and Seraphena doesn't belong to him now.

He tells Penellaphe and Holland that Kolis knows *something* is in the Shadowlands and has already sent a draken and the dakkais. He assumes that, as the Primal of Life, Kolis can't enter the Shadowlands and asks Holland to confirm. The Arae refuses to answer.

Nyktos assures Sera that Kolis is no fool and wouldn't make a move on her in front of others and risk blowing his façade as the *fair and rightful King* but promises he won't let Kolis lay a finger on her. When she reveals that she's not worried about herself but *is* worried about him, it doesn't surprise him at all. He tells Sera that he's more afraid of her running to Kolis than away from *him*.

He tells everyone that his uncle has not summoned him yet, though he expects it to happen soon, and he can only delay the inevitable, not refuse the command.

Nyktos asks Holland about the Revenants and learns they're not the only mockery of life Kolis has managed to create. There's also the Craven—which he realizes is what Andreia Joanis turned into.

He tries to tell Sera that she didn't kill her stepfather by way of fate, and explains that while the Arae are cosmic cleaners, their balancing of rules only applies to mortals, not gods. Therefore, there should be no innocent-death fallout from her Ascension of Bele.

As discussions continue, Nyktos clarifies for Sera that a Primal of Life and Death isn't meant to exist. He says that such a being would be unstoppable and able to destroy realms in the same breath they create new ones.

He tells them that Kolis wants to rule over both realms, and Nyktos imagines his uncle's *creations* are meant to aid him in his bid to take over Lasania and the other kingdoms and make mortals subservient to him.

Holland reveals to Sera that Nyktos can't save her as he is now. When she doesn't understand, Nyktos tells her that he made sure love was a weakness nobody could ever exploit and had the Primal Maia remove his *kardia*. He can care about others, but love can no longer sway him.

Discussions return to how to keep Kolis—or anyone else—from snatching Sera out of the Shadowlands, and Penellaphe tells them about a charm. Nyktos is surprised to learn about it.

After thanking Penellaphe for everything she's done, the goddess leads him away to speak to him privately, but he keeps a close eye on Sera while he talks to the goddess.

Once Penellaphe and Holland leave, Nyktos asks Sera what she's thinking. He felt her go from anger to sadness to sorrow. He tells her it's hard not to read her emotions since she projects a lot. She asks him about his *kardia*, and he's evasive about when he had it removed—telling her it doesn't matter. He says that only Maia and Nektas know what he did. He then fesses up to how badly it hurt and reveals that he almost lost consciousness. If he had, he says he would have gone into stasis. But then he explains a bit more about why he did it: he didn't want to endanger anyone because of how he felt. And he believes he actually cares more because he can't love. Caring for others is more important to him than loving someone.

Nyktos tells Sera she needs to stay hidden. No one will think her being his Consort and the power they felt is a coincidence, especially if they meet her and feel the eather inside her. If they do, they'll definitely question what she is.

Nyktos confesses that her original plan annoyed him but that's not why he's mad now. What enrages him is that she doesn't value her life at all, and hasn't since the moment they met. He tells her that him saying such a thing isn't meant to be an insult, it's just an observation. He then goes on to tell her that her safety is worth everything—even the Shadowlands, and stresses that he means it with every part of his being.

Nyktos is such a softie, despite how tough and powerful he is.

When he tells her the embers are too important to risk her, he sees the hurt on her face and realizes she was likely offended that he mentioned the embers and not her. Before he can say anything, though, Rhahar interrupts and tells him there's a problem at the Pillars.

He assures Sera they'll finish their conversation later.

After hearing about the entombed gods swarming the woods, Nyktos heads deep into them with Rhahar and Saion to round them up.

Sera gets hurt. In his Primal form, Nyktos kills the freed gods with eather, ripping the last one in half with his bare hands—something Sera admits she finds hot.

Nyktos realizes that she is wounded and carries her inside the House of Haides, feeling and tasting her pain the entire way. Placing her in an unused chamber on the first floor, he closes the door and moves a chair with his eather before lighting the fireplace.

Sera tells him about the god in the courtyard who stood by and would have let her die as Nyktos checks her wounds. He informs her that she needs blood and says that while she won't die, he doesn't want her to remain in pain, either. Plus, she won't be able to heal herself while in the Culling.

He asks her to let him help her. Even says please. She agrees, and he thanks her, then tells her he's sure she'll enjoy it. As she drinks from him, he can't stop the shudders that ripple through his body. Brushing her hair back, he pulls his wrist away and explains that his blood is making her feel the way she does—the wanton look in her eyes is obvious. He explains it will likely be the longest few minutes of his life and says he's drowning in her desire.

She tells him to drown with her.

He reiterates that it's his blood making her say things like that, not him, and she tells him she always feels this way when he touches her. He urges her to pleasure herself and tells her not to stop, even when Nektas checks on them through the door. Controlling her rhythm with his hand, he brings her to climax and sucks her release from her fingers.

Later, when he readies for the debriefing, he's surprised by Sera's request to join him. Once with the other gods, he tells Bele that he needs her in the Shadowlands where she'll be the safest. He doesn't want her to hide forever, but until others *see* that she Ascended, they can't know for sure. When Rhain suggests that Veses knows what Sera looks like, Nyktos agrees and then declares that no one in the Shadowlands would betray her identity to another Court. Sera argues the point and reminds him about Hamid.

Sera leaves the palace, only to be attacked by Shades in the Dying Woods. Nyktos goes to her, but she runs from him. He tackles her—absorbing the impact—and asks why she ran. His fury shoots out of him, shattering the trees around them and turning them to ash.

Let me tell you…it was so sexy.

Then he asks why she left and is stunned when she tells him she was trying to save him. She breaks his hold, but he catches her—long enough for her to put her blade to his throat.

He tells her to make sure to cut all the way to the spine. And even then, he'll only be down for a minute. She won't make it out of the Shadowlands.

They fight and wrestle, and he asks her to tell him that he's wrong about what she was doing. He takes his true form and slams his wings into the ground as she explains. Once she finishes, he tells her that he will gladly suffer anything Kolis dishes out so long as his blood is spilled and not hers. He reiterates that the embers are important. Sera screams in frustration, and power explodes from her, throwing him into the air.

As he's lifted, trees shatter, and the temperature drops to freezing as silvery light snaps and ripples all over Nyktos's body. Nektas arrives, sensing the conflict. It scares Sera, but Nyktos tells her that the draken isn't threatening her, he's *protecting* her…from Nyktos. The draken is worried the Primal will retaliate out of reflex. Later, Nyktos confesses that he almost did.

It takes him several minutes to recover, but he finally does. He'd assumed her Culling would be like a godling's, not a god's. Explaining the difference to Sera, he tells her that her embers are definitely making her stronger.

She asks him if he needs to feed, and he tells her they'll just make sure nothing like that happens again.

Sera changes the subject and tells Nyktos about the Shade she touched, and how it started to come back to life. They ask Nektas if that's even possible. When they decipher what the Shade said, and Nektas finishes sharing about Eythos, Nyktos realizes he never knew his father could raise the dead.

As they return to discussing Sera taking off, Nyktos tells her he'll never let her go. Whether she stays as a prisoner or as his Consort is up to her. He reiterates that her destiny is not to die at Kolis's hand, and there may yet be a way to prevent her death entirely if she gives him some time and peace to think.

After calling Odin forth, he tells Sera the horse is very unhappy with her—he would be, they are one and the same in many ways—and that the next time she puts a dagger to someone's throat, she'd better mean it. Especially if it's his.

Nyktos orders her to her room, and she outs them as lovers with her grumbling. He catches up to her on the fourth floor and warns her against another outburst. Sera tells him that if his guards knew the truth about what she attempted, they would have helped her and would be happy to see her gone—or dead. He demands to know why she thinks that, but she refuses to answer. He then makes a decision and informs her that she'll be sleeping within arm's reach from now on.

When they get closer to their chambers, Nyktos realizes she escaped her room by climbing down from the balcony. It impresses him, but he tells her she's too brave. Still, a small, twisted part of him kind of wants her to use her eather on him again.

He carries her to his chambers, but she refuses to undress. He does it for her and then unbraids her hair. After turning off the lights with magic, they go to bed—within arm's reach.

Later, Nyktos begins shaking and panting, scaring Sera awake. He makes her promise never to go after Kolis again.

The next day, Nyktos gathers everyone in the throne room and tells them that Sera tried to go after the King of Gods to protect the Shadowlands. He emphasizes that her bravery is unmatched and praises her willingness to sacrifice herself for them, believing she was the cause of the recent attacks. He whispers that none will harbor ill will toward her and will see her as she is: brave and daring. He then warns those in attendance that if they don't, any negative thoughts about her will be their last. He says he'll destroy them, no matter how loyal they are to the Shadowlands. Making sure she understands that he meant what he said, he reiterates: she's brave and strong and a Consort more than worthy of them.

Nyktos joins Jadis, Nektas, and Sera after dressing down his guards, then cuddles Jadis for a moment before badgering Sera about eating. He says the Culling will weaken her, and if she doesn't eat enough, she risks going into stasis.

He tells her that he wants to get the embers out of her, saying that if they can remove them, she'll be like any godling entering their Culling, and his blood would ensure she survives the Ascension. He then tells her the alternative is unacceptable and alludes to the fact that she might Ascend into a god.

Nyktos reveals what Penellaphe said to him in private since it's been nagging at him. She told him that Delfai would welcome Sera. He explains to Sera who that is.

When talk turns to how to find this Delfai and get more information, Nyktos tells Sera he moved the Pools of Divanash to the Vale, where neither he nor Kolis can go. That way, Sotoria could stay hidden. Sera projects her excitement, but Nyktos tells her he won't allow her to go until after the coronation—for her protection. He can't stop creatures or other Primals from attacking her until she's officially claimed.

Sera then asks if removing the embers will have the same effects on her as it did when Kolis did it to Eythos. Nyktos tells her it won't. The embers will go to him, and he'll become what he was originally destined to be.

Nyktos explains to Sera what happened to Halayna, Nektas's mate, and tells her that Nektas was the first draken, the one who helped Eythos create the mortals. Draken can live as long as Primals. Only the Arae are immortal, though the *viktors* are eternal in a different way given their constant reincarnation.

He tells her that only a few know of the plan to remove her embers—the usual suspects in the Shadowlands—and they know there's more than one ember in her and support the plan…including her Ascension. Only Nektas knows about Sotoria's soul, however. It would be too dangerous for others to know about that.

When talk turns to Kolis's creatures, Nyktos says he doesn't think the Revenants and the Craven are the same and hopes the missing Chosen haven't been turned into either of them.

He then explains that if their plan works, he'll Ascend again, and others will feel that Kolis isn't the Primal God of Life any longer. And while he is the oldest Primal alive, and they may never be able to kill him, they might be able to weaken him enough to entomb him.

Sera once again asserts that she's the key, but Nyktos denies it, stating he will never accept that as the truth.

They discuss the Rot, and he says he believes it will vanish if things work out as they hope.

Talk turns to the coronation and the fact that everyone needs someone to watch over them—even him.

Nyktos grabs the Book of the Dead, but before he can do anything, Saion interrupts and tells him there are Cimmerian at the gate. Nyktos asks Sera to remain inside and reminds her she has no protection until she's crowned, even with the charm Vikter placed on her. He urges her not to push back about his directive.

Heading outside to assess the situation, Nyktos verbally squares off with Dorcan, realizing they must have come from Hanan's Court because of Bele. A battle ensues, and he kills a Cimmerian who throws a dagger at Sera, then smiles when she kills one attacking him from behind.

He goes to her on the Rise, realizing she's been injured—he can smell her blood. While he wants to taste her, he tells her to listen for once and stay on the Rise and then goes to deal with Dorcan.

Before he gets there, Saion informs him that Dorcan saw Sera. When they speak, Dorcan tells him that refusing Hanan will end badly for Nyktos. More will come. In answer, Nyktos beheads the Cimmerian.

Afterward, he heads to his office and scolds Sera for risking both her life and Saion's since he was tasked with protecting her and keeping her out of trouble. Nyktos orders Rhain and Ector to get him some supplies to clean her wound and then tells Sera to listen to the instinct to value her life. He reminds her that it isn't an insult; he's just trying to understand how she became the way she is. He asks her what kind of life she led. When asked what he's sacrificed—referring to what Ector said to Sera while Nyktos was outside—he refuses to answer.

He sees that her wound isn't deep enough to require blood, so she need not worry he'll take advantage of her. She reminds him that he didn't before and that she's attracted to him.

Nyktos tells Sera that Taric would have tasted the embers when he bit her and took her blood, but vows that no one will feed from her again.

He feels like she wants to murder someone and asks her why. She brings up her stepbrother, and he asks if Tavius hurt her before the day Nyktos came for her. She hedges, but he knows he did. She tells him about Tavius and his proclivities and about Kayleigh, and he realizes that Sera was being punished for him not taking her as his Consort. When he learns what would have become of her had he not come for her, it enrages him. He's surprised that she defends those who knew and did nothing about it. In a sad turn of events, he realizes that he didn't give her freedom by refusing her. He says he's sorry and tells her that his sympathy and apology are there if she ever needs them.

Nyktos tells her she should rest, saying that shadowstone would have killed a mortal or godling, even his blood in her wouldn't have stopped it. It makes him wonder how else the embers are protecting her...

That night, Nyktos visits Sera in her bedchambers in shadow form, watching as she pleasures herself and reaching out to stroke her with titillating tendrils of darkness, seeking shadow fingers.

It's one of the most erotic images I've ever received via a vision. I'm fanning myself just thinking about it.

Later, Sera asks if he plans to go to war with Kolis, and he tries not to answer. Then he tells her about the Books of the Dead.

Sera goads him, trying to get a reaction out of him by mentioning other lovers. He tells her she will be *very* selective whom she spends her time with and how, so long as she's his Consort. Translation: she will be with nobody but him. He then adds that what he did to the murderous gods in the throne room will pale in comparison to what he'll do to any who dare satisfy her needs.

Suddenly, he realizes they're about to have company and asks if she has her dagger on her. He orders her to remain on his lap and apologizes for how he's about to behave.

Attes arrives, arrogance on full display and asking questions Nyktos doesn't want to answer. He tells the other Primal that Sera is a godling on the cusp of her Culling, then threatens to cut his eyes from his sockets and feed them to Attes's war horse, Setti, if he keeps looking at Sera as he is.

Attes asks Nyktos why he killed the Cimmerian and especially Dorcan, saying he thought the two were friends.

The other Primal inquires how a god Ascended in the Shadowlands, and Nyktos says it must have been Kolis. When Attes suggests that Nyktos still has embers of Life, he laughs. All the questions and insinuations make Nyktos wonder if Attes came out of curiosity or on Kolis's behalf. Then, to make an already unpleasant visit worse, Attes informs Nyktos that Kolis is denying the coronation and will be summoning the couple to his Court soon.

Nyktos tells the other Primal to leave before he needs to be carried out.

When he finally goes, Nyktos tells Sera to argue with him to distract him from going after Attes, because if he does, it won't end well. When she asks him about what will happen in Dalos, he explains that he'll lie—he's had to convince Kolis of many things over the years.

He goes on to tell her that Attes was provoking her and explains how. He reveals that only another Primal would be immune to Attes's gifts, which could out her true nature. He says it could have been worse. Kolis could have forbidden him from taking a Consort at all. While things aren't good, he once again promises not to let Kolis touch her.

Sera argues with him, telling him that she won't be the reason for more death. He pushes back and says she never was. He knows she won't hide, but he won't put her in danger.

Nyktos goes to her room later and reminds her that she promised not to go after Kolis. He also remarks that he lives in constant fear of not being able to control himself around her. He apologizes for questioning her motives earlier, then promises not to hide the summons from her.

During training later, he squares off with Sera. She cuts his hair during their sparring, and he tells her he'd never dare cut *her* hair—we know how much he loves it. As they face off, she makes a list of demands, saying he's flesh and blood and she's flesh and fire. He tells her that all she had to do was ask to train—that being her first request. He asks her what her other demands are. As she lists them, he tells her he's not just keeping the embers safe, he's also safeguarding her. He disarms her but stiffens when she reminds him that he won't claim her. Catching him off guard, she holds a dagger to his throat, and he says *he'll* be the one to train her.

Nyktos runs a bath for Sera later, telling her to use his tub at her discretion, knowing she likely still has post-traumatic stress about hers.

What a sweetie.

When she takes longer than expected in the tub, he checks on her and finds her asleep. He warms the water for her with a touch, and when she wakes, he's surprised that she lets him still look upon her *unmentionables*. As he watches her, he breathes that everything she does is seductive.

She tells him that it's her choice to want him and says she's at least brave enough to admit it. He confesses to wanting her and thinking about being with her, even when he's not looking at her. He's been dwelling on the deal she offered in his office—pleasure for the sake of pleasure—and tried convincing himself she hadn't known he was in her chambers the other night as shadows. He admits he wants her. Enjoys her boldness and rebellion. Then asks her if what he said was a brave and real enough confession.

Sera taunts and teases Nyktos, prompting him to call her *liessa* again. She finally pleasures him, and he gets into the tub. He lifts her onto the ledge and returns the favor. As he feeds slightly from her most delicate places, she calls him Ash, reestablishing some of their connectedness and making him growl. When they finish playing in the tub, he calls her beautiful and carries her to bed.

Nyktos learns that Sera was not to be known in her kingdom. She was kept hidden away as if she didn't exist. He also learns she was veiled and never acknowledged as a Princess. She was virtually a ghost. He tells her she was *never* a ghost to him.

I love that so much. All anyone wants is to be seen. Understood. Even if you don't particularly like or engage in socialization, as with Sera, we just want someone to look and *see*. We want to be alive for someone other than ourselves.

After he holds court in the city, Nyktos and Sera discuss their intimate endeavors and how Nyktos can heal the wounds he creates. They have dinner together, something she requested when they sparred, and he tells her about his day. He realizes that Sera is used to blaming herself for just about everything and reminds her she didn't fail. He states that he expects her to live longer than it takes them to transfer the embers.

Talk turns to the Pools of Divanash, and they realize that time isn't on their side. The plan is to go in three days. Nyktos confesses that he worried Sera would feel like he was trying to control her and didn't like it. He then admits that he's having a hard time finding balance between protecting her and doing what needs to be done.

They talk about her demands and discuss Dorcan. Sera tells him it's okay to have friends and apologizes that he had to kill another because of her. He argues that it's not okay to care for others if doing so gets them tortured and killed.

They discuss Kolis a bit more, and he tells her that the King of Gods treats him and all the other Primals the same, and they fall out of favor as often as he changes clothes. Sera tells him she hopes their plan works, but not because she's thinking about the future. He reminds her that he's not good, tells her not to mistake his handling of her as him being good, and urges her to keep that in mind.

He's good. He's so very good...he just doesn't like to admit it. But with Nyktos, his goodness is a strength that not many have, and countless others can only hope to achieve.

He reminds her that she was willing to sacrifice herself for others and is thus good, but there is no such thing as a *good* Primal. He adds that the embers don't make her good or bad either.

Nyktos counts Sera's freckles as he disrobes her and decides he needs to name the constellation of birthmarks on her thigh. They make love, and his appearance shifts—skin becomes harder, shadows gathering under his flesh, eather filling the veins in his eyes. He calls her *liessa* again as he finds his release.

Before she wakes, he leaves, but returns to draw her a bath and have breakfast. As they set out for the mortal realm, he promises to bring her back to her lake once it's safe enough to do so, and tells her she can go as often as she'd like. He then explains to Sera what mortals sensing him feel, and relays that their self-preservation instincts don't bother him.

Once in Lasania, Nyktos takes Sera's hand as they approach Ezra, remarking that she's holding a town hall. He scares a guard into going to the new Queen.

When Sera talks to Ezra about some of the things that have happened, Nyktos is shocked that Ezmeria seems to believe her without question.

Ezra confesses to doubting that Sera could make him fall for her and admits she thought she'd likely just get impatient and stab him, getting herself killed in the process. It makes him laugh.

Calliphe appears, and Nyktos tells her that he wanted to kill her right along with Tavius when he came to claim his Consort, but her daughter spared her the Abyss. He adds that she should thank Sera.

Later, he retires to his office and is writing in the Book of the Dead when Sera comes in. He takes her to the basement in the House of Haides and tells her about the bone chains. Then, he takes her to the pool room, knowing she'll enjoy it.

Nyktos reveals to Sera how he used to check on her before her seventeenth birthday and tells her how he was drawn to her lake. He says he's wanted to show her his pool for a while.

His plan is to draw the eather out of Sera, so he goads her into using it on him. He tells her that he finds it amusing that she hates when he says "please" and relays that he'll reward her with a swim and sex if she behaves. They fight hand-to-hand to draw out the eather.

Nyktos can feel it ramping up in Sera and knows she can summon it and use it with will alone. He tells her to do so. Eventually, he pins her to the table, and Sera tells him that she likes submitting to him. He has his wicked way with her right there on the stone and tells her she's always safe with him, calling her *liessa* once more.

They float in the pool, and he tells her about Lathan's anxiety, discussing the breathing techniques both she and Lathan used. He tells her she's one of the strongest people he's ever met, both physically and mentally—mortal or otherwise. With or without the embers. They play for a while more and then go about the rest of their day.

Nyktos trains in the yard with the guards while Sera spends time with Aios and the younglings. Later, he tells Sera about the Primal *notam* and explains why he thinks Nektas's eyes flashed blue for her when they did—it could mean she's closer to Ascending than they realize.

They ready themselves for their trip to the Pillars, and he kisses her in full view of the guards, telling her he's been looking for a reason to. She tells him he doesn't *need* a reason to kiss her and can do it whenever he wants.

He gives her a horse named Gala, thinking nothing of it since it's customary to give a gift for a wedding. When she worries that she doesn't have something for him, he tells her the embers are his gift.

The plan is to ride on Gala with her to the Pillars and then take Odin back to the House of Haides. During their journey, he reveals that he hasn't accepted his way of life and has been planning to destroy Kolis or entomb him since the moment he Ascended. He explains what will happen if it comes to that and how many will likely die. He tells her he felt incapable of avoiding war until he learned she had the embers. Now, he has hope. But he warns her that Kolis has already started setting his sights on the mortal realm.

He's confident his plan will work, and Kolis will be stripped of his glory and weakened enough to be entombed. Still, he knows he won't go down easily. Nyktos shows Sera the poppy flower he's talked to her about before and tells her that it gives him hope—like she does.

He asks her if the need to use the embers wears on her and knows she's lying when she tells him it doesn't. He confirms that having embers is enough to make Sera feel like Eythos did, and then repeats what Nektas said to her before—that she is stronger than she realizes. He adds that *she* is strong, not the embers.

He and Nektas tell Sera about the riders when they come upon them, explaining that their names mean war, pestilence, and hunger. When they ride, they bring about the end to wherever they travel because death always follows them. Nyktos is awed when they bow to Sera and says he's never seen them do that before.

He gives her two swords to take with her, just in case, and tells Nektas that Sera is very important to him. She suddenly blurts out that she wants to be his Consort, freezing him to the spot. He reminds her to breathe and stay calm, then kisses her hands and tells her he'll be waiting for her when she and Nektas return from the Pools.

Veses shows up to collect on her end of their bargain, and Nyktos finds himself on the settee in his office, white-knuckling the arm as the Primal straddles him and feeds from his throat. Unfortunately, Sera sees what's going on and doesn't take it well. She heads down to the pool chamber and loses it, nearly destroying the entire palace. He tries to calm her but is eventually forced to use compulsion on her, something he apologizes for.

When Sera wakes, Nyktos is at the Pillars, dealing with some nervous souls. He returns and goes to see her, apologizing again for the compulsion and what she thought she saw. He still won't tell her what's happening, though. When Sera lashes out, saying he was with Veses just hours after she told him she wanted to be his Consort, he flinches and apologizes again. He adds that he never wants to hurt her and reiterates that he was a virgin when they met and has never wanted anyone but her. Ever.

Sera asks him *what* she saw if it wasn't what she thought, and he tells her it's complicated. She breaks off their pleasure-for-the-sake-of-pleasure deal and tells him she wants her freedom from him once the embers are out of her.

Later, Sera comes to talk to him about Irelone and going to see Delfai where the God of Divination is with Kayleigh Balfour. Nyktos tells her she can have all the time she wants and says he's going with her—he needs to know exactly what's said so he can remove the embers correctly. However, he asks her to wait another day since Kyn's draken is near.

He reveals that other Primals know he has a sizable army, though nobody knows how big it is. Grudgingly, he tells her that he realizes he needs to learn to deal with her wanting to help and needing to fight, even though he worries every second that she'll be killed.

Nyktos informs her they'll shadowstep to Irelone since there are no gateways near that Nyktos trusts. He brings up the nymphs she and Nektas encountered on their way back from the Vale, saying she shouldn't have been able to kill one, and then remarks that he doesn't like how things have become between them. She's acting like she was trained to—empty and without emotion. He doesn't like it at all.

Kolis summons them, a reddish black circle with a slash through it appearing in the center of Nyktos's palm, burning and stinging and causing his eyes to fill with eather.

He tells Sera and everyone that Kolis will sense she's not an ordinary godling like he tried to get Attes to believe. He hopes to use the excuse that she's taken his blood to explain it away.

He reiterates that they'll go to Delfai first and then answer the summons, but Sera insists they go to Dalos first.

Nyktos realizes that things are different now, but he tells her they need to act like they did with Attes. She tells him she was never pretending to be infatuated with him. It was never an act. He asks her if it's too late for her wanting to be his Consort and to serve the Shadowlands and Iliseeum. He's not sure why he brings it up, but he wants to know why she wanted something he could never give her. He then tells her she deserves someone who will love her unconditionally and irrevocably. Someone who's brave enough to tell her how they feel.

Nyktos informs Sera there will be war if Kolis recognizes her as Sotoria and tries to keep her. He says he'll leave Dalos in ruins if the King of Gods makes even a single move for her. Sera pleads with him not to intervene if Kolis recognizes her. He snarls and tells her the embers aren't the only important thing. She is. He adds that she's asking him to do what he's had to do his whole life: leave others behind to suffer. To live and be dead inside.

He tells her that even if he had his *kardia*, he'd be unable to love after what he's had to do. If he were to leave her to Kolis, any goodness remaining in him would be gone for sure, and he'd become something worse than the false Primal of Life.

He prepares her for their shadowstep and tells her what to expect, explaining that one hundred and ten of the blood drops tattooed on his flesh are from lives Kolis made him take. He reminds her she's good and not a monster, and then they step into Dalos.

They arrive to bodies strung up, and Nyktos tries to calm Sera when she sees them, her eather running wild. She tells him to stop her, and he kisses her, calling shadows to block out her light and reaction.

Attes interrupts, and Nyktos doesn't hide his ire, telling him he seems bound and determined to lose his eyes.

Later, talking to Dyses, he reinforces that Sera is his Consort. Dyses lashes out and tells Sera to bow. Nyktos orders her not to and tells Dyses she'll bow to those deserving respect. He shadowsteps behind the male and rips out his heart, saying *he* will bow to *Sera*. Later, he remarks that, like Dyses, none of Kolis's servants have felt right for a very long time. He sensed no soul in Dyses when he killed him.

They talk about random things—Nyktos's jealousy, Dyses, the family crest, the significance of the wolf and the hawk... When Sera says she saw a silver hawk in the Dying Woods, he tells her it's not possible, insisting that not even they would enter those woods—we know that's not true, since it was Attes in his *nota* form.

Hanan riles Nyktos about the Ascension of a god in his Court and him killing those he sent to the Shadowlands, and Nyktos threatens him, then throws him across the floor. When Hanan rails about Bele's Ascension, Nyktos plays dumb, saying it had to be Kolis, and then taunts Hanan about doubting his King's power.

Nyktos helps Sera breathe and bow and then tells Kolis that Sera's father is a god, and her mother is mortal, trying to throw him off about her eather. He reiterates that Kolis is only sensing Nyktos's blood in her. When Kolis moves to touch Sera's hair, Nyktos catches his hand and tells Kolis he'll do to him what Kolis has done to those who touch things that belong to *him*, then announces that Sera is not to be touched by *anyone* but him.

Playing his part, Nyktos apologizes to Kolis for not seeking approval for the coronation. When questioned about what he did to Dyses, he simply says he didn't like the male's tone. He then tells Kolis that he, too, felt a god Ascend and searched for the source, finding nothing. He assumed it was Kolis. Hanan challenges him again, and he argues that only the Primal of Life can Ascend a god.

Dyses enters the room, alive and well, making Nyktos stiffen. Still, he tells Kolis he was surprised by the Ascension for the same reason Attes was: it'd been a long time. He states that the dakkais in the Shadowlands surprised him, as well. He's told it was simply bad timing. The dakkais were dispatched because Nyktos didn't seek approval to take Sera as his Consort.

I call bullshit.

Sera tries to take the blame, saying it was her fault and trying to intervene. It makes Nyktos furious. He's told to be quiet, or it will not be he who suffers.

Kolis plays his sick little game and asks Nyktos what the penalty is for disrespect. He answers that it's a life. Kolis explains that Sera must kill a young draken—Thad—as recompense. Nyktos tries to intervene again, but he's told to stay silent or Kolis will rip out Sera's heart, and then warns that if anyone else pays the price for her, *she* will pay with her blood.

After the horrible ordeal, and once they return to the Shadowlands, Sera asks him to take her to Vathi. He tells her that the draken are like gods; therefore, her bringing someone back to life will not result in someone else losing theirs. However, she can't do anything to help the young draken. It would be felt.

He ends up taking her to Vathi anyway and orders Attes to retrieve Thad. Nyktos tries to comfort Sera, telling her not to thank him and explaining that Kolis was making Kyn their enemy by forcing her to take the life of a draken from his

Court. When questioned, he tells Sera that it's too late for them to wonder if they can trust Attes.

Sera goes to the young draken, and Nyktos tells Attes to never speak of what he sees, threatening that he'll level Vathi and hunt the other Primal down if he does.

After Sera brings Thad back to life, Nyktos orders Attes to keep the lad hidden and then tells him to bring him to the Shadowlands where Nektas can keep him safe. He warns Attes that Kolis may send dakkais after feeling the power surge and asks why the other Primal didn't go to Kolis with his suspicions to gain favor. Attes says that he remembers who Nyktos's father was and who Nyktos was meant to be.

Nyktos tells Sera that he trusts Attes with the secret and assumes he'll keep quiet, at least until the coronation. He then asks Sera why she spoke out. He laments that she doesn't deserve to have this done to her and is surprised when she says that he doesn't either. He quips that he's used to it and is stunned when she says that she did it for *him*. He insists he doesn't deserve it.

They discuss Dyses' resurrection and the Revenants. Nyktos hopes Kolis doesn't have a lot of them. He knows Dyses isn't a demis—a false god created when a god Ascends a mortal—and is certain that Kolis doesn't have embers of life any longer. So, he's not sure what to think of his *creations*.

Nyktos remembers what Gemma said about what she saw and surmises that she encountered Revenants in different stages of creation. No matter, Kolis found a way to bring about life without the necessary embers—something to convince other Courts that he still has the power.

Nyktos knows there's no way Kolis believes that he actually thinks it was the false Primal of Life who Ascended Bele. He was only saving face. He just wishes they could have talked to Attes about Dyses.

Nyktos reminds Sera that Kolis doesn't recognize her as Sotoria. He feels rage and asks what's up, saying it felt different. Tasted different. She tells him it wasn't only her anger. It was also Sotoria's. Nyktos surmises that Holland was wrong. Sera's not the reincarnation. There are two souls in her—hers *and* Sotoria's.

Nyktos leaves to deal with a bunch of roaming Shades. When he gets back, Bele informs him that Veses knows about Sera. He blasts the other Primal with eather after telling her to shut up when she's trying to explain why she attacked Sera. He orders that Veses be locked in one of the cells under the House of Haides.

He's told that Veses wanted to kill Sera, not tell Kolis, and she freaked out after nearly killing Reaver and seeing Sera save him. After everything that happened, Nyktos knows it was Veses who set the Shades free. He then learns that she also sent the draken that attacked them *and* released the entombed gods.

Taking care of Sera, Nyktos laughs at her stabbing Veses and urges her to feed. He gets her to take blood and allows her to see his memory of her training request. He explains it to her, and then tells her he'll wait for her in his chambers.

Sera admits to Nyktos she doesn't hate him, and it enflames him. He orders her to fuck him and tells her that nothing feels like she does. She reminds him that he can feed if he wants, but he doesn't—won't—he doesn't think he deserves it.

Nyktos realizes he can't keep Veses locked up, but he also can't release her because she'll go to Kolis and likely won't respect the Court rules. He explains to Sera how Veses could feel her but not Kolis—it's because she's the Primal of the Rites.

Later, the day of the coronation, Nyktos comes to Sera and takes her from Aios, telling her to breathe and calling her *liessa*. He uses shadows to block them from view as she calms herself and informs Sera she doesn't have to wear the crown after tonight. She tells him that she still wants to be his Consort and calls him Ash. It touches him deeply.

During the coronation, he takes the crown from Rhain and then bows to Sera, surprising everyone in attendance. He crowns her, revealing her title—the One who is born of Blood and Ash, *the* Light and the Fire, and *the* Brightest Moon. The imprints appear, shocking everyone, and he declares that the Arae have given them their blessing. He explains that the imprints and blessings belong to her and admits he fibbed a little so everyone would think the Fates had blessed the union.

Nyktos tells Sera about Keella, the Primal of Rebirth. When asked if the Primal knows about Sotoria's soul being in Sera, he says he isn't sure since it wasn't really a rebirth.

Sera says she likes her title, and it gladdens him. There is some of Penellaphe's prophecy in it, but he kept thinking about her hair and how it reminds him of moonlight. When she asks about the blood and ash part, he tells her the different symbolism.

Attes asks for a moment to speak with them, and while cool in the exchange, Ash agrees and says he will make time. He feels satisfaction from Sera and asks her why. She tells him that it's because she's being included. That prompts him to say that he hates she was made to feel unimportant for so long and loathes that he ever contributed to it. He makes sure she understands that she's both seen and heard and calls her *liessa*, telling her she will always matter as he kisses her temple.

When Sera meets Keella, the Primal remarks that Sera's title may be another blessing. Nyktos is asked about his inspiration for it, and he confesses it was because of her hair. Before she leaves, Keella tells him that his father would be proud of him.

Nyktos keeps his hand on Sera's where it rests on her lap to ground her during the greetings. Finally, the crowns are removed, and Nyktos tells Sera the soldiers will make sure the road ahead to Irelone is safe. He asks her to sit with him and massages her neck. When she calls him Ash again, he tenses. She asks him if he doesn't like it, and he confesses that he missed hearing it from her.

He asks her what changed her mind about the coronation and made her want it. When she tells him, he reveals what's been on his mind: her calling him Ash in her coronation dress, seeing her out of the dress, seeing her naked on the throne, and seeing her bare with nothing but the crown on. He then wonders if he's worthy of exploring those obsessions and decides he doesn't care if he is. He's too greedy and selfish to care. When he finds her dagger, he tells her that seeing her with nothing on but her dagger has taken second place, and that first place has been replaced by her calling him Ash when she comes. It's the only thing he wants.

Sera tells him she needs him inside her and does, indeed, call him Ash with her pleasure.

They talk about her thoughts on the coronation, Vathi, the dakkais, and Keella and Sotoria. He tells her that Keella is one of the few Primals he somewhat trusts. The discussion then shifts to their meeting with Delfai, and he tells her he's excited about learning how to transfer the embers. He reiterates that her life being saved is what matters most, not him becoming the Primal of Life.

When he asks about what changed her mind about the coronation, she tells him that her emotions didn't change, only how she wanted to proceed. Sera projects, and Ash tastes chocolate and strawberries.

Love!

She confesses that she knows the whole story about Veses, and he shatters the glass in his hand. She digs out the slivers, and he asks if she's only calling him Ash now out of pity. She denies it and tells him she'll kill Veses if he doesn't. He tells her about things with Veses and how Veses really wants Kolis. He thanks Sera for simply being herself and kisses her, about to share a wish. Only he stops himself before he gives it voice.

He mentions being hungry, and she urges him to feed. He does and has sex with her, once again saying he wishes...but never finishing the sentiment.

They go to Irelone, and Nyktos comforts Sera, telling her the embers will be out of her soon. He can taste her anxiety and asks her what it feels like. She tells him, and he says he wishes he could do something to change how it feels for her.

When the guards refuse them entry to the keep, he lets loose a display of power and leaves them riches.

He and Sera meet with Kayleigh, and he apologizes for his behavior and that of others like him, then tells her who he is and who Sera was meant to be.

They meet Delfai and find him a rambling sort. Nyktos interrupts the God of Divination and explains why they came. They learn about the Star diamond and how it's used, and Nyktos is stunned to find out how easy the ember removal process is.

Then they learn that Kolis has the embers, but they're not needed to remove the ones in Sera. When Delfai refers to Sera as a *vessel*, it infuriates Ash. The god apologizes and goes into more detail on how to remove the embers from Sera. But...there's a catch. Ash will have to Ascend her, and that means she will die.

Ash is close to losing control when he learns they cannot transfer the embers without killing Sera. He refuses to believe it and argues. He then learns that his father only survived it because he was born a god and destined to Ascend. The embers belonged to him. They don't belong to Sera; they were only hidden in her.

He's told there are three options: Nyktos becomes the true Primal of Life and restores the balance to the realms, someone else takes the embers, or Sera completes her Ascension—meaning she'll die anyway.

Nyktos shadowsteps and grasps Delfai by the throat, snarling that he won't kill Sera and saying the option is unacceptable. He takes his true form and plans to send Delfai to the Abyss, but Sera pleads with him not to hurt the God of Divination and says he doesn't deserve it. And Ash doesn't deserve another mark. Finally, he drops Delfai.

Sera urges Ash that he has to do it. He refuses and confesses that he figured draining her completely was a possibility, but he knew that wasn't how Kolis did it, so he figured there was another way. He considers getting The Star and using that, but she reminds him that removing the embers will kill her either way. Still, he's thrilled when she admits that she doesn't want to die—it's about time she values her life.

She reveals she wants to live but the realms *need* to. And that's all that matters. He erupts, telling her that *she* matters, not the realms. She calls him Ash again, and he begs her not to do that when she's talking about him killing her.

When she insists that he did nothing wrong—meaning him removing his *kardia*—he gets furious. He laments that he could have saved her. She argues that there was no guarantee he would have loved her. He tells her he would have. That nothing could have stopped him.

She orders him to kiss her, and he does, loosing a soul-torn groan. They have sex, and he confesses that he wishes he'd never had his *kardia* removed. He never wanted to know love before her. His eyes glaze over in red as he cries Primal tears of grief.

Sera asks him to take her to her lake when the time comes so she can die there, and he promises.

When they return to the Shadowlands, they realize something is wrong. They're under attack. He jumps from the balcony to the ground, and Saion updates him. He checks his emotions and finds bodies in the west courtyard, stumbling back at the horror. Saion informs him where Kyn is, and Nyktos orders him to summon the armies.

He takes his true form and rises into the sky to fight Davon, the draken, becoming a storm. He notices that Sera, Rhain, Rhahar, and Saion are unable to get to the House of Haides, so he pours Primal mist out of himself, telling Sera to *run* in her mind.

As shadows swallow the courtyard, Ash shouts for Sera and sees Attes with her. He repeatedly roars and shouts for her, trying to get to her. He tears a Cimmerian apart. Vaporizes a dakkai with a touch. She is only yards away, her eyes locked on his, and then...she disappears, swallowed by smoke and shadows.

The next time he sees her, he waits outside of Cor Palace, crouched amid the trees.

As a silvery-white wolf.

He watches as Sera succumbs to Kolis's sick obsession and attacks. He ends up killing Hanan and tells Kolis to get his hands off his wife. He threatens to kill his uncle and they battle, Kolis telling him that he's started a war.

Sera compels him and Kolis to stop fighting and threatens to take her life. He pleads with her not to. Eventually, Kolis injures him enough by stabbing him repeatedly that he is taken into custody and imprisoned in the Carcers.

While in stasis, he shares dreams with Sera and tells her to make Kolis aware that only he can Ascend her. Once she does, she should then summon the Fates.

During his time in the Carcers, Kolis watches him and then incapacitates him after he wakes. He can't blame him. Not really. He was prepared to do *anything* to get to Sera.

When Sera takes Kolis down, it weakens the wards. Between that and feeling what Sera is, he escapes and comes for her. He takes out any and all in his path, and then finds her nearly collapsed.

Sera can barely talk but manages to ask if she's dreaming. He tells her it's real. When she asks if he's okay, he laughs, reminding her that she was also imprisoned and likely dealt with much more than just some retaliation and sleep.

They discuss Veses a bit and what to do about Kolis. They also talk about what happened to her in Dalos, and Sera has to soothe his anger. She tells him he needs to take her somewhere safe and remove the embers.

Elias comes in, and Ash almost kills him until Sera assures him that he's a friend and the god swears his fealty to Sera.

Attes arrives and urges them to get moving. When Ash moves to attack him, Attes pleads his case, and Sera tells Ash the other Primal can be trusted—he saved her life more than once.

She gets dizzy, and notices she'd started shifting into her Primal form.

Just as they're about to shadowstep, Sera remembers The Star and tells them they need to get it. They talk how to go about doing that, and she tells Ash that his father's soul is in the diamond. He asks if she's sure, and she confirms.

Ash can't feel the soul within the diamond, but Sera assures him it's in there. She wonders how they can put Sotoria's soul in the stone, and Ash says Keella should know how to get a soul both in and out.

He shadowsteps them to some hot springs in the mortal realm and listens as Sera relays what she knows about his father and uncle. When he asks to hold The Star, she doesn't let him, explaining that she doesn't want him to see what she did.

He and Sera take some time for themselves and get lost in each other for a bit.

As they spend time together, they talk about everything that's happened and catch one another up, talking about what things mean and what's next. They discuss his *nota* and Primal forms, then he heads to the Bonelands to get them some clothes.

Talk turns to Attes, and Ash makes it clear that he still doesn't trust the Primal, but Sera tries to make him understand why Attes could never be loyal to Kolis. Then, she tells him what Phanos did. He starts thinking of the ways he could use that to his advantage to save her, but she stops him and insists that nobody else will give their life to save hers.

He takes her to the Bonelands and tells her how the Ancients, connected to all living things, became displeased with what the mortals were doing. They concluded that mortals and the land could not coexist and chose to cleanse the land. They then created the Primals, splitting their essence between them and sharing the balance. The Primals and gods eventually joined the mortals to battle the Ancients.

He asks Sera how she's feeling, and she admits that she's tired and achy.

Sera struggles to climb the stairs, and Ash helps her. Saion and Rhahar arrive, and both embrace Ash. Then Lailah joins, followed by Rhain.

Ash tells the assembled group that Sera saved him, and Rhain says many of them wouldn't be there if it weren't for her.

They all discuss The Star, and Keella comes forward, telling them what they need to do. Sera pulls Eythos free and then falls unconscious.

Ash takes Sera to Keella's Court when she passes out. After she wakes, she apologizes to him for cutting his time with Eythos short, and he tells her his father was ready to go. He relays that Eythos told him he was proud of him and then told him to remember what they said to each other by the Red River. The problem is, he doesn't remember what that was.

Realizing that Ash gave her blood, she chastises him. They bicker as usual, and Nektas arrives, laughing that they're arguing.

Attes, Ash, and Sera argue about Sotoria, and Sera makes them understand that the soul is alive. Attes mentions how he met her after Kolis brought her back. Then they all discuss what happens if the embers die with Sera. They talk about The Star being able to hold both the embers and a soul, and what needs to happen for them to end Kolis.

Sera says there will be war, and Ash insists he only cares about her. Attes says it's way bigger than that, and Ash says she matters. Sera tells him she loves him, and he feels overwhelming emotions toward her.

Keella asks Ash if he has sensed dual souls. He says he only ever feels Sera's. Keella tells him he needs to anchor himself to his Consort's soul. He does.

Ash walks up as Sera is talking to Rhain. He reads her emotions, and she tells him to stop.

Saion comes then and jokes that they're fighting again. Rhahar joins, and they settle a bet. Saion said they couldn't go more than an hour without arguing. Sera turns to Ash and jokes that they're his friends. He says they *were*, giving them a look.

Sera tells Ash to take her to the lake, reminding him that he promised. He can do nothing but obey, even though it breaks his heart.

He watches as the gods all bow to his wife and give her the utmost respect.

Sera tells Ash there's something she wants to talk about. He can't look at her. When she notices, he tells her that even if he's not looking at her, she is all he sees.

She tells him she loves him and says it's not his fault, making him understand. He tries but then lists all the things he'd rather be doing. Anything but what they are. She continues, telling him she wants him to live. Be King. He argues that it's her place, and she tells him she doesn't want him to be alone. She wants him to love.

He gets angry, and she makes him promise. Begrudgingly, he does. Then, they show each other with their bodies how much they care and cement that their connection goes beyond the realms.

He tells her all the things he adores about her and says he never wanted until her. Thunder booms, and Ash realizes that Kolis has been found. Sera laments being out of time but tells him everything she wanted and says that he gave her all of it. She tells him that she loves him again and then says it's time.

He takes her into the water and feeds. She begins to fade, and Ash says fuck the embers and tells her to take his blood. He says he won't let her go. He'll Ascend her.

She asks what she'll become, and he says he isn't sure. She begs him to take the embers, but he tells her to shut the fuck up and says if he loses her, the realms and everything in them are gone—he'll destroy it all. He tells her not to die. Says fuck the greater good. She tells him *he's* good.

Finally, she drinks. When she wakes, a shockwave bursts free and knocks him back.

Ash tells Sera stories while she's in stasis. He tells her how unprepared he was for how alive he feels with her. He admits he could still feel after his *kardia* was removed, just not strongly. Not until her. He says he should have known from their first kiss what they were to each other.

He reminisces about their first few meetings, her bravery in going to Kolis alone, her misplaced loyalties.

When Ash says he wanted to be strong like Eythos, Nektas says it had nothing to do with strength. He talks about how Eythos was after Mycella's death, and Ash says he would have destroyed the realms and everything in them if he'd lost Sera.

Nektas reminds Ash that he saved her, and Ash tells Sera he'll be waiting for her.

She starts to wake, and Ash tells her not to rush it. He reminds her of how they are together. How they like to be. He tells her she needs him. His blood. Says he's hers.

She intones that the Primal of Life has never fed from the Primal of Death before. They're meant to be two halves of a cycle but separate. He insists that all of him is hers, and she feeds.

After, he asks if she knows him, and she says she always will.

Ash tells her he was terrified he'd lose her. She says he didn't; he saved her. He adds that he was afraid she wouldn't remember and that he'd still lose her. She insists he won't. Ever. He tenses and tells her that when he releases her, she should run, saying he needs her too much and won't be able to control himself. He'll become his other self. She says she trusts him. Tells him she's his. Urges him to take her.

He does, using his shadow tendrils to bring her extra pleasure. He tells her that he loves her and says he's not sure when it started. She says she thought she'd die without ever knowing what his love felt like. He says he would never allow that and that he'll spend eternity making sure she knows how deeply his feelings run.

Nektas asks if they're okay, and Ash threatens him. When Sera says she's now the Queen, Ash agrees and adds that he's her Consort. She corrects him and calls him her King.

He agrees.

The King then fucks his Queen.

Ash feels Sera tensing when he goes to feed and knows that more happened in Dalos than she's letting on. He hopes she will tell him eventually. He mentions that every Primal felt her Ascension and makes her understand that they'll deal with whatever comes. Together.

He comes clean about why he didn't take her as his Consort initially. Part of it was to keep her unknown to Kolis, but also because he had a dream the night she was born. It was her at her lake, smiling at him. Then, he saw her dying, and him destroying everything. It terrified him so much he had his *kardia* removed right before he brought Sera to Iliseeum.

He laments what his choices meant for her life and insists he was a coward. She denies it, but he tells her what the vision showed him. His actions showed that he'd fallen in love. So, he tried to stop it. He tells her he fell in love anyway, and she tells him she felt more than love when he held her in the lake. Ash says there's only one reason for that. They're heartmates.

He talks about how when the Arae see threads of fate joining, they cannot intervene. He says their joined souls created the first-ever Queen of the Gods. They talk about the Arae pushing the boundaries of what's allowed and what's considered interference.

When Sera goes out onto the balcony, he follows her, and they take in the life that's returning to the realm.

Ash and Sera share declarations of love, and he tells her that he wants them to trust each other, adding that he'll always see her as strong no matter what. He hints that he thinks he knows what happened to her in Dalos, and they talk more about Rhain. She urges Ash not to do or say anything about what happened when her plans were first revealed. He agrees.

Sera tells Ash what Holland really said to her the day he came with Penellaphe. That love is more powerful than the Fates. They think and talk about how powerful life is.

She asks Ash to tell her again that he loves her, and he does. Repeatedly. Happily. And then they make love.

EYTHOS †

Primal of Life turned Primal of Death
Court: Dalos/The Shadowlands

Hair: Shoulder-length. Black.
Eyes: Silver.
Facial features: Bronze skin. Strong jaw. Broad cheekbones. Straight nose. Wide mouth.
Personality: Clever. Strategic. Wise. Kind. Generous. Fair. Protective.
Habits/Mannerisms/Strengths/Weaknesses: Fascinated by silver hawks. Partial to wolves—can even shift into one. Fascinated by life—especially mortals.
Other: Not able to see souls but knew their names and lives. Things that represent him = silver, winged masks like the silver hawk.
Background: Was the Primal God of Life until Kolis switched fates; then he became the Primal God of Death.
Family: Consort = Mycella †. Son = Nyktos. Twin = Kolis.

EYTHOS'S JOURNEY TO DATE:

My knowledge of Eythos only comes in the form of stories. So, that is how I shall relay Eythos's journey…

A very long time ago, a powerful Primal befriended the dragons. He wanted to learn their stories, and being young, was rather impulsive. He knew one way to talk to them was to give them a voice by bestowing on them a godly form—allowing them to shift between the two. This Primal was Eythos, the then Primal God of Life. But the draken aren't the only creatures the young god gave dual lives to.

Eythos had an identical twin—Kolis. One brother was fated to represent life, and the other death. Eythos was the Primal of Life, and Kolis was the Primal of Death. They ruled together for eons as they were meant to. Until…Kolis fell in love. Or, more accurately, he became obsessed.

But things began even before that. It all started long before Lasania was even a kingdom in the mortal realm. It's unknown if the relationship between the brothers was always strained, or if there was peace between them at one time. Regardless, they were always competitive. And there was also an issue of jealousy.

The Primal God of Life was worshipped and loved by gods and mortals alike, and Eythos was a fair King, kind and generous. He was fascinated with all life, especially the mortals. Even when he became the Primal God of Death—which I'll get to in a minute—he was awed by everything mortals could accomplish in what even gods would consider an incredibly short time. He interacted with them, as many Primals did at the time.

Kolis, on the other hand, was respected but feared and never really welcomed as a necessary step in life, a doorway to the next stage. When Kolis entered the mortal realm, those who saw him cowered and refused to look him in the eye.

On one trip, Kolis saw a beautiful young woman picking flowers for her sister's wedding. This woman was named Sotoria. Kolis watched her, and it was love at first sight. He was utterly besotted with her and stepped out of the trees to speak with the beauty. Back then, mortals knew what the Primal God of Death looked like since paintings and sculptures captured his features, just like his brother's, the Primal God of Life. Sotoria knew who Kolis was when he approached her and ran away in fear, plummeting to her death from the Cliffs of Sorrow.

Kolis begged Eythos to restore Sotoria's life, an act Eythos could do and had done in the past as the Primal God of Life, but he had rules that governed *when* he granted life. One of those guidelines was that he would not take a soul from the Vale. Yes, Sotoria had died young and far too soon, but she had accepted her death. Her soul arrived in the Shadowlands, passed through the Pillars, and entered the Vale within minutes of her death. And Eythos would not pull a soul from the Vale. It was wrong and forbidden to both him and Kolis.

Eythos tried to remind his brother of that. When that failed, he attempted to get Kolis to understand that it wasn't fair to grant life to one, only to refuse another of equal worth. But that was also one of Eythos's flaws. He believed he could decide if a person was worthy or not. And maybe as the Primal God of Life, he could... But still.

Maybe it was hubris, but Eythos didn't realize his power could be turned on him—especially not by his brother. If he hadn't used his gift on the mortals, then perhaps Kolis wouldn't have expected him to do it with Sotoria. But Eythos's refusal to do as his twin asked with the woman he believed he loved started everything—hundreds of years of pain and suffering for many innocents. Eons of Eythos regretting what he chose and chose not to do.

Nothing happened at first, and Eythos believed Kolis had accepted his decision to maintain the balance. Eythos even met his Consort, Mycella, during that time, and life was normal. Good, in fact. But, in reality, a clock was counting down.

Kolis spent the next several decades attempting to bring Sotoria back to life, though he couldn't visit her in the Vale, at least not without risking the destruction of her soul. After years of searching, he realized there was only one way to accomplish what he desired. Only a Primal with the power over life could restore Sotoria's. So, he found a way to become that.

He was successful in trading places and destinies with his twin, though nobody but the brothers know exactly how he accomplished it. We only know it required the Star diamond and some powerful magic. Regardless of *how* it happened, the act was catastrophic. It killed hundreds of gods who served both and weakened many Primals—even killing a few and forcing the next gods in line to rise from godhood to Primal power. Many draken were also killed, and the mortal realm experienced earthquakes and tsunamis as Kolis's actions offset the balance. Many places were leveled, and pieces of land just broke off, some forming islands while others simply sank.

Eythos knew immediately why his brother had done it. He'd warned Kolis not to bring her back, stating she was at peace in the next stage of her life, and that it had been too long. He warned that if he were able to do what he planned, Sotoria would not return as she was. It would be an unnatural act and would upset the very unsteady balance of life and death.

Still, Sotoria rose, and as Eythos warned, she was not the same. She was morose and horrified about what had been done to her. When she eventually died again, Eythos did something to ensure that his brother could never reach her. Something only the Primal of Death could do. With the aid of the Primal, Keella, Eythos marked Sotoria's soul— making her destined for rebirth. Meaning, her soul would never enter the Shadowlands to be judged. It would, instead, be continually reborn, over and over. Her memories of previous lives wouldn't be anything of substance—if she had any at all. Eythos hoped that would bring the poor girl some semblance of peace.

As centuries passed, Kolis kept up his search. He knew she would be born in a shroud because of what Eythos and Keella did, so he continued to look for her in the mortal realm.

Both Eythos and Keella paid dearly for what they did. Kolis grew to despise his brother and vowed to make him pay. Eventually, he killed Mycella while she was pregnant because he believed it was only fair that Eythos lose his love just as he had. To add insult to injury, Kolis also destroyed her soul, ushering in her final death. Losing her took a piece of Eythos that he never regained.

Kolis destroyed all records of the truth—both in the mortal realm and in Iliseeum. It was then that the Primal God of Death was no longer depicted in artwork or literature. He went to great extremes to hide that he wasn't supposed to be the Primal of Life, even when it became apparent that something wasn't right. He started losing his ability to create and maintain life. The destiny was never his to wield, just as that of the Primal God of Death was never Eythos's.

When Penellaphe's prophecy emerged, Eythos took it upon himself to thwart his brother's plans and hopefully restore balance at some point. Even after the shifting of destinies, Eythos retained some of his ember of life. Just as Kolis retained some of his ember of death. So, when Ash was conceived, part of that ember of life passed on to him—just a flicker of power. Not as strong as the ember that remained in Eythos, but enough. Eythos took that ember from him before Kolis could even learn of its existence, added it to what remained in himself, and put them both in the Mierel bloodline. He hid it where it could grow in power until a new Primal was ready to be born—in the one being that could weaken Kolis. Then, he made a deal with the King of Lasania and gave the mortals and his son at least a chance to do something. To stop the fallout of what Kolis did—the unnatural climate, the Rot, the destabilization of the balance.

Unfortunately, Kolis eventually killed his brother and used what was left of his ember of death to seize his soul. When Eythos died, it severed the bond between him and his draken and upset the balance even more. So, even though Ash was born to Ascend and assume the role of the Primal God of Death, it wasn't entirely his. Not to mention, his ember of life now lived in a vulnerable mortal vessel with an expiration date.

In addition, because the state of things wasn't natural, no Primal was born after Ash. Seraphena has the only ember of life in both realms. She is why life continues. And if she dies, there will be nothing but death in all the kingdoms and all the realms. She has become what Eythos was always meant to be: *the* Primal God of Life.

MYCELLA †
Primal of Death's—Eythos—Consort
Court: Lotho/the Shadowlands

Hair: Deep, red wine color.
Eyes: Silver.
Facial features: Rosy-pink skin. Oval-shaped face. Strong brow. High cheekbones. Full mouth.
Habits/Mannerisms/Strengths/Weaknesses: Ability to read emotions.
Background: Family came from the Court of Lotho. Used to tell Aios stories.
Family: Husband = Eythos †. Son = Nyktos. Cousin = Aios. Had an aunt or uncle from the Court of Kithreia.

MYCELLA'S JOURNEY TO DATE:
After Eythos told his twin that he would not interfere in Sotoria's soul journey, he met Mycella, and she became his Consort.

Sometime during the decades that Kolis searched for a way to bring Sotoria back to life, Mycella conceived Nyktos/Ash.

Kolis took his revenge on his brother by killing her while Nyktos was still in her womb—somehow, he survived, which is why they call him *The One Who is Blessed*. Kolis then destroyed her soul, ushering in her final death.

KOLIS

Primal God of Death turned Primal God of Life
Court: The Shadowlands/Dalos

Hair: Golden. Nearing shoulder-length.
Eyes: Silver with streaks of gold.
Body type: Muscular.
Facial features: Bronze skin with shimmers of gold. Strong, carved jaw. Sharp cheekbones. Lush, wide mouth.
Distinguishing features: Golden band encircling biceps. Voice carries a sharp, bitter edge.
Preternatural features: As the Primal God of Death, he could see and summon souls (unknown if he still can). Can shift into a golden hawk.
Personality: Reckless. Wild. Entitled. Competitive. Reserved. Cold. Prefers solitude. Deceptively charming when he wants to be. Manipulative. Jealous.
Habits/Mannerisms/Strengths/Weaknesses: Hates Nektas for abandoning him. Loves the color gold. Prefers redheads and blondes. As the Primal God of Death, he claimed souls if people pissed him off. Views other Primals as annoying, whiny, sniveling brats who've forgotten the ways. Keeps his *favorites* in gilded cages for ages. Believes mortals should be in service to the gods. Has loyalists amongst the Courts.
Other: Sigil of his Court is a circle with a slash through it.
Background: He used to be the Primal of Death until he stole his twin's embers and switched fates, becoming the Primal of Life—all because of an infatuation. Murdered Halayna. (More background is detailed below).
Family: Twin = Eythos †. Nephew = Nyktos.

KOLIS'S JOURNEY TO DATE:

As the Primal God of Death, Kolis ruled alongside his twin brother, Eythos, for eons. During a trip to the mortal realm, Kolis saw a young woman picking flowers. He watched her and instantly fell in love. As he stepped out of the trees to speak with her, she got startled and ran, plunging to her death from the Cliffs of Sorrow.

After, Kolis begs his brother to restore Sotoria's life, but Eythos refuses to pull a soul from the Vale. He says it's wrong and forbidden and tries to remind Kolis of that. When that fails, he adds that it isn't fair to give life to one and refuse another of equal worth.

Kolis spends the next several decades attempting to bring Sotoria back from the Vale. As the Primal God of Death, he can't visit her there without risking the destruction of her soul. After years of searching and growing to despise his brother, he takes revenge by killing Eythos's Consort, Mycella, while she's pregnant, then destroying her soul. He believes his brother should feel the same pain he has in losing the one *he* loves. When he realizes there is only one way to do what he desires, he takes action to find a way to become the Primal God of Life and switch places with his brother.

Executing his plan, Kolis manages what he set out to do—we assume with the Star diamond he received, possibly from a Fate. He swaps destinies with his brother, making himself the Primal God of Life, and Eythos, the new Primal God of Death, then destroys all evidence of how things were. Eythos knows why his twin did it. Still, he warns Kolis that bringing Sotoria back to life is unnatural and would upset the fragile balance of life and death, not to mention she won't come back the same—it has been too long, and she's at peace in her next stage of life. Kolis doesn't listen and pulls her from the Vale. As Eythos warned, she isn't the same. She's morose and horrified by what he did.

When Sotoria dies again, Eythos and Keella intervene, marking her soul and ensuring Kolis can't find her. Still, he looks for her. Given what he knows about what was done to ensure her reincarnation, he knows she will be reborn en caul, so he searches the mortal realm for any who are.

After he takes his brother's place in Dalos, he summons Nektas's mate, Halayna, at some point and murders her to punish the draken for not sticking by his side.

The night Sera is born in the mortal realm, her father, King Lamont, summons Kolis and tries to make another deal to save his child and best the deal that King Roderick made with Eythos after he became the Primal God of Death.

Kolis retained some of the embers of death in him, just like Eythos retained some of his embers of life. And it's enough power for Kolis to capture and hold a soul. So, he does with his twin.

While Kolis's control as the Primal of Life wanes, *his* innate power does not. He is the oldest and the most formidable of the Primals. He can kill any Primal, but then what? A new one can't rise. Not without life. And he has lost that ability. That doesn't stop him from going about his cruel rule. While draken generally are bonded to Primals by choice, the bond *can* be forced, and Kolis does that often.

He also takes great pleasure in selecting *favorites* and putting them in gilded cages. He provides them with everything they want and need—except for their freedom. However, when he grows tired of them, he revels in their torture and death.

When Gemma enters the Land of the Gods as a Chosen, Kolis takes to her. He keeps her close to him and talks about the power he's felt, almost obsessing over it. He tells her he'll do anything to find his *graeca*—an old Primal word meaning love and life—though he never speaks of it as if it's a person, something living and breathing. He leads Gemma to believe it's an object, a possession. He never tells her what he plans to do with his *graeca* once he finds it, but she knows he's doing something to the Chosen. Many of them disappear and come back…not right. Different. Cold and lifeless. Some stay indoors, only moving during the brief hours of the night, and their eyes change, becoming the color of shadowstone. We know the others have eyes almost leached of color. They're as terrifying as Kolis is, and he calls them his reborn, his Revenants. He says they're a work in progress and that all he needs is his *graeca* to perfect them.

Kolis hasn't set foot in the Shadowlands since he switched fates with Eythos, though it's unknown whether he *can*. Still, it's assumed that he knows about the embers of life and thinks he can use them. It's also presumed that he knows about Taric and the other gods Nyktos dispatched, and that Bele's Ascension has unsettled him and the other Primals.

Kolis sends Attes to the House of Haides to let Nyktos and Sera know that he disapproves of the coronation, and orders them to come to him in Dalos when he issues the command.

The day Sera arrives at Cor Palace, Kolis enters the atrium, followed by the stench of stale lilacs. Gold-laced eather spills across the floor and collapses, coiling like a viper around his feet. He orders everyone to sit—everyone but Sera. He shadowsteps to her and tries to force her with eather to look at him.

He remarks that she doesn't feel like a godling as he's been told and notices she's been warded with a charm. He calls Nyktos clever. When he tries to touch Sera's hair, Nyktos blocks and threatens him. Kolis tells Nyktos that he pleases him but warns him to release him immediately.

Kolis claims to be hurt that Nyktos didn't seek his approval for his union and asks if Nyktos knows why they've been summoned. Hanan speaks up, and Kolis scolds the Primal for talking without permission, flexing his power.

As the discussion turns to the Ascension that's been felt, he confirms that he is the only one who can restore life and Ascend a god, knowing that's not true. He turns his attention to Hanan again and chastises the Primal for his lack of faith, ordering him to leave and not return until summoned. He then apologizes to Sera.

Kolis brings forth Dyses, his Revenant, and remarks that Attes and Nyktos seem surprised by him. He then asks if they have the same doubts and lack of faith as Hanan does. They both simply say that it's been a long time since the Primal of Life restored life. Nyktos adds that he was shocked by the dakkais, too, and Kolis says the attack was punishment for his nephew's failure to seek approval.

He adds that he will not let Nyktos's disrespect go unpunished. Sera says it was her fault, and Kolis calls her brave. He then turns his attention to Nyktos and says Sera must earn permission the same way he would.

Kolis turns to Kyn and asks the Primal if he brought what he was ordered to and then instructs Sera to kill a young draken. Nyktos speaks, and Kolis tells him to be silent and that it won't be him who suffers if he disobeys.

Sera inquires about what will happen if she refuses, and Kolis chuckles when Thad tells her it won't matter. Kolis then tells her to pay the price, or he will by killing Thad, her, and a draken from the Shadowlands.

Sera asks Kolis what he'll gain by making her do what he asks, and he tells her that it will tell him everything he needs to know.

Sadly, we know that's true.

Nyktos tries to intervene, and Kolis warns him again, telling him that he'll rip out Sera's heart if he does it once more. He then turns back to Sera and tells her that the draken is young enough that hitting the head or heart will do, then adds that if anyone but Sera pays the price, he'll demand she pay it with *her* blood.

Sera kills the draken, and Kolis laughs. Then, smugly, he gives the couple permission for their union and the coronation and dismisses them.

After Attes kidnaps Sera, Kolis enters through a partitioned wall and remarks that he's happy to see she's awake. He calls her brave again and tells her she betrayed him the moment she left by using what wasn't hers to snatch away the life she owed him—by going to Kyn's Court and bringing Thad back to life.

Sera asks him what Blood and Ash means. He tells her about the prophecy and has Callum recite most of it, only finishing the end. He asserts that he knows Sera's heard it. When she remarks that *he* is the great conspirator, he laughs.

They try to dissect the prophecy, and he states that he believes Mycella was the first daughter, and Sera is the second. He also thinks the middle section of the prophecy is something that will happen at some point in the future. He thinks the end of the prophecy is all about her.

He tells her she is the bearer of two crowns and he needed her to restore a draken's life to know that the embers had reached the point of power where they would ensure the rest of the prophecy came to be. He calls her clever and tells her she's just a vessel to give him what he wants.

He remarks that the Ancients didn't imagine he'd do anything to change what they foreshadowed, and it seems it was foretold that Eythos would set it all into motion. However, they underestimated him by thinking he'd just stand by and let it happen.

He says there's no need for *any* other Primals if there's one of Life *and* Death, then reveals that if he does nothing, he'll die.

When Sera asks why he needs more power, he answers, "Power isn't limitless or infinite. Another can always rise. Power can always be taken." He then grabs her by the throat and tells her that Nyktos would have taken the embers from her the moment he felt he was ready to and insinuates that he could raise Eythos if he took them.

He goes on about why Eythos hated him and confesses that if his brother had brought Sotoria back, it wouldn't have changed anything; though it would have saved all the lives Nyktos had to take in place of him. He tells Sera he's going to drain her, take the embers, and rise, completing his final Ascension. He then taunts her that she knows what will happen to his nephew when he does.

He boasts that absolutely nothing will be forbidden or impossible, not even what has been hidden from him, and then strikes, biting Sera just above the shackle on her neck. She tries to save herself by telling him she's Sotoria reborn, and he calls her a liar. Attes interrupts their exchange and reminds him that Keella helped to find her, even though he's hunted down every mortal who bears an aura. He then suggests that Kolis couldn't find her over the past few centuries because she had been reborn and reminds him that Eythos was clever and would do this just to fuck with him.

Shaking, he lets Sera go but catches her, then falls to his knees and hugs her to him with horror etched on his face as he realizes who he has to kill again—Sotoria.

Kolis tightens his hold and asks if it's really Sotoria. Callum urges him to take the embers from Seraphena and Ascend, while Attes tells him if he doesn't save Sera, his *graeca* will be lost.

A storm of gathering power builds, and Kolis sees Nyktos in his *nota* form changing into his Primal form. His nephew calls him out. Still holding his love, he watches as his nephew kills the Primal God of the Hunt and Divine Justice.

He gently lowers his *graeca* to the floor and turns to his nephew when Nyktos orders him to take his hands off his wife. He tells Nyktos he can see how powerful he's become and chastises him for hiding it. He gives him a chance to walk away, but only because they're family.

He tells Nyktos to go to his Court and tell Bele to appear before him and swear fealty immediately. Instead, Nyktos moves to pick up Sera, and Kolis knocks him back, telling him he's started a war. His nephew says the moment he strayed from tradition and faith *he* started it.

Kolis taunts him, saying he killed Eythos and Nyktos swore fealty. Nyktos attacks, and Kolis accuses him of treason.

When Nyktos says that Sera was never Kolis's, the false king argues that if she is who she claims to be, she was never Nyktos's to crown. They fight, and Kolis incapacitates Nyktos.

Attes calls to him, telling him that Sotoria needs his help. He goes to her and lifts her, then tells his guards to put Nyktos in the cells.

Sera wakes while in his arms and he tells her that she'll live as long as she is who she claims to be. He gets into the water and summons Phanos. The Primal arrives, and they talk about Sera being Nyktos's Consort. Kolis tells him it's irrelevant. As Phanos asks more, Kolis gripes that he asks too many questions and says he needs Phanos to make sure Sera doesn't die.

Phanos asks Kolis why he can't just make her a Revenant, and he tells the Primal that they're just death reborn. The Primal of the Skies and Seas asks if she's Kolis's *graeca*, and Kolis tells him he believes she is. He tells Phanos he's been holding her soul in her body, but he can't much longer.

Phanos wonders if Kolis knows what he's asking, and Kolis says he's *not* asking.

Phanos finally takes Sera, and Kolis watches as he takes her deeper and then one ceeren after another floats to the surface, dead.

When Sera comes back out, she asks him why, and he tells her that he won't allow her to die. She says she doesn't want anyone dying for her, and he lets her know she has no choice, then taunts that if she were Sotoria, she would know that.

Sera runs from him and grabs a sword. Kolis tells the guard to leave and remarks that he expected her to run.

He urges her to put down the sword and she tells him to make her. Before he can react, she stabs him in the chest.

He is not amused.

She starts to run, but he stops her. They fight some more, and he hits her, then immediately feels bad about it. She mouths off and he tells her he never wanted to be a villain. He blames his brother for that. She asks him if there's anything he doesn't blame Eythos for.

He tells her not to push him and calls her *so'lis*. To keep her in line, he threatens Nyktos. She insists she doesn't care, but he doesn't believe her and tells her as much. Upset, he grabs her by the throat, not even realizing what he's doing until she points out that he's killing her. Again.

He tells her they're going home and then compels her.

After Sera attempts to escape, he goes to see her and asks what she and Callum were discussing. Callum tells him they were talking about Antonis, who Kolis found out turned Craven. He tells Sera that they're an unfortunate side effect of creating the Ascended.

Sera points out the differences between him Ascending the Chosen and his brother, and it angers him. He tells Callum to leave and asks Sera if she's been resting. He orders her to have a drink.

When Sera asks about Nyktos, he wants to know why. She tells him it's merely curiosity. Then she asks about the armies. He tells her they haven't left the Dalos border and are still in the Bonelands to the south along the coast beyond the Carcers.

She asks him why he hasn't forced them out, and he tells her about how the mortals are becoming complacent. He says he plans to take a more active role when he's the Primal of Life and Death.

I'll just bet he does…

She then asks if him taking her will cause issues, and he tells her only if the other Primals think him taking her is worth going to war over.

He asks about her relationship with Nyktos and listens with anger as she answers. She tells him that Nyktos only wanted the embers, not her, and never knew what Eythos did. He thinks she's lying.

Not able to help himself, he asks her if she's fucked Nyktos. She tells him they are attracted to each other, so...yes. He tells her that someone doesn't go to war or kill for someone they're just attracted to. She argues that people kill all the time for all sorts of reasons. His rebuttal is that Primals don't.

He informs her that his nephew is in stasis and watches her reaction. When she asks why he didn't go to ground sooner, he explains that the earth can't get through the shadowstone in the chamber.

Sera tells him Nyktos had his *kardia* removed, and he says he believes it—it sounds like something Nyktos would do to stop Kolis from using those he loves against his nephew. Especially since he never wanted to end up like Kolis.

When Sera starts to glow and taps into the embers, it angers him and he tells her to calm herself. He orders her to sit and tells her he doesn't believe what she said about her feelings. He insists that the marriage imprint is proof that there's love. She explains the difference between loving someone and being in love with them, and he admits he loves Sotoria. Says he's in love with her.

She asks him to prove it by letting Nyktos go. He says her demand proves that she loves his nephew, and she argues that it would prove that Kolis would do anything for her. He lists for her what he's already done, but she tells him that's the bare minimum needed to show someone you love them.

Kolis asks her why she would be interested in falling in love, and she tells him that she's never known it and wants to.

He asks her if she thinks he's a fool and reminds her that she tried to kill him. She tells him that she stabbed Nyktos, too, which surprises him. He asks her what will change if he releases Nyktos, and she tells him that she will submit to him. He warns her that if she's lying, he'll own her soul in both life and in death.

Kolis has her made what he deems presentable so he can hold court in her chambers. As the gods come in, he notices how they look at her and decides to play with them a bit. When Uros looks a little too hard and long, Kolis tells the god that he offended *him* and implodes him. Feeling uptight, he excuses himself for a bit.

When he returns, Kyn shows. He asks if the Primal brought news. Kyn tells him that he spoke to one of the Shadowlands' commanders and says they're unwilling to stand down. They talk about how the forces are separated and discuss what to do about it. Kyn says something needs to be done, and Kolis asks him if he has suggestions. The Primal asks if he can take his forces and attack those to the east. Kolis warns him that they'll all die. Nektas is there. Kyn asks if he can finish what he started then and take the Shadowlands while the strongest are away.

Kolis wonders what Attes thinks, and Kyn tells him he's more attuned to accord than war. Kyn then assures Kolis he's not worried about retribution or Nektas. Kolis tells him he's brave and loyal and has his gratitude. The Primal kisses his ass.

When talk shifts to the embers, Kolis says he's maintained the balance this long and that won't change anytime soon. He asserts they won't make any moves against the Shadowlands unless provoked. When Kyn asks what happens then, Kolis says he'll do what must be done. They talk about Nyktos, and when Kolis notices Kyn looking at Sera, he tells the Primal she draws the eye and asks her to move closer. He wonders what Kyn thinks, and the Primal agrees with Kolis. He then says that if it comes out that she isn't his *graeca*, he will gift her to Kyn after he's finished with her. Kyn humbly accepts, then tells him he's happy he brought a gift, as well.

Someone wearing a black hood is brought in, and Kolis finds out it's Rhain. He remembers his father and brother and what they could do. Rhain seethes as Kolis talks about his father and calls him a traitor. He wonders if Rhain allowed himself to be captured and if finding Nyktos wasn't really his end goal.

He searches the god and finds a pouch with a necklace in it. He assumes it's his trigger object, slightly confirmed when Sera says it's hers, but insists she didn't know what Rhain could do. He listens to Kyn and Sera bicker and tells them to stop. Turning to Rhain, he says he believes Sera; therefore, he'll make his death quick. Sera argues, saying he's only being loyal to the Primal of his Court, Kolis insists he should be loyal to *him*—his King.

When Sera tells him that he should be thrilled that Rhain is worried about Nyktos, it confuses him. She explains that the gods in the Courts should care about their Primals. If they don't, how can they care about their King?

Sera tells him she'll do whatever he wants if he lets Rhain go. He asks her why she'd want to save the god, and she says she's trying to prevent a war. She reiterates that she'll do anything if he promises that Rhain will be returned to the Shadowlands in the same condition he's in now. He agrees and dismisses Kyn, then informs Sera they'll be sharing a bed.

Once Sera is bathed and dressed, he comes in and tells her she's far bolder than before, then asks if what he requested of her was a surprise. She tells him it only surprised her because he offered her to Kyn just moments before. He tells her that her advice to release Rhain was wise and shows that he's reasonable, fair, and worthy of loyalty. He mentions that the god is back home.

They go to bed.

The next day, Kolis brings Ione to meet Sera. He tells her that the goddess can see into others' thoughts to uncover truths, lies—all that is needed.

He tells Sera it won't take long and assures her that Ione will be quick and efficient. He orders her to sit. Kolis takes in her demeanor and says she seems nervous. She replies it's because a god did this to her before, and it hurt.

Callum fills Kolis in about Taric, and he asks Sera if the god found her. She says it wasn't just him, it was him, Cressa, and Madis. She wonders why he had Taric searching for the embers if he already knew where they were, and he tells her that he ordered Taric to look for his *graeca*, not the embers.

Kolis then asks Sera if the other gods fed from her, and she says only Taric did. He wonders if the god told her what he saw, and Sera says he didn't have a chance to say anything before Nyktos killed him.

Kolis watches as Ione is pushed from Sera's mind and demands to know what she saw. The goddess says the embers in Sera are strong, and he gets exasperated. He asks if Sera is his *graeca*, and Ione tells him she carries the one called Sotoria. That she is her.

He feels nothing but joy.

Kolis asks her more questions, which the goddess answers to his satisfaction

He gets all emotional, and Callum says it has to be a lie. Ione tells him she doesn't lie and has no reason to.

Discussions rise about how Sera doesn't look like Sotoria, and Ione explains why. She tells Kolis she's glad he found his *graeca*.

After she asks Kolis if he requires anything more of her, he thanks her for her assistance. When she turns to leave, she addresses Sera as *Consort*. It pisses Kolis off and he interjects that the coronation was neither recognized nor approved.

The goddess leaves, and Sera snaps that she was always telling the truth. Kolis says he sees that now and dismisses Callum. He approaches her, telling her she looks more like Sotoria when she smiles. When Sera asks about Nyktos and Kolis honoring their deal, he gets angry and can't stop himself from biting her.

He loses control and finds release. He insists it'll never happen again and begs her to say something. All she says is she needs a bath.

Later, Kolis walks into Sera's chambers and asks her and Callum why they always look like they're about to go at each other's throats. Sera tells Kolis that Callum still doesn't believe that she's Sotoria. Kolis tells her the Rev is in denial, then reveals that Callum is Sotoria's brother.

Sera continues bickering with the Revenant, and Kolis comments on their fighting reminding him of how he used to quarrel with Eythos. He then tells Sera—as Sotoria—how she had two siblings: Anthea and Callum.

He informs Sera how he went to Sotoria's family to apologize when she left him, remembering how her parents cowered. Only Callum remained unafraid. He tells her that they talked, and Callum shared details about Sotoria.

He continues, saying Callum mourned his sister and felt responsible. When Sera asks why he would feel that way, Kolis tells her that Callum was supposed to be with Sotoria but was instead screwing the baker's daughter.

She asks how Callum became a Revenant, and Kolis tells her how the boy used a small knife to cut his throat. He tells Sera how he held them both as they died, adding that he couldn't allow Callum to perish, so Death gave life.

She asks him if Revenants are demis, and he tells her they're not, adding that they'll discuss it more when there aren't more pressing matters to attend to. Kolis tells Callum to leave them.

He wants to talk to Sera about the deal they made. He tells her that Nyktos has not been released, adding that he's not reneging, but his nephew is in stasis, and that needs to be resolved.

She asks what that means, and he tells her that Ash lashed out when he woke, and Kolis had to ensure he behaved.

Sera asks how he is, and Kolis admits that telling her would likely upset her. She argues that *not* knowing will only make her worry more. Seeing her so affected by news of another bothers him. He tells her as much and adds that he practically feels the worry seeping from her pores.

He wonders what inspires her care for Nyktos and her fear for *him*, saying she wasn't afraid of him at first but that's since changed. He then mentions Eythos having heightened intuition and foresight and says he gets why she seemed frightened after he threatened someone she cares about and saw him as Death, but he doesn't understand the timing of the changes in her.

She seems shocked, and he reasserts that he apologized and said it would never happen again. She insinuates that he forced himself on her.

He says he realizes his display of love was intense, and she argues it was much more than that.

He asks what will make it okay.

She tells him she needs some time.

He gets angry and tells her that his word should be sufficient to garner trust, and she tells him she doesn't know him. That hits him hard. He gets more upset and yells that he's the King of Gods.

When she seems afraid, he pulls back and then orders her to say something. She begrudgingly utters a thank you.

Kolis apologizes once more and then scolds her for using the embers. She argues that Callum provoked her, and he says the essence does not belong to her and is not hers to use.

He takes care of some things and then watches his *so'lis* sleep. When she wakes, he asks who she was dreaming of—she was smiling. He then notices the scents of mountain air and citrus.

She says she doesn't remember her dreams, and he informs her that they'll start fresh. He asks how he can make that easier for them and tells her there's no limit to what he'll do for her. He offers her things he can think of, and she tells him she wants out of the cage.

It makes him happy that she wants to spend time with him. She asks him what he plans to do about the embers, and he tells her he'll take them and Ascend her. When she asks what Ascension will mean for her, he says she'll become an Ascended.

She wonders what will happen when *he* Ascends, and he tells her he will ensure loyalty in both realms.

Kolis lets her out after breakfast. They walk, with Elias guarding them. Sera asks if it'll be night anytime soon, and he tells her it will be in about a week, explaining that it's only night once per month. When she seems shocked she's been in Dalos for so long, Kolis tells her that she slept for several days after her escape attempt.

She asks Kolis how many live within the City of the Gods, and he tells her there aren't many left. When she asks what happened, he tells her they're dead at the hands of the Fates. He admits that he had a hand in some of the death, too.

When Sera sees all the alcoves, Kolis notices the look on her face and asks about it. She replies that it's just a lot of sex. He wonders if it bothers her, and she says it doesn't. Still sensing her confusion, he explains that being near Death makes the living want to *live*.

They get to the Council Hall, and he notices her nervousness. She says it's the crowd. He tells her she needn't worry. When she says she knows, it makes him happy that she's coming to trust him.

Kolis takes the throne, and Callum brings in a floor pillow for Sera. A server brings around a tray, and Kolis tells Sera to have a drink.

He notices Keella and says he hasn't seen her in a while. She says she's come because of Sera and knows who she is. Kolis tells her she should; after all, she knows who she *really* is. He then asks if she knew about Sotoria before the coronation.

Keella addresses Sera using her Shadowlands title and asks about Nyktos. Kolis gets irritated and says the Primal-killer is where he should be. Keella then inquires if he did it to protect his Consort. Kolis doesn't really answer but says his nephew's actions could have had lasting consequences.

Keella says another has risen. It should be celebrated and seen as a blessing. Then she asks if Kolis is going to stop what he's doing since it goes against tradition and honor.

He tells her that he didn't sanction the coronation. Turning to Kyn, he asks if he gave permission, and Kyn backs him up.

Keella asks if Sera will be released when Nyktos is, and Kolis tells her she's not going back to him at all. When the Primal asks if she is there of her own free will, Kolis suggests she ask Sera herself. Sera says she's in Dalos by choice.

Noticing an exchange between one of the servants and a god, Sera asks if the Chosen have free will. He says they've had nearly all their choices made for them all their lives, then looks at the couple and says it appears as if the servant is enjoying herself. Sera disagrees. He tells her that where they couldn't be touched or spoken to in the mortal realm, they can in Dalos. He says Sera views them as victims, whereas he sees those starved for what's been forbidden. He tells her that the Chosen have opportunities in Dalos. They can shed their veils or Ascend.

He reveals that the couple's names are Orval and Malka, and they are known to each other. She asks what would happen if they weren't, and Kolis asks her if it matters. She emphatically says it does, and he points out another couple. He mentions the servant's name is Jacinta and tells her the god is Evander. He then adds that Evander is turned on by pain. Looking at Sera, he asks her what she would do if she could. She says she'd kill him and then asks what Kolis would do to her. He tells her he wouldn't do anything.

Sera stands abruptly and asks for a weapon. Kolis calls for Elias, and the god hands over one of his daggers.

Amused, Kolis watches her walk up to Jacinta and Evander, grab the god by the hair, and tell the woman to leave. Then, she strikes.

And the screaming starts.

Kolis orders his people to remove Jacinta and Evander's body. When Naberius moves toward Sera, Kolis tells him to stand down.

Sera returns to the dais, and Kolis asks her why she thinks she knew what was going on. She clearly starts to say that he told her, so he interrupts and says he merely asked her what she would do. He never said that Evander was forcing Jacinta.

Sera argues that she saw the tears on Jacinta's face, and Kolis asks her if they were tears of pain or pleasure. He goes on to say that she only hears what she wants to hear and thinks about herself. Just like his nephew. Just like his brother. She argues some more and then asks whose Court Evander belonged to. Kolis tells her he was from the Thyia Plains.

Which means he got a little retribution on Keella for questioning him, too.

Attes calls to Kolis, telling him it's time to start court. He orders Sera to sit. He talks to two gods and decides he's had enough of disrespect. He kills the god who accused another of cheating and refused to show his King what he's due.

Sera appears displeased and asks if this is really how he wants them to spend time together. He tells her he's multitasking. He wants to be with her, but he has things to do. She adds that she never expected *this* when she asked for time out of the cage, and he asks what she means. She tells him that he's only shown her death. He questions more, and she mentions Evander. He says that's on her, and she breaks down the errors in that statement, then adds that he killed a god for calling another a cheat.

He says it's about maintaining control and balance. She questions that, and he says every action has a reaction. Disrespect is met with an appropriate response: death. She asks if *she* is to be sentenced to death, and he tells her she's different. He won't punish her.

And he won't. Unless she makes him.

He tells her to stand and come to him, ordering her to sit on his lap. He continues with what he was saying, repeating that he won't punish her but *will* rethink their deals. He asks if she understands. When she says she does, he tells her he's capable of more than just death.

He wishes people would see that.

I can't imagine how they could...

Veses addresses Kolis, and he beckons her forward. They talk for a bit.

Kolis asks Veses if she recognizes Sera. The Primal says she isn't sure, and Sera calls her out as a liar. She tells Kolis they met in the Shadowlands.

He finds that very interesting, since the Primal never told him that.

Veses and Kolis talk some more, and Kolis goads Veses, thoroughly enjoying himself. She's just so easy to manipulate. He insinuates that Veses would do *anything* he asked of her, she agrees, and he can see the distaste on Sera's face.

Good, Sotoria doesn't like the idea of him being with another.

He's delusional…

Veses asks Sera why she's there, saying she thought she was the Shadowlands' Consort. Kolis tells her she's wrong and says he never gave permission. Veses then assumes that Sera's presence must be punishment, and he corrects her. Veses says she could find something less crushing for Kolis to use to warm his lap if that's what's going on, and it pisses him off. He orders the Primal goddess to apologize and tells Veses she's speaking to his *graeca*. She says it's impossible and must be a lie, but he insists he had it confirmed.

When Kolis orders her to apologize again, Veses does, but not happily. Then she tells him she's happy for him.

He doesn't believe that for a minute.

Before she leaves, Kolis summons her back and says that she still disappointed him and must be punished. He calls Kyn over, and watches in amusement as he begins carrying out the punishment.

Sera tries to stop it, and Kolis asks her what she's doing. She says that what he's doing isn't right and asks him to stop. He pushes back, and she tells him it's the right thing to do. Furious, he rises and tells her they're returning to her quarters. Before they leave, Phanos tells Kolis he needs to talk to him. He says he'll be right back.

They return to the cage, and Kolis chastises Sera, reminding her that he told her not to question him or use the embers, yet she did both. He details what he's done for her and says she isn't appreciative. He tells her that he wanted to show her what he's risking for her and orders her to obey her King.

Weeping, he chains her, saying he wants to hate her for making him do this to her, but he can only love her. When she acts as if she doesn't believe him, he tells her she's still alive. Nobody else who questioned him would be. And that's proof of his love.

After court, Kolis reenters and releases the shackles. Sera cries out and sags into his arms. He apologizes.

The Chosen bring in stuff for a bath, and Kolis tells her to bathe, rest, and all will be well.

After Sera wakes, he comes back and tells her she looks lovely. She apologizes, and it shocks Kolis, but he tells her he understands.

He asks her to walk with him and has Callum and Elias trail along after them. He takes her into a side chamber and calls for Iason and Dyses, who bring in a Chosen named Jove.

She tells him he doesn't have to prove anything, and he insists he must show her what he can do. She tries to talk him out of it, and he simply instructs the Chosen to unveil himself. Kolis asks Jove how he is and tells him he'll be blessed.

Jove replies that it's an honor. Sera tries again to stop Kolis, and he tells her she's always had a kind heart.

He insists she needs to know why it's so important. Balance is necessary.

She asks if he can at least make it so it doesn't hurt and he thinks that's easy enough. Instead, he makes sure Jove finds pleasure.

As the steps are completed, Kolis explains the process of what he's doing and calls Elias over to give Jove his blood. He tells her that without the embers of life, the Chosen become the Ascended, but he's been working on the drawbacks, like their sun intolerance and bloodlust.

Sera wonders what happens if they can't control their hunger, and he says they're put down. He adds that gluttonous gods were killed under Eythos's rule, as well, and *he* was used as the weapon to do it.

He talks about the creation of life and how he cares. She asks about the difference between the Ascended and the Craven, and he explains that the Craven are dead, then elaborates.

He assures her that the newly made Ascended are watched. The one she encountered would have been, too, if she hadn't tried to escape and pulled the guards from their posts.

She asks what happens if an Ascended chooses not to feed, and he tells her they will weaken, their bodies eventually giving out. They discuss how everything created or born has the potential to become a murderer.

He tells her the Primal of Death is supposed to remain distant from anyone they may have to judge—all but the other Primals and the draken. He complains that it wasn't that way for the Primal of Life and goes on to say that it made sense to the Arae, and it all comes back to the balance established when the Ancients created the realms.

Sera chimes in that she thought Eythos created them. Kolis tells her that he created some but not *the* realms. The Ancients were not the first Primals, nor can any Primal become an Ancient. He tells her there must always be a true Primal of Life and a true Primal of Death.

Later, Kolis suggests another walk, and Sera asks him where Callum is. He tells her that he sent him away to handle something important. She asks about the Revs, wanting to know if they need things like friendship, love, and sex. He tells her they don't, just like they don't need food or blood. They are only driven by their desire to serve their creator.

She says she can't imagine not wanting anything, and he counters that he thinks it would be freeing.

She goes back to the subject of Callum and says he's different. Kolis acknowledges and reveals that the Revenant is *full* of wants and needs. He tells Elias to stay back when they reach the stairs and moves with Sera to them. He says he was once told that motivation plays a role in the creation. For example, feeling means becoming. He says he's not so sure because he tried with others, and it never worked.

He takes her high to look over the City of the Gods. She asks him about the Fates clearing the city, and he tells her they do whatever they like. Especially when someone upsets the balance.

He tells her he gave the gods in Dalos a choice. They could serve him as the Primal of Life or die. He killed half. It displeased the Fates, so they wiped out the rest. He admits he could have probably acted a little less rashly.

He looks at Sera and sees Sotoria in her, but everything is…amplified. He says he wishes she looked how she used to. It seems to offend Sera, and he doesn't get it. Once again, he asks what she wants or needs to forgive him.

When she mentions an irregular silver diamond she used to covet, he offers to get it for her. She replies that she doesn't think Calliphe even has it anymore, so he tells her he has one. When she asks to see it, he can't deny her. He takes her back to the cage and summons down the cluster at the top, letting it transform into its true form: a silvery diamond shaped like a star.

He tells her that it's called The Star and says it was created by dragon fire long before the Primals could shed tears of joy. He adds that he came upon it by chance.

She asks why he keeps it hidden, and he says he keeps it with what he cherishes the most. When she asks to hold it, he of course lets her, watching her reaction.

Suddenly, she blurts, "You cried," and he freaks out. He asks what she saw and rips the diamond away, returning it to its place. His Primal form emerges, and she retaliates with the embers. He reminds her what he warned and tells her that whatever happens next is on her.

He traps her, but she takes control, dismantling the cage and chamber around them. Then she attacks him. He tells her to stop, but she throws the words from her vision back at him.

He realizes she saw his brother's last moments. When she moves to stab him with a bone, he doesn't even fight her. After, she gets in close and tells him she wants him to remember that she wants nothing more than to kill him. Then, she stabs him again and again, leaving him weakened and falling into stasis.

SOTORIA †

Mortal

Here are some details about Callum's sister and the false King of Gods' obsession (I hate referring to her as such. She's a mortal. A woman—a beautiful one. One with a tragic history)…

Hair: The color of ruby-hued wine and falls to the middle of her back.

Eyes: Green like spring grass.

Body type: Slightly shorter than average height and voluptuously curvy.

Facial features: Oval face with angular cheekbones. Full, bow-shaped lips the color of berries. Strong brow. Some freckles across her nose to her eyes. Cute nose.

Personality: Timid but a fighter. Kind. Fierce. Stood up for her brother.

Background: Died by falling off a cliff while picking flowers for her sister's wedding and getting scared by Kolis. Was brought back to life and kept as a prisoner. Died again, but had her soul marked so she'd constantly be reborn. Ends up sharing a soul with Seraphena and then being transferred to the Star diamond. Is finally reincarnated—I believe Poppy is Sotoria reborn but I have not received confirmation of that as yet.

Family: Brother = Callum. Sister = Anthea †.

SOTORIA'S JOURNEY TO DATE:

Poor Sotoria has had a rough journey. First, Kolis sees her and instantly becomes infatuated. When he reveals himself to her, it scares her enough that she falls from the Cliffs of Sorrow while picking flowers for Anthea's wedding.

She enters the Vale and is fine, until Kolis rips her from there and brings her back to life. But she doesn't come back the same. She's morose and resentful. Not to mention she's kept in a cage.

She eventually dies again—exact cause unknown, though there's a rumor that Eythos killed her—and Eythos and Keella take measures to ensure she can't be ripped out of the Vale again. They mark her soul, making it so she'll be reborn over and over.

Eythos takes additional measures by placing her soul in Seraphena. But she's not reborn as Sera, they share Sera's body.

Inside Sera, she becomes enraged at the sight of Kolis in Dalos and the price he forces Sera to pay—the young draken's death. Her fury fills Sera.

When Sera is captured and brought back to Dalos, Sotoria's anger and panic fill Sera—it's a reminder of what she endured.

As Sera is held in Dalos, Sotoria emerges several times, letting Sera feel her pain and fear and panic. She also lets loose her anger and fury at times when the embers rise within Sera.

Once Sera escapes, Sotoria feels herself being removed from Sera and questions the Primal, Keella, if she will be okay. Once she's reassured, she lets go, letting herself be transferred into the Star diamond.

But on her way out, she tells Sera they'll meet again.

CALLUM

The First Revenant

Court: Dalos

Hair: Golden. Shoulder-length.

Eyes: Pale blue—almost colorless—with eather.

Body type: Tall.

Facial features: Golden skin. Delicate curve to cheeks and chin.

Distinguishing features: Mole beneath his right eye. Soft lilt to his voice.

Preternatural features/abilities: Able to come back to life. Telekinesis.

Personality: Apathetic. Flippant. Cruel. Arrogant. Thick emotional walls.

Habits/Mannerisms/Strengths/Weaknesses: Wears gold. Is often seen with gold-winged face paint—an homage to Kolis. Knows Primal magic. Wears a sword strapped to his back and a dagger on his thigh at times. Also two swords on his back—pommels down—and a black dagger strapped to his chest at others. Loves the word *scampered*.

Other: Incredibly old.

Background: Showed Isbeth how to make Revenants. Ezmeria thought he was a god. Told Calliphe how a Primal could be killed.

Family: Sisters = Sotoria † and Anthea †.

CALLUM'S JOURNEY TO DATE:

If I had to pick someone who both intrigues and terrifies me, it would be Callum. He's incredibly enigmatic, but as someone even older than I, who has been in league with some of the vilest of the vile, he admittedly scares me.

Callum first entered my radar when I saw him in the visions I had when Sera was attacked by the guards. I, like Ezra, thought he was a god at first. He immediately rubbed me the wrong way, taking obvious pleasure in Sera having killed the guards and then lying about it.

He later appears in Dalos when Kolis meets with Sera, peeking through the curtain and telling the draken Davon that they have something to take care of.

After that, I *suspect* that I caught a glimpse of him lurking in the shadows during Kyn's ordered Cimmerian attack at the House of Haides, but I don't have anything to confirm that definitively.

Callum is there when Sera wakes after being abducted by Attes, revealing that she's been unconscious for two days, and that Attes wasn't supposed to hit her so hard. He then tells her that it's no longer a secret that she's a mortal with embers of life in her, then greets her by her full name and asks if she remembers him.

Callum insults Sera, telling her she stinks of the Shadowlands and the Primal there, then warns her not to disrespect Kolis. As talk turns to her life in the mortal realm, Callum says that he got the impression the Queen wasn't much of a mother to Sera and then tells Sera he'd had regular contact with Calliphe for years and was the one who told her how to kill a Primal—make them fall in love and then end them.

He adds that Kolis knows all about her and has since the night she was born, then says Sera's father, King Lamont, summoned the Primal of Life to make another deal. He remarks that it was clever of Eythos to hide embers in a simple mortal, especially someone who would one day belong to his son.

Sera asks why Kolis didn't just take the embers. Why wait for her to be taken to the Shadowlands? Callum and Kolis reveal the prophecy and reiterate the *Blood and Ash* bit.

As they talk and explain more, Callum laughs when Kolis says how silly Sera's question is about wanting more power and then warns Kolis to watch out for Attes. He tells him that the other Primal is trying to trick him and not to trust him. Attes threatens that he knows how to kill Callum—draken blood—and will do so if he disrespects him again.

Callum keeps watch over Sera as she's held in Dalos. He doesn't for one minute believe that she's Sotoria and makes it abundantly clear to her. All the while, they argue and do things to provoke the other.

They really do fight like siblings—if that brother and sister constantly had murdering each other on the brain, that is.

When Kolis reveals that he's actually Sotoria's brother, Callum gives his sister the credit she's due, calling her sweet, and fierce, and caring. But he takes great pleasure every time Seraphena is knocked down a peg and plans to do whatever is necessary to make sure that Kolis rises to the power he was always meant to have. He owes Kolis, after all. The King forgave him for letting Sotoria down and gave him eternal life.

My next sighting of Callum is actually in my more recent visions of Poppy and Casteel. I first saw him entering the dungeon with five Handmaidens and Isbeth when the Blood Queen held Cas. He remarks that Casteel is clever when he figures out what Isbeth is and then takes interest when she asks what Cas knows about Malec.

After Poppy beheads King Jalara, Callum is a bit stunned. He's careful not to touch his head as he steps forward to confront her.

Later, back in the dungeon, Casteel threatens to kill him, and Callum quips that he's heard that more times than he can count but confesses that Cas is the first person he thinks might actually succeed. Then, he removes a shadowstone dagger and stabs the new King of Atlantia.

Casteel repeatedly calls Callum *Golden Boy*, and it irks him. I love it, and I've taken to doing it myself. He lashes out and says he's not a *boy*. When Cas attacks and stabs Isbeth with the sharpened bone, Callum looks on in captive interest. He tells the Blood Queen that Casteel needs to feed. As they try to force it, he holds Cas still, but the Atlantian elbows him in the chin, headbutts him, and throws him into the wall, causing him to acknowledge how strong Cas still is.

Callum separates Kieran and Reaver and then formally greets Poppy, telling her it's an honor to meet her. As Poppy tries to read him, she's met with only thick, shadowy walls.

Poppy threatens Isbeth, and it gives him goose bumps. He remarks that he hasn't felt power like that in a very long time. When Reaver asks how long, he only responds with, "Long." I imagine he's alluding to the fact that she feels like the Consort, Sera, whom he had loads of experience with, as well.

Callum leads Poppy, Isbeth, and Millie to Casteel's cell in the dungeon and has Poppy blindfolded once they're underground. He stares at Poppy's scars and remarks that the wounds must have hurt something terrible. She tells him that he's about to find out if he keeps standing so close to her. Callum backs away at the Queen's order.

As he leads Poppy to Cas, he warns her not to stand too close to him as he's like a *rabid animal*. Poppy tells him that she'll make sure he dies and make it hurt. When they see Casteel, and Callum remarks that he's surprised to see Cas talking since he was only foaming at the mouth the last time, Poppy tells him she's changed her mind and will kill him the first chance she gets. When she displays some of her power, letting it into her voice, he hisses and straightens his spine.

Later, he asks if she thinks Cas really deserves food, and she stabs him in the heart with his own dagger. He swears, and Millie removes him.

The next day, he tells Casteel that his arrogance is impressive and admits that Poppy stabbed him with his own weapon. He lets on that he's seen love take down the most powerful beings but has only seen love stop death once—with Nyktos and his Consort. He taunts Casteel with this, saying that love is a weakness for him and that he should have fed from Poppy when he had the chance. He then stabs Casteel, barely missing his heart on purpose, sending him straight into bloodlust. He removes the blade, licks it clean, and then wishes Casteel luck.

When the group escapes, Callum rushes to warn Isbeth and runs into Malik. They get into it.

Callum and a half dozen other Revenants confront the group, and Callum tells Reaver he thinks he knows what he is, then taunts Kieran, saying he wants to keep him since he's always wanted a pet wolf. Turning his attention to Poppy, he tells her that humanity is a weakness.

The Queen orders Malik to be brought to her, and Callum tries to warn her that it's not the right time, but she merely silences him. As everyone is distracted, he snaps forward and cuts Kieran's arm with a blade, whispering a spell as he does. Casteel stabs him in the chest in retaliation, and he remarks that it stings before falling dead.

When he comes back to life moments later, Isbeth is removing her ring, then Callum watches in amazement as Kieran knocks Malik unconscious.

After the Queen kills Clariza and Blaz with power, he tells Poppy not to bother trying to bring the couple back to life because nobody comes back from a death like that, yet he takes clear pleasure in watching her reaction to their demise.

Poppy and the group bring Malec to the Bone Temple, and Poppy makes demands. He taunts her, asking her, "Or what?" When Cas says they'll set the casket on fire and kill Malec, Callum turns his attention to Casteel.

Approaching Kieran, Callum is shocked to see the curse mark missing. Still, he uses a milky-white blade—a bone of an Ancient—to open Kieran's skin. Black smoke seeps out of the wound as the curse lifts. He then tells Kieran that not much can do serious harm to him now—indirectly referencing the Joining. The wolven plunges a bloodstone dagger into his heart in thanks.

Callum revives just in time to see Isbeth stab Malec. As things unfold, he thanks Poppy for fulfilling her purpose and doing what she was prophesied to do. He explains the prophecy—sort of—and says that as long as both she and Malec had the Primal God of Life's blood and were loved, it would restore *him*—meaning Kolis. He adds that Isbeth just needed someone from Kolis's bloodline to find Malec, but Ires wouldn't do it.

Callum didn't know that Isbeth would kill Malec until she asked for him. He figured it was a fifty-fifty chance who she'd kill—her heartmate or Poppy. He explains that Isbeth is the harbinger, and Millie was the warning. He then says that it'd take Poppy eons to be powerful enough to destroy the realms, then adds that it's time for them to bow to the True King of the Realms.

As a final taunt, he tells Poppy it should have been her on the altar and that it was always about her and Millie, promising they'd be dealt with later. He also explains that Kolis slept fitfully under the Temple of Theon but was kept well-fed. The extra Rite made him strong enough to wake up. When Poppy Ascended, it woke him completely, and when Malec takes his last breath, he'll be at full strength. Reciting part of the dark nursery rhyme Poppy heard as a child, Casteel silences him by ripping out his heart.

With a gaping hole still in his chest, he gets up and tells the group that the True King's guards are coming—the dakkais.

Callum fights with Malik and then runs off as soon as Poppy calls the Consort's name—he knows what that means.

The group promises to find and deal with him later, and I certainly hope they do. However, I fear there is still more to come as it pertains to Callum. He knows more, has experienced more, and had a stake in more than anyone. His end goal is still very much a mystery.

NEKTAS
The first draken
Court: Dalos/the Shadowlands

Hair: Long, black, and streaked with red (becomes streaked with silver).

Eyes: Blood-red with a vertical pupil (become sapphire blue with a vertical pupil).

Body type: Tall. Long legs.

Facial features: Copper skin. Broad, proud features.

Distinguishing features: Ridges along his back that resemble scales—can present elsewhere if close to shifting.

Preternatural features: Black and dark gray scales. Spiked tail. The size of three large horses. Long, graceful neck. Head is half the size of a horse's body. Flat, broad nose. Wide jaw. Pointed horns on his head like a crown. Body is at least twenty feet long.

Personality: Quiet. Reserved. Sage-like.

Habits/Mannerisms/Strengths/Weaknesses: Extraordinary hearing. Can manifest clothing.

Background: Was Eythos's bonded draken, the very first, and was close to him even before receiving his dual nature. Created the first mortal with Eythos. When Eythos died, it severed their bond, and he ended up bonded to Nyktos by choice.

Family: Daughter = Jadis. Mate = Halayna †. Distant relative = Thad. Bonded Primal = Eythos and then Nyktos.

NEKTAS'S JOURNEY TO DATE:
When Nektas first meets Sera, he wants her to pet him and is a bit hurt when she thinks he'll bite her. He has no interest in eating her or any of the gods—especially Saion. Given his bond to Ash (a.k.a Nyktos) Nektas knew when Sera stabbed him and told Ash as much, but he also knew it wasn't serious. He would have come for the Primal if it were.

After Sera is attacked in the woods, Nektas is there when she wakes. He reveals that the only reason she is still alive is because Ash used a rare antidote on her, which he actually found surprising. He is honest and says it would have been better if he hadn't saved her. When Sera questions him, he admits that he doesn't think *any* of Ash's decisions have had anything to do with the deal King Roderick made.

Nektas watches Sera and Jadis as they slumber. When Sera wakes, he tells her he was looking for his daughter and figured she'd be with Ash. He didn't expect Sera to be here, too. He adds that he's never seen the Primal sleep so soundly, even as a child, and explains that he knew Ash's parents. He makes it clear he considers Ash family, and then tells Sera that he will call her his, too, since she has given Ash peace.

After Sera brings Gemma back to life, Nektas arrives and says that all the draken felt what she did. He then leaves with Reaver.

I saw a lot of inconsequential stuff in my visions between these happenings and the things I will recount in a bit, but I will relay one takeaway from them: Nektas is an incredible father and a wonderful caretaker. He has a huge heart, and even with his stoic demeanor, that is clear for anyone to see.

In the war room, Nektas shares that Eythos was a fair King—kind, generous, and curious by nature. He reveals that it was he who gave the dragons their god forms. He then outlines what happened when Kolis switched destinies with his brother and surmises that Sera's presence alone is slowly bringing life back to Iliseeum.

During the first major battle, Nektas arrives with the rest of the draken from the west and sends fire onto the docks, beaches, and the water. He rounds on the crimson draken as it pursues Sera, Ector, and Rhain. It falls, and Nektas circles it as Ash draws near.

Nektas arrives at the palace with Nyktos and Saion. He tries to get Ash to feed, but the Primal is stubborn and insists he'll ride it out. Nektas lets it go but relays to Sera that the Primal can tip into something dangerous if he doesn't take sustenance, but even if he doesn't do that, he's still weakened and not healing and that's the last thing any of them needs. He adds that Nyktos won't feed because he was forced to do it, and Kolis did all manner of things to him.

After some thought once Sera's plan is outed, Nektas says he thinks they can get Ash to feed from Sera—he's angry enough to do it. He asks Sera if it's really her choice since they won't force her. He's relieved when she says it is.

When Sera is escorted back to her chambers, Nektas tells her he's doing as Ash asked and putting her somewhere safe. He adds that Nyktos won't answer if she knocks on their adjoining door, but he's sure it's unlocked. He then asks Sera if she would have followed through in killing Ash if she hadn't learned it wouldn't save her people.

She can't say.

Sera starts feeling pain from her Culling, and Ash goes to get her some healing tea. Nektas arrives just as he leaves and settles in to guard her, sitting on the balcony. He talks to her about the bond between the draken and the Primals and says that he likes being bonded to Ash. When talk shifts to the crimson draken that attacked, Nektas says he doesn't know if they chose to bond with Kolis because Kolis doesn't give many of them a choice.

When Ash returns, Nektas tells him that Sera is lying about feeling better. He relays that everything has a smell, and everyone has a unique scent. He tells her that she smells of death, referring to Ash, and that bathing wouldn't wash it away. He's disappointed when Sera doesn't want to know what *else* she smells like.

Sera drinks the tea, and Nektas tells her he's impressed that she downed it so quickly. He explains that it wouldn't have been a known thing in the mortal realm. When Sera tells him she thinks it's the same as the one Holland gave her, he asks if

Sir Holland was mortal and challenges her confirmation that he is.

When the vengeful gods attack, Nektas comes in through the ceiling and torches Madis. He growls a warning as Taric materializes an eather sword and then trills at Sera, urging her to use her gift. Ash tells him to be sure the guards are ready for anything, and Nektas calls out to the other draken, who answer him immediately.

Nektas watches as Sera brings Bele back to life, and trills again when the goddess draws renewed breath.

Nektas leaves to summon the Fates and then returns, waiting for Ash and Sera in the throne room. He eventually sends Reaver to get them. When the Arae respond, Nektas waits with Rhahar, Ector, Ward, and Penellaphe outside the throne room with Reaver by his side and tells Sera and Ash that they will wait—for both of them.

After the dakkais attack, Nektas checks on Ash and Sera. He remarks later in the war room that he doesn't know every draken but sensed the enemy draken was young—*too* young to be up to that kind of shit. He wonders if the other god involved in the dakkais attack saw Sera and wanted to grab her, and then tries to calm Ash when he hears that the god planned to let Sera die.

He tells them that a Primal had to be behind the attack, as no one else could command a draken. The question is, *who* would be willing to anger both Kolis and Nyktos by letting Sera die?

Nektas arrives in the Dying Woods just in time to see Sera and Nyktos fighting. He lands and crouches over Sera after she blasts Nyktos with eather, protecting her from Nyktos possibly retaliating out of reflex. When Nyktos calms a bit and lands, he nudges him and is told he's okay and just needs a minute.

Nektas shifts and smirks when Sera stares at his nakedness. He manifests some pants for her benefit. He then asks her what the Shade said and grins when she explains what happened. He tells her it's the embers and explains that Eythos could raise the bones of the dead. He says that he only remembers him doing it once, and it's not the same as restoring life to the recently dead—that's why nobody felt what happened with the Shades like they did with the other things Sera did. He reiterates that the embers are really strong in her and then asks Ash if he's better.

He tells them that he doesn't think even Kolis knew Eythos could raise the dead that way and then instructs them to go back to the palace since the Shades won't be scared off for long. He shifts back to his draken form and flies off.

Nektas spends some more time with Jadis and Sera after Ash puts the other gods in their place about Sera and her bravery. He tells Sera that he's with her because he chooses to be. When Sera asks about Davina, the draken who fell during the battle, Nektas explains about the draken's family, saying there won't be a burial rite and telling her why.

Food is brought in, and Nektas laughs and says he thinks it's funny that Ash thinks he doesn't know that the Primal lets Jadis eat whatever she wants. He then tells Sera that his daughter can have food if she eats it off a fork instead of using her grubby little fingers. When Sera gets her to eat with the utensil, Nektas stares in stunned amazement and states that everyone has tried with little to no results—even Reaver. He tells Sera that he thinks she reminds Jadis of her mother and then relays what he knows about matings and heartmates. He admits that he knows everything Eythos did and tells Sera the price always matters—speaking about her risk of going after Kolis on her own.

As Nyktos and Sera bicker, Nektas tells them it's entertaining. He insinuates that death isn't a foregone conclusion for Sera because the embers aren't fully hers until she Ascends. They should be removable until then. He adds that when Eythos was the Primal God of Life and Ascended the Chosen, they became like godlings because the eather was stronger in them. None ever became gods, but none had embers in them either. He tells Sera that anything is possible with her and reminds her that someone had to tell Kolis how to take the embers from Eythos.

As they discuss possibilities, Nektas tells Sera how they can find Delfai via the Pools of Divanash but adds that they're temperamental, and he can't be the one to ask. It needs to be her.

When the Cimmerian appear, Nektas arrives at the battle, killing one with a bite and shaking it in two. He senses the eather growing in Sera and looks up to give her a warning growl.

After the attack, Nektas brings Sera breakfast and sits with her. He asks if she wants to accompany him to check on Jadis and then wonders what she thinks of Ash's plans to remove the embers from her. He tells her the road to the Vale is dangerous. When they talk weaknesses, he says he can burn anyone to a crisp save for a Primal—no one can fight a Primal unless they attack Nyktos or his Consort.

Nektas tells Sera that Ash could hurt her if he loses his composure but won't risk it if she's close to him. He then says he thinks Kolis will use the summons as a chance to find out how the embers of life were felt and will offer his permission for the coronation in exchange for the embers.

After following her back to her chambers, Nektas calls her meyaah *Liessa*, and she calls him meyaah draken. He recognizes that she doesn't like being referred to as a Queen and says that he didn't know he was *her* draken, then tells her that she's their Queen with or without a coronation. She carries the embers of life; therefore, she *is* the Queen.

Nektas reveals how Ash has had to convince Kolis that he's submissive to him and what would happen if Kolis knew the truth. When they discuss in more detail, Nektas tells Sera that everything that's going on is personal for her because Sotoria is part of her. He then asks her why she no longer calls Nyktos *Ash* and explains that Eythos called him that. Ash introducing himself to her as that the first time means something.

Sera and Nektas discuss Ash and Court and whether Ash forgives her for what she planned. Nektas says he never said Ash forgave her, only that he understands and accepts it. If he didn't, she wouldn't be in his bed or smell of him, and Nektas wouldn't have sensed peace from Ash.

He visits Vathi to see Aurelia—Reaver thinks he's sweet on her. When he returns, Sera blames him for everything that's gone on since he left and then tells him that his eyes flashed blue. He relays that it happens *sometimes*. He mentions it to Ash and then takes the younglings away.

After their trip to the Vale is planned, Nektas says he'll meet them on the road to the Pillars. After they meet up, he tells Sera about Eythos as the Primal of Life and explains that being near the Pillars was hard for him. He then tries to get her to understand that she's stronger than she thinks and calls her meyaah *Liessa*, adding that it's her that makes him say that, not the embers.

He and Nyktos tell her about the riders. When they bow, Nektas remarks that he hasn't seen them do that in a while. When he and Sera break off from Ash and the Primal says she is very important to him, Nektas replies with, "I know."

Nektas tells Sera he knew she cared for Nyktos before she was ready to admit it to herself. She says that if she'd been able to kill Ash, he wouldn't have needed to kill her because she would have done that herself. Nektas answers that if that's true, he's even more right than he thought.

They talk about what happened in the Dying Woods, and he tells her that Ash could have fucked him up. It's another reason he knows the Primal's feelings go beyond fondness. Nyktos cares for Sera.

Nektas then details that Ash removed his *kardia*, not so he wouldn't become his father and how he grieved for Mycella but so he wouldn't become his uncle. He suggests that Sera loves Ash and tells her that love *should* be terrifying.

When they approach the Shroud, Nektas stops Sera from getting too close and tells her about the sirens. To keep her close, he takes hold of her horse's reins, only releasing them hours later to go through the passage under the mountain to the Pools of Divanash.

Nektas tells Sera he smells Ash on her but also death—lowercase *d*. Her body is dying; the Culling is killing her. He then tries to detail what life and death smell like to him.

At the Pools, he tells her what to do but admits that he's never seen it work. He hears Sera confess her suicide attempt. He calls her meyaah *Liessa* again and tells her it worked, then identifies Delfai for Sera in the Pools.

When they see where Delfai is, Nektas remarks that it's fate that he's with someone Sera knows. When Sera explains who Kayleigh was to her, the draken tells her that Ash finds great enjoyment in visiting Tavius in the Abyss and does it quite often.

As they talk more, Nektas reminds Sera that he was there when the mortals were created and helped, that fate isn't absolute, and that nothing is more powerful than the ability to feel.

After they leave the Vale, Nektas asks her if she's okay and tells her she can talk to him if she ever isn't. He'll ensure she is.

As they travel, he senses the nymphs and tells Sera to halt. He explains about the nymphs, and they fight them. Sera kills them, and he tells her that only the Primal of Life can wield the kind of eather needed to kill nymphs—it's the same as what can kill another Primal.

Nektas eavesdrops on Sera and Ash and then brings the younglings to say goodbye to the couple. He wants to go with them, but only they can answer Kolis's summons. He tells Sera he *will* see her again.

Nektas and Jadis go to the mountains. On coronation day, he returns but leaves the younglings there. Landing in front of the thrones in draken form, he remains there the entire time. Attes stops to speak with him after talking to Sera and Nyktos. He nudges Keella's arm in response to something the Primal says, and she strokes his cheek.

When the next big attack comes, he and Orphine attempt to fend off the enemy draken attacking Lethe. Nektas then fires on the dakkais attacking Ash, scorching those in front while Orphine takes those behind Nyktos.

Nektas comes to Ash's aid when he breaks free of the Carcers and goes to rescue Sera. When Ash Ascends her, he's there to help watch over her and talk to Ash as *he* talks to his Queen. At one point, he makes sure they're okay and has his life threatened by his friend.

He's pretty sure they'll be just fine.

My next viewings of Nektas were in Poppy and Casteel's time.

Nektas wakes when Poppy touches him, snarling and sniffing her and then giving a soft whirring trill.

When Poppy returns to Iliseeum the second time, he's in his god form and tells her that Nyktos has rejoined the Consort in sleep. He urges her to be sure before she speaks the words that cannot be rescinded and says that once she summons the flesh and fire of the gods to protect, serve, and keep her safe, they will be cast in fire and carved in flesh. He then asks if she wants them to destroy the Blood Crown for her and is told she wants them to fight the Revenants and the Ascended. To fight beside Atlantia, not *for* them. She adds that she doesn't want any cities destroyed or innocents killed.

Nektas asks Poppy if she plans to take what is owed and inquires whether she can bear the weight of two crowns. He also pleads with her to bring back what is theirs to protect and what will allow the Consort to wake—Poppy's father. He then adds that Malec is lost to them; he was gone long before they realized, then reveals that Malec is not her father. His twin, Ires, sired her.

He tells Poppy how Ires was lured from Iliseeum some time ago and drawn into the mortal realm with Nektas's daughter while everyone slumbered. He informs her they cannot look for Ires without being summoned, and while Ires has not called to them, he knows he lives.

Nektas says that Ires was fond of taking the form of a large, gray cave cat, much like Malec, and is surprised to hear that Poppy saw Ires and knows he's in the Blood Crown's clutches.

Poppy tells him Isbeth's claim of being a god because Malec Ascended her, and Nektas laughs. He tells her that gods are born, not created, and that she, like the Revenants, is an abomination of everything godly. He then tells her that her enemy is truly an enemy of theirs.

As talk turns to Malec once more, Nektas tells her that anyone entombed by the bones of the deities would simply waste away but they would not die. They would exist in a place between dying and death, alive but trapped.

He then tells Poppy to speak the words and receive what she came to Iliseeum for. When she does, he tells her they are hers from that moment to the last and then calls her the Queen of Flesh and Fire.

Just as Poppy goes all Primal at the Bone Temple, Nektas arrives and takes out the dakkais on the Rise. He reveals that Reaver took Malec to Iliseeum after the stabbing and that he's alive—for now. He then says that Jadis is alive and in the mortal realm.

When they talk about what happened with the mass resurrection, Nektas tells them that Poppy didn't bring everybody back to life, the Primal of Life aided Poppy, and Nyktos captured their souls before they could enter the Vale or the Abyss. But he warns there must always be balance.

Poppy announces that the Consort is the true Primal God of Life and Nektas replies that the Consort is the heir to the land and the seas, the skies and the realms. She's the fire in the flesh, the Primal of Life, and the Queen of the Gods. She's the most powerful Primal. But then he adds, "For now."

He tells them briefly about Eythos and Kolis and their true roles, relays the story of Sotoria and the aftermath, and states that Nyktos is *a* Primal of Death but not the true Primal. He was never the Primal God of Life and Death. There's never been one, and he would never have answered to that title.

Poppy argues that it's nonsense that no one can talk about—or really even know about—who the Consort is. She calls it sexist, patriarchal bullshit. Nektas tells them that it was the Consort who chose for it to be that way. She wishes to remain unknown, and Nyktos honors her wishes because of everything they did and sacrificed to prevent what just happened at the Bone Temple.

Nektas adds that if Poppy chooses to have children, they will be the first Primals born since Nyktos. If Kolis hadn't stolen Eythos's essence, Nyktos would have become the Primal of Life, and Ires and Malec would have been born Primals, but *only* if a female was born first.

He tells Poppy not to apologize for existing and adds that Malec and Ires were already well on their way to being born when the plotting that led to Poppy started. What was done to stop Kolis meant that Malec and Ires could never risk children, but Malec did it anyway. The risk, creating the cosmic restart, would allow for what was done to Kolis to be *un*done.

He then tells them that Callum knew what speaking the Consort's name would mean. They realize the Revenant is missing and agree that he must be dealt with.

Nektas says that Poppy is the Primal of Blood and Bone, the true Primal of Life *and* Death, and adds that the two essences have never existed in one being.

When Poppy reveals that she knows where Ires is, he tells her to take him there. He then sees that they all think they've stopped things and tells them they've stopped nothing. What happened at the Bone Temple freed Kolis, and they've only slowed the inevitable, preventing Kolis from returning to flesh and bone and power, but he will rise if left unchecked.

Nektas tells them they must kill Kolis, though he doesn't know how—I assume they can now since Poppy is the balance of life and death. For now, Nektas says he needs to get to Ires, find Jadis, and return to Iliseeum.

He mentions that the Consort and Nyktos no longer sleep, which means other gods will awaken, too, and not all are loyal to the Primal of Life.

War has just begun.

Nektas leaves to take Ires home, knowing he will return for his daughter.

REAVER
Draken
Court: The Shadowlands

Hair: Blond. Shoulder-length.

Eyes: Crimson with vertical pupils in the time of the gods. Blue with vertical pupils in recent times.

Body type: Long legs.

Facial features: Sand-colored flesh. Sharp, strong, chiseled jaw. Wide-set eyes tilted down at the inner corners. Full, bow-shaped lips. Not classically handsome but interesting and striking.

Distinguishing features: Faint but distinct scale pattern on the skin.

Preternatural appearance: Purplish black scales. Large but not as big as Nektas. Smooth, black horns starting in the middle of the flattened bridge of his nose and rising up to the center of his diamond-shaped head. The ones around his eyes are smaller but lengthen into sharp points that jut out from his frills as they travel up his head.

Other: Gruff voice. Can change his teeth and breathe fire while in his god form.

Personality: Aloof. Sarcastic. Easily irritated.

Background: Was young when news of what Kolis did came out. Was hidden away with the other younglings. The first draken to emerge after Poppy summons Nyktos's guards.

REAVER'S JOURNEY TO DATE:
Reaver first entered my visions as an adorable, precocious ten-year-old draken just learning to fly.

He spends a lot of time with Sera after she gets to the Shadowlands, pestering and being pestered by little Jadis and getting into trouble.

When Sera brings Gemma back to life, it affects Reaver—and the rest of the draken.

In the throne room, after Sera tries to go after Kolis on her own, Reaver lets out a staggering, high-pitched call when Nyktos says her bravery is unmatched.

Reaver waits with Jadis, Bele, and Aios when the Cimmerian arrive. After the battle, he joins Nektas, Sera, and Jadis, and the two younglings play. He insists he doesn't like Nektas's daughter, but he's so sweet with her. Like when he brought her favorite blanket to her while she was napping in her mortal form.

As time passes and Sera's embers grow stronger, Reaver becomes closer and closer to her—and more protective. He even issues a warning to Nyktos at one point, even though he knows the Primal won't hurt her. He just doesn't like Sera being upset at all.

When Veses attacks Sera in her chambers, Reaver tries to protect her and gets thrown into a wall by the Primal. His death is imminent, but Sera is able to save him. When he opens his eyes, they shift from blood-red to brilliant blue, and he calls her *liessa*.

On coronation day, Reaver stays in the mountains with Jadis.

The next time I saw Reaver in my visions, he was a huge and gorgeous, purplish black draken in Iliseeum. He's the first to erupt from the ground, roaring and breathing silvery-white fire.

Back in the mortal realm, Reaver and Kieran immediately become antagonistic to each other. Reaver almost bites Kieran when he gets too close to him while Reaver is resting, and they engage in an epic stare-down outside of Oak Ambler.

When Poppy delivers her *message* to King Jalara, Reaver accompanies her. He lands before the Revenant, letting out a deafening roar and hitting them in the chest with his spiked tail.

While in Cauldra Manor's banquet hall, Reaver is amused by Poppy and Kieran's interaction. Like usual, he spends his time staring at Kieran—likely because he knows it bothers the wolven. Kieran snaps at him, and Poppy scolds Kieran, making Reaver laugh. She chastises him, too, and he puffs out some smoke, affronted.

Vonetta asks how he managed to get into the banquet hall, and he simply thumps his tail on the floor in response.

Later, Reaver tells Poppy that she's filled with worry and every draken can feel it, even those not there with them. He confirms that all the draken are bonded to her and is surprised she didn't realize that. He then tells her that she can't communicate with them telepathically like she can with the wolven, but they will know and answer her will, adding that it's always been that way with Primals.

Reaver explains that a god can kill another god, and shadowstone to the head or heart will do, as well. He then says that a mortal stabbed with shadowstone will normally die, adding that Tawny is obviously alive for a reason.

He tells Poppy that she's the first female descendant of the Primal of Life—the most powerful being known, and that she'll become stronger than even her father, Ires, in time. He says that Ires left Iliseeum while the draken slept, though he woke one to accompany him. Reaver just became aware of what happened eighteen years ago when the Primal woke. He then tells Poppy that her birth was felt, and that's when they learned that both Malec and Ires were gone, as was Jadis.

Reaver explains about Ires and Malec and what Malec would have to do in order to stay strong and in the mortal realm—he'd have to feed and often. He tells Poppy she won't have to feed as often as Malec and Ires once she comes into her power...unless she's injured. However, until then, she needs to make sure she doesn't weaken since she hasn't finished her Culling, adding that he would feel it if she had.

He tells her that nobody can feed from the draken. It would burn the insides out of most, even the Primals.

When Reaver calls Poppy meyaah *Liessa* for the first time, it stuns her. He takes the time to tell her about the balance of power and how the fire the draken breathe is essentially the essence of the gods, though using it weakens them and slows them down. He says that even Primals had weaknesses and that only one is infinite.

As Poppy talks, Reaver tells her she sounds a lot like the Consort and confirms the Consort will wake when Ires returns. He says the gods will eventually wake, too. When asked what the Consort's name is, his reply is that it is a shadow in the ember, a light in the flame, and a fire in the flesh, and to speak it is to bring the stars from the sky and topple the mountains into the sea.

When Isbeth's *gift* is delivered, Reaver is there and emits a strange staggering call when he sees Poppy's reaction to Casteel's finger. Later, he accepts Poppy's request to join her and Kieran on their mission to save Cas.

During Vessa's storm, Reaver watches, stunned, and lets out a low, mournful sound when the draken die and fall from the sky. When Poppy goes to heal them, he tells her she cannot bring back the dual-natured and explains that only the Primal of Life can restore life to a being of two worlds. When they tally the dead, he tells everyone it was no storm; it was an awakening of death.

He explains that Vessa smells of death, saying that the Primal of Death's stench is oily, dark, and suffocating, and that's how she smelled—which doesn't make sense. When talk turns to the god of death, he tells them that he knew Rhain before he was the god everyone recognizes, and that he wasn't a god of death. There *is* no god of death, only a Primal of Death. He then adds that Nyktos isn't the Primal of Life and Death, and he was never the true Primal of Death, either— that was Kolis. However, they wouldn't know that because Kolis erased the history. He goes on to say that Kolis was interred, that no one would be alive if he hadn't been. The only way he can be freed is by the Primal God of Life.

Reaver later realizes what the Revenants are and remarks he should have caught it earlier. He tells them how the first mortals were created, how third sons and daughters are special, and about the Revenants being Kolis's pet project. He talks about the Rite, the original Rite, and how Eythos always gave the Chosen a choice.

When talk turns to Jadis, he says he believes she's dead but that one drop of draken blood, no matter how old, can kill a Revenant.

Reaver is present during Poppy's meeting with the generals, watching Valyn and getting irritated by Murin suggesting they let the draken fly over Oak Ambler and incinerate it all.

Later, he *does* take down Oak Ambler's gate with fire, then he and Nithe take on the soldiers in the inner part of the city before the wolven are overwhelmed. Next, he, Nithe, and Aurelia take down the internal Rise, and then Poppy calls them all back, telling them to rest. Reaver perches at the top of Castle Redrock and lets out a deafening roar.

Following the macabre discovery in the tunnels and the Temple, Poppy orders him to burn the Temple to the ground. He flies over, circling the structure as he does. Happy to do it.

Sharing a meal with Poppy, Reaver tells her that it's good they can't understand what the Ascended did. He stresses that Nyktos is the True King and wouldn't approve, and the Priest thinking it's anyone else is unfortunate. He adds that the Consort doesn't like limitations either and laughs when Poppy imagines the Primal of Life probably doesn't like her bringing people back to life. He tells her that Nyktos would be conflicted. He'd be happy about life yet worry about fairness, while the Consort would weigh the concerns, throw them aside, hope no one was looking, and do it anyway.

He explains that the Consort sleeps so deeply because it's the only way to stop her from doing the kind of harm that can't be undone in her rage over her sons being taken from her. With Ires in mind, Reaver reminds Poppy that they mustn't forget about him. The god needs to return home to Iliseeum.

Reaver wears Kieran's clothing—to the wolven's chagrin—as he readies the horses and the wagon of whiskey for their trip to the capital.

He tells them the truth about demis on their journey and says they're so rare he's never seen one. He explains that a demis is a god made, not born. They're mortal—though not Chosen—Ascended by a god. He says that few existed because the act was forbidden, and most didn't survive the Ascension. However, those who did make it were essentially gods with the same weaknesses as the gods.

When he sees the state of things in Solis, it saddens him. He tells Poppy and Kieran that he's been to the mortal realm before, back when this area was Lasania, though only a few times when it was necessary. He reveals that the Consort was born there with an ember of pure primal power in her, unlike the Chosen.

Reaver notices another group on the road, not Huntsmen, and offers to burn the soldiers. Poppy tells him not to, saying she doesn't want his identity revealed.

When Millie stops them, he tells her that if she wants Poppy, she'll allow him and her advisor—Kieran—to accompany her as a show of good faith.

Inside Wayfair, Reaver is in a chamber below Poppy's room but is under guard. Still, he behaves and is taken to see Kieran whenever the wolven demands it.

Poppy checks on him, and Reaver follows her to meet with the Queen. Millie escorts him, Poppy, and Kieran to the Great Hall. He stares at the statue in the center of the Great Hall. Poppy believes it's the Primal of Life, Nyktos, and Reaver tells her it isn't. Millie confirms.

He announces that he doesn't like how the Ascended look at Poppy. When she remarks that he and Kieran are beautiful and she's flawed, and the Ascended can't figure out why she's with them, he tells her that's the stupidest thing he's heard in a while, and he's heard a lot of stupid.

When Isbeth enters, Reaver doesn't bow. She comments that she doesn't recognize him, and he tells her that she wouldn't.

After meeting Callum and hearing him say that he hasn't felt power like Poppy's in a very long time, he becomes incredibly interested and asks him how long. The Revenant's response? "Long."

During their rescue and escape attempt later, he blows the stairwell doors off the hinges and emerges drenched in blood. When Poppy and Kieran look at him, he tells them he's a messy eater and then promises he'll handle any Revenants they encounter.

When confronted by the Royal Knights, he tells them he'd be offended by their threats if what was left of their souls wasn't about to be ushered into the Abyss.

Reaver revels in the battle, taking down many and commenting on his prowess.

Poppy calls the Shadow Temple the Temple of Nyktos, and Reaver corrects her. He tells her they were the Sun Temple for the Primal of Life and the Shadow Temple for the Primal of Death when it was Lasania. He confirms that the Shadow Temple is in the Garden District, however, near the Luxe, and he is familiar enough with the city to know the way.

He tells Poppy that Nyktos only sat on the throne for a short while. When the candles start responding to Poppy, he tells her that she carries the blood of the Primal and she's in his Temple, then teases her for being *special.*

Reaver suggests that they use the spell to find where to go next to find Casteel and spins as Malik arrives. He reminds them all that they don't have time for distractions and says to either kill him or make sure he can't betray them.

After they find Casteel, Reaver agrees with Poppy that Callum should be dead and helps keep Casteel in check by removing the shadowstone shackles from his ankles and neck but putting the bone chains on him.

Poppy later asks if he can break the chains around Cas's wrists. He does. When Cas is more himself after, he introduces himself and says he's glad Cas didn't bite him, and he didn't have to burn him alive.

When Cas reveals that the Revenant, Millie, is Poppy's sister, Reaver is stunned. He asks if Ires is her father, too, and then remarks that the Consort will be pissed.

Later, he confirms that Poppy is, indeed, a Primal born of mortal flesh. He says he thought she knew but then realized she doesn't know much of anything. She was able to summon the draken and has the Primal *notam.* He tells them there's no danger of her not surviving her Culling now and then congratulates her on knowing now and being able to prepare.

As they talk more, Reaver tells Poppy that only a Primal can create the mist and that her eyes are a sign that she's close to completing her Culling. He says the streaks of eather may remain, or her eyes could go full silver like Nyktos's.

When Casteel asks how a Primal is born to a mere god and of mortal flesh, Reaver says he can't answer that but tells them that Poppy is the first Primal born since the Primal God of Life, and only the Primal of Life can answer that.

Reaver wonders why the Blood Queen thinks Poppy will destroy the realms. When the talk turns to the prophecy, Reaver tells them it isn't bullshit, not when spoken by a god. And then explains that the goddess Penellaphe was close to the Fates.

After Malik shares his story about being there the night Poppy was attacked in Lockswood and mentions seeing the Consort in Poppy's eyes as a child, Reaver swears. He tells them the Consort sleeps fitfully and that things happen sometimes that partly wake her.

At Blaz and Clariza's, Nektas opens the back door to guards and roasts them. When Callum enters, he tells him he's about to find out for sure what Reaver is and puffs smoke from his nostrils. He's told to stand down but turns to Callum just as he snaps forward and wounds Kieran.

On the way to Padonia, Reaver leads the horse with an unconscious Malik. After they eat a little bit, he asks them if they're really worried about the curse Callum put on Kieran—he assumes Kieran, Cas, and Poppy are Joined. He tells them the essence Callum used had Kolis's stench.

Outside Padonia, Poppy releases Reaver to do as he pleases, and he joins his brethren, flying above the city, their calls echoing through the valley.

After scouting for the ruins, he arrives just in time to join the fight with the Craven. He takes out several trees and incinerates the remaining threats. Once things die down, he tells them the ruins are a day's ride north.

When talk turns to Malec, Reaver tells them that the documented *O'Meer* was not Malec's last name, and if he did have one, it would have been Mierel, which was the Consort's mortal last name.

As they approach the ruins, Reaver mentions that he didn't see the mountain of rock from the air and figures it must be where the forest is the thickest. When the Gyrms attack, he warns the wolven not to bite them, saying there's no blood in them, but there *is* a poison that will eat them from the inside out. He elaborates and says the ones attacking are Sentries, which are like Hunters and not like the other kind of Gyrms they've fought before. Fire won't work on them. He also mentions they're filled with snakes.

Poppy asks him if eather will work on them, and he tells her it will from her, but only because she's a Primal about to complete her Culling.

After the fight, he asks if anyone was bitten and informs them that the snakes' bites are toxic, too.

As they talk about the Unseen, he says he doesn't know what they are or how or why they'd be summoning the Gyrms. After Poppy explains more about them, he surmises that they must have come to be a thing while he was sleeping.

Before they rest, Reaver tells them the Gyrms were once mortal, those who summoned a god and pledged servitude for whatever favor the god granted them. Hunters hunt things. Sentries guard things—objects, people…usually people. Seekers, like Hunters and Sentries, can sense whatever they're searching for. Either they find said thing and bring it back, or they die in the process of defending it. He explains that the ones they saw and fought were down there for hundreds of years and tells Cas that whatever brought the Sentries wasn't tied to what Eloana did. He adds that he thinks the mountain formed as a way to protect Malec's tomb and that the Gyrms they encountered weren't summoned by Primal magic—only a Primal could have sent them.

Reaver reveals that when Malec left Iliseeum, he did so right before the other gods went to sleep and didn't do so on good terms. The Primal of Life, even if asleep, would have sensed that he was vulnerable. However, the deity bones would have blocked their ability to know where he was. Therefore, the Primal of Life must have summoned the Sentries to protect Malec.

He talks to Poppy more about Malec and says they were friends when they were younger, before Malec started visiting the mortal realm and lost interest in Iliseeum. That loss of interest meant a loss of affection for those who lived in the Land of the Gods.

Reaver comments that it's strange that Malik is so closely named to Malec, but he imagines it was a way for Eloana to honor what could have been.

Cas asks Reaver if Nyktos could have prevented Malec's interment, and Reaver says the Primal of Life could have prevented it, but Malec must have been injured or significantly weakened to be entombed. If neither Nyktos nor the Consort intervened, they must have had their reasons.

At the Bone Temple, Poppy orders the draken to take to the air to avoid the dakkais. Reaver lands and shifts to mortal form, telling Poppy to stop using the Primal essence since it's only drawing the dakkais to her. She tells him that Kolis will be at full strength if Malec dies. He responds that if that happens, they will all *pray* for death. He urges her to go and try to save him, then takes to the air again, lighting up the Temple grounds.

Eventually, he gets taken down by dakkais and dies. Luckily, he returns like everyone else when the Consort merges with Poppy. After, he takes Malec to Iliseeum.

JADIS

Hair: Dark.
Preternatural appearance: Greenish brown scales. Long neck. Oval-shaped head.
Personality: Fearless. Inquisitive.
Background: Taken prisoner by the Blood Crown.
Family: Father = Nektas. Mother = Halayna †.

JADIS'S JOURNEY TO DATE:

Oh, dear, sweet Jadis. The visions I first had of her were of her youngling days. She was such a precious little thing. But the more I saw of her, the more a miasma began to cover her visage, leading me to believe that her future was in flux. I now know why, given my understanding that she went missing, and knowing what the Blood Queen has said about the one who came to the mortal realm with Ires, looking for Malec.

Let's take a peek at what I did *see*—and do know—about this bacon-loving draken.

A precocious child, Jadis spends most of her time getting into trouble, irritating her older friend Reaver, sleeping, and begging for food. When she meets Sera, she instantly takes to her and isn't unaffected by the changes occurring within the soon-to-be Primal—like when Sera brings Gemma back to life.

The draken loves Nyktos and spends as much time curled up with him as she can.

Proving just how much she's taken to the new addition to the Shadowlands, Jadis agrees, at Sera's request, to eat from a fork, a feat nobody else has been able to do and falls asleep with her in her god form, something the draken only do when they trust implicitly.

Jadis goes to the mountains with Nektas and is left there with Reaver, which makes her incredibly unhappy when she realizes she can't attend Sera's coronation.

The bits between this and the future are murky for me, sad to say. The only things I know are supposition and piecemeal factoids. It's assumed that Jadis accompanied Ires into the mortal realm to look for Malec and was somehow taken prisoner along with the god when Isbeth locked Ires away. After that, we can assume that her blood was used for nefarious purposes since only draken blood can kill a Revenant, and Isbeth killed Coralena. It's also unknown whether or not she still lives. Isbeth says she was *dealt with*, but that could mean many things.

I certainly hope that she's just hidden away somewhere, and Nektas and Sera will be reunited with the sweet girl again so they can help her heal.

When Ires is rescued, he says that she's somewhere in the Willow Plains. Hopefully, Poppy, Cas and their allies can locate and save her if she is.

HOLLAND (A.K.A SIR BRAYLON HOLLAND)
A Spirit of Fate. One of the Arae.

Hair: Closely cropped.
Eyes: Hickory-hued.
Facial features: Brown, smooth skin.
Personality: Gentle. Kind. Compassionate. Honest.
Other: Appears to be in his forties. In a relationship with Penellaphe—a goddess.
Background: Posed as a Knight of the Royal Guard from the time Sera was seven, teaching Sera how to deal with her anxiety and taking care of her in each decade of her life. When Sera healed her cat Butters, he told her she did nothing wrong but urged her to be careful. Tavius sent him off on a ship to the Vodina Isles the day after the King died.

HOLLAND'S JOURNEY TO DATE:
Holland first appeared in my visions as Sir Braylon Holland, a Knight of the Royal Guard in Lasania. He wasn't, however, present on Seraphena's birthday when the Crown presented her to the Primal God of Death.

When the Lords of the Vodina Isles arrive, Holland is shocked by their refusal of the Crown's deal and bothered by how they look at Sera. The Queen's order for Sera to deal with them angers him, even though he's known for Sera's entire life what she's been trained to do…to *be*.

Still believing that the Primal God of Death will come for her, he carries on, training her as best he can while also protecting her as much as he is able—the Arae are forbidden from directly interfering.

Seeing—and possibly knowing—that Tavius is a threat, Holland warns her. He also asks what's going on with her. When she says she's unworthy, it surprises him, and he tells her that isn't the case at all. He says that she carries the ember of life inside her. Hope. And the possibility of a future. When he said that, it seemed he meant the deal and the Rot. However, we now know that he was being literal.

When Sera asks him why he isn't married, he responds that he just hasn't felt like doing it. The romantic in me thinks it's because he has Penellaphe. The realist in me knows it's likely because he can't.

After Sera witnesses the seamstress rising after dying from an attack, she asks him what happened. He replies that he has no idea what such an abomination would be and asks her where she heard about it. I wonder if that's true. He's an Arae. Wouldn't they know all about the Revenants and Craven?

Ezra tracks them down in their hidden spot while they're training, and Holland is a bit annoyed that she is aware of their activities—especially since he knows that Sera let the Princess follow her. He questions Ezmeria as to why she and the orphanage need Sera's aid and is irked that his training with Sera is cut short.

Sera is attacked, and Holland checks on her, then later attends Odetta's funeral. A couple of days later, he learns of Sera's headache and stomach issues and asks her if her jaw hurts. When she tells him it does, he brings her something for it. We later learn it was a tea that helps a god get through their Culling. He also tells her about Sotoria and says she reminds him of the woman. Reminds? She shares a soul with her.

After all the details were revealed to me, it was interesting to look back on the things I saw happen between these two and their discussions. Holland really was skirting the line of propriety when it came to interfering.

Once Sera is in the Shadowlands, she sees him as he enters the throne room. After her shock, he admits that he's known her for most of her life. That he trained her. He tells Sera to call him Holland and explains that he's not a *viktor*, saying, "That honor is not mine."

He goes on to explain that he knew his time in the mortal realm was over when Tavius reassigned him to the Vodina Isles. He didn't go because he knew Sera and Nyktos would want to talk to him. When she asks him how he's stayed so young, he tells her that he's ageless because of the whiskey he drinks.

I think maybe I can claim that, too.

Later, he says that he never directly intervened. He couldn't tell her the Rot wasn't tied to the deal or the pointlessness of her endeavor, though he *was* pushing it with the healing tea.

When asked why he got involved at all, Holland confesses that he knew Eythos when he was the Primal God of Life and considered him a friend, though he didn't know what would become of him. He insists that if he had, he wouldn't have been able to stand by, and would have intervened, even knowing the punishment for such an act is final death.

He then tells them exactly what Eythos did. When Penellaphe recounts her vision, he reaches over and takes her hand and says how tricky it is to understand prophecies, adding that they're only one possibility, and not every word is literal.

Gods, is that true. I have revamped my interpretation of the prophecy so many times as visions came to me over the years.

Holland explains that Sera will go through the Culling but won't survive it. As they talk more, he reminds Sera how reckless and impulsive she is and tells her it can be her greatest strength; it could have given whatever Eythos believed upon hearing the prophecy a chance to come to fruition.

He shows them the cords of fate, and as they look at the almost broken thread, the only way to disrupt fate, Holland reveals that the key is love—the only thing not even fate can contend with. He says that love is more powerful than the Fates. It's even more powerful than what courses through their veins, though it is equally as awe-inspiring and terrifying in its selfishness. He says it can extend a thread by sheer will, becoming a piece of pure magic that biology cannot extinguish. It can also snap a cord unexpectedly and prematurely.

He reiterates that Sera cannot survive the Culling, not without sheer will of what is more powerful than fate and even death. Not without the love of the one who would aid in her Ascension.

When Ash takes Sera to her lake and Ascends her, those statements become all too clear. And it moved me to witness it.

Holland then tells Sera she's had many lives, and Eythos remembered the first one: Sotoria.

As they discuss the Rot, Holland says life has only continued because the ember was in Sera's bloodline. However, she now carries the only ember of life there is, and if she perishes, everything everywhere will die with her.

He goes on to say that the Primal God of Life is the most powerful being in all the realms and that she's never been merely mortal; she's the possibility of a future for all.

When Sera's doubt creeps in, Holland reminds her that she's a warrior, just like Sotoria learned to be. He adds that he doesn't know what Sotoria originally looked like—he didn't follow her threads until Eythos asked what could be done about Kolis's betrayal—but he knows she didn't look the same with each rebirth. He then tells Sera that Kolis may have sensed traces of eather in her and thought she was a godling entering her Culling.

Holland knows what Kolis has been doing to the missing Chosen—turning them into Revenants—but states they are not the only mockery of life he's managed to create. He details what some of the gods from Kolis's Court have been up to: creating the Craven.

Not to mention the Ascended…

Holland tells them about the Craven, talks about balance, and alludes to the fact that Sera bringing Marisol back to life had consequences. He confirms it was her time, and Sera's act needed to be righted. Therefore, the Arae decided who would take her place. Holland asks Sera if knowing that ahead of time would have changed her actions, and she says it wouldn't have.

Holland reveals that what the god Madis did to Andreia was an attempt to rectify what one of Kolis's creations left behind and adds that is all he can say without it being considered interference.

He reveals to Sera that Kolis can't kill Nyktos because life cannot exist without death, and they should not be one and the same. He adds, however, that anything is possible, even the *im*possibility of a Primal of both Life and Death. He says that such a being would be unstoppable, and there would be no balance. The Fates ensured long ago that the absence of either ember—life or death—would collapse the realms. Suddenly and absolutely. He says that if Kolis kills Nyktos, he'll kill himself and everything else in the process. He ends by saying he doesn't actually know what Kolis's end goal is.

When they discuss what led to the present moment, Holland admits that he couldn't tell Sera how pointless her duty was and outlines that the mortal realm has a year—maybe two or three if they're lucky—before the Rot consumes it, but warning the people would only incite panic.

Sera seems a bit crestfallen, and Holland reminds her not to give up hope, bringing up the broken thread and saying that fate is never written in bone and blood. It can be as ever-changing as her and Nyktos's thoughts and hearts.

She reminds him that Nyktos can't love, and he tells her that love is more powerful than even the Arae can imagine.

Before they part ways, she asks if she'll see him again, and he can't answer. He does remind her of something she already knows, though: All her training wasn't a waste. She *is* his weakness. Only it's not Nyktos. It's Kolis.

OTHER PRIMALS

AND GODS

PHANOS
Primal God of Sky, Sea, Earth, and Wind
Court: Triton Isles

Hair: Bald.
Eyes: Silver.
Body type: Very tall.
Facial features: Burnt umber skin.
Other: Crown shaped like a trident.
Background: Destroyed Phythe after the games honoring him were discontinued—sent waves taller than any Rise to wash away the entire kingdom. Hunted down many of the gods who left his Court after—Saion and Rhahar only escaped because Nyktos claimed their souls.

PHANOS'S JOURNEY TO DATE:
Attends the coronation with the other Primals.
Speaks to Saion and Rhahar briefly and then walks off with Embris.
When Kolis brings Seraphena to him off the coast of Hygeia, he hates what he's forced to do—especially since he should be paying Nyktos back for stealing Rhahar and Saion from him.
He tells Sera that he should just take the embers from her and says what he's doing isn't even worth it since it's only a temporary fix. Then, he breathes life into her and has his ceeren sacrifice themselves to save her.
During court later, he tells Kolis they need to talk, and Kolis promises to do just that as soon as he returns Sera to her chambers.

MAIA
Primal God of Love, Beauty, and Fertility
Court: Kithreia

Hair: Warm blond that cascades down her back in thick curls.
Eyes: Silver.
Body type: Full-figured.
Facial features: Yellow-brown skin. Stunning.
Habits/Mannerisms/Strengths/Weaknesses: Her every move and mannerism carry an air of softness, and a hint of spice.
Other: Pearl crown of roses and scalloped shells.
Background: Removed Nyktos's *kardia* upon request.

MAIA'S JOURNEY TO DATE:
Attends the coronation with the other Primals.

KEELLA
Primal Goddess of Rebirth
Court: Thyia Plains

Hair: Curly. Russet-colored.
Eyes: Silver.
Body type: Regal bearing.
Facial features: Smoky, reddish brown skin.
Personality: Welcoming yet reserved. Believes in right, wrong, and balance.
Habits/Mannerisms/Strengths/Weaknesses: When a babe dies, she captures their souls and gives them a rebirth. Sees those she saves as her children and often follows them throughout their lives. Doesn't always believe things attributed to the Arae.
Other: Nearly as old as Kolis. Can see the souls of all those she captures. Wears a pale blue quartz crown of many branches and leaves.
Background: Was involved in Sotoria's rebirth and hiding her soul from Kolis.

KEELLA'S JOURNEY TO DATE:
Keella attends the coronation like the other Primals. When the *benada*, the *imprimen*—the imprint—appears, she smiles at Sera and presses her hand to her chest.

After, she says something to Nektas. He nudges her arm, and she strokes his cheek.

When Nyktos announces Sera as the One who is born of Blood and Ash, *the* Light and the Fire, and *the* Brightest Moon, Keella asks him about it and says that perhaps it is another blessing. As she inquires about its inspiration with an edge to her voice—not anger...something *else*, she says it's beautiful and gives the couple an old, knowing, clever smile.

Before she leaves, she tells Nyktos that his father would be proud of him.

EMBRIS

Primal God of Wisdom, Loyalty, and Duty
Court: Lotho

Hair: Curly and brown.
Eyes: Silver.
Facial features: Boyish.
Personality: Quiet and watchful.
Other: Bronze crown of olive branches and serpents.
Background: Doubts some things regarding the Arae.

EMBRIS'S JOURNEY TO DATE:

Like the other Primals, Embris attends the coronation. He spends some time with Saion and Rhahar and then walks off with Phanos.

VESES

Primal Goddess of Rites and Prosperity (a.k.a The Eternal Goddess)
Court: Callasta Isles

Hair: Long, thick, golden-blond ringlets that reach her waist.
Eyes: Silver.
Body type: Thin but shockingly endowed.
Facial features: Creamy complexion—no freckles. Delicate nose and brows. Full mouth. Apricot-shaped lips.
Distinguishing features: Incredibly beautiful. Velvety voice. Smells like roses.
Preternatural features: Can sense a god or godling nearing their Ascension, but Kolis switching fates with Eythos dulled the ability.
Personality: Vindictive. Entitled. Can be vengeful. Can become fixated and resentful. Vocal about annoyances and complaints.
Other: Very old—should have gone to sleep long ago. Crown is shaped like a jade tree and made of bloodstone.
Background: Wants Kolis but settles for Nyktos. Found out about the deal regarding the Rot and Sera and made her own bargain with Nyktos to keep it a secret—she gets free access to him for feeding and…other things.

VESES' JOURNEY TO DATE:

Veses is a hard Primal to like. I *want* to think maybe she's just misunderstood or has reasons for her selfishness and vile ways, but realistically, I know it's just that she's entitled, jealous, and bitter.

Sera arrives in Iliseeum, and Veses comes to the Shadowlands to confirm that Nyktos has taken a Consort. When she discovers that it's true, it upsets her.

Veses comes to Nyktos for their deal, to feed from and indulge herself with him, and does it in such a way that she knows they'll be discovered—which Sera does when she returns from the Vale. When Veses sees Sera, she says, "So, this is her?" before Sera flees. Veses laughs at the fallout.

Later, when Nyktos is otherwise engaged with Shades—something Veses set up—she decides to confront Sera. Ector denies her entry into Sera's chambers, drawing his sword, and she throws the god into the room. Rhain then arrives and says he'll get Nyktos, but Veses just slides him out into the hall along with Ector's unconscious form and closes herself in the room with Sera.

She reveals that she knows Sera's full first name and asks how she became Nyktos's Consort. She also relays that she believes Nyktos lied to Sera, just like Sera is lying to her. She calls Sera fat and freckled and remarks that Sera is a Consort in title only. Sera taunts her and says Nyktos called her the "worst sort," pissing the Primal off. Sera makes it worse by then calling her pathetic. Veses takes it out on young Reaver by kicking him across the room.

In retaliation, Sera plunges her dagger into Veses' eye, and Veses hits Sera with eather. As they argue and battle, Veses confesses that she sent her guards and her favorite draken to the Shadowlands, confirming she was the one behind the earlier attack. She also wonders aloud if Nyktos realizes the others likely know Taric and the other vengeful gods were in the Shadowlands before they disappeared.

Veses reveals to Sera that she felt her and knew there was more to everything—a reason Nyktos was willing to do anything for Sera. She insinuates that being able to sense her either means Sera has so much of Nyktos's blood in her that Veses is latching on to that, or Sera's a Primal in her Culling.

She then taunts Sera that she knows the difference between Nyktos's blood and something else because she's *had* Nyktos's blood—she's had all of him. Sera punches her, and they fight some more until Bele arrives.

Veses sees Bele and realizes she's Ascended, relaying that there's a bounty on her head. As Bele keeps her busy, Sera heals Reaver. When he wakes, he calls her *liessa*, and Veses explodes with shock and anger, saying she was right and asking what Nyktos did.

Bele attacks with renewed fervor, and Veses fights back. Sera throws a dagger at her, and Veses tells Sera she's going to kill her because she's an abomination.

Bele renews her attack with an eather bow and arrow and gets Veses on the cheek. Shadows fill the room as Nyktos arrives, and Bele tells him that Veses knows about Sera. He blasts Veses with eather and orders Orphine and Ehthawn to take her away and put her in a cell.

Nyktos's attack essentially puts Veses into stasis, meaning she'll be out for at least a few days.

While she's out of commission, it's revealed that she hasn't been able to sense a god or godling in their Culling since Kolis took Eythos's embers. She only knew that Taric and the others were looking for a source of energy in the mortal realm and ended up in the Shadowlands. She felt something within Sera and realized they were embers. Putting two and two together, she figured she'd deal with Sera to keep Nyktos from getting in trouble with Kolis.

Admittedly, Veses cares for Nyktos in her own twisted way, but that doesn't make me like her any better.

Veses ends up escaping when Nyktos falls into stasis and the wards on the dungeon are weakened. She chews off her arms and gets out. Once she's healed, she heads to Dalos, only to find Sera there.

She makes it very clear how she feels about her being there, and ends up punished by Kolis, using Kyn as his weapon.

Later, she blasts into Sera's chambers where she's in the cage and convinces Callum to let her talk to Sera. Once they're alone, the Primal goddess tells Sera she knows she's lying, and insists she won't let Kolis throw her aside for Sotoria again. She'd rather see him dead.

She tries to convince Sera that she doesn't mind Kyn's particular brand of punishment, but I'm not sure even she believes that. Still, Sera says she's sorry for what happened to her, but it doesn't change that she can't wait to see her burn.

I'm sure Veses wishes she'd try.

ATTES

Primal of War and Accord
Court: Vathi

Hair: Light, blondish brown that frames his face.

Eyes: Silver.

Facial features: High cheekbones. Chiseled jaw.

Distinguishing features: Scar that runs from his hairline, across the bridge of his nose, and down his left cheek. Dimples. Silver cuff around his biceps.

Preternatural features/abilities: Can manifest clothing out of thin air. Turns into a silver hawk.

Body type: Tall and broad.

Habits/Mannerisms/Strengths/Weaknesses: Uses eather for provocation, feeding emotions to incite violence or peace. Has many perverse pleasures. Wears shadowstone armor and carries a curved sword on his hip. Driven by three things: peace, war, and sex. Turned on by boldness in women. Knows how to kill a Revenant. People pray to him on the eve of battle to grant their armies cunning skill and cleverness. Can shift into his *nota* form—a silver hawk.

Personality: Strategic. Cunning. Clever. He prefers to do things himself instead of delegating.

Other: Crown = a helm made of reddish black stone.

Background: Co-rules Vathi with his brother, Kyn. Kolis killed his children in retribution for losing Sotoria. Has feelings for Lailah.

Family: Brother = Kyn, Primal God of Peace and Vengeance. Children = unknown †

ATTES'S JOURNEY TO DATE:

Attes is a bit of a conundrum for me. I wanted to like him right off; he is, after all, the ancestor of some of the most pivotal people in my current history. Yet the things I *saw* led me to be incredibly wary. I thought, even at first, that he might be playing both sides a little and working behind the scenes, but I had no proof to substantiate that, and thus kept waiting and watching.

Luckily, I didn't have to wait too long.

As close to Kolis as a brother, Attes knows about Sera and watches her. He even saves her once as his *nota* form, the silver hawk.

After Sera arrives in the Shadowlands, Attes travels there to meet her. He remarks that she's no mere mortal and says she carries a mark and an aura. When she lashes out verbally as Sera is wont to do, Attes remarks that she has bite and asks Nyktos if Veses has seen her.

When he turns his attention to Nyktos, he inquires why the Primal killed the Cimmerian, Dorcan, and states that he thought they were fond of each other. Ash answers by reminding him what Attes did to his brother's guards.

Attes asks if Sera knows not to repeat what she hears, and she snaps at him again. He tells her to mind her tone and says that while he finds her boldness refreshing and alluring, others will not. Nyktos says that Sera will *kill* those who don't.

He attempts to use a bit of provocation magic on Sera and realizes that his presence does not affect her. He then turns the conversation to the Ascension that was felt and asks how a god Ascended in the Shadowlands. When Nyktos says it had to be Kolis, Attes clearly doesn't believe him. He says he knows it was a god from Hanan's Court and guesses it was Bele.

He tells Nyktos that Hanan has been having a fit in Dalos, and the other Primals are worried. He then adds that he hasn't forgotten who Nyktos's father was or who Nyktos was meant to be. If Nyktos wasn't the one who Ascended the god, then the embers are in the Shadowlands somewhere.

Attes says he's at the House of Haides out of curiosity *and* on Kolis's behalf. He believes he was chosen to deliver the message because he was the closest—and the least likely to be thrown into the Abyss. He then drops the bomb, telling Nyktos and Sera that Kolis denies their right to the coronation. He says the Primal of Life wants it to be more formal, and that requires his permission. He adds that Kolis will summon them and then comments on Nyktos being Kolis's *favorite*. When Sera calls the fake Primal of Life a son of a bitch, it makes Attes laugh.

Testing the waters, Attes offers himself to Sera if she'd rather have a *warmer climate in bed*. Nyktos is not happy, and Sera threatens Attes again. As he leaves, he tells Theon about Sera's threat on his way out and admits he was both turned on and amused.

In Dalos, Attes enjoys the show as Nyktos and Sera kiss and then interrupts them, flirting as usual. Nyktos threatens him again and says he's bound to lose his eyes. He tells Nyktos it would be worth it.

When Dyses enters, Attes finds joy in watching the Revenant provoke Nyktos. He remarks that Nyktos killing Dyses would either annoy or amuse Kolis. He also says that he imagines there will be many heartless, dead gods by the end of the day.

He tells Sera and Nyktos that he was awaiting their arrival, saying they're better company than the rest in attendance. He also remarks that Dyses has always felt off to him and tells the couple that some of the bodies they saw were from the last Rite.

When asked why he's there, he says that Kolis summoned Kyn, so he decided to join his brother. Not to mention, he wanted to see Sera again and remind her what he said when they first met about her watching her sharp tongue.

He adds that he's only been in Dalos for a few hours and that no other Primals are there but him and Kyn.

He sets off to find his brother before Kyn gets himself into trouble. After, he tells Nyktos why he killed Kyn's guards when the Primal of Death brings it up again.

Kolis arrives, and Nyktos blocks the Primal of Life from touching Sera. Attes remarks that Nyktos is quite possessive and says that the Primal of Death has threatened to rip out his eyes at least three times.

When talk turns to the Ascension they all felt, Attes chimes in and clarifies that what Nyktos says means that only Kolis can Ascend someone.

Kolis demonstrates his *life-restoring powers* with Dyscs, and Attes sits up straighter when Dyses enters, restored. Kolis asks him if he has the same doubts as Hanan since he seems surprised to see Dyses alive and well. Attes explains that it's just been a long time since Kolis has bestowed the honor, so it was a bit of a surprise.

He lies so smoothly.

Kolis tells Kyn to retrieve what he was ordered to deliver, and Attes swears when he sees the youngling, Thad. After Kolis makes his decree, Attes brings a dagger to Sera. Once Sera takes Thad's life, Attes lifts the draken's body, the blood singeing his flesh.

Later, in Vathi, Attes inquires as to why Nyktos and Sera are on his balcony without invitation or warning. When Sera asks about the draken, it takes Attes by surprise. He explains that Kyn went to burn Thad. Sera urges him to stop his brother and bring the body to them. When he hesitates, Sera shouts at him, and Nyktos orders him to do it.

It surprises me that he'd listen given how much older he is, but his loyalties really *do* lie with the Primal of Life. And he *was* Eythos's friend.

He returns with the draken's body and is told not to speak of what he sees. Nyktos says he will level his Court and hunt him down if he does. To which he responds that he's getting really tired of the Primal of Death's threats.

Attes watches, stunned, as Sera revives the draken; so shocked, he stumbles back from the table and swears.

The couple tells him he'll have to keep Thad hidden, and Attes confirms that the gods and Primals would have felt the revival. It will be hard to keep him hidden, especially from Kyn. They tell him to bring the draken to the Shadowlands and promise he'll be safe there. Attes says he knows Nektas will take care of him.

He comments on Sera's charm, saying it won't work there, but vows that no one will learn about what happened in Vathi—he swears it. He bows to Sera and promises not to betray what she did.

Attes insists that he knew something was different about her. He had even more suspicions when she didn't react to his presence. Nyktos asks why he didn't go to Kolis with his assumptions and gain favor, and he says that he could have, but again, he remembers who Nyktos's father was and who Nyktos was meant to be.

At the coronation, Attes sees Nyktos bow to Sera and remarks that he's a man who knows his place. He approaches the dais and bows to the couple—he is the only Primal to approach them up to that point—and tells Sera that her crown and imprint suit her. He adds that the imprint was…unexpected.

He reveals that a few dakkais have been sniffing about but left without causing too much trouble, then says they need to make time for the three of them to speak in private. Before he leaves, he says he hopes their union will bless the Shadowlands and beyond and then briefly stops to speak to Nektas.

During the battle later, he comes up to Sera from behind. She swings at him, not knowing it's him, and he catches her. She thanks him—presumably thinking that he came to her aid—and he says that she shouldn't thank him yet.

When I saw this, I instantly felt rage. When things unfold more later, I felt a little sorry for him.

He tells Sera that what he's about to do is the only way and disarms her, then hauls her against him. He says that all they want is her. If she removes the charm, no more blood will be shed, and no more lives will be lost. If she refuses, his brother will leave none but the Primal standing. He reiterates that it's Sera's choice, but she needs to make her decision quickly.

Sera makes him promise that no one else will be harmed, and he swears. When she surrenders, he tells her she made the right choice.

Back in Dalos, Attes interrupts Kolis and reminds him that Keella helped Eythos capture Sotoria's soul to be reborn. He reiterates that Kolis hasn't been able to find her, even after hunting down every mortal with an aura. He then suggests that maybe he couldn't find her because she'd been reborn over and over the last few centuries and insinuates that maybe Sera is telling the truth about being Sotoria reincarnated.

When Callum disrespects him, Attes tells the Revenant that he knows how to kill him and will prove it if he speaks to him like that again.

Kolis still seems hesitant to believe what Sera said, so Attes reminds him how clever Eythos was and says that it's just the kind of thing he'd do to fuck over his twin.

Attes visits Sera in her cage, coming in as his *nota* form, the silver hawk. He explains himself, and gets her to understand, telling her that he was never really loyal to Kolis. Not after Kolis killed his children.

While he brings Sera news of what's going on and does what he can to help her, he makes it clear that while she's important, Sotoria's soul must be saved since she's the only thing that can kill Kolis.

Once Ash breaks free and gets to Sera, Attes shows up to assist. He has been working through a god from his Court, Elias, for a while and continues that by lending him Setti to transport Kolis somewhere he won't easily be found.

He goes to get Keella and witnesses them transfer Eythos's soul out of The Star, set it free, and then put Sotoria's in.

Not liking what's happening to Sera, he makes his opinion known and tells her how he feels about it. And while he still isn't Nyktos's favorite person, he at least knows the Primal understands he's on their side.

And he plans to uphold his promise to Sera to support Nyktos however he needs when she's gone, as well.

He made a vow. Even if he weren't duty-bound as a Primal to uphold it, he would.

Won't he be shocked to find out that Sera Ascended as the new Primal of Life?

Or maybe he won't.

KYN

Primal God of Peace and Vengeance
Court: Vathi

Here is some information about Attes's evil twin...

Hair: Light, blondish brown.
Eyes: Silver.
Body type: Tall and broad.
Facial features: High cheekbones. Chiseled jaw.
Distinguishing features: Dimples. Silver cuff around biceps.
Habits/Mannerisms/Strengths/Weaknesses: Extremely fond of the draken. Spends a lot of time in the mountains. Heavy drinker.
Personality: Asshole.
Background: Co-rules Vathi with his brother, Attes. Kyn's guards were taking young ones years out from their Culling to their encampments, so Attes killed them.
Other: Gods in Kyn's Court are a bunch of assholes—taking after their Primal. Crown is a helm of reddish black stone.
Family: Brother = Attes, Primal God of War and Accord.

KYN'S JOURNEY TO DATE:

Kyn arrives in Dalos before the others, already deep in his cups, and Attes quickly shoves him into a chair before he falls on his face.

The Primal of Life asks if Kyn has what Kolis asked him to bring, and Kyn moves to the hall to retrieve a young draken. Sera asks Kyn what Thad did to deserve being killed, and Kyn can only answer with the truth: "Nothing." Kolis then orders Sera to take the innocent draken's life, and he is struck down. Kyn folds his hands over his eyes during the act, unable to watch, but then glares at Sera with burning hatred afterward. Later, he heads off to find some whiskey before undertaking the task of burning the draken's body.

Kyn attends the coronation with Hanan, both of them highly intoxicated. He and the Primal of the Hunt and Divine Justice are the only two who do not approach the new couple, showing utter disrespect.

Eventually, Kyn heads to the Shadowlands looking for Nyktos and Sera, ultimately killing both Aios and Ector.

Once his brother takes Sera to Kolis, Kyn shows up at court in Dalos and gloats about Sera's captivity. He fights his attraction to her but is eased a bit when Kolis offers Sera up as a reward for his loyalty if she turns out to be lying about who she is.

He brings news about the Shadowlands' forces and offers to take them out. Kolis doesn't give him express permission, but he makes it known that he's at his disposal should he change his mind.

When Kolis calls him in to punish Veses for her failure, he gladly accepts. It speaks to his sadistic side, and he will never refuse an opportunity to let it out to play. He only wishes Ione hadn't told Kolis that Sera was Sotoria. If he hadn't, he might have had his chance to play with her, as well.

Still, he's holding out hope that the truth will come to light, because he doesn't, for one minute, believe that she is who she claims to be.

HANAN †

Primal God of the Hunt and Divine Justice
Court: Sirta

Hair: Dark.
Body type: Tall.
Facial features: Pale. Sharp and angular—beautiful in a cunning, predatory way.
Distinguishing features: Silver cuff on biceps. Deep, gruff voice.
Personality: Combative. Contrary.
Other: Appears to be in his thirties. Follower of Kolis. Wears a crown of ruby antlers.

HANAN'S JOURNEY TO DATE:

As the Primal of the Hunt and Divine Justice, Hanan rules the Court of Sirta with his gods but follows the ways of Kolis. He has a small army of Cimmerian at his disposal, which he isn't afraid to employ against the Shadowlands. At one point, he sends upwards of one hundred of them.

When Hanan meets Seraphena, he calls her "a diamond that will inevitably be shattered into tiny pieces." Nyktos takes offense and threatens to break every bone in his body and bury him so deep in the Abyss it'll take him a hundred years to claw himself out if he so much as looks or speaks to her again. Not afraid, he challenges and tells Nyktos that he knows Bele Ascended. Nyktos says that no one in his Court can Ascend a god and taunts Hanan about doubting Kolis. Still, Hanan questions Nyktos's explanation because he doesn't believe that Kolis would Ascend someone in the Shadowlands for no reason and then just leave.

Later, when everyone is together, he speaks up without permission, and Kolis reprimands and scolds him, telling him to leave his sight and not return until summoned.

At the coronation, Hanan joins Kyn in a little too much drink and disrespects Nyktos again by not approaching the new couple.

Later, Hanan comes to back up Kolis in Dalos when Nyktos busts in trying to save his Consort. Unfortunately, he doesn't succeed, and Nyktos kills him, ripping out his heart and taking off his head.

His title transfers to Bele.

RHAHAR

RHAIN

SERAPHENA

PENELLAPHE

IONE

LAILAH

SAION

NYKTOS

THEON

BELE

AIOS

ECTOR †
Court: Originally, Vathi

Hair: Curly. Fair.
Eyes: Deep amber.
Body type: Tall. Slender.
Facial features: Sharp cheeks, eyes, and jaw.
Personality: Loyal. Likes to tease.
Other: Older than Nyktos by several hundred years.
Background: Knew Eythos and Mycella fairly well. Knew about King Roderick's deal. Sometimes joined Lathan to watch over Sera—starting on her seventeenth birthday.
Family: Sister.

ECTOR'S JOURNEY:
I'm going to admit that when I started seeing Ector in my visions of the past, I immediately had a soft spot for him. And the more I saw, the more I learned by researching and viewing others, the more endearing he became.

The first real glimpses I got of Ector started when he hands Sera a narrow birch box that he was ordered to give to her—the box containing her special crescent moon shadowstone dagger.

Ector accompanies Nyktos to the mortal realm to retrieve Sera and tends to her after Tavius's assault, freeing her from her bonds and calling her stepbrother an animal. When Nyktos orders everyone out of the hall, Ector escorts the mortals.

When they return to the Shadowlands, Ector stands guard outside Sera's room, even though he feels he has much better things to do. However, he remains for her safety since he's heard that she likes to wander off into dangerous situations. He also takes it upon himself to bring her meals.

Ector accompanies Sera as she watches Nyktos hold Court, though he was against letting her come. Rhain teases him that he worries *Daddy Nyktos* will be upset and send him to bed with no dinner. When Veses arrives, he is ordered to take Sera somewhere safe and gives her the option of her chambers or the library. When she chooses, he deposits her and reminds her to adhere to what they agreed to.

Later, when Erlina arrives, Ector brings Sera to her chambers and stands guard outside. When the seamstress leaves, Ector offers to walk with Sera in the courtyard instead of keeping her in her room. He tells her that the draken understand when someone talks to them, even when not in their god forms.

Ector sympathizes with the shock Sera must have felt learning the truth about the Chosen. They discuss Gemma, and Ector tells Sera that she hasn't been in the Shadowlands long. He then reveals what Court he's from and tells her how old he is, teasing her about how good he looks for his age.

As they discuss Nyktos's parents, Ector tells Sera that Eythos loved Mycella, even more so after she died, and would never have remarried.

A ruckus arises at the south gate, and Ector asks Sera to stay put as he goes to investigate. He finds Gemma, injured, and carries her into the palace, then orders Rhahar to get Nyktos. He tells Sera to return to her chambers.

He tries to argue that Gemma isn't dead, but then he sees that she is. When the draken start acting strangely, he remarks that he's never seen anything like it and then stares in shock as Sera starts to glow. He watches in awe as Sera brings Gemma back to life.

Later, Ector enters the war room with Bele and helps to relay the tale of Kolis's treachery, how he exchanged destinies with his twin and then destroyed all records of the truth. When they discuss recent happenings, Ector remarks that it makes sense now why the poppies returned.

After Sera's secret becomes known and during the dakkais siege, Ector asks what to do with Sera but ends up fetching a hooded cloak and meeting Nyktos by the gates to the bay. He doesn't believe that Sera cares about Nyktos's safety and tells her so later when he relays that *monsters* are in the water. He adds that Nyktos won't kill her until he figures out what's up with the embers.

When the dakkais spill out of the bay, he remarks that he thought they'd cleared the harbor, and Rhain tells him they were in the process of doing it. As he watches Bele fight, he gushes that he might be in love. As the battle rages, a dakkai pins him to the parapet wall, and Sera throws a dagger at it, saving Ector's life. He thanks her in response.

Ector takes Sera back to the palace and wants to return her to her bedchambers. When he sees Nyktos, he asks the Primal how much of the blood he's wearing is his and realizes that most of it is. It concerns him. He then turns his attention to Sera and tells her that she doesn't have to pretend to care for Nyktos around them. She promptly tells him off and chastises him not to tell her how to feel.

After Hamid attacks Sera, Ector arrives with Nyktos and Saion. He kills Hamid with eather before thinking that Nyktos would probably like to question him. Sadly, there's nothing left but ash. Despite the error, he's a little surprised by how upset Nyktos is that he killed Hamid and remarks he should probably think before he acts, then goes to clean up the mess.

Ector says that no one would piss Nyktos off when he could fuck with them after they're dead. As they talk about what might have led to the attack, Ector tells everyone that Gemma is still in the palace and was sleeping when he checked on her half an hour ago.

He shares that Nyktos doesn't enjoy being touched but likes Sera's kind of touching and is asked if he has a death wish. His response? "I'm beginning to think I do."

He reminds me so much of Emil…

Ector enters the throne room just as Nyktos engages the murderous gods. When he sees that Bele is injured, his eyes turn glassy. He falls to his knees and argues when Nyktos says she sleeps, that is all. Then, with awe and fear, he stares at Sera, saying, "That is *not* all," and watches in shock as Sera Ascends Bele.

Ector and Saion pace as they wait in Nyktos's office with Sera. She asks them if they're scared of her, and Ector responds that they're more unnerved since nobody should be able to do what she did—bring a god back to life and Ascend them. He then adds that he doesn't think Bele is a Primal, but she *is* more powerful. He goes on to say that he was around when Primals Ascended.

He's ordered to fetch a bowl of water and a towel so Sera can clean up and does, then leaves to wait for Nektas. Later, he waits outside the throne room with Nektas, Reaver, Rhahar, Ward, and Penellaphe—the Arae have answered.

When the next big attack comes, and Davina is struck down, Ector stops Sera from reviving the draken. Then, he curses when Sera admits that she finds Nyktos ripping a god in half hot.

In discussions later, Ector wonders how a god was looking for Sera when no one knows what she looks like. But then Rhain implies that Veses *does*, and things become clearer.

After Sera tries to leave to take on Kolis by herself, Ector is with Orphine when Nyktos returns with her and is subsequently stunned when he hears the specifics. But maybe not as surprised as he is when he finds out that Sera and Nyktos are lovers. Later, when Nyktos tells them all that Sera's bravery is unmatched, he draws his sword and bows to her.

Ector fights with the others against the Cimmerian and then joins Rhain and Sera in the office after the battle. He tells Rhain that Sera saved his ass outside.

Tensions arise between Rhain and Sera, and Ector tries to defuse the situation. He says that she's not the enemy. When talk turns to the things Nyktos has sacrificed for Sera, he brushes aside the topic and then leaves quickly when Nyktos arrives, donning his *scary face.*

Ector enters Nyktos's office just after Attes leaves and reveals that Attes told him about Kolis making Nyktos get permission for the coronation. When they discuss what happened, Ector realizes that Attes's presence had no effect on Sera and tells her that gods and godlings are not immune to a Primal's influence. Only three things are: the Arae, the draken, and another Primal.

The time approaches for them to head to Dalos, and he is confused why everyone is so nervous. He says it's how they get permission. Though he *does* worry about something: not Nyktos but rather *Sera* not playing nice with Kolis.

After Sera's dinner with Bele and Aios, Ector escorts her back to her room. He tells her that Orphine is with Nyktos and remarks that he'll lose an eye to a draken someday, given how little awareness they have of where they are in a space. He goes on to say that there are Shades at the edge of the Dying Woods, too close to Lethe, and Nyktos and Orphine are dealing with them. He adds that the Shade issue is an infrequent one, but something that is becoming a bigger problem.

When Veses arrives, Ector refuses her entry into Sera's chambers and is thrown inside by her power, landing on and crushing a table.

Once he recovers, he rides outside Sera's carriage with Saion on the way to the coronation, until the end, when he enters the carriage with her. He notices she's pale and nervous and says she reminds him of his sister on her wedding day. He adds that he didn't believe Bele when she told him that Sera was anxious. He tries to comfort her, telling her that nothing will happen to her, and is taken aback—and thrilled—when she blurts out that she *wants* to be Nyktos's Consort.

After the coronation, Ector tells Sera that the cheers and shouts are for her and then stands by her side as the revelers greet her and Nyktos.

During the next big battle, Ector moves to protect Aios from the Primal Kyn and dies. Sera goes to save him, but Saion stops her when her power starts drawing the dakkais. She backs off, and the dakkais swarm him, drawn to the eather Sera released, leaving nothing of Ector behind but a *mess*.

Let me tell you, viewing that last battle and Ector's tragic end was enough to bring even me, someone who has seen and experienced much, to tears.

BELE

Goddess of The Hunt (in Blood and Ash timeline)
Court: Sirta/The Shadowlands

Hair: Midnight black. Shoulder-length. Often braided.
Eyes: Became silver after Ascension.
Body type: Tall. Lithe.
Facial features: Light golden-brown skin. Round cheeks and chin.
Distinguishing features: Paints her fingernails black. Wears no bands on her arms like others.
Preternatural features: After Ascension, she can conjure a bow and arrow made of eather, and her bolts of eather kill rather than wound. Powers of prosperity and fortune in Blood and Ash timeline.
Personality: Nosy. Flippant. Nonchalant. A bit of a showoff.
Habits/Mannerisms/Strengths/Weaknesses: Doesn't like crowds. Usually wears a short sword on her hip and a bow over her shoulder. Often speaks without thinking. Huntress of information. Has a knack for moving about unseen. Is often in other Courts trying to uncover information that might be useful. Helps the Chosen get out of Dalos. Has a thing for Aios. Loves fighting. Always armed.
Background: Knows many Consorts but none who are mortal. Was born after Eythos died. During her Culling, she shattered windows every time she got upset.

BELE'S JOURNEY TO DATE:

Okay, I'm just going to say it. I love Bele. She's absolutely delightful. I only wish she played a more prominent part in my visions because I enjoy viewing her every time she appears.

When Sera comes to the Shadowlands, Bele is the first to bow to her and explains why it's so important. She also reveals that some Courts are betting on how long Sera will live. After it's shared how Sera killed Tavius, Bele is delighted, impressed, and a bit surprised that a mortal Consort has a violent side.

She gives Sera advice, like not to show fear during the coronation.

Once Sera brings Gemma back to life, Ector escorts Bele to the war room, where she stares openly at Sera. She says that no Chosen are Ascended because Kolis no longer has the ability to grant or create life, so he can't Ascend them. She adds that he can't stop the Rite, though. It'd raise too many questions, so the unstable balance shifts more toward death.

When they discuss Sera's plan, Bele says that she doesn't believe Sera thought becoming Nyktos's Consort would save her people; she learned how to end the deal in the summoner's favor.

The dakkais attack, and Bele reminds everyone that most Courts likely felt a ripple when Sera used her powers, and the attack is probably because of that. She, Saion, and Rhahar go to find out what's happening. Later, they ride down the bluffs and engage the dakkais, Bele standing on her horse to fire her arrows as the others crouch. She punches a dakkai and it explodes, then follows another that made it up the bluff and into the city.

Bele doesn't think that Sera should be going anywhere after Hamid's attack, not even to see Gemma. She tells Sera that Nyktos is in Lethe dealing with an incident and then questions Gemma about how she knew Kolis was looking for Sera. When the word *graeca* is mentioned, Bele tells Sera it's the old language of the Primals and means life. During discussions, Bele realizes that Hamid thought he was protecting the Shadowlands by killing Sera.

The goddess admits that she knows nothing about the Revenants but *has* been working hard to find out what happened to the missing Chosen. As talk turns to the Fates, she tells Sera they don't know everything, though they *do* know more than most. She adds that the Primals cannot make demands of the Fates. They can't even touch them—it's forbidden in order to maintain balance. She says that it wouldn't have even crossed Nyktos's mind to go to the Arae—Kolis, either. And he has no respect for the rules.

When the gods attack, Bele throws herself over the staircase at Cressa and fights with her. She's eventually stabbed in the back with a shadowstone dagger and kicked hard enough in the head that it would have killed a mortal.

The fighting dies down, and Aios removes the dagger. Bele dies, but not for long because Sera brings her back to life. When she wakes, she says she just feels tired and then goes on to say that she saw an intense light—what she thought was Arcadia—before passing out.

After Bele awakens again, she spends some time with Aios. Everyone acknowledges that she's not a Primal. Still, she's definitely stronger, and they felt a burst of energy when she healed and rose—not as strong as when a Primal enters Arcadia and a new Primal rises, but she's still Ascended, and that's a big deal. The most significant part is that she can challenge Hanan for the Primal position of the Hunt and Divine Justice in Sirta now, and he won't take kindly to that at all.

When the draken attacks, Bele gives Sera a spear to fight with and remarks that Nyktos will lose his shit when he finds out that Sera is fighting with them. As they set off, Bele calls those they're fighting for "our people," referencing Sera.

Bele acknowledges later that she didn't recognize the god who was talking to Sera—the one Orphine killed, though she imagines that Hanan was behind the attack. She then declares that she needs to leave so no more deaths occur because of her, though she refuses to hide forever. Nyktos tells her that she's needed in the Shadowlands and it's also the safest place for her. Sera tries to soothe her, saying it's not Bele's fault. It's hers. Bele thanks Sera for saving her life.

Bele joins the others in the throne room when Nyktos tells them that Sera went after Kolis and reiterates her bravery. Later, when the Cimmerian arrive, Bele takes the younglings to Aios and refuses to leave them.

Sera returns from Lasania, and Bele trains with her for the better part of an afternoon.

Bele is with Rhain in Nyktos's room when Sera wakes from her mini stasis. She flips off Rhain but goes to get juice and water for Sera. She shares that Sera slept for four days and says it's a lot like hibernation. She adds that Sera could have been out for weeks. Bele continues to be Bele, oversharing and annoying Rhain. She tells Sera that Nyktos barely left her side and was very worried. She shares that he's currently at the Pillars, dealing with something. When Sera mentions her nakedness, Bele tells her she's okay with it.

I just bet she is…

Bele sits with Sera for dinner and tells her that not even the oldest and strongest gods could shake the palace like Sera did when she got angry at seeing Veses. She asks what made Sera so mad. Sera tells her about her Culling and her anger, and Bele calls Sera aggressively assertive. She then reveals that she knows it was the Primal goddess.

Bele says she was waiting for Aios and headed to the kitchen when she saw Veses enter Nyktos's office. She had hoped the Primal's visits would stop after Sera's arrival. She admits that she doesn't get what's going on with Sera and Nyktos and doesn't know about Veses, but she sees how Sera looks at the Primal of Death and has never seen him act the way he does with Sera. She insists it's not just the embers and tells Sera how he told them all off after the bravery speech in the throne room.

She guesses that Sera saw Veses and Nyktos together and reveals that she's seen Veses feed from him before—without sex. She doesn't get it and knows there has to be a reason he allows it, but she doesn't know what that is. She insists she doesn't believe Veses was *ever* good and tells her that the Primal supports Kolis and that Nyktos doesn't trust or even like her.

Bele and Aios have dinner with Sera in Sera's receiving chamber, and the goddesses covertly flirt. When Sera heads to her room, Bele charges in to face

Veses.

Veses tells Bele there's a bounty on her head and Kolis will rip out her heart and devour it. She flippantly replies that there are tastier things on her than her heart. After Veses hurts Sera and Reaver, Bele tells her that Sera is Nyktos's Consort, Reaver is under Nektas's protection, and things won't end well for her.

Bele engages Veses, and Veses shatters her sword and throws her back. She summons an eather bow and arrow and fires at Veses, the energy grazing and wounding her cheek.

Once Veses is subdued, Bele tells Nyktos that Veses knows about Sera. He orders her to take Reaver to Nyktos's quarters. Later, while talking to Sera, she tells her not to thank her for helping. She's been waiting to get her hands on Veses for ages.

Bele tries to keep Sera still during her gown fitting and does a terrible job. She tells Sera how big the crowd will be for the coronation and remarks how beautiful Sera is in her gown. Despite having to stay at the House of Haides for the coronation, Bele comforts Sera's worries about a few things and then warns her about dismissing her title while praising her for remaining armed. After Rhain speaks with Sera, Bele sees them off.

Bele joins Rhahar in Lethe to fight the dakkais and isn't aware of what happened to Aios.

I can only imagine how she'll take it. The romantic in me hopes it will finally force them to stop dancing around each other.

AIOS
Goddess of Love, Fertility, and Beauty (in Blood and Ash timeline)
Court: Kithreia

Hair: Red.
Eyes: Citrine with thick lashes that turn silver after Ascension.
Facial features: Plump lips. High cheekbones. Heart-shaped face.
Personality: Cheery and bright. Worrier.
Habits/Mannerisms/Strengths/Weaknesses: Is a hugger. Wears a silver chain around her neck.
Preternatural features: Powers of life, love, and birth.
Other: Can create many beautiful things with her touch—like the trees of Aios. Voice like spun gold and windchimes. Slumbers in the Skotos Mountains in Blood and Ash timeline.
Background: Was very young when Kolis killed Mycella. Was one of Kolis's favorites at one time—kept in a cage of gilded bones until she gutted a guard and escaped.
Family: Cousin = Mycella †. Second Cousin = Nyktos.

AIOS'S JOURNEY:

When Sera arrives in the Shadowlands, Aios is called to take her to her chambers and have food sent up. She's startled when she feels an electric jolt when her skin touches Sera's. She reveals that Sera's room has been ready for a while and was dusted frequently just in case. She tries to settle Sera by telling her that she trusts no one in either realm more than she does Nyktos and wouldn't feel safer anywhere else. She leaves to get what Sera needs and returns with food and a belted chenille night rail.

Bringing clothing for Sera, she tells her more about godlings and the Culling. She asks Sera if she previously knew about the deal. As talk turns to her, she reveals what Court she once served and says that she came to the Shadowlands because it was where she knew she would be safe.

Sera watches Aios help Reaver learn to fly. Later, Aios helps Sera after the Gyrm attack and brings her a robe and some whiskey. She informs Sera that Veses is gone and then leaves when Nyktos arrives.

As she and Sera spend time together, Aios tells her that Mycella used to tell her about Veses being kind. She also reveals details about stasis and Arcadia. When Rhahar and Bele return, she gives them both hugs.

After Gemma is hurt, Aios arrives just as Ector brings her inside the palace. She asks if Shades got her and runs off to get supplies. She returns just as Sera starts glowing and watches in awe as Sera brings Gemma back to life. She checks on the girl and declares that she's definitely alive.

Talk turns to the deal and the Rot, and Aios thinks Rhain is on to something about the deal and the Rot being linked. The mortal realm is more vulnerable to the actions of the Primals and should have been affected long before now. She wonders if maybe the ember being in the Mierel bloodline protected it in some way, but once Sera was born, it was in a vulnerable vessel that carries an expiration date—Sera's death. Or maybe it's weakened in a mortal body and can no longer hold off the effects of what's been done.

When Gemma wakes, Aios comes to tell Sera. She says that Gemma claims to have no knowledge of what Sera did, but she thinks the girl is lying. She wants Sera to confront her. Aios tells Sera it's clear that she didn't want to do what she believed she had to do—make Nyktos fall in love and then end him. She adds that she disagrees with her actions and is disappointed but that everyone has experience carrying out terrible deeds because they believed they had no choice. She says she's done worse than Sera—all of them have.

Aios takes Sera to see Gemma and learns what she told Hamid and why. The girl says that Sera is who Kolis has been looking for.

As they talk about Kolis more, Aios tells Sera that *graeca* also means love, and she's afraid that Kolis somehow found a way to create life.

When the murderous gods attack, Cressa throws a bolt of eather at her and takes her down. When she wakes, it's to go to Bele. She removes the dagger and cries as she rocks the goddess. She begs Nyktos to let Sera try to heal her, shaking as it appears not to work. But then it does. She stays with Bele as the now-Ascended goddess recuperates.

Aios continues watching over Sera, doing everything she can to ensure everyone is safe. When Sera starts fretting, Aios tells her she did nothing wrong by bringing Bele back and asks if knowing the outcome will change her actions in the future. She imagines that Sera doesn't really have a choice. It's part of her makeup and driven by instinct.

Later, in the throne room, Aios stands next to Paxton as Nyktos tells them how Sera tried to go after Kolis on her own to protect the Shadowlands and that her bravery is unmatched.

When the Cimmerian arrive, Nektas brings Reaver and Jadis to Bele and Aios for safekeeping.

Aios spends time with Sera and the younglings, talking about how draken only sleep in their mortal forms when they feel safe, and the coronation being delayed. They gush as Reaver is sweet, bringing Jadis a blanket, and then discuss Aurelia and what being sweet on someone—as Reaver put it—means. Aios blushes when Reaver insinuates that Bele is sweet on *her*.

Later, Aios asks Nyktos if he thinks Kolis will be able to sense the embers in Sera. Before they leave, she helps Sera pick out an appropriate gown for her meeting with Kolis and remarks that she is like Bele in stashing weapons everywhere. Aios inquires whether Sera will go after Kolis while she's there and asks why she thinks she can take the Primal. Sera tells her that she's Kolis's *graeca*. She is Sotoria. As they talk more, Aios asks Sera why killing Kolis and being Nyktos's Consort can't *both* be her destiny. Then, she reveals details about her time in Dalos when she was Kolis's *favorite* and kept in a cage.

Sera apologizes and tells her how strong she is. As the discussion wraps up, Aios tells Sera that she's wrong about what she can do because Kolis has no weaknesses—he's incapable of love.

Aios and Bele have dinner with Sera and Reaver in the receiving room.

Before the coronation, Aios does Sera's hair and makeup. Later, she takes Sera from Rhahar and escorts her to Nyktos with the guard, Kars. She asks if Sera has any questions. Sera asks her if she's been in love, and Aios says she doesn't think it feels the same for everyone. For her, it was like feeling at home in an unfamiliar place. Like being seen, heard, and understood for the first time in a way you never were before. She tells Sera that you know you're in love when you'd do anything for someone. Then she hands Sera off to Nyktos.

During Kyn's attack, the Primal kills her. She had just gone outside to help when he takes her down. Despite her mangled chest, Sera restores her. She wakes and is confused. Kars helps her inside.

Eons later, when the gods sleep, Aios comes to Poppy in a dream and keeps her from falling from a cliff in the Skotos Mountains.

PENELLAPHE
Goddess of Wisdom, Loyalty, and Duty (in Blood and Ash timeline)
Court: Unknown

Hair: Honey-colored.
Eyes: Bright blue—like sapphires that become silver in Blood and Ash timeline.
Facial features: Light brown skin.
Preternatural features: Powers of intelligence and will.
Other: In a relationship with Holland—an Arae. Slumbers under the Great Atheneum in Carsodonia in Blood and Ash timeline.
Background: Was young when she had her first vision. The source of Poppy's prophecy and her namesake.
Family: Mother was a God of Divination.

PENELLAPHE'S JOURNEY TO DATE:
Penellaphe goes to the Shadowlands with Holland to discuss Sera. When she arrives, she bows to Nyktos and tells him she's come about Sera and brought an Arae.

As the group chats, Holland tells Sera that he's ageless because of all the liquor he drinks, making Penellaphe laugh. When they discuss what she saw and what has happened, she tells Nyktos that Holland didn't technically intervene by being *Sir Holland* to Sera and that their years together were very long.

I feel this deep in my soul. Being away from those you love can feel unending, indeed.

They talk more, and Penellaphe tells Sera the Arae can't do anything to affect her fate. At least, not anymore. But she clarifies that Sera has the essence of Eythos's power, and it could be recognizing its source in Ash, signifying soul mates.

Penellaphe reveals that she had a prophetic vision before Eythos made the deal with King Roderick. It had never happened to her before, and she wasn't sure what she saw or heard. And while she didn't understand the words, she knew they carried purpose and were important. She told Embris, and he took her to Dalos. Kolis questioned her extensively as if he could force understanding or clarification. Eventually, he gave up. Afterward, she went to Lotho, figuring if anyone could make sense of what she had seen, it was the Fates.

The prophecy:
From the desperation of golden crowns and born of mortal flesh, a great primal power rises as the heir to the lands and seas, to the skies and all the realms. A shadow in the ember, a light in the flame, to become a fire in the flesh. For the one born of the blood and the ash, the bearer of two crowns, and the bringer of life to mortal, god, and draken. A silver beast with blood seeping from its jaws of fire, bathed in the flames of the brightest moon to ever be birthed, will become one.

When the stars fall from the night, the great mountains crumble into the seas, and old bones raise their swords beside the gods, the false one will be stripped from glory as (NOT UNTIL) the great powers will stumble and fall, some all at once, and they will fall through the fires into a void of nothing. Those left standing will tremble as they kneel, will weaken as they become small, as they become forgotten. For finally, the Primal rises, the giver of blood and the bringer of bone, the Primal of Blood and Ash.

Two born of the same misdeeds, born of the same great and Primal power in the mortal realm. A first daughter, with blood full of fire, fated for the once-promised King. And the second daughter, with blood full of ash and ice, the other half of the future King. Together, they will remake the realms as they usher in the end. And so it will begin with the last Chosen blood spilled, the great conspirator birthed from the flesh and fire of the Primals will awaken as the Harbinger and the Bringer of Death and Destruction to the lands gifted by the gods. Beware, for the end will come from the west to destroy the east and lay waste to all which lies between.

While talking to Sera, she offers her some information about her paths, saying that knowledge is power, and then reveals that Sera always dies before the age of twenty-one. She says there are many *ways* she can die, several at Ash's hands. She then tells them the only way for Sera to survive is with the blood of the Primal the ember she carries belonged to—Ash—and remarks that it's unfair to both of them but that love, life, and fate are rarely fair.

As talk turns to Eythos, Penellaphe tells them that he wanted to keep Ash safe but also save the realms and take his revenge. So, he stashed the ember, hoping it would grow until a new Primal was ready to be born, and hid it with the one thing that could weaken his brother.

When Nyktos and Holland say that Sera is the Primal God of Life, Penellaphe confirms it and tells Sera she can't afford to deny it. She reveals that other than Eythos, only Embris and Kolis knew the prophecy. Then she says that prophecies are confusing, even to those who receive them, and mentions the Gods of Divination and the oracles, explaining to Sera who and what they were and are.

Penellaphe offers that her mother was a God of Divination, which is likely why she could share a vision. However, she doesn't have any of her mother's other skills like the ability to see what is hidden or unknown and has never received any additional visions. She assumes that with the passing of the oracles and most of the Gods of Divination, that other visions have either been lost to time or are only known to the Ancients since prophecies are their dreams.

The group discusses what may come, and Penellaphe tells Sera that Bele's Ascension would have been felt. She also says that if she looked like Sotoria and Kolis already saw her, he would have taken her on the spot. As they discuss how to keep her safe, Penellaphe says that becoming Nyktos's Consort will offer some protection, but until then, any god can make a move against her, and he'll have no support from others if he retaliates. Even the coronation poses a risk since some like to push the limits, though Kolis doesn't usually make a habit of attending such events.

And if it was done in the Shadowlands, he may not have been able to attend anyway.

Penellaphe remarks that Kolis sending the dakkais was a warning, letting Nyktos know that *he* knows something in the Shadowlands can create life. She believes he hasn't responded to Bele's Ascension because it caught him off guard. She then asks Nyktos if he's been summoned yet.

They discuss Kolis's quest to create *life*, and Penellaphe says that's not their biggest concern right now. What they should be worrying about is that he will do anything to get the embers of life, and if he finds out that Sera has Sotoria's soul, he will stop at nothing to have her. He'll burn the Shadowlands to the ground if that's what it takes. She knows precisely how cruel Kolis can be.

When it's revealed that Nyktos had his *kardia* removed, it stuns Penellaphe. She tells Sera that it is the piece of the soul that allows others to love irrevocably and selflessly. Then she says that having it removed must have been terribly painful and that he is genuinely unable to love.

Penellaphe offers to help prevent Sera from being taken from the Shadowlands against her will. As the Goddess of Wisdom, she knows things others do not, like spells that can prevent that. When she brings in Vikter to help with the charm, she reveals that he was the first *viktor* and is the only one who remembers his past lives. When Vikter shrugs off some praise, Penellaphe tells Sera he's too humble and says that he saved the life of someone very important and paid a steep price for doing so. The Fates decided to reward him and later realized they could give aid without upsetting the balance. Wishing there was more she could do, Penellaphe apologizes and then leads Nyktos away to speak to him privately.

The next time we see her is at the coronation, wearing white and speaking with Keella.

RHAHAR

The Eternal God (in Blood and Ash timeline)
Court: Originally, the Triton Isles

Hair: Dark. Cropped short.
Eyes: Silver in Blood and Ash timeline.
Facial features: Rich brown skin.
Body type: Broad shoulders and chest.
Personality: Impetuous.
Habits/Mannerisms/Strengths/Weaknesses: Uncomfortable with hugs. Often speaks before thinking.
Preternatural description: In Blood and Ash timeline, he is said to oversee deity and Atlantian afterlives and have the powers of death.

Background: Left the Triton Isles after Phanos destroyed Phythe. Nyktos found him in Dalos awaiting sentencing for defection shortly after Eythos was killed. His soul was taken with his cousin's, saving him from punishment.

Other: Slumbers in Stygian Bay.

Family: Cousin = Saion.

RHAHAR'S JOURNEY TO DATE:

Rhahar isn't a prominent feature in my visions—or in my research, truth be told. I don't even know what he represents in present days, even though it's clear from depictions that he became an important figure since he appears with others such as Saion, Aios, and more. His Temple is located in the foothills of the Undying Hills, and he is often depicted in artwork and literature with Ione.

As for his history…

Rhahar arrives at the House of Haides with Bele after Nyktos brings Sera to the Shadowlands. He's impressed that she is a fighter and admits that Saion told him what Sera did with the whip and Tavius.

When Gemma gets hurt, he brings her to the palace and sends Orphine to get Kye, the Healer. Inquiries arise, and Rhahar confirms that Shades attacked Gemma. He goes to get Nyktos to tell him what happened, thus missing the miracle that is Sera restoring Gemma's life.

Later, in the war room, Rhahar stares openly at Sera, not hiding his curiosity or wariness. During discussions, he wonders aloud if mortals would be so afraid of death if they viewed it as a beginning, not an end. When they discuss Kolis, Eythos, and the embers, he says there's more to Eythos's actions than giving life a chance.

The battle with the dakkais commences, and Rhahar is sent to retrieve Odin for Nyktos before joining him, Saion, and Rhain as they ride into the fight. He engages the dakkais as they advance toward homes, crouched on horseback and firing arrows.

When the Arae arrives, Rhahar waits outside the throne room with Nektas, Reaver, Ector, Ward, and Penellaphe.

Rhahar interrupts Sera and Nyktos in the Primal's office to let him know there is trouble at the Pillars. He then accompanies Nyktos to deal with that.

Rhahar witnesses Nyktos telling everyone that Sera tried to go after Kolis on her own and that her bravery is unmatched among them. Like the others, he draws his sword and bows, saying he will endeavor to be deserving of such an honor.

As the time for the couple's meeting with Kolis approaches, Rhahar finds the idea of Sera playing nice with Kolis amusing and tells her that she can't threaten Kolis like she did with Attes.

Before the coronation, he remarks that Sera's gown looks like starlight. After the ceremony, Rhahar stands by Nyktos's side as the couple meets with the revelers.

When the dakkais infiltrate Lethe, Rhahar fights them with Bele. As he attempts to return to the House of Haides, he joins the others in the courtyard just after Sera's outburst and swears when he sees there's no safe path to the palace.

Bleeding from a wound on his face, he and Saion go to help Nyktos as the dakkais swarm him.

That's about all I know when it comes to Rhahar. I'm actually a bit anxious to find out more. I would like to know which Primal's seat he assumes—if he does. Given that most of the gods of present times have taken the titles of the Primals of yore, it stands to reason. But one never knows.

RHAIN

God of Common Men and Endings (in Blood and Ash timeline)
Court: The Callasta Isles/The Shadowlands

Hair: Golden red.
Eyes: Dark golden-brown that become silver in Blood and Ash timeline.
Facial features: Wheatish skin tone.
Personality: Purposefully contrary at times. Loves to push people's buttons. Easily amused. Sarcastic.
Habits/Mannerisms/Strengths/Weaknesses: Can't use compulsion. Can use thought projection.
Preternatural features: Powers of death in Blood and Ash timeline.
Other: Said to sleep deep below Stygian Bay. Queer. Has a home in Lethe.
Background: One of Nyktos's guards. Was born after Eythos died.
Family: Father = Daniil †. Brother = Mahiil †.

RHAIN'S JOURNEY TO DATE:

When Nyktos returns to Iliseeum with Sera, Rhain meets them by the stables and knows who Sera is. He inquires about the incident that led to Sera being there. When *he* is asked why he's still there, he says that he decided to annoy Ash in Saion's absence but came to talk to Nyktos about something important. He finds it highly amusing how Sera and Ash bicker.

As Ash holds Court, Rhain hangs out with Sera, teasing Ector about fearing that *Daddy Nyktos* will send him to bed with no dinner. When Gemma goes missing, Rhain leaves with Saion to investigate.

Just as Gemma dies, Rhain arrives from Court. He then watches Sera bring her back to life.

The story of what Kolis did to Eythos is shared, and Rhain is in the war room for it. Learning that Sera reminds Ash of temperamental poppies makes him laugh. As talk turns to the Rot, he says that it's likely just coincidence that it showed up after Sera was born, though the ember *could* be triggering something. However, he has no idea why it'd cause that.

After Sera's secret comes to light, Rhain becomes extra protective. At one point, he tells Sera not to die because Nyktos wants the honor of killing her.

When the dakkais attack, Rhain is the first to see them emerging from the pitch-black water. He tells Sera that Kolis sent them, and they've come for her. When Bele executes one of her amazing feats during the battle, he calls her a showoff. Then, he switches his attention to Theon as he fights and remarks that he thinks he's in love. As he runs out of arrows and the dakkais continue to come, he realizes there are too many.

The draken get involved, and Rhain grabs Sera, shielding her as the draken rain fire down on the dakkais. He then explains that the draken aren't bonded to all Primals and can attack other Courts, especially since not all Primals play by the rules.

After the fight, he takes Sera back to the palace, wanting to put her in a cell. He's relieved when Ash at least takes her dagger from her. When he asks Nyktos why his wounds aren't healing, Ash asks him if he wants to die. He then tells Sera that they can't get Ash to feed and that he just hopes the Primal rides it out.

Hamid attacks Sera, Ector kills him, and Rhain arrives just after. Stunned, he asks what happened and remarks that he's surprised there wasn't a guard outside Sera's door. He adds that there is no way anyone betrayed Nyktos and says Hamid likely learned of Sera plans. She corrects him and tells him it's *planned*, past tense; it is no longer the case. He has Aios sit with Gemma and then searches Hamid's house and the bakery.

Just as Nyktos engages the murderous gods in the throne room, Rhain enters. Bele is injured in the melee and Rhain tells Nyktos, only to find out that she's dead. When Sera brings her back to life, Rhain can only stare in wonder.

Rhain thinks about how many Primals would actually be bold enough to pull a stunt like the attack. When they discuss Veses, he implies that she knows what Sera looks like, and Nyktos confirms. He then tells Sera that Hamid was different. He was trying to protect the Shadowlands. Lailah agrees with him. Despite what Sera has done, he still feels a certain way about her and openly glares when she touches Nyktos.

After Sera tries to go after Kolis on her own, Rhain is in the throne room, witnessing Nyktos tell everyone that her bravery is unmatched among them.

When the Cimmerian attack, Sera saves Rhain's life. Later, he begrudgingly thanks her, but it's clear that he doesn't care that she doesn't actually plan to kill Nyktos. She's not the true Primal God of Life, she's a vessel. He then mentions what Nyktos has endured and sacrificed for her but won't go into detail. Ector finally de-escalates things between them before Rhain offers to go and get supplies for Nyktos and makes himself scarce. He asks if Ector wants to go and get scarce with him.

It surprises Rhain when Sera disarms Saion and asks to spar with Nyktos. Still, he settles in to watch, reluctantly amused.

When Sera loses control below the House of Haides, he tells Nyktos to stop her before she brings down the palace and kills herself, urging him to use compulsion on her.

Later, as Sera wakes, Rhain is in the room with Bele. He asks Bele to grab water and juice. She flips him off but goes to get them. He helps Sera sit up and is obviously concerned. Their touch creates a shock, and he's surprised by its strength. It makes him hiss and jerk away.

Sera jokes about him trying to get her naked, and he replies that he has no interest in that. Saion or Ector, on the other hand…

I have to admit. I've seen depictions of those two and I'm utterly on board with that, as well.

Rhain then tells Sera he's never seen anyone do what she did—not even a Primal in their Culling. He says she's powerful and asks her what happened.

She asks him why he's being nice to her since she knows he doesn't like her. He doesn't exactly address that, just tells her not to lose her shit like that again or she might not wake up. When Bele returns and begins oversharing, he gets annoyed and knocks her feet off where the goddess has them resting on him. He then goes on to relay that Nyktos has been worrying. To the point Rhain thought the Primal might kill Ector—at least five times. After, he brings Sera bath water and has food sent up.

When Sera comes to see Nyktos in his office, Rhain is there. He's concerned by how polite she's being since it is utterly against her nature. He thinks she's unwell and says as much before heading out to the Rise.

Later, when Kolis summons them to Dalos, he tells Sera that she must do whatever Kolis demands of her, no matter how distasteful or vile, and adds that there are only a few things Nyktos can refuse on her behalf. He also makes it known that delaying in answering Kolis's summons will make Kolis incredibly angry, and it *will* cost them.

Rhain goes to check on Sera and finds Veses in Sera's chambers. He apologizes and offers to let Nyktos know that she's arrived, trying to lead the Primal away. She tells him that she's not there to see Nyktos and it scares him a bit. After she attacks Ector, Veses sends Rhain skidding out of the room with her power, along with Ector's unconscious body. He rushes off to find Nyktos and inform him of Veses' attack on Sera.

Before the coronation, Bele retrieves him at Sera's request so he can be her escort. He confirms that, as the Consort, she will have authority over Nyktos's guards, and he has to answer her honestly. Therefore, when Sera asks what he meant by Nyktos having to sacrifice, he first tries to backpedal but ends up telling her about Veses and her deal with Nyktos. He's concerned the Primal of Death will murder him for sharing that and is not convinced he won't find out.

He goes on to say that Eythos kept his deal with King Roderick a secret for a long time, and so did Nyktos. Still, it was discovered a few years back, and he doesn't know how. Somehow, Veses found out about Sera but nothing else and threatened to tell Kolis. Rhain tells Sera the price Nyktos paid for Veses' silence. He adds that he believes Veses may have tried to take Sera out to prevent blowback on Nyktos, but it was more likely because the agreement was about to end. He also tells her that only he and Ector know about the deal with Veses because they found Nyktos in bad shape once after a feeding.

As he feels Sera's fury build, he tries to calm her by grabbing her face and making her focus on him. He knows he can't stop her like Nyktos did before without hurting her and is stunned when Sera claims she'll kill Veses.

He blocks her from going to the Primal and tells her that Veses will be dealt with. The moment the embers are in Nyktos and he Ascends, Veses is done for. Then, he stuns Sera by calling her *Your Highness* and saying she will be and has been his Queen.

When he asks Sera if she loves Nyktos and she can't answer, he realizes what it means and confesses he thinks he was wrong about her.

On the way to the coronation, he falls into step behind Rhahar and Sera with Ector, followed by Saion and the twins. As Nyktos and Sera enter, he addresses the crowd and tells them to bow. During the ceremony, he hands Sera's crown to Nyktos. Afterward, he appears at the door to their carriage with the shadowstone box for the crowns. When they arrive at the House of Haides, he takes them to put them away.

When Kyn attacks with his dakkais and draken, Rhain leads the guards on the Rise. He sees Ector taken down and kicks away a dakkai, only to see the mess that is left of his friend. He can't hold back and vomits. At one point, he grabs Sera and asks if she's okay after her blast of power, only to swear when he sees Nyktos drawing the dakkais away with Primal mist. Sera tears free of his hold.

After Sera is taken to Dalos, Kyn captures Rhain and brings him to Kolis. Kolis taunts him about his father and brother and susses out that he has the same gifts. He figured it would happen, but he still manages to talk to Sera in her mind and tell her to take the palace down like she did at the House of Haides.

Sera makes a deal with Kolis to spare his life, and they return him to the Shadowlands. He isn't sure he'll ever be able to repay her. When she's finally free, he makes sure everyone understands that she's the reason many of them are still alive and free.

When it's time for Nyktos to take Sera to her lake to extract her embers, he kneels and extends his sword, drawing blood before destroying the weapon, pledging himself to her forevermore.

SAION

God of Sky and Soil—is Earth, Wind, and Water (in Blood and Ash timeline)
Court: The Triton Isles/The Shadowlands

Hair: None. Bald.
Eyes: Black that turn silver in Blood and Ash timeline.
Body type: Tall.

Facial features: Deep black skin.

Personality: Snarky.

Habits/Mannerisms/Strengths/Weaknesses: Doesn't believe that anyone is genuinely benevolent throughout their lives and thinks that long life contributes to that benevolence waning.

Preternatural features: Powers of elemental control.

Other: A seasonal god. Temple in Saion's Cove off the Cliffs of Ione. Older than Nyktos.

Background: Born in the Triton Isles. Helped to create the pool under the House of Haides. Left the Triton Isles five decades after his Culling, so about two hundred and fifty years before Sera comes to the Shadowlands. Was in Dalos awaiting sentencing for defection from Phanos's Court after Eythos was killed. Nyktos saw him in a cell and took his soul so no other Primal could claim him.

Family: Cousin = Rhahar.

SAION'S JOURNEY TO DATE:

Saion accompanies Nyktos—then going by *Ash*—to the mortal realm to retrieve Sera when the Primal feels her distress. When he sees what's going on, he remarks that calling Tavius an animal is an insult to animals. He notices no blood despite the brutal appearance of what Tavius had been doing and then laughs when Sera remarks that Tavius is too weak to break the skin.

Saion frees Sera of her bonds by simply placing his hand over them, then settles in to get his daily dose of entertainment. When Nyktos makes his move, and Ector comments on the Primal of Death seeming angry, Saion replies that he has been moody lately and they should let him have his fun.

After Sera kills Tavius with the whip, Saion is hard-pressed to contain his surprise. As he escorts the mortals out of the Great Hall, he remarks that he's in the mood for whiskey and then finds a cloak for Sera.

In the Shadowlands, Saion retrieves Sera to take her to breakfast with Nyktos. He mentions that he told Nyktos that the Primal should be watching over his Consort himself and then reveals that he was threatened and told Nyktos would feed him to Nektas.

Later, Saion waits for Nyktos when they exit the dining hall. He takes Jadis and is told to rock her but warned that she's been able to cough up sparks and flames lately. He awkwardly soothes her as best he can.

As Nyktos holds Court, Saion waits with Sera and teases her about fidgeting. He tells her that no part of Nyktos doesn't know exactly where she is at all times. When word comes that Gemma is missing, Saion joins Rhain and leaves after a signal from Nyktos.

When Sera attempts her escape, Saion escorts her back and is told to grab Rhahar to check the tombs. While they're returning to the palace, Saion realizes she's hurt and sniffs her wound, snarling.

Saion reappears just after Gemma dies, his head jerking up when he hears

Ector remark that Sera is glowing. He then swears and asks the room at large if they can sense what he's feeling. Finally, he watches as Sera brings Gemma back to life.

Afterward, Saion stares openly at Sera in the war room and tells her that the power to give life is both a blessing and a curse. He acknowledges that it's a strength and not a weakness because most would not realize how quickly that power can turn on them. He then adds that bringing back the dead doesn't just sound impressive; it *is* impressive. As they discuss the past, Saion agrees with Rhahar that there was more to Eythos's actions in putting the embers in a mortal line than just giving life a chance.

Saion, Bele, and Rhahar go to check on word of a disturbance and find that something is happening along the bay. He informs everyone that a ship capsized. He adds that anyone who goes into the water usually doesn't return.

Later, he, Rhahar, Theon, and Nyktos ride out of the gate and head down the bluffs, engaging the dakkais as they advance toward the homes. They all crouch deftly on horseback, firing arrows.

Saion arrives at the House of Haides with Nektas and Nyktos and states that at least twenty died, but they're still checking to see if any in Lethe perished. He also shares that Nyktos was swarmed at the docks and the dakkais got a lot of hits in. When Sera leaves to try to feed the Primal, he flashes her a thumbs-up and tells her she has his thoughts and prayers.

Smartass.

After Hamid attacks Sera in her bathing chamber, Saion arrives with Ector and Nyktos and hands Nyktos a towel for Sera—one that wasn't touched. He tells Rhain that Hamid tried to assassinate Sera and questions if the mortal's motives may have to do with what Sera planned.

As Nyktos deals with the murderous gods, Saion checks on Sera, and she tells him to go to Bele. Once Taric moves his attention to Sera after being told not to look at her, Saion remarks that the fallout will be good.

Sera Ascends Bele following the attack, and Saion paces in Nyktos's office with her and Ector. He mentions that he wasn't around when the Primals Ascended, then tells Sera that not every god she brings back will Ascend. They'd have to be fated to hold that position. Nyktos agrees. He then learns that Sera may have had *viktors*, though it's been a long time since he's heard anything about them. He states that it would make sense if she did have them given what Eythos did.

Escorting Sera back to her chambers, she asks him if he wants revenge for what she had planned. He tells her that if he thought she was a real threat to Nyktos, he'd snap her neck, even knowing he'd be killed for it. He adds that Nyktos is attracted to her, but that's as deep as it goes.

Sera reminds him that she's a threat to all the Shadowlands while she's there, and he asks her if he *should* snap her neck, then. She invites him to try and urges him not to be a coward and wait until her back is turned. She adds that she won't make it easy, and he replies that he wouldn't expect her to.

Saion reminds Sera that she'll be the Consort in a few days. She asks him if she'll be *his* Consort, and he doesn't answer her. He then introduces her to Orphine, who's there to make sure Sera is safe in her chambers—it's protection more than punishment.

He joins the others in the throne room when Nyktos shares that Sera tried to go after Kolis to protect the Shadowlands and says her bravery is unmatched. He mirrors Ector, drawing his sword, bowing, and saying he hopes they deserve such an honor.

When the Cimmerian storm the gates, Saion interrupts Nyktos and Sera in the Primal's office and tells them about it, adding that they're from Hanan's Court and there are about a hundred of them.

He's ordered to stay with Sera and make sure she doesn't leave, and he responds that he's honored to obey such a command. He then ribs Sera by talking to her like a child, mentioning snacks and naps.

Saion asks if she really tried to go after Kolis. When she confirms, he states it'd be dishonorable to talk about harming her now and suggests that he should bow to her since she's technically the Primal God of Life—but he won't.

He wonders how good Sera is with a bow and then orders her to remain unseen, telling her that the Cimmerian don't know what's inside her and will kill her. He adds that if Nyktos is overpowered, she is to go inside to Aios and Bele. He also says that Dorcan would take her head to Hanan on a spike without hesitation. He then leaves to join the fight, jumping off the Rise. Later, he tells Nyktos that Dorcan saw Sera.

Saion takes his turn guarding Sera's room and then goes to breakfast in the first-floor receiving room with Reaver. Sera asks him if the other rooms are ever used, and he tells her that other than Jadis and Reaver exploring them, they aren't. She asks him who keeps them so clean, then, and he tells her that Ector does, in memory of Eythos. When Sera asks Saion where he's from originally, he tells her about his past and how Nyktos saved both him and Rhahar.

He informs Sera that they train for a few hours every morning but says he won't train with her. When he reiterates that and she disarms him, he's shocked. He confesses he'd have to think about which he'd prefer: babysitting Jadis and Reaver or following *her* around. As Sera spars with Nyktos, Saion takes a seat on a nearby boulder to watch and then escorts her to her room afterward.

Following Veses' attack on Sera, Saion is ordered to keep an eye on the Primal with Theon and tells Sera that Ector will be okay.

The day of the coronation, Saion remarks on how pretty Sera looks in her gown and then drives the carriage to the ceremony. After, he falls into step behind Rhahar and Sera with Ector, Rhain, and the twins. Still later, he opens the carriage door for Nyktos and Sera, addressing them as *Your Highnesses*, ending with a bow and a wink.

After Kyn's attack, Saion informs Nyktos of what happened and tries to block them from seeing the bodies in the west courtyard. He tells Sera that she's starting to glow and points out to Nyktos where Kyn is. He's ordered to summon the armies and runs to guard on horseback.

Later, Sera has him help her get Aios down from the pike. He tells her it'll make it worse and orders Sera to grab her head before it detaches. When Sera seethes and says, "Fuck the dakkais," when she's warned not to use eather, he tells her that he likes her.

Saion watches in amazement as Sera restores life to Aios and is relieved to see the goddess once again alive. He orders Kars to take Aios inside and then informs Sera that the dakkais are over the wall. He tries to stop her from saving Ector, knowing it'll just make things worse with the dakkais, and physically keeps her away.

The battle rages against the dakkais, and Saion is injured. He tells them they need to get inside and then goes with Rhahar to help Nyktos when he's swarmed by dakkais.

LAILAH
Goddess of Peace and Vengeance (in Blood and Ash timeline)
Court: Vathi/The Shadowlands

Hair: Shoulder-length. Braided straight back.
Eyes: Wide-set. Gold. Become silver in Blood and Ash timeline.
Facial features: Deep, rich brown skin.
Preternatural features: Powers of strength, tactical prowess, and logic.
Other: Wears white armor.
Background: Said to be Nyktos's child—proven untrue. Said to rest with Theon beneath the Pillars of Atlantia in Blood and Ash timeline.
Family: Twin = Theon.

LAILAH'S JOURNEY TO DATE:
When Nyktos arrives with Seraphena, it takes Lailah aback a bit. Like her twin, she immediately teases Nyktos about taking Sera against her will, asking if he's taken up his ancestor's habits of kidnapping young women.

While Reaver is learning to fly, Lailah takes him for his *airtime* with Theon. It's absolutely adorable.

After Gemma gets injured, Lailah enters the room and witnesses Sera glowing as she brings Gemma back to life. She then follows Theon with a basin to clean the girl as he carries Gemma to recovery.

Lailah isn't present when Sera's original motives are revealed, she just hears about it later. From what I saw of her, she didn't seem to hold it against Sera quite as much as some of the others. Perhaps that's because of the Court she originated from. Who knows?

When draken from outside their Court enter the Shadowlands, Lailah asks

Nektas if he recognizes the tan draken. She also agrees with Rhain about Hamid: that his attack on Sera wasn't to protect the Shadowlands; it was to threaten it.

Later, after Nyktos calls them all together and announces that Sera tried to go after Kolis to save the Shadowlands and states that her bravery is unmatched, she—like the others—bows, saying she hopes to be deserving of such an honor.

Lailah tells Seraphena how Attes told Theon that Sera threatened him. It seemed to tickle her. And I think it might, given her chemistry with the Primal of War and Vengeance.

On coronation day, Lailah exits Sera's room and asks Sera and Rhain if they felt the manor shake.

THEON
God of Accord and War (in the Blood and Ash timeline)
Court: Vathi/The Shadowlands

Hair: Braids along scalp.
Eyes: Wide-set. Gold. Become silver in Blood and Ash timeline.
Facial features: Deep, rich brown skin.
Personality: Funny. Sarcastic. Flirty.
Preternatural features: Powers of strength, tactical prowess, and logic.
Other: Slumbers with his sister below the Pillars of Atlantia in Blood and Ash timeline.
Family: Twin = Lailah.

THEON'S JOURNEY TO DATE:
When Nyktos arrives with Seraphena, it surprises Theon—he knew nothing about her. He and his sister immediately tease Nyktos about kidnapping her and tells Sera to blink twice if she's a captive.

He takes Reaver for his *airtime*. I just love watching him with his sister and the youngling. It makes me feel all warm and fuzzy.

When Veses arrives at the House of Haides, Theon announces her arrival.

After Gemma gets injured, Theon enters the room and witnesses her passing. He also sees Sera start to glow and watches as she brings Gemma back to life. After, he carries Gemma to recovery.

Theon isn't present when Sera's original motives are revealed, but when the attacks start, he's there to tell Nyktos which direction the water attack came from and what happened and then joins Bele, Nyktos, Saion, and Rhahar as they fight the dakkais.

When draken from outside their Court enter the Shadowlands, Theon announces that three gods were involved and states that he didn't recognize the two he saw. He theorizes that Sera's been seen, and it wouldn't be a stretch for anyone to deduce that she's the Consort. He also states that Hanan could have given the order to take Sera and Bele.

Later, after Nyktos calls them all together and announces that Sera tried to go after Kolis to save the Shadowlands and states that her bravery is unmatched, Theon draws his sword and bows, saying he hopes to be deserving of such an honor.

Theon reveals that Attes told him about Sera's threat and that he was both amused and turned on by the news. He quickly apologizes when Nyktos gets prickly over the comment.

Reaver sticks up for Sera with Nyktos, and Theon comments that it's wrong for the draken to take her side.

When Nyktos orders that Veses be kept under guard, Theon and Saion assume the responsibility.

IONE

Goddess of Rebirth
Court: Thyia Plains

Hair: Chin-length. Reddish brown.
Eyes: Silver in Blood and Ash Timeline.
Body type: Tall. Slender.
Facial features: Medium brown, beigy skin tone. Sharp features.
Preternatural features: Powers of life and birth. Can root out memories.
Habits/Mannerisms/Strengths/Weaknesses: Can see into thoughts. A bit shy.
Other: A seasonal goddess associated with spring. Temple is in the foothills of the Undying Hills. Often depicted with Rhahar in artwork.

IONE'S JOURNEY TO DATE (AS KNOWN):

I didn't see much of Ione, truth be told. Not until Sera ends up in Dalos.

Kolis summons Ione and brings her to Sera's cage. She has a rare gift to sift through and root out memories from someone's brain, and Kolis wants to know the truth about Sotoria.

Playing both sides, she does as she's told, but makes sure to stretch the truth when relaying what she saw in Sera's head. In her mind, Seraphena is Nyktos's Consort and that's the way it should be.

She hates that she had to put Sera through the pain of doing what she had to do, but she hopes that putting herself on the line will make up for it.

I imagine I'll see much more of Ione soon. All the gods and goddesses are waking up, and there is too much backstory still buried.

I can't wait to find out more.

PERUS
God of the Rite and Prosperity*

Here is what people *think* they know about the *god*, Perus…

Hair: White.
Facial features: Fair.
Background: Perus didn't exist. The Ascended created him, though nobody knows why.*

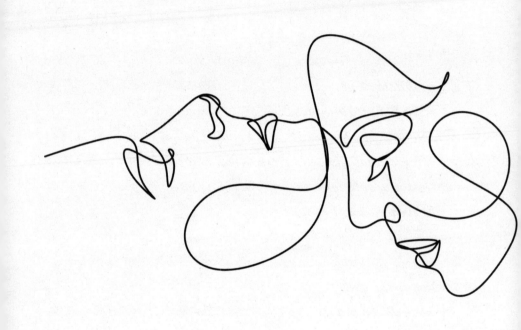

A NOTE FROM MISS WILLA

So, that's as much as I've been able to amass thus far. New things come to me almost daily, and I pick up information tidbits in my travels, as well, so I don't expect this story to end anytime soon.

Big things are on the horizon for Poppy, Cas, and their allies, not to mention the fact that the gods are waking, and timelines are about to converge in a way nobody expected, uncovering fallacies and fleshing out prophecies even more.

Enemies still lurk around every corner, and I have a feeling the Primal of Life is about to make her opinion known on how things unfolded while the gods rested.

For now, all we can do is prepare—for the best, the worst, and the unknown—and wait to see how things play out.

And despite being a Seer, I have a feeling even I will be surprised.

-Willa

From #1 *New York Times* bestselling author
Jennifer L. Armentrout comes the thrilling
conclusion to her beloved Flesh and Fire series...

Born of Blood and Ash
Flesh and Fire, Book 4
Available May 7, 2024

DISCOVER MORE
JENNIFER L. ARMENTROUT

From Blood and Ash
Blood and Ash Series, Book One
Available in hardcover, e-book, and trade paperback.

Captivating and action-packed, From Blood and Ash is a sexy, addictive, and unexpected fantasy perfect for fans of Sarah J. Maas and Laura Thalassa.

A Maiden…

Chosen from birth to usher in a new era, Poppy's life has never been her own. The life of the Maiden is solitary. Never to be touched. Never to be looked upon. Never to be spoken to. Never to experience pleasure. Waiting for the day of her Ascension, she would rather be with the guards, fighting back the evil that took her family, than preparing to be found worthy by the gods. But the choice has never been hers.

A Duty…

The entire kingdom's future rests on Poppy's shoulders, something she's not even quite sure she wants for herself. Because a Maiden has a heart. And a soul. And longing. And when Hawke, a golden-eyed guard honor bound to ensure her Ascension, enters her life, destiny and duty become tangled with desire and need. He incites her anger, makes her question everything she believes in, and tempts her with the forbidden.

A Kingdom…

Forsaken by the gods and feared by mortals, a fallen kingdom is rising once more, determined to take back what they believe is theirs through violence and vengeance. And as the shadow of those cursed draws closer, the line between what is forbidden and what is right becomes blurred. Poppy is not only on the verge of losing her heart and being found unworthy by the gods, but also her life when every blood-soaked thread that holds her world together begins to unravel.

* * * *

A Kingdom of Flesh and Fire
Blood and Ash Series, Book Two
Available in hardcover, e-book, and trade paperback.

Is Love Stronger Than Vengeance?

A Betrayal…

Everything Poppy has ever believed in is a lie, including the man she was falling in love with. Thrust among those who see her as a symbol of a monstrous kingdom, she barely knows who she is without the veil of the Maiden. But what she *does* know is that nothing is as dangerous to her as *him*. The Dark One. The Prince of Atlantia. He wants her to fight him, and that's one order she's more than happy to obey. *He may have taken her, but he will never have her.*

A Choice…

Casteel Da'Neer is known by many names and many faces. His lies are as seductive as his touch. His truths as sensual as his bite. Poppy knows better than to trust him. He needs her alive, healthy, and whole to achieve his goals. But he's the only way for her to get what she wants—to find her brother Ian and see for herself if he has become a soulless Ascended. Working with Casteel instead of against him presents its own risks. He still tempts her with every breath, offering up all she's ever wanted. Casteel has plans for her. Ones that could expose her to unimaginable pleasure and unfathomable pain. Plans that will force her to look beyond everything she thought she knew about herself—about him. Plans that could bind their lives together in unexpected ways that neither kingdom is prepared for. And she's far too reckless, too hungry, to resist the temptation.

A Secret…

But unrest has grown in Atlantia as they await the return of their Prince. Whispers of war have become stronger, and Poppy is at the very heart of it all. The King wants to use her to send a message. The Descenters want her dead. The wolven are growing more unpredictable. And as her abilities to feel pain and emotion begin to grow and strengthen, the Atlantians start to fear her. Dark secrets are at play, ones steeped in the blood-drenched sins of two kingdoms that would do anything to keep the truth hidden. But when the earth begins to shake, and the skies start to bleed, it may already be too late.

* * * *

The Crown of Gilded Bones
Blood and Ash Series, Book Three
Available in hardcover, e-book, and trade paperback.

Bow Before Your Queen Or Bleed Before Her...

She's been the victim and the survivor...

Poppy never dreamed she would find the love she's found with Prince Casteel. She wants to revel in her happiness but first they must free his brother and find hers. It's a dangerous mission and one with far-reaching consequences neither dreamed of. Because Poppy is the Chosen, the Blessed. The true ruler of Atlantia. She carries the blood of the King of Gods within her. By right the crown and the kingdom are hers.

The enemy and the warrior...

Poppy has only ever wanted to control her own life, not the lives of others, but now she must choose to either forsake her birthright or seize the gilded crown and become the Queen of Flesh and Fire. But as the kingdoms' dark sins and blood-drenched secrets finally unravel, a long-forgotten power rises to pose a genuine threat. And they will stop at nothing to ensure that the crown never sits upon Poppy's head.

A lover and heartmate...

But the greatest threat to them and to Atlantia is what awaits in the far west, where the Queen of Blood and Ash has her own plans, ones she has waited hundreds of years to carry out. Poppy and Casteel must consider the impossible—travel to the Lands of the Gods and wake the King himself. And as shocking secrets and the harshest betrayals come to light, and enemies emerge to threaten everything Poppy and Casteel have fought for, they will discover just how far they are willing to go for their people—and each other.

And now she will become Queen...

* * * *

The War of Two Queens
Blood and Ash Series, Book Four
Available in hardcover, e-book, and trade paperback.

War is only the beginning…

From the desperation of golden crowns…

Casteel Da'Neer knows all too well that very few are as cunning or vicious as the Blood Queen, but no one, not even him, could've prepared for the staggering revelations. The magnitude of what the Blood Queen has done is almost unthinkable.

And born of mortal flesh…

Nothing will stop Poppy from freeing her King and destroying everything the Blood Crown stands for. With the strength of the Primal of Life's guards behind her, and the support of the wolven, Poppy must convince the Atlantian generals to make war her way—because there can be no retreat this time. Not if she has any hope of building a future where both kingdoms can reside in peace.

A great primal power rises…

Together, Poppy and Casteel must embrace traditions old and new to safeguard those they hold dear—to protect those who cannot defend themselves. But war is only the beginning. Ancient primal powers have already stirred, revealing the horror of what began eons ago. To end what the Blood Queen has begun, Poppy might have to become what she has been prophesied to be—what she fears the most.

As the Harbinger of Death and Destruction.

* * * *

A Soul of Ash and Blood
Blood and Ash Series, Book Five
Available in hardcover, e-book, and trade paperback.

Only his memories can save her…

A great primal power has risen. The Queen of Flesh and Fire has become the Primal of Blood and Bone—the true Primal of Life and Death. And the battle Casteel, Poppy, and their allies have been fighting has only just begun. Gods are awakening across Iliseeum and the mortal realm, readying for the war to come.

But when Poppy falls into stasis, Cas faces the very real possibility that the dire, unexpected consequences of what she is becoming could take her away from him. Cas is given some advice, though—something he plans to cling to as he waits to see her beautiful eyes open once more: Talk to her.

And so, he does. He reminds Poppy how their journey began, revealing things about himself that only Kieran knows in the process. But it's anybody's guess what she'll wake to or exactly how much of the realm and Cas will have changed when she does.

#1 New York Times bestselling author Jennifer L. Armentrout revisits Poppy and Casteel's epic love story in the next installment of the Blood and Ash series. But this time, Hawke gets to tell the tale.

* * * *

A Shadow in the Ember
Flesh and Fire Series, Book One
Available in hardcover, e-book, and trade paperback.

#1 New York Times bestselling author Jennifer L. Armentrout returns with book one of the all-new, compelling Flesh and Fire series—set in the beloved Blood and Ash world.

Born shrouded in the veil of the Primals, a Maiden as the Fates promised, Seraphena Mierel's future has never been hers. *Chosen* before birth to uphold the desperate deal her ancestor struck to save his people, Sera must leave behind her life and offer herself to the Primal of Death as his Consort.

However, Sera's real destiny is the most closely guarded secret in all of Lasania—she's not the well protected Maiden but an assassin with one mission—one target. Make the Primal of Death fall in love, become his weakness, and then…end him. If she fails, she dooms her kingdom to a slow demise at the hands of the Rot.

Sera has always known what she is. Chosen. Consort. Assassin. Weapon. A specter never fully formed yet drenched in blood. A *monster*. Until *him*. Until the Primal of Death's unexpected words and deeds chase away the darkness gathering inside her. And his seductive touch ignites a passion she's never allowed herself to feel and cannot feel for him. But Sera has never had a choice. Either way, her life is forfeit—it always has been, as she has been forever touched by Life and Death.

* * * *

A Light in the Flame
Flesh and Fire Series, Book Two
Available in hardcover, e-book, and trade paperback.

The only one who can save Sera now is the one she spent her life planning to kill.

The truth about Sera's plan is out, shattering the fragile trust forged between her and Nyktos. Surrounded by those distrustful of her, all Sera has is her duty. She will do anything to end Kolis, the false King of Gods, and his tyrannical rule of Iliseeum, thus stopping the threat he poses to the mortal realm.

Nyktos has a plan, though, and as they work together, the last thing they need is the undeniable, scorching passion that continues to ignite between them. Sera cannot afford to fall for the tortured Primal, not when a life no longer bound to a destiny she never wanted is more attainable than ever. But memories of their shared pleasure and unrivaled desire are a siren's call impossible to resist.

And as Sera begins to realize that she wants to be more than a Consort in name only, the danger surrounding them intensifies. The attacks on the Shadowlands are increasing, and when Kolis summons them to Court, a whole new risk becomes apparent. The Primal power of Life is growing inside her, pushing her closer to the end of her Culling. And without Nyktos's love—an emotion he's incapable of feeling—she won't survive her Ascension. That is if she even makes it to her Ascension and Kolis doesn't get to her first. Because time is running out. For both her and the realms.

* * * *

A Fire in the Flesh
Flesh and Fire Series, Book Three
Available in hardcover, e-book, and trade paperback.

The only thing that can save the realms now is the one thing more powerful than the Fates.

After a startling betrayal ends with both Sera and the dangerously seductive ruler of the Shadowlands she has fallen madly in love with being held captive by the false King of the Gods, there is only one thing that can free Nyktos and prevent the forces of the Shadowlands from invading Dalos and igniting a War of Primals.

Convincing Kolis won't be easy, though – not even with a lifetime of training. While his most favored Revenant is insistent that she is nothing more than a lie, Kolis's erratic nature and twisted sense of honor leave her shaken to the core, and nothing could've prepared her for the cruelty of his Court or the shocking truths revealed. The revelations not only upend what she has understood about her duty and the very creation of the realms but also draw into question exactly *what* the true threat is. However, surviving Kolis is only one part of the battle. The Ascension is upon her, and Sera is out of time.

But Nyktos will do anything to keep Sera alive and give her the life she deserves. He'll even risk the utter destruction of the realms, and that's exactly what will happen if he doesn't Ascend as the Primal of Life. Yet despite his desperate determination, their destinies may be out of their hands.

But there *is* that foreseen unexpected thread—the unpredictable, unknown, and unwritten. The only thing more powerful than the Fates…

On Behalf of Blue Box Press,

Liz Berry, M.J. Rose, and Jillian Stein would like to thank ~

Steve Berry
Doug Scofield
Benjamin Stein
Kim Guidroz
Chelle Olson
Hang Le
Chris Graham
Tanaka Kangara
Jessica Saunders
Malissa Coy
Jen Fisher
Stacey Tardif
Laura Helseth
Jessica Mobbs
Erika Hayden
Dylan Stockton
Kate Boggs
Richard Blake
and Simon Lipskar